Welcome to Vidia, a once great realm now becoming methodically undone by a group of idealistic clan warlords called the Kunn. Led by their Father, the Ahga, the Brotherhood undermines the sovereignties of the realm in its great and obscure endeavor to fulfill the will of the Divine One. Eroded and conquered from within, the city-states fall to the wealth and influence of the Brotherhood, plunging a just realm into despotism and clan violence. Going before the clan is the power of the Mari, an ancient religion providing its true followers with extra-capabilities. Through their harsh code the Kunn rises quickly to power, displacing its competitors and becoming the leading force in the region.

Enter Damian, a timid farm boy from Tirien captured by the Kunn. After years of toil he escapes from the slave mines of Khala with the help of his best friend Cam. Alone in the desert they are miraculously empowered by a divine being to confront the Ahga and his uncanny Brotherhood. Aided by their mentor, a mechanical genius named Riman, the three form a unique resistance. But they discover there is more to this conflict than they imagined as they soon find themselves a part of an old feud and legend, pitting one deity and its forces on earth against another in a quest for domination. To counter Damian comes Tog, the super adept of the Mari who strives with him and attempts to lure Damian to his side. Filled with espionage, politics, history, philosophy, and adventure on land and sea, *Ratarra* is an exciting exploration of good and evil and the spiritual forces behind them. Join Damian and Cam as they embark on their mission of justice, discovering not only who they have become but what this clan is really searching for…

EMMA,
SO NICE TO MEET YOU AT BOSTON COMIC CON 2016!
THE WILL OF THE DIVINE BE DONE …
Nushvan
8/14/16

ACKNOWLEDGMENTS

I would like to thank my loving wife Kim for all her hard work, dedication, and encouragement, and my mother Joan and sister Catherine for their unquenchable faith. I would also like to thank the Oneail family for their editing and artwork contributions, and Leonard Perkins for tech support. You have all made this project become a reality.

Library of Congress copyright registration 2008
Printed by Createspace, Inc
Artwork by Jeremy Oneail

Table of Contents

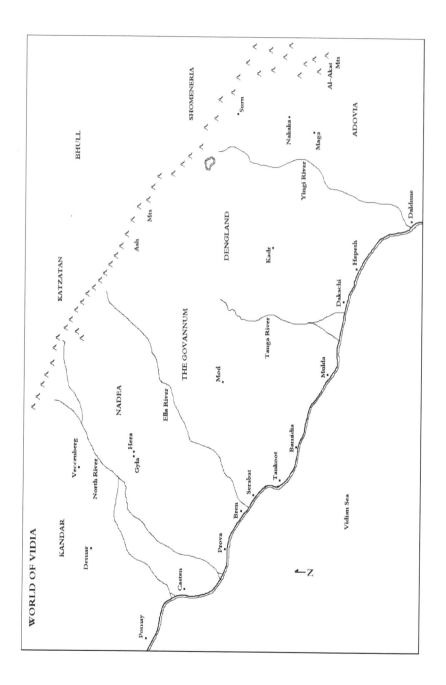

WORLD OF VIDIA

KANDAR

BHULL

SHOMENERIA

KATZATAN

Denur

Veccenberg

North River

NADEA

Gyla · Hera

Ash Mts

DENGLAND

Surn

Nakaka ·

Maga ·

Al-Akat
Mts

ADOVIA

Ponay

Casten

Prova

Bren

Serabat

Taukoot

Banidia

Ella River

THE GOVANNUM

Mod

Tanga River

Kadr ·

Yingi River

Hepesh

Dakachi

Mulda

Dakume

Vidian Sea

N

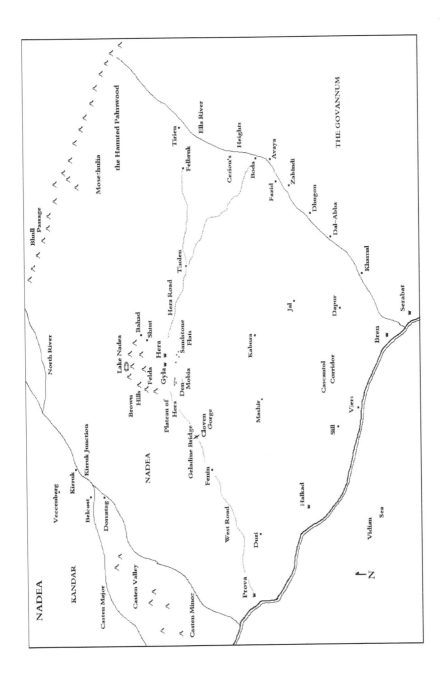

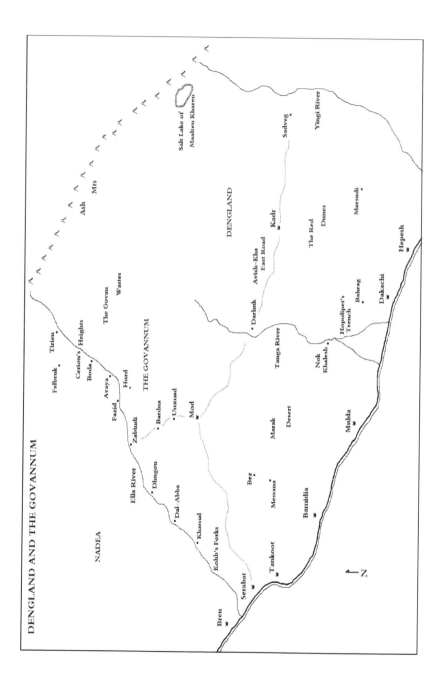

DENGLAND AND THE GOVANNUM

NADEA

THE GOVANNUM

DENGLAND

Bren
Serabat
Tankoot
Kohlb's Forks
Khamal
Dal-Abba
Dingon
Ella River
Zabudi
Fazid
Avaya
Hurd
Bardua
Ummad
Mod
Boda
Cerion's Heights
Tirien
Felbruk
The Govan Wastes

Messaui
Bez
Bamidia
Marak Desert
Tanga River

Mulda
Nok Khalesh
Hopolipet's Trench
Bahrag
Dakachi
Hepesh
Darbuk
Avish-Kha East Road
Kadr
Sadveg
The Red Dunes
Marsudi
Yingi River

Ash Mts

Salt Lake of Maalten Kharen

N

8

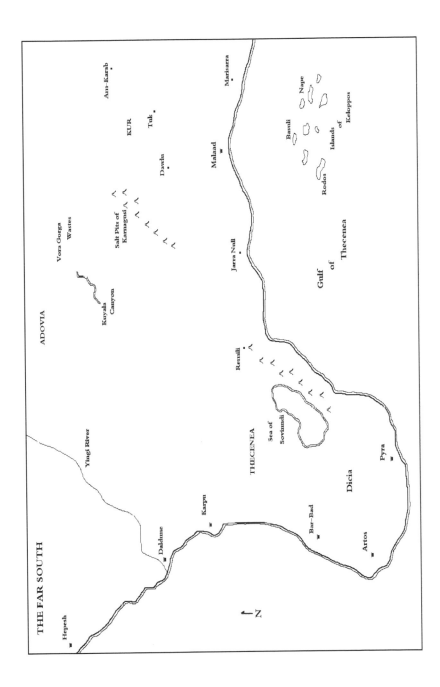

THE FAR SOUTH

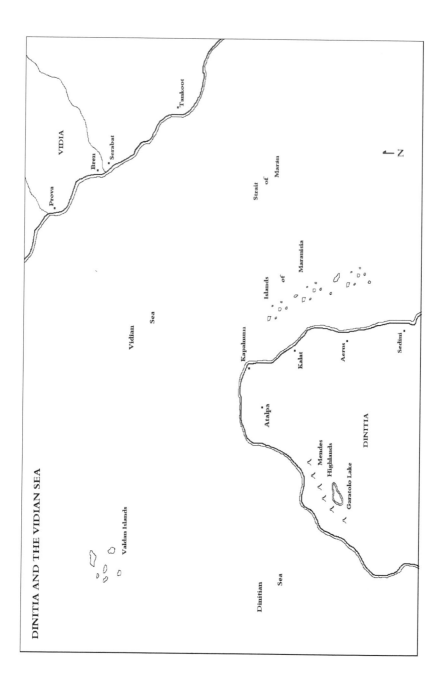

DINITIA AND THE VIDIAN SEA

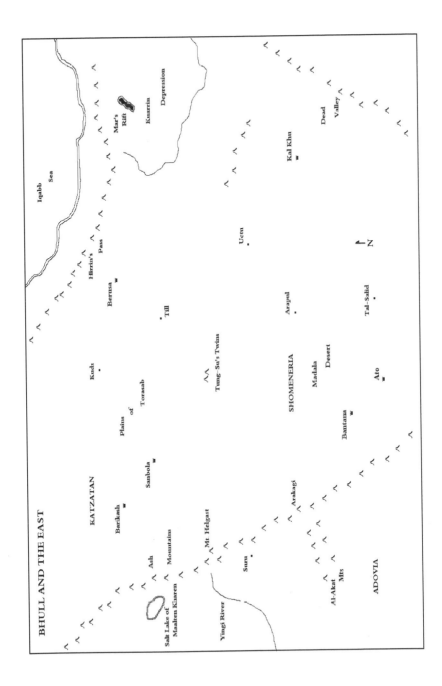

BHULL AND THE EAST

Iqabb Sea

Mar's Rift

Kuarrin Depression

Hirrin's Pass

Berusa

Till

Uctu

Kal Khu

Dead Valley

Kudx

Plains of Torasab

Tung-Sut's Twins

SHOMENERIA

Madala Desert

Ato

Arapul

Tal-Salid

KATZATAN

Barikash

Sambola

Ash Mountains

Salt Lake of Maalten Kharen

Mt. Helgast

Yingi River

Suru

Arakagi

Bantana

Al-Akat Mts

ADOVIA

N

11

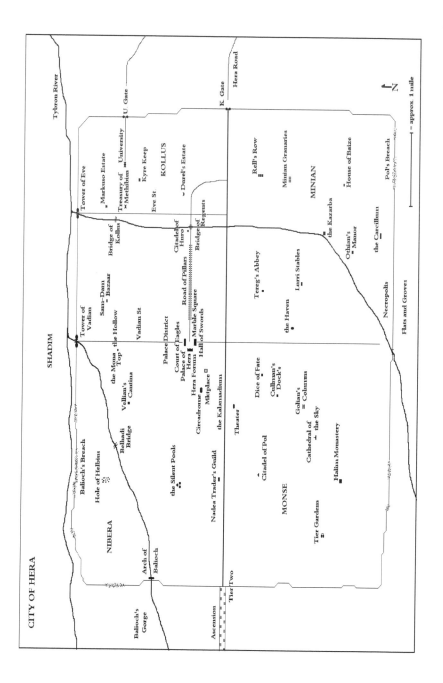

CITY OF HERA

Tybron River

SHADIM

Baliocli's Breach

Hole of Helbius

NIBERA

Baliocli's Gorge

Arch of Balioch

Bellind Bridge

the Silent Pools

Nadea Trader's Guild

Ascension

Tier Two

Citadel of Pol

MONSE

Tier Gardens

Halun Monastery

Cathedral of the Sky

Golian's Columns

Dice of Fate

Culbnan's Dock's

the Kalanadium

Theater

Circadrome

Palace of Hera

Court of Eagles

Palace District

Hera Forum

Mktplace

Marble Square

Hall of Swords

Vellian's Cantina

the Mona Top

the Hollow

Vadian St.

Sam-Dam Bazaar

Tower of Vadian

Tower of Eve

Bridge of Kollus

Markuso Estate

Treasury of Methibius

University

U. Gate

Kyre Keep

Eve St.

KOLLUS

Durel's Estate

Citadel of Huro

Bridge of Regents

Road of Pillars

the Haven

Tereg's Abbey

Larri Stables

Rell's Row

Minian Granaries

MINIAN

Othian's Manor

the Kazarba

House of Baize

the Carcillium

Necropolis

Pol's Breach

Flats and Groves

K. Gate

Hera Road

N

= approx. 1 mile

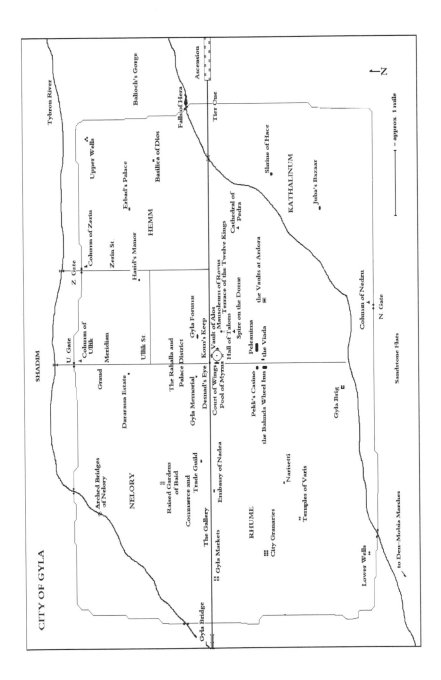

CITY OF GYLA

SHADIM

Tybron River

Balioch's Gorge

Falls of Hera

Ascension

Tier One

N

= approx 1 mile

Upper Wells

Erbad's Palace

Basilica of Dios

HEMM

Column of Zerin

Zerin St

Hamd's Manor

Z Gate

U Gate

Column of Ullik

Meridian

Grand

Ullik St

Dararassa Estate

The Rahalla and
Palace District

Gyla Forums

Komi's Keep

Gyla Memorial

Desnad's Eye

Court of Wings
Pool of Myrna

Vault of Alos

Mausoleum of Rovus
Terrace of the Twelve Kings

Hall of Talons

Spire on the Dome

the Vaults at Ardora

Cathedral of
Pedra

KATHALINUM

Shrine of Hace

Juba's Bazaar

Peleanima

the Viada

Column of Nedzu

N Gate

Sandstone Flats

Pekl's Casino

the Baluda Wheel Inn

Gyla Brig

NELORY

Arched Bridges
of Nelory

Raised Gardens
of Baid

Commerce and
Trade Guild

The Gallery

Gyla Markets

Embassy of Nadea

Nariaetti

Temples of Varis

RHUME

City Granaries

Lower Wells

Gyla Bridge

to Deni-Mobia Marshes

To all those who long for righteousness in an unjust world...

EPISODE 1
RETURN TO KHALA

CHAPTER 1
THE MINES

The boy looked out at the stars from behind the bars of his cell. There was no demonstration happening on the ground below tonight. That enabled him a night of peace. The guards of this prison performed many demonstrations on the prisoners in the area below him for all to see, various tortures and humiliations, all horrible and unthinkable. They called it the 'reinstruction pit.' Kurg, the great Mogoli chieftain of this facility enforced his strict laws and sought pleasure in making examples out of the disobedient prisoners. On these nights the boy would cower in the back corner of his tiny cell.

And that indeed was the cruel intent of the cell layout here at the Khala slave camp. The prisoner blocks were carved into the sides of the huge U-shaped rock formation on this side of the mountain, closely positioned, directly across from each other, with the cell blocks facing inboard. This semi-circular arrangement compelled the prisoners to witness the horrors not far below. Kurg plainly wanted the effects of his punishments felt by all.

The boy, Damian, had witnessed far more of these than he cared to in his eight years here. Once, a man working in the slaughterhouse not far from the stables where the boy worked each day, bolted and tried to climb the stone wall. He was quickly shot by a guard and staked in the pit. Kurg released his kelgan steeds and the boy would never forget the man's cries as the beasts ate him alive. On another time, when Damian was much younger, a human and an accomplice guard were hung in the pit by their legs all night. Damian later learned the guard sold food to the prisoner for gold he must have found mining. The guard, one of the Hidari race, was later executed. Kurg could not afford collaboration with the prisoners, the result of which would be fatal. Obtaining sympathy and favors from the guards would undermine authority and be detrimental to his purpose. Besides, any gold found here at Khala was strictly for the benefit of their cultish following, the Kunn, and their leader, the great Ahga-Rosh, or Father.

Everyone here had whip marks. Some even had hideous holes under their back bones from suffering 'atonement'. The Kunn soldiers called it the *ruk-mesh*, a brutal ritual the clan itself underwent as a rite of admission. Here it was implemented as a punishment for the prisoners. Kelga fangs were driven under the victim's back bones which were then strung to a wooden beam. The victim was then lifted into the air and hung and left for what seemed like an eternity. Damian himself bore the scars of his own atonement experience. Shortly after his arrival, the starved boy had been caught with smuggled meat from the slaughterhouse. He lunged at the guard when his food was confiscated. Damian was beaten and strung, but watching the guard eat his food and jeer at him while he suffered was even more painful. The quiet in the pit below tonight was actually somewhat peaceful and Damian tried to find comfort and hope in the stars above on this cloudless night.

But hope was scarce here at the Khala mines for this factory was a great source of gold, gems, and metal for the Kunn warlords, in particular a metal called garvonite, which could be found in abundance here. This rare metal was the material of choice for its hardness and unsurpassed resistance to corrosion and decay, and therefore was of great worth and widely coveted. Weapons and gold were in high demand for the Ahga was ever in need of materials and wealth to sustain his growing power and ranks. The Kunn, which meant 'The Fist' in their old language, relied on steady output from Khala in the form of gold, tradeable stones, metal and meat for profit. The prisoners were not allowed to make usable weapons here, of course, but shipped out the procured goods in raw pieces which they crudely manufactured on site and in turn sold on the market. Withholding of any precious metal or stone was a serious crime, and Kurg and his chief taskmaster and strongman, Belósh, a huge one-eyed half-mog with an evil smile, saw that rules were enforced.

Damian could never forget his first fateful encounter with the Kunn that autumn day eight years ago. He grew up in a farming settlement called Tirien with his father, mother and sister. He was a sturdy but timid boy with dirty blond hair and hazel eyes, and learned the meaning of labor at a very young age. They lived on a farm, self sufficient for the most part and making their way in the world, selling their crops at the local village market. He helped his father on the farm, raising crops, milking the cattle, slaughtering the livestock, storing the harvest and feed, and otherwise assisting with the various tasks, of which there are many. He was, therefore, a bit stronger than other boys, his young muscles accustomed to burden and toil. He excelled at athletics or any other sport or task which required physical strength and stamina but was markedly humble and generous, seemingly oblivious to the power he possessed over others, and undesirous of such an advantage anyway. His father had given him a young horse of his own and he proved himself to be a skilled rider and often rode to the village market on an errand, or to a friend's house when he could. He cherished this horse greatly and treated it like the gift that it was, earning its respect and obedience in return.

He was returning from such a ride one afternoon in his twelfth year when he saw them–a small troop of Mogoli, green skinned and fanged humanoids, well-statured and muscled, armed and fearsome, bearing the token red bandanas and armbands of the clan known as the Kunn. Their bodies they had daubed and disfigured with paint and cruel piercings to make them look fierce. Stripes were branded into their girthy necks. These strange thugs of the desert countries to the south rode onto the farm mounted on kelgan–fast, fierce, four-legged beasts of the barren lands. His father, Darren, went out to meet them with fear in his eyes. These clan bandits had been here twice before, he remembered, demanding a portion of the harvest and slaughter. These times Darren had paid them out of fear for his family's safety but this year had brought a drought and the harvest was minimal. The family stood a fair chance of starving before next spring unless they could find work and Darren could not afford the request, or demand this time. His father knew that opposition or defiance to the Kunn would result in death or enslavement. Damian would never forget the terrified look in his mother Loren's eyes as she clutched his ten year old sister, Lilia's, hand as she peered out from the window behind the front porch of their small home. They all seemed to know what would happen as Darren descended the steps and approached the clan chief, called an *ulak*. This chief was a larger, stronger mog having only one eye and an evil smile, a smile that found pleasure in others' pain, a smile that would torment Damian in sleep and in waking life, a smile that Damian was forced to see daily for this clan thug was none other than Belósh himself, the taskmaster, the executioner, the genius of torture and pain here at Khala. Damian hesitated on his horse, frozen with fear and uncertainty. Dread weighed down on him like lead as he watched not a stone's throw away in the pasture.

"I have nothing to give you," stuttered Darren nervously to the ulak, halted before him. The ulak offered no reply but dismounted. He approached Darren and paused for a moment in front of him. There was a silence, then Belósh motioned to the woman and child in the window. Darren glanced back at his wife and daughter and their eyes met, then he reluctantly faced the ulak again with a desperate look. Belósh laughed.

"Please," begged Darren , "we have no food."

The smile on the ulak's face vanished. Such an answer was unacceptable. He drew his sword and beheaded Darren with one swift stroke.

Loren immediately ran onto the porch, screaming hysterically, followed by Lilia.

"NO!" Damian cried from his horse.

"DAMIAN!" cried his mother now completely overcome with grief and terror. She reached desperately for her son who was beyond her aid. She took a few steps toward him but was arrested by the strong grip of Kunn henchmen. Belósh turned towards Damian and their eyes met for the first time. He growled and Damian fled in terror, but the mounted riders were already close on his tail.

"Run Bish, run!" Damian urged the fleeing horse but it was in vain. The soldiers with loaded crossbows quickly brought the small horse down. Damian fell in the grass and found himself in the clutches of the villains. He was dragged back crying violently, delirious from horror, and brought before their leader. Belósh regarded the boy closely for a moment and ordered him tied. The cruel, one-eyed ulak then grabbed Damian by the hair and pulled him close.

"You come with me, *Ratarra,*" snarled Belósh and all went dark.

Damian crawled back into the corner of his cell, wrestling with these painful thoughts, cursing himself yet again for his cowardice. He always felt like he should have done something that day, but what could he do? An unarmed boy against a troop of clan gangsters? There must have been something, he told himself, but this brought him no comfort. He would never live down this great personal failure. He watched helplessly as his father died and he never was able to learn the fate of his mother and sister. Probably killed or taken captive like him, he thought. Their cries haunted his dreams. He cursed himself again.

He was relieved of these dark memories by the arrival of his neighboring cellmate, Cam. He heard the door to Cam's cell open and close with a clang. He waited for the footsteps of the guard to fade down the hall before approaching the bars where he could communicate carefully with his friend on the other side of the rock wall that divided them. They were careful to avoid alerting the guards to their friendship. Friends could be a problem here and any that were discovered would be separated and moved to another cell, so they communicated as secretly as they could. Cam just ended his shift and was probably pretty tired but Damian longed for a relief to his miserable solitude. But also the two were genuinely concerned for each other. Each day was always an unknown, with death and torture always a possibility, and one never knew what might befall him from one miserable day to the next. When all was quiet Damian tapped twice on the wall with a rock, then waited for the reply. He heard one tap from the other side. That was Cam then, their secret password, two taps then one.

"Cam?" called Damian quietly to the adjacent cell.

"Damian, I brought something for you." A hand reached over from the other side of the wall through the bars with a lump of bread. "The guard was too busy watching Reese get whipped."

"Cam, you're a miracle." Damian said thankfully as he reached and took the bread with difficulty through the bars of his cell. Their two cells were close enough to allow, with some difficulty, the passing of objects from one hand to another, a circumstance enabled only by a dislodged rock between their cells outside that otherwise would have rendered any transaction impossible.

The Khala mines were dug into not so much a mountain as a huge, lone, isolated rock formation located in a vast wasteland. Khala could not rightly be called a mountain for it was not high enough, only reaching about eight hundred feet, but was deep and wide, measuring four miles in circumference in what was strangely close to a perfect circle looking down from the sky, and had a flat, plateau-like top. The word originally meant 'crown' in the old Slovidar tongue, for such was its regal appearance and almost comely shape on the vast desert floor. The sides of Khala were of a sheer and virtually unclimbable, unforgiving rock, extending upwards at right angles to the earth, a brown, grassless, unfriendly and ominous giant, an island of towering defiance in a sea of nothingness that did not seek friendship, preferring rather to be left alone to bask in its power. Khala was the keep and the throne, and the earth and its lowly inhabitants were its subjects, crawling and vying for survival on the barren, flat terrain that worshipped its master. This tower of independence, however, boasted riches only a king like Khala could procure, and promised resources in abundance to any who dared venture and delve into this mysterious, rogue landmass, and the Kunn wasted no time capitalizing on what proved to be a great find, and claimed it for their own. Veins of a fiery substance from the earth were discovered here and engineered to use, dangerous but possessing vast potential, and it was called the Underlight, the Red Pit; the clan soldiers called it the Firemouth, after this strange but useful resource they found burning in perpetuity within. Surely this hidden expedient was a gift of the Divine One, a means to their ultimate purpose, and the clan seized it for their great objective. There was nothing the Ahga could not tame and he bled Khala like a beast, and like a beast, he bent it to his will, removing its treasures for his profit.

The cutout which formed the inlet of the Khala prison camp was located on the western outermost side of the mountain, and had an advantageous semi-circular shape, and this is where the cells and mine entrance were situated. This inlet formed a unique, arced barrier that provided optimum detainment of the prisoners that would be necessary to perform the work the Ahga-Rosh demanded. The prisoner blocks were carved into the sides of this curved inlet, facing inboard directly across from each other, as previously mentioned, arranged in rows, ten cells each, on three ascending levels on each of the two opposing rocksides. With the inlet facing definitively west, these prison blocks were simply referred to as 'south block' or 'north block.' Altogether there were usually between sixty to seventy prisoners here at any given time, and more than half that in guards and personnel.

There were three main tasks performed here: the mining of useful ore and stones, the processing of these goods for transport, and the slaughtering of cattle for the sustenance of the prisoners and personnel. A portion of this meat was also packed and preserved for export and picked up regularly by supply wagons and brought to the city and sold. This facility ran itself, a fully functioning slaughterhouse and gold mine, only requiring food to be brought in from the outside in the form of livestock driven in routinely by the desert herdsmen from distant parts, salt by the block, and bread. More luxurious commodities and trinkets were imported for the use of clan personnel, of course, and upgraded food sustenance. The Ahga wanted his gold mine well cared for. Water was obtainable by wells dug down to the underground river that ran underneath Khala. Kurg was careful not to allow mining in this direction as it might provide a means of escape. But Khala was located in the barren wilderness, many miles away from the nearest city or town, or food, and so even this possibility of escape was not of great concern to him. He kept the prisoners tired and hungry enough, only feeding them twice a day, so the thought of an escapee making it anywhere alive was fairly inconceivable.

The rest of the facility, however, was almost completely self-contained, all work performed happening underground with the exception of the slaughterhouse, which was located outside in the inlet underneath the prisoner blocks. This crude, meat processing facility was surrounded by a high stone wall and had a dual gate system that allowed for the admittance of livestock for slaughter. Then of course there was the reinstruction pit, on the ground in the bowl formed by the rocksides, apart from the slaughterhouse and in full view of the prisoner cells. There was also the stable, where Damian worked, which was located on the first level, two levels below where he now crouched, inside the mountain underneath south block where Damian and Cam were both kept. The stable was where the fleet of kelgan was housed, just inside the cave's main gate, needed at times for long distance errands or possibly defense against rival clans. The Kunn had its competitors, and Khala was an attractive prize. Also fresh kelgan were kept as replacements should any messengers or herd drivers from afar need one. The smithy and furnaces were located behind the base of the circled inlet, inside the mountain, only accessible through the main gate on the outside. Inside the prison this main work room was accessed by hallways that led to the prison blocks on either side, connecting them. This is where the majority of the prisoners were forced to labor each day unceasingly, mining, running the furnaces, hammering and shaping the metal and stones. The mine shafts extended in an eastward direction from this great work room, all waste rock being brought up to the top rear of the mountain on the east side and dumped over the cliff some five hundred feet below.

And so one miserable day of toil and fear brought another. Escape was ever on the minds of these utterly oppressed and forsaken inhabitants but a means of escape from this dungeon was elusive and futile anyway, so hopelessness was a disease, and everyone had it.

* * *

Damian ate his bread ravenously. He'd tried unsuccessfully to steal bread several times before by pickpocketing the guards or pilfering rations, which is difficult and dangerous enough, but desperation drove these poor souls. He was brought down to the reinstruction pit, tied to the post and whipped each time. On the last attempt a guard had hanging from his belt a coveted *delling* rat, a delicacy in these parts even to the powerful, but to a hungry prisoner it was the treasure of the world. For this memorable failure he was deprived of his precious evening meal. Damian had seldom known such hunger, even here. He needed every morsel of sustenance he could get his ever-soiled hands on and could not afford to forsake any of it. That night he curled tightly on his cell floor, clutching his abdomen and weeping with pain and weakness. He never tried stealing again but also could never figure out how Cam did. Perhaps it was because of Cam's much shorter stature which Damian learned about only by Cam's own admission, for the two had never once actually seen each other in all their years here. Cam worked the mine, Damian the stable, and with conflicting shifts and routines, and of course the thick rock wall separating them, visual contact between the two was impossible.

But where sight is deprived, improvisation will be employed for communication, which they did carefully each night. They spoke to each other from the closest corners of the cells, passing news, telling stories past and present, sharing thoughts and words of encouragement. They even played a game called shoot, a dice game Cam had learned as a young boy back home, but here they adapted small rocks for it.

Cam grew up in a coastal town called Bren. He was an unusually small, thin boy with dark hair and eyes, and a dark complexion as the result of his frequent exposure to the sun in that warm, seafaring town far away.

23

He had no knowledge of his parents, being orphaned almost at birth. He spent his early years being passed from the care of various guardians until he voluntarily departed on his own to survive and make his way on the streets and along the busy waterfront. He eventually established a lasting friendship with an old fisherman who noticed the lone, small boy running along the wharf every day or swimming in the shallow harbor, salvaging fish scraps dumped by the fishermen alongside the seabirds who vied with him. The old seadog took the scrawny, bright-eyed child under his care and, needing some assistance and endeavoring to help the destitute orphan, allowed him to assist with the deck duties and maintenance of the ship, or the sorting and disposal of the catch, all this much to the delight of the remarkably energetic boy who accepted the offer of work for food. The old man became his mentor for a time, teaching him the trade and showing him the wonders of nature and the sea. Cam was very short as a boy, and he was still even at nineteen. His lack of stature made him the object of amusement by the other boys he happened upon and he became uncannily adept at hiding or climbing to avoid them, when he was idling ashore or the old man didn't require him or didn't dare take him out. And so it was often that he found himself playing alone, chasing gulls, skipping rocks, or running nimbly along the wharf's edge by the seaside where he knew his only friend's boat soon would come. Sometimes he would climb under the wharf and swing from the crossbeams at low tide, looking out at the horizon until sunset before heading to his home on the street. Sometimes he would race along the numerous, busy, seaside streets and alleys, climbing on the palm trees or buildings or stacks of fish traps and supply crates to avoid the other boys.

One day, when he was eleven, during his prowls, he came across Kunn thugs making some kind of deal with what appeared to be a city official in a back alley. Money was exchanged. The strange scene brought a feeling of unwholesomeness to the boy. Although he had seen many other peoples and races of this world before in the busy city and on ships which came from across the sea, he had only heard of clan villains and gave a gasp at the sight. The official's bodyguard discovered him cunningly hidden under a staircase and they had the uncomprehending, confused little boy shipped off to Khala to silence him lest he heard anything incriminating. The old man hadn't seen him since.

And so, by what little good fortune they could claim to have, these two life-deprived boys from different backgrounds but sharing the commonality of grave misfortune and brute victimization, found themselves almost together, separated, but close enough to give each other the humanity and companionship they needed to make it through each day. The two quickly became desperate friends, a lifeline to sanity, each providing the other a brief respite and relief from the daily pain and anguish, two co-dependent sparks of life, invisible to each other but as close as brothers staring at death only an arm's length away.

"Cam, I don't know how you do it," Damian said munching his bread.

"A gift from the Creator," Cam replied. "Poor Reese was getting it from Belósh again, always a good opportunity. Think I'll get some for Reese next time, I feel like I owe it to him." Cam had a proficiency with stealth and concealment, partially by his size, partially by necessity, and he used his abilities whenever he could for the benefit of himself and his friend.

Damian had heard stories of the Creator before from his mother and father as a young boy. They would tell him that a place existed where everyone loved each other and where gifts were given to those who treated each other fairly. "Do good work for the Creator, Damian," they would say, "and you'll be rewarded." Whenever his mother especially imbued him with faith he was filled with a hope and spirit that was always memorable. There was something different about her, a soothing love in her eyes and an uncanny tranquility in her healing touch. But that was so long ago now for him it seemed like a strange dream in another world in another time. That was a life that was difficult for him to relate to, as if it never really happened. Being a miserable work boy for the Kunn machine was all he could now relate to and identify with, there was no other world, only Khala, and this was the beginning and the end. Even imagining another life became more and more difficult as the years wore on and the labor and hunger broke him, until his mind and soul became host only to helplessness and despair, completely unable to entertain the idea of a better life existing anywhere. Thoughts of happiness only existed for the purpose of worsening the misery, like the vision of an oasis to the thirsty: ever viewed, ever beyond reach.

What belief he had in any divine being withered greatly from year to year until it was driven out by feelings of utter despair and abandonment, and anger for such an abominable circumstance as his. Certainly he felt if there was a Creator, He could not have meant this to be. He ultimately concluded that no such thing could possibly exist, that such a notion was nought but the ravings of the delusional. But something inside told him otherwise, a dogged entity deep within him, beaten, half strangled and clinging desperately for life, but somehow barely alive, a common feeling shared by any who are oppressed. Beyond all this, on the other side of this fetid window, there must be something, he conceded. Cam and Damian had many discussions on the subject. The Kunn were fervent believers in what they called 'The Divine One', and boastfully purported to do His will here, but Damian couldn't believe it. What his parents said of the Creator and what his captors claimed of the Divine, though purportedly the same, were, to him, two very different things. This obvious conflict of beliefs, ostensibly of the same idea, only served to confuse the boy and further douse what spark of faith he had. For the most part Cam felt the same way, that such a notion was too fallible, even preposterous, especially under their circumstances, and long ago decided to take matters into his own hands. If things weren't going to get better, if life wasn't going to offer him an alternative, then he was going to make one.

"So, how goes the bloody furnace room, Cam?" Damian asked after finishing his bread, a little moldy but he wasn't complaining. "Reese and Belósh are getting along as usual, I see."

"You know Reese, he's like an untamable horse, even half starved as he is though I can't say that I blame him. If I get my way I'd take an axe to all those Kunn maggots, especially Belósh. I'd burn him alive." Cam gritted his teeth.

"Shh!" warned Damian. "Not so loud. You remember what happened last year to that blacksmith?"

"Yeah, cut his hands off for plotting an uprising, though can't see what good he is to Kurg now. He was a miner, now all he can do is work the well, that is, until Kurg has no further use for him. Then he'll probably throw him over the cliff. Belósh nailed his severed hands to the smithy room wall. Can't see what good I'd be without my hands." Cam folded his arms and shuddered. Kurg was known to have informers and any word of disdain toward or about the guards or the Kunn or even the mention of rebellion or escape overheard by unfriendly ears would result in punishment of the worst kind. For this reason the prisoners mostly were silent and subdued, not daring to utter a word, or spoke in low, inaudible, hurried whispers. Belósh, ever suspicious, would stalk to and fro among the workers as they labored, pounding metal and flesh, rather hoping to find some excuse to harass, torture, and humiliate a slave, and usually doing so anyway.

The guards were always on the lookout for friendship or alliances among the slaves, and for the prisoners having one was a dangerous, tricky business. Cam and Damian never crossed paths so they were generally safe. But there were guards down in the pit below them, they could see two of them now and in the towers across from them, one of which was only a stone's throw away, so even their secret arrangement could be discovered and undone. These two watchtowers were located at the entrance of the camp inlet, one on the north wall and one on the south, both with a good view of the empty plain beyond and the road that led to the city of Mod, a hundred miles or more southwest of Khala, where their supplies came from. They could see the banners of the Kunn stirring gently but hauntingly in the warm, night breeze, a black fist in a red field, hanging from the towertops. These towers were crudely constructed of logs and beams and were only just higher than the third level of cells. The two friends were also on this level and the farthest over, at the westward end, and therefore closest to the south tower. The tower guards mostly served as lookouts, sounding the horns when necessary to herald errand riders or herdsmen approaching on the road, but were also close enough to keep an eye on the prisoners in their exposed cages. But there was no front gate into the yard itself, only the main gate into the cave. Khala was little known to the outside world save in a rumor, for the roads into the desert were far away, and with the prisoners adequately locked inside Kurg felt it unnecessary to have a gate. Even if folk were aware of the existence of this rock they would never have guessed what the Kunn had done with it. Kurg half wished one of those useless, filthy rats would escape anyway, he thought. It would give him an excuse to release his kelgan and go on a manhunt. A break in the monotony would be almost welcomed.

Damian and Cam lay quiet for a moment, watching the guards in the tower and listening to the guards below in the pit, bickering or joking at times as they paced. They looked to their left, westward as they often did, this direction alone and the view of the plain left visible by the gap in the encircling cliffs. They dwelt ever on the view of that beautiful emptiness and drew from it some strength each night. They could read and write but had only vague geographical knowledge, and had no idea where they were. To them that vast, open plain was freedom, the road that for them held the only possibility of hope and any promise of a better existence, and they could only guess and hope that somewhere out there, far away, their loved ones, what remained of them, were faring well. Damian wondered if his mother and sister looked out at the same night sky as he did. Perhaps they were searching for hope and strength in the stars even now. He felt sure of it.

"If there was some way we could just get outside the cave we might stand a chance," whispered Damian. From this point and no fence or gate blocking the entrance to the camp, the view they had made freedom seem almost attainable. Beyond the slaughterpit the yard was clear and open. "If you could smuggle me some metal shards I bet I could make a saw and cut the bars. All I would have to cut is one. Are you still digging that hole alone Cam?"

"Yeah, they want another air duct dug for the furnace room. You can't breathe in there. Of course I have my own ideas. Kurg's mighty upset with the prisoners dropping like flies in that hotbox. Hurts production." The guards used Cam as a pilot digger because of his ideal size. He's been working for weeks on another air vent. This required him to dig from a higher elevation, three levels above and in front of the furnace room, in a downward direction, but Cam made sure he was the only one that could fit down it. The hole was only a foot in diameter so it became *his* hole, and where he was actually digging to was his own business.

"See if you can get me a length of shaved metal and I'll break us out of here," said Damian, grasping the bars in frustration. Cam, being a miner, had more access to tools and metal than Damian, but what few tools they were allowed to use, under strict supervision, had to be turned in daily. Metal or instruments of any kind was considered contraband and they were subject to strict body searches at the termination of each shift.

"It's easier to get food than metal, you know that," replied Cam. "They only let me use a hammer, chisel and a pick, and I have to turn them in. Besides, how would you survive out there?" They looked out onto the miles of barren waste below them. "Even if we did get out we'd need a fast horse, too. Escaping alone isn't enough."

Damian sighed. "What I wouldn't give to ride a horse again. Kelgan are nearly impossible to control. Dendu racers are too unpredictable. Riders have to train with them. There are a few open bays in the stable, though. Maybe we'll get to keep a horse again sometime. It's happened before."

"Yeah, for those humans and Hidari who work for the Kunn. They prefer horses to kelgan." This was rare, for although many of all races were in the service of the Kunn the Ahga only disclosed a secret like Khala to his most trusted agents. Though there were rumors in the populated areas of this diverse world of a secret slave camp in a mountain far away, few knew anything of this dreaded place, much less its location. The Ahga intended to keep it that way.

"It seems hopeless, then," said Damian and he sighed. "You can't count on horses turning in here, and even if the guards got their hands on one they'd probably make it dinner. Mogs and Turuks love horsemeat."

"Well you'd know before I did," Cam said. "If we do get one let me know." Just then the tower guard turned his attention in their direction.

"Guards," warned Damian and the two of them instantly retreated to the rear of their cells. The tower guard grunted something to his companions below him and the sentries on the ground ventured toward them suspiciously, looking upward. The two friends didn't dare make another sound the rest of the night. Nothing was worth their discovery and they turned to their precious allotment of sleep.

* * *

Damian was awakened by footsteps. He heard the familiar sound of the key fumbling in the lock of his door, a sound he dreaded. Another miserable day of toil was about to begin and Damian began the day with downcast eyes, reluctant to leave what peace was allowed him. The thick wooden door creaked open and two guards entered, a mog and a tall, sturdy Hidari.

28

One of them flung a chunk of bread at him before leading him out and down the hall. He passed Cam's cell on the left but didn't dare even to look at his door. He passed the other cells, still closed and occupied. Kurg insisted Damian start his labor earlier to feed his precious kelgan land steeds. Funny, Damian thought. Kurg could have cared less for his beasts, as much slaves to him as were his prisoners. The door to the last cell on this level was open, however, and Damian could hear the unmistakable sound of Belósh interrogating the unfortunate detainee of that cell. It was unusual to be conducting such questioning this early, he thought. Perhaps it was of some importance. Damian instinctively slowed his pace somewhat as they passed to perhaps catch a few words that would provide him with an idea as to the nature of the brutal questioning. But this came at a price. The escorts gave him a shove for his apparent sluggishness and he tripped and fell down the stone stairway that opened up before him to his left, which descended to the lower levels. He lost his grip on the bread and it fell down the stairs ahead of him. Damian watched it roll down the stairs horror-stricken, fearing the permanent loss of his meager breakfast. Unclaimed bread must mean that no one wanted it and was taken away. The guards loved to make the prisoners 'lose' their food, and Damian was sure this time was no different. He immediately scrambled for the precious loaf but this was stepped on by one of the guards who was leering at Damian with a smile.

"Oh, he must not want this," joked the escort as he picked up the flattened bread. "Ratarra's moving a bit slow today. Let's see if he can pick up the pace a bit. If you can get the bread before I do, you can have it back, you sluggard *insal*." He flung the bread down the stairs and onto the landing below. Without thinking Damian sprang forward, a filthy, starved creature, haggard and desperate, clothed in rags. With what strength he had and a look of utter terror at the risk of losing his sustenance, he flew down the steps. The guard only took a few token steps behind Damian to enhance the amusement and laughed as he slowly descended the rest. Damian pitifully shoved the mangled bread pieces into his mouth. The burly guards laughed at him, picked him up and continued.

They stopped at the bottom, turned right and passed the *kumitam,* a small worship shrine for the Kunn. They passed this space, continued down the hall and unlocked a door. They proceeded through this and continued down another passageway on their way to the well. This hall also led to the main work room and furnaces further on, and another connecting hall branched left to the slaughterhouse and meat yard. They stopped at an opening to their left and entered. Inside this small room there was a prisoner doling out water from the well, which was extracted by chain and bucket. The prisoner had some difficulty turning the windlass to the well for he had been deprived of his hands some months before and was reprimanded to this duty. The Kunn often maimed their victims, not just here at Khala but wherever they were. It served as punishment and a warning but also as a mark, or brand, a cruel means of supremacist proclamation. Someone once told him that this particular prisoner, who was of different race–a blue Harikan of the south–was a member of a competing clan, somewhere out in the wide world, and was captured and enslaved for the Kunn. Like the Kunn this fellow had crude brand marks on his face to make him look fierce, insignia of clanhood. But all this didn't convey much to the boy. Damian tried to learn as much as he could about the mysterious group of villains who captured him and unfathomably ruined his family forever. He asked questions about this subject of the other prisoners when he could but all he could gather was that they were the dominant clan in some bordering country and were trying to encroach into and gain power in these parts. They were always seeking strong laborers for their various workshops around the world and slaves were certainly more economical than paid workers. The once peaceful and prosperous days of this province were over. The Feud of Adin lived on, they said, in their time. The Kunn believed the great riddle would be solved and the hidden city would be theirs again in all its glory. Since the fall of Karius and the collapse of the Old Alliance no one would be safe for long. But all this meant little to him. These vague thoughts ran through Damian's innocent and uncomprehending mind while he watched the maimed arms of the unfortunate prisoner turn the crank and pour his serving of water into a large bowl which his parched mouth accepted greedily. He was then led back down the hall through another door and outside to the meat yard.

He began his daily ritual feeding the kelgan which first required him to retrieve meat from this bloody facility. The slaughter yard was surrounded by two stone walls with a gate, the mountain itself serving as the rear wall. A handful of guards armed with clubs paced about. Several stone slabs in the center of the yard served as work tables. Some prisoners were already at work in here. The cattle were brought in singly from the holding pen and killed by sledgehammer, which was chained to the rock wall for security. The carcasses were then chained to winches and pulled apart for the guards would not allow them the use of knives or saws. The prisoners had to make do almost without tools, sacking or boxing the meat in large chunks and salting them for preservation. All waste was brought to a huge burn pit in the far corner. The smell of this place could knock one down if he was unaccustomed to it and a nauseating residue dwelt ever in the mouths of the inhabitants, all but depriving them of taste. Damian bore it as best he could and made his way across the open yard to the stacked and stained bags of meat against the wall. He hoisted one of the heavy bags across his shoulder and walked back inside through the two doors he came through, down the corridors again, past the staircase which led back up to his cell, until he arrived at the double doors to the stable. Belósh had him specifically assigned here due to Damian's obvious connection and experience with animals and his skill as a rider. "You work here Ratarra," he remembers Belósh saying to him on his first day and he was thrown into the stable. 'Ratarra', he later learned, meant 'rider' in their tongue, and this became his name here. Only Cam knew his real name. Indeed he could understand the old Sloviad language fully, having been here so long and shouted at constantly.

Damian could hear the wailings of the kelgan in their cages anticipating their meal. Some guards threw open the heavy double doors for him and he stopped in front of the first cage, dropping the sack before his feet. There were fourteen cages in all in this extensive torch-lit chamber, seven on each side, each unit separated by a rock wall. Not all the cages were occupied all the time. The steed count could change from week to week depending on the needs of the errand riders and cattle drivers. This week there were only ten, less than usual. He began flinging chunks of meat from the bag into the cages, one by one, until he was out of meat. It usually took him three to four trips back and forth to feed them all depending how many there were, and he headed all the way back outside for another bag. The guards at either end of the room paid him little heed, bickering and joking at their posts or playing *suka,* a popular card and dice game. They left Ratarra to his task which he knew so well, only checking on him occasionally through the exiting portcullis at the westward end of the stable chamber. Through this portcullis, across from the stable was a guardhouse, well stocked and manned, for this was the main entry foyer to Khala prison, ready at all hours for the acceptance of guests or prisoners. Up the ramp from the guardhouse, northward a short distance, lay the main gate, another portcullis drawn by chains and pulleys. This arrangement facilitated quick release of the kelgan steeds, the stable being located in close proximity to the main gate. All traffic besides cattle entered through these two series of gates. Damian was the sole prisoner working the stable so this arrangement usually made him privy to new information. He was oftentimes the first to report any news of interest to the prisoners, but close as he was to the main entrance the view outside was blocked by the turn in the passageway.

Damian was finishing his first task, feeding the last of the beasts, making his way closer to the gate when an unexpected sound caught his attention. To his left, the last two cages on this side were empty as far as he knew, but something was definitely stirring uneasily in this last pen. Damian approached curiously and to his utter disbelief and surprise beheld a horse, very great, thoroughly black and fiery, untamed. The poor beast, without saddle or reins, was chained around the neck to the rock wall beside him and sprang in alarm at Damian's approach.

31

"Whoa, my friend," Damian whispered softly and stepped inside. The horse calmed somewhat, perhaps perceiving that this creature would not mistreat and abuse him so horribly as the others had. The horse's uneasiness and whinnying abated slowly as the young man approached. The horse, longing for amiable companionship, let him caress his forehead and then his flowing black mane. Damian's comforting, understanding presence and soothing words intoxicated the captive horse. Damian wondered why he was here and for what cruel purpose. He could not recall any guest of import arriving recently. Officers from afar would sometimes make visitation here for inspection. The horse must have been brought in by request on yesterday's livestock delivery and Damian sadly concluded that the he was probably going to be eaten at a feast or banquet for Kurg and his senior officers which they had as often as they could. Damian welcomed the change, however, and took great interest in his new friend. He brushed aside thoughts of its likely fate and tried to raise its spirits.

"I am a prisoner here too, my friend. I had a horse once. Can I call you Bish?" Damian stroked his neck. What he wouldn't give to ride this great steed, he thought, but without stirrups Damian doubted he could make the jump to mount him anyway. He couldn't recall ever seeing a horse this magnificent when he was a farmboy and it pained him to think that it would probably be dead or gone very soon. "Well, I imagine you'll want something to eat." Damian turned slowly and stepped out of the cell just in time to see Belósh and two other guards right in front of him. Damian was immediately knocked to the ground by a full feed bag which Belósh threw at him. The fearsome mog placed his huge green, clawed foot on Damian's chest as he lay prone, shaking with fear.

"This is for the pig. And don't bother making friends with him Ratarra, he'll be on the spit in a week," Belósh warned him, bringing his hideous, one-eyed face close to Damian's, his hot breath and fangs pressing on him. "Your only job is to keep him fat. Hurry up you slob, these kennels still need to be cleaned. Keep moving like a miserable snail and I'll shove this under your nails." He pulled out a long, curved knife. "I have ways of curing laziness." Belósh pulled him up by his dirty blond hair and shoved him against the wall before exiting with the other two.

Damian, shaking, picked up the bag of feed and applied it to the horse. Not for a moment doubting Belósh's threat, he quickly took leave of his new friend and immediately set to work cleaning the kennels. This messy task involved removing the waste and bones, all of which was brought outside to the burn pit in an emptied sack. At the end of each day the guards doused all the animal waste with oil and set fire to it. His work in the stable took about half his day, after which he went outside to resume work in the slaughterhouse, stacking meat in two different piles, a portion in the ready wagons for export, the rest against the inner wall for Khala's use, to be brought inside for storage. Later in the afternoon, after another water break, he again delivered meat to the stable for the evening feeding, one heavy cumbersome bag at a time. He joyfully reunited with the horse one last time for the day, filled him another feed bag from a barrel in the corner and took his leave. He received another water ration and some meat and bread for supper as he was thrown back into his cell, exhausted from work, his arms and back aching from the labor.

He sat in his cell, looking up at the stars as he often did. Dusk set in slowly and he felt the warm breeze. The weather in this southern, drier part of the world was very warm year round, fortunately, except for the summer which could be brutal, Khala being located in the hot barren lands. Even the nights were warm enough not to freeze the exposed prisoners, and it seldom rained. Damian remembered spending a few miserable nights, cold, rainy and sleepless a few years ago, and occasionally a sandstorm would blow through, but otherwise the weather was steady and predictable. The sun burned bright and hot in a clear sky overhead most of the time. There was nothing going on in the pit below him, thankfully. The guards went about their business as usual, pacing or occupying themselves with mundane tasks. His thoughts strayed to the doomed horse down below and what he overheard in the interrogation this morning. He couldn't wait to tell Cam. This was an unusual amount of news in one day.

Cam returned some time later. As before, Damian waited for the footsteps to recede before approaching the corner. He once again enacted the tapping code, and Cam acknowledged. They took their code very seriously and never failed to use it for the danger of informers was so great. Kurg liked to shuffle the prisoners around without warning, and he also had his plants. He'd prevented several major uprisings with the effective use of his informers. Many bones of past rebels still adorned the ground around the whipping post down in the pit. Miraculously, Damian and Cam had been kept here side by side their entire eight years here though many others had not. They checked to see that the guards above and below were not observing them.

"Cam you won't believe what turned up today," Damian said as loudly as he dared. "I was feeding the kelgan this morning and found a horse in one of the kennels."

"Just what we need to get out of here," replied Cam. "Do you know how long he'll be here?"

"Belósh said a week. Looks like the warden's having another banquet. I hope he doesn't have another 'guest of honor' like last time. Some poor fellow tried to take a swing at a guard with a pickaxe. The guard got too close, I guess. They chained this fellow's hands to the spit and burned them beyond recognition. I'll never forget the screams. Kurg himself later tied him to the stake and executed him. That's some pile of bones building up down there."

"Kurg keeps them there as a reminder," replied Cam. "Yeah I remember him, about two years ago, an Irendi named Mori. Worked in the mine, from Hera, wherever that is. He was moving in on Kunn territory in that city, so the story goes, a big seller of kuth weed and hyr to all the cities around, especially Bren, my hometown. Had a fair amount of influence with the underground there. Kunn scum told him to find another market, they were taking his buyers. Told him to move to Demar, up north. The gutsy fellow killed the lead thug right there before he was captured. He went down fighting. Most of the guards know better than to get too close to a slave with a tool. That's why they ball and chain their feet down there, and after that incident Kurg doubled the guard. That was a close call. With the way the Ahga takes care of him, it's no wonder he's so desperate to keep his job. If anyone escaped it would be Kurg's head on the stake down there. So what's this horse like?"

"He's without a doubt the greatest horse I've ever seen, here or when I was a kid on the farm. I don't think I could mount him if I tried. But that's not all. I overheard Belósh interrogating someone in the first cell this morning. He mentioned a missing chisel. Been gone for a while. Wants to know who's got it. He was holding the poor man up in the air by his throat. Belósh seemed pretty serious. Maybe it really is missing. Of course I got it for trying to listen. I was surprised they didn't throw me in there to join him."

"You know what that means," said Cam. "It's a matter of time before we're all drilled and the place scoured. Probably tomorrow. Been gone a while you say? That's not a good sign. I got a bad feeling something's about to happen. You're better off not knowing, it's safer. Otherwise you're considered an accomplice. We'd better stay sharp."

"Yeah, I'm scared. No one's ever escaped here as far as I know. I guarantee if someone did, we'd all pay. But I sure wouldn't begrudge the clever bastard."

"Anything's worth the risk as far as I'm concerned," replied Cam. "I can't take this pit much longer. I swear I'll either be dead or gone by my tenth anniversary. That's a promise."

"Agreed, and I'm going to take one if those vermin down with me when I go." Damian clenched his fists and gritted his teeth. He could never forgive or forget what the Kunn did to him and his family and vowed that if he ever did escape, the Kunn would pay. He felt the same way as Cam regarding his tenure and had been embracing the thought of death as a desirable alternative to this barbaric captivity. It would not be difficult to arrange, it was the attempting that held him back, some dogged will of self preservation uninterested in the suffering of the body. There were many times when Damian wished he had the strength to overcome that will.

Cam must have been thinking the same thing because his voice and tone changed, became more serious. "Damian, promise me if you ever get out of here you'll do something about these villains. I know if I can somehow manage it this bunch is going to pay. I swear I'd be the worst little menace these slugs ever had making their lives miserable, though it looks as if that could be put off permanently." Cam paused a moment and sighed as if contemplating the possible impending circumstances. "In the meantime, keep an eye on that horse."

Something about the way Cam said this made Damian uneasy, and he too had a foreboding feeling. Something stirred in Khala, for good or ill. Something felt like it was about to happen and Damian readied himself for it. He slept uneasily that night. Thoughts of impending torture and merciless interrogation kept him awake. The guards played mind games with the prisoners frequently, but if there really was a tool missing that would spell doom for them all.

* * *

Damian awoke to the horrible sounds of torture, whipping, beating and screaming. Certainly it was early in the morning, he felt like he'd hardly slept. The stars were still visible in the early dawn sky. The guards were conducting a mass interrogation and search of the camp, and started with everyone on this level. There was much commotion and noise, yelling, running of feet, and opening and closing of doors out in the hall just outside his cell. He could plainly make out Kurg's thundering voice, barking orders and beating the walls and doors in anger with his trunk-like fists. Kurg was definitely on a rampage. He must have received the news and set out without delay to attempt its resolution. Damian cowered in his cell in terror, shaking and sweating with fear, his heart pounding with anticipation and dread for he knew his time would come very soon. They were making their way down the hall, cell by cell, and to his horror he could finally hear them in Cam's cell, and his turn came. No, thought Damian, he's a tiny thing, have you no limits to your cruelty? Oh, will not someone or something halt this atrocity? He grabbed the bars of his cell and looked skyward longingly, searching for intervention but found none. Damian squirmed and clutched the bars in rage and fear as he bore witness to Cam's agony, the tears rolling down his lean, haggard face in torrents. He could not bear to let his friend suffer like this. The agony of helplessness writhed his body, he stomped, he panted, he beat the walls, he swore and tore his hair, then flung himself to the ground in terror when he beheld the one who he despised and feared the most, his solitary eye of pain and punishment bore into him like a brand: Belósh had come, and it was Damian's turn.

The whole camp was thrown into commotion and chaos that day, for word had spread like fire that the inconceivable had been accomplished: someone escaped. The rumor that the prisoner named Reese escaped was confirmed. The chisel was found, along with a mog corpse at the base of one of the watchtowers, apparently strangled with a length of broken chain. Several mounted kelgan had been dispatched but had not as yet returned. The daily ritual was postponed until the conclusion of the searches and questioning, and to complete Damian's horror all the prisoners were relocated, including himself. This was by far the worst punishment they could possibly exact on him. He was moved down to the second level, the tears running down his haggard face as he passed Cam's cell, probably for the last time. This time he inhabited the cell farthest east, closest to the smithy and just above the meat yard. Of his friend he heard nothing, and where he was or even whether he was alive was left to Damian to ponder in his new seclusion. He may never see him again. The familiar cutout in the rock wall just outside the bars they used for the transfer of acquired goods was not there, nor were his small rocks for shoot. Everything he had come to look forward to each day was removed, leaving a total loss and emptiness as Damian sat by the front corner of his cell, in the same relative position he sat in every night to communicate with his only friend. He placed his hand on the right side wall, the other side of which his friend since boyhood resided unseen, a faceless voice that became his source of sanity. But it was like placing his hand on a corpse–cold and lifeless, unresponsive. He shuddered and withdrew himself, wondering if he would ever see his friend again.

The rest of the day was spent in their cells, idle and lonely as the guards concluded their relocation of the prisoners. The morning meal was also postponed, and Damian was aching and bent with hunger by the time he was fed in the afternoon. They finally, to his great relief, released him to resume his task of feeding the kelgan, who also had not been fed. This would also mean he would receive his water ration at the well downstairs. His mouth was so dry he couldn't talk, but he was also eager to see the horse again if it was still there.

Damian was escorted into the stable, as usual, and when left immediately proceeded to the far end to check on Bish. The horse appeared very ill tempered and restless. His dislike of captivity and the kelgan so close, howling and gnarling, also ill tempered and hungry, was very evident. The horse, however, became very tranquil and sedate at Damian's presence. His temper subsided and he grew content, even relieved as he was slowly approached. The great horse allowed Damian to place his hand on his head and flanks. Damian himself found his mind at ease, his anguish abated. He was reminded of better times as his mind wandered, of his boyhood and his short life at a happy home, running along the stream, hunting in the groves or along the crags with his father, riding his old faithful horse freely on the shrubby hills. He felt not only the obvious connection with this unfortunate animal but also a need for the relief it brought him, and with his best and only friend gone, now more than ever the pain and sadness the death of this horse would bring weighed on him heavily. He begged and wished that somehow this doom would not come to pass and wearied his mind in vain for ways to prevent it. Then he cursed himself for being such a fool. After all, he himself was a helpless prisoner too. He could not save this horse any more than he could save himself. He leaned against the horse and sobbed.

CHAPTER 2
ESCAPE

The next day he was woken abruptly. Visions of his only friends disappearing forever dominated his dreams, and he was, as usual, very hungry and thirsty. But he learned to his horror that water rations were being withheld until someone came forward with information about the escaped prisoner, who was still at large. The kelgan hunting parties had returned empty-handed. Kurg was no doubt growing impatient and angry and the camp would feel the effects of his rising wrath. The daily ritual would continue as normal, no food or water was to be given until information was presented or the prisoner was found. Someone had to know something, Kurg insisted. The prisoners fell to their knees and begged, and the guards had to drag them out of their cells and beat them. Damian was brought downstairs and led immediately to stable first instead of the well. He panted and fell, looking longingly down the hall that led to the precious liquid he so badly craved. He clasped his face with thirst and would have cried if he had tears. He could only sob as he collapsed onto the floor. The guards gripped him fiercely and dragged his prostrate body through the double doors to the stable and kicked him in.

"Same workload Ratarra," one of them yelled. "We need strong kelgan to catch runaways. *Stalat uruz al-Medu* (we give for the Divine)." Damian heard them say this many times here. They closed the door with a clang.

Damian weakly pulled himself up and initially sought to feed his friend first. He filled the feed bag, and when the guards at the other end weren't looking, fed himself, knowing that this might also compromise not only his food ration for later, if there was one, but the horse's as well. The guards perceived the friendship between the two and would punish the horse for his missteps, Damian doubted not. This act of desperation was not fortunately observed, however, and he proceeded to feed the horse who awaited him and the food eagerly. As he entered Bish's kennel though, his hand was arrested, quite suddenly, by Belósh, who was waiting for him there.

"Oh no, Ratarra, no food for him either," said the tyrant and he yanked the bag out of Damian's hands and threw it across the floor, spilling it in full view of the hungry, chained animal, then he kicked Damian to the ground. "No food for the prisoners, and that includes the pig." He glared at Damian but the eyes that stared back at him were full of rage instead of terror and fear as they usually were. Damian's eyes grew darker and colder as the horse's angry thrashing and neighing tortured his ears. Damian picked up the feed bag, threw it in the barrel unused, and began his ritual of feeding the kelgan. Belósh laughed heartily as he watched Damian trudge away to the meat yard with anger. His plan delivered the intended effect.

Damian, bristling with wrath, threw the meat chunks into the kennels, cursing to himself. He continued to suffer with the horse's unabated whinnying and pulling of the chain in its fruitless attempts to free itself. Listening to his friend suffer tore his heart and he vowed to himself again that if he were to escape, he would see to it that no one or any fair beast would suffer like this again at the hands of another. He would shut down the Kunn and any who oppressed or tyrannized others. Whether there was a Creator or not, Damian would make it his life's mission to halt these horrendous injustices wherever they were to be found, to help the simple who were abused by the powerful, to even out the horrible odds in this world that seemed to favor the wicked, to fully rid the world of the unjust, whatever it took. That the peaceful many always suffered at the hands of the corrupt was a sickening reality he would attempt to change. The timid, broken, and forlorn soul within him was quickly waning and giving way to courage and determination. He entertained the possibility of escape. One prisoner had done it and thus far was successful. Perhaps escape was possible after all. But surely he thought he would have to take Cam with him, but how it was all to be accomplished he did not know.

He was finishing the afternoon feeding when he came across an overly large-sized bone in the meat sack he was working with. It was the size of a large club, the bloody leg bone of a slaughtered ox he guessed it was. He checked to see that the front gate guards were occupied and quickly hid the bone under some loose hay in Bish's cell. He had a feeling that would come in useful.

That night he was thrown into his cell without water or supper and immediately collapsed onto the floor with weakness. This intolerable thirst took its toll on him and he found himself almost wishing that the guards would discover the accomplice, if there was one, or that someone would come forward with information in order to lift the water ban. He crawled, exhausted and malnourished to the bars and looked west, onto the plain in the distance. It was another clear night but it brought him no comfort. Memories of the stream not far from his home tortured his mind, his breath came in gasps with visions of pools and wells and even the bitter Khala well water would have been more than welcome to him now. He tried diverting his thoughts, and instead focused his attention on the incoming supply wagons approaching in the distance. His view drifted along the watchtowers and their ever watchful sentinels, looking out onto the lonely road that wound its way out of sight in the west. He observed the execution stake down in the pit below, now closer that he was moved, and the many lit torches that were spread out along the inner, circular rock wall that illuminated the entire enclosure, the better to observe the emaciated, pitiful prisoners leaning on their bars, also looking inward idly. Damian looked across and beheld them, half starved creatures, clothed in filthy rags like himself, some near death, panting with weakness and hunger. Just then several Kunn riders galloped into the inlet, yelling and jeering, their weapons held high. Some yells of delight went up and the guards on the ground cheered. Something was happening down there and Damian watched closely, expecting the arrival of some guest, perhaps the Ahga himself, he thought. A guard below opened the main gate and ran inside, probably to alert Kurg of the mysterious news. The wagons rolled slowly into the enclosure surrounded by mounted, cheering guards. Damian watched and waited.

As the wagons pulled to a halt all the guards came running over, encircling one in particular with great interest and still more yelling and shouting. Damian wondered what could be so amusing and whether he wanted to know. Some moments later Kurg emerged from the front gate and approached with authority. The cheering subjects made way for him and he reached inside the wagon. He removed and held aloft the body of a man. The guards yelled and chanted as Kurg paraded it around the pit in full view of his encaged slaves. He held the body high and triumphantly in his mighty arm, and Damian recognized it as that of Reese. So, the prisoner has been retrieved, found dead from exhaustion and hunger by the wagon drivers. Poor Reese probably followed the road hoping to run into a traveler and beg for food. To Damian's horror he saw Reese's skeletal body and face, his mouth covered in grass and shrub stains, testament to his desperation. Damian felt sickened and angry by this disgusting display but felt too weak to crawl away. He leaned his head on the bars of his cell as utter hopelessness conquered him, for now was acknowledged the bitter truth: there would be no escape from this dungeon, that his life was reserved strictly for this punishment. He was singled out by fate for this purpose and this purpose only. The freedom that he had so come to crave, a virtue of life only a prisoner can fully appreciate, had cast its last dying light upon his withered soul. He purged himself of thoughts of escape and vengeance and justice and helping others, for such things would not be taking place. Those were just dreams, a yearning of the soul, but he henceforth decided to abandon these forever. They were not for him, only

Khala and a life of perpetual misery and forced servitude. Hope only served to engender perpetual disappointment; without such perhaps some acceptance would finally arise, he thought. And still the guards cheered outside.

He ultimately resolved to somehow find a permanent exit from this world, but letting his hands fall he felt a strange sensation as his hands slid down the bars, some foreign object that immediately alerted his attention and interest. Prisoners are constantly on the lookout for anything out of the routine, however minute, and will take in it a keen interest and even a pleasure, having little else to demand their attention. He scrutinized this object more closely and it appeared to be some kind of cloth that had been tied around one of the bars of his cell. He could not account for it being there, it certainly wasn't there earlier, and he concluded that his present fatigue and preoccupation prevented his observing it. He quickly untied it and opened it, and there, written in what appeared to be coal or some dark, gritty substance, were scratched a few strange words: MEET ME IN STABLE. What on earth can this mean, thought Damian and he repeated the message to himself. Then his heart leaped. Cam, that slippery little worm must have emerged from some tiny, overlooked, crack in the earth again and somehow spawned right in front of his cell. He's the only one that could have done this, Damian felt sure. His pace quickened, his hope rekindled, a light and fire in his eyes ignited. He suddenly felt more invigorated then ever before, the energy surged through him as a mixture of terror and excitement took hold. Yes, Cam must have some escape plan, Cam the pickpocket, Cam who walks and stalks unseen, Cam that cunning little phantom somehow managed the impossible. Feelings of hunger and thirst were immediately forgotten and he clutched the dirty cloth and held it close like a treasure. Yes, thought Damian, it was time.

That night, to Damian's relief, the prisoners were marched downstairs by level and allowed their water and bread ration. Damian felt sure it was only because Kurg was returning to business tomorrow and expected production now that the disaster was averted, otherwise he would have happily left the miserable back-stabbing rats to die of thirst in their cages. He could spare them, replacement slaves were readily available. The Ahga always had victims that he had no use for. Service at Khala was a fitting reward for those who opposed him, enemies or rival clan members, and a good riddance. Why not only would they no longer be a nuisance, their belligerence would be made to fill the pockets of the Kunn with gold. He was proud of Khala's reputation as inescapable, a place to be feared, a bargaining chip to acquire what goods the Ahga demanded from those he chose to coerce. But those who were sent to Khala rarely returned, unless the detained perhaps had a change of heart, deciding finally to acknowledge the wisdom of the great one they once rebelled against. Kurg intended to uphold Khala's prestigious title and reputation, somewhat out of fear, but mostly to profit from the favor of the one he served. His standing with the Ahga and the Kunn was very high, and he received bonuses frequently for his unsurpassed detainment efficiency and better than satisfactory production levels. The recapture of the escapee brought him not a little relief, and he hoped it would go unreported.

When Damian reached the well he was the only one among the line of starved with a half distracted look on his face, as if he was somewhat hopeful about something and too preoccupied to care much about his overpowering thirst. His physical debilitations seemed to have little effect on him at the present, or perhaps there was aught which marginalized these bodily encumbrances. No one noticed the strangely content prisoner, however, and Damian gulped down his bowl thankfully, taking his fill with the rest, took his supper, and returned to his cell.

He spent the night upright and tense, his heart racing with anticipation. He didn't know exactly what was going to happen or when, but felt it must be soon, perhaps tomorrow. He put all thoughts of punishment aside, if their plan was foiled and they were caught, and resolved that a chance to escape was well worth whatever torture they would receive after. He had nothing else to live for anyway, nothing to lose, but he also knew that he and Cam would only have one chance, there would not be another. After what they would do to their bodies if caught, escape again would be a physical impossibility. He thought of the maimed prisoner at the well. Damian shuddered, took a deep breath, and set his will to attempting it, whatever happened after.

The next morning the guards were a little surprised to find Ratarra up and for once eagerly awaiting his labor for the day. They shoved a small loaf in his gut, pulled him out and marched him downstairs again for water, then to the stable to commence the day's service. Damian's anticipation and excitement grew as he approached the stable entrance. He successfully restrained a burning desire to rush in and find his friend, and upon entering proceeded, somewhat distractedly, with his daily ritual. As usual he filled the feed bag for Bish, who to his shame he had somewhat forgotten about, thinking only of Cam and what possible scheme he could be up to. He carried the bag to the far end where the horse's kennel was with a feeling of intense curiosity, but also dread. He half expected the kennel to be empty and the appetites of the guards well satisfied from the prize, but lo, to his relief, there was the horse. Damian restrained a gasp for the guards were just outside the stable gate to his right. Then he did actually jump for he heard a hiss in his ear and turned to see Belósh's hideous face pressed up against the gate bars.

"Give the pig his last feeding Ratarra," he growled. "His banquet's tonight. He'll be feeding some big boss from Mod, one of the Baccád. He's on his way." Belósh looked at the horse and chuckled, licking his lips, then walked up the ramp to the front gate.

Now Damian was truly afraid and shook from limb to limb. It seemed Bish had less time to live than they thought. He thought he had at least three more days. Whatever stunt they were going to pull, it better happen soon or they'd be walking out of here. Where was Cam? Damian wished there was some way to contact him, but Damian didn't even know where he was. If Cam left another message tonight it would be too late. He swallowed hard, digesting this untimely information and approached the kennel with mounting anticipation and newly heightened fear. A horse may not arrive here again for a year as far as he knew, and it looked like he may just be waiting that long for another one. He slowly entered the kennel expecting a surprise of some kind but found nothing out of the ordinary. He searched the walls and floor for a message or weapon but found none. His hope ebbed momentarily but he fed the horse and checked to see that the bone was still stashed in the near corner, then he went about feeding the kelgan. He made his trips back and forth to the slaughterhouse and performed the necessary cleaning tasks, constantly alert for some surprise from Cam, but alas, still nothing. Then he remembered that Cam's shift started later than his. After midday he went out to work in the slaughteryard which was backlogged with work from the inactivity of the day before. He spent the afternoon collecting and bagging the meat, the whole time thinking of Cam and what he could possibly be up to.

That afternoon in the meat yard, when the labor of the prisoners was intense and consuming, and the guards were nearing the end of the daytime shift and therefore less alert, no one had presence of mind to notice a small figure drop from a tiny hole in the rock wall above the burn pit in the far corner, a hole no one ever recalled seeing before, and like a cat the figure quickly crawled out of sight.

Damian finished his shift outside and was just about to head back in with meat for the kelgan evening meal when he heard a hornblast from the watchtower heralding an arrival of some kind, supplies or cattle, a guard relief detachment, or maybe even a few new slaves. Damian quickly brought his load inside, his heart pounding with fear. He didn't know what guests or goods just arrived but he had a good idea. Belósh was probably right. It was getting late and time was growing short. That horse they needed so desperately wouldn't be there much longer. He quaked with intolerable anxiety.

43

He was on his third or fourth trip inside, practically running each time to the bewilderment of the guards, when, with a fresh bag of meat over his shoulder, he heard a voice. He thought someone whispered his name so he paused and quickly looked around. There was no one in the stable but him, the guards he could hear arguing just outside the front gate around the corner, probably over the delivery or whatever it was. Damian took another step and heard it again and stopped. He looked around again, even upwards, but still saw no one. He stood for a moment befuddled, then the sack he was carrying began to shake of its own accord.

"Damian, I'm in here."

"Cam!" he recognized the voice of his friend.

"Shh! Get us over to the horse quick." Damian hustled into Bish's cell with Cam over his shoulder. The horse sensed the newcomer and pulled at his chain uneasily. Damian quickly set him down and untied the bag, looking over his shoulder and expecting to see Belósh again, glaring at him from behind.

The two beheld each other for the very first time in all their eight years together, but they needed no introduction. They immediately recognized each other as the desperate, suffering, captive brothers they were, and clasped in a moment of joy and fear, excitement and terror, like two brothers reuniting after years of forced separation with escape or painful death just moments away. They regarded each other momentarily: Cam, a filthy, skinny little thing with dark hair and eyes, lucky to be four and a half feet tall, and Damian, a full six feet tall, or would be if his back wasn't bowed from hunger and labor, dirty blond, equally filthy with animal blood covering what rags he had left, smelling of excrement. The circumstances allowed little delay, however, and the two hastily and quietly oriented themselves.

"How did you find me?" asked Damian, unable to ever figure how Cam did anything.

"Easy, you're always looking at the stars. I could see you from my hole. It took me four months to dig it. Your new cell is right across from it and I was able to climb over there and leave you the message."

"Well you finished just in time," said Damian. "This horse is going to be on the spit tonight. Some leader or boss just showed up."

"How fitting," replied Cam. "Maybe we'll get to run him over on the way out." He chuckled at the prospect.

"If we make it. There's three guards right around the corner. Maybe you should have left on your own."

"I couldn't. I need a ride. Plus some help with those three villains. I think you could help me with that. Besides, I'm not leaving without you."

"We don't have any food." Damian already felt weakened with hunger. "We'll just have to trust to luck."

"And we can't get caught. One chance is all we've got."

"Well I'm not sticking around here regardless," Damian resolved, plucking up courage. "I know you feel the same."

"Agreed. We can do this." Cam was itching to go and flexing his fingers.

"Well, what's our plan?" The two quickly organized a risky and dangerous breakout which called for luring the guards in and eliminating them. They only needed the first gate opened. The front main gate could be opened from the inside. There were at least three guards in the foyer and they would need all their strength and speed, not to mention surprise and luck, to eliminate them before any reinforcements arrived. There were more guards outside in the pit yard. And both gates would have to be disabled to delay the release of the inevitable kelgan pursuit if they were to get anywhere. It was definitely a desperate longshot, a plan with little chance of success, but nothing was going to stop them from trying it. If they could just pull it off fast enough...

"Ratarra!" called one of the guards from behind the gate. It had been some moments since they had seen him working, and they knew he wasn't done yet. The guard looked around into the stable for a moment and unlocked the gate with his keys and entered.

"Ratarra you slug!" he called and paced the stable room. "If you're so much as sitting down I'll string you up in the pit tonight! We'll have some entertainment for our guest. Azag loves that stuff. You'll be one miserable rat tonight! Ratarra!"

Damian's heart was racing and beating so loudly he thought the guard would hear it. He watched the fearsome Mogoli of the Kunn from inside Bish's cell with anger in his eyes, knowing what was about to befall him. This was the same guard that ate Damian's food tauntingly while he suffered his atonement years ago. Damian could never forget the anguish he felt being strung and the jubilant look in this tormentor's face in his moment of pain and humiliation. Damian stepped just outside the cell and in view, leaning on the rock partition. *Your time has come at last*, he thought.

"Ratarra!" called the guard with rising impatience and fury. He was about to assemble some friends to search for the filthy stable rat when he noticed Damian standing stone-still just outside the last cell with an obstinate look that infuriated him even more. Why, the rat was actually *leaning* against the wall. The mog pulled out his whip with a crack and lunged for Damian, who backed into the cell and out of sight.

"You want to play games Ratarra? We'll play games alright! We'll play games until you're nothing but a bloody mess! Come here you little snake!" The mog jumped inside the cell and raised his whip at Damian who was just to the left of him, but another voice to the rear of the cell, behind the horse, caught his attention and he turned to look. Damian wasted no time breaking the ox bone over his unhelmeted head with a crack. The mog fell dead without a sound.

"Need some help, Barag?" called one of the guards from beyond the still open gate. They could not have failed to hear the shouting of their companion and endeavored to help him. "Ratarra playing games again? I'm in the mood for some sport. I'll hold him down for you! Come on, Zerga!" he called to the others, "Looks like Ratarra's slouching. Get Rigash too!" he laughed.

"Quick!" said Cam, just above a whisper. He grabbed the keys from the dead mog while Damian armed himself with his sword. Cam unlocked the horse's chain.

The first guard rounded the corner with a whip but his laugh vanished as he was brutally trampled by an angry charging horse. Bish, wild with freedom, passed through the first gate and into the foyer, followed by Damian brandishing his sword. Cam immediately closed the stable gate behind him and attempted to lock it. Zerga and Rigash ran down the ramp from the main gate they just opened and were knocked over suddenly by a horse they certainly weren't expecting. Bish galloped up the ramp to the open gate in full view of his freedom but stopped, as if perceiving his master's need, and with incredible force of will he actually waited, even at the risk of losing his freedom that was so close. He yearned for it desperately but his will held and he turned back, just inside the gate for his friends. Damian slashed Zerga across the shoulders as he was trying to stand up and he yelled in pain, but Rigash was up.

"RATARRA!" he yelled and aimed a spear thrust at Damian who dodged and used the big mog's momentum to throw him against the stone wall. Rigash growled and spun around but Damian came down with the sword and buried it in his chest. The intensity of the moment drove Damian to incredible strength. His weakness seemed to have departed.

"Damian, look out!" yelled Cam, still fumbling with the stable gate. Damian spun around to face Zerga who got up and threw his club at Damian, hitting him on the side of his head. Damian cried out and felt the blood ooze down his neck but what he saw next filled him with even greater terror. Another mog, and especially large and cruel one, emerged from the guardhouse across the stable gate with a short stabbing spear. It was Belósh, and he was right behind Cam.

"CAM!" yelled Damian. Cam was just finishing with the lock on the gate, a vital part of their plan for they would not get far being chased by kelgan if they made it out. The threat of mounted pursuit had to be neutralized, but Cam, being occupied, was unaware of his serious danger.

Belósh shoved his spear into Cam's gut as he turned around. Cam yelped and slowly crumpled to the floor.

"NO!" screamed Damian. More then enraged and with even greater desperation he dodged a blow from Zerga and beheaded him with a swing that would have felled a young mona tree in one stroke. Belósh placed his foot on Cam who groaned and twisted with pain, removed his spear and charged up the stone ramp at Damian with a hideous yell, half of anger, half delight. Ratarra would meet his end here for pulling such a stunt and slaying his friends. He had endured this stable rat long enough. With tears of anger running down his bloody face, Damian dropped his sword and yanked the spear from Rigash's cold, lifeless hands. With a yell of rage Damian gave the spear a mighty heave. It sailed a short distance through the air and exploded through the chest of the detested tyrant. Belósh fell backwards down the ramp and landed in a heap at the bottom.

"Bish!" yelled Damian as he ran desperately to Cam's side at the bottom of the ramp. The horse obeyed and knelt beside Cam's prostrate body. Damian picked him up carefully but quickly and placed him on the horse in front. He could hear guards yelling outside the front gate: an alarm went up. The skirmish in the foyer had not gone unnoticed and was being investigated. Damian ran a short way, grabbed the sword again in his right hand and with his left grabbed the chain around Bish's neck, and with his last remaining strength, swung himself onto the great horse. The figure of a guard stood upon the threshold. He beheld the carnage and gave a shout. They could now hear alarm horns sounding in rapid succession and a rushing of booted feet outside. Now Bish really panicked and sped up the ramp, running down the lone guard on the threshold, and with his sword Damian swung and struck the catch that suspended the portcullis which then fell behind him with a crash. They were outside now and the only thing between them and escape was a handful of Khala guards in the pit charging at them. It was then that Damian realized he must have dropped his sword back at the gate. But it was of little matter. Bish, tasting his freedom at last, galloped wildly out of the gate, heedless of the oncoming assailants and the flying darts and spears they were hurling at him, and sped like an arrow out of the inlet, past the watchtowers, and onto the hard plain beyond. Damian, breathless and exhausted, lay flat on top of Cam, clutching the horse's chain for his life.

* * *

Bish sped across the plain for about an hour, without direction or destination. They didn't know it but they were headed northwest, crossing the Govan Wastes and beyond sight and reach of the suburb of Bardua, now about fifty miles directly south of their current position. The Khala road, which they left behind them, dipped southwards toward the desert city of Mod and its satellites and was long since out of sight. Damian, exhausted, held on as best he could with Cam, mortally wounded, in front. They heard no sound of pursuit yet but with the stable gate locked and the main portcullis closed and no one behind to man it they knew it would be a while before Kurg could release his kelgan. Cam was fading in and out of consciousness and it wasn't long before Damian also noticed Bish had slowed his pace somewhat. He became concerned for the horse and looked up for the first time since they fled. Damian had energy and presence of mind only to hang onto the chain for dear life with his eyes closed tightly out of fear. He rubbed his eyes clear and gazed about him. The land was very flat and barren, dotted occasionally with low rock rises and scant shrubs and grasses. Patches of sand and dust were spread across the dreary landscape, increasing in abundance further to the south. All of the Govannum was laid out before him in its emptiness and desolation. Some carrion fowl were circling in the distance to his left. The stars and full moon were soon becoming visible as dusk drew nearer and an unfriendly twilight set in. Damian couldn't see any sign of traffic or even a road for that matter, not even a river or mark to steer by that showed any sign of promise. His happiness of freedom was greatly offset by feelings of fear–fear of survival, fear of the open world he was just now experiencing for the first time in years, and grave concern for his friend who lay motionless and dying in front of him. Even Bish was causing him doubt. Certainly the horse was showing difficulty running and he seemed to be having difficulty breathing as well. Cam had been unconscious now for a while and Damian decided the time had come to risk a brief halt.

He brought the horse to a slow, clumsy stop and dismounted. The horse was coughing and staggering. He placed his hand around the horse's neck in a gesture of affection for his friend and it was then that he discovered a dart or bolt lodged in deeply, possibly in the horse's throat. Cam's own blood had coated a significant portion of the horse's neck keeping Damian ignorant of the wound. Bish stumbled and lowered himself. Damian felt a surge of panic watching the horse fall but before Bish fully succumbed he quickly but carefully pulled Cam off and placed him on the ground, his small frame weighing heavily and lifeless in his fatigued arms. Bish laid himself fully on the ground beside Cam and continued to cough blood and sputter. Damian felt the tears coming as he tried to comfort the horse. "I knew you'd wait for me," he said sadly, then checked on Cam, turning from one dying friend to another. He couldn't believe this misfortune, to be losing both his friends like this at a time when he needed them most. They had helped him achieve his freedom only to be denied it themselves. He scanned the barren miles and darkening horizons in fear. Not only were his friends gone, he was hopelessly lost without the faintest idea which direction any kind of civilization lay. His youth had been robbed and knowledge of the world with it. Kurg will have begun his hunt by now and it will only be a short time before he was caught and dragged back to that accursed hellhole. There, they would perform unspeakable acts of punishment on him and there would be no escaping again. He could only imagine what the prisoners there were already suffering at the hands of an angry Kurg due to his escape. Soon he would be returned to them for his plight was utterly hopeless now. He had finally stepped on the threshold of life only to have it taken away yet again. He didn't bother to plea to the stars for help. They had abandoned him at the end and from them he would seek no further consolation. Instead he crawled away, clutching his stomach with hunger, choked with tears, overthrown by exhaustion and despair. His last breath of faith was spent at last, crushed under the foot of fate and prolonged dejection and was now withered and lifeless. With his one last ounce of energy he found vent to utter the words *help me*, then collapsed into a white mist.

He woke immediately, he thought, though he may have been unconscious for a while. He couldn't tell. He found himself surrounded by a white light that flowed about him like a mist, though deep night had set in beyond. He looked up puzzled, then felt himself being lifted effortlessly from the rocky floor, as if he had no weight. All feelings of hunger, pain, and fear were forgotten. Only peace and tranquility seemed to exist in this strange and wonderful place enveloping him in its sphere. He wondered where he was and if he was dreaming and where his friends were, for they were nowhere in sight, but then these thoughts became irrelevant when he saw a brighter light approaching him. He felt himself pulled toward this brilliant light which seemed to emanate peace and vast energy, but also understanding. He felt as though this presence had an intimate familiarity with him and was aware of his past hardships, and that they did not go unnoticed. He saw the light shower him with brilliance and felt it flow through his emaciated body like water, fulfilling him, restoring him, empowering him. He felt an energy course through his body. All his cares and pains seemed to be washing away and he felt cleansed and new as the energy repaired him and gave him incredible new life. He felt himself stronger, much stronger, invigorated, confident and more capable and fearless than he could have even imagined. He felt as though he would burst with energy and life as he floated in the presence of this wonderful light. The experience was unbelievable. Presently he perceived the completion of this indescribable renewal. He was placed gently upright on the ground after his cleansing and the light withdrew itself from him slowly. The transformation was complete. But Damian felt the light had left behind a part of itself in him and was not wholly gone, as if some piece of energy and power remained though the rest had withdrawn. The light lingered for a moment, as if regarding Damian before leaving, imparting a wordless message of a thousand sensations, and started to fade as if in farewell. Damian beheld the light with awe and eternal gratitude as tears of understanding and thankfulness swelled his eyes, his faith renewed. He followed this presence with outstretched hands, reluctant for it to leave, and saw behind it in the distance two familiar figures running toward him through the receding mist as if in slow motion. Damian couldn't believe his tear-filled eyes, for there could be no mistake that there indeed, as though they were freely given gifts, were none other than his best friend Cam and his loyal, courageous horse Bish, both likewise restored and cleansed, running to him in the distance. The three clasped with joy and disbelief, then turned to regard the light with happiness and gratitude. A moment later the light and mist vanished, melting imperceptibly into the clear night sky, leaving behind only a bright star in the horizon. The dark, empty plain lay motionless and quiet about them and the warm night breeze was stirring, just as before. They felt as if they were in a dream and had awoken, refreshed.

The two friends gazed at the sky for some moments, blinking in speechless awe. Neither could describe what happened. Then they regarded themselves and each other as if trying to convince themselves of the wonder. Yes, there could be no doubt, for their physical appearance changed greatly as a result of the strange experience. They were cleansed and clothed for one thing. Their filthy rags were replaced with simple clothes; Damian wore a black laced tunic over a simple white shirt, black pants and light, black boots; Cam wore loose khaki pants with a dark brown sleeveless shirt and soft shoes of leather. They both stood upright and strong for a change instead of half bowed as before. Cam had a fire in his eyes that begged action and felt an explosive strength and speed that he had trouble holding in check. He looked as if he was ready to pounce on something. Indeed he felt as though he could leap onto a high precipice or swing from high trees and would if there only was one near at hand for him to subdue. Damian stood tall and strong to his full height, his body musculature well exceeding normal capacity, and his eyes had a stern, focused gaze, full of purpose, completely purged of any previous fear and timidity. The look they now bore was fearless and determined, but also held a memory of a great sadness, an injustice suffered. His young boyish features, which prolonged captivity and malnourishment prevented from developing, were replaced with full maturity in body and wisdom in his eyes that belied his mere twenty years. In fact they both looked somewhat older and wiser for their age, more fair and fell to behold and ready to burst with energy. It was with some difficulty that they recognized one another.

Their broken bodies had been replaced with newer, far more potent ones, possessing seemingly unearthly capabilities. But their memories remained unchanged. For many minutes they could say nothing.

"Well Cam, looks like we have another chance to finish what we started," said Damian finally in a voice he almost didn't recognize. The voice he now spoke with was unhindered by fear and desperation, deep and clear. "Let's not waste a moment." He hopped lightly onto Bish, whose chain had been replaced with light reins. But he still had no saddle or stirrups. "The Kunn has a new enemy," he declared and clenched his fists. "No one will suffer at their hands again. They must be stopped."

"That's what I was hoping you'd say," said Cam with a smile, relishing the thought of action against those villains. He ran a few steps and flipped into the air and after several somersaults landed squarely on the back of the great black horse. Damian, however, was not surprised by this impressive display of acrobatics. They both felt greatly empowered.

"We need knowledge and armament first, in order to achieve this goal. Run, Bish!" Damian yelled. "Follow that star!" The two riders leaned low and braced themselves. Bish reared and neighed and sped off like an arrow, following the star in the northwest. The night rushed past them quickly and the wind was in their hair. They looked ahead eagerly, a light was in their eyes, the joy of freedom and purpose on their smile. But they also couldn't forget the severe hardships they had suffered. The memory of their cruel captivity ached them like a deep wound that would never heal. Damian's purpose and will were set. The blessing and gifts that he had just received were to him confirmation of this objective, and charge to pursue it. He was now on a lifelong quest to fulfill his vows of justice and rid the world of this evil organization, however long it took. Memories of the atrocities inflicted upon him and his family at the hands of these villains drove him to ride even harder as the night flew by.

CHAPTER 3
A RESISTANCE CONCEIVED

Just at daybreak, following the star, they arrived at a river flowing southwestwards. The land had changed considerably during their journey. They were unaware that they had traveled well over sixty miles in a single night, because of the great speed of the horse or the strange experience, they didn't know, and the dry barren lands seemed to be well behind them. The light revealed a land that was less dusty and hard but became more grassy and hospitable, with a thin graduating layer of low, deciduous trees, among them date and palm groves, gini stalks, and thick, lush, fruit-bearing shrubs spread out before them, foliage and land features indigenous to these semi-tropical and arid regions of this part of the world. The groves and reeds increased in density and vitality to the north and west. The dry, cracked, rocky plains and dunes of the Govannum eased into an arable region. They had come to the muddy and rocky banks of the Ella River and reined their horse to a halt. This river flowed through the outskirts of the great Palmwood to the north, originating in the Ash Mountains beyond. On the northern bank the land was more thickly forested and fertile. It also became less flat and the low, rolling, hillsides before them were covered in thick, tall grasses and wildflowers. It was as if they had left a world of desolation and hopelessness behind them and stepped on the threshold of fertility and life, and they looked upon it with wonder. This land had a familiar feel to Damian, bringing memories of home to mind, the smell of the grassy breeze along the river and the forgotten flowers stirring his memory. Even the broad leaves on the palm trees, stirring in the morning breeze, held their attention for such things had been forgotten.

They turned their focus to the river that they had to cross and sought for a low point to ford it. They found a suitable place further north where the river seemed to thin to less than a hundred feet across and forded here. The cool water felt refreshing and cleansing and they took pleasure in its forgotten touch and felt an indescribable appreciation for it. They spent a moment drinking and basking in the precious liquid that was denied them so long, that not long ago they would have done anything to get. Never again would they take such a vital necessity for granted. Even Bish gulped and splashed as he crossed.

They reached the other side and climbed up a low, grassy hill, at the top of which they beheld a village not a half mile below them. Damian halted a moment and peered more closely. There could be no mistaking the place even though it had been eight years.

"Tirien," he muttered to himself, and he looked up at the star which then disappeared. He didn't know what else to say, for this village bore memories for him both great and sad. He was reminded of his father, mother, and sister, and filled with a desire to find them and perhaps learn their fate he quickly approached the village below.

Tirien was a small but busy farming town, consisting mostly of the presiding farmers and their large tracts of land to the east used for the production of crops, meat and dairy, and the village main square to the west of town. This area, which they approached curiously, was where most of the crops and goods were brought for wholesale distribution. Buyers would come from Felbruk mostly and from there it was shipped to the city—Hera, Gyla, and even Prova on the coast some seventy miles away. Demand for food in these vibrant cities was very high so the small village market of even Tirien was fairly busy most of the time, especially during the harvest. During this time travelers would have difficulty finding lodging and would be compelled to stay with anyone who would take them, but for most of the year the several inns this small frontier town had sufficed. Damian and Cam found themselves in the village square in the heart of the busy season. The main road through the market was clogged with wagons, horses, strange steeds of burden they had never seen, and folk bustling about on business, running in and out of the many closely placed buildings, shops, and storehouses. These were built of either wood or lashed cane stalk, or else beam-reinforced clay or stone and roofed with the broad, dried leaves of the trees and plants of the region, or wooden shingles. The buildings were low, reaching only one or two stories. Barrels were being rolled down ramps of large storage bays, crates of foodstuffs were being stacked onto wagons or near the road for pickup: nuts, figs, dates, fruits and vegetables of all kinds indigenous to the hot southern hemisphere of this world. Laborers carried boxes and crates of spices, meats and skins. Robed, important-looking merchantmen were haggling. Milk wagons pulled in drawn by yoked beasts of burden. Deliveries were coming down the road to the east where the many farms were located, dotting the fertile, rolling hillsides in the near distance. Everything seemed to be making its way to this focal point from east and west. The weather and climate was warm in these southern parts and the year had brought abundant crops, so the farmers here were expecting good business.

Damian and Cam pulled into the village square on the road and stared about them for some moments in the middle of the commotion, trying to ingest this strange civility and make some sense of their first interactive experience with free people since their escape. The preoccupied, however, took little notice of the mounted strangers. Folk of Tirien were accustomed to travelers and foreigners, having residence near the frontier. The fugitives were about to inquire of some news and information from one of the locals when suddenly a yell went up from further down the road, suggesting fear or danger. To the west they thought it came from. The business and activity ceased momentarily and all eyes turned westward. Cam could hear galloping in the distance, approaching quickly, but the trees in the direction and the bend in the dirt road to the left prevented them from seeing what it might be.

"Horses don't gallop like that," said Cam. "Only kelgan make those footfalls. But there aren't too many of them." Suddenly around the bend in the distance six mounted riders emerged and approached the village square. They appeared to be of the Mogoli and Turuk race. They were armed with curved swords and wore thick leather armor. They rode into town in full view of the timid onlookers, riding not so much quickly as proudly and brazenly, apparently with the intent to intimidate and subjugate as they rode through the now silent and still market. The villagers beheld them with fear and anger, some even retreated out of sight. Damian and Cam could hear the murmurs of the nervous onlookers as they watched the dusty riders approach.

"It's those villains again," said one.

"What can they want this time?" said another. "They're going to drive the business right out of here with their constant demands. Don't they have enough money to take care of themselves?"

"Cursed highway robbers and gangsters, that's what they are," said a milkman nearby. "They're the warlords of Blado, come back from the dead. They don't come by here often but if you don't give them what they want, they'll kill you or worse. You mostly see them in the desert cities to the south from what I've heard, but they're making their way up here." They all watched the riders in fear as they rode by, eyeing the villagers with disdain. Damian recognized the head and armbands at once and he tightened his grip on the reins. Here indeed were riders of the Kunn.

"They burned a family's home a couple years ago when they wouldn't give them money," said a crop salesman, "and killed a farmer and took his boy when he wouldn't let out any of his harvest a number of years ago. No one's seen him since." Damian could feel the tears coming at this remark. He had little wonder of whom he referred.

"Yeah, and his wife and little girl," said a milk vendor, "probably taken as prisoners or something. Don't know what was so important they had to have from them, or what brought them this way. We didn't have these problems when Karius reigned." The riders rode past, continuing up the road eastward towards the farmsteads in the distance. "I don't know what they're up to this time but it can't be good."

"I hear they're good for business in the cities," said a butcher in front of his shop, "but it comes at a price. If you cross these fellows it may be the last thing you do. You're better off paying up."

"I don't care what the Herites say," said the salesman, "or the scum from Mod. These Kunn are villains, whatever supposed prosperity they bring to these parts. They're in it for their own purposes. They've turned into a bunch of warlords and thieves, overrunning the realm in its state of decline. They have so much power and influence they take as they please, and the Guard won't touch them. Who knows how many unfortunate folks have had the privilege of their cruelty."

"And none shall have it again," declared Damian and the onlookers regarded him with a look of surprise and new awe. Who were these fair strangers making such a declaration? More rogues and troublemakers, they thought, just what we need, and they looked doubtfully at Damian and his smaller but fearsome companion who had held themselves reservedly long enough. Damian and Cam watched the clan thugs ride through with rage in their eyes and the sight of these malicious extortionists in Damian's hometown, presumably with the same purpose or worse, stirred the already vengeful emotions within them. If these thugs thought they were going to commit some similar atrocity here they were about to discover otherwise, even if everyone else stood by and watched. Save for some independent men-at-arms at the service of the merchants, few seemed to have much for weapons or were disinclined to use them, Damian noticed, and neither did they for that matter, but that wasn't going to stop him. He called to Bish and they bolted after the now distant riders. The townspeople abruptly made way for the great steed and shook their heads in wonder.

The clan riders picked up their pace once they passed the square and continued east down the main road. The land here was slightly hilly and mostly open and grassy, with treelines spread here and there and lining parts of the dirt road. This bent occasionally left or right but held its main course east, toward the far edges of town. They passed several roads and lanes to either side which led to private farms and smaller residences. Damian kept some distance back from the party and could see them finally turn left down a lane not far ahead.

"Looks like they're heading for that one," Cam said, pointing to a lone farmstead at the end of an extensive, winding lane. A low stone wall, they could see, had been built near the house on the southern side. A large herd of cattle was visible grazing on the wide hillside beyond the house and barn. They had a good view of the settlement and its layout from their position, halted at the turn. They could see the riders pulling into the front yard of the ranch establishment.

"Bish, wait here," said Damian, and he pulled the horse off the road behind some trees after they dismounted. They stole through the small patch of trees and brush noiselessly, making their way quickly to the stone wall to the right of the lane.

"I'll break off," whispered Cam. "Meet you up there." Like a squirrel he sped nimbly and silently off to the left, seeking to flank them. He crossed the lane and made his approach from behind. The Kunn riders had dismounted and were casing the area. They had weapons drawn and were calling someone's name, evidently searching for someone.

Damian quickly searched the ground and found a suitable branch with which to arm himself and crouched behind the stone wall. He could see one of the thugs on the front deck of the house, pinning someone up against the adobe brick wall with a sword to his neck, questioning him. It seems they found who they sought. Damian could hear every word, he was not even a stone's throw away. The mog was using the common tongue of the realm, forcefully grilling the farmer who was shaking and struggling under the grip of the fearsome questioner. The other five riders stood somewhat apart on guard, swords drawn, waiting.

"Where is he, Malik?" demanded the clan leader, pressing the man against the wall. Malik was a slender, older farmer, dirty from work and unarmed, probably by choice. Resistance to the Kunn was widely considered not worth the risk by these people. The Kunn was not something anyone wanted as an enemy, for revenge would be swift and certain. There would be no place to hide from them if one defied them.

"You were friends with that backstabbing thief, Malik," the questioner continued. "You should know better than to associate with fugitives of the Kunn, especially this one. After the stunt he pulled every bounty hunter in Nadea is on the hunt. Of course you're a useless two-faced liar like him yourself. I'd love to be rid of your stench. You were part of his network. Where have you put him? Where's he hiding?" He pressed his sword close to the terrified farmer's throat, drawing some blood. "Is he here?" Malik shook and gasped and murmured something inaudible. "That so?" the mog replied. "He lives down the road you say? You're probably lying. A poor old fool like yourself may keep him hidden right here. He's got money. Search the area!" he yelled to his troop.

Damian picked up a stone the size of his head that he found lying at the bottom of the rock wall. The leader punched the man in the gut and kicked him as he fell down. Now that the two were apart Damian flung the heavy stone at the Kunn thug with all his might. The mog's skull was crushed upon impact and he fell lifeless onto the porch floor, right beside Malik who looked up shocked. Three of the remaining thugs had circled the house to the north, out of Damian's sight, and searched the backyard and barn which was adjacent to the house. Two of them circled south, right

56

in front of Damian, who saw him throw the stone from behind the wall and gave a shout. Damian jumped over the waist-high wall with a yell, brandishing his tree-limb club high. The nearest of the two raised his sword and swung downward at Damian's head. He dodged and planted a savage kick into the mog's side that lifted him clear off the ground and sent him flying into his companion, knocking him over and landing on top of him. One of them got up and charged at Damian, but to everyone's surprise fell dead with a cry, a crossbow bolt sticking out of his back. Damian looked out into the trees to the west to see whence the shot came, and so did the other mog who stood up and looked about fearfully. Damian seized his opportunity and broke the branch over his head (I keep breaking them, he thought) while he was distracted. Damian didn't give it another thought but grabbed the sword and ran to the back of the house to aid Cam, wherever he was.

Cam ran swiftly but quietly across the lane and darted from tree to tree, watching the raiders carefully but failing to notice the phantom archer perched motionless in a tree just above him. He quickly made his way to the other side of the barn as the man on the porch was being questioned. He passed by a parked wagon and entered the barn through some open double doors and he cast a hurried glance around. There were tools in abundance and variety inside the barn and Cam spotted some horseshoes hanging pegged to the wall. He grabbed a few of these and climbed up a short ladder to a landing with an open window. This landing merely served as a shelf for grain and feed, and Cam readied himself as he peered out the window. The barn was located directly behind the house and the opening afforded him a good view of the front and rear of the land. He heard the leader shout to his friends and saw three of them round the corner directly below and in front of him. He heaved a horseshoe which caught the lead runner on the side of his head, a Turuk, knocking him out. The other two stopped dead and looked around, then pointed a finger up at the open barn window above them, but Cam had already jumped down inside and grabbed a pitchfork.

"Check the barn!" yelled one of them and they dashed around the corner to the open double doors. They entered quickly but cautiously, swords drawn, one going left, one going right. They looked around inside the barn but saw no one. The one that went left moved closer to a haystack and looked up at the landing and window where he suspected the projectile originated from, but no one was there.

Cam was hiding in the haystack, pitchfork lowered under the hay, watching them enter. One of them stopped right in front of him and looked up. The villain didn't notice the charging, pitchfork-wielding, undersized berserker not six feet in front of him suddenly emerge from the haystack until it was too late. The little berserker impaled him in the chest and drove him back against the wall and stuck him there, upright.

The other intruder saw his friend's plight and picked up a large knife from a workbench and drew back to throw it at this little demon. He flung it at Cam's head from across the room but Cam flipped in the air, backwards and up, landing on the shelf above and behind him. The knife whistled through the air and stuck into the far wall. The mog growled but cried in terror when, to his left, he beheld the tall imposing figure of Damian, sword raised, his fate in those vengeful eyes. Cam jumped down as Damian finished this last thug with a blow and pulled the knife out of the wall.

"There's someone else coming," said Cam aiming the knife at the barn entrance.

"Yes, we're not alone," said Damian, readying himself with the bloody sword. All the Kunn attackers had been accounted for but someone else was approaching slowly. They could hear slow, heavy-booted footfalls just outside the barn doors. The two poised themselves for a new threat.

He appeared before them slowly and deliberately, one black booted foot at a time. With black-gloved hands he aimed a small, loaded crossbow at them, surveying them curiously with his dark, unforgiving and distrustful eyes. He looked to be in his fifties, a tall man with grey and black hair about his hooded head and beard, a man of experience who possessed wisdom and perception. He was dressed and cloaked all in black, as if the better to conceal himself and move unseen. A remarkably fine sword, they saw, was sheathed on his back along with a small quiver for his bolts on his side. There was a moment of silence as the three gazed at each other tensely.

The stranger slowly lowered his weapon first. "Seldom have I seen such fierce resistance to the Kunn," he said. "You perhaps do not know your peril by so doing. I am impressed, however, and maybe there is hope after all. But then I perceive that there is something unusual about you." He regarded the two with some wonder, for they obviously exhibited unique and rare abilities and hidden power unfounded in mortal race. One of them was tall and uncommonly strong and hale, the other small and light and possessing amazing speed and agility. Arriving unarmed they eliminated foes with grace and efficiency. Certainly better than most everything he'd come across before. These weak village folk were of little use to him. Perhaps he had found some worthy companions at last.

"My real name is Riman," he said, unloading his weapon. "I can see that you are an enemy of the Kunn as well as I. I have a home, a hideout really, not far from here. It would be well for you to come. It would also be wise to leave the area immediately to avoid the inquisitive. The Kunn have informers and spies here. It will not take long for them to bring report of three rebels in Tirien. Will you not come?" He stepped away a few paces and whistled to his hidden horse which then emerged from a small, rocky rise to the north within calling distance. The swift brown horse pulled up obediently to his side.

Damian and Cam had lowered their weapons and looked at each other. "Wait," Damian said. "What about the farmer, Malik. Where is he and what is his connection to you?"

"I'm afraid I had to put an end to him," replied Riman. "I suspected him of being an informant for some time. He knew who I was and where I was hiding. He'd do almost anything for money or under threat, having financial difficulties. I feared my exposure. If the Kunn found me, well..." He paused a moment. "Let's just say I'm the most wanted man in this province, perhaps the whole country. I learned of this excursion to Malik's house through a reliable source and staked out the place. My only plan was to eliminate him then you unexpectedly arrived." Riman mounted his horse. "Come now. We should leave. You'd better call your horse. He's by the road, I believe." He looked down the lane.

Damian and Cam emerged from the barn cautiously. The Kunn riders were killed and there was no sign of their steeds. Damian looked out into the distance where Bish was hidden and called him by name. Bish neighed and came galloping up to Damian's side.

"A magnificent animal," observed Riman, "greater than any beast I can recall ever seeing."

"The greatest I believe you'll ever see," replied Damian and he mounted the horse. Cam mounted in his usual fashion, by running and jumping onto his back. After a moment's debate they concluded that they had nothing to lose and were probably guided here to meet by design, so they decided to follow him. He had proven himself to be a capable adversary to the Kunn, and that, it appeared, was difficult to come by. Courage around here, it seemed, was scarce, brought by a false feeling of peace and security, or simply blind complacency. Damian felt they needed a base, an organization, a place from which they could strike, a foundation for their resistance, and information and armament. They knew little of the geography or the politics or the history of the area or from where the Kunn operated and could be found. Certainly some valuable information and a reliable connection to it would be beneficial to his purpose. Perhaps this man was the source of knowledge and information they were looking for. "How far to your hideout?"

"About a mile from here, east, down the road," replied Riman and they started off.

"Can't be far from my old home," thought Damian as they headed down the lane toward the main road. They passed the house and looked back to confirm what Riman said about Malik, sensing some possible deception. Cam wasn't thoroughly sure of Riman yet, and neither was Damian, but they could see the farmer's body slumped over the porch railing, a bolt piercing his heart. That put some of their concerns to rest.

They took a left at the end of the lane and continued to follow the main road. Damian remembered this area well. He knew that most of the farms, in fact most of the town was behind them and there could not be much farther to go. There was no east road that would take one out of Tirien. It simply ended at the edge of town, just before the last hill along the northern bank of the Ella River which Damian and Cam crossed to get here. Beyond this the hillsides eased into the borders of the vast and dangerous Palmwood. Damian knew little of that mysterious realm for he had never ventured there as a boy. It was rumored that it was haunted, that there was an unrest within. Strange folk dwelt there, it was said, ghosts that danced in the night beneath the moon in the old hidden city, somewhere deep within. Though Damian was curious about that dense land he avoided it. They encountered no traffic thankfully, and Riman told them that he didn't expect any. They were on the outskirts of town and most of the farmers were down in the square doing business, but there was seldom anyone about this far out anyway. Most of the villagers congregated in the square. This part of the road was used mainly by the landlords themselves and there were less homesteads here. It definitely seemed like a place that one could hide from the general populace, if he desired it. The trees grew thinner as the last of the few settlements drew nearer. They passed one more lane to the left and Damian was fairly sure, though it had been a long while, that there was only one more lane to the right, and it was his.

Riman stopped before the turnoff and looked behind him to see that they weren't being observed, and rode in. Damian felt a sickening feeling as he was quite sure he was riding down what was once his own driveway. He saw the house and farm he grew up on for a short time drawing nearer, and the yard he and his sister played in when he was younger. It certainly hadn't changed much and vague memories of his childhood were aroused, cheerful and pleasant, but these were superimposed by the haunting memories of that fateful day when his life was ruined and his family scattered. He saw the fenced yard where he rode his first horse and the cropfield he worked in the distance. It looked like it had been quite some time since it had been tended for now it was covered in tall grass and low shrubs. The barn where the pigs and sheep were once kept was closed and silent. The well was dry and had even shifted, leaning to a side, and their old tree swing was missing. The house was dark and dreary and in a state of disrepair. Damian's old home fell quiet and sad since his departure and he felt a mixture of grief and dread as they pulled into the entryway.

Riman led them to the stable which was behind the house and they dismounted. They noticed that the inside was deceptively well kept and clean though the outside was disheveled, and they also saw a large covered wagon parked against the back of the house. This wagon was concealed in a newly constructed wooden shelter attached to the roof, unnoticeable from the lane. They saw to it that the horses were well fed and closed the stable doors before going into the house. Riman, as usual, looked about him first before opening the door. He entered the kitchen and lit several lanterns, for though it was now midday the shades were closed and it was dim inside the house. Damian and Cam saw that this was also well maintained and servicable on the inside, and was well stocked and provisioned. Fresh food and drink of all kinds adorned the countertops. Riman offered them whatever they wanted and they arranged a hasty but very satisfying meal. They seated themselves at the table.

"I keep the place closed and dark most of the time," said Riman. "Suffice it to say there are some people I don't want knowing I'm here."

"And how did you come to be here?" asked Damian, still concealing his secret.

"Malik brought me here four years ago, for a price of course. Said it was abandoned. I met him in a cantina in Felbruk. Told him I needed a place, out of the way, and I was in a hurry. I needed a place I could hide and work where the Kunn would have difficulty finding me. The city grew dangerous."

"Seems like they got pretty close," remarked Cam, munching on some seasoned meats.

"Yes," Riman acknowledged. "Perhaps it is time again to return to my alternative residence."

"What cause do you have to flee them?" Cam asked.

"First tell me your names and whence you come," replied Riman, "and why you go about weaponless slaying their members so fiercely? Perhaps you have also suffered at their hands?"

"My name is Damian, and this is my comrade Cam. And as you are the guest here you should identify yourself first. For this is my father's house." Cam looked at the man across the table with a grin. Riman looked at Damian wide-eyed and speechless. Damian was not overly concerned that his house had been given over to someone else, even if it was given illegally to some potentially friendly fugitive in need. He had long ago given up his family as forcibly displaced from here and had no intention of returning. His mission, he knew, lay elsewhere, probably in the cities, and that's where he ultimately intended to go. He figured the Kunn had little interest in this castaway town on the hills. But the sight of some stranger seated at his table and benefiting from his family's labor and absence irked him slightly.

"Tell me the names of your family," demanded Riman.

"Darren and Loren are my parents, and my sister Lilia," answered Damian.

Riman regarded him with wonder. "Then this is your house. I've seen the names, including yours, here inside on old records and letters. It was not my intention to intrude. What price do you demand of me?"

"Aid," said Damian, "but you need not fear. Any sworn enemy of the Kunn is welcome here."

"Very well then," Riman replied. "Aid in the destruction of this organization you shall have, for it shall benefit us both. I shall then tell my tale, from the beginning. Let us comfort ourselves a little more."

CHAPTER 4
A HISTORY DISCLOSED

They finished their meal and gathered their stools around the large rear window which looked out upon the acres of pasture on the hill. They relaxed themselves while Riman spoke. He was absent-mindedly chewing a stick of *hypsan* cane, drawing the plant's sweet excretions occasionally as he oft did when he had need for thought and contemplation.

"I was a young blacksmith and metallurgist, being crafty and compositionally inquisitive by nature, working in the city of Hera, selling my contrivances from a pushcart in the city's open marketplace, but also weapons, of unique sort, to put it modestly, being a craftsman and inventor by nature, and products of engineered compounds of my own creation and experiment. I lived in a cellar not far from the city center which I rented from a man in the trade. I provided fabrication and treatment services of every kind, making, repairing, and cutting gems, metal weapons, tools, armor, also elixirs and elemental contrivances of a secretive nature. I eventually had an extensive workshop of my own and a large clientele. My income was increasing and thankfully I was able to move into my own residence right in the city. I married and had three children in close succession and my own enterprise. I invented new ways of forging, deviating from traditional laws of metallurgical processes and established doctrine of refinement, and created new kinds of weapons and armor, from different materials mostly, with my own mixtures and treatments, making them stronger or lighter. I improved ballistics and engineering of missile weapons and made bows, darts, arrows and shooters of different materials and composition in attempts to improve them, but I make other more interesting devices and chemurgical compounds as well, things you won't find anywhere. I guess you could call me an improvisor of sorts.

"My unique innovations earned me high renown and the lord of Hera, Lord Karius, purchased many items from me for his militia and guard, and employed my talents wherever he needed them. The years passed with good fortune, my children growing with them, my house and estate more grand. Hera was a beautiful city and prosperous under the just rule of the Old Alliance, with her twin, Gyla. Goods and wealth from these cities reached as far north as Demar, in Kandar Province, to Mod and Dakachi in the south, some two hundred miles away, and further still, and traders from all over would make the journey to purchase our technology. So the cities of Hera and Gyla left their mark everywhere in this southwestern part of the world. We are only surpassed by the city of Prova in regards to shipbuilding, but much of our tools and raw materials are exported to that great seafaring city to the west. And I do not begrudge them. For the wealth of the sea they return to us is payment enough.

"And so the cities of Nadea Province thrived for centuries, providing each other with the fruits of their labors. But the blossoming days of the Alliance began to fail. The ill effects of societal and economic breakdown drove traders further from the pocket of routine commerce. Income had migrated to other parts where here it faded, and its effects were soon felt. Greater wealth, many thought, could be acquired from elsewhere in the more distant parts, namely Govannum and Dengland, and business should be resumed, some said, with the clans and warlords who wielded power there. The Kunn began their Brotherhood there, in the unstable countries to the east and south, creating their wealth through tyrannical and criminal means, crushing opposing clans or rival powers in that strife-ravaged region. But many less than reputable tradesmen and greedy politicians felt we should conduct commerce with them, open our lands to the ways and black markets of those foreign capitalistic warlords who grew in power as order at home and around declined. They would have little choice, they said, under the worsening circumstances, but to recognize these clans and commence trade relations. We could not ignore them forever. But the Lord Karius forbid it, hearing only ill of such folk, and kept them at bay, upholding the policies of his predecessors and defending the realm from these thugs and highwaymen of the east and desert states. But some years later Karius died and was succeeded by his competing legionary, the now Lord Helbek. That was thirteen years ago. Helbek espoused the common idea of transprovincial commerce with that dubious clan organization known as the Kunn, the most powerful and emerging of them, along with Lord Kom of Gyla, who, at nearly the same time, succeeded his uncle Alos who strangely died shortly after his brother, Karius. There was mystery surrounding the deaths of the allied brothers but official inquiries were forcibly quieted by the new government, which was hastily implanted. It has always been my belief that they were murdered intentionally to remove them and their obstructionist policies and to make the way clear for their intended and sinister alliance. This suspicion was reinforced when I saw these Kunn agents for the first time in Helbek's stronghold, the Palace of Hera. I was still one of the primary suppliers of the Hera Elite Guard and militia, and would at times make trips to the keep for pay or consultation to the lord himself or his designated subjects.

"Well, the clan was kept at bay and denied all residence and even passage through the realm while the Lord Karius and his predecessors were in power. The Guard prevented them crossing the border of our fruitful province and was constantly watchful of their spies. The warring factions and competing clans of bordering lawless territories could remain in the despots they came from, the lord said. I couldn't have said it better myself. But shortly after Karius' death dispatches arrived from Mod to proposition the newly crowned Helbek. The Kunn desired to establish a business foundation in Hera and their leader, the Ahga they call him, offered attractive profit bonuses and incentives for allowing them to operate in his city. The same was true for Gyla where Lord Kom had an alliance with Helbek before they even rose to power, I believe. These new governments were too eager to accept, for the Kunn was and is, a powerful, wealthy organization. They are by far the most notorious and feared of all the clans in this part of the world, for the territories as a whole are weak and comparatively undeveloped. The open lands to the east and south are little policed and lawless thugs thrive there. This scenario breeds lawlessness and there are those who will capitalize on that weakness and become dangerous and powerful. The Kunn emerged dominant in this unstable environment and therefore were sought. They control much of the food and raw material distribution in the region. Their mining and gold production is unparalleled, and the rare jewels and precious stones they bring from beyond Adovia cannot even be found in this part of the world, not even in the Ash Mountains far to the north. Their pursuit of metallurgical and chemical technologies is persistent and considerable, profitable–and to be feared. The Kunn had incredible purchasing power and businessmen and traders were impatient to benefit from it and seek protection under their widening sphere of influence. The principles which kept the realm in safety and prosperity were abandoned and forgotten by this latter generation. The old wisdom quickly eroded; foolishness has supplanted it, to our detriment.

"Rumors abounded about the Kunn's brutality and barbarism but these were dismissed as simply effective business practices and were considered fair play, an easy sentiment for the naïve and ignorant to embrace. After all, folk thought, the Kunn didn't rise to wealth and power by being kind and foolish. If they had a questionable reputation then the commerce they brought would negate it. Traders were ready for a new source of wealth, the politicians political leverage with which to acquire their dubious interests, so they eagerly began conducting commerce with the Kunn. Some foul folk even sought to join the ranks of the Brotherhood and adopted the lifestyle of the gangster and savage ideologue and thus earned enrollment and status with them. The Kunn had already established a solid chapter in the city of Mod, to the south in Govannum province, and had proven beneficial there after years of solid commerce and trade, so they said. The people there boasted of their new wealth acquiring capabilities and representatives and dignitaries from Hera would return from that city with news of a great new trade partner. But others with sterner judgment told another story. They would speak of murders and coercions of lords and masses and eliminations of competing clans and anyone foolish enough to be indebted to them. The Kunn's viciousness and intolerance of any competing power was little known at the time in these northern territories for few who were targeted by the Kunn were ever seen again. The isolationist policy instituted by Karius, whatever protection it may have lent, led to a degree of ignorance, and many were eager to forsake the ethical lord's reclusive ways and strict doctrines, especially after his death. The level of destitution in foreign realms to the south caused by these ruling thugs and their strife with other clans was too little known. But these favorable circumstances won the Ahga the monopoly he wanted for his cause, and consequently, vast wealth."

Riman paused a moment and sighed. "I remember well my first encounter with Kunn henchmen. I was making a routine visit to the new ruler, Helbek that is, to receive his orders for the month when two clan members entered his chamber along with a particular human who worked for them. Tura was his name. Helbek seemed to be waiting especially for me and I was introduced to the newcomers, but I was wary. He told me that now I would be reporting to them for all my business and that a Kunn 'representative' he called him, would now be my person of contact, that I was no longer needed to come directly to the governor. 'And what if my firm chooses not to do business with them?' I asked. Helbek smiled warmly and came amiably to my side. He put his hand on my shoulder and told me it would be in myself and family's best interest to do whatever these kind gentlemen asked of me–these were the words he used. He assured me of my illimitable worth to the realm and praised me for my vast contributions and innovations to the Guard, a benefaction he hoped would continue. The lord did his best to win my favor and cooperation when the meeting was over. I took my leave feeling unsure of things. Members of the Kunn had begun to be seen quite regularly in the city now and many businessmen foolishly pursued them. The militia and general populace had mixed feelings about this strange and troubling influx at first, but the leadership in Hera, and Gyla as well, was always open and lenient with whatever happened in the marketplace as long as taxes were levied.

"Militia and Guard presence in the city was generally minimal and subdued, except in the vicinity of the palace, of course. The Guard was dispatched only routinely in those days for there was not much unrest to quell, really. Folk were content with the prosperity and mild taxation. The governments didn't overly involve themselves with the trade and commerce of the land and people preferred it that way. But the lack of oversight paired with the disintegration of the ideals that provided our prior success did lead to some lawlessness by overzealous capitalists who sought to expand their riches through questionable means, and this, in my opinion, is what led to the desire to have greater diplomatic and commercial access to the warring clans, by businessmen and leadership alike. This indulgence, for which many had waited but for the passing of the obstructing rulership which restrained them, has jeopardized the security of the citizenry and ruined the sanctity of what Nadea province was founded upon. Their greed and ignorance made them blind to what the Kunn really was—a clan made up of gangsters and creed-adherent villains who acquired their wealth by theft and forced servitude and acts of terror and monopolization, a means they claim as some divine directive, and this too conceives some accord and draws interest among this latter generation eager for change and a divorce from the old ways. So there is a clash of ideals going on, a wave of philosophical rebellion and tenetal revolution, and the clan, in fact, enjoys widespread favor. And upon this wave of societal introspection and perceived divine charge the clan has achieved their success with remarkable rapidity, and this, too, has afforded validation for the clan's claims. Their philosophy of force, however, was simple but effective: provide traders and governors with sufficient motivation to divert a disproportionate amount of funds to them in order to ultimately seize control."

"Manipulation for a grand objective," said Cam.

"Demagoguery," added Damian, "and conquest by force, and to tax, as it were, as an overreaching governing body unbound by land parameters. More efficient, perhaps, than traditional polities bound by codes."

"There are numerous ways to secure their goals," Riman continued. "They often seize control of goods shipments and vital delivery routes, starving a target governance into compliance. Piracy, bribery and extortion are rampant. Assassinations are commonplace. If they had enough of a foothold or influence in a city they would have a non-conforming politician or lawman 'removed' and he'd conveniently never be seen again. And, as the Kunn paid handsomely for steadfast loyalty and cooperation, their tactics, however brutal at times, were overlooked and hushed by a sympathetic society or governance. But these dark tactics were little known at the time for their Brotherhood was still largely alien. The previous governments were right to forbid them, but they no longer had majority support.

"Anyway, I conducted my business as usual. My firm, as I mentioned, was now quite extensive and my clientele numerous. All races and creeds from afar and dignitaries of all states came to Hera to purchase my esteemed goods. I, and some close friends with whom I shared secrets of the trade, forged our prized creations in the seclusion of my shop. Our products were widely considered the best in the industry and demand for our goods was high. I sold not only to the realm but also to private businessmen and other firms, some local, some abroad. It was this matter that my Kunn friends wanted to clarify on their first dreaded visit to my shop at the end of the day, one summer's eve ten years ago. The three of them boldly entered, uninvited, as if to wrest ownership from me. I would hardly have been surprised. The man, who I remembered seeing at the palace before, introduced himself as Tura, and he spoke on behalf of his Ahga-Rosh who was temporarily in the city to convene with the governor on business matters and to overview his fledgling chapter in Hera. The Ahga was very personally interested in me and my operation, he said. My name and products had singular reputation and my talents were wanted for the Kunn.

"But Tura remembered my cold reception of them at our first meeting and he was prepared for it again, which he did receive as anticipated the second time. He then demanded that I forsake all present relationships and divert my business dealings instead to certain individuals–their agents– names of which he would provide me of course, and that a minimal portion of my earnings would have to be transferred to the Kunn local cache, and that it would be necessary to relieve me of certain goods for the Ahga had need for them. These customers, he said, would compensate me and I would gain favor and gratitude from the Ahga himself. I refused again, saying to whom I sell and buy is my own business and is of no concern to him or his precious Ahga. I had many friends in the business and did not wish to cut off trade with them like that, and, I added, I was quite satisfied with my income and didn't trust or expect them to make a change worth my while, even for this new wealthy entity. The Kunn was obviously aware of my profitability and enviable technological advantages and wanted them for themselves. 'You mean to rob me,' I said, 'and take over my operation. You must be a fool to think that I will accept these terms.' You can imagine his reaction to these remarks, especially the way I scoffed about his Ahga. His two strongmen grabbed me, as I was alone at the time, and Tura struck me low. I coughed and gagged and was led out the back door to an awaiting carriage and driven to an unknown location.

"They brought me into a mansion, blindfolded until my arrival. It was a beautiful estate, I remarked. It looked similar to one of Lord Karius' old unused palaces, probably lent or given to the Ahga for his pleasure by the new governor. There were many thugs of the Brotherhood there, some on guard, some obviously of great importance, advisors and elevated agents of his, members of the Baccád most likely, his most trusted and deadly servants. My escorts brought me before a large room with open doors. The Ahga was expecting me, they said. After a moment he called me in by name as if I were a dear friend. I obediently entered the chamber which was extensive and lofty, and lavishly furnished. Their Ahga was seated and ready behind a large wooden table. He was flanked by several intimidating and armed bodyguards, trained in the harsh martialities of the Brotherhood. The doors were closed behind us but the guards still had a grip on me. He was an extraordinarily larger and older mog, the Ahga, the Father of the clan in its new right. The strength of giants he had, acquired through the training of his code, quite fearsome and venerable looking, and dignified. He sat alone in a large iron chair and was dressed and robed as the royalty of his following, the black and crimson garb of the Brotherhood, though he projected a feeling of death so strong it made one sick with fear. The demeanor in his face and eyes belied the professional countenance he tried unsuccessfully to convey. Rumors I had heard of this kingpin of crime regarding his brutality and murderous ways I doubted not after being in his presence. His palace in Mod is built from the bones of his victims, 'tis said. His many loyal henchmen will do anything for their Ahga, even slay one of their own at his bidding. Needless to say I was not at ease standing before him."

"You have seen their Ahga?" asked Damian in disbelief.

"Many times as you'll see," replied Riman. "Always a most unnerving experience. He expressed great displeasure in my refusal of their business requests and was giving me one last chance to reconsider. The location of my estate and names of my family were known to him and his agents, he said, and it would be most unfortunate to have to use them as bargaining tools to achieve his purpose. My continued rebelliousness against his generous proposal might compel him to resort to unpleasant methods of persuasion, that of course, he felt were distasteful and maybe even barbaric. Perceiving his thought, and fearing for my loved ones, I reluctantly agreed. At first he was only relieving me of some of my income but due to my unfortunate reluctance to acknowledge the wisdom in his generous offer, as he put it, he was now forced to ask for more. He wanted my state of the art devices and technology for himself and his men, especially my ballistical innovations with improved range and accuracy, and armor, materials I forged out of garvonite for its strength and lightness. He was also interested in what engineered compounds I may have discovered 'productive' uses for. A fitting term for murder and mass destruction. He wanted his servants to be better equipped than any adversary they might come across in any province or city where they operate and this is why the Ahga wanted me for himself.

"But little did he know of what else I created, thankfully. There are only a few known engineers capable of properly forging and treating this rare element known as garvonite for the process is unknown to most. We few keep it secret for it raises the value. I only sold items of this material to the governor himself for use of the Elite Guard and some close wealthy friends of my own, so they were not widely distributed and of great value. The Ahga wanted these for himself and his hierarchy, and I was forced to oblige. He was pleased then with my change of heart and ordered me to my task. They discharged me to the back door of my shop, which they forced me to close to the general citizenry, and informed me of their next rendezvous and made delivery arrangements for the goods. These goods I kept locked and secret in a vault under the shop, accessible only to myself, and I prepared them. I did not inform my family of this coercion or their risk, for I did not want them to live in fear unnecessarily. Losing my wife and children was not worth this risk and decided that when the time was right I would strike back and make my escape. In the meantime I conceded to their every request which grew somewhat more demanding as time wore on. The Ahga oftentimes would require my professional opinion on precious black market stone or gem shipments and I was brought to his palace many times to evaluate them. I was also asked to price these goods and negotiate deals with buyers. I ultimately became the chief buyer and seller of precious metals and gems for the Kunn in this province. I traveled abroad frequently to arrange deals and seek out new buyers. I eventually became somewhat of a diplomat for his organization, easing the clan into the favorability of doubtful and uncertain lords and leaders. The Ahga was very impressed with my services and was very pleased with the growth and wealth I provided the Kunn. But he also ordered me watched closely. I was reminded of agents that had constant watch over my household, a fact I still concealed from my loved ones. My every move was watched, even more so now that I myself held power and status within the ranks.

"During my forced eight year tenure the Kunn made riddance of several of my closest friends, the last of those who were knowledgeable of garvonite and improved balsan-based pyrotechnical treatment. He had them hunted down and assassinated intentionally to remove its secret from all but himself. This of course meant that the Kunn was now the only supplier of garvonite items in the world, and this won him wealth and power indescribable for princes and lords all over greatly desired it and paid him in gold by the horde. You can now understand my singular worth to the Kunn and the objective the Ahga succeeded in achieving. I was closely guarded and watched, and afraid, for there were others I knew who were either killed or enslaved. I had, at times, heard rumor of mysterious slave camps or prisons far from the cities where they would ship dissidents or their kin to silence any who dared defy or oppose them. I do not doubt that unspeakable atrocities were committed in these feared places and that the prisoners were exploited of their labors, whatever they were, for their own profit. I lived in constant fear for my family and my own life as well if I did not serve the Ahga satisfactorily. I would receive threats from time to time to remind me of my peril and where my allegiance lay to ensure my loyalty."

"Couldn't you go to the governor or Guard for help?" asked Cam.

"Lord Helbek is on the Ahga's payroll and under his auspices, and the militia and Guard fear the Kunn. The Brotherhood had fairly free reign in the city and control of the underground. They were virtually untouchable but also careful to keep their dark operations quiet at first and mostly unobserved by the populace to avoid resentment on a grand scale. Fear keeps mouths shut and swords sheathed. But there were many who profited by the Kunn so they were not wholly ill-favored by all. Only those who have dared to resist them have cause and reason to despise and seek vengeance upon them, those who have suffered cruelly and unjustly at their hands, those whose families have endured hardships and grievances unwarranted. If the general populace was at first ignorant to their brutality, that played in the Kunn's favor."

"Where did they come from and how did they acquire their power?" asked Damian, burning for knowledge.

"The Kunn began simply as a small, secret brotherhood and crime gang," replied Riman, "a reborn offshoot of their former bygone relatives, the Slovidars, who traced their lineage to Adin himself, a lord of legend, if one believes in that nonsense, but eventually evolved into a clan of thieving warlords whose reign encompasses most of the region. In its latest form it was founded by the Ahga about thirty years ago in Dengland, in the city of Kadr. The Kunn claim a rightful succession to the legacy of that defunct clan and from them are derived their ideological means and perceived formal entitlements to carry on that dormant ascendancy. Their fantastical objective is to restore the greatness of something called the Consortium of old through economic and geographic conquests, dominance of existence, as commanded by their code, and relocation of lost relics to reassemble the missing pieces of their cult to win their city back. No one knows the Ahga's real name, or it is forgotten. It is the title he has declared for himself, as though he shed his former being to embrace this new pilgrimage. He began his following with only a handful of his most loyal and trusted friends, his Baccád, who follow the strict and secret code of life of the clan, passed down by the various teachers of the ages, one that promises earthly gifts to its adherents. They call it the *Mari*, and from it they claim to derive some level of power, one which will be restored in its entirety if they are successful. Verily they seek the strength of gods. Ideological rubbish in my opinion, the all-too abundant fancies and notions of similar cultists and theosophic adherents pursuing some ridiculous and inconceivable end, though I cannot deny an uncanniness about them, and you as well, I might add," he said looking the two strangers over again. "Perhaps there is some truth to the old legends after all."

Damian and Cam simply looked at each other.

"Whimsical piety aside," he continued, "control of the earth and influence over its people have always been priorities for the clan, objectives of the code. The Brotherhood needs money to achieve this long-term goal. Their means of monetary generation includes, but is certainly not limited to silk trade, spices, salt certainly, beer and wine, kuth weed, rare ivories and skins, gambling and assassinations of course, food in the way of cattle, products of scientific study, and precious stones. Any commodity or service that yielded high revenue, usually illegal or dangerous. Whatever the Ahga felt worth his while. They need money to achieve their dubious objectives which bring them to all corners of creation. They pirate the seas from the Gulf to Dinitia like wolves. They create most of their own goods to sell abroad, mostly through slave-run production camps, but also through extortion. If a trade or mercantile firm was profitable enough in their eyes they found a way to overtake it or extract monies from it through extortion. Any trader unwilling to cooperate was dealt with severely by threats, murder, family endangerment and the like. The constabulary element, what remained of them after the fall of the Old Alliance, provided no assistance in the matter, being under the influence of corrupt leadership. Most traders simply gave in, felt it wasn't worth the trouble. Money sources that were less than lawful and counter-operative to attempts at reestablishment of order benefited, for the Ahga provided them his protection. Others, like myself, would have nothing to do with his evil ways and practices but had little choice. I took a heavy hit, but some were eager to take part and engage transaction with the Kunn for their wealth was vast and cooperation made that wealth accessible to themselves. But the Ahga made sure any local Guard or militia superior was compensated for his blind eye toward these unlawful matters. Implantation of influential operatives in sovereignties and their respective political circles is elemental of their grand design.

"But not all cities were so corrupt or easily bought. Gyla and Hera, for example, the twin capital cities of this province, held out long against the Kunn. It was not until the deaths of the ruling brothers and change of governments that the Ahga could finally move into this region and expand his control and monopolization. They follow a harsh creed and code and this lends to their success. Those who desire power are drawn to them. And as his income grows so do his ranks, though admission into his organization is very difficult. One has to prove his loyalty and worth, usually through some kind of initiation."

"What are his legions made of? Who are accepted into their ranks?" asked Damian.

"Any that are considered worthwhile to the purpose of the clan and demonstrate sufficient dedication and favor to the code. There are many races under his authority, Hidari, Human, Irendi, Harikan, Mogoli. His ranks are comprised mostly of Mogoli due to their existential predominance in the far eastern countries, where the seeds of the Slovidar lineage originated, but his servants are as diverse as Vidia. Those who are accepted need only renounce their former loyalties and embrace their code, the Mari, and prove their strength and worth to the clan's purpose of expansion. The Ahga seeks to expand his riches through the vibrant markets our cities boast, which brought them here. The peoples of the east and west are not at war or dispute and trade openly and mix societies with each other, so that the mutual co-existence of all peoples has become commonplace in these latter days. But there is no open war, unless it is between any warring clans and factions in the undeveloped and lawless regions. And their despotisms adversely affect all. Verily our beloved city is now drawn into that abyss. The peoples buy and sell across the land, money being the common goal. The black market especially thrives for there is little law enforcement anywhere except in Kandar province to the north. The cities of Demar and Pomay, being of higher principle and scrutiny, have a strong guard and border watch and the Kunn have no power there. Kandar province is solidly united and strong, and that territory was used as a model for the eager and ambitious lords of Hera while they were in power and they succeeded in some part to achieve this. The provinces in this part of the world are now made up only of independently sovereign city-states and total reunification of them remains elusive. The cities and their subsidiaries became realms unto themselves since the lamentable breakup of the Old Alliance and are governed and ruled independently, but also continue to trade freely abroad. Once the territories were unified and strong, but that is long since past. The greatness of old is fast crumbling and we have since been in a state of regression. Kandar is the last of the united territories and therefore a target. The Ahga has an especial enmity for that land.

"But great wealth is attainable for those who acquire it in wrongful ways, and this is what the Kunn do. The weakness in these cities and the lack of unity among the citizens provides the Kunn and other crime entities their opportunity to take by force, to use their power to gain the wealth and influence they seek with little repercussion. Despotism and moral dissolution facilitate their progress. The people are weak, bickering unceasingly and concerning themselves with pettiness and selfish endeavors while they abandon the principles that once kept them strong, and these things are leading to their own demise. And now that our once great province is again becoming a den of thieves, these foreign clans and villains have taken up their throne here."

Riman took a draw at his hypsan stick and shook his head in disappointment. "But those who cooperate with the Kunn receive just punishment for the Ahga is conniving, deceptive, and abusive. An entity that he is displeased with or has no further use for is robbed and eliminated. The Ahga will not risk letting a former contributor become a future competitor. I have no doubt that I would have been murdered and my shop and secrets destroyed if my services were no longer needed. The Ahga's distrust in me grew as the years went by, my resentment growing with them. I believe I only just escaped in time. It is the murder and extortion of decent folk that adds to their despicability. It is when the labors and sufferings of the simple are exploited that they are to be most despised."

"How did you escape?" asked Cam.

"My wife died unexpectedly in my fiftieth year, the year 613, and as my eldest son was eighteen I felt the time had come to make a move. I not only wished to flee but to send a message to the Ahga that he would not soon forget."

Riman paused a moment before continuing. "The Ahga, as you now know, dealt heavily in the precious stone black market. In his relentless search for lost relics, he also ever sought gems and crystals of greater and greater value. He and his clan have a fancy for legendary heirlooms, feeling them necessary for possession to edify and legitimize their clan. Among these gems was a stone called the Siryn Crystal, one of the Eyes of the East, a collection of five, two only of which have been accounted for though one is believed to be buried in the city of Hera. This crystal was beyond price for it could not be found in this part of the world. It came only from a far distant country, well beyond even the land of Bhull, and held far greater value than any other crystal or gem obtainable in this hemisphere. His pursuit of this crystal, and indeed the entire collection, became an all-consuming obsession for him over the years, believing it to propel his organization and purpose incalculably, as a directive from the Divine One as the Kunn say, and he sent agents abroad to every corner of the world to retrieve one somehow, that he would pay anything for it. His possession of this crystal would bring him wealth and an even greater status and fear, a status and worldwide prestige he greatly desired. The lords of the lands would no longer be able to ignore or thwart the Kunn, but indeed with the possession of this almighty crystal they would instead bow to him, and he pressed his agents abroad for the finding of one.

"Well, one day the Ahga was expecting a large shipment of gold and gems coming from somewhere in the east. He was very anxious and impatient for the arrival of this delivery for it took well over a year to reach his temporary palace in Hera, and it indeed was rumored to contain some of these crystals. Word had reached his ears that one of the legendary Siryn had at last been obtained and was even now on the Ahga's front doorstep. A small caravan, under heavy guard and cover of night, was on its way to his palace. I was expected to be there for negotiations and verification of the shipment, but instead of riding my horse as I usually did I took one of my large carriages. The gate guards admitted me and I parked my carriage in the undercroft of the palace where I knew the shipment would also be parked temporarily for unloading. This underground vault, of course, was very large, able to accommodate many carriages and even had a stable for all the horses. Several carriages pulled into the compound late that night and remained on the grounds, underneath the palace. I inspected the goods which consisted of much gold and gems, and evaluated its worth, which was very great. The Ahga, of course, was right by my side along with his top agents and fellow brothers of the clan and impatient to behold his treasured crystals. One of the foreigners, who was of strange race and seemed to be the chief ambassador of the whole delivery, finally brought forth a large and heavy metal case and presented it to his purchaser. We all gathered round as he opened it, and there inside was one of the finest and venerable crystals I had ever seen, and I have seen many. There indeed was the Verdstone, the Emerald of the East. It was the size of one's fist and was of a deep but dazzling and hypnotizing green color, eerie in fact, changing hues and shades as one turned it before his bewildered eyes. I verified its authenticity and could not doubt that its worth was what it was rumored to be having beheld the wonder so close.

"The Ahga took the case and returned with his friends to his suite upstairs for wine and refreshment after his payment. The foreigners were invited to stay in the palace overnight, of course, and the Ahga lent the party a well furnished and comfortable apartment to use. I was assigned the task of unloading the remaining cargo in the under-vault with the guards, but, knowing the Ahga was well occupied and intoxicated with his new treasure, leaving myself rather free to wander, I instead informed them that we would be unloading in the morning and that I was departing for home. They did not question my authority so they left to their rooms for the evening, leaving behind only one guard and myself. When left alone I knocked the guard unconscious with a drug-soaked rag which I had hidden in my cloak, another of my more simple concoctions, ideal for quiet operations, and concealed the body. I then pulled out a long coil of rope from within my carriage. I made my way quickly but secretly to the outside rear of the palace, careful not to alert the guards which were posted along the outside walls and at the front gate. I finally reached the third floor outside balcony which was at the backside of the estate. The Ahga's chamber, I knew, was on the fifth and I looked up at the open window. I threw my rope and hook in and scaled up the wall. The Ahga was in another room of the suite entertaining his guests, and the case of crystals was locked in his desk. This was girthy and heavy, an adequate safe indeed, virtually impenetrable to most. Not to me. I broke into it with some of my own tools, crafted especially for my unique purposes, picked the lock for I had designed it myself, and stole the almighty crystal and made my way stealthily back to the vault avoiding the guards. I also quickly took several crates of gold and gems from the other carriages as I dared to that time and circumstances allowed, and departed.

"I drove my loaded carriage out and bade goodnight to the gate guard and fled for Felbruk. I met with what remained of my family previously that evening to make arrangements for our flight. My children also fled that night as planned, the Ahga's watchful agents being called to the palace for the occasion allowing them their escape. They headed north to Veccenberg, and ultimately Demar, where I knew the Kunn could not seek them. I saw them off for the last time in years that afternoon before my long awaited engagement with the Ahga. I gave them much gold, in fact I gave them my entire life savings for I knew that after tonight I would not need it, so I know they are well off. I bid them luck and health and told them painfully that we would meet again sometime, but that now I had a purpose I must see through and in the meantime I wanted them safe. That is why I dwell here out of choice, in the territory of those I seek to rain justice upon and perhaps save those who would become new victims, indeed the whole of this falling realm, in my own small manner. The crimes of the Kunn must be answered. These gangsters must be driven back into the foul realms where they came from, their creed undone. I passed through Felbruk and into the rurals of Tirien where I felt I could hide. And because of this great theft and wound I inflicted upon the Ahga, not to mention my extensive and dangerous knowledge of his inner workings and crimes, he placed a heavy price on my head and sent bounty hunters and agents to capture me. They have been scouring the neighboring suburbs of Gyla and Hera, and myself and others have kept a close watch. The loss of his precious crystal must have been a heavy blow to him. So much the better, a fitting retribution. One day I hope to somehow return the crystal to him, as a final farewell when this is all over. And here in Tirien I have been hiding and working since, and keeping an eye on Kunn operations, all the while in a house previously inhabited by another who has a score to settle with them. But perhaps it was fated to be so."

"So it would seem," answered Damian.

"For am I not correct in perceiving that you also have a grievance?" asked Riman.

"More than a grievance," answered Damian, "for Cam and myself have undergone severe injustice and that is why our feud with them is so bitter." Damian and Cam recounted to Riman their entire tales from their capture to their escape, painfully recalling every cruel episode in detail with tears of anger and sadness in their eyes. They could not forget even the minutest of details, so engrained they were in their minds. Riman leaned back in his chair and chewed his hypsan thoughtfully while their tale unfolded and the afternoon wore on.

"And in the end Cam and my horse Bish died, and I was close to death myself, delirious with hunger and grief," Damian said, nearing the end of his tale.

"And you returned to Tirien thus clad and nourished?" Riman asked, looking them over in wonder, not for the first time.

Damian paused a moment, distracted. "We had a wondrous experience in the wasteland," he said, his eyes looking skyward and seeing something that was not there. His face brightened momentarily and painful memories melted away, his thought replaced with something indescribable.

"We were saved by a light!" spurted Cam, unable to contain his vast energy and clutching the arms of the chair with profound excitement as he relived this unbelievable but unforgettable memory.

"We were inexplicably blessed and restored by some divine being or power," said Damian. "We were diverted from death, fulfilled and returned home."

"If that is what you believe, then it is with pain that I admit you may be right," said Riman. "I must concede there was something unusual about you when I first beheld you and your unique abilities. The old tales seem to have come alive again to disprove the agnostic and cynical such as myself. It is apparent that you have experienced something remarkable, blessed as you say, and returned perhaps to fulfill some great purpose."

"And we intend to see it through," said Damian.

"Then perhaps you would like some tools to help you accomplish that?" suggested Riman. "I cannot furnish the fire and thunder of the Divine but I can give you what I have." He motioned them to follow him outside and he led them to the barn. He unlocked the chained double doors which slid open to reveal a surprisingly sophisticated and well-equipped blacksmith and forging shop. Damian's old barn had been gutted and completely remodeled on the inside for the purpose of wood and leather working, chemistry, and metallurgy. There were precision tools of every kind hanging neatly on the beams. There were grinding wheels, hammers and anvils, burners and mixers, supplies and ingredients in glass vessels for various purposes, probably secrets of the trade for they looked expensive and foreign; urns and vats for mixing, some filled with strange solutions, a large indoor mill-wheel which purported to turn an array of gears, and many tools and devices also for the shaping of wood placed about. A large furnace with bellows was in the middle complete with a newly constructed chimney. Suits of armor of various makes were carefully hung. There were stacks of molds and casts, blocks of various unshaped metals, and piles of scrap in a corner. This pile consisted mostly of broken or experimental devices and weapons of all types. Several spears, arrows, swords and bows were neatly stacked or hung against a wall. Damian and Cam examined these closely.

"I see you've spent your time constructively," remarked Damian, fingering a large sword. This new friend was obviously a gifted craftsman and inventor. Cam was trying a short bow and eyeing some arrows with interest.

"Those are some of my better creations I decided to keep," said Riman.

"Better?" asked Cam in surprise. "This is excellent craftsmanship, far better than the crude weapons the Khala guards use. Theirs is fodder by comparison."

"Then you cannot have seen many," Riman contradicted, "and you know little of them, but maybe that is well. They are well equipped and strong in the upper ranks of the Order, and well trained, make no mistake. You will meet them soon enough."

"Perhaps, but I must agree with Cam," said Damian, brandishing the sword with both hands. "You take pride in your work. It is no wonder your skills were so coveted by the Kunn. However they compensated you it could not have been enough."

Riman growled to himself at the mention of this and walked over to a small locked room against a side wall made of brick. He opened the heavy metal door and with their help carried out several large wooden trunks which were also locked. "Shall we venture outside?" he asked and the three walked out to the back yard with their burden.

"I keep my best creations in here," Riman said as he unlocked the trunks. He opened them to reveal arms of various kinds, some of which they couldn't even identify for they had never seen things like this before, and all obviously of excellent workmanship and made of a strange metallic composite. One of the trunks held a large bow of this metal and several dozen arrows of the same make, nothing like Damian and Cam had ever seen. Damian picked up the large metal bow and inspected it with great interest.

"It's so light," Damian said. He tried the string and saw that it was uncannily strong and made of a strange material also unknown to him.

"It's made of garvonite," replied Riman.

"*Keplag*," added Cam, looking over some knives and short swords. "That's what the tormentors at Khala call it."

"That's what they call it in the east. Known for its strength and lightness," said Riman, "and its deceptive dull grey color and forgeability. Strong but also remarkably tractable. It is even proven to be marginally flexible if properly fabricated. It's very hard to find. Now I know from where the Kunn derive it. They rule the market on that material."

"Khala has a fair amount of the raw ore," said Cam. "No wonder they mined it so aggressively. I remember when a guard tried to steal a sizable piece of it on his last day. Kurg caught him and fed him to the kelgan."

"Always a concern in this trade," Riman acknowledged. "It does not surprise me that the Kunn have to keep a close eye on their own members of the lower planes of the clan. Inside theft has always been a plague to the Ahga, despite his imparted discipline, a consequence of hiring scum." Damian removed a garvonite arrow from the box and fitted it to the bow.

"Capable of piercing most armor types with this bow, though it is virtually impossible to draw. My ambitiousness, I'm afraid, led me to over-fabricate the tension. It would take a kunga to draw it. I have been hoping to find someone with the strength to—" Riman said but was cut short. Damian drew the great bow fully back with ease and released, sending the arrow clean through a young palm tree fifty feet away. The flexible wood split asunder right through the middle. Riman actually raised an eyebrow and Damian cracked a satisfied grin. Cam discovered a small case within the trunk containing a large assortment of throwing knives, stars and spikes. With amazing speed Cam removed several of these and sent them flying en masse into a wooden fence post some distance off. Thrilled, he pulled out all the remaining spikes and faster than the eye could see flung them all, in succession, into the same post which consequently split in several places from the deadly barrage and crumbled to the ground a disintegrated heap of splinters and chunks. Cam growled triumphantly and grinned from ear to ear. He eagerly sprinted out to retrieve his new beloved weapons and surveyed the destruction he caused with excitement. Riman produced a special carrying case and belt and handed them to Cam.

"You can put them in this," he said, happy to give them to a worthy keeper. "This is designed with friction clips so that they're easily placed in and removed." Cam fixed it to his belt gratefully. Damian pulled out a large two-handed sword and drew his finger along the sharpened edge, appreciating the skill and craftsmanship the weapon boasted. He was surprised at its strength and lightness.

"I think you'll find it durable and sharp, and quite able to—" Riman was cut short again as Damian brought the mighty sword down onto the thick wooden crossbeam and cleaved through both the top and bottom with little effort.

"Yes," acknowledged Damian, "I believe you're right." He inspected the blade which did not bear the slightest marks or blemishes from the impact. Riman gave him a sheath for it and a quiver of garvonite arrows for his bow. Cam also took a pair of short swords which he strapped to his back and a garrot of leather.

"Useful for quiet infiltration," Riman said, nodding to Cam. "I also have this." He removed some thick studded black leather armor, complete with skirt and shoulder plates and handed it to Damian. He tried it on and found it quite tough but light and comfortable and flexible, and fitted his weapons over it with straps that Riman provided him. It was surprisingly unencumbering.

"I'm afraid I don't have armor small enough to fit one of your size," Riman said turning to Cam, "though whether you need any is doubtful."

"I do not think he will have any," Damian replied. Cam smiled, sprinted a few paces and jumped high in the air, performed several somersaults without effort and landed squarely in a handstand on a feed barrel by the fence. He did a backflip to dismount and folded his arms smugly and smiled before his amazed friends.

"I see your point," Riman agreed. "Now you are armed, what do you intend to do? The Kunn grow in power in the cities and are becoming ever more brazen and criminal. Even the common folk are becoming more aware of their true nature and are increasingly victimized by them. The Kunn no longer restrict themselves to the underground but steal, threaten, and murder where they will. Roving gangs of Kunn warlords are now more regularly seen in this part of the world, and they bring their competitors with them. Wherever they roam now people cower and hide lest they become victims themselves. Their pleas for help go unanswered for the powerful seek the benefit of their presence. The people desperately seek outside help but there is little to be had, or it is weak. Local militias feel helpless or ill-equipped to thwart them and the Kunn know this. Their chapters in Hera and Gyla are now thoroughly established and thriving. The roads connecting the provinces of Nadea and Govannum are now trafficked regularly by highwaymen and thugs of the Ahga who will waylay and extort goods or money from unsuspecting travelers unfortunate to cross paths with them. Businessmen now fear to travel abroad without armed escort. And rumors continue to grow of this dreaded place you hail from. Your courage and strength are needed. With some reliable friends at last I long to return to the city with them."

Damian listened with anger in his eyes. The thought of others also suffering injustices burned in him. He was sure others had undergone the same fate as they had, or were even now. What other children had been captured and enslaved, innocent and ignorant, robbed of their youth and families, forced to work and be subjected to cruel punishments, all for the wealth of this despicable brotherhood? He thought of his own robbed youth and his slain father and missing mother and sister, and what possible cruel fate they had been met with. He thought of simple folk being harassed and exploited or worse, forced to give up the fruits of their labors to these thieves, and the many brave or destitute individuals slain or imprisoned for noncompliance. He could see in his mind the filthy, underfed prisoners in Khala, some near death, working away under fear of pain, and now, knowing what further evil the ill-gotten fruits of the prisoners' labor brought and enabled the clan, enraged him even more. These villains were making a fortune from the backs of their oppressed, enabling them even greater crime and power, all justified by their creed and code. One thing was certain, old or young, the prisoners must be freed. Not only to remedy a personal score Damian and Cam held against their former captors, but also to slow the great engine of the Kunn. The destruction of their former abode of captivity would greatly weaken the Kunn wealth and power machine. No, it would not completely defeat them or halt all their operations but it was a blow that must be dealt. This deed would undo many of their wrongs and slow the machine that drove them. Khala must be shut down.

"We have a personal dispute to settle with them first," Damian said at last. Cam nodded in agreement. "We must return to Khala. Never again shall the Kunn victimize a being in such a manner. We will send the Ahga a message as well. His criminal activities have created some formidable enemies."

"Very well," said Riman. "Then allow me to assist you even more." They took the empty crates and gear back into the barn. Riman equipped them with rope and hook for climbing, a pack containing a week's worth of hard rations, water skins, torches and oil, and other traveling necessities. Riman laid out before them on a table a large map of the area and over the next hours gave them instructions of navigation and taught them all the names of all the places in this western and southern hemisphere of the world, and the numerous peoples and their ways, and the states and their allegiances. Damian and Cam found themselves at last modestly acquainted with their geopolitics and socio-environment.

"I cannot tell you how to approach the mine for it is not charted," said Riman. "Folk do not travel out that way. There is no road thither. You know your own business best. But if I understand your escape correctly then I judge it to be in this area." He pointed to the map. "Somewhere in the Govan Wastes, northeast of Mod. If you travel too far south you'll run into the East Road and the outskirts and suburbs of Mod, namely Bardua, and that is Kunn territory."

"It will not be hard to find," said Cam. "There are no other hills around it for miles. I got a look out the back several times, where they dump the waste and scraps." Damian acknowledged this fact. Cam had further reign in Khala being a miner and knew his way around the facility better than he did. But then there were other things Cam knew.

* * *

They ate a large supper that evening and made their final preparations for their departure for Damian wished to leave without delay. He hoped to arrive there by late tomorrow night, with the help of his speedy horse, under cover of darkness and so make his infiltration. How exactly that was to be accomplished he did not quite know yet, but he felt more than confident they could do it, even if he had to bash his way through Kurg's front door and confront all those accursed guards at once, the thought of which actually appealed to him. His feelings of revenge and justice and a desire to undo this great menace that was quickly gaining power in his own back yard drove him like an engine that wouldn't slow, tireless and powerful. He and Cam both knew the purpose of their refulfillment at death's door and eagerly sought to achieve it.

They withdrew themselves separately for a few moments of solitude before their departure for this moment held great meaning for them. Cam found a length of thin black cloth, and, kneeling, wrapped it around his head as a bandana in a personal ceremony mixed with solemnity and determination. *This will not be removed until my deed accomplished or death take me, so be it.* He remained kneeling outside in the grass in a long moment of meditation, tears running down either side of his round, dark face, for henceforth he was now committing himself to a quest of justice. Damian ventured about his old house momentarily, reacquainting himself and making silent promises in front of old and dusty family portraits before stepping back out. He arranged the portraits and mementos in a small shrine on a bureau in one of the rooms. He looked long upon the pictures of his loved ones, family he was deprived of blessing with the gift of his presence for they had been removed from him so soon. This home to him was a victim of an inconceivable ill, a symbol of a rising new tyranny, a shadow of the oppression sweeping the land. He knelt and placed his head on the hilt of his drawn sword, tears of anger welling in his eyes, he gritted his teeth, his powerful muscles tense and shaking with potency below his sleeveless armor. *This vow I make to you: with the power vested in me this world will be cleansed, their own brotherhood dissolved, their creed broken. This clan shall be undone; this realm set aright.* He looked up and detached himself. His youth here held only superficial sentimental value to him now. He had a new life and destiny. This home now would serve a different purpose. His will was set. He stood before the precious portraits and bowed. They loaded their supplies without further delay onto Bish and mounted him. Riman gave them a map and a star chart to steer by and bade them farewell.

"May the blessing of The Divine One be upon you." said Riman.

"It is," answered Damian. "We shan't be long."

"I doubt it not," said Riman, "I eagerly await your return. Deal them a heavy blow my friends."

"Of that you can be certain," answered Damian and with that they sped away into the deepening dusk.

CHAPTER 5
RETRIBUTION

Leaving Tirien behind they traveled in an easterly direction over the low hills and quickly reached the Ella River. Once again they sought a suitable place to ford the shallow water. Still being late summer they found the water cool and refreshing. Bish quickly emerged and sped up the southern, opposite bank, which was flatter and more firm. Damian and Cam leaned low for Bish was running with the wind and his speed was greater than mortal capability. The full moon waxed brightly in the clear early night sky, dimly revealing the rapidly deteriorating landscape of what soon would be the Govan Wastes. The lush, groved countryside of Tirien failed to spread its fertility to this barren, rocky land. The fertile, soft soil quickly gave way to a hard rocky floor where low grasses and shrubs strove for a foothold. The land was mostly flat but shallow depressions or low rises occasioned the unyielding earth. The visibility was fair thus far and they could see well ahead of them and all around. They saw no sign of a rider anywhere and expected none, for there were no roads here. All traffic was south of Khala, far away, and headed either to Mod or back to Dengland, south and east, but Damian had little doubt the Kunn or other vagabonds would possibly use this flatland as a shortcut to reach the suburbs and villages on the perimeters of Nadea, such as Tirien and Felbruk, especially now that they travel and roam more openly. They kept a sharp lookout, Cam peering ahead with his far seeing eyes, but they took advantage of the flatness and rode swiftly. They rode on well past midnight before they camped and slept until morning.

They awoke eagerly, ate a quick breakfast, and emerged from the shallow pit where they camped and looked around. The sun rode up quickly to a clear sky: typical Khala weather, Damian noted. The weather didn't seem to change much here and the clime and the overall feel of this desolate place helped intensify the painful memories they bore. The land and sky they had so often looked out upon each night brought them a sick feeling, for now they were treading upon it. Heading back to that accursed rock of misery and being in its domain brought no feeling of comfort, only further bitterness. They looked with disgust about them. The land didn't look much different in the light, but they reckoned themselves to be about halfway there. That was exactly what Damian wanted, hoping to arrive within sight of Khala at dusk that day and therefore plan a break-in in the dark. They consulted the map, packed up, and galloped off.

The sun was riding into the west when they halted for a brief meal. The land passed below them as it would have a swift bird. All about them as far as even Cam's eyes could see lay a stony wasteland with hardly a tree to disturb the monotony. Now being many miles from any civilization and a source of food or water they felt the solitude that a vast wilderness can bring, but it suited them. Not a rider or traveler of any kind had they seen thus far but they also knew the road leading to and from Khala would probably have some traffic on it when they got there. If they were lucky maybe some guest of the Kunn hierarchy would once again be visiting Khala. Maybe he'd even be there for some duration, overlooking the evident lack of security and poorly executed detainment of the prisoners. After all, they did only escape two days ago. The Kunn did not want a dark secret like Khala disclosed to the general populace and maybe Kurg was even receiving chastisement for letting two prisoners escape. Damian smiled to himself. *And if this officer was there he will be honored to be buried in Khala with the rest of them,* he thought. The more the merrier. They finished their evening meal and rode off in haste.

It could not have been much more than an hour later of swift riding when Cam pointed in a southeast direction. There was a lone landmass far in the distance, its vast bulk jutting upward in a sea of flatness. From here it looked like a vague shape, a brown shadow taking form in the hazy horizon. Soon even Damian could see it. There could be no mistaking this accursed place. The loathsome shape of the Khala mountain loomed up before them some fifteen miles away. Damian halted his horse and dismounted.

"Cam, can you see anything?" asked Damian while he surveyed the land. Being this close to Khala meant that riders may be near and the two friends stood a fair chance of being discovered. Their figures would be an easy mark against the flatness of the plain.

"There is a road," replied Cam, standing on a rock, "on the southern side of Khala, heading south." He scanned the road in a southerly direction until it was lost from sight. "I can see no one on it. Nothing else moves on the plain. The opening to the mine is facing our position and we are in full view of the watchtowers, although I doubt the sentries could see us this far away."

"We had better wait here until nightfall," said Damian and they all cowered low in a shallow depression to avoid being espied from some errand rider from Khala. "Even then walking unseen to the front gate through the pit will be difficult. It is always lit and well guarded at night, more so now that we escaped. They will be more on their guard now, perhaps they are even still searching for us. I am sure we could take out the tower lookouts easily enough but the entry gate is always locked at night, unless of course they're having a prisoner exhibition in the reinstruction pit. Then we could charge in. We'd have half of them slain before Kurg even knew what was going on. Some of the guards would even be off duty and idle in their barracks. Surprise is going to be key. We've got to neutralize the opposition quickly before they have a chance to organize. Even with our newfound abilities challenging thirty or forty clan soldiers at once will be dangerous. We've got to speed down the halls eliminating them in two's and three's, and we'll need a set of keys, too. Or maybe we could lay in wait by the road and waylay a herd or wagon driver and drive right in."

Cam had been listening to these ideas silently, unconsciously fumbling with some small rocks at his curled up feet while Damian deliberated, and felt it was time to tell his friend his secret. "I do not suggest we approach by the front," he said. "There is another way in."

"Another way in?" Damian asked, incredulous. "How do you know this? The only opening on the back side of Khala is five hundred feet up. They don't mine in close proximity to the exterior. You said yourself the tunnels are not accessible from the outside, only through the furnace room on the inside. The hole you dug originated above the holding cells and brought you out above the meat yard, just far enough to allow you to drop within its enclosure. Unless there's something else you discovered." He turned to Cam.

"That's not the only hole I dug," replied Cam smugly. "I stumbled upon a room to my left while I was digging to the right, trying to gain access to the slaughterhouse area, which I knew would put me behind the gate and from there I would make my way to the stable in my own fashion, where I knew you would be. I was only waiting for a horse to somehow arrive and speed us out of that place. My hole was finished there and while I waited for the arrival of our deliverer I did some exploring. After a short, steep descent I only dug my tunnel six or seven feet inwards before I ventured in a sideways direction, and many times I thought I heard voices coming from the other side of my tunnel while I dug, on the inner side, above the prisoner cells. I knew I was fairly high up so I knew it could not be on the prisoner level that these voices came from, and figured that there must be a room or passageway behind the rock wall of the tunnel, that there must be a fourth or fifth level to the factory unknown to the prisoners. I listened to them many times throughout my tenure in that rat hole, to which I was lowered daily by my guards by means of a rope around my waist. I decided to eventually discover this room when I had completed my original tunnel of escape. I dug very carefully in an inward direction instead of left to right like my other tunnel, which was done, unbeknownst to them. The guards questioned me about the slow progress of my digging and I came up with some interesting excuses to prolong the project. If they pulled me off it before a horse arrived I was doomed.

"Anyway, I had only to dig a short way and I opened a tiny hole in the wall in the upper corner of this mysterious room. This hole enabled me to view the room in its entirety but I dared not make the hole larger than was necessary for my eye and studied the room and its traffic carefully. The Kunn had evidently discovered some kind of fire-gas in the mine, learned its uses, how I can't figure, probably some poor engineers like Riman working for them, and channeled this substance to the furnace room from secret depths within the mountain itself. I always wondered how they kept the furnaces running for they never brought any wood or coal in for the purpose of fuel. It is some dangerous though. I know a few miners that were set afire by its unpredictable and apparently uncontrollable character, and several times at least we had fires in the tunnels and workrooms. The mountain is aptly named. Almost made me glad I was a digger. This room, however, provided access to these channels fashioned out of the rock itself which seemed to direct or pump this gas substance to its desired destination, the smithy, which was directly below this gas room. A guard or two, at the end of a shift or when the fuel was not needed, would turn some kind of wheel or lever to stop the fire."

"Khala is nothing if efficient," observed Damian.

"Yes," replied Cam, "but that is not all I discovered. Eventually I made the hole large enough for me to enter. By now I knew when the guards would make their rounds here so I knew when I could dig. Fortunately my hole of entry was low enough to the floor of this room that I could easily climb down or up to it. I saved stones and form-fitting rocks in my tunnel to conceal the opening, which was very small, and prevent its discovery when not in use. I wished to enter this room not only to study the art and control of this substance but also because there was an opening in the room to the far right, just out of view from my position in the hole, a dark and seemingly unused chasm in the rock which I could only see with difficulty, for its position was parallel to my own, and as you can imagine the presence of another passageway excited my curiosity exceedingly. I never saw the guards go to or come from that way, they always entered by means of a door to my left which left this new chasm a mystery, and I had to satisfy my curiosity on this point. Perhaps this hole would provide us another means of escape, or maybe it was a barren tunnel in the past and was now blocked or abandoned. I had to find out.

"One night I waited for the guards to come in and turn the wheels, which they did as expected and left. I knew it would be some hours before they returned. I removed the stones carefully from my hole and for the first time dropped down into the gas room. They kept this room lit at all times, of course, by means of a torch which I took with me as I approached this unexplored recess, otherwise the utter and impenetrable darkness inside the mountain would have rendered my excursion dangerous and almost impossible. I discovered a tunnel, crudely cut, and descending at a fairly steep but manageable angle, which I descended at once with caution. I couldn't tell you how far this tunnel wormed its way downward, in what must have been a south-easterly direction, but after some time of climbing one-handed and spider-like down this rough shaft I heard the distant but unmistakable sound of running water. With what excitement and curiosity it is needless to say, I proceeded further and threw the rays of the torch as far as I could in front of me. I soon found myself on an almost flat ledge that jutted itself outward above what appeared to be a subterranean river, flowing underneath a great cavern. My wonder and excitement were extreme, and my heart leaped as I stood there aghast. But I had not time on that opportunity to explore this river further for I knew the guards outside that monitored me would soon return and would grow suspicious at my long absence. I climbed back up the tunnel to the gas room and replaced the torch. I should also mention this room provides access to the high outside balcony which overlooks the entirety of the Khala prison. I climbed up the short ladder to it several times when I was able to and had a look around, laying flat on the balcony, careful not to be seen by the watchtower guards which were actually below me from that high level. It's a good view up there, you can see the whole empty plain in front of you. I saw one of the herds being driven in once. I even saw Kurg talking with a strange caravan-driver from somewhere far off. Probably buying himself some hot loot. They always bring interesting trinkets and dainties from the cities for the guards.

"Anyway I climbed back into my hole, which I repaired with the greatest care, and terminated my excursions for the evening. The next day, however, I was able to return to the ledge and I sought for a way down to the stony river bank. Due to the roughness of the cavern wall, climbing down to the floor was fairly easy, which was about fifteen feet below me, and I stood on the bank holding aloft the torch. I immediately took some water to drink and had my fill, then followed the river. After walking a short while the cavern abruptly ended and I had to swim in order to discover the water's destination. I placed the torch upright in a niche in the wall near my point of departure and plunged in. There was, thankfully, a gap of about a foot above the river and between the low cavern wall, so I could breathe as I clutched the rockside desperately for fear of being carried away, but I did not have far to go. The water did not flow overly fast but it carried me to the exit."

"What, to the outside of Khala?" exclaimed Damian in disbelief. Cam's proficiency as a sneak was amazing even him.

"Yes, to the outside and freedom," sighed Cam, relishing the memory, "which looking at the map and the site before our eyes must be located somewhere on the eastern side of the mountain. There is a small but enterable crack in the rock just above the running water. The river, however, continued from that point and turned right and downward under the earth again. I had to cross the river to the other side which was frightening enough for a weak, little starved thing as myself, but I managed to scramble onto the opposite bank before the water took me under the earth and certain death, for there was no longer clearance for air past that point. I pulled myself up through the magnificent opening and to my unbelieving, blinking eyes, I beheld the open world. The feeling of joy and triumph at the sight of the sky and the open plain was indescribable, and I breathed in deeply the free air. I just wanted to run like an animal across the plain until I collapsed. At least I would have died happy. I did not enjoy my rewarding excursion long, though. I knew freedom was useless if it meant dying of starvation in that vast wilderness and besides, I needed to take my only friend with me. I made my way back with difficulty but felt as one with renewed strength and newfound hope. I waited in my hole for some time before emerging to dry. I had in the end made only a few trips to that wonderful crack of freedom, for it was dangerous and risked my discovery. I can only conclude that the tunnel to the river was originally dug as a mine shaft and they stumbled upon the river and cavern accidentally, but it was not without profit. They found their water source, though they do not use that tunnel for it. The Kunn no longer excavate that way for obvious reasons and they certainly do not let prisoners in there or the gas room. Besides myself I don't think any prisoner is aware of its existence. I couldn't tell you these things for your own protection, you understand."

"Have the guards discovered your tunnel?" asked Damian.

"The hole outside to the meat yard, yes," replied Cam. "They will have discovered that by now, but it won't do them much good. No mog could fit into that hole, not even Kurg's little scribe Morish the Turuk, I made sure of it, and since the hole to the gas room is still concealed, since I did not escape that way, I must also assume they don't know about it. If Kurg knew about my access to the water-tunnel he would have it undoubtedly blocked or barred, but I think it is still an accessible underground entrance. I propose we go that way."

Damian looked out into the distance, the ominous shadow of Khala marking itself plainly against the miles of nothingness that surrounded it. He digested this new information carefully and his mind walked him through every hall and crevice he remembered about Khala, trying to think of other possibilities of infiltration and execution. Whatever they were going to do, they weren't traveling closer until deep nightfall for fear of being seen. Sentries or riders were a distinct possibility being this close to the mountain and they could not afford premature discovery. The land was so open and the sky so clear it was perilously dangerous to move. They found a small pit to rest in while the remainder of the afternoon carried on slowly, and they laid low and took turns watching. Damian had the first watch for he could not sleep anyway, being undecided about how best to proceed. Certainly infiltrating the camp by surprise and from underground was preferable to knocking down the front gate and taking them all on at once. Why this tunnel would bring them right into the heart of the whole facility without alerting anyone. They could probably sneak right into Kurg's own chamber as he was sleeping, Damian thought. A fitting wakeup call indeed. He was liking this idea and heartily accepted it after some deliberation. Another thought occurred to him and he wondered if he could make use of it. He woke Cam for his watch when the time came and posed a last question.

"This substance you speak of creates fire," Damian pondered aloud.
"Yes," replied Cam.

* * *

A clear dusk was setting in, though nightfall was still some hours off. Cam sat up at the lip of the pit, watching the horizon to the east for some time while Damian napped. His far seeing eyes thought they caught a hint of movement on the plain in the far distance. It was not traffic on the Khala road, for that was to the south. This movement was on the opposite side of Khala, to the north, so Cam figured it could not be errand riders or herd drivers. Besides, there weren't many of them, whatever they were. Whatever these beings were they must have a specific purpose and were not just wandering about. They had to be looking for something or someone to be out here. The figures seemed to be moving steadily in a westward direction, towards them, and Cam watched intensely.

The figures drew closer, now probably two miles out and Cam could discern the unmistakable silhouette of kelgan, and yes, Kunn riders. He stiffened. There were four of them and something else even further off, moving more slowly. It looked like some kind of horse-drawn wagon but it wasn't keeping up with the fast moving kelgan, who were moving quickly in side to side directions, well separated as if the better to cover a greater area. At this rate and if they maintained their present course the riders would be upon them very soon. He woke Damian.

"Must be a Khala hunting party," said Damian, peering at them over the pit edge. "Must still be looking for us."

"We'll have to take them out," said Cam. "They seem to be almost heading right for us. If they see us they might send word and spoil our sneak attack."

"Yes, they must be destroyed. It doesn't seem as though they're altering course. They can't know we're here by the way they're riding but it won't be long for the kelgan to pick up our scent if they haven't already, though they'll probably smell Bish first. Those kelgan are well trained and experienced." He looked down at his horse which was crouched tensely, waiting for a command.

"Just wait until they come a little closer," said Cam, holding back an intensifying impatience. He couldn't wait to attack but they would have to be eliminated quickly. Maybe one of them even whipped him just the other day, he thought, during that horrible interrogation, whipped him until he passed out. His back no longer bore the scars but his memory did. He ground his teeth and flexed his fingers, itching to pounce. He eased the swords on his back and readied his throwing spikes. Damian watched their progress tensely and kept his hand on Bish who sensed in his master that action would be called for very soon.

After a short, tense wait the riders were not more than two hundred yards away. They had just turned slightly southward, apparently trying to circle an area, and were no longer facing the escapees directly but still were drawing nearer. Damian could see their merciless faces and cruel fangs, their thick leather armor and banding, their swords and bows at their sides. They did not seem to be speaking at all but were scouring the area quickly and quietly, riding in a wide, four-man front and communicating with hand signals, hoping to surprise the ones they hunted. The hunters turned their heads from side to side and covered the distance quickly and skillfully. The kelgan must have caught their scent because they suddenly and simultaneously turned west again, heading right for them. This was the same party that would have dragged Damian back to his prison when he was found, he thought. And what would they have done to him upon his return? He growled and drew his bow. When they were a hundred yards off they sprang their trap.

This hunting party had been dispatched from Khala a day before at Kurg's orders, relieving the first that had returned empty-handed. Finally, some action, they thought. The stunt these prisoners pulled made them all look like fools to the Ahga. Oh, they would pay, pay dearly. These riders rode with a vengeance, seeking to avenge their fallen captain at the hands of these two miserable little rodents. They knew the names and faces of those they hunted, knew them well. And a reward of twenty gold pieces went to the group that found them. That would buy them quite a bit of loot in Mod the next time they were there. They could pick up some more *rovola* teeth from the vendor in the marketplace to adorn their armor with. Those rare and expensive fangs would make them the envy of the unit back at Khala. Only Kurg could claim to have a few of them, very prestigious. This tight group of devoted clan members was looking forward to this, and you could be sure the filthy prisoners would be caught. Kurg needn't worry. They had trained with these kelgan on hunts many times. They would drag the escaped prisoners triumphantly back in the meat wagon they had brought with them and some level of honor would be returned to their tainted detachment and Kurg would be saved from dishonor.

The hunt was not going well thus far, though, and this intensified their anger. They had already circled the area several times before but came up with nothing. The runaways couldn't be that far off, no one could even survive out here. Maybe someone had picked them up, some agent from Kandar sent to rescue them. How dare they defy the Kunn. The clan was always having problems with those obstructionists to the north. And didn't they just imprison some official or diplomat from that rebel country? No, it couldn't be. Wait, the kelgan picked up something. Maybe those fools are just over that small rise…

Bish launched himself forward like a projectile out of the depression at Damian's command and charged the kelgan head-on. The distance was not great and at this high rate of speed that distance would be closed in a matter of seconds. Damian already had his bow drawn on Bish's back and the first Kunn rider was down before they even knew what they were up against. The hunters gave a surprised shout and drew their swords but it was too late to do them much good. Cam, standing on the back of the great horse, threw a spike at one of the oncoming riders, puncturing his throat and dropping him to the ground with a tumble, then jumped on the back of one of the steeds as it passed them. Damian replaced his bow and drew his sword, wheeling around as he passed the two that were left. Cam, on the kelga's back, stabbed the rider with his short sword and dismounted, jumping high into the air and landing firmly on the ground. There was only one left and, dismayed at this effective surprise attack and seeing his slim chance of survival, he was attempting to flee. He wheeled his kelga steed around toward the east again, back towards Khala, but Damian and Bish were close on his tail. He looked back in fear at this determined and swift rider closing the gap quickly behind him, sword drawn, and desperately urged his swift mount to even greater speed. But there seemed to be no outrunning this horse. He saw the futility in escape and brought his steed about, charging his pursuer. Cam stood stone-still on a rock and watched Damian's sword break clean through the curved sword of the mog on their impact and clove through him in a single blow. The kelgan fled Damian's wrath and he returned immediately to pick up Cam.

"Easy enough," said Damian. "I just hope we weren't seen, though it is getting dark."

"Didn't have much of a choice," replied Cam, "though I can't say I didn't enjoy it."

"Didn't you say they had a wagon or something with them?" asked Damian.

"Yes, it's over there." Cam pointed to the cart in the distance, parked about a half mile back. This crude wooden cart was equipped with chains and shackles for the purpose of prisoner transport and the hunters had brought it with them for this intent. It was unmanned and drawn by a lone mule. "Why do you ask?"

"I have an idea."

* * *

As the night sky grew darker they made one last pause for a meal before they attempted their infiltration. Khala was still almost ten miles away but the reluctant sunset in this open land made moving too risky. They waited for deep night to finally set in, and when they felt it was safe to move they again mounted Bish but rode more slowly and carefully, riding northeastward towards Khala, seeking to encircle it from the north and reaching the back unseen. From that direction they would not have to cross the road to their right. To present themselves on the road, even for a moment, would be perilous. The sky was clear, as usual, and the stars and moon provided some light. They were exposed to view by the watchtowers but at this distance even Cam's eyes could not make out any figures or riders within the circular enclosure, though he could make out some smoke rising above the mountain from what could only be the burn pit. Looks like the day's toil is over, thought Cam. They decided to ride more northward some way to make line of sight inside the camp impossible and eliminate this danger while they were still far away, then ride more quickly eastward, flanking it. These last few miles passed tensely but uneventfully. Damian and Cam looked around them constantly in fear and anticipation of being espied by some errant rider or scout. The dark giant shadow of Khala drew closer and more ominous, filling the twilit skyline in front of them. After a time Cam said the entrance and watchtowers were no longer in sight, that they had circled the mountain to the left sufficiently and they should no longer be a threat.

When they were finally only a mile away they dismounted and walked. The entrance to the camp was to their right and drew closer, just out of sight around the bend, but the light from it projected forth and illuminated the road and ground in front of it. They looked upon this accursed rock of misery rising quickly before them with disgust and anger, heightening their already potent emotions and state of alertness which thrilled them to intense excitement that increased with each step closer to this place of fear. The loathing that this place once held for them though was replaced with desire. They no longer viewed Khala as something to be avoided and fled from; now it was an enemy, a target that demanded elimination, a beast that must be taken down. Like hunting cats with their prey in sight they crept silently by the entrance, now only a hundred yards to their right. They crouched low and stealthily, sidestepping cat-like and silently closer to the vertical rock wall. They could distinctly make out the familiar voices, mog and Turuk, a sound they despised, probably the tower sentries around the corner, bickering or joking at their posts. They had listened to those voices for years, cramped in their cells, and the fact that those cells they once occupied were almost within reach and sight made them shake with a mixture of excitement and dread. A sound in the distance alerted Cam and he signaled to Damian to lie down. Damian whispered to Bish at his side and the horse immediately dropped to the ground next to him. Bish remained while Damian and Cam crawled on the hard rock floor toward the road somewhat. Damian could now hear what could only be a small herd and supply wagons approaching down the road toward Khala, but they were still quite distant. The supply trains often traveled at night to Khala, using the darkness as cover. They had time to hide behind a low fold in the earth beyond the light that streamed forth from the mine entrance. A horn blast and calls sounded from within and they could see several guards emerge onto the road awaiting the delivery.

"Look Damian, livestock delivery," whispered Cam.

"Yes, the prisoners will need food and steeds for their journey home. This is good." Several wagons finally pulled in with the livestock and disappeared into the camp, along with the Khala guards.

Damian and Cam crawled back to Bish and continued to make their way carefully and quietly around to the outside of the mountain and out of sight. When they were out of earshot of the front entrance they again mounted their horse and rode along the steep rock wall, looking for Cam's hidden river. The clear sky enabled the half moon to shed some light but this side of Khala was not facing the moon and therefore cast into shadow. They didn't dare light a torch for they would be seen, and they knew that over five hundred feet up, somewhere on the rock wall, there was an opening for waste deposit. Though it was probably not in use now the guards occasionally would venture there when they were not on duty, passing time idly. The view must have been impressive from that high vantage. Cam couldn't remember exactly where the opening in the earth was for the river but he felt he would probably hear it before he saw it anyway. They continued to tread around the back side of Khala, listening for running water.

It must have been over an hour later, creeping along the edge of the rock in a southward direction when they finally heard what they sought. Cam went running ahead and Damian followed, leading Bish. They had almost completed the circuit around the mountain when they found the small cave entrance, not much larger than a burrow of some large, wild animal, on the southeastern side of Khala. They stood upon the brink and peered inside. What little light there was allowed them to see a narrow river several feet below them, running towards and past them in a small, dark cavern. Somewhat further downstream it plunged back under the mountain and into total darkness. Damian decided to go first and would pull Cam in later with the rope, along with their pack of supplies. Entry would be dangerous and difficult for the current flowed out against them and Damian would not have the benefit of light until he reached the bank on the inside. They debated that Cam would have to hold a torch within the cavern as best he could until Damian managed to venture further in. The front entrance into Khala was still a considerable distance away, about a mile, and the chance that the light would be seen was improbable, but it was a risk they may have to take. Discovery now was not an option, however, and Damian finally decided that he would just have to feel his way in, crawling hand over hand on the opposite bank, against the current until he found the ledge which Cam assured him could not be more than twenty or twenty-five feet upriver from here. Damian pulled the pack from the horse and removed the rope. He tied an end around his waist and plunged in feet first. He swam to the other side of the river, which was about twelve feet across here, and proceeded to feel his way down the rock and into the thick darkness beyond. Cam lowered himself into the water next, holding himself stationary onto the rock listening for Damian's call, feeding the rope upstream.

After a few moments he could hear him, he had gotten through to the inner ledge. Cam climbed back onto the ground outside. He tied the remainder of the rope around his chest securely and dug out a torch and lit it, using the enveloping shroud of the cavern to conceal the light as best he could. Attempting passage through the cavern in the dark would have been impossible, as would lighting the torch on the inside bank, so Cam risked momentary exposure. Once the torch was alight he carefully lowered himself in again, holding the torch high and calling to Damian who began pulling him in with the rope from his end. Cam looked over his shoulder fearfully, half expecting a wandering guard to discover them. He pulled Cam in quickly, the torch lighting up the entire cavern on his way over. Cam handed the torch to Damian who was standing on the inside ledge and Cam went back for the pack which held the food and more torches. The current quickly brought him back. He climbed back onto the ledge outside, gave instructions to Bish and bade him farewell (*that horse is some smart,* he thought), took one last look around, and again plunged into the cave with the pack held high above him. Damian again pulled him through against the current and they at last arrived together on the ledge in the cavern and proceeded carefully inside.

Cam led the way along the rough and noisy river edge for some way, slowly navigating around anomalous subterranean rock formations in their path, when Damian stopped and looked up. He noticed a narrow shaft cut into the uneven rock ceiling above him ascending upwards in a straight line. It could not have been formed by nature so uniform were its dimensions and angle, it had to be carved by hand but it was too narrow to climb into and without rails or ladder. Damian had little doubt Cam could climb it but suddenly he rushed forward and shaded the torch.

"That must be the well shaft," he whispered. "We must be right under south block. I wonder if that poor handless fellow is still there, or if Kurg finally killed him." They hurried forward with their revealing torch, hoping no one above noticed the strange light that lingered in the well shaft momentarily.

"There it is," said Cam a few moments later and pointed upwards. There was the elevated ledge, about fifteen feet above them, just as Cam said. The cavern continued onward for some distance in the darkness until it ended abruptly further upstream.

"I'll have to leave the torch here," said Damian. "Probably a good idea to leave one here anyway. We don't know under what chaotic circumstances we may be making our escape." He jammed the torch in a crack in the wall above his head.

"Let me go up first and have a look around," said Cam, and he lightly hopped his way up the rough wall to the ledge, beyond which lay the steep tunnel that led to the gas room. He groped his way up this tunnel a short way and listened in the darkness for any sign of guards or activity in that room above, which at this time of night could be expected. Cam judged that the shift must be over by now and the guards would be cutting off the fire if they haven't already. Not hearing anything nearby he climbed further up nimbly in the dark, feeling his way up the steep but rough tunnel. It was only a few moments of climbing when some light from the gas room became discernible. Cam quickened his pace and soon reached the top of the tunnel and peered over the lip of its floor, listening. The torchlight from the room threw its rays somewhat around the bend in the hall, dimly illuminating the water-tunnel, but he still saw or heard nothing. Cam stood up on the level floor and silently walked toward the light. He had once again entered Khala, but not as a prisoner this time, emaciated and praying for escape. This time he had actually sought entrance to this detested hole of misery and destitution for he was on a mission of justice and he grinned with each step, savoring the thought of dealing a heavy blow to the Kunn and having a personal hand in what he intended to be their ultimate downfall. This will be but the first blow, he thought, and slowly looked around the bend in the hall. Now he could hear voices coming from the right and he soon saw two mogs enter and immediately carry on with the turning of the wheels, of which there were several, spread out along the wall horizontally. The nearer one finally got to within ten feet of Cam's position, just around the corner. Cam could see the other guard at the far end of the room, busy with his own task. He lunged at the first one, leaped fully onto his back and looped the garrot around his neck, tying it and dragging him backwards around the corner. The mog dropped to the floor quickly and quietly, unconscious. This silent task completed he dragged the body into the darkness of the tunnel. The other guard turned to leave and almost opened the door out when he noticed the absence of his friend. He turned back and walked toward the water tunnel with a grin.

"Playing around again, Brogga?" he asked as he came closer. "Did you find the runaways? Or did you find ol' Tolbog's rotting corpse down there? Har, har, har," he laughed. "Hurry or we'll miss the show." He turned the corner but the smile on his face vanished and his career with the Kunn ended suddenly when a flying spike crashed through his forehead. Cam pulled his body into the shadows next to the other one. He ran into the gas room and took a quick look around. He listened at the door and heard nothing close by, grabbed the torch off the wall and hopped back down the water tunnel to get Damian.

Damian had climbed up the ledge and waited while Cam was away. He was just about to climb up after his friend when he saw him descending the tunnel with a torch and calling him quietly. Damian shouldered the pack and climbed up the lit tunnel.

"No one's here," said Cam when Damian reached the top, "well, no one alive anyway."

"I see," replied Damian noticing the bodies lying neatly on the ground. Cam brought him into the gas room and showed him the tunnel he had cut into the wall when he was still a prisoner. It was undisturbed, fortunately. Cam then showed him the ladder which he had previously spoken of, that ascended to another tunnel and to the balcony outside.

"That will bring you to the balcony that overlooks the whole inner yard," said Cam. "I suppose we should take a look."

It was late at night and Kurg was having his usual prisoner demonstration down in the pit below. Many fires were lit and most of the guards were present, attending the function and making some noise. A single prisoner was tied to the stake in the middle of the pit, receiving his treatment. This prisoner had dared to voice disgruntlement and even opposition to the Kunn in front of the other prisoners and in Kurg's own presence. He even went so far as to denounce the organization and declare their deeds evil and unjust. One day, he said, a hero would rise up and put an end to their tyranny, that the people of the lands would live in peace and without fear of their brutality. The Kunn's days were numbered, he said, and the Divine One would punish them. These words so enraged Kurg he had him gagged and bound on the spot and dragged outside to the stake where he waited all day in the sun without water for his execution which was to take place that evening. Such rubbish must be silenced. The Kunn was proclaimed to be favored with the Mari; unbelievers would be destroyed in time. Well, the prisoner had received enough punishment from the whip by now to satisfy even Kurg, and he was at last ready for its conclusion. He was about to give the order of termination when one of the tower guards gave a shout. Everyone paused and turned toward the front entrance to see what it might be. A delivery or something was here, but that was strange because it had already arrived. Maybe the hunting party had finally returned. They'd better have caught them, those slugs, or there would be hell to pay, thought Kurg. It's about time they found them, what was he paying these useless guards for anyway? They can't even take down a couple of starved boys and his hunters that he had once bragged about to the Ahga were certainly not living up to their reputation. Ah, looks like they caught them. Here comes the meat wagon now.

The wooden prisoner cart rolled in slowly and unescorted, which was odd, drawn by the mule, the frightened animal having no place else to go but back to his home. As it came closer and into the light the lighthearted faces of the onlookers changed to uncomprehending and confused stares. Not only were there no kelgan escorts, the bodies that the cart carried were not of starved boys at all, but piled with dead soldiers of the Kunn, four of them to be precise. Wrapped around the downcast head of the mule, as if in mockery, was a red bandana of the clan. A hush fell and glances of perplexity were exchanged. Kurg's face twisted with rage and disgust as the cart rolled slowly by within reach of his shaking hands. *What in Vidia is this? The prisoners cannot behold this!* He glared at his lieutenants, seeking an explanation, but they cowered at his anger. He was going to break something. With lowered ears and solemn step the mule sadly and calmly dragged its burden to the holding pen, right through the speechless guards who drew back and made way for it as if they were afraid to touch it. Poor Kurg could find no words of explanation either and after some time of trembling with anger simply bellowed, "EXECUTE THE PRISONER!"

Cam scrambled up the ladder like a squirrel and crept down the short hall that brought him to the ledge outside. This ledge, or balcony of rock, being in the exact center of the 'U' of Khala, and being four levels high overlooked the entire inner yard of the slave camp, which was well lit at all hours to keep an eye on the prisoners. Cam's eyes scanned quickly the entire area from left to right. First he viewed the slaughterhouses and meat yard below, quiet and vacant, except for the livestock which were chained up in the holding pen, stirring uneasily. His gaze moved upwards to the prisoner levels on south block, all now filled. Hands clutched bars, feet dangled over the edges of the cells, all quiet and subdued, ten units to each of the three levels. Then he saw the guards in their distant watchtowers on either side of the Khala entrance, amusing themselves with the festivities below. His eyes shifted to the right side prisoner cells, or north block, a mirror image of its counterpart, the haggard prisoners in a similar state. They are all in for the night, he thought to himself. Good. That would keep them safe though there was certainly a fair amount of wailing and yelling going on down there in the middle, and he cast his glance downward to the pit where there was much activity. It looked as though there was a prisoner tied up down there, probably receiving some unwarranted treatment. *I remember what that was like,* Cam thought and his face grimaced. Kurg was down there with most of his guards, also good, and the poor fellow was barely alive before them. Cam couldn't tell who it was for he was slumped over, clinging to life. He was only held slightly upright by the bonds around his wrists, fixed to the post. That's strange, everything suddenly went quiet. He looked more closely down into the pit and saw the mule pull in. He had difficulty holding back a chuckle at the look of the lost faces down there. His grin changed to fear though when he heard Kurg bellow out his order. A guard with a spear took a place directly in front of the doomed soul and the other guards made way. His back was to Cam.

"Damian! Damian!" screeched Cam above a whisper. He couldn't contain his terror and was shaking and jumping uncontrollably. "Damian come quick!" Cam was hissing with intense fear. Damian rushed up the ladder and down the hall and beheld the impending carnage. The powerful mog guard raised his spear...

"I don't think so," growled Damian. He jumped fully onto the rock balcony outside, beyond caring that he was now in full view of everyone in the camp. The emergency admitted him no delay. With amazing speed his great bow was in one hand, an arrow in the other. He loaded it, drew it back, and released one of Riman's specially crafted garvonite arrows across the yard and down into the pit.

The guard pulled his spear back and prepared to throw. They were all glad to be ridding themselves of this nuisance prisoner, and after what just happened they needed some vengeance. But suddenly the executioner let out a hideous shriek as an arrow went through his back. The spear then fell from his grasping hand as he collapsed lifeless before the feet of the prisoner, who looked up astonished. The guards froze again in silence and awe, then they looked around to see whence such a deadly shaft could possibly have come. What was happening? What is all this trickery? The prisoners in their cells, also witness to these goings-on and no less astonished, actually stood up behind their bars, trying to make sense of the miracle and discover their deliverer. In the next moment, scores of fingers pointed to the balcony where stood Damian, under the stars with the breeze in his hair, nocking another arrow. The moment of silence where time seemed to stand still was immediately followed by total chaos. Cries of joy went up from the prison blocks while shouts of rage bellowed from the guards.

"INTRUDER!!" shouted Kurg and his great booming voice echoed throughout the enclosure and shook the earth. "GET HIM!!" he thundered, and utter chaos and hysteria commenced: Kurg shouted orders to his men who seemed to be flying in all directions and bumping into each other; a rush was made for the main gate on the first level; alarm horns from the watchtowers sounded; the prisoner was forgotten (to his relief); the prisoners were screaming and shaking the bars of their cages and pounding them with rocks, making a great noise and clatter. The prisoners, for the first time in too long, were filled with a heretofore unknown energy and excitement. The half starved skeletal creatures actually became hysterical with rebellion, their hunger and pain forgotten. The guards had to beat them back with sticks and clubs through the bars in a vain attempt to subdue them. Everyone seemed to feel that the Khala slave camp had come to an end and that the moment of deliverance was upon them. Damian picked out Kurg from the frenzied crowd and shot an arrow at him. Another guard, instead, crossing in front of Kurg on his way to the gate caught the arrow in his throat and dropped dead at Kurg's feet. Kurg looked up at Damian with rage and cursed. He knew that arrow was intended for him. But then there was definitely something familiar about that face that glared back at him. He watched this mysterious rebel dive back down the hall and out of sight as a thicket of arrows and darts pounded the high balcony wall where he once stood.

"So much for a sneak attack," Damian said as he ran down the short corridor followed by Cam, hopping with energy at the deadly excitement.

"Nice shot," he said. "We can still do it." They flew down the ladder and burst through the door that exited from the gas room. They could still plainly hear the horns and chaos echoing outside.

"Careful," said Cam, "the guard barracks are right below us." They bolted down the hall which turned left. They saw a door straight ahead of them and a hall that branched off to the left that seemed to head downstairs. "That door has to belong to the warden's chamber," Cam said. "I'm curious to see what he's hiding in there."

"Maybe on the way back," replied Damian. They stopped at the end of the hall and looked left around the corner to see if anyone was coming. The heavy metal door to Kurg's chamber was locked, so they turned their attention down the hall, where a carved staircase descended. The Khala mine was not overly large or complicated so they knew that the guards knew roughly where they were and would not take long at all to reach the intruders they sought. Damian and Cam wanted to get into the heart and larger areas of the mine to prevent getting trapped in the upper, smaller levels. They needed to descend rapidly to the areas where they could hide or fight before they were caught, and to fulfill their delicate and daring plan.

"I hear guards down the hall to the left," said Cam and they hustled down the staircase. "I think it must be their barracks. Maybe those inside are off duty or sleeping and don't know what's going on yet."

At the bottom of the stairs was a landing and a set of open double doors to the left. Not interested in taking things slowly and quietly anymore Damian jumped in front of the doors to find two mog guards right in the doorway, attempting to leave after hearing the alarms and gearing up for action. The guards ran to the doorway and stopped dead to find a large, powerful, unchained and well armed human not quite cowering in terror and fear as expected. They paused and looked at Damian dumbfounded for a moment; in the next Damian smashed their heads together, dropping them instantly. Several other guards from the distant rear of this large room cried out and rushed forward past rows of racks for sleeping. How did a prisoner get up here? Cam rushed in and together they grabbed the swords of the prostrate guards, closed the doors which opened outwards, and quickly jammed the swords under the doors locking them in. The guards inside banged on the door and yelled. Damian and Cam didn't give it another thought but were already bolting down the stairs. They had to reach the huge work room on the first level and stage an attack before Kurg and his soldiers did.

"That should hold them for a while," said Damian. They reached the bottom of the stairs and were now down to the first level. They turned left and found a closed wooden door. Damian tried the handle and from this side it required no key. It opened to a small room which happened to be simply a buffer between the furnace work room/smithy and the staircase passage that led back to the sentry barracks. The guard on post in this room turned toward the intruders casually, expecting his replacement, but all he remembered was a large, incoming fist and two figures rushing past him before the world went dark. Cam stopped to take his keys while Damian unbolted the door. This heavy wooden door had a barred cutout for viewing the main work room and anyone trying to enter the upstairs barracks.

Damian couldn't see anyone in the work room yet and swung the door open.

"Looks like we beat them to it," he said. "There's no one here yet, but they'll probably be here any moment. Let's give them a surprise." They ran into the empty and quiet main work room of Khala. This room was huge and had a lofty ceiling. It was dim now despite the many torches which lined either wall, and the room was so big only Cam could barely make out the distant opposite wall to the south. There were several large furnaces against the western wall and iron tables of large size and thickness for metalworking placed about. Huge vats of steel were suspended from the roof by heavy chains, moved and adjusted by massive pulleys which traversed the room on overhead rails, by gears and heavy wheels. Large wagons of rock and dirt were parked in front of the two mine shaft entrances on the east wall, boring their way deep into the mountain and below it in an eastward direction. The entrances to the tunnels flanked the large, locked room where all the tools of the Khala mine were held. The tool room was always carefully manned and guarded during working hours but was now quiet.

"We need to get in there," said Damian just outside the tool room door. He pulled at the heavy iron door momentarily.

"We won't have time now," said Cam by his side. "They're coming." He looked expectantly at the door on the far southern wall on the other end of the room. Many booted feet were rapidly approaching.

The guards burst into the furnace room from the south, wielding torches and swords. They quickly spread out in the huge room, making their way to the far end. Kurg entered barking orders and was in very ill humor. He had run his subjects like cattle trying to get here in hopes of beating his intruders but he knew they had a shorter run than they did. Those rebels must have made it here already and could be anywhere now—the prisoner blocks, the mine shafts, or even somewhere in this vast room where two villains could easily conceal themselves among the gear and heaps of clutter and junk. Wonderful. First a dual escape, a *successful* dual escape, and now two bold rebels broke into his previously perceived impenetrable and inescapable fortress of rock with the obvious intent to sabotage it, maybe even break out one of his prisoners. He did have in custody several high profile prisoners, captive individuals of wealthy or prestigious backgrounds, enemies of the Kunn which the Ahga felt necessary to have removed from his society. In fact he just recently jailed a northerner, some dignitary or spy from Demar who had vital information the Ahga didn't want disclosed, but with whom he would negotiate at a later time. Kurg remembered the arrival of this foreigner, sent to Khala with a specific letter to Kurg from the Ahga himself. *See to it that he speaks to no one,* the note said. Kurg had him locked in solitary confinement, no questions asked. Perhaps that's what this was, word had reached the cities of the north of this official held captive here and some mercenary or agent of the Hattél, was dispatched for his release. How could such a secret find its way to enemy territories so quickly? His guards were too easily bought. When he found out who leaked the information he'd cut the traitor's tongue clean off with the bastard's own knife. It had been a while since he'd made an example of one of his own, and this is the price he paid for his leniency.

Furthermore, someone must have also revealed the secret underground river-tunnel. None, absolutely none of the prisoners could possibly have known about that. The fragile weakness of the mine must be kept secret. If a prisoner discovered that vital weak point it might be exploited, and that would spell doom for certain. Kurg knew that cursed hole would bite him one day if he didn't block it, but he left it open as an emergency escape. That hole will be the death of us all one day, he said to himself many times, knowing the mine's volatility, though he often went down there himself if he ever needed 'a word' with one of his men. The tunnel was well isolated, however; no prisoner would have any hope of even reaching that perilous shaft located upstairs behind the guard barracks and all these locked doors. But nothing seemed to be going right for him these past few weeks. He'd already received a visit from an officer of the Baccád, the closest and most trusted members of the Kunn, very dangerous, who clearly made it known to Kurg the Ahga's dissatisfaction with his recent handling of the facility. Decreasing production and runaways, why the mighty Kurg, it seemed, was losing his touch, he said. He was told in no uncertain terms that he was one more mistake away from expulsion. And the Ahga did not permit life beyond service to members that are expelled. The possibility of an excommunicated Kunn member turning against the Ahga was real and must be forcibly prevented. He certainly was on his last leg and how he was going to prevent this last episode from reaching the ears of the Ahga, he did not know. He had, however, taken matters into his own hands with regards to the Baccád dispatch. He wouldn't be telling the Ahga anything too soon. One small blessing was that the prisoners were all locked up still or he'd have a riot to deal with as well. Those filthy rats were making so much noise upstairs some passing nomads from Mod might hear them. He shook with rage then remembered the prisoners he still had. The rebels weren't here so he broke up his troop and assigned them prisoner blocks to guard, each with a lieutenant for supervision.

"Find and eliminate those rebels," Kurg shouted to his crew before they departed. "A week's leave in Mod to the one who kills them. No one gets in, no one gets out. Seal off the cell blocks!" he roared. The guards fled his wrath and two groups of ten each headed for the cell blocks, one group to each side of the facility, but ten remained. Kurg was not finished in this room and still hadn't explored the mine shafts yet. Eight of the guards took places around the room and doors. Kurg and two others began an extensive search of the room. There were only two of the rebels and this room was quite large and equipped enough to make their discovery difficult.

The guards had paced up and down the room for a few moments, searching under work tables, looking in the furnace cavities and prodding piles of scrap metal and rocks, shadowed closely by Kurg. He was always more concerned with speed than tidiness around here and now it became a problem. Clutter and debris were everywhere. One of the guards came close to one of the rock-carts. He stopped and looked in, only to be suddenly beheaded. Damian jumped out of the wagon with a roar, his bloody sword held high. The guards, not accustomed to this level of fierce resistance and seeing an armed, bold warrior with fire in his eyes in their midst, actually paused a moment in fear and wonder. Kurg let out a roar and they all charged in.

The melee that ensued was fast and deadly. One of the guards at first threw his spear at Damian who caught it in mid-air and launched it at another incoming Hidari, impaling him. Cam jumped out of the roof-suspended vat in which he was hiding and somersaulted his way through the air onto one of the guard's shoulders. The surprised guard found himself stabbed in the neck by a dagger-wielding demon. Damian lopped off an arm of another one who swung at him. Two guards were charging Damian from behind but they were quickly felled by Cam's throwing spikes. Damian nodded gratitude.

There were four guards left, and Kurg, who seemed slightly disconnected, and was approaching the scene slowly and deliberately as if relishing the moment. He thought he had recognized this rogue outside when he first saw him, and he was right. The faces of these two rebels could not now be mistaken though their physical forms had benefited from some unaccountable alteration. There, before him, he watched his two escapees eliminate his guards at first with a burning curiosity, then with an evil, satisfying happiness as their identities were slowly revealed to him. Here indeed were the two runaways who had caused him grief and fear these past two days, fear of the Ahga and his punishing henchmen, fear of what unspeakable repercussions would certainly befall him because of these two rats. He didn't know how they affected their escape or how they returned, and under what gift or power or guise they were thus so quickly fulfilled and blessed by puzzled him greatly, but he did know he was going to take great pleasure in their impending ruin which he would personally bring about. He dismissed the mystery of their return. Their strange resurrection was but trivial now. The deeds of these two ingenious rogues brought into

104

question Kurg's competence and his name was now associated with weakness and foolishness. Ratarra and his little imp friend soiled his almighty name here and among the Kunn. I remember him, thought Kurg, that imp was used as an advance explorer and dug the air duct tunnels. He remembered asking for a very small boy some years ago for just such a purpose. And how could he forget his beloved Ratarra, that filthy, weak, teary-eyed, animal-loving fool? He would pay dearly for the death of his prized lieutenant and strongman. How that starved boy managed that he couldn't figure. A lucky shot perhaps, but Ratarra's luck had run out. Belósh would be avenged. Kurg enjoyed making an example of that pathetic, kelgan-fodder toting, stable rat before, but if Ratarra thought that was painful what Kurg was about to do to him would make him screech like a pig that was being burned alive. He smiled to himself. He even remembered what became of his mother and sister. Belósh had told him the day Ratarra was delivered to him for service. He had also received and updated confirmation of their interesting fates some years ago by one of his connections abroad. *A fitting end for their defiance.* These two fools were but petty nuisances now, like mice in his breadbox that had eluded him before but now were trapped and beyond help. Their capture would save him.

He grabbed one of his remaining guards. "Get the others!" Kurg pointed to the southern door which led to south block. Another of the guards, perceiving his thought, ran to the northern door and went in to call the reinforcements. Damian picked up a Turuk and hurled him through the air at Kurg, but with his trunk-like arm he simply swatted the bodily projectile and redirected it toward Cam who acrobatically evaded it. The Turuk went crashing into an iron table. Cam jumped into the air, grabbed a chain suspended from the roof and swung on it toward Kurg. The monster just backhanded him too, sending Cam spiraling into the same iron table. The Turuk was just getting up, rubbing his bruised shoulders but Cam drove his head into the anvil he was using to help himself up. Kurg tore from the floor and picked up one of the iron tables and held it high. The last guard and Damian were exchanging blows in front of the tunnel entrance but Kurg threw the large heavy table at the both of them. Cam called out and Damian kicked the mog off him and into the path of the massive projectile. Damian rolled to the side but the guard was flattened by the now crumpled metal table which crashed against the wall with a deafening screech. Kurg picked up a large steel vat and aimed it at Damian.

"You should not have come back, Ratarra!" Kurg shouted and heaved the huge iron jug across the room. Damian again dove out of the way and the vat splintered into pieces against the stone wall with an equally loud reverberation. Cam considered throwing a hail of spikes but felt it would have little effect against this monster. Kurg was a giant among the sturdy

Mogoli race, considerably larger than most. Instead Cam leaped over the table that separated them and landed beside Kurg as he threw the vat at Damian. Cam drew his one of his swords and drove it into Kurg's leg. Kurg howled and picked Cam up in his fist and would have crushed him but a metal arrow suddenly impaled his arm forcing Cam's release. Kurg kicked the tiny figure at his feet and Cam went skidding across the floor and crashing into the tool room door. Damian had shouldered his bow, drew his sword and charged the brutal beast, yelling with rage. All the memories of Kurg's viciousness and unparalleled heartlessness and cruelty to himself, Cam, and the other prisoners drove Damian like a madman famished for justice and lawfulness. In the past it was Damian who cowered in fear, Damian who groveled and begged at the feet of this master oppressor, Damian who avoided the eyes of his cruel masters. But now he had returned like a vengeful ghost that had been wronged, he had respawned like a scorching light in this dungeon of darkness, cleansing his former abode of captivity and servitude. The house of his abductors would fall and all those who dwelt there and abetted the atrocity would perish with it, ridding the world of their heinousness. So it was with tears running down his face and indomitable strength and determination that Damian clashed with Kurg in a final bout of unreserved melee.

Kurg drew his heavy mace from his thick hide belt and parried Damian's powerful blows. Kurg found Damian a formidable foe, one that nearly matched his own strength, but Kurg felt he had the upper hand. He was a huge mog, greater in height and stature than even Damian, and he had to be the mightiest human he had ever seen. But Kurg chuckled with glee inside for even Damian's improved strength didn't quite surpass Kurg's. The great mog swung his deadly mace recklessly, shaking the air with the crashing and banging, breaking tables and opening craters in the stone floor and walls with his blows against Damian, who evaded and countered unceasingly.

Cam fumbled with the keys he had taken as he lay prostrate on the floor, his ringing head resting against the tool room door. He stood up and tried the key in the lock. The door swung open and he rushed in. He found the biggest hammer he could, of which there was one in particular of excessive weight and dimension, and he laboriously dragged it out amid the thundering combat around him and started pulling it toward the northern door where they intended to make their escape. He happened to turn around on his way to check upon his friend and beheld Kurg being thrown into a pile of rock and metal chunks. He pulled the mammoth hammer onward. It wouldn't be long for the rest of the guards to arrive. *We don't have much time, Damian.*

Kurg and Damian managed to lock their weapons together for a moment in front of the far southern tunnel. Their mighty arms held each other fast.

"You won't escape again, Ratarra," Kurg growled and pressed his huge, fanged head into Damian's. "You and your friend grew up here and you'll perish here, too. There is no escape. My guards are on their way."

"The Kunn will fall!" Damian growled back, "You will all perish along with your Ahga. Your despicable Brotherhood will pay for its crimes. I will bring down the Kunn. I shall see to it myself. There is nowhere you can hide!" These bold words enraged Kurg and he kicked Damian square in the chest which sent him tumbling across the floor and into the tunnel. Kurg chased him, his mace held high for a blow. Damian rolled out of the way just in time as Kurg let fall his weapon and it buried itself harmlessly in the cratered floor with a crash. Damian pulled himself up but Kurg, unrelenting, swung again to the side. He ducked and took a few steps deeper into the tunnel.

"I never told you what happened to your mother and sister," Kurg revealed to him with a hint of pleasure as he approached. Damian looked at him with an even greater anger mixed with shock. "You'd be surprised." The giant swung again and Damian desperately darted to the outside and Kurg's mace struck the wall with a crushing blow but had embedded itself slightly in the rock and became momentarily stuck. Damian's sword came down that fateful instant, completely severing Kurg's right arm.

Voices and the sound of rushing feet in the nearby southern hall forced Damian's withdrawal from the tunnel entrance. He left Kurg to his agony and saw Cam across the room with a hammer opening the northern door.

"You found one," said Damian running up.

"They're coming!" Cam pointed to the opposing doors from which the sound of the remaining guards came forth. Damian sheathed his sword and relieved Cam of the massive steel hammer.

"You go ahead," said Damian and Cam sprinted up the stairs that led back up to the barracks. At that moment the guards burst through the doors and spilled into the work room simultaneously. Damian slammed the heavy door shut and rammed it with the hammer, bending the door slightly and jamming it. He didn't feel it would hold them for long though. There were tools and hammers aplenty in the tool room down there, but if it could just keep them occupied long enough...There was another small door exiting the rear of this room but he left it open as he bounded up the stairs.

The guards pounded on the door below with hammers and pommels as Damian ascended. Cam was standing on the landing in front of the barrack's doors that they had previously jammed shut. The guards in there had only succeeded in opening it enough to get a hand through and see Cam peering at them through the split.

"Perfect," observed Damian when he saw it. The two left them and ran up to the last and highest level. They reached the landing. To the left was Kurg's chamber, to the right the gas room. They faced the door and exchanged glances.

"Suppose it's time," said Cam.

"Let's see what's in there," Damian resolved and lifted his hammer. After several swings the heavy steel door was thrown down in a crumpled mess. They stepped in and looked around.

Kurg's chamber was fairly large and well furnished. In the corner was a rack for sleeping and in the opposite corner was a dual bunk rack, probably for his frequent guests. Several chairs and benches were placed about, along with a small table for card and dice games. The Kunn were frequent gamblers and swindlers, indeed gambling was a major source of their income. Against a wall was a well stocked wine rack and many empty bottles lay on the floor. In the middle was a large desk and connecting table. On the desk were numerous books, apparently for record keeping, and a large chest, they noticed, was locked underneath.

Damian moved the heavy chest and gave it a shake, revealing the tell-tale jingle of coins inside. With the hammer he smashed it open, spilling the wealth all over the floor. "A gift for the prisoners," he said, and turned his attention to the volumes on the desk. Cam looked on as he turned the pages. "Written in the Mogoli tongue. Let's take them with us." Damian quickly unshouldered his pack and placed the books in.

"Damian!" said Cam in surprise. He was facing the rear of the apartment and it was just then that Damian noticed a corpse in one of the guest racks. They approached it with interest.

"Probably done in by Kurg himself," said Cam. In one of the racks lay the body of a mog, older and powerful looking, bearing the standards and brands of the Kunn. Indeed he looked to be one of the Ahga's own captains. His body was arranged flat and orderly, his hands and feet tied, ready for disposal. Its throat was slit.

"Kurg must have had a dispute or other with him," thought Damian aloud. "Maybe a competitor or a replacement, murdered him in his sleep after some intoxication." They gave the room a last look over and exited toward the gas room. Just then, down the staircase two levels below, they heard a crash and a roar.

"They've broken through!" yelled Cam, "Come on!" They fled down the hall into the gas room, leaving its door open behind them. Cam picked up the torch from the corner wall and ran to the far end, toward the water-tunnel. Damian beheld the many crude wheels and levers against the wall which controlled the flow of the mysterious and volatile Khala fire-gas. He raised his hammer and wasted no time smashing them one by one, heading back toward the escape tunnel. A strange, vaporous substance spewed out of the wall with a hiss as craters opened from the hammer swings, indeed the wall almost in its entirety was crumbling and falling from the heavy impacts. Damian coughed and choked in the acrid mist as he neared the completion of his work of justice. But there were thundering footsteps heard and felt just down the hall.

"RATARRA!!" thundered a voice that Damian knew too well, a yell of rage with a hint of haste and agony, both physical and mental. Damian, at the far end of the hall, spun around to see an enraged, one-armed monster crash into the room. Kurg stopped and gagged, looking left and right for the enemy he so desperately had to destroy. He now had an idea what Ratarra was up to and knew how little time he had to stop it. He had underestimated this former slave of his and now the shock of what his adversary obviously intended to do drove him to desperate madness. If this rat knew about what secret substance fueled the furnaces, and he probably did if he entered the mine from that horrible tunnel, it is possible, however unlikely, this fearsome and determined warrior could put an abrupt and destructive end to them all. This volatile substance was just another blessing found in Khala to complement the wealth of others there. The Ahga lost a score of his best engineers trying to tame it, enduring frequent fires and collapses, but it was well worth the expenditure. Such risks must be made for capital, and Khala made good on its promise. But now this lucky coward was about to use this dangerous discovery to destroy them. The magnitude of his failure made him swoon with fury. Maimed arm and all, Kurg had torn down doors and leaped up staircases in his rage, shaking the very roots of the mountain with his bellowing voice. No one would embarrass him like this. He would not go easy this time, attempting to capture him and exert slow pain for his own pleasure. This time he would kill with speed and brutal, beast-like strength. For Ratarra to even think such a deed warranted the very worst death Kurg's horrible imagination could conceive, but he had to reach him before he could succeed with his stunt. He lunged up the stairs and down the hall with the speed and strength of a charging bull.

"RATARRA!!" Kurg roared and charged down the hall toward Damian, followed at a distance by his remaining troop of guards, some twenty-five or so altogether.

"DAMIAN!!" yelled Cam, seeing that they had run out of time. Damian dropped the hammer and fled the fumigating hall past Cam and dove down the water tunnel as Cam flung a lit torch over his head into the gas room.

Cam and Damian, tumbling wildly down the steep tunnel in their desperate attempt to escape did not witness the final fiery destruction of Kurg and his men. The massive, resulting fire caught their clothes as it chased them down the tunnel and singed their skin as they fell heedlessly off the ledge and into the river far below. The fire momentarily spouted forth from the ledge and lit and scorched the entire cavern before it quickly receded. Inside, the entire upper levels exploded and collapsed two floors down into the main work room which consequently blew the entire western wall completely off the face of the mountain. It was as if the mountain was purging itself of the parasite that had fed off it like a leach all these years. Through the numerous exhaust ports flames spouted into the dark sky. Large chunks of rock were thrown for hundreds of feet, landing on the road and plain outside and bringing down the watchtowers like they were made of toothpicks. Fire shot out of the balcony that overlooked the yard before crumbling. Anything that was alive in the mine was consumed by an angry flame that wound its way through the tunnel like a searching worm, but failed to reach the prisoner blocks which were away from the epicenter and sufficiently sealed by the closed, heavy metal doors that protected them from the mountain's wrath. The blast could be heard miles away and the flame that the mountain spewed forth in its act of self-purification lit the early morning sky like a giant torch that vanished almost as quickly as it came on.

* * *

The cleansing of Khala was complete, but word would not reach the ears of the Ahga for some time for all the guards were destroyed and no rider rode abroad at that hour to bring swift report of this bold deed, the first of what would be many against the Kunn. Even if it was witnessed no one would know what to make of it for the Kunn had no known adversary capable of delivering such a blow. Until now. The Kunn were unaccustomed to resistance from the weak that they victimized, so fierce and swift was their brutality, and this despicable act could only at first be met with a lack of comprehension, then anger, then vows of swift revenge. The Ahga would put forth all his energy and resources to the destruction of these daring rogues, new proclaimed enemies of the Divine One. His many agents would comb the lands and cities in search of them. No hole in the ground could hide them from the inevitable and inescapable wrath of the Ahga. He had powerful destructive weapons of his own in his arsenal and he intended to use them. Problems like this would be dealt with. And be brought to justice they would...

Damian and Cam, by the light of the flame in the cave, swam breathless to the exit under the mountain, pulling themselves onto the ground outside in the early dawn. And so it was that Bish found them, soaked and singed but smiling faintly, as if satisfied of some great deed and heedless of any hurt. They reunited joyfully and finished the circuit around Khala to the road and front entrance. They rode slowly into the open front yard and pit triumphantly, surrounded and deafened by the thunderous applause of the prisoners who beheld their deliverers and former brothers. They saw them stride slowly into the entry enclosure and they suddenly recognized the champions who had bled and starved beside them only days before, and now had returned as heroes to save them. The riders stopped in front of the prisoner still tied to the stake, alive miraculously but covered in dust. His weary eyes looked up and regarded them as almost unearthly, and his emotion was that of a man with eternal gratitude and awe, for he knew he had been saved by the deeds of these men. He could not forget their faces. His rescuers dismounted and cut him loose and the ecstatic onlookers cheered all the more. The three marched into the huge, gaping hole that once served as the work room west wall. Damian climbed over the debris to the doors on either side, clearing a way as he went. The doors that led to the prison blocks, being damaged and partially melted by the blast were easily kicked in or destroyed to gain entrance. Cam handed the keys to the prisoner who took them with a smile. Many grateful tears rolled down his hopeful face, once lean and drawn. The lines of torment he once bore were washed away and did not return. He praised the names of his rescuers and disappeared through the door and up the stairs to the cell blocks to release his friends. Damian and Cam walked over to the slaughterhouse to ensure that the livestock had survived and the wagons and carts parked there were intact for the prisoners before mounting Bish one last time. One of the stone walls had partially collapsed there but otherwise everything was alive and serviceable. Even the mule was alright, still attached to the wagon and covered in dust but strangely fiery and restless as if sensing a positive change of fortune. The riders waved to the prisoners as they headed out to the plain and they chanted their names. *Ratarra! Cam!* they cried, and Damian looked upon them for the last time. *Ratarra! Cam!* they chorused again and the two galloped beyond the confines of the encircling rock. They rode out of earshot of the mountain and Damian checked his horse to a halt and turned around. They looked again upon the rock that had been their abode of misery for years, now vanquished and cleansed. The early morning sky was clear and the sun shone fully behind the mountain from a horizon of hope. Almost it looked like a halo from where they watched.

"Doesn't look as loathsome," said Cam. "The beast has been slain. The deed that has been done and the more that will follow almost makes our suffering and imprisonment understandable."

"True my friend," replied Damian. "Our past hardships will drive us to relieve others'. For as long as I draw breath I will not permit this injustice to continue. The crimes of the Kunn will be answered and their great plot on earth undone. The oppressed will be justified. Tyranny, oppression, victimization of the innocent–these are my enemies. The realm must be set right again."

"There is a great satisfaction in this victory against the Kunn," said Cam.

"It is but the first," said Damian and they rode home.

EPISODE 2
ENTER TOG

CHAPTER 1
TESTIMONIALS

The boy ran desperately down to the village square. He saw them again–armed and mounted Kunn soldiers, swords and bows at their sides, those distinguishing headbands above their cruel and evil eyes that made the boy sick with terror. And he saw *him*, he was sure of it, and the boy recoiled at the painful sight. The bones and clan marks adorning the mog's neck and that white stripe in his banded black hair was a sure giveaway. They were riding onto the premises of some local landlord here in Tirien, and after what they did to him and his brother his vengeance drove him to act, even being only ten years old and terrified.

Not a moment went by that he did not relive the events that forever changed his life last year, indeed it was impossible to forget, though he wished he could. The sight of those hateful vultures riding about on his own lane brought the painful memories back to his consciousness full force as he sprinted to get help at the bottom of the hill where he knew everyone always was, his sad eyes crying with fear, his young heart beating fast and hard and his stomach turning.

It was only last year but it seemed an eternity of misery and slow and painful recovery since. They came for his beloved elder brother, came right into his house and murdered him, *he* slew him with his own cruel knife, then seeing the younger brother hidden behind a chair this same unforgettable thug grabbed the horrified child, held him down and cut out his tongue. The young boy didn't understand the elder brother's important connection to that violent gang, being an informant of the Kunn, providing them with times and routes of Guard patrols and important and valuable merchant shipments along the local highways, presenting these caravans for sacrifice to these robbers and thieves, making them easy prey. His informational services had become more necessary lately due to the greater care with which the traders took to travel these past few years, owing to the increasing likelihood of ambush. He worked as a young laborer in the busy village market and acquired departure and route information from the cautious farmers and merchantmen who had been using alternative roads and times to reach the city. The wealthier ones even hired guards to escort them. The clan to which these villains belonged paid him well for his tips, far better wage than what he earned stacking crates of raw produce and meat. And the tyrannical and violent lifestyle that the Kunn lived began to appeal to the young man. He developed a taste for the power their methods brought and wished to further his usefulness to them, but he kept his involvement secret.

The boy also did not witness what befell his brother some few days before the tragedy when another group of thugs found their informer and beat some information out of him. Apparently these were looking for *him*, and the brother, under pain, gave the information they desired. And when *he* found out, that cruel mog returned to the home of the informant and killed him, then not only viciously deprived the younger brother of forever speaking anything that this clanster might not want revealed, but also to exact further punishment on the family of the traitor, regardless of innocence. The innocent but traumatized child could never understand why a being could do this to another, or what gangs were and what they did, and why anyone would want to embark on such a life. He would not understand that the elder brother endangered the life of the younger simply by association and criminal involvement, a possibility the former learned too late as he watched with his dying eyes the maiming of his younger sibling and would take the guilt of his selfishness and foolishness to the grave with him.

The boy recovered slowly, adapting himself to his new handicap, but his life was changed forever for it was a wound that went beyond the flesh. He became withdrawn and distrustful. His previous light-heartedness and blissful, spirited character was supplanted by a deep-rooted fear and timidity. An emptiness existed in his mind and soul created by an unspeakable horror, and his eyes held the sadness of the world. He avoided people and spent most of his time alone, hiding in the groves and walking along the river, asking questions of the world, seeking an escape from the horror and society in general, a world in which one could do evil and hurt to another, a world he did not understand. Making sense of the crime would take many painful years, years that quickly hastened his wisdom and opened his eyes to injustices and why they existed, for it was on these that he dwelt as he gazed thoughtfully across tall, quiet grass fields and fruit groves near his home and splashed solemnly in cool waters by himself. But he also learned that this evil must not be allowed, injustices like these must not continue, and he looked for strength and courage from his guardians and the folk of the town. Some greater power must exist somewhere, a role model to emulate and draw wisdom from, but any and all such virtues forebore to present themselves in this sleepy and ignorant village. Such things must lie elsewhere, he thought, and he continued his quiet search.

The townspeople, however, ignorant of the true events that befell him, eventually called him 'the mummer' because of the way he sounded when he attempted verbal communication, humming, grunting, and hand signals used being deprived of his powers of speech. An inevitable end for one who involves themselves with those villains, they said, and they ignored him. Some would give him bread out of pity or send him on an errand for some money. Others would aim a kick at him if they ever saw him scampering about, feeling that he and what was left of his family were a plague to the land and his injuries were deserved. "It's the Mummer!" the cruelest would say, "Get him out of here!" and the hurt child would flee and seek the solitude he craved and trusted.

Today, however, he defied his craving for isolation, for he knew that someone was in need of immediate help just up the lane behind him. Wherever those thugs were, trouble must also be, and a poor victim in need of assistance. The boy set his fear and general dislike of people aside and strengthened his will. He must find some help though he knew most would laugh at him. Someone down there would help him though, and he rounded the corner of the road and burst upon the busy village square like a madman. He ran to and fro among the preoccupied villagers, waving his hands, pointing up the hill, grunting and barking as best he could with fear and desperation, pulling on sleeves and boots of tall riders who paid him no heed. The more principled looked concerned and grew pale at the reference to those familiar gangsters but mostly the villagers ignored and even rebuked him. The cold and uninterested reception he received from them all drove him to greater distress and terror, and in his chaos he ran right into a drunk farmer passing by who knocked the boy over and into the muddy roadside. "Watch your step, Mummer!" the man laughed and walked on.

The impressive determination in the face of the impending disaster and the sober and brave presence of mind the impaired boy demonstrated so profoundly in the square caught the attention of two mounted riders who viewed the scene before them. Seemingly out of nowhere the unnoticed riders suddenly launched themselves through the thick and crossing traffic with many a vexed and confused stare, knocked over the intoxicated farmer like an angry bull and headed straight for the crying boy who sat up hopelessly and alone by the lane in the distance. The boy rubbed the tears from his eyes and saw these great strangers charge right for him on their mighty, black, and powerful steed. The man in front was tall and strong, his stern eyes fixed, and his blond hair flew in fury behind him. He swore he was mistaken but he thought he saw the man lean out and reach for him as he rode by, and the entranced boy found himself easily lifted off the ground and placed gently on the horse in front. He looked amazed behind him to see another boy that could not have been much older than he by his looks riding in the rear, smiling back at him with excited and commending eyes. He looked about him as if he were in a dream, riding horseback with two great warriors full speed up the lane to counter those vile and hated thugs.

They could see them up in the distance, attempting with haste to depart with some stolen horses. They had evidently bound and tied the farmer of that plantation and robbed him of his prized horses, horses that *he* felt necessary to have, probably with the intent to give as gifts to one he intended to impress or simply to have for himself to increase his prestige, so great and valuable were they. The boy could see the riders of the clan approaching the lane from the farm towing their prizes. The mysterious warrior halted a moment and picked him up from the horse and set him upright on the ground to the side for safety.

"I thank you for your bravery," said the stranger. "You are strong indeed. You will find the answers to your questions. Put your gifts to good use and you will find the comfort that you seek. Farewell." The boy stood stone-still as if an enchantment dazzled his eyes and mind. He had never seen these two before and felt as though he had finally found his heroes. The horsemen galloped off to apprehend the thieves, and on the way the smaller rider on the back of the horse turned around and gave a confident smile and a signal to the child as if to say *all will be well, watch this.* The boy ran up a nearby dirt mound to watch the unfolding action. All he could see through the cloud of dust in the distance was the swords of the avengers rising and falling with a wrathful vengeance, the thieves scattering and fleeing before them and the boy gaped in awe. Something was finally being accomplished about this menace, he thought, and he began to jump up and down with excitement. Several of the survivors managed to break away, flying down the lane on their kelgan steeds, and the boy was sure that among them was the cruel stripe-haired one he detested and feared most. He watched the strangers chase after them down the road until they were all lost from sight. An expression one could call happiness formed on the face of the child, the first in a long time.

Firindi watched the gang of Kunn bandits ride into his village. Nothing was the same around here since the Lord Karius was killed years ago. The entire region had disintegrated into a lawless hellhole. Bandits and ruffians were everywhere. The new regime that had taken over in Hera was fraught with corruption and deception. The local Guard had kept a close watch on the borders of this province and all its subsidiaries in the past, including the small crossroads village of Tholen on the Hera Road, which was the midpoint between Hera and Felbruk and also branched off to Tirien, farther east. But a rapid disintegration in the leadership of the realm and its executory branches that had taken place over the recent years severely weakened what infrastructure this lesser but once prosperous province could claim to have, and its small defense was thrown into disarray. The traffic on this road was heavy year round, and businessmen from the cities and the rurals to the east made their way back and forth along this vital route and spread their prosperity like seeds on the way. So it was no small wonder that a village like Tholen would spring to life here, providing the travelers with lodging, food, and other necessities, including services such as metalcrafting, wood, and leatherworking or care for mount beasts and the like, for a small price of course. These villagers made their modest living from the traffic they serviced and therefore depended on it for their livelihood.

But the traffic and business here had lessened of late. Since the arrival of these gangsters and their frequent raids on shipping and the exorbitant duties they imposed on the many supply caravans that passed through regularly, business had only trickled through this past year. Firindi's small leathershop and equipment enterprise had suffered as a result, and the old man looked upon the incoming thugs with disdain.

He himself had several unfortunate experiences with these thieves in the past. He remembered them pulling in here some eight years ago, shortly after Karius' death, and terrorizing folk, demanding money or goods. The Kunn, they called themselves, and they wore thick leather armor and were fearsome, bearing cruel swords and daggers, wearing red headbands and taking and killing as they pleased. The terrorized would pay them what fee they demanded, fearing for their lives or their families'. Once, a man refused to give up his potato load to them for he had labored greatly for it and his family back home in Tirien needed the payment the sale of it would bring him in Hera. The cruel gangsters kicked him and beat him to the ground, relieving him of what money he had and riding off with his horse and loaded wagon. Another time they came and robbed the blacksmith, stealing his horse, probably for food, he later learned. Horses certainly weren't cheap and it was a heavy blow to the poor blacksmith, who was only two small shops to the left of Firindi's home where he worked. Everyone had been panicking these past years and calling for the Guard but they were nowhere to be found. Indeed it seemed as though the Guard no longer existed or ceased to care for any outlying towns or villages. Demands for protection went unheard. A breakdown in the government seemed to have taken place with the new lord and his cabinet, and as a result, the militia as well. Inquiries to the new governor about such matters went unanswered or ignored. Protests were quelled. Helbek, the old man recalled, that was the one who ruled Nadea now. Because of the many folk that came through here and the evident lack of enforcement, these Kunn raiders realized their opportunity and roamed about at will, making more frequent visits to this weak but prosperous little community. They returned often, here or along the Hera Road, taxing or extorting goods from the now desperate businessmen, risking life and capital to continue their diminishing livelihood. But it was one extremely unnerving instance in particular that forever ingrained itself into the wounded mind of the old man, and it was on this that he dwelt as he watched with fear the approaching Kunn raiders.

One day, just last spring, as Firindi finished up a long day's work, he heard screaming outside in the main road, right out his front door. He ran out front and there they were again, committing yet another atrocity, only this time they had in their possession a young child that had been forcibly removed from her hysterical mother who had committed the horrible crime of withholding what bread she had left in the small hut her poverty compelled her and her four children to inhabit. Her husband had died of some sickness shortly after his children were born and the exhausted mother was struggling with her now twofold burden of working and raising her still very young children. Times had certainly become more desperate very quickly of late, and all the locals felt it. These villains had dared to demand food from this poor family and when refused, simply took one of the children instead. They were always looking for able-bodied slaves to work for them at production camps, usually the young, male or female. The bandits beat the frantic woman down with their fists and were about to ride off with the child when Firindi threw himself on his knees in front of the clan chief and begged his mercy, imploring him to spare the child. The old man would pay anything, they could take all the bread in his cupboard now. The clan chief, or *ulak,* regarded him furiously for a tense moment, debating on whether to run him over with his steed or take him up on his offer. The world seemed to stand still and everything fell deadly quiet in that fateful moment where doom hung just over the head of the imploring and humble old man, knelt in the mud, who didn't dare to even look into the eyes of the enraged oppressor. Suddenly the ulak dismounted and held his sword to Firindi's lowered head, greatly desiring to destroy this man who had dared face him. Draga, that's what they called him, and the old man would never forget it. Draga's name was well known in this area and held fearsome reputation owing to the horrible deeds he committed regularly to the inhabitants here. He grabbed Firindi by the throat and pinned him to the ground, squeezing him tightly so that he couldn't breathe.

The man looked up with terror-stricken, bloodshot eyes into those of the ulak's.

"You can have it your way, old man, *ardin-ub-mukkaba!*" Draga snarled, and led his troop into Firindi's small house, looting and destroying the inside of it, turning over tables and chairs, breaking windows, tearing books and portraits, breaking pottery, and otherwise completely and irreparably ransacking what he called home. When they were finished they threw all his food into a cart and departed, throwing the terrified girl into the mud with her mother who had passed out from shock. Firindi crawled toward them on the other side of the road. The mother and child reunited and the three of them embraced each other, crying from the horror and the incomprehensibility of the deed, pleading for help from above. The heavens opened and it started to rain, as if in sorrow. They went into the home of the grateful mother who insisted on his staying there for the evening, and fed him. After the incident the two became close friends, helping each other when they could for they shared a common memory and experience, a grievance and understanding. The old man by no means regretted his act of generosity and he was even strengthened and emboldened by it. Firindi, who lived alone, would at times care for her children and teach them, relieving the woman of the great burden she carried and she was grateful, making him supper often. The children looked up to the old man, especially the little girl, and they all became like family, supporting and caring for each other always, easing their pain and poverty. The bond of friendship and strength between them has followed them since.

Firindi withdrew himself from his reveries. He stood in front of his lowly hut dreading the approaching raiders, his painful memories invoking vengeful and angry emotions as they neared the square, which was only sparsely populated right now. Just then the bowed figure of a hooded beggar, wandering in the lane in the middle of the junction caught his attention. He must be blind as well, thought Firindi, for he is walking slowly and waywardly, with a stick before his feet. My word, but have times gotten that bad, he thought. Surely this poor soul will become a victim of these thugs, they love to prey on the weak. Firindi ran out to the beggar, for he was only across the road, and sought to divert him from the inevitable harassment which awaited him.

"Hello, my friend," accosted Firindi, clutching the shoulder of the stranger amiably. "Let us move off the road for you are about to fall into a ditch." Firindi placed his arms around him and tried to guide him to the side of the road, beside the front porch to the crossroads goods store. But he found the beggar sturdier than he anticipated, or else his old strength was failing, and he called to a boy who happened to pass by for some help with the burden. The boy, who he couldn't recall seeing here before, running about in the village, obediently and happily lent the old man a hand and grabbed the other side of the beggar, guiding him over.

"Thank you, thank you," said the beggar, "and what is your name so that I know to whom I am indebted?"

"I am Firindi, and you owe me nothing my good man. But who are you and what are you doing here for I have never seen you in these parts before? Do you not know that you are in danger?"

"My name is–," started the beggar. "Bless me but what is all that noise? It sounds as if we'll get run over by the cavalry. What is going on?"

"Clan riders," replied Firindi. "We'd better go someplace else."

"And what do they want? Do they come through here often?"

"Yes, and they hold up travelers and storekeepers, highway robbers they are, curse them, I myself was a victim."

"Where do they come from?" asked the beggar.

"Hera and Gyla of course, and south of the river, up from Mod. Ever since the deaths of the brother lords of our capital cities corruption of all kinds has been drawn here. Thugs and thieves seem to have free reign now and their deeds go unchecked. Rumors of bribery and payoffs in the palace are as abundant as these Kunn raiders and agents. The new lords must have made alliances with these villains from distant parts for their own gain. The people have no longer representation in the Court. What was once a just and prosperous realm is now tainted from within and the effects of the disease spread abroad like a plague. Nadea is not as it once was."

"Such contamination will destroy a people indeed," replied the beggar and he looked up. Just then the thugs stopped in front of the crossroads storehouse and some of them walked up the few stairs, led by Draga. There must have been twenty in all. What few people there were in the road or in nearby buildings and houses paused to witness but the intimidating thugs held the inquisitive at bay. The store owner had been hit before and was ready for them this time, and angrily went out to face them with an axe. Before the riders even said anything the owner aimed a swing at Draga, but the mog ulak actually laughed at the feeble gesture and merely dodged the blow from the old man, kicked him in the gut disarming him and lifted him up with both hands.

"Now you know better than that, Gabe," said Draga, holding him high. The old man gasped and wheezed under the grip of the tyrant. "Don't make me do worse than I did before." While he was saying this the beggar broke away from Firindi, against his quiet warnings, and had fumbled his way up onto the porch unnoticed. The distress on Firindi's face was quite evident as the beggar ascended the steps. Draga threw the old man to the floor and was about to strike him when his hand was abruptly arrested by the beggar, who had quietly come up from behind.

121

Draga turned around to face this strange threat and attempted to release himself from it, but found he was unable to. This beggar had an iron grip on his wrist that he couldn't break free of. The ulak had never known such strength from a human and beheld him wide-eyed.

"I am Ratarra," he said, "and I am putting an end to you." With his free hand Damian punched him in the chest so hard the mog went flying off the porch, taking three others down with him. Firindi and the several bystanders gaped in wonder. Damian threw back his hood and drew his sword, cutting through the bandits in front of him like a scythe through grass, instantly killing the half dozen on the porch. The other riders sought to attack this warrior but the boy that was beside Firindi a moment ago darted into the fray like a wild ape, hacking with his short sword, hopping, leaping and dodging like a cat, killing these clansters left and right, and there didn't seem to be anything they could do about it. They could hardly see the boy he moved so fast. The whole thing was nothing like anything anyone here had ever seen, and the onlookers gathered round in increasing numbers and curiosity. The sword of this mighty warrior before them came down on them all, breaking right through their weapons and armor like they were made of silk. Draga and what few remained of his troop mounted their steeds in a hasty retreat and fled. The cloaked warrior whistled a strange note and a great black horse emerged from behind a house nearby and pulled up to him. He leaped off the deck and onto the horse, the boy also mounting behind him in an airborne fashion and like the wind they flew away into the west and disappeared, leaving the crowd in utter bewilderment. And when Firindi placed his hand in his pocket a moment later he was surprised to find a gem of great worth, but how it came to be there he could not fathom.

Báyed sat upon the wagon seat, miserable and angry. He had been forced to accompany his father to Hera, delivering the family's valued spices from Tirien. He, being sixteen, had been brought along not only for his assistance which he very reluctantly and rebelliously provided only because of his unrelenting father, but also as protection. They were blockade running, making every attempt to avoid the thieves which had been operating on the Hera Road with increasing frequency and boldness. His father and his friends had been hit before en route and the thieves only took all his money the first time, which was almost a year ago now, but of late these Kunn robbers demanded far more, even your life if they were not satisfied. They had been reportedly raiding these parts in greater numbers and frequency, ambushing caravans and travelers, riding forth on their swift steeds from their many hiding places on the way, watching the road seemingly at all hours so that one could not avoid them. Times as a result had become more desperate and the once wealthy farmers and tradesmen, and the many who depended on the fruits that they brought forth, found themselves quickly impoverished by the stranglehold placed upon that vital supply route called the Hera Road. Oh, some brave wain drivers fought back. They had all heard stories of some valiant farmer and his hired hands who stood up to the savage thieves and defied them, only to be all slain or taken captive by the bloodthirsty villains and never seen again. Circumstances necessitated boldness, however, and the father today was taking a great risk in the early morning, hoping to safely complete the worst and last stage of the journey between Tholen and Hera. He had wisely traveled in the early morning hours until just before midday, at which time he and his group would seek concealment, in a village or in the wild. They had only ten more miles to go before they reached the city gates where they could envelop themselves within the hundreds of other traders and merchants, for the gangsters would not show themselves or their deeds to the many this far north, and so bring their valuables to the busy city market. Báyed wanted no part of what he considered an unnecessary measure. There was nothing to fear here. He fingered a little gold chain in his pocket, a gift that he picked up from a passing Govan nomad in Tholen.

Something strange caught Báyed's eye to the side of the road in the distance, just before a bend which began an uphill climb. It looked like wreckage and dead beasts or something, heaped like corpses, broken and unmoving. His father saw it too and he called quietly to the others and they halted their four laden wagons, surveying the ugly scene before them. They gasped in terror.

"Let's see if there are any survivors," said the father with fear and dismounted, followed by his son whose expression had changed at the sight. There, just off the road, were the remains of five burned wagons sitting like charred hulks, still smoking, and to their horror they found the bodies of the horses laying on the ground in front of them, excessively hewn and disfigured as if the culprits took pleasure in the unnecessary butchering of the beasts. Strewn about all over were the bodies of the wain drivers, plainly clad and simple, farmers and husbands, their fellow countrymen. Several bodies of the raiders were also found and Báyed's father removed a red bandana, a token he had been dreading to see. They all surveyed the destruction with an expression of disgust and disbelief.

"Looks like there was fight," said the father. "They were heading for the city. Their loaded wagons weren't fast enough for the swift steeds of those scum." Just then one of the other hired drivers gave a shout and they all came running over.

"This one's still alive!" he said, pointing to a man crumpled by a dead horse. They carefully sat him upright. His chest had been pierced by a bolt and he coughed and wheezed as he tried to talk.

"They came on us at nightfall." he struggled to say, "Kunn bandits…must have been twenty of them. I think they waited for us up there in the road." Báyed looked at the maimed and bloody corpses sprinkled like fodder all about the charred and stained earth. His mouth was gaping with horror at the sobering sight of his first experience with real and vain death as he glanced speechlessly about him. The wounded man continued. "There's a turn in the road and a small cliff that conceals it. I think that's where they came from." He pointed westward toward the rising slope and coughed at the exertion. "We almost made it, curse them. They got my brother and son." He began to weep. "Who are they? Why do they do this? We have to stop them. Be careful, I think…" But he said no more.

They all looked around them fearfully and made a move for the wagons. A mutual panic and dread set in immediately. They were alone and beyond aid and their desperate gamble failed. They felt eyes upon them from the hill up ahead and hastily boarded their wagons for flight. But it was too late. Thundering footfalls could be heard from the dreaded direction further up the road, coming down the hill like a rockslide: they had been seen. Some raider scout must have been watching them from behind the small rocky cliff that bordered the low hillside, waiting for new prey, surprised to see some daring riders about at this hour. That man was right, they thought. This is a good place for an ambush and now they too were caught. Báyed panicked in his seat and his father tried desperately to put the wagon into motion but it was in vain. The raiders were upon them, a dozen or so. The farmers drew out spears and made a brave but fruitless attempt to defend themselves. Báyed saw them drag his father to the ground and he tried to break away in terror of the oncoming thugs who were coming for him. Their strong arms reached for him and he could see his own death in their cold, soulless eyes and he jumped from the seat, shaking with a new and heretofore unknown fear and realization. But his hand was in his pocket, and, losing his balance and unable to break his fall, he fell bodily onto the ground and was caught and struck down as he tried to stand. Many cruel swords were pointed just inches away from his throat as he lay shaking and panting with fear on the earth.

"It's been a busy day," said one of the raiders, apparently the leader. A distinct white stripe, the boy noticed, ran through his thick, banded black hair. The branded black marks on his neck, or *shukk* marks, held all the disgust of this idealistic clan. He stepped on Báyed's wrist, forcing the release of the little golden trinket which the boy had unwittingly procured from his pocket in his attempt to flee and had forgotten about. The ulak caught sight of it and held it up curiously before him. "Well, well, what do we have here? This is pretty." Could they hear a horse galloping? The mog gripped the boy's trembling body and pulled him close with a smile of sinister intent. "What else do you have?" The ulak began to search his clothes. Just then one of the villains dropped dead with a shriek from an arrow, then another. They all spun around to see a charging horseman, sword now in hand, blond hair flying in the wind. Something flew off the back of it, a young boy or something, no one could really tell for he moved too fast, leaping and yelling through the air wielding dual daggers, attacking the raiders like a frenzied beast. The horseman clove through the bewildered gangsters with his sword and ran them down with his horse, with a vengeance and ferocity the boy had never seen. The whole affray was over in seconds, only one remained, the leader, and Báyed watched the dismounted warrior pin the Kunn leader to the ground by his throat, right by the boy's side so that he could hear.

"We meet again, Draga," said the stranger. "I leave you alive, you understand, to tell the other fools you consort with of their peril. Your reign of terror here is coming to an end, I'm afraid."

The striped raider laughed as best he could under Damian's fierce grip on him which he actually loosened and stood him up for the familiar ulak to speak. "You're too late Ratarra," growled Draga, and Damian listened to him angrily. Cam came up by his side, sheathing his bloody daggers. "It cannot be done. This is Kunn territory now. I have power here. Do you really think you and your little friend are a match for the weapons of the Ahga? By the will of the Divine One the Kunn supervenes. It will take more than a strong grip and a sharp sword to better what will come your way. Have you been beyond this territory? Have you had the pleasure of meeting his more colorful henchmen in Mod? Are you wise only to the ways and strengths of his lowest subjects? Mark my words Ratarra, the Ahga has friends that will make you squirm like a mouse being crushed by giant talons, and your pathetic companion will be of no help."

Cam, challenged and insulted, took an angry fighting stance.

Draga continued. "If you think *suchuk* fighters are fierce and cruel..." He chuckled a moment in Damian's face. "We are but the lowly obedient pawns of the Kunn, though oft overlooked, servants of the Divine whose favor we have rightfully earned, unlike the many faithless, and we are blessed with His hand until the great task is done. Azandium will be ours again in its full right and the enemies of the Kunn will be swallowed up into the pit of oblivion with the last of the Five Heretics on the Last Day. This has been foredoomed according to the great Book. But the higher adepts of the Mari dwell elsewhere for the time and I will one day be among them. Woe to you when you have the pleasure of their acquaintance. The Mari will not be overruled. Sacrifices are an acceptable and necessary vehicle for a desired end, and the Kunn is willing to procure. You are just another rebel *insal* pig that will be sacrificed along with the others who amused the Ahga for a time, only to be crushed under his fist when he'd had enough of them. You may have succeeded with smaller matters of late but there will be no victory for you. Even now he knows of you and is making preparations for your destruction. Oh yes Ratarra, the whole of the Kunn knows of its latest pest. The youngest of the Kadali rides forth to renew their failed legacy! Ha! But do you think the Ahga is sitting idly by while you live out your delusional acts of vigilantism? It is but the pause of delight before the axe of the great one falls. You'd better keep an eye over your shoulder." Draga ended and chuckled with delight.

Damian growled and gripped the vermin tightly again, enraged by the venom he spewed. "I look forward to the challenge!" Damian hissed. "Your precious Book is nothing but a pile of lies. But I warn you, Draga, the next time we meet will be our last." He lifted the ulak clear off the ground and angrily shoved him to his awaiting steed which he consequently mounted after a groan from the impact, and with an evil chuckle and one last look at Damian sped off westward, up the hill toward Hera.

Báyed, his father, and the others picked themselves up and gathered near the strangers, but kept some distance for they did not yet know what to make of these heroes. Angelic they seemed, holding a power not only without but within. Energy and strength seemed to emanate from their formidable and robust figures. Thought and wisdom lay upon their brows. They seemed unearthly, emissaries from another realm. So it was with awe and sobriety that Báyed beheld his rescuers, knowledgeable and powerful, mounted once again upon their mighty steed. They paused upon their horse and the warrior addressed them.

"This road is safe for now along with the villages east of Hera. You may complete your journey. But as long as the waywardness and disunity of the people continues the plague of terror remains. Hera has become weak."

Word quickly spread in the cities and villages all over of a cloaked warrior and his shining sword and his amazing sidekick by his side, who galloped around the countryside fending off raiders and highwaymen and villains of all kinds, rescuing the oppressed, defending the innocent, driving the Kunn back into the mud where they came from and cleansing the land of this new menace with a speed and power that left the citizens in shock. They arrived out of nowhere and vanished like the wind, leaving the saved aghast and in wonderment, and everywhere they went the hearts of the witnesses were cleansed and filled with renewed hope and vigor. They wondered where these two came from for they were unlike commoners in speech and deed, and the people concluded that the fearless riders must be from some foreign country far away, over many hills and rivers, and had come to save them from the dark times that seemed to have befallen them.

Victims of the new oppression felt their time for justice had come at last and just in time. Ratarra has come, they would say, and they cheered. That previously unheard name quickly became the topic of conversation in the territory. But not all those who heard of this new stranger were pleased...

* * *

The Ahga sat in his iron chair with the members of his Baccád in his private chamber on the top floor of his palace in the city of Mod. This grandiose estate was purchased of the lord of Govannum province himself, the Lord Thuliak, a half-mog, a twisted, power hungry, vain and corrupt swindler, no less detestable than the Ahga himself, but possessing far less intellect and perception. Thuliak achieved his power solely by inheritance and reputation, his position being passed to him as chief beneficiary of the death of his far more intuitive and determined predecessor who had reigned this gluttonous and vile capital city for decades before him. The powerful that absorbed wealth here did so by any means and the Kunn long ago easily bought their way into the governance. Thuliak was easily swayed and also deceived, as long as those who proposed to him brought wealth in their wake intended for his personal profit. He was ignorant of the dark deeds that went on around him, being blinded by his own pride of his fanciful image as a strong and decisive leader, feeling that his title and representation alone would win him obedience, loyalty, and whatever riches or goods or favors his rulership demanded. The hierarchy with which he surrounded himself operated independently in the shadows of the many dark corners within the labyrinth of his immeasurable domain of carved and decorated stone, and would humor the dictator for their own sake for their own survival would depend on it. But when the Lord Thuliak learned of deeds done or decisions made without his precognition that he found disagreeable or were decidedly lacking in his personal profit he would become reputedly enraged and vengeful, feeling insulted and that he had been exploited, and his subjects would become the pitiful victims of his unreserved acts of terror, and those that were present would flee his undousable temper. Thuliak would go so far as to execute any being at hand to satisfy his sudden fury, guilty or innocent, and for this reason alone his flattering and deceptive subjects feared him. Because of the corruption permeating this domain and the filth of which spread forth throughout, this extravagant castellated residence of two towers had assumed the unofficial new name of Harásh, or lair, and was referred as this by the royalty and common folk of Mod alike–Mogoli, Humans, Turuks, Harikans, Irendi, and all other beings that dwelt in this diverse and dangerous city terrorized by scum. So those that dwelt or lobbied at the Harásh would do so carefully, balancing greed with compliance.

The Ahga, however, dwelt in a separate inhabitance of the compound when he resided here, the Olóbid, a tower of little less splendor and size, well suited to the austere taste of the one it housed, with notably less décor and art of ingenious engineering and architecture like its counterpart, the Alád, which was only a lengthy courtyard away in the vast palatial compound. The Ahga, achieving his wealth and power through far more tyrannical and coercive means, but which required strategy and intellect nonetheless, held little respect for Thuliak, who was a faithless and spoiled fool in his eyes, an antithesis to the pious ideals of the clan. The Ahga grew his enterprise from the withered seed of his predecessors, a small band of cruel and remorseless but loyal brothers, dedicated to him and his dogmatic cause, sanctioned by the Divine, and over the years had created his empire with their perseverance. The Ahga knew he had earned his success by work and divine right where Thuliak had not, risking great capital and life, wealth, success, and conviction to pious duty answering for brutality and barbarism. The road to the Ahga's power was paved with the blood of those who tried to defy or deceive him, even his own men, and he therefore was infinitely more respected and revered. When one entered the chamber of the Ahga, he was greatly feared and venerated; Thuliak, pitied and despised. The Ahga himself in fact greatly despised Thuliak and secretly dreamed of his demise, but smiled in his face when in his presence for the Kunn, not yet dominant in this state, were enabled their nascent operations in Mod by Thuliak's authority. The Ahga had long ago bribed Thuliak to allow the Kunn virtually unlimited free business reign in his realm, and the profit percentage Thuliak received as a result was generous, increasing with the power and expansion of the Kunn under his jurisdiction as the years passed. As much as the Ahga yearned for the day when this palace fool would dwell forever in a box he was at the mercy of this volatile puppet, only to a degree of course, and walked Thuliak's delicate line for the common good, and the Ahga, knowing who held the real power, despised him all the more. But the Ahga sought to satisfy his quiet detestation, which was shared by all in his Baccád, and he found ways to fulfill his feelings of vindictiveness. The deeds he committed against the blind fool who dwelt only a paved courtyard away brought the Ahga the satisfaction he felt he deserved, and though Thuliak brandished his rule the Ahga chuckled with glee inside even as he promised obedience.

A small problem, however, one of utmost urgency and import, had arisen recently which threatened the fragile cooperation that demanded immediate resolution, and for this reason he convened in haste and secrecy with his most trusted and proven subjects, and had included, due to the severity of the situation, a special guest of fearsome repute and expertise.

"We have an issue," addressed the Ahga to his servants seated easily but attentive in his upper-story suite. The ambience was austere and foreboding, dark and bellicose; the stone walls were unadorned; the dim light cast a grayness into the lofty vault; the echoes of grim words reverberated gloomily in this joyless council hall in which were discussed issues of great weight and secrecy. The Ahga introduced a certain man, of unkept and shoddy appearance, looking as though he had just spent a month in the wild. This man, he said, had just arrived early that afternoon and was his spy at the now defunct Khala quarries, and he had some interesting but disturbing news for them all. Even Kurg was unaware that he had an informant of the Baccád operating within his domain. The only plants Kurg ever used were within his own circle of allies for his own purposes, but the Ahga, ever distrustful and suspicious, needed an independent assessment of the situation at his prized but secret wealth factory and had him imprisoned under cover. The individual unfolded in detail to them the events at Khala that had taken place over the last few weeks of its existence. They all listened with shock and anger at the news of the destruction of their factory, which they all had worked hard to build, and the complete looting and ransacking that took place by the crazed prisoners after the Ahga's guards were killed, and their subsequent exodus to the cities. He also confirmed the murder of one of the Ahga's chosen, Azag, intended to be Kurg's replacement. This especially invoked rage among the assembled for this great mog had been their brother and a captain among the Kunn, a more suitable and trustworthy chieftain to supplant the former for his failures. He went on to speak of the two strange heroes who had made their remarkable escape from the camp and then inexplicably returned, changed somehow from the way he remembered them, and killed all the guards and destroyed the mine in one vicious blow. These two rescuers possessed rare and inhuman abilities and their destruction would require unconventional means. The prisoners all hailed them as their new deliverers, new servants of the Mari, he said, and how the Kunn was to deal with this new threat he did not know.

"We will speak of them later," interrupted the Ahga. "I have something special in mind for them."

"There was a certain prisoner who escaped among the rest," the man added, "one of great value or who held information vital enough to warrant his strict confinement. He had no contact with the others, nor did he perform labor. I don't know for what purpose he was guarded so rigidly. Kurg ordered him closely watched and placed in isolation. He has been found and captured in Hera by some mercenaries as a ransom-hold. Apparently someone discovered his worth to the Kunn."

"It is not necessary for you to know why," replied the Ahga and he dismissed him. The informant obediently left the room. The Ahga motioned to his *ghad-hesh*, his second man Gathmug, who continued.

"This character in question is a certain Gadrin of Demar, an agent of the Hattél," said Gathmug, another large and older mog, like the Ahga, but not older in the sense of being frail and feeble, rather powerful and exceedingly deadly owing to the wisdom in their eyes and their unyielding and remorseless demeanor. The poisonous and penetrating gazes that shot forth from their lethal eyes demanded respect and invoked fear. Volumes could be written from the innumerable deeds committed by the villains in this room, atrocities that spanned the provinces in the creation of their vast underground empire, and their eyes held the experience and wisdom of these things. Just being in the presence of these loathsome monsters would make one nauseous with fear, acknowledging a certainty of his own death. These clan gangsters were experts at what they did, passionate professionals of coercion and assassination. Supremacy and divine benefaction was a creed they believed in, a road to wealth and divine favor they enjoyed treading. One could not doubt or question a threat posed by one of the Kunn for execution was certain. Weakness did not exist here for the Ahga and the Kunn did not sow such a defect, purging the inferior of the clan through harsh trial and rituals of pain, and he bred and chose his officers based on the proven attributes he demanded of his men, none of which could be a liability to the cause, such as weakness. The clan members in this room had proven themselves over the years with succession of these trials and their unwavering obedience to the Ahga, and they listened intently and respectfully.

Gathmug continued. "This Demarian spy knows of our theft and sabotage of Thuliak. How he penetrated our network and discovered this incriminating information will be made clear in time. But now he is in the hands of some opportunistic vagabonds who are aware of his dangerous worth to the Brotherhood. His secret cannot be disclosed. This is dangerous information." This induced some grunts and uneasy looks. Their situation was in evident peril. Apparently nothing more needed to be said. They were all familiar with this circumstance.

"Gadrin must be retaken," said the Ahga and he stood up and walked over to the window that overlooked the Harásh across the courtyard. "The Kunn will not be held to the mercy of some rogue bandits who dare blackmail us. This is our assignment in which we cannot fail. The recapture of Gadrin is our priority and the subduction of those who attempt to undermine us instilled. This secret cannot be divulged, for the time of our unveiling has not yet come. All must be done according to the will of the Divine. But we also seem to have some interesting new friends to deal with, some offspring of the Kadal it would seem, and for this I have requested the intervention of our mentor." He turned around and nodded to one of his men who opened the door to the hall outside where a familiar figure stood waiting.

The being that entered held familiarity among all for they had required his services in the past, though who he really was and what great role he had to play in the quest of the Brotherhood remained a mystery to many save the great here assembled. Only the Baccád knew his true purpose and stature. Mystifying, he was, possessing a nameless ethereality that superceded the boundless perception of the clan's most ardent and learned adepts. That he had been dispatched to earth by the Divine, with powers exceeding even those of the Baccád, to lead his lesser servants on earth to complete a specific but great task they doubted not. But his was another charge for which the Brotherhood contributed only their reserved and allotted portion; the realm of the Kadal and the Consortium was not theirs in which to meddle. Tog entered slowly and quietly and all eyes turned in recognition. He wore thin black leather armor over like-colored clothing and soft, flexible, high-topped and laced form-fitting leather boots. Several black pouches were strapped about his body, strategically placed, all hand tailored to suit his fit and deadly purposes. A straight and single-edged sword in a black sheath was strapped to his back along with a long dagger at his side. He had other weapons as well, throwing blades and poisons, but they were all well concealed and placed to facilitate easy and stealthy movement. He wore a black hood over a red bandana and thin, fingerless black gloves of leather which only partially revealed his dark, thick skin, more like hide. Little else of his features could be seen under his dark exterior, but his stern and potent countenance and red eyes of disdain and perception left the beholder little doubt of his veiled ferocity and strength. To some it seemed that a faint red aura outlined his frame.

He did bear a small strange badge on his left breast, a vertical line intersected with a perpendicular ray to one side within a circle, the *rumjad*–dominion–the token of the ancient Hakai, a strange race dwelling in the cold mountain country of eastern Adovia. The original Hakai were an alien species, unlike other races of this world, a conception resultant of some catastrophe or divine curse or declaration. They were of darker color and slighter but no less powerful build than mog or even Hidari, dwelling in the cold mountain caves and canyons in the deserts of the far east of this continent, though it was also said that they sometimes haunted the eerie realm of Mosethulia. They lived in small, reclusive tribes, seldom to be seen unless one happened upon their rituals under the stars at night, and it was amid the darkness that the phantom folk were said to have run across the earth to their haunted domain in the perilous Palmwood. Their strange tribe was very spiritual and disciplined, ritualistic, trained to hunt, track, and kill, beast, bird, humanoid, or otherwise, and their spiritual, monastic lifestyle honed their bodies into machine-like beings, feeling neither pain nor fear, nor fatigue, pushing their incredibly capable bodies beyond original design.

The origin of this singular breed was shrouded in mystery and the subject of speculation. What few remained of these reclusive alien beings hunted their food in the caves they inhabited, seeking large and dangerous prey in the quiet dark, and they often hunted alone or in pairs, perfecting the art of stealth and surprise as they stalked in the night or waited motionless hours or days at a time for their moment to strike the unwary. They spoke seldom for it was said about them that they could communicate telepathically among themselves. Words were unnecessary for Tog for a glance was sufficient for him to understand. The Hakai were valued for their strength and unfaltering physical endurance, but more so for their stealth and perception brought by their unique and ancient spiritual discipline and beliefs which they still held. It was rumored that the Hakai had a connection with the unseen, sight and hearing developed so far beyond mortal capability that visual contact with others was virtually unnecessary, true wielders of the Mari. Other beings regarded the Hakai as a strange nocturnal race and feared them, thinking they were part ghost, the damned children of a vengeful deity, running wildly through the night wreaking havoc and fear with their barbarous rituals in the dark, killing silently and unseen in their host darkness in the mountain or wood. Though the particular assignments and spheres of operation of Tog and the Kunn differed greatly their overall objective was mutual. They found common purpose long ago and fused their functionalities for the greater goal of their ideology.

The Ahga welcomed him with a gesture of submission and obeisance. "We meet again, my friend."

CHAPTER 2
THE ROGUES OF HERA

"Looks like there's six of them," said Cam, poised attentively behind one of the many small statuettes which adorned the balustraded rooftops of this stone mansion. "They must have sent some of their best, they're actually being quiet about it. They must really want this noble eliminated."

"Riman has good information," agreed Damian right beside him, lying prone on the floor behind the rail that decorated the balcony, bow in hand. They had taken a position on the raised ceiling above the front entrance and vestibule to the stately cityside residence of a certain Vid Markuso, a local and wealthy politician of considerable rank in the Hera Council. This powerful and influential lawmaker's dislike of the Kunn was well known and he used his vast leverage to thwart them at their every attempt to gain more of a foothold on the city or buy more influence among the executives and royalty. Markuso was one of the last of the original supporters of the late Lord Karius, and he witnessed the infection of his beloved city with the arrival of the new regime. He had also witnessed the strange and methodical disappearance of his fellow supporters and colleagues in the Council and the Court over the past few years. He felt he was the last of a vanishing breed of the defenders of righteousness and justice in the realm, a threatened and targeted icon of resistance. Karius and his courageous supporters had carried the wondrous legacy of the realm's ruling predecessors and had brought their province to heretofore unknown flower and prosperity, and worked diligently to maintain the cohesion of the whole realm, but fell short of his ultimate but elusive goal of reunification for which he and others yearned so desperately. The fall of the once great and indomitable Old Alliance was slow but inevitable, its framework corroded to virtuous emaciation from within. Robbed of that goal would be a more accurate term, Vid thought, robbed by these very villains and corrupt, grasping leaders which he must face daily and divert of their unjust schemes. Markuso alone held the power to accomplish that, being a Council member himself of Hera's Second Pillar, a political faction among a delicately balanced trifecta, and how he had managed to survive among these thieves and cronies these past few and increasingly dangerous years he did not know. Fate perhaps. He was suspicious of his senatorial associates and feared his death with each new day he found himself alive. But the inevitable could not be far off, he felt, and that fear increased daily. He hired some extra men-at-arms for his protection which went about with him and guarded his lavish estate, but had not as yet actually needed them.

The Ahga, however, with his ambitious sights on this vestigious city, among the latest to fall of the Old Alliance, had had enough of this defiant and incorruptible obstructionist who spoke out vociferously against the Kunn and all forms of organized criminals in his city, spoke without even any fear on the floor of the Council, and the corruption and detriment to the common folk these villains and their bought representatives brought to his once just realm, he hesitated not to point out. Just the other day he dared to openly declare Helbek and two of his highest subjects 'vipers and pawns of the Kunn, spewing their filth and vomit on the High Throne of Karius.' This haughty old fool had breathed his last holy words. Helbek and the others had enough. Markuso was dangerous and must be removed, and the Ahga authorized the raid. But the Ahga didn't know there was a spy in the Hera hierarchy and his intention tonight was foreseen...

"They're breaking up," whispered Cam. They could see now the assassins climbing ever so quietly in the night over the gated iron fence which encircled the entire grounds of the broad estate, the multi-leveled mansion being toward the center for security reasons to afford a view of any approach. They broke up into groups of three, seeking to infiltrate from either side. Riman knew the guards at the Markuso estate were probably insufficient and endeavored to lend some aid, but he wanted to deliver this vital representative a special favor, a gesture of gratitude for his steadfast courage in the face of adversity. He wanted this to be a surprise from a faceless friend, dispatching his new secret weapons, and Damian and Cam made sure their presence would be unknown to the one they protected, arriving in the early dark right before the assassins.

"We'd better split up," Damian whispered. Cam headed to the far left side of the low roof, crawling spider-like. Damian moved likewise to the opposite end, bow ready, never taking his eyes off the quietly approaching attackers. The stone balustrade that bordered the balcony provided them sufficient cover and concealment. They were dressed all in black like the thugs which stalked like cats in the night right below them in the well-manicured yard of desert shrub and palm foliage, dimly illuminated by the few lanterns that surrounded the whole of the architecturally superior building. They were a little too distant for a sure shot with his bow but that would change quickly. The assassins moved separately and noiselessly, taking cover behind the several well-groomed palm trees and low, broad-leafed shrubs that lined the symmetrical yard. They avoided the semi-circular driveway that curved its way around a sculpted fountain from the front gate to the front doors. They must be making their way to the first level windows, thought Damian. It's almost time. The nearest assassin was crouched behind the nearest tree, looking about him and at the windows above for a moment before he made a dash across the open to the building. *That tree won't save you...*

Cam had already jumped down onto the soft, sandy turf on the other side, waiting not for the enemy but happily going out to meet them. Cam snuck around the trees and hedge like a shadow which melted into the darkness, flanking them unseen and positioned himself behind the last of the unaware intruders. He could see the lead assassin, crouched momentarily behind a sculpted stone fountain before he too made his final approach. The attacker in the rear dropped to the ground with a soft thud, felled by a metal spike. They weren't wearing helmets for this stealthy mission and Cam took advantage. At the same moment another one, to the front, fell from a well-aimed shaft. The soft tree leaves he used as cover didn't protect him from that deadly shot in the dark. The Kunn raiders froze a moment in indecisiveness, sensing an ambush and trying to find their enemies. They were not expecting attack from behind and they grew frantic. Cam strung a garrot around the throat of another. The assassins, perceiving sabotage but desperate for success, made a dash for the arched windows near the ground level. A cloaked figure dropped down on them like a phantom from above, and they looked up with fear.

Aroused by sounds of altercation outside, Vid and his men rushed out for action, torches and swords in hand, but when they arrived on the front threshold all they found were several dead bodies littering the front yard and a single raider, still alive and struggling, strung to one of the columns that supported the stone balcony above, right in front of the door. They heard around the corner the sound of a horse galloping quickly away in the night. They looked stunned at the captive assassin, writhing and twisting beneath his bonds, then at each other.

* * *

Their hideout in Hera was an underground vault derived from none other than the ground level tenement Riman rented in his younger years, working from a mere pushcart in the busy and crowded city's center. The old building, which was old even in his younger days, located in the city's northwest and poorer quarter of Nibera under the shadow of the hills beyond Shadím on the outskirts of town, still provided fairly close access to the open marketplace being about two and a half miles away. Now the building, indeed a greater part of the block, was lately abandoned due to the notoriously unstable foundations underneath this row of stone structures perpetrated–it was believed–by overdevelopment in and underneath this part of the city which seemed to cause or exacerbate a subterranean shift in the land itself, weakening the foundation in a wide radius. Furthermore, the Plateau of Hera, resting fitfully along a fault line, was renowned for its periodic shifting and gradual absorption of surface structures and was not entirely trustworthy. To worsen the situation, the many and winding underground waterways had compromised the stability of the fragile earth here and the structures themselves were crumbling from within as a result, slowly collapsing into the widening chasms below the surface, and the leadership had no interest in rebuilding or repairing the ruins of that sector for the present. This sector of buildings and foundations, called the Hole of Helbius, was deemed hopelessly condemnable and became forgotten and deserted, and none dared venture into the stagnant, muddy pools that enveloped it. That cursed old strip under the cruel eyes of the Hills was volatile and dangerous, they said, and would one day be the bane of the city. It was only a matter of time before the very streets collapsed from under them, they thought. Verily one could watch the foundations here sink into the shifting earth, or a crack form in a wall, if one had the patience. Due to its decrepit, subterranean characteristics this improvised refuge was referred to simply as 'the Cave'. It was indeed an ideal hideout for fugitives and revolutionaries if one dared to dwell down there.

Underneath Riman's old dwelling was an access tunnel to the underground waterways. A river ran down from the fertile hills to the north, the great Tybron, and the cities were built around it, channeling the water throughout for their purposes. Rather than repair the disintegrating tunnel it was simply bypassed with a new one and the water was diverted from its original course, and the old tunnel fell dry and empty. A chasm had opened in the tunnel wall that ran along and abutted the basement and undercroft of the old building and they crumbled into each other, providing one mutual access, and they found themselves with a limited system of relatively dry and empty arched or rounded tunnelways at their disposal. Riman had kept it secret and hidden these years, knowing that one day he would probably need it for refuge in this city of thugs ever becoming more loyal to the Kunn, and improved it on rare occasion whenever he left Tirien and returned to the city for business or espionage. Though the moral fabric of the city fell more into decay, still there were many who lived honest lives and were well worth the protection. The spirit of Karius was not wholly expelled from the salvageable city and Riman sought to heal it in his own way. Keeping his treasured hideout secret and inaccessible was priority so he had built the lone interior door to the basement undetectable, but also very strong and impassable by force, remaking it of heavy and solid steel, locked and fitted, with tedious care, to the thick stone floor. But it was also quite large enough to admit their highly valued steed which could descend beyond this via a stairwell. He had also placed reinforcing columns about the recess inside to supplement structural stability, doing his work at night over time by torchlight to prevent his discovery. The vault inside was extensive, lofty, and habitable. Some weeks after their return from Khala and their adventures in the Tirien area, Riman had brought Damian and Cam here under cover of darkness and restocked it afresh and furnished it sufficiently for dwelling. They had left Tirien behind for the present, bringing some of their valuables and necessities with them.

There was only one other person who knew of the existence of their secret outpost and he was present with Riman when Damian and Cam returned from their skirmish with the Kunn assassins. Riman inquired of the operation and introduced the stranger. Damian and Cam looked at him suspiciously. Marcus Galnum was a man of roughly the same age as Riman, slightly shorter but thickly built, dressed in regalia of the Council partially concealed under dark robes for his occasional returns in the night to the vault. He obviously worked around important people, a legislator of the state. He looked not only stern and serious, as were all those here, but also seemed a bit nervous at present and notably shaken than the others, as though he had just eluded discovery and death once again. His daily routine of information gathering in that rats' nest of the Palace of Hera was extremely dangerous and unnerving. He could swear that Helbek and the others suspected him as he inconspicuously and coincidentally presented himself in every room of the palace at seemingly just the right moment to overhear something of import, a presence the lord and his higher subjects certainly found irritating as they attempted to convene in secret. He was of substantial rank among the upper hierarchy of the Council, a representative of status of the Second Pillar, one who swore loyalty to Helbek with his words but without his eyes. Members of his family had been murdered in the past and he had evidence to believe the Kunn and their puppet Helbek were behind it. Rather than flee his post and seek continuing justice with the sword, which would undoubtedly jeopardize the usable authority and leverage he enjoyed, he felt he could better serve his desire for vengeance with the informational access and influence his political posture enabled him. He had worked with the sword in the past but now he wielded a different weapon. He had been close friends with Riman during the just days of Karius and with their mutual detestation of the corrupt regime they found in each other a supplemental means to achieve their purposes. He feared his ultimate exposure but reveled in the small victories his espionage won them. Even the steadfast Markuso was unaware of his own ally by his side at the Council and his true mission, one who showed obedience and loyalty by day and delivered secrets at night. Marcus' desire for justice trumped the fear his dangerous and delicate work brought, and he

137

eventually learned to live for the excitement and terror of it and the rewards his bravery delivered. News recently brought by Riman of some very helpful new allies in their resistance was gratefully accepted and Marcus was excited to be finally meeting them this evening, in person.

"This is Marcus," Riman said. They exchanged greetings, with looks of awe and wonder coming from the stranger. They look like some capable adversaries, he thought. Finally. Perhaps Riman is right. Maybe now we can get some real work done. "He is our agent in the Hera Council and has been my friend for many years. He it was who provided us the information about tonight, among other things. But we will discuss his worth later. Our Council leader is still alive, I trust?"

"Markuso will live a bit longer," Damian informed him, "though he will now require even more protection. Helbek will be surprised to see him on the floor tomorrow."

"He must be preserved," Riman said. "We need him where he is. The last steadfast voice of justice in that accursed assembly. Even now he is mustering his revolution in secret. The Guards of Karius, though outwardly disbanded, still lie hidden and ready, waiting for the moment when their lion calls them forth. The power of the Second Pillar hangs by a thread, and if Markuso falls any chance of revival will vanish irretrievably. Markuso is this city's last hope. But I fear you're right. He will need close watching."

"Not a problem," said Cam, flexing his fists. "We have fun doing that."

"It will have to be postponed," Riman said, "for we have an interesting development." Cam looked up, ever more hopeful, the fire in his eyes brightened. "An escaped prisoner from Khala, it seems, has been found and captured."

Damian and Cam looked at each other. "Only one?" asked Damian. "He must have been of importance if only he was found out of the many that escaped. What can the Ahga want with him?"

Marcus, the newcomer spoke up. "This particular individual holds information vital to the Kunn, no one seems to know exactly what, and someone found out about him. Some loose tongue at Khala must have mentioned something to someone, hoping to make a profit from it. He was making his escape to Kandar with the help of some Demarian agents of the Hattél, but a bounty hunter captured him in the hills beyond Hera to the north and sold him to some independent entrepreneurs, mercenaries unassociated with or looking to blackmail the Kunn. The word is the Ahga in Mod is desperate for his recapture or death and is paying these villains handsomely for it."

"Klavék and his gang," Riman answered. "He can always be counted upon for competency and seizure of opportunity. It is perhaps better that they found him before the Kunn did. But their secrets are unlocked with payment. Klavék has interest only for money, not the ideals of either the Ahga or revolutionaries."

"Do we know when or where this will take place?" Damian asked.

"The Ahga has assigned his lead ulak in Hera to the task, Mozep," Marcus answered, "a Kunn brother of very high standing in the clan, very deadly, a gangster of despicable repute. He is the highest ranking member of the Kunn in the city, holding as much power as Helbek himself, and is well trusted. The Ahga does not want failure here; this is an important purchase, though it is likely the Kunn will attempt a counterattack. The Ahga does not take well to blackmail. The deal will transpire on neutral territory, somewhere in the Monse District. The final arrangements have not yet been decided upon. I will try to get the latest information tomorrow. Tura is not an easy agent to glean. In the meantime I must depart at once. I have already been here too long. There is great activity in the streets now, even at this hour, and I hope no one has observed my movements here."

"There is little concern of our discovery," Riman assured him. "I planted a little surprise at the door for unwanted guests."

"No doubt you did," Marcus replied with a smile. "Your ingenuity and craftiness can always be counted upon my old friend. Put it to good use. But my days at the Palace become more difficult. I have to be more on my guard now than I ever did in the past. I am being followed, I can feel it in my bones. I would not be surprised if some spy of Helbek followed me out of the Palace this evening. I suggest you be prepared for the very possibility of unwanted guests. I will not come here again for a while, for our own protection, and will make the necessary adjustments to thwart pursuit on my end. I will communicate in my usual fashion though our routine will need modification. Personal contact is no longer feasible. Further use of coded transcript has become increasingly necessary." He turned to Damian and Cam. "And to you I say this: your heroism is a welcome friend, your courage and deeds I acknowledge as a much needed blessing. Riman has told me of you. But beware the henchmen of the Ahga; do not underestimate his loyal servants. He has skilled mercenaries and assassins at his fingertips. This spirit-creed they follow breeds a zealousness that is to be feared. And if you find this man they're looking for, find out what they want with him. A secret of theirs can be used as a mighty weapon against them."

"We will find him," answered Damian with a note of determination, "and what he knows, of that you can be assured. Cam and I will see it done."

Marcus took his leave and exited the vacant and dark building from the side instead of the back as he usually did. The warm night was deep but active, and he could hear the distant voices of the revelers and musicians and other restless folk mingled with thugs and thieves making a commotion in the dense city center many blocks away. He could feel eyes looking for him in the dark and he hustled away by quieter roads to his home across the city.

Damian looked at Riman curiously. "What is his position in the Council, and what do we know of him? He must be of great import indeed if he knows of our refuge here. Can he be trusted?"

Riman was leaning against a large work table in the room, working on some kind of new spring-loaded trap device. His work table was cluttered with small metal parts, gears and tools for precision metal working. Instruments of metallurgy and ingredients for chemical composites lay about for constant use. Magnifying lenses, vials of unknown solutions, and small burners complimented the unusual assortment. Prototypes of various weapons and devices lay about in different stages of completion. Cam was eyeing a strange cylindrical-shaped object with intense interest.

"That is what guards our front and back doors," Riman said. "Even you would be challenged to avoid the peril this device projects, my speedy friend." Cam looked up at the craftsman curiously and gingerly placed the object back on the table. Riman turned to Damian. "His brother's family owned a very large ranch and farming plantation outside Felbruk years ago, one of the largest in this province, very profitable. The Ahga of course was interested in a portion of their earnings and production, and ultimate takeover, and sought his usual forcible extraction of what he desired. Instead they were going to immediately inform the Guard of the coercion and had a representative of the Council, with whom they had connections, about to dispatch troops for protection. This was during the latter years when Karius was still in power and the Kunn had no established power and influence in the territory yet, but that didn't stop the Ahga from expanding his monopolies across the borders of weak realms and probing into conquerable profitable endeavors. When the Ahga discovered their intent he had Marcus' brother and wife captured and murdered before the Guard arrived, then fled. If the Ahga can't have what he wants of you he takes your life instead. He will not be gainsaid.

"The Kunn still have not achieved power over the plantation yet, even to this day. The family can afford protection but you can imagine how it affected Marcus. He took matters into his own hands, seeking to eradicate the problem before it came here. He and an independent group of individuals, friends of his from the Guards of Karius, staged their own raid against Kunn villains encamped near the southern border of Nadea who had been raiding supply lines and attacking villagers who dwelt nigh the river. The Kunn threatened to capture citizens of the realm to try to pressure

Karius into dubious negotiations. Marcus and his band tracked the murderers all along the border near Dal-Abba and waylaid them in the night in a daring raid. He was outnumbered but he was victorious, and placed the head of the ulak in a basket and sent it to the Palace of Mod where he knew the Kunn was strengthening their presence and the Ahga often dwelt. He wrote a message to the Ahga warning him to stay away. He also personally assassinated a certain Kunn member who he proved was spying on Karius and by this I believe the death of the good lord was postponed. Because of his deeds and proven worth Karius personally appointed Marcus a position of representation in the Council. Through our covert methods of communication he has provided me information of Kunn intentions and movements for years now, long before you arrived to help us. Yes, I trust him."

Two individuals had followed Marcus after his late departure of the palace that night. They had been shadowing him now for weeks due to Helbek's growing suspicion and dislike of him. Several of his schemes of late the lord found had been strangely thwarted or upset. The abduction of a prestigious statesman had somehow been foiled. This individual was close to presenting evidence of wrongdoing on his part, which he intended to disclose to the Council which still held sufficient power to keep the lord partially in check when necessary, by majority consent. This rebel needed some persuasion to keep silent. Though Helbek was promised the delivery of this character, for he was watched and his whereabouts were well known, his agents could not account for his location when they arrived at his residence for his apprehension, nor could they find him the following days. They searched the city desperately for him before he could make public his incriminating evidence but the elusive individual was nowhere to be found. He had strangely reappeared at the Council some days later in the presence of a certain noble of stature who Helbek recognized as a man he had cheated out of payment in a land deal. The lord was seen to be convulsed with rage when the two paraded triumphantly up the broad steps and through the huge doors to the Council, to whom he was modestly accountable, and, being exposed before all, he had to pay the sizable sum. Now how did he escape his agents? It was as if he suddenly and inexplicably realized his impending fate and fled just in time, conveniently eluding his many searching watchmen in the process. Helbek felt that was too much of a coincidence. Someone must have helped him.

Then there was the time he planned to raid the estate of a competing nobleman on the other side of the city, in the district of Minian, seeking to relieve the daring dissenter of some valuables in order to cripple his enterprise and buttress his own. All was ready the day before the raid, his agents informed him, the money and goods on location, but the next night when his men broke in they found the abode deserted and the vault empty. Odd. He must have gotten word somehow. Many of the Hera government were bought Kunn representatives, and those that weren't were coerced into compliance anyway. Who was leaking this information? There was a rat with ears right in his own chambers. Being proficient with deception himself, Helbek, always suspicious of his own, did not find it difficult to suspect several individuals possible of these undoings. Those adept at evil will ever be perceptive and paranoid of the same and are doomed to be forever on their guard against reciprocity. Helbek could read deception and the evidence he had suggested several individuals including Marcus, and he was determined to finally catch the elusive culprit, whoever he was.

The two stalkers tracked their target along the winding and dark city blocks for some time, deftly avoiding the populated center, they noticed, and thought they saw him turn quickly into that abandoned and tilted building just around the corner. This particular sector, the Hole of Helbius, they knew, had been condemned and vacated due to its instability, a creeping epidemic in this old city becoming victim to widespread erosive decrepitude. The very river that nurtured the city's inhabitants was eroding it steadily. Now what could he possibly be doing in these filthy ruins at this hour? An esteemed member of the Council, gallivanting about in the dark among thieves and rascals? Convening with rebels, no doubt, and dispensing dangerous secrets. Marcus was still inside, they assumed, for he hadn't yet been seen emerging. They planned to catch him in the act. It was a rumor among the Kunn that a small but effective resistance and agency of espionage was organizing in the very city and gaining strength. Perhaps now the hive was found at last. Maybe Helbek will pay double for the find, they thought, and reward us with promotions, and they became giddy with their thoughts of grandeur. They waited a few moments before making the mistake of venturing into the quiet structure where they noticed him enter. They crept down a hall on the first floor and opened a door, a door that in the dark they didn't notice was concealing some strange depressions in the floor just beyond the threshold. One of them stepped on what must have been a plate of some kind which subsequently made a metallic clicking sound and he felt a sprung tension, like something which held considerable potential energy had just been released or opened. They couldn't see the two strange canisters project vertically from the floor about eight feet apart from each other and about six feet off the ground, spinning with such a speed that the multitude of tiny metal fragments embedded loosely inside were ejected in all directions with a deadly velocity, peppering the faces and eyes of the intruders with poisoned spikes...

CHAPTER 3
A DUAL EXCURSION

Damian and Cam departed their hideout early in the morning and sought for a place where they could hone their skills before the day's activities. They rode horseback, swiftly passing the many stone and brick structures, fair colonnades and public forums the prosperous and architecturally advanced city boasted. Tenements of stone and white brick under the sun were packed densely in blocks on either side. Shops of all kinds lined the many roads and avenues, and folk of all walk and race soon would be upon them in droves. The riders flew along the streets of Nibera district, heading southward. After a few miles of galloping down the still quiet and intersecting stone-paved streets they arrived at the Kalamadium, the main east-west road through the city. They followed this grand throughway until they met with the abrupt termination of the city of Hera. This level of raised earth was known as 'Tier Two.' The sister cities of Hera and Gyla were built on abutting plateaus, Hera being at slightly higher elevation than its counterpart, Gyla, a circumstance conceived by two competing plates of earth which strove with one another along an active fault line. Rocky ascents lined the northern sides, the Brown Hills; low and easing cliffs and rough flats bordered the southern. Between these two tiers, however, a narrow gorge and ravine opened, into which spilled the Tybron River, and from here continued its journey through this second, lower city. From a distant bird's eye view the two cities looked like one giant metropolis on two levels, separated by a long man-made incline connecting them.

The steepness of the rise in the land between the two cities necessitated an improved system of rampways to provide easier access for the heavy commerce which passed through back and forth daily, and a great connecting road was cut right into the rocky slope. This masterpiece of engineering was called 'The Ascension' by the Lords Karius and Alos who built it mutually and jointly in the early years of their rule and took fifteen years to build. The wide paved stone road, carved out of the sloping rock at a fairly easy angle, zig-zagged its way up the rise from Gyla, broken at intervals with a smooth, flat level space before the road rose again at the next point. These level sections served as easy passage points for the

143

multitude of wagons and carts which labored their way up and down the incline, an exertion the engineers of this great and ingenious construction sought to ease. A wagon rider would travel a full two miles side to side before he reached Tier Two. For those on foot a single wide stone staircase was cut on either side of The Ascension, wide enough to easily accommodate heavy traffic, also broken at intervals with level spaces for rest and easy passage before it again ascended. There was no gate at either end of the magnificent road for travel and commerce was open and unrestricted, encouraged toll-free by the allied brothers of the twin cities, although there was a large archway of polished stone at the top and bottom of the prodigious stair, one at either end with words of welcome engraved along the chiseled archways inviting travelers to the respective cities. This awesome project served a dual purpose, as the removed stone was utilized in the recent improvement and as yet unfinished construction of the cities' walls.

The road was, however, well guarded at most hours, especially during the day when traffic was heavy, and had recently seen an increase in guard presence, a presence the citizenry found unnecessary and intrusive. The new regime, buttressed propitiously atop the fruits of the old, wanted to keep an eye on the road and apprehend any dissident or fugitive sought by them, and Helbek ordered the captains of his Guard to be watchful for these certain individuals and would have them secretly arrested if found. These captains had in their possession names of interest and would frequently stop and interrogate travelers and inspect their goods, a practice rarely employed under the rule of the cities' former rulers. The citizens had seen some unpleasant changes suddenly and strangely put into effect recently and were compelled to subject themselves to them, and a mood one could call fear and paranoia set in among the contributors and providers of the populace.

Damian and Cam sat upon their great steed wide-eyed beholding the spectacle. No obstruction was there to impede the breathtaking view of the great stair and its magnificent descent to the city below, and the two avengers paused and gaped, halted right below the huge stone archway threshold of Tier Two. The words 'Welcome' and 'City of Hera' were inscribed with skill upon the westward face of the entablature, and a statue flanked either side. One was of a man holding a sack of grain, the other a hammer, both symbolizing hard work and reward. An open book, they saw, was engraved at the top center of the entablature, symbolizing knowledge. Upon the left page were the inscribed words PROSPERITY THROUGH ADHERENCE. And upon the right: DISSOLUTION THROUGH DEVIATION, a bold warning and reminder from the city's founders long ago. The sun rose fully and clearly behind them in the brilliant blue sky and shed its light on one of the province's greatest creations. They scanned all within the horizons in awe. They could see already travelers upon the road of wonder, paved and crafted with skill and pride for the lords whom the men of the time served with happiness and vigor. They could see the stone city of Gyla laid out not far below them on the elevated plateau, white walled and potent, eager for the morning. The pride these cities once boasted, if only for a limited time, was very evident but its splendor was now tainted with a distrust and watchfulness, a sadness and discomfort that could be felt, a memory of a greatness that was.

Damian broke the silence. "For this alone the realm is worth saving," he muttered to himself. They spent a moment in reverence for the once great and vestigious city, then they rode down the massive winding stone ramp.

They reached the bottom after a lengthy descent and turned right, passing through another like archway greeting travelers to Gyla. The few guards on duty about the entrance eyed them curiously. They looked fairer and more fearless than the nervous folk that traversed the cities daily, cowering in fear and distrust under the unfriendly stares of the guards. They asked the strangers no questions though, and Damian and Cam headed northward through the city streets and soon exited the city. They were heading for the hills that bordered the outskirts of Gyla to the north. They could see before them crop fields which stretched for miles slowly upward to the east, past Hera, and scattered farmsteads and villas in the fertile valley of Shadím below the rising hillsides. The river Tybron ran down from the hills and valley and wound through the cities to the south and beyond to the low plains. Further to the west and down the decline they could see the cavities in the hills which comprised the Quarries at Felda, the source from which the cities were largely built. Great yoked boro steeds could be seen in the distance far below pulling heavy wagons of stone slabs. Cam spied a likely place further to the north that would suit them for today, a low point between the hills and past the farmsteads which seemed to form a small secluded valley, lightly forested and rocky, some four miles or so away, they guessed. Bish carried them quickly from the city limits, crossed the bridge over the river, through the fertile fields, and into the climbing wilderness beyond. They felt they needed a place to vent their thoughts and discuss the situation at hand alone in a physical interactive forum while their enemies concealed themselves during the day. Training and upkeep was considered vital to their purpose and they intended to pursue it regularly. Preparedness for melee had to be maintained.

They soon pulled into a grove of mixed trees and shrubs located in a wide craggy bowl of the hillside. This inhospitable piece of landscape could not hope to be used for any kind of civil purpose; sharp boulders and broken trees protruded dangerously in all directions. This would work well for them. Cam was the first to dismount, shaking with energy and impatient to tame this exciting new territory which would serve as their training arena. It was now past midmorning and they were more than ready. Damian jumped from the horse and quickly climbed onto a ledge with broken rocks. Bish sprang free and leaped and ran along the untamed and diverse landscape on his own, darting over the rocks and gullies like a huge mountain goat on his home turf. Damian smiled after him as he watched the tireless horse soar along the hillside. Cam hopped and sprang onto a fallen tree that made a bridge across a chasm in the rock. He flipped in the air and jumped and somersaulted mid-air back and forth along the thin tree and held himself up with one hand before flipping upright. Damian was pulling loose head-sized chunks of rock from the ground and heaving them across the uneven depression to the other side, aiming for and breaking off tree branches. Cam stood upright and tense and gave Damian a taunting look. Damian gave him an evil smile back. *Very well you squirrel...*

"Let's see what you can do," Damian challenged and picked up fist-sized stones in either hand. Cam grinned and poised himself for action. Damian started flinging them at Cam with both hands, ambidextrously and in rapid succession, and with great speed picked up more stones to continue the hail. Cam nimbly dodged the salvos, flipping all over the narrow log like a crazed ape.

"That pick-up has to happen soon," said Damian as he threw a huge, ten foot palm log at his elusive target.

"Maybe tonight," said Cam as he sprung high into the air and kicked the log as it passed by him. Cam caught the high branch of a nearby tree and swung on it.

"There'll be lots of them," said Damian and he flung a broken tree branch as a target toward him.

"Half the Kunn gang in Hera I would imagine," Cam replied and leaped through the air, sword in hand and split the branch with it in mid-flight. He landed on a rock below him and likewise threw a chunk of wood high across the depression. Quicker than mortal eyesight could see Damian drew his bow and fitted a black garvonite arrow.

"Maybe even an accursed member of the Baccád," Damian growled and shot the hurtling projectile. It split in two and fell in pieces on the ground in front of him. Cam picked up a seven-foot stick of solidly petrified cane plant from a patch and quickly evened out both ends to serve as a weapon. He threw it at Damian like a spear and pulled out another cane for himself. Damian replaced his bow and caught the stick weapon and charged his enemy. Cam, pole arm in hand, sprung into the air toward Damian and they clashed.

"And we must wonder who these other criminals are," said Cam as he rained swings at Damian. "Apparently the Kunn isn't the only enemy."

146

"Rogues of all kinds stalk these lands," replied Damian, blocking the lightning-quick blows from his supernaturally adept comrade. "Villains have become emboldened by the decline of defense and enamored with chaotic entities and ideologies such as the Kunn live by. The Order of old is now non-existent. The folk are afraid." The two fenced fiercely for some time with the poles, blocking, striking, evading, and the dell echoed with the great noise of the rapid ceaseless cracks.

"I wonder what this fellow knows anyway," said Cam.

"Hopefully something we can use to destroy the Kunn. We have to get him. I'm sure he has something interesting he could tell us." Damian swung down on Cam, splitting Cam's cane in two with the impact of the block. Cam, thrilled, wielded the two halves and Damian braced himself, anticipating the next and even more dangerous mode of attack.

"Taking on so many will be quite a challenge, not that I wouldn't enjoy the privilege," said Cam as he wielded dual sticks against Damian who countered and blocked with even more speed, a speed and strength not given to his fellow mortals of like race. The cracks from the impacts sounded like an avalanche of stones in an empty canyon.

"It will be dangerous, even for us," acknowledged Damian. "Maybe Riman can help us with that."

"Yeah, one of his spring devices. I wonder what else he has in his arsenal of gadgets. Did you see what they did to those intruders?"

"Impressive," acknowledged Damian between breaths, defending against Cam's barrage with some difficulty. "The crafty old man knows his business. We are lucky to have him as a guide." Cam was undaunted by the tall, intimidating stature of Damian and used his small size and amazing speed to challenge the brute. He hopped back and forth, flipping over Damian's head like a jumping spider, all the while showering him with accurate and deadly blows. They both relished the exercise and alternately laughed and growled at the empowering exertion. To an onlooker the simulated fight was very impressive and he would have had difficulty convincing himself of their mortality: two highly trained and disciplined warriors of an unknown fighting art and capability, one great and strong, one small and adept, finding in their supplemental abilities an equalizing power and deadliness, sparring like professionals up and down the rocky depression, seemingly oblivious and unhindered by the rolling and broken landscape which they traversed with ease while they fenced. Cam finally caught Damian on his back with a controlled glancing blow.

"Ha ha!" blurted Cam triumphantly, then seeing Damian's wrath, fled and sprung back onto the fallen tree.

"A lucky shot you little rat," growled Damian and he angrily removed an oversized stone weighing a few hundred pounds. He held it aloft with one arm and prepared to throw. Cam's eyebrows went up and his permanent, confident and challengeful smile faded momentarily. *That's a big rock...*

Cam leaped as the hurtling rock split the tree in half. The former bridge burst and fell into the shallow rocky chasm it once spanned. Cam landed on the side of a nearby tree and perched there momentarily. His jaw dropped when he looked down upon an aimed feathered shaft and met the playfully vengeful eyes behind it.

"And hopefully tonight we will have such luck," said Damian and he whistled for Bish. The great black horse came flying over, eager to serve his master. Cam leaped down and Damian released the arrow, hitting the very spot where Cam crouched a moment ago. "There is something afoot. Come, Cam! I am sure the Kunn has not been idle." They both hopped onto their horse and sped out of the rocky dell and back toward the city. But Damian and Cam were not the only ones out honing their skills...

* * *

Tog hung from a tree, upside down as he always did when he hunted, sensing prey below. His feet and legs he had made just as capable as his arms and hands. He would put to use all the gifts *his* Creator gave him to kill and he would improve his capabilities beyond that of others'. Through years of intense and rigorous training, and incredible physical and mental discipline he had transformed his body into that of a versatile, silent, deadly, killing machine, weaving muscle onto muscle, bone onto bone, his flesh thickening into layers of nearly impenetrable hide through his merciless training and livelihood of terrestrial unison and ethereal perception. To live in accord with the earth was his gift, to utilize its energies as though they were his tools and subjects, and he was duly rewarded by its fruits. He was the living paradigm of an adherent of the ancient code of the Hakai, *the Mari,* the code of energy and life by which his folk lived. The Mari was an obscure and decidedly harsh but rewarding dogma carried through successive generations of clans claiming exclusive rights to it and that which it promised. Being of that brotherly lineage it was little wonder that it was also adopted by the Ahga and his Baccád, claimants of Slovidar inheritance, a once great but bygone clan of a continuing objective, one that the Kunn sought to fulfill, though it was speculated that there may have been some divine involvement in the Ahga's formation of his organization. But it could not have been considered a vain endeavor. The Kunn had grown in power exponentially in a remarkably short time. The code they followed, established by a divine entity as the old legend of Adin went, demanded what the unbelievers considered impossible: unlimited capability and power of both mind and body. There was nothing beyond the ability of mortal power if one has only the patience and discipline to overcome it. These weak and faithless mortals of other creeds considered certain tasks or feats impossible, such as elemental manipulation or even flight, and never bothered to train themselves into the realm of superior strength or the paranormal. Such things may have been oft referred–insultingly–as 'conjuration' or 'elementalism' by the faithless who deemed the vague gifts of this religion naught but enchantments by shamans and ghosts of the haunted realm of Azandium. Superstitions abounded among unbelievers of the legend of Adin and its disbanded brothers who strove with one another for the treasures of that strange domain. But those such as Tog knew that one's own weakness of will was his own inhibition, thereby rendering a being woefully impotent. To a true student of the Mari, such as the Hakai, and the blessed aspirants of the Kunn, the challenge of breaching mortal parameters was a mere obstacle of the flesh and mind the Mari demanded conquered.

The code clearly stated that all mortals are blessed with infinite power not limited to the perceived confines and restrictions of this world and are called upon to use them, an inherent ability of which they were previously ignorant, an ignorance caused by an inferior connection with the material and thus rendered to be dormant. Anything was possible to Tog, he had his own extraordinary powers to prove it, and no one and nothing could tell him otherwise. Denial of unlimited power was espoused by the faithless which seemed to surround him and he despised them for their incomprehensible ignorance and conscious rejection of greatness. There was no room in this world for these blasphemers who insulted the Divine One with their failure to acknowledge and utilize the full potential that was obviously bestowed upon all, and he had no problem ridding the world of them. In the end he and his earthly subjects would conquer them all, thereby gaining ultimate divine favor as promised by the Great Book. He obviously belonged to a far superior species, the eldest and most fell of his kin, and was the beneficiary of the gifts of his unseen master. He would fulfill the great mission of that deity here in this material realm along with the Ahga, the only mortal with the courage and wisdom to continue the broken pilgrimage of the Slovidar clans and create a new following based on principles which he shared and held dear, and that principle was supremacy and domination, a gift so reservedly and uniquely indigenous to this world of material. For his proven dedication and abidance to the teachings of the Mari, Tog long ago chose the Ahga as his earthly partner, and to him the religion was especially imparted. Tog put to use the supercapabilities thus bestowed by dedicated adherence, thereby ridding the world of his proclaimed enemies–the Kadali monks and was promised the ultimate reward his creed and folk had long sought. To destroy the supernal enemies of the Hakai and their institutions on earth was his charge. The Kunn was a mortal hand to assist him in this.

Tog felt his own virtually limitless strength flow through him as he hung motionless from the high tree branch for hours, coalescing with the powers of the earth, seeking prey through energy detection, a gift of unique strength and ability he earned and deserved; others did not. They would reap the punishment for their gross ignorance, he thought as he hung still. This weakness and waywardness lived by so many, this rejection of proffered blessing, stirred the hatred within him, a widespread despicability of all beings that grew in strength and intensity as the years passed. How backwards this world is and how it must displease He that sits on the divine throne unseen. The Ahga and the brotherhood Tog invited to join and assist alone understood him and this great purpose, and for this they were chosen to aid him in his great dual-faceted quest. In this symbiotic fellowship Tog found a means to pursue his objectives effectively in the wider world, through this shared idealism, and therefore complete the great assignment. The Kunn was an earthly pawn, faithful of the code and worthy of divine favor, and with this joint association their dual objectives could be achieved. But the Mari was not a creed to loosely proselytize. It chose its interested applicants with care and kept its blessings to itself, doling them selectively to its most ardent and worthy adherents. Though the Ahga infused the beliefs of the Mari into his organization, Tog was of far loftier mold and could not be properly replicated, undoubtedly being a descendant of Adin himself, a member of some higher order and echelon, worshipping his beliefs and practicing his ancient rituals and meditations to such a degree his underlings wondered at him. But they certainly feared him. Whatever practices and disciplines Tog was eagerly subjecting himself to he certainly benefited from, in ways other students of the Mari could not, and what few members of the Kunn perchance crossed his paths would dare not offer words of mockery to the revered and mysterious dark assassin of the Divine One. Efforts were made to avoid his piercing and disapproving eyes which seemed to look down upon all with disdain and expose them as ignorant and unworthy. But they avoided him out of fear and Tog kept his reproachful thoughts to himself.

The Ahga, however, emulated Tog's excessive idealism and devotion, which he exalted as the model paradigm of the code's exemplar. Though the clan followed the Mari with earnestness, eager to reap its blessings, there was little doubt that Tog possessed certain uncanny abilities his fellow striving brothers could not claim: a rare, bestowed gift of the Divine One perhaps, maybe he was even an object of Divine Selection. There was obviously something unusual about this servant of the

Mari. Were the Divine One himself to assume an earthly form, so it may have been, and thus he was regarded.

Tog sensed an energy in the forest below him and he opened his red, reptilian eyes, the first time he opened them in hours as he meditated high above the forest floor. Eyesight to him was an unnecessary sensation. These other paltry, subordinate mortals mistakenly considered this to be a vital and superior sense, relying on it too often and therefore failed as a result to tap into greater gifts ignored and unused. The full transformation to that of a higher being was hopelessly beyond the ability of the faithless. There were far more reliable and sharper senses he had learned to harness, and he merely employed what he considered to be a lesser sense to confirm the type of prey and its exact location. He had reached the lower groves and flats just south of Hera, arriving in the early hours on foot, running the night away all the way from Mod at the urgent need of his cause and the speed of the Divine: the Imposter had borne seed to another. The Feud of Adin had entered a new chapter. Thither he sped. Steeds or any other type of artificial transportation were an unnecessary and unwanted burden to him, his machine-like legs of hide and iron being more than sufficient and trustworthy to him and certainly more versatile. Mechanical help of any kind supplanted that spiritual connection which he craved and lived by and displaced him from the subjects he trusted most: earth, mind, body, spirit, the elements of existence, all which could be culminated, if one only attempted, into provisional forces disposed to mortal servitude and manipulation, and he drew strength from the vibrant earth as he pounded it relentlessly below his merciless legs while the night rushed past him.

He closed his eyes again for the prey was not yet close enough and he did not wish any earthly distractions to ruin his deadly ambush. This was the main reason he preferred to do his gruesome work alone and by so doing derived far greater personal satisfaction as a result, a satisfaction he lived for. He did not trust others, preferring his own solitary powers and control. Other species could not hope to understand his methods and would be a hindrance. He returned to his meditation, listening to the earth and hearkening to its energies, hanging motionless and silent, hardly breathing, seeing the creature with his mind's eye. He focused on its movements and behavior. He watched it forage through the brush, stepping cautiously and warily. It was obviously a creature of herbivorous characteristics: four-legged, fairly large in size, long-necked, small-toothed, hooved, overly cautious as it explored the forest floor, sniffing the air and looking about constantly.

The strange, furry creature was within Tog's supernatural springing distance and his body curled imperceptibly, preparing for an angled lunge from the high tree-top. He contorted his body into an incredibly tense statue, holding himself unmoving and outwards almost parallel to the flat earth in the direction of his perceived victim. He could see and feel it draw steadily closer. It was time. He opened his eyes.

He projected himself from the tree limb noiselessly, flying rather than falling at a slanted direction toward the animal who stiffened somewhat, as if it suddenly detected something, an ability Tog and his kindred the Hakai could relate to and identify with, and respect. This alerted reaction, however, only endeared itself to its master predator. This creature indeed, and the thrill and satisfaction it brought Tog made its destruction far more valuable in the heart of the killer and glorified himself all the more to the One and the creed to which he belonged. The ignorant animal didn't even know what hit it as it was suddenly and fiercely gripped by unforgiving and vice-like arms which twisted its neck so completely and absolutely it never even saw its silent conqueror.

Tog gave thanks and finished his meal and looked toward the city on the rising distant plateau. He had a new enemy.

* * *

Riman ventured out into the market later that day. He wore a close-fitting hood and eye patch today to conceal his features. He was, after all, in his home city and there were many in the trades and black market that were still familiar with him. This city was crawling with scum loyal to the Kunn and there were many who knew his looks and would recognize him. Among the many the Ahga sought, Riman was most valuable, and the gangsters and mercenaries would love to sell him back to the clan. Riman still had many customers and acquaintances. Then there were many in the Hera governmental spheres that worked with him closely in the recent years. The price on his head for his daring and insulting stunt years ago was still attractively high, indeed it increased as time passed without his capture and the wrath of the Ahga grew with it. Bounty hunters from all over combed the cities with their discerning eyes from dark corners and asked questions of his whereabouts, his aliases, his many guises. Folk seemed to know who he was but as far as they could tell he vanished some years ago, fell into a hole or was tied and thrown overboard some pirate vessel in the Dinitian Sea, or was robbed and killed by some Cerrulian gem thieves in some distant country. He was always traveling about, they said, he must be long gone. Didn't he work for the Kunn for some years? Some kind of metallurgist and gem peddler or something. But the vagabonds and thugs that were questioned in holes and dens of ill repute had no real idea of why this rebel was still being sought so aggressively, nor did the hunters. Probably insulted the Ahga or killed one of the Baccád, they said. One rarely committed murder against them without repercussion, they had eyes and ears everywhere. The Kunn was always looking for someone and had bounties out on numerous characters, rebels or assassins wanted by the Ahga, even high profile merchantmen or politicians who had defied him and fled. The return rate of these bounties was very high and if one made the list his death or capture was all but assured. The Ahga could afford the best and their desire for more of his wealth returned them to his presence often.

These dangers did not daunt Riman, however. His passion for justice was too great for these trivial fears to be of overwhelming concern. His knowledge of the underground in the city combined with his genius carried him safely to his vengeful objectives. He was aware of hunters daily who sometimes passed by him so closely as to brush against him in the street or taverns and he sought ways to divert or avoid them, staying one step ahead of them all the time. He liked this recent change of habitation, however, to have returned to the city, and was glad to leave rural Tirien behind for a while to allow his scent to grow cold there. His dangerous predicament necessitated him becoming a master of disguise, and he roamed about the city running his necessary errands dressed and acting in accordance with a variety of different personas; one day a foreign count, another a drifting gambler, another day found him a venerable diplomat or ambassador, the next a kuth dealer of the south. Today he was simply a common passer-by of Hera for he did not intend to stay out long. Whatever his needs of information gathering or sabotage against the Kunn and Helbek called for on a particular occasion, he found a way to fit the mold and smiled to himself as he, with the help of Marcus, foiled plot after plot and thwarted Kunn intentions in the city, one small but memorable deed at a time.

The marketplace of Hera was a huge open space on the southern perimeters of Nibera district, nigh the Kalamadium and the massive Circadrome arena. The market was lined with ranks of open tents and pavilions. Carts, wagons, and tables were arranged in rows which could change daily and even hourly as the business wore on and sellers departed and new ones arrived. The huge palace of Hera and its adjoining compound and other structures of government were not far away and well in view, consuming most of the skyline to the north and east. Though it was surrounded with a high wall and gated at several points, many guards were always present there outside in the streets and in the busy market below, keeping an eye on the masses and heated activity. Riman made unnoticeable efforts to avoid them as he merged himself with the diverse crowd which was comprised of numerous and different humanoid and mount creatures from the nearby territories. Tribes and folk from all over convened here for business and lately crime. Caravans from the plains of Halkád and Jal, and even as far as Mod and Serabat rumbled their way onto the grounds and established their venditions. He wound his way through the loud and challenging vendors as he usually did, taking careful note of certain individuals he saw as he passed: a human, northern-looking, probably a businessman from Kandar, scouting rare skins and cloths of the river settlements of the Ella; a half-mog, twisted and unfriendly looking, from Mod perhaps, maybe even within Thuliak's corrupt family circle; he looked wealthy and was bartering for jewels, probably that pig Thuliak's half-brother by the looks of him; a Hidari and his caravan drawn by *taulkas*—tall, camel-like steeds of the mountains pulling wagons of rare silks and fabrics called *volia*, made from the same plant in the distant country of Adovia, his van well guarded by others of the same race, light-skinned humanoids with long black hair and beards, large and thickly built; an Achellan, a tall, dark-skinned and haired being and his table of expensive ivories, meats, skins and ornaments of unknown beasts from his home island of Dinitia to the west in the Vidian Sea; a trio of armed Turuks by an open pavilion, obviously Kunn thugs intending to intimidate the passers-by while they awaited orders from their superior who was undoubtedly dealing coercively with the tenant inside—Riman detoured away but was followed at a distance by another human, tall, cloaked, and sinister who eyed Riman suspiciously from his watchful position outside the nearby tavern. Two other foul-looking fellows went with him.

Riman kept his destination in sight the whole time and finally made it there: a large open bazaar, fairly populated at present where among trinkets and odds and ends from all over one could purchase books and tomes from a collection at a back corner. Riman slowly made his way to the farthest tables where old and mostly unwanted literature and scrolls were arranged and stacked. He sought and found the book where he and Marcus currently concealed their correspondence. *Allegiance of the Fallen* was its name, the memoir of Sevinian, a lord of the realm long ago and a historian who recounted the fall of the kingdom of Dengland by clans from the south who subversively undermined and eventually overthrew the corrupt governments there in his tome. Confident no unwanted eyes would peer curiously into this book, the two conspirators chose it for the transfer of their classified communication. Shame, thought Riman as he opened the old and worn book. These people in the realm who become ever more foolish and ignorant might learn something from it. He found page 604, the year Karius died, and he let the encoded parchment fall into his open tunic pocket. After a few moments he replaced the book and began making his difficult way out of the marketplace.

He quickly left the crowd and noise behind, taking refuge from the eyes in an alleyway several blocks away from the chaos. He made it a point to stop in his travels and quickly change disguise to throw off any possible pursuit. He ducked in behind some stacked and empty casks and jugs to make some quick appearance adjustments before reemerging.

Riman's pursuers had divided themselves, two mogs coming from behind him through the back of the alley, the human seeking to cut him off at the top end. These three had been tracking Riman for many months now, through the rurals and farmlands of the eastern province and back to the city again, and they were pretty sure they finally had their man. The money they would pull in after this catch would make their tedious search well worth the trouble. They would carefully watch the marketplace and the traffic on the Ascension daily, taking note of interesting characters they observed, and any bribed guards or scouts of the Kunn throughout the city would bring any report of interest. Though he looked different every time they saw him, through repetition and deduction, and a few tips from the knowledgeable underground, the hunters felt that there was definitely something interesting about this fellow who dodged his way regularly about the marketplace and to the same open pavilion with few words and departed. No one seemed to know who he was and he certainly didn't work for the Kunn or any other criminal organization as far as the pursuers could tell. They alone decided this character, whoever he was, was worth a look, and today intended to arrest and interrogate him once he was alone. Something about this drifter alerted suspicion and it did not take long for his possible true identity to take shape in the minds of the persevering hunters, and the excitement of the possibility made them reel with greed and determination. Could this possibly be he that the Ahga seeks so desperately? And what was the current price? It was doubtful but this character was certainly strange; he looked too sinister and street-crafty to be simply a farmer or herder. His eyes were keen, scanning everyone and everything in an environment with an uncanny wit and perception, memorizing it all in an instant and hastening away. They decided only days ago the next time they came across this slithering and ever-changing character to find out for sure, and now they had him, alone.

The two mogs came flying around the corner and nearly crashed into an old and limping, long-haired, half-drunk and bent sluggard of a fool right in their path, heading back out toward them. The drunk cursed as he fell over and spilled his open bottle on the narrow, cobblestone alleyway. The hunters angrily kicked him out of the way with some scolding words and hastily searched the remainder of the cluttered and dirty walkway. *He can't be far away,* the old man heard them say. He slowly pulled himself up and limped out to another side-street that ran along the marketplace on the southern side.

Riman continued down the side street which eventually overlooked an open waterway. The small rivers that fed the cities flowed from the Brown Hills to the north and the architects of old built stone ducts and walls to channel this vital substance throughout various parts of the city. He limped his way to a small, secluded stone bridge that crossed to another street on the other side of the channel. There was no one else upon the bridge at the moment and with the exception of the running water below the whole area was relatively quiet. He was almost halfway across when a man jumped onto the bridge from behind a wall on the far side. He wore no armor underneath his cloak to facilitate his much needed speed, but was armed and had an evil look, a scarred face with sneering and greedy, bloodthirsty eyes, eyes that saw through a trick and smiled at a prize that soon would be his. A sword was at his side and a small loaded crossbow was in his hands, aimed at the drunk and ready. He held the weapon steady as he approached.

"We meet at last, old man," he said. "You may have fooled my associates, who possess some less wit than most. I am not as easily deceived, though I am impressed. Perhaps I will keep all the reward for myself as punishment. You may stand up." Riman straightened and looked into the eyes of the stranger. "Well, well. What the Ahga wouldn't give me to get his hands on you," he chuckled. "Riman, isn't it? The price on your head grows ever greater. Maybe I'll keep you in my care for a while just to see how high it goes. You are one slippery little snake but I crave the chase. All over the countryside and towns I tracked you like a hound for months. I just missed you making a pickup from one of your spy friends in Felbruk. Your pathetic hideout in Tirien was lately deserted. I alone found it, putting some tips together. You need to be more careful. Did you think you could just scamper about at will without anyone at all knowing of your activities? We are not so blind. Folk spoke of some new heroes riding about the realm, giving ol' Draga and his boys quite a time. I've never seen him so angered. I guess you could say he's bitter. Word is he's brewing up his revenge, he, he. I won't get in his way. I've got what I want. And suddenly these two enlightened newcomers were reported recently heading for the city. I also heard the hit on some Council member the other night was mysteriously broken up. Seems like the Kunn has some new enemies. More work and money for me. They wouldn't happen to have been involved with that would they? I wonder how much they're worth and where I could find them? You wouldn't know anything about that, would you?" He chuckled smugly to himself. "But now," he said coming closer, "hand over that message."

Riman slowly reached to his pocket and unfolded the paper. The captor reached to take it with his free hand but failed to see a small, cylindrical, spring-loaded weapon which Riman withdrew from a side pocket and used the paper to conceal. Just before the man could take the message he was shot in the chest by some kind of propelled knife and with an amazed look in his eyes at Riman he fell backwards into the water behind him with a splash. Riman replaced the message, took a quick look around, removed his artificial beard and reversed his hood for a quick disguise change, reloaded his weapon and carried on as if nothing had happened. He crossed the bridge and walked across town into a residential area. He still had one more stop to make.

* * *

Damian and Cam rode back down the rough slope of the hills, passed through the farm villages of Shadím, and quickly reached the outskirts of Gyla. They passed through one of the northern gates and wove their way through the buildings and city blocks, patrolling, observing the activity that commenced, looking for any signs of trouble or Kunn presence. But the city was quiet and strangely uneventful at this early afternoon hour. The guards about the streets seemed tranquil and the passers-by content. But it was a peace that did not bring comfort. A feeling of foreboding set in their hearts, an ominous premonition of trouble to come they could feel as they looked about them curiously. Whatever the Kunn was up to today they kept themselves out of sight for the time. The two galloped down the streets, sought out the great stair, and began their climb to Hera.

They were stopped just below the last ramp to Tier Two by an armed guard who called out and held up his hand to them. Damian halted his horse and looked upon him as he approached.

"Who are you and where are you headed?" the man asked, looking them over with fear and wonder.

"Our names and destination are our own business. Why do you ask? Is it customary for travelers to be interrogated as they labor back and forth along the great road?" Damian countered disapprovingly.

"We have orders to halt riders and inspect their goods if they are deemed suspicious or are wanted by the Lord Helbek," he replied.

"You mean the Kunn," Damian replied. "And whom do you serve? Are you loyal to them? You wear the old garb of Karius' Guard of the City. Did your previous lord demand such an order of you?"

The guard looked uneasy and turned behind him to see if any of his fellow men were watching him. His friends being occupied farther up the ramp he turned back to Damian and spoke in a more melancholy tone. "Things have changed. Our orders are different now. Ever since these Kunn gangsters have acquired some sway in the city we have been ordered to be on the lookout for some of our own fellow citizens, nobles and lords even,

157

officers of government, but what their crime is I cannot say. We caught a merchant just the other day, pulled him from his cart of goods and bound him. His possessions were confiscated. He was wanted by *him* for failing to fulfill some business promise or other, so it was said. More probably he had information or money they were looking for. That's how these new fellows operate. They offer threats and punishments if their demands are not met. You'll give them money or goods without a word or they'll take your life, burn your home, or mark your loved ones for death or capture. The Guard now takes orders from Helbek whose allegiance and judgement is questionable, but they are loyal to him. The Guard was once considered the protectors of the realm, but the people now fear the Guard and the two are estranged. Folk now are afraid of us and are distrustful, fearing that they'll be jailed or turned over to a crime gang that grows in power here. But not all of us agree with their manner or swear allegiance. I for one wish them gone and the greatness of the past returned, but alas, I have sworn loyalty out of ignorance."

"Fear not, their days are numbered," growled Damian. "They have a new enemy. They will find themselves faltering and every deed undone, hindered by an unknown wrath and vengeance that will follow them to their destruction."

The guard stepped back a pace and gazed at them with understanding. He had never heard words like this. The strangers seemed to change before his eyes. A look of hope kindled in his sad eyes. "I have seen you before, just this morning passing through and I remarked to myself how you two fit the description." He came close and his voice sunk to a whisper. "Tell me, are you the ones that folk speak of, the one they call *Ratarra*? If you are then you have come just in time and are an answer to our prayers."

Damian looked at him. "What is your name?"

"Derrol," he replied.

"Well, Derrol, be comforted and vigilant. Do not fear or hide. Keep your eyes and ears open. Be alert, for things here may change quickly. I may need you. Ratarra could use some allies." Damian smiled at him and sped off toward Hera, and the guard watched them with amazement.

Riman brought the message to his work counter in their underground hideout. Owing to the many spies and bounty hunters in this increasingly wretched and dangerous city, and the ever-paranoid tyrant who presided over it, he and Marcus employed a diverse means of coded communication. Their small detachment of city watch and espionage operated with extreme fragility, passing their enemies in such close proximity they could hear one another's words, could view one another's writing, and one minor breach would collapse the network and inculpate them all to those upon whom they so secretly spied. The information for this particular encoding was contributed in part by agents afield, for Marcus, who operated primarily at the palace and offices of government, had not direct access to the specifics of this event, but arranged the transmit, as his authority and direction saw fit, in his turn.

Centurion Zera,

This is to inform you that your presence is requested at the Circadrome at the Last Hour this evening for the viewing of the popular spectacle Dorza's Dozen. I know it has always been one of your personal favorites. I have secured our seating between rows 40-50 for the best possible viewing of Cullman's Chargers when they burst forth from the gates with the prisoner. I'm afraid there was substantial competition for the prize and the bounty was high indeed, almost more than I could afford. Considering the view and its revelations I consider it to be worth the expenditure, as do many aspiring bidders. Fear not, my friend, such a crowd may be worth the risk! Meet me at the west concourse and be sure to bring stock for indulgence!

Yours in brotherhood,
Minias

Riman smiled and leaned back in his chair. Marcus had apparently taken a very direct approach in this particular message. The haste with which this had to be delivered may have compelled him into simplicity in this case. From the words–references to locations and directions, inferences and accentuations, quantifications, all inconspicuously concealed in a mundane letter hidden in an old book–a definitive covert communiqué could be easily derived. He consulted his map of Hera, which was spread upon the table, and made some notes. He had a mission for his new friends.

CHAPTER 4
VENGEANCE OF THE RIVAL

Draga sat a moment upon his high seat in his hideout in the hills, tense and impatient, occupied with his thoughts of revenge and a return to a former greatness. He had been waiting all morning in his secluded and castellated abbey for his scout to bring report of this latest and much rumored trade that must be taking place very soon down in the city below. He knew who it was that was being ransomed to the Ahga, an agent of the Hattél, the hated Demarian spy network, and what value he was to him through his many contacts, and he intended to capitalize on this golden opportunity, not rectifying one personal score which ate his wounded pride but *two. So, my old rival of the Baccád will be there himself,* he thought–Mozep–the one who snatched what should have been rightfully his for all his hard work, a place among the honorable circle of the Ahga himself. For that theft that spineless swine will pay with everything he has to give, and from him will be wrested this interesting asset for Draga himself. The one who shows real loyalty and service to the Ahga and allegiance to the Kunn will triumph. His perceived tainted reputation among his former fellow warrior brothers will be set right once again, indeed it will be exalted as before his unfortunate and unintended secession. Though he had been unofficially separated from his clan, through what he considered to be a grave misunderstanding, he intended to mend this unfortunate rift with the opportunity at hand. His grace and patience in this bitter matter will have paid off.

And then of course, to undermine his rise and further his rage, there were his two new friends who had undisputedly made a mockery of him in the countryside, driving him out of the territory that he himself secured for the Ahga, the land and settlements that provided Draga most of his own wealth. This great impending plan of his would conveniently solve that problem as well. Ratarra the hero indeed. That self-righteous fool will meet his end also, in a way that made the injured Kunn gangster grin even amid his present unease. And his little mouse friend? Ha, ha! He has hopped his last. Draga knew that he would require some help to bring about the destruction of these two newcomers, obviously gifted with the powers of the Mari, who disgraced him in front of his associates in the past, but it was an end that was not entirely impossible to meet. Proper planning was all that would be necessary. Even the great *kungas* of the north can be taken down. Even the offspring of Adin are not wholly indestructible. The fog that seemed to have filled the eyes and minds of his Kunn superiors lately will be lifted with this latest and greatest of his deeds, and the anxiety of this upcoming event and the eagerness to embark upon it drove the great embittered mog to intense agitation. He had been pacing about the place, yelling orders, readying kelgan and weapons, arranging his troop of rogue riders for swift departure and battle. All had to be ready for this vital skirmish and his well experienced detachment was itching for the word. His ingenious plans of revenge were set and waiting for their execution. The bait he so desperately needed to fulfill them would soon be his. All he needed was the time and place of this gathering. Ah, the scout has returned and brought the news he'd been waiting for. *Revenge at last.* He and his veteran squad were bolting down the hillside within the minute.

Damian and Cam returned to their vault under the building that afternoon. Riman was busy at work on some unique weapon or mechanism at his bench. He didn't even look up at them as they entered.

"The prisoner purchase will be transpiring tonight," he said. "From what Marcus hinted at, it should be an eventful exchange. You've been provided with a map showing the location and your best likely approach points. The highest member of the Kunn in Hera, Mozep himself, will be making the trade with Klavék. This is a critical task. You can be assured of his entire force also being there, some forty or fifty, for they do not trust these unknown and independent captors and failure is not an option. It is also likely that they may attempt to take the prisoner for themselves without barter. The Kunn does not take well to blackmail ransoming. The Ahga does not suffer subjection by a competitor and Klavék is risking much on this venture. You may see some action this evening. The number of the selling party is not certain, but from what I know about Klavék and his hired hands they are skilled and crafty hit men and bounty hunters, experts in the trade, not to be underestimated. Their successful capture and concealment of their prisoner for this long in Kunn territory is testament to their proficiency. Mark my words, the Ahga's agents have been looking everywhere for him. Take what you will for weapons, you'll need them."

He stopped what he was doing for a moment and approached Damian solemnly. "I also found out something else," he said. "In the interest of haste I turned in Kurg's books to a translator I could trust. I know that you press for information regarding your lost kin. Records were kept of the prisoners and names and locations of close relatives, probably for bargaining or ransom purposes, but it is possible that the fates of your mother and sister are documented there. It will take some time before we know for sure. In the meantime we have an important mission this evening."

They spent some time in the Cave before emerging, eating and reequipping themselves for what could be a great and dangerous fight. Damian restocked his quiver with more of Riman's custom fabricated metal arrows and took a pair of small daggers which he placed in his boots. Riman gave him some black bracers to wear over his wrists. "Made of garvonite," he said as Damian snapped them on. Cam was given a pouch of caltrops and some small, lightweight, metal climbing gloves which fit perfectly over his small, dexterous hands. They were studded with small spikes for improved grip. They were almost weightless and slid on or off with ease and speed. "These will allow you to climb the rough stone walls that most of the buildings in this city are made of," Riman told him. "Approach from a greater height can have its advantages." Cam refilled his supply of throwing stars and spikes. He withdrew his small swords and swung them around with great speed before he strapped them to his back.

"You'll have to be careful," warned Riman. "There will be many. My only advice to you tonight is focus primarily on the prisoner. Follow Mozep to see where they take him. Perhaps you could waylay them on their way back to the palace or wherever they go. They may even try to go back underground. Also there is reason to believe that there will be more than one interested party. Keep your eyes open. You may just get to meet more than one form of scum in Hera."

Damian and Cam went through their individual rituals and personal meditations while they waited for the evening. Once again they were about to embark on a mission against the Kunn, one that would undoubtedly prove difficult and dangerous, and they met it with eager determination, but also caution. Cam ventured off into another division of the spacious vault to be alone and so practice his skills. He tightened the bandana on his head and knelt on the stone floor for some time, eyes closed tightly, tense as a coiled spring, his explosive muscles holding in an energy and speed that increased with intensity, crying for release. *Give me the speed and strength to dominate these and all villains.* With that he propelled himself into the air backwards, drawing his swords, swinging skillfully at imaginary foes while he somersaulted and flipped about. The air was loud with his yells and the beating it received as he sliced and kicked it faster than eyesight. Damian knelt tensely before his drawn sword, gripped by the merciless hands of one who has sworn destruction to a clan that has taken the lives of his loved ones and plagued and corrupted the land with their reckless thirst for power and wealth. Many bitter drops of sweat fell to the stone floor as his tension built, his muscles flexing to the point of creating a veritable iron skin. *There are many that depend on me. This land must be cleansed. The wicked must be purged. Help me use my strength to achieve this. The Kunn must fall. This is my charge.* He stood up with a yell and brandished his sword, swinging it through the dusty air of the vault, the walls echoing with his anger.

* * *

A large cantina, a gambling hall, an inn and its connecting mount stables and storage bays, along with several other tall structures adjacent to them were arranged in such a way as to form a large square city block, spread sufficiently apart to create a wide, vacant space in the middle, and this is where the trade was to take place. This particular location, in the southern quarter of Monse in the city of Hera, often called Cullman's Docks, was widely considered neutral territory by the various scum that ruled the night in other districts of the city. On occasion, when a trade or negotiation was necessary between lawless factions, this area was utilized. There were several small inlets providing one access to this rectangular and well isolated area, two alleys to the north separated by the cantina and the inn, and three other alleyways to the south on either side and in the middle of the dwellings adjacent to the stables and across from the hall. But these were all narrow and not commonly used, and with these buildings facing outward the recess between them all provided the unlawful an optimum and well concealed space with which to conduct their dark deeds away from prying eyes. The few simple folk about at that hour that happened upon the incoming gangsters and thugs in the vicinity fled. Doors were shut and windows closed, and all light from the inn and nearby homes went out. The cantina fell suddenly quiet and many silently departed as a feeling of dread and fear spread like an evil spirit that could be felt as it passed like a dark mist through the whole district while it followed the incoming riders of the Kunn down the dark, quiet streets. The riders of the Kunn were afoot on this night, called to an urgent engagement, and as the hideous host passed the citizens trembled and hid themselves and crouched in dark corners, praying for their own deliverance and destruction of this plague that rode, murdered, and committed acts of thievery and extortion just outside the locked doors of this unchecked city, phantoms of the night, offspring of the underworld, seldom seen during the day but spawning seemingly everywhere from unknown origins and depths of the winding and multi-leveled municipality. Mothers clutched the young and the old hid themselves in their helplessness. Decent men writhed in anger and frustration and pleaded to a greater power above, but dared not venture forth. What has become of our once great realm, who are these villains that ride upon our streets in the night, they thought as they peered cautiously from behind fastened shutters with faces pale and forlorn.

A tense, quiet watchfulness filled with fear and uncertainty fell upon the district as Mozep and his squad of Kunn suchuks pulled into the dim and empty seclusion. The light from the several lanterns which hung about vaguely illuminated the backdoors and loading areas of the businesses and dwellings here; crates and sacks of stacked grain and salt stood upon a large dock behind the stable to the north; a ramp and stairway ascended into the cantina back room where the foodstuffs were locked; empty barrels and casks of various liquors and drinks were arranged in rows by the rampway, ready for exchange; all four stories of the various windows were darkened and a feeling of fear could be felt from the inn to the east; more ramps and stairways led up to the large, closed wooden doors of quiet storage bays to the west; the two separated tenements to the south inaccessible from this side, their alleyways to the main road outside concealed from view by tarps and cloths hanging from cords spread across the divisions so as to form an awning shelter for the narrow alleys and upper windows, providing a makeshift roof and protection from the powerful sun and elements for the streetside business that was conducted there. Mozep and his troop of kelgan-mounted thugs pulled in loudly and brazenly through the main way by the cantina. The band of twenty-something quickly spread out and secured the area before reconvening around their fearsome leader, awaiting the planned arrival of those they intended to make a careful purchase from.

Mozep and his gang of ruffians looked especially fearsome and dangerous: bands of leather or metal were about their bare arms; studded collars were worn about their necks; heads were shaven or carved into foul stripes or patterns; paint adorned their eyes and faces, the marks of the gangster lifestyle; rings and other crude and vile piercings of the body were visible–all done to invoke fear and disgust and to remove from all doubt their perceived greatness and strength. Indeed they seemed to radiate an evil that sickened as though it were a visible vapor of darkness which they breathed and which followed them, empowering them, and to the simple who beheld the host in their vileness a feeling of disgust and fear at once welled in their timid souls and they withdrew in horror, falling into the pit of despair and helplessness which these and all gangsters spread over the city like a leprous disease. An aspect of terror and recklessness went before them, an arrogance beyond description, an unrestrained condemnation and regard for all else which was below them and their might.

They waited upon their steeds, armed with all types of melee weapons, some obviously modified: clubs with spikes, swords with serrated edges, multi-pronged throwing blades, chains and three-piece staffs swung in anticipation. Separable bladed staffs and one-handed bolt and dart shooters also complimented the sickening assortment. Some fingered their throwing knives, itching for a target. A few stationed themselves to the rear, armed with crossbows, eyeing the high windows and balconies suspiciously. Mozep sat upon his steed, waiting with a look in his cruel, fanged face that would have sent the most jovial fleeing in terror. The innkeeper and some pale men-at-arms came out, inquiring about the strange goings-on and accosting the vile assembly, but when they saw the fearsome Kunn riders with their familiar red bandanas and armbands coming to him to silence the brave fool, the innkeeper and his friends quickly retreated in fear, feeling intervention would be futile. The foul assembly looked about them for some moments in tense anticipation.

They soon heard footfalls coming from the southwest and a moment later saw a diverse group of strangers pull in on horses and *pads*–hairless, light, four-legged creatures from Dinitia and beyond to the west, named for their large soft feet. Klavék and his gang drew in. This group of about a dozen consisted of almost every race this continent was home to, humans, mogs, half-mogs, Hidaris, Turuks–green-skinned, smaller, sleeker, mog-like beings, and even a Harikan, quiet and watchful, bringing up the rear, studying the assembly before him as they halted a short distance before the Kunn. The two groups watched each other carefully, brandishing their weapons and each attempting to intimidate the other: one, a gang of organized and well-financed robbers and henchmen, creed-followers, relatively new to this particular territory, coming to power only in the last decade or so to complete some great idealistic task of their ludicrous conception; the other a tight group of bounty hunters and assassins, well trained in the arts of murder and secrecy, responsible to no one and answerable only to themselves, independent and roaming opportunity seekers. They eyed each other thoroughly, studying one another, trying to read strengths and weaknesses, ready for a deception or sudden trick. One gang stood tensely before another on the dim street. No one moved or made a sound for a short moment. Finally Mozep urged his steed a few paces forward.

"Well," the Baccád ulak growled, not inclined to favor a band that had arguably embarrassed the Kunn and their Ahga, "you know what I want. Bring the slug forward. I've got better things to do than meddle with a group of fools like you, as quick to hide as to take."

"I don't need to listen to this fodder," said Klavék, a human, dressed well in brown and black with a long brown cape and a high collar that partially concealed his bearded face. A keen wit and intellect lay behind his black eyes that suggested cunning and perception, a well experienced and established mercenary-hunter and negotiator. He was the spokesman and had taken a position directly in front of Mozep. "Let's see the money and you can have your man."

"The Kunn can be trusted to deliver, and then some, my faithless friend, as no doubt you know," Mozep returned, eyeing him with dislike. "Why else would you be here?"

"I'm not interested in your loyalties or your devotion to that big-headed slouch you worship in his pompous stone hut. Is he too greedy and important now to do his own dirty work? Or is he too busy chanting to the ghosts of his fancy with the fools he surrounds himself with? The Kunn may have some newfound power in these parts but not all need bow to its beliefs or the Ahga. Azandium is a wasted investment but you are free to pursue that dead legend as long as it doesn't interfere with me and my enterprise. There are other profitable ways to earn one's keep besides taking up the harsh ideology you fools still live by. Not everyone fears you or submits to your demands. I'm sure your Ahga informed you of other competing parties, or did his pride in his shadow army cause him to forget? But I shouldn't complain. You folks keep my pockets full. All I want is his money."

These words sounded like a hiss in Mozep's ears and his hand gravitated toward the huge mace on his belt. "When our kingdom comes into its own the faithless will be purged from the earth, the heretics pulled from the sight of the Divine One. Your time will come." The clan chief eyed him for a moment in restrained wrath, longing to crush him with a blow but decided this faithless parasite wasn't worth it. He then signaled to one of his men who brought forth a case which they laid on the ground by their leader's feet and opened to reveal much gold. Mozep never took his eyes off his adversary who looked upon the wealth. A satisfactory grin crossed his face and the mercenary also gave a signal. A pair of sturdy Hidaris in black armor pulled a bound individual from a mount in the back and escorted him forward. He looked to be a typical Demarian human: mid-thirties, dark brown haired, of average height and build though he looked ragged and weary and even a little malnourished. He wore no armor and was weaponless but a fire of defiance existed in his courageous eyes. Mozep looked hard upon the prisoner. He certainly fit the description.

Draga kept his troop hidden a block further down the abandoned street. He peered out from around the corner of a building, waiting for the signal from his trusted scout. He was about to stop in on this gathering uninvited. He thought of the revenge he was about to take, now only a few tense minutes away. He forced himself to be patient as he relived that disgraceful day in his mind, expelled by the Ahga and watching his rival instead ascend to the coveted rank within the Brotherhood. Draga was about to put an end to him: Mozep, that fool who was chosen over him, once his equal and brother and now his detested superior. The two had risen through the ranks of the Kunn together, serving the Ahga well during the constructive years of the new organization, each secretly vying for the favor of the Ahga and ultimately the most honorable and sought position: admittance into the Baccád. Then Draga, seeking higher recognition and hopefully a greater personal gratitude and reward, set out on his own, creating a detachment that would secure the northern territories and bring the Ahga the service, loyalty, and wealth he desired from these profitable lands. And rape the land he did, but not in a manner that was necessarily in concurrence with the Ahga who was brought report of Draga's overt and rash methods that prematurely tainted the name and distorted the reputation of the Kunn to the new regimes the Ahga intended to methodically penetrate and seek assistance from. More to the point, thought the Ahga, this overly ambitious and rogue subject of his was clearly withholding unknown wealth for himself. Draga had clearly run away with his freedom and over-zealousness and needed to be reigned in.

Mozep, meanwhile, dutifully obeyed his master and executed his precise orders in the careful infiltration of Hera and its government. Removing the head of the snake covertly and securing influence stealthily proved far more beneficial than enraging the masses, however weak and selfishly preoccupied, with the outright tyrannical modes employed by Draga before the Kunn had a proper foothold. Wealth and power will inevitably find its way to those who possess the methodical and patient state of mind necessary to acquire them, a promise of the Mari. Draga would pay for lacking these prized qualities and refusing the wishes of the Ahga, seeking rather to impress him with his ambitious independence. He could remember quite vividly that infamous moment in the presence of the assembled Baccád high atop the palace in Mod early last year when he was denounced before the Brotherhood, essentially demoted, and was returned to his detachment to pursue the Ahga's original intentions for him which was to find a way to infiltrate the lands to the north, in especial Kandar, which defied and fought against the Kunn, and home of the detestable Kane, the Ahga's old rival. In the meantime he was to live in the hills apart and unassociated until he could again prove his worth and loyalty. The Ahga knew he was only in the business for himself and was excluding his brothers who had helped him to his present power, and said so to Draga's face before the assembly. His anger and disgrace were indescribable but when he learned later that Mozep was invited to undergo the brutal initiation and join the elite ranks of the Baccád and learn the secrets of the cult, the outcast mog became more than infuriated. The insult exacted upon him with obvious premeditation was unbearable and drove him to a vengeance that surpassed madness. But it was a madness that bred determination. Draga retreated to his domain high up in the hills and pondered his eventual return. He had not completely forsaken the Brotherhood though they had him, and he planned a comeback that would prove beyond doubt his dedication to the Kunn and who he still considered to be his master. For many months he paced about his lofty seclusion, and with a partial view of the city far below him and this strange stroke of luck he arrived at his bold scheme. Mozep was but a fortunate and chance inclusion in it all, and Draga relished the unforeseen blessing.

"It's time," he snarled, and deployed his force.

"That must be Mozep," said Cam. They watched the Kunn mog in front approach and have a few words with who must have been Klavék, the leader of these unknown rogues. Damian and Cam climbed into and hid themselves in the low tenement building to the west, empty and good for ingress, as Riman accurately instructed from the message, and peered out of the open window at the dangerous gathering right in front of them. The Kunn riders had pulled in right in front of their position and were facing east toward the strangers, so all Damian and Cam could see for now was Mozep's back as he consulted with his adversary. But they could also plainly make out his unmistakable insignia of the Baccád, the four black shukk marks on either side of his thickly muscled neck distinguishing him from the rest as one of the hierarchy. Presently one of the Kunn brought forth a case of gold. Then the mercenaries presented their highly valued prisoner and they all looked upon Gadrin for the first time.

"So there he is," said Cam, "he looks like he's had quite a time of it all, too, but not ready to drop just yet."

"And it looks like you got your wish, Cam. There's plenty down there to satisfy even your appetite."

"Indeed there are, an entire lot full of wriggling vermin!" Cam sighed with delight and became giddy. "Scum ripe for the picking. And more than one bunch of thugs, too. Looks like my services are needed elsewhere as well. The Kunn wouldn't mind a little competition, would they? Well, I suppose it's time." He loosened the swords on his back.

"I do not discriminate between scum," Damian replied, studying the scene before him. "It looks like we'll have to take the direct approach. Let's split up. They'll most likely leave the way they came in. These bounty hunters have the other exits blocked. And watch for the sharpshooters along the sides. They have every angle covered. You watch the alley to the south and I'll move north. Try to send them my way, they'll probably try to avoid confrontation and seek only to flee with their captive. If they get away meet me with Bish. Don't let them kill him. I'll see you after the war, Cam." With that they set off, Damian quickly moving through the building to cover the main entrance to the street and Cam stealthily darting over to the adjacent building in the dark and seeking a good cutoff point from that position.

Tog climbed to the roof of the inn that night, using his animal-like, clawed hands and feet to scale the rough wall like a crawling black spider in the night. Ropes and ladders and other climbing tools were not necessary for him. It was as if the elements of the earth–stone, wood, air, or otherwise–succumbed to his wishes and allowed him passage. Elemental utilization was a gift promised by the Mari. He came tonight not only to survey this interesting situation but also in the hopes of it perhaps drawing his enemy hither. He had specifically given orders early that day on his arrival at the palace which passed through the command chain of the Kunn, an order to withdraw themselves and maintain reduced conspicuousness. Starve the cat and he'll come out to hunt, was the strategy. If this new and interesting rival of his at all lived up to the rumors he heard then this indomitable warrior would doubtless present himself in such an opportunity. Perhaps Mendiviam had conceived another offspring to take the lead of his ragged order. The doomed Kadali had been reduced to desperation. For this, the newcomer must be destroyed. He looked around. The moon shone fully in the east behind him amid the stars and the cool night breeze stirred. He sensed the fear and tense energy in the fabric of the air as he viewed the surroundings from a high point. He looked forward to a greater challenge and thought of his past accomplishments as he perched silently and patiently on the flat stone rooftop, unseen by those below.

The destruction of this rumored hero would be but another great achievement to add to his reputable list, and he pondered over them as he waited. He brutally assassinated a Baccád brother in the distant city of Kadr years ago, one of the Ahga's own who helped him establish their organization in its beginning but eventually became envious of the Ahga's power and favor which he felt he rightly deserved. This member threatened to oust the Ahga and the overseeing mentor ran forth from the wilds of Adovia in swift interference to show this prideful swine no mercy. Tog could respect ambition but not at the expense of his chosen subject. Tog found the challenger alone one night after a meeting, soon after he had made his blasphemous declaration before the Ahga, and ambushed and strangled him to death after a brief altercation, a hideous murder. Tog himself carried the body and placed it before the iron seat of the Ahga in his counsel room of Kadr that very night, placed the body in such a way that the arm of the corpse appeared to be reaching for the high chair, the pinnacle of power, but failed to reach it in his foolish attempt, an endearing touch of Tog's instructive design. This display was left for all to see the next day when the Ahga's henchmen reconvened, and the Ahga-Rosh looked upon the silent and understanding faces of his followers. Lesson learned. Tog also partook in the much desired elimination of the lord of Darhúk, the Lord Krishtag, who, because of a sizable gambling debt to the

169

Kunn, attempted to pay off the Ahga in *volia*, that incredibly valuable and rare silk, but after the shipment was received closer examination revealed it to be a counterfeit substitute. The Ahga, already infuriated with this fool's perpetual deception and intolerable lack of punctuality prepared the coffin for this scheming snake. Tog secretly broke into his mansion late one night and snapped Krishtag's neck with his bare hands, hands he had used in the past to crush prey in the cold dark. He had fastened himself to the arched ceiling and hung there like an awaiting beast until the arrival of his target. He then strung the body from the balcony in the hall for all to see. But he would not be satisfied with his death alone, so Tog killed the brother as well. A small group subsequently looted the vault of the empty dwelling in a planned raid and fled. Message delivered, payment received. Tog's real name was difficult to pronounce, being of the ancient tongue of the Hakai, and because of his abilities and mysterious ways the Ahga and the Baccád reffered to him as *Tog* which meant 'cobra'.

Tog had since conducted numerous other hits and assassinations, sometimes even within the Kunn itself, but his greatest accomplishments to date in the earthly realm involved none other than the lord brothers, Karius and Alos, the bold leaders of the Hera biumvirate who dared defy and oppose the Kunn, poisoned them to make their deaths look natural. Their removal was a critical component of their grand design. Oh yes, the credit for the removal of these two belonged to Tog alone, and Tog insisted to the Ahga that he be honored with the secret privilege for this task went beyond simply the murders of two foreign lords, but was a deed that sparked the evolution of something vastly more important. Tog was not simply a mentor of the Ahga and his clan, performing small but vital services to the earthly auxiliary with whom he worked in cooperative function, but was an instrument of something far greater, a mover of events in this world, relevant to the master will of the Divine, an effective manipulator of the spiritual powers at work across the lands he was an important and designated executor of. And he perceived that the fabled creation of this new and yet unfamiliar rival which he eagerly sought was also of something greater than flesh, perhaps even similar to his own mythical and supernal league, but represented the desperation, in his mind, of an opposing force to counter him and his ascending organization and all that they stood for. Facing this new adversary would also be of a necessity that Tog alone could fathom the vast importance of, and he gave thanks for the heavy and honorable responsibility and the new wisdom he found himself possessing. *Indeed I am worthy of this charge, I alone have earned this great responsibility as chief representative of my consort,* he thought as he roamed about within his deep reveries and sought worlds unseen. So it was with great eagerness and anticipation that Tog carefully surveyed the scene before him, employing his superior senses in the hopes of detecting the one they call *Ratarra.* Where was this new warrior of Adin they all spoke of on this clear night?

As if in answer to his thoughts he felt a presence somewhere in the crowd below, or maybe it was beyond, in one of those buildings. It certainly was a signature he'd never felt before and he felt a struggle and a spiritual disorientation as he tried to identify it and pin it down, discover its exact location. He knelt and closed his eyes in patient meditation below the stars, alone and undisturbed on the building top, tuning himself to the energies of the earth and the spirits that roamed it until he had him at last. Yes, that *must* be him.

Damian had acquired his new position at the far northern end of the building, bow in hand, with a good view of the inner yard and the main entrance to it only one story below. Cam poised himself in the dark open window of the building to the south, parallel to Damian, shaking with excitement, unable for the time to choose between his throwing stars or his swords, waiting for a move below. The three alleyways out were all to his right but were partially concealed by the awnings which canopied and flanked them. Mozep and the band of mercenaries had concluded their transaction, miraculously without bloodshed thus far, and were carefully preparing to leave. Damian and Cam were ready to attack and the gangsters were withdrawing from each other when the sharpshooters suddenly cried out. Shouts and rushing footfalls echoed from the two alleyways to the north and all eyes turned in surprise. The street shook with the thunder of it; the attack had come. Out from either side of the cantina powerfully emerged the first of Draga's rogue force, two dozen at least, mounted riders with swords and spears, yelling as they charged upon their steeds. They fell upon the assembly like a great wave upon the sand, but it was only a feint. Yells went up and ignited the previously quiet night like a thunderclap. Mozep was screaming orders at his men who began fighting Draga's. A sudden, intense, intra-rival combat took place and a great noise went up. The Kunn found itself fighting against its own former but now estranged brethren, and upon each other the highly trained warriors of the Ahga turned. Klavék and his bounty hunters, only interested in their payment, quickly sought flight from the premises, closely guarding their gold and retreating in haste. Some of Draga's faction were shot by Mozep's sharpshooters perched high in the rear. A few had been dismounted and were fighting among the street clutter of parked wagons, barrels and crates, breaking them over their heads so that they burst. Torches were shoved in faces, chains and blades swung, blood was spilled. A fire exploded on one of the docks. Bolts and darts and spikes flew through the air. Windows were broken, pieces of roadside debris and concrete were smashed over heads. Draga's charging cavalry took a few down with spears but held their position behind the cantina and stable, intentionally drawing Mozep's forces toward them.

Damian jumped down from his spot in the window, seeing clearly that some attempt to steal the prize was obviously under way. To see the Kunn fighting each other was strange. Perhaps there was some enmity among embittered compatriots within the clan. He ran toward the fray with a yell, sword in hand, keeping an eye on Mozep and the prisoner Gadrin the whole time. *Khala will be avenged!* he yelled. Cam was about to do the same from his position with the same thing in mind when he thought he heard something to his right, more approaching marauders perhaps, just below him, and he turned his attention in their direction. He looked back to see Mozep retreating with his bodyguards and the prisoner, seeking an escape and heading for one of the alleyways to the south, trying to get away. That was what Draga was hoping for.

From behind a canvassed alley to the south, right underneath Cam, burst forth another sortie of mounted thugs, about ten, which headed straight for the escapees. Cam let fly a carefully aimed throwing star, piercing the skull of a rider below him before he too jumped down and drew his dual swords, charging the chaos. The newcomers cut off Mozep's escape and the desperation and anger in his eyes intensified. He stopped cold, realizing he'd been set up and prepared to fight his way out. There was still another exit, on the opposite corner and this is where he desperately renewed his retreat. Delivery of the prisoner was his mission; confrontation was too risky a possibility here and had to be avoided though he was prepared to lose all his men in the process if necessary. The prize must be delivered to the Ahga or suffer an unspeakable punishment at his hands he would. He and his outflanked gang made a dash for it on their steeds with the still tied prisoner, slung over the shoulders of one of the sturdy bodyguards. Escape for a moment seemed almost possible but yet another small sortie burst upon the site from this last alley on the far end. This last group was led by Draga and Mozep found himself driven right into it in what proved to be a well coordinated attack. *An impressive cutoff indeed.* He was now completely surrounded and Mozep saw defeat beyond any doubt and let out a hideous yell of anger with the acknowledgement of his failure. Draga led his troop forward bearing the red standards of the Kunn, followed by a kelgan-drawn open wagon. Draga's men quickly shot Mozep's fearsome guards with their crossbows and surrounded the targeted Baccád mog in a hasty circle that was momentarily protected by Draga's others, forming a shield, fighting in the front and keeping the others at bay to allow their captain his revenge. Gadrin had been searching for an opportunity to break free in the chaos but quickly found himself in the clutches of this rogue Kunn detachment who were obviously contesting with the others of the established Hera chapter. Mozep found himself surrounded by a pack of vengeful wolves and looked about him in defiance, glaring back at his encircling conquerors with his cruel eyes. The monster was about to lunge at a weak point and break free when he was struck down with a staff of some kind, which broke across his chest in a shower of fragments, for he was a mighty Mogoli, and he was knocked to the ground. He knelt up and looked into the eyes of one he knew well but it did not bring him comfort. Mozep's eyes widened in anger. He knew what this was about.

"The Ahga's pet indeed!" cried Draga who had pulled up in front of his fallen rival, "a fitting subject for the Father! Welcome to the Baccád, ha ha!" Draga swung a heavy mace and crushed the head of his enemy in one fatal blow. Not wasting another instant all Draga's loyal followers ceased their melee and simultaneously bolted from the place on their steeds in all directions, some heading out to the main street to the north, Draga and the others with him flying down the alley to the south with their prize captive in tow, thrown in the wagon like luggage. Draga's retreating laugh could be heard over the clamor as they escaped out onto the street and rode away in haste with what remained of their force.

Damian rushed into the tumult, cleaving through his foes like a charging ram, the whole time keeping in his sight the prisoner who seemed to be pulled first this way then that, his captors obviously attempting a hasty escape with him, and Damian's frustration grew as he found his objective increasingly difficult to reach. Draga's gang, under strict orders to prevent the mission's undoing even at their own ultimate sacrifice, flocked to the newcomer and surrounded him closely to slow his advance. They knew who Ratarra was and upon his not unexpected arrival sought to suppress this greatly feared swordsman and sworn enemy of the Kunn, declared wanted at any cost by the Ahga. At first sight of him one of Draga's lieutenants shouted his name so that his men could hear, even above the tumult and they understood. *Ratarra! Ratarra is here!* he yelled, and the host rushed over. Damian found himself sufficiently challenged by a surprisingly determined horde of the ones he detested and his wrath increased with each desperate swing of his mighty sword. Thug after thug fell before him and he cursed them as he fought, yelling as he heaved his sword, but being surrounded he also became the recipient of bodily damage himself: a bolt from one of the sharpshooters pierced his lower leg; glancing blows from spiked clubs and chains bounced off his tough leather armor and grazed his exposed elbows and knees with some effect; kicks and punches of the trained martial combatiers knocked him down or back. Damian hacked the legs completely off a Turuk who hit him across the chest with a three-piece staff, almost knocking him over.

173

But all the short while his objective became seemingly further and further away from him, won by a determined foe with an effective, well executed plan. Damian watched in the unattainable distance as Gadrin was seized by what seemed to be another faction of the Kunn, or perhaps a competitor. He could see the marks of the clan upon them all. Then he shouted in terror and disgust as he recognized the apparent victor as none other than Draga himself, the one Damian had just purged of the lands to the east and made an example of to the Kunn. Damian felt sure this was some sort of planned revenge by Draga as he caught sight of his distinguishing striped hair from the vile and loathsome crowd, just up ahead but out of reach. This supposition was confirmed when he fancied a wry smile from the familiar gangster as the eyes of the two actually met across the bloodied battlefield. Draga's triumphant laugh in the distance pierced Damian like a dagger, and Damian's fear and distress grew to an intense fury as he watched his rival ride in at the last moment, despite desperate attempts to stop him, and slip away with the prize the next. Suchuks, the apprentice fighters of the Kunn, fell like young trees in a wind storm but Damian could only taste failure as he watched Draga escape down the alley. The objective thus achieved, his enemies before him fled in all directions, suddenly uninterested in him, and Damian looked about for his sidekick and called for his horse. In his rage he chased the last of the thugs onto the street, drew his bow and shot one of the rearguards before they were lost from sight around the corner. He sprinted back to Bish who met him obediently on the road. Cam came flying up behind him.

"They put up a good fight," he said, mounting the awaiting horse. Damian jumped on and they wasted no time but started off after the group. "You'd almost think they knew we were coming," Cam continued as Bish thundered down the streets and turned corners. "I took down a few before they surrounded me. Haven't had that much fun since the work room in Khala. I had to take on five or six at once. One of them actually struck his own when I jumped out of the way of a spear thrust. Ha! They did get me a few times, though, and when I saw our old friend making off with the cake one of the wounded ones on the ground managed to grab my leg and trip me before I could get to him. Looks like they outsmarted us this time."

"By the effective use of numbers and avenues of approach," Damian angrily ended in acknowledgement. They bolted down the stone-paved streets after Draga's gang with the fury of the night wind.

Through his masked eyes Tog watched the unfolding action below with great interest, lying prone and hidden from view behind the stone lip of the roof. Very interesting, he thought as he studied and watched his enemy perform. Some other will is undoubtedly at work within him, providing him his unearthly abilities. His fearlessness and the wrath with

174

which he executes it are remarkable. He is blessed indeed, a new servant of the Mari. But not invincible. Ratarra, in fact, seemed largely ignorant of the abilities he possessed. He was yet young and inexperienced, despite his apparent divine inheritance. He had much to learn, and this perhaps could be exploited. A naïve and ideologically inclined opponent can be carefully turned to the understudy of a nemesis. The friend with whom he operates is also deserving of consideration. His skills and speed make him a potent enemy, one to be feared, an adequate addition to the team, but he directed most of his attention and thought to the one who wielded the hammer of his forefathers. He possessed ability and strength certainly, but so did Tog. Mere obstacles that were easily overcome which led to higher achievements. The petty combat below him and the trivial dealings of the organization he served were of lesser concern to him. Tog perceived a much larger picture of what was at stake in this world and the forces which influenced weighty outcomes. The deeds these two could accomplish were of a quantity and magnitude so great Tog felt an urgency at the thought of the potential. Without a doubt the Kunn had some formidable opposition, two gifted and influential vigilantes worthy of respect. The Ahga was right to consider them a viable threat, one that required special elimination. But not just here, though. Tog worked alone and the methodical and usually tedious assassinations he performed were very personal to him. His work to him was an art form and he preferred solitude for its implementation. The greatness of his enemy called for a meeting, at an especially desirable location, a setting capable of providing the satisfaction he sought in the destruction of his enemy and worthy of the final and dramatic elimination of what could only be some kind of avenger dispatched from above, a new son of Adin, sent to drive out and dismantle the Brotherhood. If it was one thing Tog possessed it was patience, and he prepared himself for the slow and deliberate pursuit of this earthly avenger, a pursuit and confrontation that would more properly offer such a prize to the masters he served. The activity below him reached a quick conclusion and he began his chase, leaping from buildingtop to buildingtop, shadowing his enemy like a black ghost floating closely above.

* * *

Damian continued his pursuit, following after the fleeing riders as best he could down the dim, quiet streets in the direction they thought Draga took. Cam offered his assistance, listening to their retreating footfalls and relaying his information to Damian, for they could not see those they pursued. The Kunn riders had enough of a head start to safely elude their pursuers down the dark, winding and intersecting streets and across small bridges of wood and stone which echoed with the pounding of the kelgan

175

as they madly sprinted past quiet blocks of buildings and forums. They knew pursuit was inevitable. Draga had briefed them all of his plan thoroughly before the raid though, and his obedient servants, what few remained of them, maintained strict silence, using only hand signals to communicate as they rode. They did not wish to rouse the Hera Guard which probably even now was rushing to the altercation. Damian thought they had caught up with them but Cam suddenly became confused and disoriented.

"I think they split up," he said. "I'm hearing them on different streets."

"They must be trying to make a break for it with the prisoner," said Damian.

"We have to follow the right echo," said Cam. "I think the wagon went this way." Cam guided him around some blocks and turns. He felt as though he were chasing a phantom stampede through a graveyard.

"There's the wagon!" said Damian. They could see the small wagon that Gadrin had been thrown into heading down a small, narrow street and its pace seemed somewhat to have slowed. They couldn't tell in this light and at this distance how many riders accompanied it, if any, or whether Draga was among them. Damian urged Bish to greater speed and the horse bolted after them in a final attempt to overtake them. As they drew nearer to the slowing cart they perceived that it was driverless and completely unescorted. Damian drew his bow and shot the kelgan steed that was harnessed to it. The beast crashed to the ground and the wagon came to an abrupt and noisy halt. Cam was already in the air before Damian stopped and landed in the open box with both swords drawn.

"Empty!" he cried, looking about in distress. Damian pulled up and growled in disbelief.

"They must have made off with Gadrin and sent this as a decoy," he grumbled and clenched his fists, his increasing failure evoking even greater anger. Cam jumped down and Damian lifted the wagon in frustration and threw it over to the side of the road. It flipped several times before striking a stone wall and splintering. "Draga got away," he admitted under his breath.

"Well he can't be far," Cam offered.

"To the Ascension!" cried Damian. "Maybe we can see something there." They immediately mounted and bolted off.

When they arrived under the tall stone archway at the top of Tier Two they found the great road below them and all about quiet and empty. Several lonely travelers could be seen slowly laboring up or down the torch-lit ramps in the night. They looked like insects crawling up a great staircase at this distance. The night sky above them was clear and the stars shone. The air was cool and mildly breezy, and it brought them no report. The tenseness that Damian felt in the Monse District with the presence of the villains there could be felt no longer. The city behind and below him on the distant plateau fell silent and sleepy. They looked around and listened for some minutes at a loss, Cam employing his far-seeing eyes to comb over the hills to the north, dimly lit by the luminous night sky. Their name was the Brown Hills, but folk simply called it the Northwall for they bordered the twin cities that were built under their shadow, and they ran roughly forty miles in an east-west direction. Paths and roadways had been cut into them to allow passage to the lands beyond, namely Kandar, though travelers from the south were often turned away so strict and distrustful was the border guard of that grand province on the other side. Of late rumors had been whispered of pirates and bandits establishing their secret abodes high up in those secluded hills and within the valley, descending from their peaks at night to raid the unwary. One must be brave indeed to tread that way. But Cam could see nothing distinctly on the distant hillsides under the night sky and he sighed in frustration.

"Looks like they succeeded in making a well coordinated escape," he said.

"And who knows how we're going to find them now," replied Damian, giving thought to some options. "The city is vast and concealing. They could have an underground hideout like us and eventually we'll have to find it. We need more inside information." He thought of Riman and Marcus and what possible information or assistance they may have to help them on this matter but Damian didn't want to admit defeat and return to their Cave empty-handed. He could painfully hear Draga's triumphant laugh play over in his mind. Just then he turned around, for he heard footsteps, and saw a man approaching them.

"You said you needed an ally," said he. It was Derrol.

Draga detoured through the city, making his way to his ultimate destination in a roundabout manner, snaking along streets after switching his prisoner's mode of transportation in a planned stop and disposing the decoy. His several detachments fragmented in various directions to confuse any likely pursuit and facilitate his escape with the prize. When he felt he had sufficiently eluded them he headed east, out of the city through University Gate. Here he had a spy awaiting his troop, opening the gate for them at that late hour. They passed quickly through the fertile lowlands of Shadím and began the climb up the mountain road to his abbey in the Brown Hills. Everything had gone fairly well thus far. He couldn't believe the ease with which he wrested the prize from his unsuspecting enemies. The fact that he lost just over half his muster in the process was unfortunate but when he considered what he would gain with the heavy purchase he felt by far it was worth it. He carried an agent, he was sure, probably of Demar, a key into the dark labyrinth and twisted underworld of the Ahga himself, a vital piece pulled along in his van with no one left to stop him. Why else would the Ahga want him so desperately? The knowledge this operative would soon provide him would undoubtedly prove valuable, perhaps even present him with some unlikely opportunity to represent his worth afresh to the Ahga. But all in good time. Only one obstacle remained to be removed lest his great plan be foiled in the end. He had some final preparations to put into place for the inevitable aftermath. It was time for part two of his plan.

CHAPTER 5
LAIR OF THE VULTURE

"I will take you to the highland road," said Derrol, retrieving his pack and water skins from the guard shack nearby. He had just finished his duty for the evening and gathered his belongings and packed them on his horse, hastily readying himself for departure.

"You do not need to put yourself at risk," said Damian.

"That is of no matter," Derrol replied. "I will service that corrupt lord and his foul henchmen no longer. I am fairly sure of where Draga resides. I have been there. He has likely returned there with this prisoner. It is the safest place for him. We can probably reach it in the morning. If what you say is true and he has suffered heavy loss we must depart at once before he has time to reinforce himself or flee. The hills are unfriendly. He has friends there." Derrol mounted his horse. Damian looked at him astonished.

"You are a true ally indeed," Damian said and they followed after him. But just then Damian felt a strange disorientation within himself, confusion of the mind mixed with feelings of fear and of a detected power of determined counteraction. A sense of merciless intent and an acknowledgement of a greater, detectable resistance without troubled his soul, an existence or power affixed specifically to him, a will Damian somehow felt certain was bent on his presence, his doings, his whereabouts, and ultimately, his elimination. He knew this strange new sensation could not be associated with his present vexations for it was new and unknown and presented itself abruptly and with potency, almost making him sway on his horse, indeed he half stopped and turned about. He stopped in his tracks and looked about him suddenly. Over his shoulder and along vacant rooftops and dark windows and cluttered sidestreets his glance was hastily thrown for an instant. Something was there, he felt certain, something watching him, but nothing was to be seen. He consequently shrugged off what he concluded could only be an induced dream of some kind, but a faint lingering premonition of fear and intent pursuit behind him and out of sight dogged him as he galloped thoughtfully on.

179

They left the city through the Tower of Eve and began their climb up the easternmost side of the Northwall. Utilizing the Hera Road would have exposed them to the many eyes that kept watch along that main entrance to the east so they turned as quickly as they could to a lesser used road, one that quickly dissipated into a rough path northward, through the outer fields of Shadím and toward the hills. They soon reached the hill-path. This was rocky and winding but proved not too steep or difficult for the horses. They trudged along this as the night wore away. This path, in fact, was frequently used by the few travelers who journeyed often to Kandar but looked to cut the distance by using the highland roads instead of the Hammén Passage further east. These traders of late, however, feared to use these roads for the bandits that dwelt in the confines of the hills kept watch there and waylaid them. So the folk instead were compelled to travel through the city and out the main entrances, either through Gyla if they were traveling west, or east through Hera, and seek easier and well-peopled roads through the flatlands before they reached Kandar's southern cities or even distant Prova on the coast.

But they met or saw no one on the narrow path. The night passed and the light of the early morning broke in the east. Like a golden orb it rose above the Ash Mountains to bring its radiance to Nadea. They were watchful and stopped often and listened, or Cam would dismount and look about, or around rocky corners and across chasms that dropped into forested ravines dimly lit by the waxing morning light, and so form an idea of the road ahead and hopefully spy anyone on it. Derrol told them this road was used often by villains of all types, including Draga and his henchmen, outcasts of the Kunn who dwelt up here, establishing a separate detachment by themselves it would seem, and descended to the city or the main roads to the north on the other side of the hills to extort money or goods from the unarmed or weak caravans using them.

"There can be no other likely abode for him in this area," Derrol said as they trudged on. "This road leads to an outpost at one of the peaks, positioned, by design, in such a way to afford it a grand view of the roads to the north but also the cities below it to the south. It is difficult to see until you are upon it for it is constructed of the dark rock that surrounds it on one side, cut and formed from the hill itself so that it blends almost invisible. The tower is built adjacent to the dark cliff that rises up behind it on the west so at a distance it seems, in fact, to be a part of the hill face itself, hence its effective concealment. It is likely that hallways and tunnels have been bored into the cliff or underground to expand the dwelling since its construction long ago, but I have never actually been inside. Who knows what Draga has done or created within for his dark purposes during his tenure there. Some years ago, before the Kunn brought its plague to the realm, I journeyed twice to this outpost for it was a watchtower in the days of Karius, keeping the hills free of the very brigands that now dwell in abundance here, and small garrison and store of arms and provisions were kept. The Crest of the Eagle it was called. But soon after Karius' sudden and mysterious death what guard was kept there was disbanded, by dubious governmental decision, and they reluctantly returned to the city. Some rubbish about its defunction and purposelessness was offered as reasoning for this abandonment. It was rumored that the dwelling was given over to the Kunn, bribed from Helbek for their use, a probable truth. The price must have been great but the corrupt lord who rules Hera can be bought. Because of the mounted raiders who dwell in that tower it has been named anew the Crest of the Vulture, for the havoc that descends from it to the folk below."

"Then it is well that we are headed there," said Damian. "The nest of these vultures needs to be cleaned."

"If I am right and Draga dwells there you must beware," Derrol continued. "It is also rumored that he has a fancy for beasts and strange pets, for he often purchases or steals horses or other useful or valuable creatures, sometimes at considerable price for his amusement or some wicked purpose perhaps. Who knows what resides in his abode, locked behind cages and released to do his bidding."

"You seem to know much about a thug who operates in the dark hills," said Damian.

"I am a seasoned guard of the city," he replied. "My duties take me through the realm and even the palace and I have acquaintances. Many are familiar with the Kunn, they have agents and influence within even the Council. Even soldiers talk and I have connections in the Court and Hall. There is much that I know."

"That is well," said Damian.

They traveled up the rocky slope for a few hours as the sun climbed into the sky. They stopped and ate some food from their packs, eating in a hole apart from the road before continuing. Derrol said it had been some years since his journey up here, but it couldn't be much farther and they could expect to see it soon. They continued on for maybe another half hour during which Derrol seemed at a loss, when they emerged from around a high rocky bend and suddenly saw it: a tower of black rock against a tall cliff of similar hue which rose up behind it to form the peak, only hundreds of yards away, overlooking all the lands to the south, east, and north, the view to the west blocked by the high cliff that from here seemed almost a part of the tower itself but was not. They quickly retreated out of sight of its many open windows which looked out upon the lands like a watchful giant and dismounted for a better look. They crawled some way from the road and took cover behind some rocks and trees which occasioned the steepening slope and looked upon the scene more thoroughly.

From their new position they had a better view of the tower and its connecting curtain walls which branched out from it in an angled and rectangular shape, lower in height than most, declining and curving slightly with the contours of the land below and closely hugging the cliff behind it. These walls enveloped what could only be large, open courtyards within. The three, hunched low against the steep rise in the land, could see several Kunn guards watching attentively on the parapets of these walls, and this seemed confirmation enough of Kunn presence here. The tower was of a thick square shape, dark and uninviting, rising from the ground at what they judged to be only about six or seven levels high with the walls of the connecting courtyard being significantly lower. The inner baileys ran only some two hundred feet from the tower. On the whole, not an overly extensive domain, a low and inconspicuous hilltop outpost and looking tower, built to blend well with its surroundings which consisted of high rocks spread about and scant trees and shrubs. Nothing stirred about the place besides the wall guards, walking the lengths of the courtyard on the parapets above and surveying the lands below. All seemed quiet and dead, no one or riders were about and all was eerily silent. An atmosphere of dread and fear seemed to have overtaken the hilltop. The air fell stone-still and silent and a spirit of tension seemed to form an invisible ring around the peak that could be felt, a watchfulness and ominous premonition that seemed to dim the sun, now striving with the newly gathering clouds to shed its light. The once fair and warm morning seemed to dim and cool while it held its breath, a breath and stillness that whispered of impending doom, something far larger than mere altercation. Something of consequence was about to happen up here; an engagement awaited. A misty darkness seemed to seep into the sky. Their eyes followed the rough road which wound its way up to the tower stronghold. A pair of massive, heavy wooden doors at the base of the tower, they saw, was fastened tightly shut and seemed the only way in.

"Doesn't look like I could break through those," said Damian.

"There must be another way in," said Cam. "I think I could climb those walls. They look rough enough. The builders must have set the unchiseled stones in their places as they were for a good, natural look. Blends right in. Let me climb in and find another door and if not, open the front ones."

"Let's not forget about the guards," said Damian.

In the end they decided to simultaneously eliminate the guards along the walls for Cam to make his quiet infiltration. If the guards managed to raise an alarm they may make an attempt to kill the prisoner rather than let him fall into the hands of another. Then he would explore the inner areas and find a door to open and together they would scour the establishment and eliminate any opposition. Damian prohibited Derrol from proceeding further for it would be dangerous and they would be well outnumbered. Draga had suffered heavy losses lately and was probably desperate. He was not likely to fall easily and would die before accepting defeat, and Damian felt certain Draga would probably make this last stand a daring and deadly one, especially with the prize in his possession. He may even have some trap or defense in place inside for further protection. Damian did not wish for him to be placed at such risk. More importantly, said Damian, Derrol was needed in the city and his cover should not be compromised. Ratarra will return soon, he said, and would again need friends knowledgeable of Kunn activity. Derrol reluctantly acknowledged the wisdom in this and departed with words of gratitude and encouragement from Damian and Cam.

They didn't dare bring Bish any closer so Damian hid him in a grove of thick trees at the bottom of the rise with instructions to await his call. The horse nodded and obeyed, and found a place to rest while his master fulfilled his mission. The two then continued on foot, climbing the northern, steeper slope, approaching the courtyard walls from that side. From this angle the tower and its eyes were furthest away, and the shortest length of wall in front of them.

They waited for the guard at this end to slowly make his way to the far corner before Cam sprinted across the open ground from his hiding place and reached the wall. He removed the metal climbing gloves that Riman gave him and quickly slipped them on, thinking of the old man and his genius and how much they relied on him. He was thankful to have him as their leader, crafty as well as wise. He immediately began the climb. The rough wall was only about thirty feet high and he ascended with ease. Damian watched him scale the wall like a spider, smiled to himself, and then slowly and carefully repositioned for a sure shot at the guards above. There were three of them, spread out evenly along the parapets, one at the smaller, northern end where Cam was and two along the eastern wall which overlooked the approach from the road. Though the guards were alert, owing to the previous night's activities, the strange new darkness, afforded by the eerie onset of clouds, together with the rising wind, seemed to offer concealment and sound cover to that which moved cautiously below. Damian planned to first eliminate the sentry closest to the tower, leaving the other two to Cam, which should be no problem for his proven comrade. Damian crawled carefully along the rough, rocky ground toward the road and hid behind a high fold in the inclined earth, drew his bow and fitted an arrow, waiting for Cam to reach the top and make the first move.

Cam scaled the wall in a matter of moments, quickly and silently. Damian could still see him around the bend in the wall though the view from his new position in the road made line of sight more difficult. Damian was now facing the front of the ominous dwelling and Cam was climbing the wall to the side, and he looked like a small bug high up on a wall from there. When he reached the top he paused stone-still just below the very top of the battlement and listened before slowly raising his head up slightly. He didn't need to see the watchman pacing toward him. His booted feet thudded slowly along the wooden floor of the parapet just on the other side. The thuds drew closer. Cam froze without breathing and could now feel himself practically underneath the sentry. Cam could hear him breathing and muttering occasionally, unaware of the armed insect clinging to the battlement next to him, suspended high above the earth and within his arm's reach. Cam didn't dare even peek at the passing sentry, but when the footsteps finally surpassed his position flipped over the merlon and onto the wallwalk right behind him. Before doing anything Cam risked a perilous but necessary moment to scan the inner courtyard. *No one else here. Good.*

The sentry thought he heard something and stopped, peering over the wall. These were Draga's henchmen who had just returned from action in the city, which one could actually see indistinctly from up here and were still quite alert, but he was backstabbed before he was able to see his intruder. He slumped over on the narrow floor and his two companions on the front wall turned in surprise. At that moment Damian emerged from below, took careful aim and shot one. The stunned mog fell far to the ground within and crashed into a wooden well frame with a clatter. The last guard gave a shout and attempted to run toward the stairwell. Cam chased him a short way and felled him with a spike. The guard tumbled down the stairs and fell below. Cam waited tensely a moment before doing anything, looking within and listening. Still nothing, no answer. He signaled to Damian below to wait and pulled off his climbing gloves while he stealthily descended the long stairway to the courtyard, constantly alert for more trouble.

Like a spy in the fortress of his enemy Cam prowled silently around the enclosure. Everything still seemed incomprehensibly quiet–no sound or life could he detect within the courtyard or the tower which was now very close to him and in full view. Vaulted openings there were on each level that only revealed darkness within, black windows masking any possible observer, and each seemed to watch him as he crept skillfully closer. He looked up at them distrustfully and sought ways to avoid their unfriendly stares. The grounds inside the courtyard were fairly cluttered with piles of stone, wood, metal, and other necessary building materials which looked as though they had been recently used, along with piles of refuse. The courtyard looked as though it had once been fair but Draga had turned it into a dumping ground. Cam kept these obstructions between him and the rising and ominous tower which he watched with increasing suspicion and unease. The dark and lifeless edifice rising forebodingly before him seemed to project some silent doom and its original architecture seemed to have been modified or altered in places by its domineering inhabitants, refaced to that which would have evoked fear in the beholder. He grimaced but crept onward and undaunted, passing the corpses of the guards at his feet, their bodies broken from the fall. The level floor which approached the tower, he could see, was paved with smooth stones, laid with skill and led to a broad stone staircase of few steps, rising easily to a large, smooth, platform of rock beyond. Columns held up a heavy stone roof and balcony above this floor forming a portico, the fair inner entrance to the tower, and cast this grand threshold into a darker shade. Through the darkness Cam could see a high arched opening located well behind the columns. Miraculously, its twin doors were open. Cam finally stole up the smooth steps and through the uprights, pausing a moment to look upon a fallen statue which lay in pieces in a far corner of the threshold, some unknown leader or politician by the looks of him. Cam concluded it was probably Karius or one of his subjects for the Kunn which had overtaken the fortress would have no favor for that just ruler. This was a lookout outpost in earlier years, built to keep watch upon the highland roads. He turned and approached the archway into the tower and listened. Still nothing.

He shuffled down a short hall, his soft shoes of leather making no noise. The room beyond, he could see, was dimly illuminated by a single torch on the wall directly in front of him. Now Cam could hear something, low and whispering it seemed to him, horses inside, the smell of which supported this probability. Must be the stable, he thought, and entered. There was hay spread out along the dirty floor and shelves along the wall with various dry feeds. A lengthy, windowless chamber stretched its way to Cam's left which led to a pair of locked and heavy double doors, barely visible in this light, the tower main ground level entrance. He snuck past the many occupied bays toward the doors. The beasts housed inside paid him little heed as he passed like a mouse. Cam studied the huge doors a moment, looking behind him and expecting Draga's thugs to jump on him. The stillness was unnerving. He removed the braces which held the doors fast, grabbed the iron ringbolt and pulled the door inward. It swung open slowly, creaking slightly. He peered over his shoulder yet again then placed himself just outside the door, looking for Damian. His awaiting friend came running up to the door from his place outside and Cam darted back into the darkness.

Damian halted suddenly, right before the massive door and yielded again to an inexplicable desire to glance behind him and into the land beyond. That strange sensation he felt in the city earlier gripped him once more. He could swear something was following or watching him in the rocks and thickets beyond the road. He thought he could sense a presence in the hill somewhere, hiding, its thought focused on him. Damian couldn't account for it, decided he didn't have time anyway, and at Cam's urgent beckoning stepped inside, locking the door behind him. He caught up with Cam.

"Haven't seen or heard anyone," he whispered to Damian.

"Let's look around before we do anything," Damian replied. "I don't trust this place, something strange is at work. I feel like I'm being watched. Don't underestimate Draga, he seems to have some wit. I don't fancy being backstabbed in this dungeon before we can get away."

They passed back along the rows of bays and looked upon the tenants: horses mostly, some rather unkempt by the looks of them, probably for food, but also various mount beasts from distant lands, ones they had never seen before, some obviously rare and valuable and well kept by contrast. Probably stolen from traders at knifepoint, Damian thought. Mount beasts were expensive. He drew his sword angrily and slowly proceeded deeper into the tower.

At the further end of the room were two flanking staircases leading up to the second level, rising along the wall across from each other and meeting in the center at the landing above. They were about to ascend when Cam gave a gasp. He discovered a rather large wooden trap door on the floor. The straw which surrounded it was parted for access. Damian pulled the handle and the door swung upwards on its hinges to reveal a wide rampway descending at a fairly steep angle into the quiet darkness below. They looked at each other.

"That may be a dungeon-keep," said Damian, "maybe where they're holding Gadrin. I don't want to go there just yet, it's probably trapped. Let's secure the upstairs first. I don't want any surprises." They quietly but quickly sped up the stairs, swords drawn and ready.

They reached the floor of the second level and halted, peering over it. The weak sunlight struggling through the eastern windows revealed to them what seemed to be a mess hall and kitchen. Two large tables were placed in the middle surrounded by wooden chairs. Ovens and storage cabinets lined the southern wall. Several torches burned separately in far corners. Platters and foodstuffs of different kinds lay about disorderly, as though the inhabitants had departed recently and in haste. They could see no one and ran inside. They looked out the windows on all sides, scanning the grounds around the tower for activity. The northern wall held doors which opened onto the outside balcony that overlooked the inner courtyard. Cam quickly ran out to have a look. Still nothing. They bolted up the stairs to the third level.

This room was wide open and lofty and was apparently the sleeping quarters. Dual wooden bunk racks were arranged in rows throughout the room. Small piles of clothes, trunks for storage, and other personal effects lay about. No one and nothing of interest. They stole through the room suspiciously and as before quickly looked outside through the windows before climbing the stairs to the fourth level. Nothing special there either. At the top of what they thought must be the last staircase they found a single locked door. They stopped just outside and listened. Not a sound, not even the wind. Being a light, interior door of wood, Damian drove his booted foot right through it, sending it to the floor in pieces.

"This must be where Draga spends all his time planning his dirty deeds," said Damian as they entered the empty chamber. They searched the room carefully, poring through parchments and drawers of a large table against a wall. They found maps and some old records on his desk, some old bladed weapons in a drawer. Probably kept for sentimental purposes, Cam thought disgusted. He wondered who was unfortunate enough to have been the victims of them. He closed the drawer. Damian searched his bunk and some chests on the floor. All were unlocked and empty of valuables. They both looked puzzled at each other.

"This isn't right, Damian," said Cam, shaking his head. "Draga's pirate tactics are well known around here. His power covers a great territory. There must be somewhere in this castle where he keeps his loot."

"Perhaps we'll find the answer below it."

They reached the ground level again without incident and approached the trap door in the floor. They opened it and again peered cautiously down the dark decline. Taking the torch from the wall Damian descended the stone ramp. They could immediately smell the change in the air which became staler and dustier but also moister as the ground level above became further away. They kept a sharp lookout, expecting attack any moment. They still met no further opposition and this only increased their suspicions and fears. The ramp ran fairly deep into the earth, several levels at least, and the torchlight revealed to them a huge subterranean vault, the roof of which was suspended by two rows of thick stone columns, crude and in need of repair for they were crumbling, ascending to the ceiling now distant and cast into shade. Fungus and mossy growths sprouted from cracks and corners. The light from the torch grew weaker in the thin, damp air of the vault and the visibility was reduced to only about a fifteen foot radius. A faint foul smell arose to their nostrils which grew stronger as they descended. They finally reached the bottom and stepped onto the floor. The overall shape of the apartment was rectangular and they strode cautiously across the lengthy floor, weapons ready, spread apart, their heads turning this way and that. They could hear something at the far end and their pace quickened. A few moments later they could distinguish the shape of a

187

person against the wall, apparently chained or bolted to it. They soon recognized it as that of Gadrin, the very man they were looking for, bolted directly to the rock wall by iron braces around his arms. His clothes were filthy and he looked ragged and weary as though he had spent some time in hostile captivity. Damian and Cam approached him.

"Who's there?" Gadrin called out with an effort, his eyes blinking from the light.

"I am called Ratarra," Damian answered cautiously. "Where are Draga and his men?"

"Ah, so you're the one who destroyed Khala?" Gadrin said and his eyes lit up, regarding the stranger with wonder. "That was a bold move. We all hailed your name at that hole. I made my escape because of you, though it didn't do much good. Here I am chained up again. Yes, I heard him mention you on the ride up here, and not with much favor as I recall. The new enemy of the Kunn, eh? I'm surprised you haven't already met the same fate as the rest as foolish as you. You need the right weapons to fight against that group. Maybe you've got them. I certainly hope so, they grow ever in power and we are all beset. Kandar can't right everything by itself. So much for the Old Alliance. Anyway, they blindfolded me on the ride up here and threw me onto the back of a kelga. I must have been right behind the old villain because I could make out almost everything he said."

"What did he say about me?" asked Damian.

"That he finally got his revenge and that you would no longer be of concern. He seemed to feel as though his problems had come to an end, probably because of me and that old acquaintance of his he slew so ceremonially down in the city. He just needed to communicate with some of his friends who live nearby."

"So he's not here?"

"No, he left with the handful of his thugs that were still alive after the skirmish in Monse. Probably to make contact with some of his hill-dwelling neighbors. That's what he said anyway. Could be lying."

"How many were left?"

"Couldn't be more than a dozen or so. Imagine about fifty gangsters all fighting over me. Must be their whole force in Hera. Of course an operative of the Hattél like me is worth it. Too bad for Draga he'll never get anything out of me."

"We need to get you out of here," Damian and Cam came closer.

"No!" he barked suddenly and they halted, perplexed. "You can't touch me. Draga's got me rigged to some trap or other. If I'm moved it will be the death of me. I can't die just yet. I have some information that absolutely must be passed on. There's no time anyway, he'll be back soon." Cam checked over the iron loops carefully, searching for any means of release or mechanical linkages and spring mechanisms. Damian continued the questioning.

"What does he want with you?"

"I'll probably be dead soon so I had better tell you. Under the circumstances it seems I have little choice. After that stunt you pulled at Khala you sound like a trustworthy ally. I'm a spy for Lord Kane in Demar, an agent of the Hattél. I pose as a diplomat to Mod, trying to reduce tariffs along the East Road and raids on goods from Kandar. Trade to the south becomes ever more problematic. I met with Thuliak in his palace many times over the course of several months, negotiating with him or his close subjects. A nest of vipers they are, curse them all. The strange characters from governances all over come and go like cattle, swindling and bartering who knows what with that serpent Thuliak behind his closed curtains. Those conditions were, however, advantageous for information gathering which was my real purpose there. The Ahga resides in Mod most of the time lately and I was able to slowly work my way into his circle as well, though it was more difficult. The Ahga keeps a far better watch over his domain and security was very tight. Anytime I was capable of presenting myself to the Kunn representatives for negotiations of sorts I was closely accompanied by a pair of escorts per orders of the Ahga. He is especially distrustful of foreigners but even more so of myself who hails from the only region he has thus far failed to achieve influence in. He seems to harbor an especial enmity for our realm. Even his spies have difficulty there for the Lord Kane breeds good virtues in his realm and the people are wholesome as a result and strong. A spy there with ill intent will have trouble hiding among the wise and prudent.

"But I could also tell the Ahga was trying to use me to facilitate or bring about just that objective. So there was a mutual manipulation going on. I was trying to discover what schemes or intentions he had in mind for the penetration or coercion of Demar and he pried me for sensitive information as well, gleaning what he could from my guarded and vague revelations of my capital city and its ruler. Most of what little I leaked over the numerous conversations I had with him or his higher subjects was useless or intentionally misleading. But little could I learn of him or the Baccád, but one day I was approached by an agent of Thuliak who had watched me for some time and perceived my intentions. This character endeavored to recruit my help. He offered me his information on the Ahga and his latest and great plan of the Kunn if I helped him execute a certain task. Thuliak evidently is also untrustworthy of the Kunn. I was to help him uncover the mystery behind the recurring disappearances of certain valuables purchased abroad, which turned out to be mostly volia from northern Dengland where the Hidari have settled and manufacture it, an element called *balsan crystals,* used to mix with other composites to make fire, and *platilin,* a shiny, malleable metal used in décor. Not practical for armament but visually appealing and tractable for embellishments, valuable for merchant sale. A predictable purpose for that vain fool but it was very valuable nonetheless, and he grew more enraged with the strange disappearances of these goods which he paid handsomely for. His men were constantly changing delivery arrangements and locations to deceive opposition, even down to the Tanga, but it was to no avail. These cunning thieves were always aware of his designs and able to craftily acquire his precious goods.

"Well, this friend of mine had gathered some interesting information, how he wouldn't say, though I doubt not that he risked his life in the endeavor for agents of the Ahga certainly would not reveal information of this sensitive nature. A purchase was again going to be attempted and when the time came we planted ourselves at the secret location. This particular deal took place in an old temple in a small village east of Mod. We hid in a corner under a collapsed portion of the roof to witness the transaction and perhaps discover the clever culprits. The representatives of both parties arrived as planned later that day, Thuliak's armed guards and a group of Hidari and Turuks with their shipment of several carriages. These were all ambushed by clansters of the Kunn who emerged upon the scene quite suddenly and with obvious precognizance. All Thuliak's men and the vanguards were slaughtered in a quick ambush but myself and my accomplice were captured. I thought the whole thing strange because the Kunn and the clan-oriented Hidari and Turuks generally seem to have an understanding with each other. Perhaps this issue was exclusive of any existing treaties or alliances with them, but there you have it: it's the Kunn that's robbing Thuliak. And if he finds out you can bet the palace of Mod will be stained with lots of Kunn blood, he, he. An efficient way to eliminate the crime lords there, mutual extermination. If we can just tell this to Thuliak…Good riddance to the whole lot of them. They executed my conspiring partner on the spot but held me as valuable to the Ahga and the Kunn. They seemed to recognize me as a northern agent. The Ahga could make use of me, they said, and I was brought to that secret slave camp in the wilderness to be held until further notice, and, I might add, to loosen my tongue."

"And what of Demar?" Damian asked. Cam gave up on the iron bars and looked around impatiently.

"Yes, he told me. A certain Lord Ralen of Pomay, a politician of high status and influence and Kane's own nephew, is to accompany a party of officials to the coastal city of Prova for business matters and negotiations with the rulership there."

"That will be a long journey by carriage from Pomay."

190

"He's going by ship, ordinarily a safe means of transport and the Ahga is counting on this. The Kunn now also have substantial power at sea. The Ahga has lately realized the potential of piracy by sea as an added method of acquiring riches and theft of goods and intends to use it to pry what he wants from the province he hates most. A pair of ships under the flag of the Kunn lays in wait off the coast, moored evidently in some rocky cove with a good view of the approach to the city by sea. They plan to raid the ship, which is only lightly armed and carries mostly passengers and some cargo, and take this lord and all his associates aboard captive for a ransom-hold to place pressure on Kane. Apparently my lord has in his possession something which the Kunn greatly desires, or perhaps it is merely his regal stature which they intend to use for some ill end. My country is very prosperous and attractive to wealthy businessmen and so we can expect this kind of envious reception from the southern despotisms. But we will not allow his scum admittance there. You can imagine how this would affect one with such pride as the Ahga, being repelled so insultingly, and ever he seeks ways to remind us of his competing power. Prova is not an entirely trustworthy state of the province, non-affiliated and independent, a fair medium for trade and commerce if you know your business, but neither are they fully under the shadow of the Kunn or any other dominating criminal entity. If they can accomplish this abduction it may force Kane into talks or dubious deals. The Ahga greatly wants a foothold in Kandar, not to mention some revenge against him especially, and this may deliver him at least some of it."

"We should have some time to thwart this attack. Pomay is a fair distance away."

"Nay, the ship may have already departed by now. My attempt to bring them warning of this danger has failed."

"What is the name of this ship?" asked Damian. Gadrin was about to respond when they suddenly heard a familiar laughter behind them and they all turned in surprise to look.

"Well, I think we've all heard enough." It was Draga, with a smile, who had strangely appeared at the shaded rear of the room. They could barely make out his hand in the distance which seemed to be placed on a lever or handle on the wall. "I found out all I need to know, ha ha!" He threw the lever downward and the floor beneath them all opened suddenly under their feet. Cam, by some inert reflex, flung himself high in the air, beyond the reach of the yawning pit and landed on the floor to the side in safety. Damian, however, caught off guard, fell helplessly through the aperture which was wide and virtually unavoidable if one stood before that particular part of the wall. Draga used this trap door as a means of prisoner ejection, the doors below being linked to the iron shackles on the wall so that they opened simultaneously at the pull of the lever. The iron loops around Gadrin's hands opened and he would have also fallen but Draga took the precaution of chaining his waist to the wall by means of a thick leather belt which he had placed around his prisoner earlier. Draga felt sure he could still make use of Gadrin after he inevitably divulged his secrets and Ratarra and his friend fell to their deaths. So instead of falling with Damian, Gadrin remained suspended to the wall above the pit and struggled in vain against this impediment. Cam and Gadrin looked about them in a blind panic for now they could not see their own hands waving in front of their faces. Damian held the only torch and his abrupt disappearance through the floor and down that horrible tunnel took all the precious light with him, plunging the entire room into thick, impenetrable darkness. There was an alternative purpose behind, or underneath Draga's deadly trap door besides ridding himself of unwanted men or beasts. He had an animal to feed.

Draga's plan had gone almost perfectly. He had successfully delivered the spy to his hideout, making sure he was close by on the journey to clearly overhear the lie about leaving for reinforcements as soon as he arrived. He prepared his domain for the inevitable arrival of his foes, intentionally sending three of his men to their deaths with the assignment of guarding the outside walls, a task Draga knew would result in their elimination but was a necessary feint to provide these heroes some level of token resistance and therefore lure them in. *Stalat uruz al-Medu.* He had displaced the remainder of his force to his inner cave, locked the front doors which he knew they would probably find a way around, and made the trap door to the dungeon clearly visible to ensure its discovery by his hated rival for which he so desperately yearned vengeance upon. But it was a revenge that demanded thoughtful patience and it had paid off. And after his usefulness Ratarra had fallen into his trap as anticipated. He knew this veteran spy would not easily divulge his precious secrets, not to him anyway, and Draga didn't feel he had much time to wait for it. Ratarra had served this purpose well. When the Ahga received report of the catastrophe he suffered at the hands of his unfavored subject he would throw all his might at him. Draga would not hold out long against the onslaught that awaited him, one which would soon come to pass, that even now was undoubtedly under serious consideration. The miles between him and his unhappy master were inconsequential. Draga could taste his own demise now stronger than ever but it did not daunt him. He now wielded a new and powerful weapon. His courage and determination had yielded unbelievable results. These shocking and incredible secrets he had just learned about the Ahga were power enough to blackmail him into submission, or at least bring Draga the newfound respect and standing he was looking for when he exploited them. He was sure no one outside of the Baccád could know of this issue. In the matter of guarding secrets they demonstrated unparalleled competence. It was rumored that the Ahga removed the tongues of those closest to him as a requirement of service. Nay, this interesting secret indeed would bring them all to their knees. Draga now held all their backstabbing throats by a cord and relished his newfound influence. Thuliak may be a weak and useless fool, one who Draga himself wouldn't mind spilling all over his polished floors, but he held great power nonetheless, power to cripple or drive out the Kunn in that territory. Now the Ahga would listen to him.

One small problem remained, however. Of Ratarra he was no longer concerned. Even he had undoubtedly met his bloody fate and Draga's only misgiving was that he would be sadly denied the look on Ratarra's face just before his life was hideously ended. His imagination would have to suffice, for now it seemed he had a slight dilemma because he could hear Ratarra's filthy little comrade somewhere still in the room. He must have avoided his trap for he could hear him feeling his way about on the floor like a lost, panicking mouse. With his night eyes Draga could still see Gadrin in the distance, clutching at his restraints in vain. But the little one whose agility Draga had underestimated he could not see from his present location. He replaced the lever in its original position and the floor reaffixed itself, grinding back into place. Gadrin stood himself up again on the floor but was still otherwise helpless. Draga took his bow in his hand and in the dark began the quiet hunt for his small enemy.

Damian felt the floor under him suddenly vanish and he was pulled helplessly down a shaft whose sides and face were crafted almost completely frictionless by some unknown art, denying him and any previous victim any hold. But he did not have far to go. He fell straight a short distance before the shaft angled somewhat. He could see some dull light from outside peeking through from underneath and suddenly he departed the shaft, fell freely a short way and landed hard on the rocky floor outside. He immediately jumped to his feet and looked around.

He appeared to be in a large, open bowl, oval in shape, surrounded by high rocky cliff all around. A horrible smell immediately arrested his notice. All about him were bones of various creatures strewn about and piles of filth and vomit which gave forth a stench. He looked up and could see the tower high above him, the bottom of which must have been about fifty feet distant from here and so therefore were the rocky sides of the bowl below it. Damian judged that he was behind the tower and under the cliff behind it which was undercut here and invisible from view to the front. Looking up Damian could also see a railless bridge of black steel which spanned the chasm overhead, poised against a dark and swiftly moving sky, connecting the tower to the entrance of a high and otherwise inaccessible mountain cave behind it. So, thought Damian, Draga does have an extension to his hideout and that must be where he locks and conceals all his loot, and where his men are probably hiding now. *No wonder we couldn't find anything. He lured me into his trap like a rat,* he thought and grew enraged at his own blindness and its resulting plight. He should have destroyed this slug when he had the chance in Tirien. Draga will pay dearly for this. He grit his teeth and his hand went to his sword. His only consolation was that Cam was still up there, safe hopefully but also well out of reach.

He had only a moment to consider all these things for the hungry beast was already upon him. It shook the very ground as it hastily emerged from its shelter of overhanging rock to surprise and take advantage of its stunned prey, which this time, to the beast's surprise, was already standing and armed before him with a sword. Damian looked upon the beast in utter amazement and shock for his worst imaginings could have not conjured a more hideous and deadly predator. It was a four-legged beast of vast bulk and height, dwarfing the pathetic and doomed prey before it with its immense head of hide and its widening mouth with rows of teeth that looked like mounted knives upon an engine of death, designed with the sole intent to tear and rend flesh in its insatiable desire to destroy all and feed itself with the inhabitants of the earth which it crushed under its immense weight and girth. It was covered in thick brown hair of light hue as though it hailed from the far north, each as thick as spines and stained with blood. A deep bellow escaped its cave-like mouth as it charged, echoing within the chasm and shaking the foundations of the earth in its hunger and rage.

Damian could only stand still for a moment, paralyzed with shock as his very legs were shaking from the mere impact of the beast's colossal feet upon the sandy floor. Of a foe like this Damian possessed no skill or experience and he stood his ground a moment, cursing the deceiver who delivered him while searching the grounds about him for anything that might provide him some advantage and trying to formulate a hasty plan. Tog would have been able to inform him of his peril and even the name of the beast. Even he would have agreed that this was a monster to be avoided in a disadvantageous scenario such as this. But Damian had little concern for the creature. The elimination of Draga and delivering the spy was his mission.

Fortunately Damian had enough presence of mind in the imminent and dire circumstances which environed him to take notice of a small door against the cliff at ground level about thirty yards across the chasm and underneath a narrow rocky overhang that promised escape and entry. He also noticed several large rocks laying about and purposed to make use of them. That door across the floor of the arena became his focus and destination and he bent his will to gaining it at all cost.

At the first pass of the monster Damian bounded to the side and dragged his garvonite sword along its trunk-like leg, gashing it. The beast howled, not anticipating this level of defense. It was accustomed to unarmed and weak prey, refuse sent down to it by its master, stolen beasts or prisoners of all race that he had no use for other than providing Draga and his followers entertainment as they watched the gore with glee from the bridge high above. Also at times an effective means of discipline for his men, Draga might have added. On this occasion, however, the beast had no spectators for its master was inconveniently occupied in the tower dungeon above and therefore deprived of the ultimate vindication and humiliation he so craved to witness. And his few remaining men he had removed to the cave complex would not receive his alarm when the time had come to take part in their victory celebration. But it was of little matter. Ratarra was doomed either way.

The creature, in reflex to its injury, jerked its leg upward and outward, knocking Damian over as he attempted to bolt past and reach the door the beast knew its victim sought. All his victims tried to flee for that door in the past and he was ready for it again. He turned about and quickly placed himself between the door and his foe. Damian was knocked a distance by the blow but quickly regained his feet in time to ward off the huge seeking mouth which seemed to engulf him. The beast managed to knock Damian over and into a loose boulder. Damian immediately raised a large rock in front of him to defend himself from its oncoming colossal jaws. The beast bit down too fast, biting instead the massive rock held aloft in its face and in its fury snapped off several of its own front teeth in its attempt to kill its prey. Blood sprayed from its mouth and it bellowed in rage. Damian seized his moment, sprinted a few yards while the beast was stunned and lifted up another boulder which he heaved at the bloody face of his newly charging enemy. The huge projectile struck upon its wounded mouth and it staggered back a pace from the impact which was heavy enough to influence even this great creature, and it rocked the earth in anger and disbelief. No victim in the past had ever fought with this strength or made injury like this to him. Damian hesitated not a moment but sprinted for the door, desiring only escape. The thundering titan was already at his heels as he reached the low cave overhang and finally the door. Though the mouth of the beast was pressed into the small recess that denied its full admittance, its huge and ghastly blood-soaked tongue shot out, sweeping the hole in its desperation to finally arrest its hated prey and it howled in anger as it searched. The door was of wood and just out of reach of all but the creature's searching tongue. Damian waited not for deliberation. The door burst asunder as Damian leaped headlong and projected himself bodily through the closed entrance. He rolled safely to a halt in the tunnel beyond, out of reach of the beast. He sprang to his feet and looked about, hearkening to the cries of the monster outside.

The tunnel quickly bored its way to a small empty room at the end of which was a closed door. There was no light here and even this short tunnel was very dim. The scant light outside barely made the door against the northern wall visible. Damian took his sword in his hand and pulled it open with the other. He stepped into the pool of darkness and almost tripped onto a staircase beyond, cut into the rock and ascending to the north. Now Damian could see nothing but climbed the steps carefully, feeling his way blindly. He was sure this tunnel must lead to the thieves' inner hideout and endeavored to discover its destination. The walls were fairly smooth and even here as were the steps. He replaced his sword and felt his way up on all fours. Looking back he could barely see the tunnel he came through. He could make out nothing at all ahead of him but his burning desire to regroup with Cam and Gadrin overruled his concern for safety and he groped his way in the dark up the stairs in blind haste. He felt he was running out of time, that the scheming villain Draga had probably killed Gadrin and captured Cam by now. He felt it likely that his comrade was in need and Draga was already escaping down the hillside with his potent secrets. Damian ran blindly up the steps which continued onward for a considerable distance as far as he could tell in the dark. He eventually came to a level platform, and still feeling about felt an obstruction directly in front of him, preventing his advance. In his haste and anger he pounded this wall with his fists thinking the tunnel had been blocked to prevent escape but suddenly almost fell inward to his left. He groped about in this direction and felt nothing. The passage, it seemed, turned left here at the top of this stairwell. He placed his hands within the recess and felt himself inwards. He encountered another stair in this new direction and again felt his way up quickly but carefully, step by step. He finally reached another level space and could now discern some light in the distance. He thought he must be approaching the habitable inner chambers. He carefully proceeded down the hall which was illuminated by distant torches on the walls much farther ahead. His thoughts went out to his comrade who he hoped was well. Haste drove him to quicken his pace until he heard voices up ahead.

He approached slowly, sword drawn. Two doors became visible to his right, separated some distance from each other on the same wall. He placed himself in front of one of them and listened to the voices within with detestation, hearkening to their idle speech. Kunn murderers and thieves, more gangsters and henchmen, he thought, curse them. Interpreting their exchanges he could tell they were not aware of the presence of intruders. Perhaps Draga is still occupied with Cam, he thought, and some hope was kindled. He was just about to burst through the door and introduce himself before he slew them all in a rampage when something down the hall, further to his left, caught his eye. The lighting was better here, not only from the torches behind him but also what Damian was sure must be some weak sunlight partially illuminating a vast room at the end of the hall. Leaving Draga's men to their fruitless business for now he paced cautiously down the hall.

A huge room presented itself slowly to Damian's eyes as he drew nearer. The tunnel ended openly into a deep and lofty chamber, apparently uninhabited at the moment, which seemed to house a large quantity of boxed and crated items and bulk goods of value. Heavy chains hung from pulleys high over his head attached to iron hooks driven into the rock ceiling. A steel bridge well overhead projected itself from the southern wall, without rails, stretching its way into the center of the room where it ended. A large wooden structure was built at the termination of this bridge, a tower of criss-crossing logs and beams ascending to it and even above. Damian looked more closely and determined this tower to be some kind of elevator used for the lowering of loot into the chamber by means of a thick wooden platform of logs raised and lowered by ropes and pulleys operated from the top. He could see the platform in the midst of the tower now, resting at the bottom, currently in its lowered position. Ladders were also mounted along the sides of the bridge to provide one a quick ascension of about thirty feet to the top. Damian followed the bridge with his eyes until it disappeared through a wide arched opening toward the main tower outside, and the bridge he saw earlier in the arena below came to mind.

He looked about at ground level and saw more closely the crates and piles of goods which lined the floor all around. He examined them curiously and determined them to be the booty Draga and his despicable bandits robbed from others and stored in his secret vault to be undoubtedly dispersed for their own profit later. Disgust and anger welled up in his soul. He was sure it was all forcibly confiscated from the hard working farmers and craftsmen in the lands about who were just trying to make a living and contribute positively to society with the fruits of their labors. He ripped the top of one crate off and looked inside.

"Must be volia," he said to himself as he examined the contents. He held up the prized material before him and did not doubt its worth. "Probably stolen from a Hidari caravan," he said disgusted and lifted the sizable crate over his head. Thinking of a way to send a surprise to the villains down the hall and hem them in while he destroyed the valuables, he threw the large wooden crate down the tunnel. The wooden box smashed into pieces with a crash and cluttered the passageway with its contents, the noise echoing within the chamber. He looked into some more crates. The presence of so much of the Kunn's stolen loot invoked not a little disgust, but it also provided him an opportunity to impart some retribution.

197

"Animal and cabskins from distant parts," he said and again heaved them down the narrow hall. He continued his exploring.

"Looks like fabrics and woven cloths used for clothes and tarps, crafted with skill by the looks of them. The Kunn has good taste." The crates burst as they crashed down the hall. A pile of rubble was quickly forming on the floor.

"Dried herbs and spices, even kinsweed. Must be worth a fortune. A sore blow to the farmer no doubt. I wonder how much work was necessary to grow and harvest it all?" A thundering reverberation and echo down the hall. Wood splinters and goods spilled everywhere.

"Salted meats, probably for Draga himself. I hope he feasted often on fruits raised with toil and slaughtered by another only to have it removed from him with a sword at his throat." Much crashing and banging as the loot was heaved down the hall, now greatly cluttered and blocked with debris. By now Draga's guards from within emerged to inquire of the strange noises behind their doors. Damian in his anger nearly completely blocked the passageway with the debris of their ill-gotten gains. The stunned guards cried out in disbelief and surprise and busied themselves with the hasty removal of the clutter to apprehend the intruder. Shouts and calls went up.

"More preserved foods and grains, probably stolen from a poor farmer in Tirien trying to feed his wife and children. I wonder if he's still alive? Probably murdered and his family robbed of a decent father. Would Draga mourn the loss?" This thought invoked great personal sentiment. In a fitful rage he drew it back in his mighty arms and smashed it all on the floor and added to the pile now writhing with the angry and shouting sentries. Damian could hear them cursing in their struggles to free themselves but heeded them not.

"Rare potteries and useful items crafted of clays, decorated and embossed with gold and silver, for Draga's personal use no doubt. Expensive looking." More crashing.

"Plates and items fashioned of precious metals. I wonder how much gold these would have brought the Ahga." More screeching and ringing in the destruction of these items.

"Ah, fresh breads and foodstuffs to adorn Draga's filthy table. Do you suppose the Kunn would take the time to create all these fair items with their own hands or do they simply feel free to remove it from the possession of worthy folk?" He thought of the desperate farmers and merchants down in the city working hard every day to earn an honest living, providing his fellow being with the necessities of life with his own toil and sacrifice, a principle with which the Kunn was in disagreement. His enemies preached a different ideology, one that allowed its followers the use of force to acquire from the inferior who believed in the necessity to create and build these things themselves and with pride for their own livelihood and the betterment and happiness of their society. To the Kunn and those like them this was an unnecessary and tedious way of life which required sacrifice and labor, something they were not willing to undergo and instead embraced the desirable alternative: power. Damian himself bore the emotional scars of their brutal recalcitrance and relieved himself of some of his rage.

He concluded his destructions. The sizable pile in the hall kept the guards back for the moment. He discovered some large jugs of oil among the goods and supplies and smashed these lastly over the rubble. Some sparks dripping from the torches on the wall managed to ignite the combustible mixture and a raging fire quickly consumed and overtook the tunnel. A couple of the guards caught struggling through the rubble were unfortunate enough to be devoured in flames themselves. Damian turned and departed, quickly climbing a ladder to reach the bridge.

* * *

Cam seemed to land in a sea of impenetrable darkness. He had sensed something was amiss in the vault, that they were being observed while Gadrin disclosed his information, but it wasn't until that hated voice sounded and the floor jerked suddenly that his suspicions were confirmed. Through a reflexive ability he knew he could not claim as his own he answered what he knew was some call from his subconscious, and without thought leaped to safety. But instead of beholding the predator which now began its slow and deliberate search for him he was met with a thick, blanketing darkness, one that not only blinded but seemed to remove from memory all visions once beheld by the eyes. Anything Cam had ever seen immediately became distant and irretrievable memories, as though a rift existed in his mind preventing him ever accessing them again. He began to have difficulty convincing himself of their actuality as his sense of sight seemed completely and permanently removed, indeed such things became irrelevant here. For almost immediately upon recognition of the perilous circumstances around him Cam had abandoned this crutch known as sight and shifted his concentration to the spiritual and instinctive. He knew he was now set against deadly opposition, one that wielded a distinct advantage and would certainly use it: Draga could see in the dark. Cam knew he had to adapt or be killed and without alternative trained his mind and spirit to overcoming his deficit, to equalize the odds against this stalking phantom. His survival depended on this vital counterbalance. He began intensely to feel the room with his mind, to implement his keen sense of hearing and strain it, to see the predator within which searched slowly for its meditating prey, pacing with measured step the lengthy vault from column to column which seemed each to take shape and visibility in Cam's mind as his meditations deepened and his powers grew more adapted to the new stimuli.

Cam had remained motionless and still behind a tall column in the northern far corner of the vault since the sudden disappearance of the precious light, tense as a spring, reorienting himself to the impediment, listening, his head slowly turning as if mapping the room with his mind, his eyes closed and forgotten. Even his breath he had brought under control until it seemed tuned and in synchronization with the energies of his surroundings, animate and inanimate. He could feel the sweat dripping from his face from his intensity and concentration. He straightened ever so slowly as his adaptation waxed and the mental construction of the vault became complete. He could feel the presence and location of the night-eyed stalker, tuning in to his quiet footsteps only some rows across the colonnaded vault. Cam could feel his will bent on him, like a ghost that hunts a mere mortal within its own tomb, patiently, methodically. There would be no escape from this prison of darkness, he would die here. Gadrin he had tuned out for the moment to hearken to more demanding needs but now could be heard again. Gadrin seemed to also recognize the danger and kept still and silent, hardly breathing. He had one last secret to tell before Draga put an end to him, if he felt the little human would be the victor, or take him away never to be seen again, to be used as a pawn for the Ahga. Cam knew he could not hide long in the dark from Draga who could spot him from a good distance. Cam felt him getting closer and made the first move. He quit his place and leaped like a cat toward the opposing column, hopping evasively to finish the distance. It was just in time. Draga drew back his bow and shot an arrow at the very spot Cam was only a moment ago. The noise of the arrow slipping along the floor and splintering into the wall echoed throughout the quiet vault.

Draga was impressed. "I suppose you are as quick as they say," he called aloud in his hoarse, mog voice. He drew another arrow and crossed the floor slowly to Cam. His words echoed throughout the lofty and spacious chamber.

"The quickest," Cam replied. "The better to slay you and your filthy friends." He felt the stone column he stood next to. He had a good mental fix on Draga, especially since he spoke words, and made a lunge for him, swords drawn. Draga evaded the passing blows from this acrobatic squirrel, fending him off with his bow. When Cam passed the mog aimed another shot at him but missed. His target leaped and clung high to a column like a spider with four legs. How this small human was able to accomplish that feat in the dark he did not know. But he liked it. Draga was loving this hunt and a wicked smile crossed his face. He fitted another arrow.

200

"I hope your friend is as quick," he said antagonizing. "Ratarra will need speed. All the strength in the world is useless against his fate."

"What have you done to him?" Cam cast himself downward at the mental image of his foe, swinging his dual swords. Draga managed to block the quick blows from his blind but adept opponent. He kicked Cam in the chest and he rolled across the floor. A perfect shot opportunity. Draga quickly aimed and released. Cam pictured death traps and engines of torture and machines of merciless mortal destruction unimaginable somewhere below the vault at the bottom of that mysterious pit, and became enraged at the thought of his dear friend, however blessed, trapped helplessly and murdered in some vile fashion. He could all but see the lethal projectile speeding towards him. As quick as a cat he flipped upright, swung his swords with a yell and deflected the arrow in mid-flight toward the ceiling. Draga yelled in anger and threw his knife at him in frustration. He watched Cam flip away, putting some distance between them for another attack. Draga tried a different tactic.

"You can forget about Ratarra," he said loading his bow, "and you can forget about this spy, too. No one else needs to hear what he has to say. I've heard enough for my purposes." Gadrin recoiled at these words, guessing his intent. He gasped and stiffened for some unknown imminent death, and he began writhing within his bonds for escape. Draga drew back the bow and placed a well aimed shaft into Gadrin's heart. Cam, horror-stricken, could hear him in his death throes as he slumped slowly in his restraints. But he dared not cry out. He was well hidden for the time, hopping back toward the southern end. He intended this pass to be his last. This Kunn barbarian, which he regarded now with even further disgust and abhorrence, would meet his end without further delay. No more close engagements in the dark which put himself at risk. Cam prepared himself for the final blow. He cast himself back into deep, motionless thought again, perceiving his surroundings and the pacing monster in his mind. He fingered a throwing star.

"I'm afraid he still had a few more things to say," Cam added, provoking a mental duel.

"So there was more to the story?" came the goading. "That's alright. You'll never leave here. I'll just leave you to meet the same fate."

Cam changed the subject to divert his thoughts. "I saw what you did to that kid," he growled with a distinct note of anger. Cam could never forget the brave boy in Tirien and his wounded eyes. Draga turned suddenly for the voice seemed to come from a completely different direction and he headed toward it. It took Draga a moment to isolate this particular atrocity in his mind from the abundance of others he committed. He chuckled at the memory.

"So you saw, eh?" he said jovially after a moment. "He wasn't the only one. That's my standard method of instilling silence. He got off easy, far easier than you will, you little rat." Cam could hear some growls escaping through his clenched teeth and a hiss. Draga was clearly running out of patience. That was good–his slow, deliberate methods were somewhat compromised. He obviously didn't want this rodent escaping with the secret. He needed to put an end to this frustrating little foe and he grew tired of the tedious hunt. This was all supposed to be over. His caution lessened. He paced more quickly between the columns, right down the center of the chamber he strode now. Right where Cam wanted him.

"You didn't see what I did to his brother," Draga continued. "Gutted that backstabbing slug like a pig. He got what was coming to him. You'll look the same when I'm done with you." *Keep talking you filth.* "He wasn't the only one. Did I tell you about the time I relieved a fellow of his eyes? Of course that's a polite way of saying it, ha ha!" *Concentrate.* "Cut 'em right out for spying. He was a Guard member, one of the old Elites, Karius' boy, scouting out my hideout some months back. He was about to tell his friends where I was and what I was about. Oh don't worry, he didn't suffer much." *Couple more steps.* "I threw him down that hole your friend just dropped into to finish him off, ha! That's where I send all my prisoners and you as well!" Draga paused to appreciate this thought more fully and chuckled with glee. "Ha! Ha! You and that fool Ratarra will end up as a smelly pile of rotting filth yourselves, heroes indeed, you'll be nothing but a–" he started but was cut off. A throwing star cut through the darkness from nowhere and found its mark. It pierced Draga's forehead and he fell to the ground with a sickening thud. Cam listened to his enemy on the ground for a moment, assuring himself of his death. He relaxed himself a bit and breathed more freely. He had not time to search in the dark for the slain spy but murmured some respectful words of parting and saluted him, for this agent he had only known for a moment had risked his life in the pursuit of undermining this same enemy and in the end had given it. He was reminded that there were allies in this cause, though he knew them not, and he gave thought to their sacrifices. Cam took comfort in the final words he passed on though. His efforts were not in vain and his words had found ears capable of bearing them some fruit. *You may rest easy my friend, this will be put to use.* Cam took his leave and spent some time searching the floor until he found the rampway out and began his crawl upwards.

CHAPTER 6
ENTER TOG

Damian reached the top of the black steel bridge and was met again with that strange sense of foreboding, though it felt nearer and more certain than before. He drew his sword and began to pace the bridge. He left Draga's goons below to their struggles. He could hear them cursing and heaving fiery wreckage down in the tunnel. He was fairly high up, at least thirty feet off the floor of the inner cave. He looked back and could see the framework of the elevator at the inner end of the bridge, reaching and affixing itself to the cave ceiling for support and stability. He approached the arched opening and ventured outside. The sky was grown dark indeed, it was as if nightfall had come to the earth even in the early afternoon. The hills and gullies all around were visible up here. Nowhere in the sky could Damian even find a hint of sun, only dark, swirling clouds above urged into motion by a rising tempest which blew his hair. Directly below him, underneath the bridge, about fifty feet or more now that he was outside the cave, lay the rocky floor of the enclosed domain of the great beast he had narrowly escaped. He could hear it somewhere below, growling to itself and rummaging quietly in its shelter of overhanging rock, unseen for the moment. Directly in front of him, across the span of the chasm of about twenty yards rose the tall black tower. The black clouds, he could see, raced behind it in the low, ominous sky.

At the end of the bridge, right before the back entrance to the tower, as if waiting for him, stood a lone figure dressed all in black save for his eyes beneath a bandana of scarlet. Damian had never beheld eyes like these before. Reptilian they seemed, alien almost, and perceptive, as though he did not come from this earth and therefore beheld things beyond it. A thought and discernment dwelt in those eyes, as if they could penetrate the minds of others if it was weak enough. Damian somehow knew he could not hide from them. A black mask crossed his lower face just over his inhuman nostrils. A belt was wrapped around its waist, black and barely visible and Damian could tell weapons or alternative devices were secretly housed within small recesses and pockets along it. A drawn sword of cold, indomitable steel was grasped in one hand. But all these invoked little interest, for the power that seemed to emanate from this ethereal beast in human form made even Damian tremble slightly and he almost moved back a pace. He perceived that this being, standing like a statue of immovable iron at the bridge's end, unblinking eyes fixed upon him, was not merely some hired assassin or feared henchman of the Kunn, armed with typical earthly weapons. He could not even be one of Draga's acquaintances or lowly subjects. He projected too much strength, of the physical and spiritual, a potency that could be read merely by visual contact, not merely of the flesh but far more, and Damian perceived that he held a power within beyond that of mortals. Draga could have no such servant or mercenary like this at his call and command. Indeed Draga was a lowly subject by comparison, a foolish and weak expendable foot soldier next to the veiled might of this silent destroyer. This being awaiting upon the bridge before him was undoubtedly a member of some supernal association or league of which Damian was not yet fully knowledgeable, and yet there was a hint of some familiarity between the two, as if they shared some common purpose or standing. Here indeed was the foremost of his enemy, the leader of their unknown association. They looked hard at each other for some time as if reading one's thought and character.

Damian's thought strayed to his encounter with Draga in the foothills of Hera some days ago and his prophetic words to him before he departed. Perhaps Draga was right, there were other beings of greater capability in this world that Damian still was little familiar with, similar to him even, and had yet to become acquainted with them. He did not feel quite so alone and unique in his blessing. There were obviously others who bore some kind of elevation, bestowed by an unseen force–or forces. These thoughts of fear and doubt, however, only drove Damian to greater courage and determination. He knew of a life and a power, which lay elsewhere, one that watched him and expected of him, and of his own paltry life and existence Damian cared little for in light of the larger purpose and majesty within this power. The unforgettable memory of his experience in the wastes stirred within him and he felt uplifted and accepted, and he looked upwards at the heavens, now swirling and twisting in its ferocity, and perceived a struggle without, beyond his sight, but building with such virulence and imminence below him in the deep chasm and all about the hilltop that it could be felt, and Damian sensed that it was like a storm ready to explode with its combat and envelop the whole of the peak in its fiery and unavoidable destruction. As if in confirmation of this premonition lightning began to flash sporadically in the tempestuous sky and Damian began to understand, what was happening and what he was facing. This adversary was more than some petty mode of earthly obstruction but was something far greater, an emissary of other plane performing the bidding of its own master, to counter his, the depth of which took several moments to fully grasp. Far more was involved in this struggle than he could ever have anticipated. This was not only some personal contention with just another clan of violent thugs, imparting injustice for a short season then withering away with their inevitable demise, but was a critical, yet finite, part of an enduring spiritual struggle in the world of material. The purpose of his blessing became more apparent. Many tense minutes passed while the two brought themselves to a more thorough understanding and reading of one another during which the very air between them seemed charged with a flickering energy.

A mutual perception ensued. Damian's enemy was now known to him. He shed all doubt and at last stepped more closely onto the bridge and squared with his adversary. Tog took a few steps toward him and they halted a safe distance apart. Damian could hear words in his mind that he knew came from the being and meant for him though its lips moved not.

We meet at last, young one. I have heard much about you. Among mortals I am called Tog. In my own circle I am called by other. I give to you my namesake so that you may know who it is that will be credited with the annihilation of one as commended as you. I look forward to ending your young and meaningless existence. You will not leave here, and the errand for which you have been dispatched will fail.

"My life has just begun," Damian replied aloud, distracted slightly by the unusual communication but still focused, "and taking it away will be beyond your capability. I have too much cleansing to do here. Your master has created a dark plague which spreads like a disease and the souls of men diminish. I have come to bring light to this realm of darkness you have created by removing its perpetrators. My purpose will be fulfilled."

Ah, so you are as naïve and deluded as I perceived. You sound like a Kadali monk I eliminated long ago. He also preached change and cleansing and intolerance of what he called 'rogue entities'. You must know the Ahga and myself could not allow such speech to persist. The Kadali are finished and you cannot resurrect their misguided designs. Though you possess the Greater Mari, a gift soon to be fully bestowed to the true adherents, you will not reverse the Great Disannulment. The last bastion of the faithless upon earth will be destroyed by the gift. Unbelievers of the Mari must be removed.

"Brave soul. I know not the fellowship to which you allude but that which shares similar virtue can be called an ally. I hope he succeeded for his part which I doubt not was great. I may be new to what I perceive must be an old contention but those who have struggled before me are my brothers. As for myself mine is yet to be done, though I eagerly accept the task. I assume the role of punisher now. I am Ratarra, named so by the same evil I seek to destroy. I am the Cleanser, the Vanquisher, the wave of light which will cast out this evil on earth. You and the foul thugs which follow you and your Ahga will be destroyed by my sword!" Damian perceived that his sword glowed yellow with these words. He held it aloft and assumed a challengeful fighting stance. He glared at Tog with ferocity and bared his teeth, his powerful muscles exposed. Tog hissed back at him and his words sounded like an evil whisper in Damian's mind.

There is no hope in that foolish road you tread and therefore I name you Pún-ghat, lost child, and you are deluded indeed, under the influence of other power which has no jurisdiction here but pathetically persists in imposing itself nonetheless, seeking vengeance and allegiance in a realm to which it does not belong. Its ways are proven to fail and bring nothing more than perpetual toil to an existence of folliness in pursuit of just such an end. One need not be shamed by earned advantage, willingly wielded where others abandon. And you are also invited to yield to the call within us to indulge for yourself the desires you seek for such things are granted here to those few worthy who obey it. The Kunn will take what it needs from those it chooses without concern for the likes of you or others who stand in our way. The Kunn is a worthy pawn of the Divine One, strengthening His rule over the world with their deeds of conquest over the weak who ignore Him.

Damian growled and cringed for he could not believe the words he was hearing.

"You! And all those who heed that call will be doomed to feel the wrath of the one true power and partake in their ultimate destruction as punishment for their crimes and failure to acknowledge and hearken to its righteous demands! The path you and your master tread is paved with the spoils and blood of others. Though you follow an ideology that deceives you into superiority and inheritance your existence would not be possible without the labors of those you call weak. You derive your false happiness and possession from those same unworthy you feel entitled to persecute and subjugate. Your false supremacy has deceived you into a boundless ethical freedom. It is little wonder you find it so appealing. You have misused the wondrous gifts bestowed upon you. Your ideology is a parasite, leaching from the fruitful to satisfy your selfish and bloodthirsty desires while they suffer from the painful burden you place on their backs and souls, creating fear and chaos, misery and death, all because you are too interested in a false fulfillment which blinds you to the truth. And that truth is there is no reward derivable from this power over others, nor do you have the authority to wield such, though the voice within you to which you hearken would have you believe this."

Tog himself growled and gnashed his fanged teeth and brandished his sword. Indeed he seemed to recoil from these words and almost convulsed with anger and disbelief. It took him a moment to recover.

You sicken me, Pún-ghat. I offer you wisdom and a choice of roads which I lay open to you so that even a misled child like you with your blindness may see the real fulfillment in existence that you are voluntarily forsaking. There is another code of life, the Mari, which calls us to challenge your questionable principles and seek fulfillment through our own means and for ourselves, for we are wise enough now to pursue our own interests as we please. And to add ultimate insult to myself and the Mari you claim to be some kind of chosen divine warrior who will somehow destroy the greatest power and influence on earth? It cannot be done, its power is anchored here in this world. Your foolishness and willful disobedience disgust even me listening to you make such a claim, Pún-ghat.

"I have not that wisdom, though I will attempt this overthrow nonetheless. There is another power, one far greater and everlasting, and it has taken up a throne here to unseat the rebels who have caused grief untold with their atrocities which they feel entitled to commit. Your conviction does you credit but has twisted you to your undoing. You have become corrupt with your beliefs, believing the world and its people exist to provide you with power and you are blind to the darkness you create with the crimes your creed falsely entitles you to indulge upon but which tears down all of society with its disease and corruption. Your destructive ways and power are coming to an end, by my might you will be expelled and the lands made clean again!" Damian drew himself up and clenched his fists. Tog countered immediately and brandished his sword.

Fool! Those who submit to this false power are like weak cattle, abandoning gifts bestowed to all and demanded of the Divine One to be used to increase His strength. You and your kind that you claim to defend are like sheep, and so, therefore, are your beliefs and this intruding power you claim to be a representative of. How can you possibly believe the filth it preaches? Ultimate power is given, already provided, and all you could ever desire is yours simply for the taking for those strong enough to shed the weakness within and pursue that strength which is available to all. Yours is a life calling to be conquered and so will those that follow it. And what is this other power that thinks we are not capable of our own fulfillment and seeks to restrict us with its irrational principles? Does it fear challenge from the lowly subjects of the earth it claims to, but cannot, dominate? Or is it too reluctant to release us for fear of us discovering its weakness and falsehood and perhaps overthrowing it from its masked power, that same power it forbids us from wielding on our own? We have that power as well, Pún-ghat, and woe to those who do not use it. The Imposter must be expelled.

"I will listen no more to this venom!" Damian brandished his sword and pointed his finger threateningly at Tog. "We are bound to the principles the power sets upon us for our own good, but you are too blind to see that. Those who choose to misuse the gifts freely bestowed will receive just punishment. To those upon whom greatness is entrusted a greater capability of service is expected; likewise greater transgression is achievable, unduly suffered by the submissive. The Kunn and its evil will be erased and the lands made free of their oppression again! Leave now or you will also be honored to learn the lesson at my hands!" Damian raised his sword to the sky and it became alight with an angry yellow flame. The figure of Damian on the bridge seemed to emanate an even greater immortal strength, one that came to his aid in this vital moment, and he became gripped and strengthened with a power that was not of this earth. Damian seemed to grow and swell with its potency and gave forth a light on the dark hilltop and the surrounding violence seemed to have little effect on him, and around his frame a yellow aura glowed. But Tog stepped forward and pointed his sword. Lightning seemed to flash behind him suddenly as if answering a call or need from within.

You will not pass, Pún-ghat! You have no destiny! Those who are not worthy of an exalted existence because they fail to understand and heed the one true power will meet their end here! Great reward awaits me, the Mari has proclaimed this, and I will not let you upset the will of the One who will provide me with it! I also have a task, Pún-ghat, and now I see that I have been called upon with great honor to bring about your humiliating destruction! I will obey such a command to my honor. You cannot be allowed to reign here! I stand in your way. You are but another thread in the great fabric of time that will suffer its eternal degradation. You will share in the fate of the Kadali. You are ended now, Pún-ghat!

Lightning flashed and Tog's cruel sword lit with a potent red light and powers of the earth seemed to gather around him and bless him with their strength and place themselves at his command, and around him a ruddy aura glowed. Damian roared with rage and his green eyes glowed with ferocity. Tog growled and tensed his powerful frame, releasing a blast from his unseen lips that shook the bridge and echoed in its hatred all about the hilltop. The two clashed in the center of the bridge and light and energy sparked and flashed as their swords collided with each other in a desperate combat, each warrior despising the other with a passion and seeking to rid the world of not only the enemy he loathed but also the unfathomable creed he stood for. They each had blasphemed the other with their opposing words, words neither could tolerate in his ears, and a mutual detestation beyond explanation arose within them for each other. The air all around shook with their savage fencing and the elements, already heightened, drew themselves up to an even higher and more potent degree, making themselves felt and drawing together almost in a whirlwind which wheeled around the peak in a barely perceptible vortex with the unearthly warriors in its midst.

They each paused a moment in their fencing and grappled with each other, trying to pressure the other over the railless edge and down to the awaiting beast below who was now aware of them on the bridge and stomped about impatiently with his huge, gaping, and sounding mouth upturned as he expected a victim. Their faces were close and they glared at each other with mutual hatred.

You will submit to the Mari or perish!

"You follow a false power, one that promises reward but only delivers emptiness! You are nothing but an empty shell, devoid of any soul for it has been ruined forever."

You, Pún-ghat, will be my greatest sacrifice! Tog managed to strike Damian with such a blow that he was knocked back fully into the cave and the sky flashed with the light of his fury. Damian landed near the far end of the bridge. Right behind him was the elevator of wood reaching the ceiling. Tog advanced and looked upon his enemy who was pulling himself up. He withdrew a handful of small metal spikes from one of his pockets and sent them flying at Damian. Still trying to stand Damian was punctured in several places and wounded. Tog looked about and beheld the large chains which hung to the distant floor below and were in reachable proximity to the bridge. These chains were used for the raising and lowering of heavy materials and were anchored to the rock ceiling with massive iron bolts, one on the left side and one on the right. He sheathed his sword and approached them. He took one in each hand, gripped them with all his extraordinary might and bellowed so that the whole of the cave shook as he pulled on them. Even as Damian regained his feet Tog ripped the heavy chains from their anchors in the ceiling which broke and cracked in places from the overpowering exertion. Tog wielded the great chains and swung them about as weapons. The air hissed with their rapid revolutions.

You are too weak to stand against this power, Pún-ghat. You are no adversary here. Tog swung the chains at Damian and he was struck with a heavy blow. He flew backwards and crashed right through the tower elevator behind him, breaking boards and beams before he began his thirty foot drop to the floor below. He landed on a pile of loot which snapped and broke under him. Tog strode to the bridge's end and peered over. Still wielding his chains he simply leaped over the edge and sailed down to the cavern floor unaffected. He approached his enemy who was slowly recovering from the impact. Damian's clothes were slightly torn in places and blood and wounds spotted his body from the splinters.

You see, Pun-ghát, you will not be the victor here. He swung his chains and chased Damian as he eluded the blows which broke through the clutter and gear and smashed any equipment in the way with much noise and clamor. Damian dodged the relentless onslaught, leaping over carts and crates which splintered in their destructions behind him. He took cover for the moment behind the subterranean tower.

Mindless and weak cattle you are, Pún-ghat, like the frail fools you claim to protect, all of whom are a disgrace to the Great One.

"His is a voice of deception and lies!" Damian yelled back. "And those who heed it will be swallowed up into the emptiness that awaits them as punishment for their crimes!" Tog raised his chain to swing but Damian gripped the high wooden elevator near its base and began to push it toward Tog. Lightning flashed outside and thunder cracked. Tog stopped and looked up for the lofty construction in its entirety was breaking away from its anchors with the sound of splitting and cracking wood and began its thundering descent right at him. Tog tried to leap and evade but Damian grabbed the idle chain which Tog still had a grip on and pulled him back into the trajectory of the cascading tower. It landed with a crash on top of him and broke asunder into pieces with a mighty yell. Damian took the chain and quickly wrapped it around Tog's foot which alone protruded from under the heap of splintered rubble and hooked it tightly. He pulled on the chain which drew Tog's partially buried frame out and swung him around, making sure he impacted with the walls and bounced off rubble. After several revolutions and numerous injurious impacts upon rock and beam, Damian flung him upwards toward the bridge and watched him collide with the arched ceiling before he dropped prostrate onto the bridge above. Damian could see the guards in the tunnel finish their labors and were now rushing for him. He ran up one of the several ladders and quickly gained the bridge again. He wanted to conclude his business with Tog.

Tog raised himself slowly and struggled to overcome the injuries which stunned him. Never before had such a foe delivered harm like this to him. Only the Kadali monks were capable of this immortal energy. The thick black clothes which enwrapped him were in tatters and torn. The bandana of the Kunn around his forehead bore the scars of the swinging rampage. Various wounds were sprinkled about his head and body but he stood again and the fire in his eyes was rekindled. He drew his sword and again clashed with Damian on the bridge. The cries from the guards in the cave could be heard. Tog seemed slightly diminished in power for Damian rapidly forced him back outside with the rageful onslaught of his sword. The dark tempest was in full swing and seemed to be reaching a decisive point, where the struggles beyond sight no longer held each other fast and immovable, gripping each other with equal force, but had now tipped in favor of the victor and was about to unleash its verdict of doom. Damian relentlessly forced Tog back toward the tower and had reached the middle of the bridge again. The monstrous creature below was directly underneath them, bellowing in its hunger expectantly, its bottomless voice rising above the tumult of the hilltop. Draga's guards had climbed up to the bridge now and were making a rush for Damian, about six of them. Damian broke Tog's sword with his own in the struggle and there was a crack and flash of light as it was destroyed. Damian lifted him up by his throat and held him fast above his head and glared into his eyes for his final declaration.

"Those who bring evil and chaos into the world will meet their fiery end!" He spun around and slammed Tog to the bridge which split crossways in a shower of sparks and light. The cave side of the bridge collapsed, taking Tog and the last of Draga's guards down into the horrible pit below where the great beast was ready and eagerly waiting.

Damian stood upon the outthrust brink for a moment, watching his greatest foe fall into the stormy darkness below. Then he turned and ran toward the tower to finally check on Cam and his situation. Damian found a wheel on the tower wall by the huge door which led into it. Turning it with haste, the door opened outwards and he was surprised to find Cam standing behind it, swords drawn, expecting attack. But then his eyes widened when he saw Damian bearing wounds and evidence of a bitter struggle. But Damian's eyes were alive and his voice was strong, though he looked somewhat vacant and thoughtful as he strode into the tower. The two took a moment to communicate the events they encountered.

"I was looking for another way out," said Cam. "Apparently Draga made a secret door here in the stable room which led to his cave hideout." Cam stepped onto the threshold and took a look outside behind the tower for the first time and below into the chasm. He heard the sound of the monster in its thrashings and saw the bridge which was completely missing halfway out. "What happened here?" he asked.

But Damian was not in a mood to speak any further after the deadly struggles he wrestled with. What he had just experienced left him with much to digest and the revelations about himself and the opposing powers at work in the world left him at a loss of words for some time, and he could only gaze about thoughtfully now that the exhilaration was over. He was informed of the fates of Draga and the spy and what Gadrin had to say in his last minutes to Cam. They departed at once, riding down the hillside on Bish, leaving the empty tower behind them. Damian felt the strength which temporarily possessed and bolstered him for the occasion depart slowly and he lessened slightly to his normal sturdy self. He felt some satisfaction in his victory but his mind was troubled and he rode in thoughtful silence. Something told him his quest was far from over, that he would have other rivals of comparable power to challenge and that his task, whatever it was, had only just begun. From this engagement he learned that his knowledge in this apparently complex and ancient affair was woefully limited, and who he really was after all now mystified him. His failure down in the city reminded him that his superior might alone was not enough to consider victory beyond all doubt. The power he sought to destroy had a significant foothold in the realm and of Tog and his mysterious consort he still had yet to make real acquaintance. Damian knew they had their work cut out for them. But more importantly he began to understand his importance and his vital role in the world that a greater power eagerly required of him. He could see now that he was not simply a lowly warrior restored from death to selfishly seek his own vengeance but was an instrument in bringing about a certain change in the world, to deliver aid and protection where it was needed but also to restore an order to earth as part of some divinely ordained prospect. Though he had only taken a step or two upon what he doubted not would prove to be a long and unique journey he saw the larger picture, and the importance of his deeds and role drove him to even greater eagerness and determination. His wounds were forgotten and his strength and ambition waxed anew as he looked ahead with lightened and yearning eyes and urged his horse to greater speed.

Cam seemed to feel strengthened as well, brought by a sense of achievement and the knowledge that he was fulfilling a necessary purpose even though setbacks at times would be suffered. His sadness for the loss of Gadrin, who he felt personally responsible for failing, was giving way to satisfaction and ambition. He knew they didn't have much time to put his risky and dangerous labors on earth to use and must honor his life on this point. Cam's desire to deal another defeat to these villains swelled and a smile crossed his face as he gazed over the lands below with his far seeing eyes. He felt as though he looked upon a world of hope as they galloped down the winding path.

The storm eased behind them and the sky slowly lifted. The clouds dissipated and the winds subsided, leaving the hilltop in peace as though a serious dilemma had been resolved. The sun slowly peered out from behind the thinning and weary clouds in the west and cast its sad light on a scene which slightly dampened the revived spirits of the triumphant riders, and they were reminded painfully that their successes came at a price. They came across the bodies of a human and a horse near the path. It was that of Derrol, apparently strangled with skilled and merciless hands, killed while returning to the city earlier. Cruel claw and slash marks could be seen about the corpses. Damian looked up and gritted his teeth as a familiar voice wrestled its way into his mind.

You have not seen the last of me, Pún-ghat.

212

EPISODE 3
THE WRATH OF CARA

CHAPTER 1
PATHWAYS

The streets of Mod were covered in a fine dust blown in from the dry lands to the south and Boli bolted across them as fast as he could. He concluded his business in the dense street market behind him and fled. He felt sure he was being watched by unfriendly eyes through the thick crowd which packed the busy street, teeming with passers-by from all over and vendors and their goods. The ordinarily nocturnal city of Mod was alive and rambunctious already even though it was now only just past mid-day. The bright sun blazed hot in the clear blue sky, visible directly overhead, the view of which was only obstructed at times by the many arched spans of clay roof or waving awnings of canvas and hide above, providing shade and relief to the diverse folk moving about in the heat below. Music and laughter could be heard all around, echoing along the winding avenues lined with closely conjoined stone and clay structures and their open doors and windows. Cantinas and open bazaars filled with customers cast forth their noise: buyers were haggling with vendors; animals for sale or slaughter were locked in cages of woven wood and reeds, screeching in their discomfort; Human and Mogoli, Hidari and Turuks, Achellan and Irendi, and all other beings of this southern part of the world emerged from or entered into archways for commerce or business of unknown nature, all with a sense of haste as if they held to a specific purpose and had little time or inclination for distraction; bells or gongs sounded in the distance, probably from some auction or other, slaves perhaps; folk carried baskets on their shoulders; Hidari pulled taulkas along with their goods and supplies; nomads pulled kelgan and other strange beasts of burden, great *boros* from the deserts to the east, huge four-legged reptiles accustomed to the arid lands, used to haul heavy burdens great distances, from Serabat and even Darhúk on the other side of the Tanga; men rode by on horseback; a fowl of some kind bellowed and writhed in agony on the chopping block for a moment, it was mealtime. It was a typical busy day in the desert city. Soldiers of the Kunn stood guard in places and in the open here, and Boli came upon a guard troop at the top of a private and sealed off street, no admittance there. It was the estate of the notorious warlord and gangster Rash-Haba. The young Hidari knew this fearsome group had at least some ties to the Kunn, and though he was a Hidari himself and an aspiring Kunn fighter he knew better than to even show his face in that hostile territory, and departed past with a look from the guards of mixed race. Boli felt that they recognized him and it brought him comfort, feeling that the phantoms behind would not pursue him here. His heart eased a little as he darted through the crowds and beasts and neared his destination which he knew would provide him some level of safety. The open streets could be perilous for a lone child of his affiliation.

He finally turned into a building farther from the commotion. He passed through an enclosed arched passageway, the length of which was cast into dark shade and well concealed from view. The far exits on either end were bright and well lit from the sun by contrast. The clamor of the activity far behind him quickly lessened so that he could actually hear his breathing and footsteps, now echoing in the quiet, dark, corridor of stone. He stopped at a locked door and knocked, looking back fearfully at the street where he came for eyes which he expected to peer at him from around the edges. A small sliding door for viewing was opened above him and the eyes of the guard behind it recognized the boy. Boli could hear the disabling of the heavy bolt lock and the door was opened. He burst in, desperate for the safety it provided. He was allowed entrance but needed no escort. He passed inside, seeking the ulak. In this particular vault the Kunn was at work here manufacturing their secret burning pitch, powders, and other volatile substances and mixtures from their vials and flasks of unknown ingredients. The techniques and methods used in the creation of these potent compositions were undoubtedly stolen from an unfortunate engineer from afar, his mode and craft seized after he was killed, or simply purchased for use of the Kunn. The finished product was stored gingerly in barrels or kegs along the walls for their own use or sold to certain customers, foreign princes and lords or assassins with money and connections wishing to make an interesting and advantageous purchase for themselves. Clientele of the Kunn reached far and wide, and the Ahga took care of his paying customers. Boli found the ulak and delivered the large pouch of *kuth* weed which he purchased in the street. The boy had a prized pipe of his own on a necklace, the winnings of a bet some time ago, with gold letterings and engravings on the handle, very valuable. He was taught the potential of risky gambling and thus far had been successful. As payment for his petty services he was given some small amount of money and a portion of the weed for himself and he departed.

Boli believed the lies he was told about the Kunn, how enrollment in this clan was the path to tread if one wished to live. Many of the people here espoused the same ideas growing up on the streets and demanded allegiance or at least support of this rising clan. During his early childhood years he made it a point to establish his dominance and strength over others, and to thwart such aggressive behavior toward himself became his justification for his increasing recklessness. A force inside him preached a different mindset, one of peace with others, but in this hopelessly hostile atmosphere that was easily dismissed. He remembered a boy about his age one day, years ago, warning him against embarking on such a life and that the road to clanhood he was treading would surely lead to his early demise and a wasted life. These were words that would undoubtedly result in one's own cowardly death on these mean streets, if he hearkened to them. To become the object of subjugation and terror by others, as he had in the past, was an unacceptable alternative in this riotous city overrun with scum. To join the Kunn meant survival in this strife-ravaged region. The violent streets upon which he grew drove him to seek an organization from which he could derive strength and protection, and a source of purpose. He enjoyed the liberating feel of the power his criminal behavior and camaraderie brought him. His crimes troubled him little; life here necessitated and justified such. The streets he once tread in terror he now boldly strode without fear and dominated. Revenge against rival clans and gangs became his passionate mission. He would help uphold and strengthen the dominant force in the region against these weak trespassers. The Kunn will destroy them all in the end. The Divine One has proclaimed this.

Being young and new, however, and merely an aspiring apprentice to his fellow street thugs, he was not wholly trusted yet and was used to run errands or make small purchases for which he received a token payment. Once, about two years ago and before his reputation with the Kunn was established, Boli espied what he thought to be individuals of a different clan, Harikans of the Bará, rivals of the Kunn, trespassing suspiciously about the streets one evening. The Bará were mostly of the Harikan and Irendi race, a clan from the south who vied with the Kunn for dominance in the territory but were mercilessly crushed by the far superior clan. The Ahga possessed wealth and forces enough to easily exterminate competition and his brotherhood was far more organized and loyal. The Kunn also possessed their greatest weapon, their spiritual zealotry, a distinct advantage most other clans failed to claim, and this served as an anchor for their creed. The Bará were weak and disorganized by comparison, mere annoyances beside the greatness of the Kunn, and the Ahga drove them out of his new city and routed them to the sea or into the dunes of the Marak desert where they came from with ease. Their numbers were drastically reduced and what pathetic structure they had was almost completely obliterated, but they somehow survived and persisted, a

216

perseverance perpetuated by this cycle of vengeance. Lately they had experienced a bit of a resurrection right here in the Ahga's back yard. Either way, the rare sight of a handful of the Bará making their way about the Kunn-occupied streets of Mod in the dusk drew the boy's notice and he immediately informed an ulak with whom he was familiar. This earned him some thanks and Boli decided then that he would provide these villains with whatever services he could in the hopes of one day being fully accepted. The legend of the Mari was known to many and he desired its enviable and mystical possession. This belief became a driving force, the impetus of all in the clan. To join the ranks of the Brotherhood would deliver him to this great end and he sought to assist them in any way.

He continued to keep watch for these foreign rivals, and sure enough, on another evening of fear and tension, caught a glimpse of them again and followed them. This time they seemed to be heading away from the center of the city and the grand Harásh in the distance, where he knew his future lord dwelt. The boy watched them turn into a strange building. He waited outside for some time but the Harikans did not emerge and the boy concluded that this dwelling must be what they were inhabiting or conspiring in for the present in secret. Very daring to burrow so close to their enemies. Boli returned to the mansion where he knew he could communicate this information. The boy and his revelations were well received and a detachment of Kunn soldiers was dispatched immediately. The boy led them to the location and the clan quickly destroyed the Harikans.

Because of his continuing services and trustworthiness, and professed interest in the creed, Boli was granted some acceptance within some of the lower circles of the Kunn. He was sent on scouting missions and was successful in routing out any competitor activity in the city. The Bará had, in small measure, lately reestablished some presence in the urban areas of this unstable region. Mod and its many suburbs and slums saw a rising but still weak rival return like a stubborn disease, and the conflicts here which had experienced a brief respite during recent years reignited with their return. But folk were accustomed to it here and the sparse fighting between the clans went ignored by most. Boli enjoyed the power and position he held being a spy and runner for the dominant and more popular clan and the fear his presence invoked in others. The thugs on the streets he grew up on no longer harassed him but avoided him out of fear, for his association with those ruthless killers was now well established. The everyday folk in the city he once feared he now beheld with disdain and he hesitated not to victimize them as he attended brazen patrols along the streets or shows of force and acts of coercion in establishments in which the Kunn had business. He laughed at the wounded faces that he was met with by his victims and the weak common folk of his city which had no choice but to concede to the demands of his fellow oppressors, should they encounter them, and though some viewed him and his criminal brethren with passionate contempt and dared offer him opposition he chuckled to himself and returned their opinion with his own. Lambs and cattle, these multitudes are, he thought, how dare they offer me insolence. Boli would take what he wanted from whom he pleased and slay whatever lowly fool even looked at him in a manner he found displeasing or lacking in the humility and subservience he greatly desired from these too-outspoken subjects who thought they knew something of life and survival and the will of the Divine. His prolonged loyalty and dedication to the Brotherhood he worshipped delivered him the respect on the streets and the reputation and obedience he sought. The fear he had of one day being a victim himself, now that he was targeted and marked by other thugs who had reason to seek vengeance upon him, did increase greatly but went largely ignored. Boli was strong and the rest of the world would bow and obey him, for now he was one of them. His reputation would act as a shield to protect him.

But today that Hidari boy who had disclosed the aggressive and unacceptable activities of the trespassing Bará henchmen who now recognized him was being stalked. The informings of this interesting young member resulted in the deaths of many of their desperate comrades and impeded the defeated clan's attempts at some reestablishment in the city. The price on this ignorant fool's head was already high. He was followed at a distance through the clamorous streets until he united with some more of his bandana-clad associates. It appeared to be a golden opportunity, there were only a few of them, idling it seemed. While they congregated for a time outside a small cantina the rival thugs put a plan into effect to capture or kill this miserable Kunn rat.

The sun was sinking into the west and the evil day was drawing to a close when Boli and his Kunn friends concluded their business and departed for their separate dwellings. But when they looked up they saw armed Harikans heading straight for them down the dim and depopulated street. Boli could see their pale blue skin and long black hair and green eyes from a distance, swords drawn, their bodies adorned with rings and hideous metal piercings and ornaments to make themselves look more fearsome, not unlike the Kunn. There were six of them, double the strength of Boli and his two friends, and with nowhere close by from which to draw additional strength they immediately bolted in the opposite direction. The Harikans chased them down alleyways and narrow side streets, urging them into a planned route at the end of which the Bará would make their kill. The various folk and travelers paid them little heed but made way for them. Such violence was commonplace here and few would dare put their lives at risk to interrupt the crime, whatever it was. Boli found himself panting with fear as he and his friends were cut off from a sure escape and diverted into an alley by the arrival of another sortie of Harikans. The gang of about a dozen cornered Boli and his older and more experienced brothers in that dark, narrow alleyway from which there seemed no escape. Walls loomed up on three sides and the Harikans approached slowly, weapons drawn, calling Boli's name as if hungry for him, and he trembled at the sound of their taunting. He didn't think it would come to this. He thought his was a life well protected and never feared he himself would end a victim of revenge for the crimes he had committed. As he fended off death momentarily he turned to see his companions climbing over the wall to escape, leaving him to the victors who obviously had little interest in the other two. Boli looked up into the eyes of the friend he trusted and reached with his hand for assistance but instead was repulsed, denied passage and offered as sacrifice to allow the others their escape. *Uden og Kabba,* he said, a common phrase uttered by the clan, success or sacrifice, except this time it was meant about him. They didn't need this child, an expendable apprentice in their eyes. Boli's eyes went blank and his soul trembled at the realization that he had become the object of the same terror that he endorsed and propagated here. The warnings he had once disregarded as misguided and foolish and undesirable now made themselves known to his crying soul one last time and he finally submitted to them. But it was too late. He wondered how he let himself get persuaded into this nonsense in the first place. Before his eyes darkened permanently he thought he could see, beyond the chanting and rushing mob which reached for him, the face of another boy his age who he vaguely recalled some years ago warning him about such an end if he ran with those rogues.

Yalu was awoken that same morning by the whining of the old man's dog. The scrawny animal poked at its friend and the boy arose from his makeshift bed. He resided underneath the home of the old man which was nothing more than a scant shack of clay walls and scavenged wood pieces lashed together. A sizable hole existed underneath the hut, a small cave-like entrance only accessible from an opening in the floor of the dwelling. Previously it was the den of some wild beast of the desert but fled or was killed by its invaders. It was small but livable and therefore quite valuable in this slum. To the boy it was a castle of stone and quiet peace, his safe retreat from the elements and the insanity he witnessed daily, a hole he gratefully crawled into at the end of each day. He would not hesitate to eliminate another aspiring occupier. His hole was that precious to him. Everything Yalu had, including his meager but valuable shelter, he had worked and struggled for and he treasured what little he possessed like they were priceless. He bled for his survival and so would any other competitor who attempted to wrest these things from him, for he relied on it all for his own desperate livelihood in this hellhole.

But he considered himself well off for a lone teenage slum child. He had some hand tools including a knife which he used mainly to skin and fillet his food, some of which he caught himself, a small ceramic jug to hold water in his hole, a water skin for his daily traveling, a small gini stick for defense and walking, and a sizable pack which he sewed straps onto for easy carrying. He also had improvised candles and some small tools for the purposes of construction or repair of wooden or metal objects, or even leather, the remnants of which he dared not discard for they might prove useful. He even had a hammer and clamps and a file for simple metal work. Any piece of raw material or scrap can be used in the creation of something else, something he could use to make some needful object for himself or to sell on the streets, and he kept a small stash of these things hidden in his refuge. For Saipa, like the other slums of Mod, demanded the survival of its destitute inhabitants on its streets.

He stepped off his bed of wooden planks and onto the stone floor. These few salvaged planks of wood he had lashed together with some thick plant fibers which dried and solidified, a trick the old man taught him. This bed alone held great worth for the boy, not only in its use but because usable wood was scarce here. Desert trees were not ideal for most building, hence dwellings were constructed of clay. The Kunn seized many material shipments imported to these parts and little of it could be found anywhere unless one stole it. The folk long since stripped the barren lands of what few usable trees there were here and now they had to search farther and wider for this rare resource, unless one could afford to purchase it of the Kunn. For this reason most things were made of animal bones, earth or reeds, or stone, and the boy possessed ceramic items of his own and quickly learned the art of making them.

He hastily gathered his necessities for the day including things he wanted to sell, and slung his pack onto his back. The dog followed him out eagerly. The boy first grabbed the old man's water bucket. He always made it a point to reach the water hole early to avoid the crowds and he was rewarded by his punctuality and discipline. He drank his fill at the well, which was not far, filled his water skin and the bucket, and carried it back with some difficulty to the hut. The old man allowed Yalu his habitation under his hut for the boy offered him some level of living assistance, being old and half blind, and he delivered food and water and ran the necessary errands into the city. It was a small price to pay for that wonderful abode the boy loved, better in his opinion than these hot, smelly, bug-infested shacks everyone else lived in. It also provided him good concealment from the warlords which rode through the dusty roads on their steeds and kelgan-drawn chariots called *bahndas*. The Kunn often patrolled the slums and villages outside the city for suspects or rival clan members which may be seeking concealment in them, the Bará mostly or even the Hōsh, though these were rare, but they also extorted goods or food from homes and families. They would kill or enslave those they sought and those who concealed them, or anyone else they felt they needed for that matter, and the boy would cower in his hole and weep with terror and disbelief whenever they should ride through. Stories of people being buried alive or maimed for resistance were abundant. To see someone missing a hand or foot was not uncommon. Villagers and farmers were especially targeted and terrorized. Herds were stolen, looted granaries were burned, and the farmers forced to relocate, often to the city. Abductions were common. Strong laborers were needed constantly for the secret workshops of the Kunn, and the young especially were prized. He had a friend some years ago who was taken away by that fearful clan. Of the fates of those unfortunate souls he had heard rumors which kept him up at night, and the boy was more than careful to avoid crossing paths with those terrible, scarlet-clad riders.

It was still dark and the sun was just peeking over the horizon when the boy set off for the day. He left the old man a small loaf for breakfast along with his water. Yalu fed himself with another as he jogged along the dirt road to the city, still quiet and empty save for an occasional wanderer or scavenger in search of the same things he was. He found a rat trap in one of his numerous secret locations. He partially buried them in strategic places where he hoped no one would find them, under low shrubs or rocks, although he had lost a few to thieves in the past. He cleverly built them out of metal scraps and fashioned them in the shape of boxes with one end open for entry. It had a catch, which was the norm anyway, the vermin being in abundance, and he gave it to the dog to eat. He reburied it, being sure to rebait it with a fragment of his bread, and moved on to the next one. They all had catches and he placed the prizes in his pack. This would certainly fetch him a little money. Today was going to be a good day, he thought.

The city was a few miles away and he walked along hastily. He passed clusters of shacks and huts on either side. Tents of animal hide and canvas stirred gently in the cool morning breeze. Some caged fowl or creature made its voice heard somewhere. He passed a smoldering hulk to the side of the road, the home of some unfortunate victim of the Kunn probably, burned last night in a raid. Some corpses lay about, pondered over by some early bystanders. Piles of refuse lay about wantonly, scoured by carrion-fowl and stray animals. The scrawny black dog followed him silently, sniffing about at times in the hopes of finding some scrap to eat. Yalu could see some other boys ahead, gathering around something lying on the ground. It was a dead taulka beast, he could now see, a large one, probably expired from exhaustion or malnutrition. Yalu watched them enviously as he passed, dragging the find back to their hut for salvage. He could have made some use of that. Then he saw that this group had confiscated the prize from someone else who lay on the side of the road, beaten. The dog at Yalu's heels paused a moment to witness one of his fallen animal brethren and a look of sad understanding could be read in his fixed eyes. He turned away sadly and followed his master who he trusted to bring them both the necessities of survival. His master was unfailing in his arts of scavenging a living in this unforgiving place, a haven of villains and anarchy, and the dog rarely left his side. Yalu wanted to arrive at the market early to sell his goods and buy what he wanted before his competition beat him to it. He was not the only clever little scavenger in this impoverished neighborhood.

The boy looked upon the silhouette of the palace, visible even at this distance, its high turrets outlined by the rising sun. The four obelisks that surrounded it spiked upwards like obscene pillars of defiant power and independence. But the sight of it brought him no comfort. It was an abode of thieves, he knew, a symbol and shape that did not incite wholesome virtues at all such as justice, knowledge, and strength to defend its beloved people who were forced to worship it beneath its feet but instead filled the boy with terror and disgust, a repugnance of its corruption and disease, a symbol of the inevitable outcome of the oppression perpetrated by the ruling tyrants and their obedient overlords, it was. It was no mystery to the boy why his fellow countryfolk lived in perpetual poverty and unabated violence, products of their foolishness for which they cared not or were too weak to remedy. The folk were molded into a character symptomatic of this inescapable despotism. The reasons were all around him, and he looked at the approaching city with indescribable abhorrence and detestation.

The rulers of this rats' nest and their obedient henchmen were not the only ones to share the blame for the despotism here, however. The citizens themselves were certainly at fault as well, though they were ignorant to it. Their orphaned children ran about, scarcely clad, the by-products of widespread fornication and the innocent victims of the lack of principles and discipline by their elders who were held in unworthy esteem and followed. This fatherlessness lent to the gravitation toward thugs and warlords of power by the young, and a life of victimization and hopelessness by those who did not. Humility or compromise were not virtues that were practiced or even heard of here, only victory and survival. Clans and gangs strived constantly with each other for power in an endless cycle of atrocity and revenge, and most sided with one of them rather than denounce them all as the scum and criminals they were. Ever they sought redress against their bitter rivals, retribution being the prevailing code, casting all of society into the abyss of utter destitution. Things must be, the folk said regarding the plight of violence and poverty, and 'for such is the will of the Divine One' was all too readily procured as the usual justification to exempt themselves from due blame. The idea of abandoning petty differences and past grievances and forsaking foolish alliances which festered the misery and unrest was impossible for these incomprehensible heathens to even fathom and the boy had contempt for them all, shaking his head in disgust and frustration whenever he looked upon these mindless masses concerned solely with retribution and respect in their fellows' eyes, established through acts of violence and domination in the streets. And so this endless pattern of vengeance unaddressed by the corrupt government and espoused by the many resulted in their own misery and demise. Pride and unquenchable vindictiveness yielded perpetual destruction. Rampant poverty, widespread sickness, hunger and destitution were the reapings of the wicked as well as the simple, and despite this–to complete the boy's utter disbelief and disgust–an envy was harbored by these vile folk for those who were well in possession, those who had good fruit to show for their adherence to the principles their own fellow beings had abandoned.

Not all these folk were deserving of a fiery destruction, the boy knew. One day they would rise up against these criminals who had terrorized their lives and crushed their souls until they became prisoners of the hopeless society thus created. Those who felt as he did and held their homeland in self-inflicted and deserving disgrace were but the few unfortunate beneficiaries of the disease spawned by the corrupt and powerful, a power that was unjust, both the thugs of the streets and the royalty above who wielded and vied for it, and who cared for so little but their ever-growing hordes of wealth acquired by foreign lords and clans their city both above and below them festered with rot until it became a writhing pit of virtual anarchy. The boy knew he had no representation from the iron throne to which he was subject. He was a mere flea among a lowly swarm undeserving of the vast riches within the precincts of the Harásh which jutted outwards and upwards deep within the city. The lair indeed, muttered the boy, an estate of vast splendor in stark contrast with the endless sea of hovels which surrounded it. This derogatory name, however, was not to be uttered in the presence of the lord's subjects, but as they were rarely seen this far beyond the palace this danger was of little concern to him. The soldiers of the Lord Thuliak limited their activities to carrying out their lord's vain and spontaneous orders which merely had the best interest of himself and his contemptible regime at heart, and the territories beyond the concern of the maniacal ruler became the forgotten jurisdiction of the clans. Only within the heart of the city was any form of order kept. Thuliak cared little for events beyond his well protected circle of splendor. The masses could fend for themselves and the warlords could settle their own disputes, so long as the regime itself wasn't directly threatened. The boy muttered angrily to himself and continued his short journey to one of the street markets for the morning's business.

The boy spent his days literally living off of the highly trafficked streets. Anything of value he could find he collected, repaired, stitched, and sold. His rats always earned him some steady income, not only for their food but for their skins. He was always amazed at what the foolish of the city discarded or abandoned. One would think folk would be more careful about assuring themselves of possession of small necessities in an unpredictable environment such as this. But perhaps these vile people cared little. He was always picking up objects, for his eyes were downward, and his pack was almost always full of trinkets he could use or sell. It seemed as though positive fortune followed him where it abandoned others, for he held ideals unlike the folk which surrounded him daily. He believed in good fortune if one walked a life in accordance with just principles, that one had a choice to breed good or evil and by this establish what he was and what he proliferated in the world, the product of his character, and to help and fairly treat others was also favor received. Several times he had given a portion of his hard-earned food or money away to some other street orphans, like himself, but less fortunate. During times such as this, though he yielded to an inner call which forced him to show kindness, he felt as though he suffered an incompensatory loss but was always mysteriously re-met with sustenance and fortune, usually more than was necessary for him. Perhaps he was favored by some intangible power or force which protected and delivered him to some greater end that would soon come to pass. It may be that some grace and wordless guidance was granted to this singular and thoughtful boy, surviving among the disdainful, and was worthy of the lone ray of light which sought desperately here for a flower to shine upon which may bring forth good fruit. He spoke his thoughts on his beliefs at times in the past to certain individuals he came across in his many romps. Taking up arms for selfish and vengeful purposes with the clans as an alternative to a futile (in their opinion) honest life will bring only more death and misery to all, he told them when confronted about his allegiance or whether he would join the ranks of the warlords one day. But to those who craved the bloody justice and fruitless victory they eagerly sought, words like these were quickly hushed and extinguished from thought.

He trudged on doggedly through the city which he was very acquainted with, selling what he knew he could to buyers seeking it. He purchased what he needed for himself and his two dependents, all the while steering clear of the trouble which erupted around him at times. Often he was even paid to run an errand or two for a vendor or lord he trusted, and found ways to acquire some food for himself and his little faithful friend in the process. Overall, despite the embedded chaos and foolishness surrounding him he somehow made it through each day with minimal difficulty or misfortune, indeed he usually succeeded well with plenty to spare. But he did not let this soften his discipline or resolve. Anything extra he earned or collected was saved to give him a fighting chance the next day.

Well his scavenging for the day was coming to an end. The sun was westering. He closed his pack which contained some new items along with a fair amount of food for himself and the old man. He saw some commotion a few streets ahead in the fading sunlight. It must be some unfathomable clan violence again for he could plainly distinguish some Harikans of the Bará abruptly rush down an alley out of sight, and from it some bystanders fled to leave the gangsters to their bloody business. The boy hid behind a stone upright, trembling, his eyes filling with tears of anger and fear. Will this lunacy ever end, he thought, and he wept. He turned again to look a few moments later and saw the heinous villains rapidly emerge and depart, looking about them with their filthy blades drawn, undoubtedly watching for a Kunn death squad for this was deep in their territory. They retreated through the streets quickly, close enough for the trembling boy to see their jubilant faces as though they accomplished their raid. They disappeared in a twinkling and the boy arose. He jogged in the direction whence they came. He turned into a closed alley and saw a body on the ground at the far end. All was quiet save for the distant echoes of the vile music piping from the numerous dens of filth in the city.

He ventured a closer examination of the corpse, driven by his instincts of scavenging and recovery. A Hidari, he thought, probably the Kunn, and they should be here soon. The possibility of the body holding something of value was worth a risky look. He hastily pored through the bloody clothes. The Harikans must have taken his money for there was none, but Yalu did find an interesting gold-embroidered pipe of ivory on a necklace that had displaced itself to the back of the body and fortunately went undetected or ignored. It was still intact, miraculously. He didn't have much time. He could hear cries in the near distance, dangerously close, just around the corner and he shook with terror. He placed the pipe around his own neck and scrambled over the wall to escape the inevitable Kunn counterattack. If he was found near the body of one of their own the boy would be seized and questioned, then killed or enslaved. He could hear and feel the vile voices of the thugs coming closer and he fled in terror, his breaths coming in gasps, until he was a safe distance away and carried onward, hoping no potential informer observed him in the vicinity of the murder. His thoughts went to the dog he had no choice but to leave behind and abandon on the spot. The boy didn't dare even turn around to find him. The dog knew his way around and he could only hope that it escaped the gangsters and was now jogging home alone. Perhaps he would meet it again in the morning and be awoken by its endearing cries. But in the meantime he felt as though · he were being pursued and he hastened homeward with many a fearful look over his shoulder. The red sun went down behind the Harásh and the boy could see it plainly imposed in all its grotesquery. Another day of survival drew to a close, and as he fled for home he wondered if he would see another and if it would always be this way.

* * *

Damian and Cam finally pulled up to the disheveled and disintegrating old stone building below which lay their hideout, the Cave. They spent the previous afternoon and well into the evening galloping along the winding paths of the Northwall en route to Hera, and by the early morning light rode in haste down the hillside, their great steed leaving a trail of rising dust in its powerful wake. They turned over in their minds the events of the day before at Draga's tower and the secrets they received there and in what possible fashion they could be best put to use. Little did they know of the circumstances of the sea to the west and even less of the great ruler to the north or his subjects abroad, and the relevance of it all. From what little they gathered in the perilous environment of the tower high above and far behind them their enemies were afoot even in the seas, and undoubtedly sowing some chaos and destruction there. The Kunn, it seemed, knew no boundaries or limits in its quest for prestige and wealth and would use any weapon or means to acquire it. *The Ahga is versatile*, thought Damian as he tore through the breezy night. *My objective carries me even to the distant shores of this country and to the sea. And what is it they seek there?* Seafaring folk of all origin have already been the victims of their tyranny, he doubted not. And the matter of the disclosed secret of the Ahga and the lord of Mod would have to be postponed for a time due to the apparent urgency of the present situation which called them to the west. They would need a plan and a means to effectively exploit that dangerous information anyway. In the meantime consultation with their advisor was clearly necessary to properly digest and process these heavy tidings, and a course of action to decide upon. They passed unseen through the porous confines of the city in the early dawn and reached the debris-encircled first floor archway of the old building, standing eerily vacant in its abandoned and isolated row of a host of others.

They passed through the foreboding, dark entryway and continued down the wide hall, still mounted. The halls were wide and lofty for several to ride mounted easily. A small host could be concealed here were the structure not so severely compromised. Chunks of stone and bits of rubble

226

lay about on the shifting floor and the rats made themselves at home. Cracks existed in walls, small fissures opened in places above or below the riders, and water dripped incessantly, forming pools in dark corners and along the seams of crumbling partitions. Large pieces of the stone ceiling above them had fallen onto the first floor, blocking certain areas from access. Light struggled to find its way in from the outside and the darkness and poor condition of the structure made one feel as though he were entering a forgotten tomb. The riders used the side entrance which was virtually invisible to view from the front and other sides owing to the debris which littered the outside of it. The front main hallway beyond the entrance was booby-trapped with spraying spikes, activated by pressure plates spread about the floor, and a pit which opened suddenly before the feet of the unsuspecting intruder, should he elude the hidden plates, and ejected him into the newly constructed underground waterway which ran alongside the small cluster of ruined and condemned buildings which comprised the Hole of Helbius. Had not the secret inhabitants taken the precaution of reinforcing key areas of the structure with steel columns this crumbling old tomb would probably collapse one day soon, along with the others, into the watery deep. They felt it fitting, somehow, that their campaign should be launched from such an inglorious habitation.

The riders reached the end of the hall and turned left down some narrow steps until they came to a large open room with a heavy steel door mounted on the floor. They dismounted and Cam turned an inconspicuous metal ring bolt located on the distant wall. This released the long, heavy metal arms connected to and protruding under the floor in a parallel direction from the steel door which acted as a counterweight underneath to open it. The heavy door, without handles or grip of any kind, slowly pivoted on the thick steel pin which served as the fulcrum and rose steadily until it was at right angles with the floor. The two descended into the secret passageway revealed beneath, climbing down yet another flight of stone steps, followed by their black horse. Due to the weight and length of the steel arms affixed to the door and the leverage they provided, these counterweights were effortlessly pushed upward into the recession above them and back into place, securely latched with mounted, retractable metal hooks linked to the ring bolt outside and easily detached manually from the inside. The massive door to the underground vault shut slowly and silently behind them. The grim passageway within was illuminated by oil lamps placed on the walls at intervals to either side. They soon arrived at the landing several levels below the building. A large opening was made in one of the walls of the spacious vault underneath and the figures passed through this and into the compartment beyond.

They found themselves alone in the underground dwelling which they had transformed into an adequately furnished and habitable living quarter and base of operations. Their dwelling was well concealed though it was actually not far from the main activity of the city center which lay almost two miles away. The horse had a room of his own and it was into this that he entered without guide for his rest and nourishment. Damian and Cam tended to their wounds with some of Riman's elixirs and ointments. These potent and strange mixtures, in numerous vials on the several shelves along the walls, many of which held vessels and pots of various plants and herbs, were effective enough to heal the worst wounds in a short time. They disencumbered themselves and took some food and rest until Riman returned.

He returned some hours later carrying a crate of various and strange ingredients and small metal parts and tools. He placed it on one of his workbenches, cluttered with his odd projects and vials of strange compounds. Damian emerged with Cam and Riman looked up.

"Things went ill with Gadrin, then?" he asked. "I did not expect you back so soon." He donned an eyepiece which magnified the small objects he began to piece together.

"Not wholly," replied Damian. "We were able to discover the information he was carrying. Seems the Ahga is robbing Thuliak in Mod."

Riman nodded to himself knowingly. "This does not come entirely as a surprise. The Kunn in Mod has been under suspicion of that for some time," he replied while filing some pieces, small springs and gears they looked like, for one of his prototype crossbows, "and now it is confirmed. We need to make Thuliak aware of this in a fitting manner. Using one foe to cripple the other is an efficient way to eliminate them both."

"He also mentioned a new target," said Damian, "a certain Ralen from Demar. He's a Demarian officer and diplomat of high status, evidently en route, by ship, to Prova. The Ahga wants to capture him and his associates aboard in the hopes that Kane will finally seek compromise with him."

Riman stopped and looked up at Damian with a look of doubt. "He could be utilized for far more than just that," he added. "I find it difficult to believe that the Ahga knows so little about him. Or perhaps he chooses to overlook his greater value, very unlikely. Or maybe the spy didn't tell you everything."

"How so?" Damian asked.

"Why the Lord Ralen is the favored diplomat to Dinitia," Riman replied. "He has great favor with the rulership of that country. I'm sure the Ahga can find a way to pry something more valuable from such a man. Secrets of the *Tarsh,* or ruler there, the riches he conceals which the Ahga would love to gain access to, and his policies, with whom he has dark allegiances, if any, or even ransoms or business coercion possibilities, can all be discovered and exploited. Dinitia is a powerful trade force in the area.

228

Though on the whole Dinitia is a respectable country, one that would not readily ally itself in any way with a band of organized thugs such as the Kunn. But the Ahga could discover from him someone who would. Ralen is well acquainted with the nobility there."

Cam spoke for the first time. "Gadrin did mention something else of interest," he said, stepping forward, "one final revelation before he was killed. He said the Kunn have lately taken to the seas to pirate sea faring vessels in the Vidian Sea, and in particular are focusing their activities in the Marán Islands. Reports of ships of prey ambushing unsuspecting merchant vessels in the area have surfaced. He impressed upon me that he felt certain the Ahga was up to something there, something considerable, that there was an operation of some kind ongoing more than simply looting ships but perhaps planning an attack or move of a much larger scale. Something big is going on out there." He fingered some new throwing stars.

Riman paused and thought a moment and considered this. "He can't mean the fortress and treasury of Spen Mala," he said finally, removing his eyepiece. "It's too heavily guarded. The Ahga must be ambitious indeed if he thinks he can pull that off. Did he lose a bet to one of his scum friends in Darhúk? Perhaps there is aught within that he seeks. But there can be no other obvious explanation. Wealth in abundance lies within the treasuries of the Tarsh." He paced about and shook his head, lost in thought. He looked up at the confused stares of his young comrades.

"Spen Mala is an old fortress built into the great cliff that overlooks the inlet cove on the island of Paladica in the Marán island belt, about fifty miles off the east coast of Dinitia. These islands are part of Dinitian jurisdiction but are quite large enough to hold settlements on the greater of the land masses. There are actually scores of islands that make up Maranisia and the people there are referred to or are at least considered separate and somewhat independent of the mainland. Ports there are on several of the islands, Paladica being the largest and most frequented of them. Trade and commerce is conducted routinely there, and exchange of goods and money. The Marán Islands are governed almost independently, being but a state of Dinitia, and they have their own affairs and livelihood. They keep their own wealth on the premises, locked and guarded in Spen Mala. A fair company of guards is barracked there for it is rumored that artifacts of old and relics of the past are locked secretly within the fortress' precincts, probably remnants of the ancient civilization which existed there thousands of years ago, before modern-day Achellans, and have long since been extinct. Temples and tombs and other ancient structures and dwellings exist on all the islands, above or below them in some cases. Though they are assured to contain gold and riches few venture into them for it is said that they are cursed, and those that dare disturb or delve into

229

the secrets within are never seen again. So the natives say. As for the old fortress I have little doubt that much gold is stored there, and gems and plates and other items the Kunn would love to have, conveniently unearthed and stored by a people the Kunn would love to injure. Attack there would be difficult to be sure but perhaps a determined force with speed and surprise might stand a chance. And the Kunn certainly have the means and determination such a near futile undertaking requires. Perhaps Gadrin is right, Spen Mala is an attractive target, though there certainly are others. Maybe the Ahga *is* up to something over there. And he hopes to somehow utilize Ralen in this endeavor? It is plausible. He must be sailing out from Pomay then. Has he departed?" Riman continued his constructions.

"Possibly," answered Damian. "Gadrin wasn't able to deliver his warning."

"And what ship will carry him?"

"It is called the *Advent.*"

"Of course, one of the lord's own flagships." Riman stopped dead and looked up again. "If they can somehow manage to capture a prestigious ship of the line with the standards of Demar, carrying diplomats and probably a small host of other dignitaries, who knows what they can accomplish or demand. They could sail right in. But no, they can't have the means yet to do it."

"It seems the spy was right, then," said Damian. "We don't have much time. Not only do we need to speed to Prova but we also need to arrange for passage aboard a man-of-war with a crew willing to help us. We may have a confrontation on the seas on our hands."

"Finding a ship will not be so difficult," replied Riman, and he resumed work on his prototype. "As I understand it, piracy and rogue vessels in the Vidian Sea are suspected of being behind the mystery of some disappearing ships of late. Based on the testimony of Gadrin and his apparent urgency in the matter it is reasonable to assume the Kunn are behind it. The Achellans have recently renewed their efforts against this elusive plague, with some help from Demar for they share a common interest. They have always patrolled the Strait in the past but do so more aggressively now due to this new threat. I think the chances are fair that you could find a captain willing to assist you in your attempt to thwart this danger and eliminate it. It is in the mutual interest of both parties. Perhaps all you'll need to divert him from his routine is some monetary persuasion."

Riman walked over to the safe he built into one of the niches which occasioned the walls. These niches were only some few vertical gaps in the stone walls formed by columns which supported the heavy floor overhead and were easily large enough for a man to walk into with space to spare above and to the sides. The amount of wealth he had locked within necessitated two heavy steel doors which opened to the walk-in compartment, equipped with shelves and racks to hold the great quantity of coins and gems carefully arranged inside. Riman still manufactured items of garvonite, the value of which had inexplicably and exponentially increased due to a recent supply shortage. He knew of the reason for this, though he kept it to himself, and seized the advantage his mysterious craft would bring him in time of short supply. He still had his customers, unaware of his secret purposes of course, and they left him in little want of money. Riman removed a small portion he felt would suffice, including other possible expenses for their journey, and gave it in a small case to Damian.

"I see you have wounds," he said, looking them over. He produced from a cabinet two vials of unknown substance which he made them drink. "More potent than hyr by all accounts. My composition includes *tylia,* a rare herb found only in the mysterious jungles of the Palmwood, with a dose of kinsweed concentrate. A month's pay apiece, they cost to make, but you'll see that they're well worth the expense."

Once again they reequipped themselves with the novelty items of Riman's secret stockpile. Damian made sure his quiver was full, again closely examining the arrows. *You sure can't find arrows crafted like this,* he thought, placing them carefully inside. He also placed in his pack several vials of Riman's healing elixir. They packed more food for they would be gone for days at least, possibly weeks, though they could resupply in Prova once they arrived there. Riman looked over their blades and applied a small level of treatment to them. He carried them as though they were his children and were precious, for he had labored to create them. Damian's sword actually bore some scars and other signs of intense struggle and Riman looked over it with concern and scrutiny.

"This has undergone some use," he remarked. "It takes abuse of the worst kind to leave marks such as this on a blade of garvonite. Against whom or what has this weapon been pitted?" He looked hard at Damian.

Damian's eyes became removed and went cold, as if a heavy memory was being relived in his mind, an aching of his soul was reignited. A grim look of concern crossed his face for a moment and he took a breath before his eyes again met Riman's.

"An enemy of unprecedented power," he said finally and with some difficulty, "not limited to this earth, such as I myself possess, one which I shall have to face again and ultimately eliminate, this I know in my heart." Damian turned and took a few paces aside and looked upwards, clenching his fists and challenging something, a memory within, and he gritted his teeth. Cam looked up with understanding at his friend. Damian would not describe in detail to Riman the events that took place on the bridge the day before or the deadly foe that stood against him and set wound to his flesh, one which undoubtedly possessed powers such as Damian and favor from an unknown force or being which presided over him. The incredible relevance on earth these two held was a subject he was not sure an agnostic realist like Riman could properly appreciate, and he felt, for the time being, that this should be concealed from him. He thought of the unearthly storm in all its rage about them in their memorable moment of deadly struggle, seemingly prearranged and eagerly anticipated, and knew he and his foe were centerpieces utilized by forces which lay elsewhere but which strove with each other. Gifted executioners and subjects of their respective powers, they were. The mere existence of this foe alone and the unfortunate necessity of the destruction of it and all it represented brought great sadness to Damian's tearing eyes. Such things should not be, though they were allowed nonetheless by a being which endowed all with a free will, even to rebel if chosen, and Damian felt an incredible sympathy. Only with Cam did he confide about the conflict on that high bridge with what he doubted not would prove to be the greatest of his foes. On the ride homeward he assured Cam that another meeting would inevitably take place and that care was needed. It was not the enemy himself or even death that Damian feared, for he had already partially experienced that which lies beyond, but failure under the eyes of the power that saved him. And a heavy failure it would be indeed, one that mortals even as wise as Riman or perhaps even the Ahga could not fully grasp the importance of. Damian could claim a victory over him to be sure, but it was only momentary. Their first engagement was decisive but he could not be sure he would triumph over this matter in the end, a matter which grew in complexity and depth. He began to question and ponder this evidently deep matter into which he had become involved, and who exactly Tog was, or even the Ahga, he realized he didn't quite know. Since his encounter with Tog and the words he had Damian found himself with more questions than answers, and the familiar rumors of ancient legends now drew sober consideration. He did know his enemy was not destroyed but was undoubtedly preparing his inevitable counterattack, one that would be more prepared and focused this time. Even now Damian could perceive a will, distant and subdued, but stealthy with a hunger for vengeance, bent upon him.

Riman looked sidelong at Damian but at length withdrew himself and took the great weapon from him and set to work on it. Cam offered to change the subject.

"What news of Marcus and the Council?" he asked as he refilled his case of heavy throwing stars. "Any word on the outcome of the altercation the night before?"

"Indeed yes," Riman replied as he filed and ground the blade. "The clan in Hera is all alive with the news of the appearance of and first real encounter with their new great enemies. Our network is realized. They'll be looking for us. The assassination attempt on Markuso has failed, though there will be others. Marcus will keep an eye on him. Our sly intruders of the other night will not be speaking of their discovery to anyone. Marcus has maintained silence these past couple of days since he has eluded discovery once again by those in the chambers of the palace. He fears his disclosure but he is sly and cunning. The highest ranking member of the Kunn in Hera, and himself one of the Baccád, is slain. Helbek must be beside himself with wrath, as must be the Ahga. The Baccád will have to select another to fill Mozep's place here. The Ahga will probably send a sortie of his trusted diplomats from Mod to knock a few heads over at the palace, Helbek included. The Ahga does not tolerate disorganization of this magnitude, but we can also take advantage of this moment of undersight. The betrayal of Draga will enrage him most. Were it not for his treasonous attempt to capture the prize for himself, the secret may have remained safely concealed. Mozep was given orders to slay the prisoner Gadrin should his attempts to bring him fail or be threatened. He did not succeed in this matter either."

Cam interjected here with a question. "I noticed some distinctive stripe marks on Mozep's neck. What is this an indication of?"

"It is a rank designation awarded by the Ahga for his closest following. When a member completes a number of given tasks and is successful in his next *chun-vok,* or test of spirit and strength, they are branded on the sides of their necks with a *shukk* mark for services and proven loyalty to him and the code they follow."

"The Mari," said Damian under his breath.

"Yes," Riman replied with a look of astonishment at Damian. "It seems you know something of them, a lesson learned on your adventure perhaps? It is said that the Mari can only be truly practiced by the Adovan race, the Hakai, but the Ahga and his followers have taken up the cause of Adin, the conceiving founder of the creed, bethinking themselves rightful possessors of his legacy. It is not simply a band of common villains we strive against. The Baccád of the Kunn is practically a cult following. The Ahga chooses only the most dedicated and ambitious of his followers for admittance consideration. But this is extremely rare. The number of the Baccád is strictly limited to thirteen. The chun-vok is an extremely brutal and painful ritual and anyone that survives it is mighty indeed, many have even been killed in the process. But the clan practices many rituals and trials, and so the Ahga weeds out the weak. Indeed they are to be feared. But the less you know of them the better. Of Draga's force in the tower, were there any survivors?"

"None," answered Damian. "They were all destroyed."

Riman looked again at him doubtfully. "In that case it is to be hoped that the Ahga will not discover that someone is aware of his crimes against

Thuliak, someone who could put this information to use to destroy him. Yes, the Ahga will be enraged at this gross failure. That is well." He handed Damian his sword once he had finished with it. "Otherwise Kunn activity remains fairly routine. The Ahga is expecting a large shipment of Ceneaen gold and gems from Thecenea, a country south of Adovia, and kuth weed and ivories from Dengland. These goods will be brought initially to a checkpoint in Mod for his inspection, then redistributed here in the north. Marcus and I will monitor these supply movements while we formulate a plan to hopefully spark a major problem in Mod between the Ahga and Thuliak." He handed Damian a map. "Find out what the Kunn is up to over there. Seek the Semáris, the sea-dragons of Marán. They will help you."

CHAPTER 2
THE SCOURGE OF THE SEAS

It was just after mid-day when Bish burst forth from the watery and shifting Hole of Helbius and galloped through the streets carrying his masters who chose the swiftest way through the city and out to avoid eyes. He sensed that his master had great need of haste and could not risk being delayed, and there were enemies who could do just that if Ratarra was spied. Though the multitudes who received the astonishing news of a strange new enemy of that despised brotherhood called the Kunn which had infested their lordship and city and enchanted the unwary would cry out in elation if they saw and recognized the horse-backed heroes riding past them, there were many others with a keen eye who would find their presence quite interesting. It was widely known that there were agents eagerly willing to pay for information such as this, and that assassins of the Ahga in search of a bounty combed through the city and countryside. But of the deeds committed by those phantom killers folk could only guess at and fall silent. The unusually bloody and high profile engagement which took place only nights ago, however, could not be concealed despite efforts, and word was indeed spoken within certain circles of knowledgeable individuals of an incredible setback suffered by the Kunn, indeed it was a shock, caused by the introduction of these interesting new characters. The great horse sped in haste along quieter roads to exit the city to the north. They passed through Vadian Gate, through the verdant uplands of Shadím, and finally rode with haste upon the West Road to Prova and its suburbs. The cloaked and hooded riders could only hope they didn't draw any unwanted attention for their purpose and could not allow for any delay, indeed they felt there was little chance of beating their enemies to their objective.

They quickly raced down the declining road and left the Brown Hills behind them. After passing the obstructing walls of the cliffs which comprised the Plateau of Hera they could see the great sister-city of Gyla behind them and soon that became distant. They had descended to the flatlands below the Plateau and expected a hasty journey to their destination. The land from the coast eased slowly to the east for almost a hundred miles before it gradually steepened into the Brown Hills and

Plateau of Hera and dropped again to the south before the Ella River. From here it quickly leveled off to a dry and hard wasteland stretching beyond to the east into Dengland. The land to the west of Hera and north of the river was fairly fertile and hospitable and the main road held its lone way for many miles before it began to branch occasionally to the left or right to smaller villages and settlements. Nomads and herders could be found out here on the plains, driving their flocks and cultivating their wares to eventually sell in the city. Their blessed horse carried them tirelessly and as swift as the wind, requiring neither food nor rest, and the miles fled behind them faster than time could seem to keep pace. They soon crossed the great Geladine Bridge, which traversed the perilous Cloven Gorge, a dry, rocky ravine and split in the earth which ran several miles in a north-south direction. They paid their tolls to the guards and quickly departed without questions or taking time to look upon the spectacle. The riders galloped for hours more without rest or incident, though they passed many other travelers on the way heading to east Gyla. By evening they finally reached the village of Duri, fifteen miles east of Prova where they sought lodging for the night. They found a shabby old house called the Crossroads Inn, stabled their horse, and afterward entered the common room for they needed information and hoped they could find one of the locals with whom they could converse. The assembly was sizable enough with a fairly even blend of travelers though the place looked as though it could hold far more. A slow night, they guessed it was. They seated themselves at the bar and ordered some supper before posing a question to the bartender.

"Tell me my friend," said Damian, "how are events here of late?"

The barkeep stopped before them and looked them over for the first time. "Good, very well, thank you," he replied. "But I must admit the mood of my patrons has notably changed for the worse these past couple of years. Since the deaths of the rulers in the twin cities corruption and secret alliances with dark foreign powers have bred nervousness and fear. The scum that has apparently achieved some influence in the twin cities have none out here, so far at least, though they are often rumored of. Businessmen from Prova and Bren trade heavily with those inland cities and there has always been growing concern about possible business affectation. But of these foul characters there has been little presence thus far in these parts thankfully, though the day cannot be long postponed and people are fearful. The corrupt have money and power and can do as they please. Travelers will bring report, but as most of them are wealthy they seldom make any journey without armed escort. They are aware of the brigands in the east that have set up roost here and travel prepared."

"What of the seas to the west? It is brought to my attention that some strange piracy or other is at work there and that ships have disappeared with no report. Can you tell us anything?"

"Nothing for certain," the barkeep replied. "Some Dinitian sailors stopped in some weeks ago speaking of such a thing. They do have a handful of ships from what I've been told, patrolling the Strait, trying even now to counter the problem. I wouldn't be surprised if it was pirates, it's happened before. Good luck to the captains and their crews, I certainly hope they do catch the scum behind it all. It's going to hurt business."

"Where can I find these crews and captains when they are ashore?" Damian asked.

"Normally they stop in to Prova for resupply and there are several inns and taverns of course along the port, one in particular called the Wharf's Edge. I think you'll find the best captains there."

Damian placed a gold piece on the bar, offered his gratitude and the two retired to their room for the evening without further event.

They awoke early, ate a quick breakfast, and sped off again on the main road. The landscape remained fairly flat with occasional low ranges of tree- and brush-covered hills which the road wound through or around. They encountered many lesser roads now which branched from it in either direction. These and villages became more frequent as the city and coast drew nearer. They passed nomad riders and caravans heading to or from Hera. Folk seemed decent enough, offering words of greeting or simply a nod as they passed, hard workers seeking commerce. Damian and Cam soon found themselves among a small crowd heading into the city. The road rose up steadily for a time before it dipped back down again in an easy decline before the sea on which the city was situated. The riders slowly reached the pinnacle by mid-day and saw before them the layout of the port city of Prova stretched out in a semi-circle along the entire waterfront which was visible from the high point where they halted. They could see many paved streets climbing throughout the sea of tall structures and apartments of white clay stone, and many folk and beast traversing them, making their way up the incline or down to the heart of the city. The entirety of the settlement descended along a vast ramp, rounded in a wide half-circle. From this vantage point it looked as though they could walk along the brown and orange tinted roofs of mortar and clay plate tiles until they reached the water far below. At the bottom of the descent, jutting out into the sea adjacent the waterfront, were several islets upon which stood the keep of the city, the Tower of Opulis, pointing up like a cylindrical watchpoint to observe the sea and its ships. Gulls and seabirds circled about and wailed. Many moored ships could be seen in the wide harbor with their tall masts and furled sails, tied along the many docks which branched out from the lengthy boardwalk.

Damian urged Bish forward at last and they plunged into the city with the other folk. There was no wall around it for the rocky rise at the inward or eastern end served as a natural protection from land raiders, offering defenders a shield and point of defense at the apex, and here a garrison was stationed on guard. The difficult slope denied riders on horseback or other mounts little other means of ingress due to the steepness of the decline below it, though this was not much of a threat anyway. The rulers of the city funneled all traffic through a few inlet roads carved into the rocky pinnacle to allow one access to the port below, and around the entrances to these roads were guardposts, well manned at all times, with barricades of stone and entry portcullises. Prova was a strong and wealthy city and well defended, still preserving its independence from its somewhat estranged sister cities which the folk here knew had been lately penetrated by a powerful foreign clan. The rise in distrust was evident. Many armed guards were present due to the recent increase of threat from abroad and they paced about on duty, on the ground or upon the thick, low wall where they overlooked the travelers and supply vans. Many folk were stopped and questioned briefly about their intents and purposes here and carriages were inspected. Scribes there were with thick scrolls seated near the points of entry logging in names. Guards inspected goods and checked names of travelers against their books, looking for fugitives and men wanted by the state, but on the whole it was not overly intrusive. This level of security actually suited the two mounted strangers well and they were pleased with it. Damian and Cam were halted before the entrance and questioned momentarily.

The guard looked over the cloaked strangers quickly. "What are your names?" he asked.

"Adus of Tirien," Damian responded, "and this is my nephew Senzu." The scribe beside him went to work.

"What is your business here?"

"We seek to rendezvous with an old friend from Casten. He's coming by boat and should have arrived recently. We are to meet at the Wharf's Edge, a common gathering place as I understand it. Could you tell me how one arrives there?"

"Simply follow this road to the bottom," the guard replied and pointed down toward the waterfront. "You'll find it on the boardwalk, right in front of that Ceneaen galley, the three-master with the red standards on her stern, yonder. Just pulled in yestereve with a load of silks and leathers. You can see a brave soul working on the high royal now, must be eighty feet up. They should feel lucky to have escaped the phantoms of the Strait. They've been a bit of a problem lately."

"I seek to end that as well," muttered Damian under his breath. The guard didn't quite hear him but Damian simply offered his thanks and was waved through.

They found the Wharf's Edge with little difficulty. The road from the city entrance held its main course directly to this main point of attraction. The boardwalk was vast and deep, running the entire length of the inlet that formed the wide Port of Prova, also called by sailors City on the Sea, for the mass of buildings and homes built on the inclined crescent were visible from a great distance and structures were built right on the boardwalk which protruded from the land, and a multitude of docks and berths accommodated the fleet of different ships that were moored here. The entire wharf and dock area was easily longer than two miles from horn to horn including the dry docks and repair yards located to the south where a handful of ships was always present for refit or maintenance. Masts and rigging of tall ships nearly blotted out the sky to the west and sailors from all over performed their duties of unloading, embark or service. Damian and Cam stood upon the boardwalk in front of the establishment for a moment looking about them before heading inside.

"Reminds me of home and my early days as a wharf rat," said Cam scanning the area, his eyes blinking in the bright noon sun. Damian looked at him with understanding. Cam told stories of the sea to Damian when they were prisoners in Khala, but it could not convey the beauty and majesty that Damian's first experience and view of the ocean revealed to him. It did not daunt him, unless it was the vastness and respect that the sea demanded, but he rather felt drawn to it, an invigoration, excitement and mortality commonly felt by those who behold the power and awesomeness of the great and moving water. Cam's exciting and wonderful boyhood tales were feeble indeed in view of the greatness in front of them, and failed to properly portray the arresting spectacle though he loved to listen to them then. Those stories helped deliver him away from the horror which beset them, and Damian yearned to listen to Cam's descriptions of an exciting place he had never seen. Now the ships which floated idly before him seemed to call him and he felt a desire to leap onto the high masts and command them with the churning sea rolling beneath. He shook his head. His enemies would find a way to corrupt even this great avenue of delight, he reminded himself as he looked out into the distant blue horizon. Already the sea, which he had only beheld for a moment, seemed less friendly and more threatening.

He shrugged off his reveries. They turned away and brought their horse to the corral outside and Damian gave him instructions to wait, whispering to him in a passive voice. Tying or tethering a blessed and intelligent beast such as Bish was not necessary, nor would Damian have it. He wanted immediate availability to his steed in time of want, unshackled. He purchased some feed from the stable boy, informing him that this horse would need care for an extended period of time. Damian tipped him well, to the boy's surprise and delight, saw to it that his horse was cared for and went inside.

They looked about them upon entering. Many of all race were present, from far to the south in distant countries like Thecenea or Hepésh, or from Pomay to the north, along with Achellans from across the Strait and Maranisia, here for layovers between stops along the coast and the midday meal. An Achellan, of seemingly elevated status and experience by the looks of him, slowly approached as if to leave when Damian courteously accosted him and sought to learn information.

"Pardon me friend," Damian said as he approached. "I understand the Strait is under siege of pirates. Do you know whence they come and what kind of people they may be?"

The Achellan stopped before Damian and his friend and nodded knowingly, and not with a pleasant look. "Yes," he replied heavily, "it is rumored that brigands of the Kunn prowl the waters of the Strait, between the continents, foul folk from far to the east and south of the mainland. Whoever it is, these phantoms of the dark sea have struck six times this year alone, and of the victims or their ships there is no sign or tale, nothing to discover that might explain this strange plague."

"How then do you know the Kunn may be behind it?" Damian asked.

"One who claims to have survived a raid brought us revelations of these unfortunate events. Though there are many who doubt his tale of ghost ships beating down the Strait in the dark, unseen all this time, I for one can believe him. His eyes are convincing."

"Who is this person?"

"Vadro Alladakis is his name," he responded and pointed to a corner where a lone man sat, "the captain himself, sir. You'll be wanting to speak with him." He departed with words of thanks.

Vadro was one of the Achellan folk and was seated at his meal, seemingly deep in thought as he dined alone. He wore a thick overcoat despite the warmth of the large and well occupied room. An old curved sword was at his side. His experienced eyes had a deep, expressionless look in them, they gave nothing but saw everything, focused and grave. Injury he had suffered, a sadness experienced. It had been a while since a look of happiness had crossed his weathered and dark face. He held within a powerful determination and seemed to cast a grim and serious presence, as did the two strangers who approached him, evincing a desire to speak. They exchanged greetings and he invited them to join him.

"Please join me, my friends," he said in a slow, deep voice and motioned to the empty chairs in front of him. "Tell me how I can help you."

"We're investigating the disappearance of merchant ships in the Strait of Marán," said Damian after they were seated. "We're also looking for a group called the Semáris. I believe you could help us with that."

240

"If you are looking for the Semáris you have found them," he replied. "I am captain of the *Cardela*, that means Sea Dog, a sturdy brig-rigged vessel lately adapted for battle among a few others that are charged with the safety of the Strait. The Semáris were established recently by the Dinitian rulership to halt these accursed preyings on unarmed merchant vessels. We have recently been honored with the task of seeking out these dark hunters and making the channel safe again. And so we scour the island waters in search of them. Thus far, however, we have been unsuccessful for these cunning pirates are elusive and know their business. I believe they have a safe haven or hideout somewhere in the island belt where they conceal themselves and can facilitate their next attack. But I will not rest until I find and destroy these bloodthirsty villains. They took captive my brother and crewmates. I myself was a victim." A shadow crossed his face and he paused a moment before continuing. Damian and Cam waited patiently.

"I recently owned a small cog of one hundred-twenty tons which my brother and I, with a small crew, sailed back and forth across the channel to the cities of the east carrying cargo as far north as Pomay and to cities as far south as can be found in Thecenea and its island provinces. With the absence of war or strife between the various states, commerce and travel across and along the Strait was safe and prosperous for many years. Until recently one could travel without fear or escort.

"Among the island belt of Maranisia is a twenty mile stretch of rocky islands, positioned in such a way as to actually funnel the westerly offshore wind and advantage any vessel sailing toward the mainland continent, which we call Vidia, and it was routinely used by merchant captains crossing the channel. The islands themselves are nothing more than tall cliffs projecting up from the water some twelve-hundred feet and seem to face each other. From a distance it looks as though a giant clove his way through the rock with a mighty hammer and chisel and so carved a clear path through the water. The early natives of Maranisia call it Agon's Pass, after the mighty giant of their legends. It is through this unique and narrow avenue that vessels seek to reach Vidia and the northern cities, for one can run easily between the lengths of islands with a good stern breeze and even well beyond, especially if one travels northward beyond the Pass, for the moment a vessel succeeds the last cliff, which we call Agon's Gate, and is brought out onto the open sea, she is struck by a wind which comes more from the north, and can run quite speedily at beam to Pomay. The distance between the continents is a good three hundred miles and if one utilizes Agon's Pass it reduces the sailing time substantially. On the return trip we simply bypassed the route, steering around it with the breeze steadily amidships. With this accommodating route, trade was vibrant and commerce steady.

"It was the benefit the winds of the Pass created that these villains sought to exploit. It was late one afternoon, six months ago almost to the day, when we were unexpectedly ambushed by these strange pirates. The last of cliffs, the Gate that is, was quickly coming upon us when our lookout gave a shout. We all looked and there, about three points off the starboard bow, suddenly a strange ship appeared from behind the Gate to the south, almost to leeward. It was a small, two-masted square-rigger, rather crude looking I thought, heading right for us, beating into the wind with reefed sails down the pass against the current which was exceedingly odd for no vessel would make any headway at all against that sturdy breeze, attempting to enter the Pass from the east. But we looked more closely and to our utter terror and disbelief, with the waning sun astern, distinctly saw many oars rapidly stroking the three foot seas. A Ceneaen bireme, it looked to me, oared by slaves. This explained the overall lack of sails on the vessel and its consequent proficiency of upwind propulsion and maneuverability. And this hideous craft appeared to be floating across the water as if by magic right for us. The gap between the cliffs can be no more than five hundred yards wide so we had little room to evade this collision, for undoubtedly this is what the villains were attempting to do. It was only a moment later when, with a glass pressed to my terrified eye, I could plainly distinguish the shapes of armed thugs upon the deck and behind the ballistae mounted on the bulwark.

"I cannot properly articulate my feelings in that moment of terror. I dropped the glass and seized the helm from my beloved crewman in a spasm of fright. I brought her hard to larboard attempting to outmaneuver the bandits, hoping the stern wind would push us through to the Gate and eject us into the open sea beyond. If successful I had little doubt escape would have been achieved for this crude, under-rigged vessel could not hope to overtake us with the wind of the Dinitian Sea swiftly pushing us eastward. But this was a heavy gamble due to the deadly proximity of the enemy ship. At best we would have passed her bow with but a yard to spare, but all this became quickly irrelevant. They immediately turned with us as if expecting and indeed urging us to turn northward. We managed to evade the collision to our starboard but looking ahead saw another ship of like craft emerge from behind the northern cliff just as we were coming up on it. I could now see the design of our enemies. The first ship was but a decoy to drive us into the jaws of the other. With the north breeze astern the second, escape was now virtually impossible. It would only be a perilous moment before we were alongside it and harpooned.

"I shouted to my crew to brace for impact for I was not going without a fight, and seeing the futility of the situation I presumed us doomed for we could not withstand these many armed foes. They immediately shot their roped harpoons into our prow. These missiles are made of heavy steel for momentum but with a small tip on the end and are capable of puncturing most unarmored hulls at close range. They didn't need any help pulling us in though. With the speed at which we spanked directly for the fiends, I drove us right upon them. The bowsprit crashed upon their starboard side with a thundering crack, just afore amidships, throwing some of the bandits overboard for they were not expecting this. The bow dragged along the gunwale and we took down most of her rigging and smashed half the oars on that side before we came to an abrupt halt, and we could hear the cries of the slaves below decks. Our bowsprit was torn clean off in the pass and the jib and foresail rigging and headstays became afouled with theirs, tearing off our foremast which consequently fell onto the deck and killed my young helmsman who had been lying prone for protection. The first ship quickly caught up and they threw their grappling irons onto us and hemmed us in tight on the port side. In the next moment gangplanks were thrown down by both ships and they stormed upon us. We fought them off with what we possessed for melee weapons but it was to little avail. My small crew of fourteen was no match and most were quickly killed before the rest surrendered. Among them was my brother.

"As for myself I fought off one of them with a broken piece of spar, for my sword was below, before my desperate eyes met those of my brother's. I was astern, and he, the bow, captured with the rest of the crew that remained, some six or seven of them, alas. I would not be held prisoner by any and would seek my own death as an alternative, especially perceiving the seriousness and cruel manner of my new enemies. I resolved to attempt a risky escape in the hopes of one day affecting the discovery and rescue of my crew and brother who were all unfortunately beyond my aid. I knew someone would have to bring news of these secret and dark deeds to my friends and authorities back home, and this strange new enemy, otherwise my men would be forsaken to an unknown fate. I feigned injury to the head when struggling with another of my victorious captors and fell overboard, imitating that of a corpse floating in the water. The pirates paid me little heed thankfully, only laughing off my death as they corralled their new prisoners and prepared the prize for towing, to be looted later and in secret.

"I slowly and imperceptibly made my way to the severed bowsprit floating near me in the water and concealed myself under the flotsam and rigging, viewing the hasty completion of the capture beneath the wreckage. By means of cutting tools they quickly disentangled themselves from the fouled rigging and beams which they cast into the sea, and made some hasty modifications to their damaged vessel enough so that they could sail before they were discovered by a Dinitian patrol ship. I watched them quickly row away with my beloved old boat in tow as the sun sank behind the pass to the west. To the south they sped, before the wind, but they were soon lost to sight on the open sea. I was carried out beyond the Gate with the swift current despite my desperate and fruitless attempts to remain within swimming distance of it and perhaps climb upon the rocks for safety. I might as well have been trying to swim for the fleeing horizon. The Gate became quickly lost to sight as I became hopelessly adrift and my eyes closed themselves out of despair, and the vast empty night and the chill of the water were my only companions.

"Three days and nights I drifted on the dark sea, and I was soon taken by strange dreams and visions and tortured by thirst indescribable under the hot Marán sun. I tied myself to the wreckage with some of the rigging for my strength was quickly failing and I doubted not that the time would soon come when I would inadvertently depart my savior of buoyant wood and finally engage in my inevitable death throes with the water. I despaired and felt a fool, feeling that death in combat with my accursed victors would have been far preferable to this slow agony. I wondered what possessed me to commit such a futile move, thinking I could somehow find and discover my friends against these heavy odds. Foolhardiness. I busied myself with the phantoms before my eyes which danced unceasingly upon the moving water. I yielded to insensibility and resigned myself to that fate which claims many doomed sailors.

"A Sedinian fishing vessel picked me up, when exactly I know not, and it was on a cot in the captain's quarters that I found myself, barely alive and delirious with hunger and thirst. It was some time before I could even speak. I communicated the entire story as soon as I could and they could scarcely believe it. Two days later I was brought home.

"Six times this year these Kunn pirates have struck that we know of, though lately their presence seems to have lessened. Nowhere has their plague been felt in well over a month. Perhaps they have moved on to hunt other territories or are preparing for an attack of larger scale. Some do not believe my story, and I do not blame them, and they credit the misfortunes of these ships to foul weather or the wrath of the sea. The weather in the vicinity of Marán is notoriously unpredictable and can be dangerous at times, especially to the south where the crosswinds are so strong one can make little headway. But no sign or remains of any attack have been discovered except one. The vessel *Phelidan* was the only victim to have been accounted for, found washed up on a sandbar close to the island of Krata, abandoned strangely with no sign of the crew anywhere though blood was spilled upon the deck. And these were our brothers, riding a man-of-war such as we have in search of the same predators. With so many islands in Maranisia so close together it is common belief that a hideout must exist in one of them, enabling the pirates a fairly rapid attack and return without detection. The Semáris from Dinitia have scoured many of them without success. For three months now I have searched the belt with no fortune, not even a sighting, though others have claimed to see rogue vessels at night like passing phantoms that disappear before one can make certain their identity. Our search is cursed and we grow weary of it. These folk are cunning and disciplined. They strike seldom so as to remain invisible, wisely never desiring to overexpose themselves. They operate only at night, it would seem, and during periods of foul weather to mask their movements. It is my belief also that they have an information source on the mainlands for they choose their targets with care and with precision timing."

"Verily I can assure you of that," acknowledged Damian. "The Kunn have spies and henchmen aplenty."

"Little do we know in the far west of this foul clan you speak of," said Vadro. "These villains which seem to follow some kind of harsh creed and divine directive have not fortunately plagued these lands with their terror before and therefore we know not by what we are besieged. We do know that great loot and goods they must have acquired in all their stealthy raids, and that our crews are presumed dead or captured. Merchantmen and shipping firms alike speak of their woes and none now dare cross the Strait without escort. And the pirates obviously do not use the ports along the opposing coasts for no one has seen these thugs and brigands anchor there for resupply. I believe they must have a supply ship of their own which returns from a city in the south loyal to them and delivers unnoticed in an unmarked or inconspicuous vessel, or else they return to their territory far to the south."

"Are all the islands populated?" Cam asked.

"No, not all," Vadro replied. "There are hundreds of islands in the belt, so many that some do not have names such that we know of or use. The natives of course knew them. The islands of rock that make up Agon's Pass have lately been called the Valley of the Wolf and few dare tread there now, for the pirates prowl especially in that advantageous vicinity. It is conceivable that the Kunn are hiding in an island within striking distance of the pass, completely uninhabited and adopted for their uses."

"Then I suggest we find it," offered Damian.

"And how do you propose we do that?" Vadro asked.

"No doubt you are familiar with the fortress of Spen Mala?" Damian asked. Vadro looked up and his eyes widened as this stranger told his own disturbing tale.

At about the same time Damian and Cam were conversing at the Wharf's Edge with Vadro about the tactical situation at sea and the necessary logistics of their immediate departure and sailing, the bartender at the Crossroads Inn unlocked the door to the empty bar and went inside for his daily preparations before his patrons arrived later in day. He didn't open his shop until noontime though it remained open until the next morning and he utilized an hour or two to make any necessary preparations. He closed the door behind him, locked it, and entered the as yet unlit and dim main function room. He sought the lantern on the wall and attempted to light it when his hand was arrested quite suddenly by that of a hidden assailant. Before he could even shout two more figures emerged from the shadows which brutally gripped and silenced him. He was shoved backwards against a wall and held fast.

"What is the meaning of this?" he demanded, taking some breaths. "What do you want with me?" Then he stopped and looked up breathless into the eyes of the fourth figure which stepped before him. This figure seemed to radiate a power within itself that cast great fear upon the man, and he was seized not by his powerful gloved hands but by his mind and eyes which seemed to have some level of control or penetrability over others, a mental manipulative power and perception other mortals could not claim to possess. He felt his mind breached by the interrogative probe of another. The man shrunk in terror before him as he approached. "Please," he groveled, "I'll tell you anything."

CHAPTER 3
RAID ON SPEN

The *Cardela* was strangely alone at her mooring. It was a small, sleek vessel compared to most, a brig modified for battle. It was a two-master with a full compliment of square-rigged sails with jibs to fore and a gaffed-spanker to aft. The whole of the exterior was black and steel plates of armor were bolted along the sides. Large, heavy, torsion-powered ballistae of crafted steel composite were mounted in places along the armored gunwale, two each to port and starboard, one to the stern on the poopdeck and two on the bulwarks of the bow. The crew of a dozen had completed the resupply and the ship was ready for departure. Vadro accepted the offer of help from Damian and Cam, who also offered payment for their expenses, and welcomed them aboard. They seemed to share a bond of grievance. He was very pleased to have with him some help also knowledgeable of this strange opportunistic and driven enemy. With a small, tight crew there was plenty of space for the newcomers and the grim but friendly Achellan sailors welcomed them and introduced themselves. Two more very capable hands were accepted heartily; indeed the vessel could easily demand a few more. They all seemed focused and grave, committed to a purpose of ridding the seas of these new foreign wolves, and were willing to sacrifice of themselves in this vital objective even at their own peril for the protection of their lands and to once again make safe the Strait. Dinitia was a just and decent country and these unprovoked raids by a vagabond clan from far away, overly hungry and invasive in their thirst for wealth and influence, inflicted an undeserved wound upon them and all seafaring folk who traveled the Strait which touched them deeply, for all had been affected by this hostile piracy. Everyone was familiar with loved ones or friends who had lost someone in the secret raids, with no word of report. The only concrete testimony any of them had about the mysterious fortunes of the victims came from the gruff captain before them all, stepping hastily onto his vessel and shouting orders to his obedient and disciplined crew, and upon him lay all hope and trust by his mates who believed him and countrymen back home.

247

The sailors quickly made ready for immediate departure. The captain barked at his men for he felt time was against them. The shocking revelations he received from his new friends drove him to desperate haste and unease. Even the thought of his new enemies attempting such a bold move, however futile, enraged the already fuming captain. The Maranisians were his brethren and any injury suffered by them would be shared by all Achellans. First they attack his beloved ship and abduct his crew and brother in a cowardly and undeserved raid, an ambush even, then they plot to strike closer to home at a government complex which proudly housed treasures pertaining to the history of his homeland and its colonization long ago. The villains, he thought, have they no honor? Will they stop at nothing to fulfill their desires of power? What grievance have they suffered at the hands of my country to warrant these acts of terror?

"Helmsman!" he shouted, "steer us out of here with all haste. Set a westerly course. We're heading to Spen, without stop or rest." The crew all paused a moment in their duties when they heard this and exchanged looks of concern and wonder. The captain went below to consult with Damian and his first mate, Erius. Cam stayed on deck to partake in the duties of sailing the ship, which he did have some experience with, and no doubt to familiarize himself with the high rigging which seemed to call to him. He leapt up the stays and ran along the ratlines with the agility of a monkey. The profound abilities of their new under-statured friend made all on deck turn their heads in wonder.

* * *

The *Advent* had been on course not for Prova anymore, but for Spen Mala for a good two days now after several days' layover in the secret island hideout of the Kunn pirates. The Demarian ship had been successfully abducted by those pirates who prowled the seas here and waited like hunting cats for the scheduled arrival of their target vessel. Their information proved to be accurate. Whatever the Ahga was paying his informers it must have been enough, for the doomed vessel appeared on the northern horizon precisely as calculated. Under the cover of darkness aided by a cloudy night sky and the three Kunn ships in full black-out posture they sprung their trap. The Demarian ship suddenly found itself flanked and bombarded with hooks and ropes by an experienced foe that was almost invisible until it was upon them. The call to arms came too late and attempts at evasion were unsuccessful, for the three ships skillfully closed in and surrounded the vessel which was heading right for them, running along at a good pace with the northwesterly wind at her stern. There was some brief melee and some few of the Kunn pirates were slain by the handful of Demarian guards stationed on the ship but the crew and passengers of the *Advent* were quickly subdued and captured by the overwhelming force. That crew had been exchanged with a troop of Kunn sea bandits which completely resumed new control of the captured ship. The prisoners were hastily relocated to each of the three attacking vessels for holding and to serve as replacement oarsmen for their slave-enhanced propulsion. By midnight all four vessels were sailing under a new heading.

The first part of their bold scheme had gone surprisingly well. Mellinak, the trusted captain of the Ahga, expected far greater loss, perhaps even one of his ships and for this reason brought along all three, bribed from a friend in the distant city of Artos to the south. A prestigious ship such as this from the great and envied realm of Demar was not expected to fall easily and the success of the raid brought the villains not a little elation, and it was with glee that they mocked the almighty prisoners. Once perceived as indomitable they were now spat upon. Demar and Dinitia shared a strong trade alliance and this blow that was beyond the wildest imaginings of those softening and spoiled officials, too blind to the growing menace that festered along their borders, would deflate their once proud and unbreakable bond of friendship and unity. That was precisely what the Ahga was intending. To the despots in the east these countries were perceived as arrogant, belittling and humbling their less developed and strife-plagued counterparts to the east with their veiled but detectable and ever-present conceit and disdain for its folk. But those underestimating proud fools from the north were not aware of any Kunn existence in these waters or that the clan in the east and south which grew steadily in power would have any here, much less on the seas. So it was unawares that the *Advent* and its crew were caught and little did they know of the greater purpose.

Mellinak strode the deck of his captured vessel with a satisfied grin. It was late in the afternoon, almost evening in fact on the seventh day of the abduction when the lookout confirmed the visual on their target island– Paladica, the largest of Maranisia and home to the royalty and governance of the island belt country and its capital city of Spen Darak, at the northern foot of and right behind Spen Mala. It was in this great cliff that these rulers dwelt and conducted business and civil affairs, that old fortress which was also the treasury and keepsafe of gold and currency and other valuable novelties and heirlooms, relics and artifacts, one in particular that the raiding party hidden below deck was assigned to remove from the premises for the necessity and prestige of their esteemed lord. And it would be delivered. Mellinak looked up at the unique landmass in the far distance, not for the first time, and heard his lookout herald the approach of two smaller vessels with the green and black colors of Dinitia and yellow flags of Marán waving in the stiff breeze. *Good,* he thought. *My escorts have arrived.* He motioned to his conspirators to remove themselves from sight, and all but a few of the human and Achellan ambassadors he captured were brought above in their place. It was time for his feint and all his actors were in place. The prisoners had received their instructions. Any deviation from these or noncompliance with the captain's specific wishes would result in the murders of several of their valued associates, their fellow noblemen who were held quietly below with blades to their throats should those on deck fail to cooperate. They were all promised release upon completion of the task and the captain assured them they were only needed momentarily to ensure their admittance into the guarded cove behind which rose steeply the cliff of their destination. And for this admittance to take place some small persuasion would be necessary to execute the ruse. Mellinak himself was a Mogoli, older and larger, with spiked bracers upon his broad wrists and thick brown leather armor upon his girthy frame and a heavy sword at his side, one that had seen much use. The red bandana of the Kunn which he proudly displayed across his banded grey hair would be an easy and revealing mark. Everything about the ship had to seem unaltered and routine, undisturbed. All marks and signs which might give rise to suspicion had been removed. He took one last look about him, saw that his actors in charge on deck were ready with the planted diplomat decoys at their sides, squinted one last time at the approaching ships through his glass, and hurried below.

* * *

Damian peered anxiously forward over the bow, rising and falling with the waves as the ship crashed through them. The spray from the broken water rose well over the prow and soaked the deck. It was late in the afternoon and the heavy breeze from the northwest had steadily increased. The ship began to heel to leeward, straining the masts, and the captain ordered the partial reefing of the sails for what he expected would be a turbulent night. They were headed for the islands of Maranisia to the southwest with all haste but those were still quite a distance away. It didn't seem as though the ship could speed there fast enough and he felt time fought against him. He looked to stern and saw Cam conversing with one of the sailors who couldn't understand how it was possible for one to simultaneously run along a slick gunwale and swing two swords as the boat heaved in the heavy seas. Damian would have smiled if impatience and worry didn't dog him. The sky was clouded over and the darkness of night came quickly. It looked likely to rain that night.

He thought over everything Riman and Vadro had said to him about this interesting island they were heading for and how it was quite possible the Kunn even now could be in the very process of executing a raid against this fat target. The spy in Draga's tower seemed worried. Inquiries Vadro had an errand-runner make in Prova regarding the whereabouts of the *Advent*, before they set off, were answered with voices and gestures of concern. That ship, they all said, was expected to have arrived at least two days ago at the latest, but that no word or sign had anyone received of its location. It was presumed that it may have been met with some misfortune or that they had deviated from their course unexpectedly. Damian and Vadro doubted that. They had a good idea of what probably happened to that ship, but Vadro decided that seeking it in the open sea would be futile and decided rather to resign it to its fate and instead head off the probable intentions of the captors by speeding to their next likely destination. A risky move. Then again it could all be a mistake, or that Gadrin received bad information and they were all alarmed over nothing. But the timely disappearance of the *Advent* was too much of a coincidence and seemed to confirm suspicions. Something was going on. There was little doubt the Ahga had his eye on a treasure hoard like Spen for some time. They all just hoped to arrive there before the Kunn did and send word. But they didn't know that Mellinak and his men were a full day ahead of them. After some hours of attempting to alleviate tense helplessness and restlessness by assisting with sailing the tall vessel and urging it to greater speed with his profound strength and determination, much to the gratitude and surprise of the sailors who made way for him, Damian eventually went below and tried to rest the remainder of the night.

The island of Paladica was positioned farthest to the north of all the islands of Marán and was also the largest, measuring about thirty-five square miles altogether though the land itself was more in the shape of a pear, the cliff mountain making up almost half the southern portion which sloped downwards to the north where it also narrowed on the sides. Behind the cliff, at the foot and termination of its steep slope lay the city of Spen Darak. It was a small and lesser city compared to the vast and more advanced municipalities of those on the mainlands such as Hera and Demar, nor did it have the flow of traffic or variety of peoples these more prestigious cities boasted. The folk of Maranisia were mostly and comfortably isolated from the chaos of the Vidia mainland. The city was constructed of either clay or wooden structures, low level and simple homes and buildings only visited by merchantmen and diplomats from peaceful territories. The climate was hot this far south and one could find many things built of cane or bamboo and stalks of trees that were far more flexible than the wood found in the far northern territories. The Maranisians built small bridges of lashed cane stalk over their streams, or lined the roofs of wooden huts with the broad leaves of lush tropical plants and built walkways over the mud with thin logs tied together. The land was lush and wet with many streams traversing the dense landscape that quickly leveled itself to the north. The people of Marán carved their living metropolis from the jungle island upon which they dwelt, full of caves and small rivers that one could see stretched out among the rugged but verdant landscape.

From the top of Spen Mala the city below looked like an assembly of log huts and walkways that was transformed right out of the earth and foliage beneath it. Wisps of smoke spiraled upwards in places. Narrow dirt roads wound like a multi-headed snake amid the rows of reed and stalk huts and clay buildings. People could be seen on them, villagers carrying bundles of long sticks or leading beasts of burden with loads on wheels. Large tracts of fertile farmland to the east were worked and tilled. Fishermen could be seen in the streams and along the beachfronts to the north, spreading their nets or spearfishing. Small boats paddled about and larger, tall ships were also visible, coming to Spen with metals, timber for building, and gold, or crafted hardwoods, or even some of the secret volatile substances and chemicals of an incendiary nature from the chemists and engineers of the east, or going from the island and heading back to the mainland with loads of spices and skins and fruits, textiles, healing herbs, and husks of rare plants and wood and other materials not found in Vidia. The peoples complimented and provided each other with necessities the other had and the sea traffic was steady.

One lone road departed from the labyrinth of others and ascended the incline before the cliff until it reached the high main topside entrance of the fortress on the northern side. This is where a host of the Honorable Guards of Dinitia stood watch, keeping the elaborately gated entrance to the cave-fort and admitting welcomed guests and rulers. From here they plunged into the mountain and proceeded down the main hall, which was on the eighth and highest level of the holding facility though the cliff itself rose far higher, and descended a vertical winding staircase cut into a spacious shaft until they reached the function rooms and halls of the lower levels, or wherever they wished to go. This winding stair descended from the top main entrance straight to the first level far below where a small but effective dungeon also was positioned, used for the incarceration of the most feared criminals and enemies of the realm. There were only four habitable and functional levels in all, however, besides the top which burrowed its way to the southern and opposite high side of the cliff which overlooked the whole of the cove below it, and this peak was used as a lookout. Here one was capable of viewing not only the entirety of the circular inlet cove right below him but the whole of the ocean to the south and to either side as far as a good glass would permit him. So ships were sighted far off, and directed by escort into the cove harbor where it would be docked with the others along the moorings below the cliff. The cove stretched in a semi-circular direction at the foot of Spen on the southern side, and it was down here that the ships were unloaded onto the lowlands beneath. The cove itself flowed into the great cave under the cliff and this was where guest ships of royalty were admitted, as this was the under-entrance to the great cave fort. A massive steel portcullis raised its colossal jaws a full hundred feet high to allow the entry of especially chosen vessels into the huge cave entrance. Beyond this mighty gate was a docking platform on the right side where esteemed guests and lords of distant lands were allowed to disembark their vessels within the cave itself, and proceed with dignity through the wide doors and be ushered into the lavish chambers above. And the great gate would close behind them, its great wheels rumbling and echoing in the deep chasm until it reached the stony floor under the water with a muffled clang. And so entrance both above and below was closely supervised and restricted.

The more frequented areas inside, however, were found from the fourth to the first levels. The fourth was where the guard barracks and officers' quarters were located, and the living necessities therein. The third was where the offices, chambers and suites of the lords that ruled were, just down the hall from the several large assembly halls, used for convergence and council on civil affairs and the like. As one descended the smooth stone steps to the second level he found himself suddenly impeded by a locked and guarded gate, for this level was off-limits to most. This was where wealth in abundance was stored, along with other great valuables secreted and prized by the island-realm, locked in a separate and extensive vault of many divisions. Among these prizes was an ancient heirloom called the Etar, a mighty round plate of gold measuring five feet in diameter, embossed with gems and decorated in places with silver and bronze. Made by the original Maranisians it resembled the sun, with hieroglyphics and historical carvings upon it etched with skill by that extinct folk. This masterpiece of craftsmanship and history became the Seal of Marán and its value was staggering. The Maranisians treasured it as an artifact and it was displayed on the wall in the vault with honor, viewable from behind its guardian portcullis for it was placed in the exact center of the vault which ran in right angles and in either direction of the short, gated hallway which led into it. This gate was drawn by a guard in an adjacent and normally locked room in which the wheels and gears that drew it up were safely concealed and at his control.

The Etar, however, was locked in place on the wall by an array of barely visible steel fingers which protruded from the circular mount behind it and kept it in place. This inconspicuous retaining hold was easily unlocked by means of a key which was in the possession of the guard on duty inside the vault, fastened securely around his wrist with a locked metal cuff. This unique key, along with the other in his possession, opened all the numerous sub-vaults which held a variety of riches, and was passed onto the relief at the end of his shift when the guard in the other room opened the gate and allowed him in. The theft-deterrent mentality of this arrangement was that the guard inside may have the key but could go nowhere anyway, being helplessly locked inside, and if one managed to kill him he would have a difficult time cutting the key off his armored and cold wrist, hopefully allowing for the arrival of reinforcements to thwart the theft.

But Mellinak was aware of all this, only too well. For the past two months he had been planning an infiltration of this very facility and preparing his squads for its execution. His ranks were not filled with common and expendable servants of the Ahga, the *suchuks*, but with elite fighters of the Mak-Baccád, or *under order*, and were specifically deployed to Mellinak's small but efficient pirating force to be an effective, undetectable and disciplined unit on the seas which the Ahga sought to selectively rape. There were riches aplenty out there, heirlooms and relics the clan needed for its great quest. Spen held one in particular the Ahga was looking for, and in this raid his secret soldiers were more than capable. There were only sixty men in his entire force, discretionally dispersed to the three ships and their secret island base which was yet to be discovered by those pitiful searching vessels which sailed by regularly. Under cover of darkness he deployed a small scout contingent of four of his best men, chosen specifically for their small size and stealth and thieving proficiencies, who sought to find ways to penetrate the impregnable fort and perhaps discover a vantage point that could be exploited.

For days his scouts looked upon and observed the cliff and its surroundings, well concealed in their position in the dense jungle of the unused strip of lowland beneath Spen on the right side of the cove, opposite the docks and ships which were directly across from them and well beyond earshot. It was in this location, one day, that the four were able to notice a single broken tooth on the bottom of the otherwise impenetrable gate that might allow one access. The smallest of them, Badai, a Turuk and a personal favorite of Mellinak, endeavored to learn more of this defect. One night when the moon was low in the far north, behind the cliff, he crawled into the calm water of the cove, and no faster than the gentle breeze swam undetected across the harbor and right up to the gate. Without a ripple he swam to the bottom and discovered a gap between the broken tooth and the solid rock floor of about a foot. That lone foot would be all he needed. This fort was his now. He made the attempt and found he was able to fit himself through the gap and infiltrate the cave-dock. From there he silently swam to the enclosed mooring, where there was usually a guest ship of some kind about once a week, and carefully pulled his slight and stealthy frame onto the stone landing. He spent days learning the ways of the place, avoiding the few night sentries (though during the day it was far more peopled), creeping along the darkened and quiet halls, learning the routines and shifts, probing ever deeper on each successive night until he formulated a possible break-in plan. He even ventured up the spiral stair shaft, and with great patience and discipline darted from shadow to shadow until he reached the pinnacle and took in the breathtaking view of the cove where he could perceive the shelter of palm leaves and brush where his friends were hiding far below, waiting for his return. And as he looked downward, with a nodding guard within his arm's reach, he discerned that this lofty lookout could very well be utilized in his great plan.

He slowly retraced his steps, cautiously, patiently. It would take him hours to reach the enclosed port where he made his ingress. Just before dawn he slithered his way back to his awaiting friends to update their scheme. Mellinak returned each week with food brought by rowboat under the night sky, and on the third week brought them back to camp where they drafted detailed schematics of their target and devised a way to penetrate the beast and deliver the prize to their beloved leader far away.

Mellinak continued his voyage to the cove. His Dinitian escorts had made an adequate visual of the *Advent* and a momentary communication with the accordingly attired delegates on deck. It was late, and with the night coming quickly below the clouded sky they were instructed to anchor within the cove harbor and remain there until the morning when a sortie from shore was able to inspect the vessel, for it had arrived unexpectedly, though the familiar ship would be welcomed by the usual Maranisian delegation at mid-morning the next day when they resumed their duties. Mellinak gladly proceeded as instructed. The escorts followed his captured ship until they reached the cove at which time they signaled the lookout atop Spen, using lights and shades, received the confirmation signal, and resumed their perimeter patrol outside the island.

Mellinak resumed his post on deck and studied the surroundings carefully. The harbor was quiet and calm. The docks and wharfs to his left which ran along the curvature of the lowland beneath the looming shadow of the quiet cliff were largely uninhabited, save for a few idling or intoxicated sailors or landsmen, enchanted by the sleeping effect of the dark and peaceful cove and yearning to yield to its hypnotizing voice. There were only a few ships moored to the dock, the mog captain noticed as he paced about and they crawled slowly by in the calm and shallow water. Good. They could see several lights shining from within the cave mouth, projecting forth between the great tines of the closed mammoth gate. A torch was alight far above in the lookout and he could barely perceive the presence of the guard on duty there. Mellinak looked hard at him. That high perch and its fearful alarm required capture. He cast his scrutinizing and analytical gaze to the right where the narrow beach and thick foliage was undeveloped. Nothing there. Little seemed to be happening. The cove of Spen had all but fallen asleep under the twilight. After ascertaining their safety he whispered some orders below, and without so much as a cough that might echo in the quiet harbor the prisoners were ushered quickly below and the hidden crew reascended to the deck to stabilize the vessel in the harbor with poles and by positioning the boat abeam to the wind to prevent its moving until they received the signal. They weren't dropping anchor.

Badai finally reached the top level of Spen and peered over the floor of the lookout room. It took him longer than usual to get all the way up to his favorite perch. The governor had turned in late and his royal guards had to delay their liberty. He became anxious, hiding in the shadows of the multi-leveled tunnelways he knew so well. Mellinak had redeployed his secret scout force to the island only three nights ago and now it was finally time. The whole operation was on his capable and cunning shoulders. The body of the guard was lying off to the side under the alarm bell, a large round shell of hollowed steel suspended from the rock ceiling. An easy kill, the ignorant slug didn't even know what hit him. Badai waited for him to finish with his coded light signal to his friends across the lagoon before eliminating him. It appeared he was right on time and he smiled with satisfaction. He could see their vessel below, still rigged, being steadied in the shallow water, waiting for entrance into the cave. He took the two torches off the wall and put them out before throwing them over the edge and into the water far below. That was the first signal, and Mellinak saw it. The bell room was captured and silenced. The infiltration was about to begin. He waited tensely for the next one.

Badai's three associates swam like water snakes under the night sky of the cove and crawled under the gap in the gate, making their ingress into the cavern. The control room for the great gate was a quick climb up a ladder on the near side of the dock within, and capture of this was their first assignment. They slithered without a sound or bubble into the cavern. There were two ships docked here; one was a Dinitian patrolling vessel, unutilized for the moment, and the other was some foreign brig from a distant city, Artos by the looks of her standards. The third berth was empty as predicted. Not for long. The mog scouts slowly made their way to the stone deck and climbed level with the floor, peering over the damp edge. The floor of the dock was mostly neat and unobstructed save for a few small rows of crated supplies and chests of gear and tools or thick, coiled rope. This was the grand and privileged entrance of the great fort, used by the esteemed visitors of the island and it was kept clean and inviting and well lit by many lanterns along the walls. Beyond the dock, which was a raised platform chiseled from the stone itself to serve as a place of mooring stretched along the rightside cavern wall, opened a wide hall which led to a broad staircase they could see leading upwards and into the chambers above. The ships were uninhabited and silent, rocking gently in the low waves, and besides the two guards at either end no one was about. One of them was not ten feet in front of the three silent killers, pacing slowly and unaware. The other was at the far northern end. The scouts separated, two heading for the far end and one remaining behind to eliminate the first. Simultaneous elimination would be critical. They could not allow the alarm to be raised at any cost or the entire, fragile operation would be greatly jeopardized. The plan called for a quick, silent infiltration and as quick escape. But these were the superfighters of the Mak-Baccád, highly trained and disciplined and well equipped. Little was beyond their abilities.

When his friends were in position at the far end he carefully leveled a small, loaded crossbow at the guard right in front of him. The metal, armor piercing bolt penetrated and impaled his throat, sending him to the floor a corpse instantly. The distant guard turned and was about to give a shout when he was suddenly strangled by two assailants who emerged from behind the shadows and he fell with hardly a scuffle under their iron grip. They looked about them a moment and listened up the stairs for noise or alarm, gave each other some hand signals, carefully lowered the bodies into the water, and climbed up the ladder which led to the winch and gear room that would open the gate for their ship, controls they needed. They reached the top and paused on the small landing. There was a closed door beyond which most likely was an attendant or sentry. They readied their crossbows and adjusted their weapons before proceeding. One of them opened the door and this suspicion was confirmed. There was a lone attendant in this small, enclosed room who miraculously managed to give a shout before he was shot.

There was a door to the east and behind it they could immediately hear footsteps approaching. The room behind the door, they knew, must be the long hall which had many windows and openings cut into it that looked upon the cove below. In this great hall a strong defense could be staged against invader ships and it was equipped with large, mounted missile-projecting weapons and slits cut into the rock from which one could seek cover while firing upon any possible attacker. An identical hall for the defense of the fort was built directly above it on the third level, and atop the flat peak of the cliff above were placed catapults for the casting of bursting and flaming missiles. A good defense against a large scale attack from the sea to be sure, but these raiders didn't intend to attack in such a foolish, obvious manner, but sought infiltration from underneath and through stealth. The approaching guard opened the door to the winch room and looked about him. Seeing and hearing nothing he was about to turn away when he was struck over the head with a heavy metal tool and knocked unconscious. One of the raiders ran out into the long hall to secure it and ventured further down the exiting shaft to the north. No one around, all was quiet. He closed the door and returned to the hall of defense to look out into the cove and acknowledge the signal from his awaiting ship. He peered into the darkness and could clearly see the lone light draped over the edge of the bow on the cave side. Just what he was looking for. His crafty little friend upstairs in the bell room must have accomplished his mission. He ran back down the hall and into the winch room to help his friend who was in the process of preparing the great gate for opening. Within moments the gears and cables were revolving and grumbling in the cave entry on the other side of the wall. With the guard barracks two levels up and deeper within the cave to the north, it was doubtful that the moaning of the gate would be heard by the many sleeping guards and officers within, but this possibility is what the third of them was now in the process of protecting them from.

The scout quietly descended the short ladder and ran across the quiet dock. He sought the case which Badai assured him contained a short length of thick chain. He found it, drew it out, and headed up the stairs with it. He reached the second level and immediately turned left up the next flight of stairs where he knew the second level gate was closed. There was no one about. He wrapped the chain around the gate, which swung outwards, and the steel fixture which secured it to the rock wall opposite the hinge side, removed a lock from his pouch, prepared in advance especially for this purpose, and locked the chain with it. This would prevent the host upstairs from using this advantageous route to arrest the crime, as they were now locked in. He then headed back down the stairs for the most difficult part of the operation.

He turned left at the bottom and headed east, toward the holding vault which was just down the hall to the left. But directly across the long hall was a small guard shack, manned at all hours, with a barred window for making visual confirmation of anyone going into the vault which was located just to the left and beyond the locked gates of this guard shack. Within this room, the scout knew, were the unlocking mechanisms for the dual gate which led into the vault. But the barred window overlooked the long hall which led to it, and the mog cautiously peered around the corner in the attempt to view the sentry behind the door. He could see the top of the guard's head. It looked like he was sitting down, rocking slightly as he idled, probably reading or repairing something but definitely awake and alert. His head was turned slightly to the side but an easy glance to his right gave him an unobstructed view of the hall. This approach would be difficult, one that tested his well-earned skills, but it was nothing his training in the fighting fields of his home in the east and practice pits of the Ahga couldn't prepare him for. He couldn't believe his clan was hitting a target this big and prestigious in a distant territory. Compared to the great powers and armies of the west his clan and following was small by comparison and largely unknown in the wider world. This would be their biggest raid in the western territories and one of his greatest personal accomplishments to date, if he survived. So far it looked as though things were going favorably for them. The Kunn would be feared indeed, the world over. But no one would know that for a while at least, would they? Not until they were far away, if they even discovered the real culprits. *Stalat uruz al-Medu*. This was all a necessary step for the Divine One. The mog pulled back around the corner, cast a nervous glance up the hall and listened again, checked his gear, made sure his small, one-handed metal crossbow was loaded and ready, along with his other small weapons and tools on his belt, and lowered himself to the floor. His clan provided him with the best equipment their unlimited money could buy, from organizations of dubious repute near and far, and he would put it to use. He began his forty foot crawl slowly across the dim hall toward the distant guard shack, crossbow in hand.

The huge gate grumbled open in the cavern. The two mogs worked furiously to crank the wheels. The assembly of sturdy gears and large counterweights were forced into motion. Mellinak wasted no time. He brought the ship around and his crew immediately muscled the boat onward. The *Advent* ruddered her way clumsily into the opening cave mouth.

Badai crept silently down the deep, winding stair shaft toward the upper guard quarters. This great shaft was minimally illuminated at night by burning torches placed in niches in the walls, one every two levels or so and staggered. From any position in this deep shaft one was able to view the stair in its entirety by following these lights which were spread evenly throughout the vertical chasm. If one peered over the railless edge from the top level the first was visible far below, and the view was breathtaking and daunting. He knew that escape through the lower levels would be impossible once the action started and he quickly descended the familiar steps. It was possible that this heist could be accomplished without misfortune but he wasn't counting on it. If something alerted the host of guards above the halls below would be swarming. He needed an alternative mode of escape, and he found one, one which suited his taste very well. He just hoped it was still there.

He stole down to the fourth level where he knew a storage locker lay. This small, dirty, and unused room was located at the far end of the row of living quarters and became a space for the men to store their refuse, gear, weapons, or any other odd or petty materials without a permanent place of residence. He stopped at the fourth floor landing and took a few steps in. He thought he could hear something, someone walking idly within. The steps came closer and he withdrew into the shadows of the dim, cylindrical, subterranean shaft. A man appeared, either on duty or apparently up for the night and bored or unable to sleep, taking a leisurely stroll about the place. He stepped onto the edge of the landing and casually peered over the edge below and then high above, not noticing the small, black-clad figure carefully gripping the dark wall behind him. Hardly breathing, Badai slipped past and into the tunnel.

He sought the long coil of thin rope from the shelf of gear within the open locker just around the corner, threw it over his shoulder, and headed slowly back out, listening and looking for the guard who he hoped had returned to his quarters. To his dismay he was still out on the ledge, humming to himself and idling. He had to creep past this increasingly annoying and persistent sentry but that would be difficult with him in such close proximity to the hall entrance. Badai had little choice but to move on. His friends below would spring their quiet raid any moment and he couldn't be caught up here in the chaos. He advanced noiselessly until he was almost right behind him, then stopped. The guard turned suddenly, hearing or sensing something, an unfriendly presence drawing closer. He looked behind him and met eyes with an intruder, the likes of which he had never seen. Shorter he was to be sure, but undoubtedly deadly and skilled by the looks of his eyes and his black, tailored attire and gear he possessed. That seemingly ceremonial black bandana around his head seemed to signify an unknown allegiance or following. There was a dangerous creed and zeal evident in his visage. Before the Guard of Dinitia could even shout alarm he was rushed by this dark phantom and pushed over the edge into the deep chasm below, his loud cries echoing in the shaft.

And then it began.

The guard in the shack beside the vault stood up when he heard the distant and muffled cries, and he peered curiously down the hall. He was about to call to his fellow guard locked in the hold around the corner when his eyes suddenly widened with fear. The mog scout with the aimed crossbow lying prone on the floor halfway across the smooth hall was prepared for this possibility. The guard was struck in the throat and knocked back to the floor within before he could make any sound. A small hand lever on the weapon allowed for a rapid reload, and the mog stood up, shuffling to the corner. To his left lay the entry to the vault.

260

Badai rushed up the stairs to his perch on the top floor bell room and readied his rope for a hasty escape. The *Advent* below had reached the inner dock and the raiding party was unleashed without delay. Every member of the small team knew his specific duty, rehearsed well in advance. They divided and bolted in two different directions. One group stole up the stairs toward the vault, bringing with them the handful of delegates from the ship, gagged and bound, coming from behind. The other stayed behind on the dock for a different task.

The mog looked around the corner to see if the guard within the vault was aware of the events, but he was beyond sight. He could be heard from somewhere within, pacing. The intruder didn't have much time. He knew that just inside the barred window of the guard shack was the release lever which opened the gates, just beyond reach of the window. He leapt onto the bars and drew his leather loop, readying for a short toss. He reached his arm within the window and looped the release. He then withdrew, letting out the length of leather rope as he reconcealed himself behind the corner just as the guard inside the vault to his left came within view, thinking he heard something. The guard would let out a cry when the time came, the pirate knew, but it would be too late to do him much good. He was in position and his fixture ready. He just needed to wait until his friends arrived, which should be any minute.

Just then a team of Kunn soldiers burst silently upon the long hall, searching for their comrade to see if all was ready. The signal was immediately received, and they hastily proceeded to the vault entrance. The mog stood again upon the threshold of the window, placed his foot upon the rope enabling a downward pull, and yanked at the cord, pulling the lever within and releasing the dual gates. In they all rushed, and the guard indeed succeeded with a shout of surprise, but it was all he could manage before he was brought down. With cutting tools, the removal of the keys locked on his wrist was but the work of a moment. The whole group moved straight for the Etar, suspended on the wall directly in front of them, and they positioned themselves for its removal. They had no time for removal of other riches, but nor was there need. This was wealth enough and their discipline held. The key was utilized and the multitude of steel fingers which held it in place for years undisturbed rotated, releasing it. They gently placed it, with difficulty, onto a stretcher of sturdy poles preassembled for easy carry of the massive and awesome artifact which they quickly strapped into place. Without further delay they returned upon their steps, toting the prize down the hall, then down the stairs, and finally onto their awaiting ship. Another small group passed them and led the Kandarian prisoners of the *Advent* back up and into the tunnel. These were to be used as decoys in the last but very important part of the mission before they could finally flee triumphantly.

The guard host upstairs was alerted by the strange sounds heard about them, odd noises in the night which stirred the reposing personnel. Suspicion of foul play was quickly aroused. Some shouts went up and within moments many booted feet could be heard above and the guards of Spen were flying down the stairs to the lower levels. They didn't need to be told which one.

Mellinak was the last to board the vessel. His presence was necessary to assure himself that the final part of the operation was completed. He looked upon the burning ships docked next to his. There would be no pursuit. His men did their work well, indeed he was impressed with their performance. Reward and incentive, virtues preached by the code. They could now hear distant cries up the stairs and his team shoved off with haste. The guards of Spen had encountered the chained gates which opened to the stairs leading to the dock below, and to their dismay found it impassable and had to detour the long way around, their shouts of anger echoing in the tunnels. The ship approached the mouth of the great cavern and the very last of his men, his prized secret scouts who preceded the attack, were the last to come running onto the dock from the winch room on the second level. The mechanisms were sabotaged to prevent reopening of the gate, and due to the lack of speed control which the gears ordinarily provided, the gate began a rapid and unregulated descent even as they proceeded underneath it. Mellinak couldn't afford to stop the vessel. The last of them made the leap onto the deck and Badai, up in the bell room, perceiving his opportunity as the bow of the emerging ship became visible below him outside the cave, swung down on his rope from above. He landed amidships just as the mammoth gate crashed right behind the vessel, close enough to fan the stern with the wind of its crushing cascade, and sending the water high into the air with a deafening splash.

Without a murmur from the crew the *Advent* sped away into the night, leaving its maimed victim to bleed behind it. The signal that sounded from the bell tower, disturbing the peaceful darkness of the quiet cove, was far too late for the heavy hammer used to strike the hollowed steel was missing along with the usual lights and shades for distant coded communication. The ships patrolling the outskirts of the island were nearer to the northern side and well out of sight of the desperate lookouts. All the frantic searchers could discover of the culprit vessel as they helplessly watched it sprint for the open sea were the Demarian standards on her stern, the sight of which brought speechless disbelief and caused a deep wound and anger that would not be easily mended. Only when Mellinak had reached well beyond the island did he finally allow himself a satisfying laugh. He sped towards home with his prize, leaving only the night in his wake. *Stalat uruz al-Medu!*

CHAPTER 4
GHOST HUNTERS

The *Cardela* sped onward toward Spen all that day and into the next. Damian and Cam looked ahead into the horizon impatiently, hounded by uncertainty and fear that they would arrive too late. They felt in their hearts that the *Advent* had fled beyond their aid and that they would have to resign it to its fate. They still had no idea where the Kunn pirates delivered their loot and if they didn't miraculously prevent their intentions at Spen, whatever they were, Vadro felt there would be little chance of ever discovering this elusive abode. Damian cursed the ill fate of the agent in Draga's tower. If he had just been able to communicate his secrets sooner the important passengers aboard that doomed vessel would have been delivered from the fate that awaited them.

Damian was finishing bracing the yards and securing some lines to the pinrail and Cam was climbing down the rigging that afternoon when Vadro emerged from below. They had a moment to take ease and the captain sought to converse with them. After some trivial courtesies they discussed the serious matter at hand.

"Tell me of this clan which we hunt," asked the captain, "for in this part of the Vidian Sea we know little of them. What is it they seek? Do they desire conquest of land and dominion of its people?"

Damian paused a moment at this perilous inquiry. He thought of his encounter with Tog on the hilltop and all that he had to say to him, little heeded at the time, now, with the certainty of his enemy's continued existence and pursuit, and the wisdom imparted, more thoroughly considered. Evidently this creed-following association sought something far greater, whether they knew the full immensity of it or not, and were effective pawns in that great endeavor, the gravity of which Damian himself had yet to fully appreciate and understand. If Tog was correct, if his supernal citations bore any truth, and after what little extraordinary events he had witnessed thus far Damian began to entertain the possibility that they may, then to even speculate the implications…No, he could not yet bear to even fathom such incomprehensibilities. Such complexities were not his to analyze. He chose his words slowly and carefully, for if

264

Damian himself did not yet fully comprehend, certainly this ordinary mortal could not, however wise.

He produced his answer with deliberation. "They seek conquest to be sure, but not in the usual sense. There is something far greater at work than mere domination of sovereignties and realms. If one would say domination of earth to in turn affect that which is withheld from view, then I would say that he may be closer to the truth. From what little I have come to understand of them they seek to resurrect the greatness of their creed, as it was of old, now scattered and lost, and to carry its greatness on in these latter days for their own zealous purposes. How that is all to be accomplished I do not yet fully know. They claim, with some degree of accuracy, to possess the favor of the Divine, and from Him they exert their abilities over others to fulfill what they believe is His will. They exist only for themselves, serving no one but extracting service, acquiring wealth and strength to destroy their enemies, competitors or vengeful rivals seeking to overthrow them. Earthly wealth is necessary for success of their various objectives, which involve all within its broad sphere of threat, and this is the stage upon which they now operate. It is the peaceful who stand in their way that will be doomed to be subjected to their indiscriminate tyranny.

"The prestige the Kunn has earned for itself is coveted and despised by other powers envious of it. The lands from where they hail have little organization in the form of broader government such as you have in Dinitia and Kandar, and those rogue entities with strength will inevitably rule in such an anarchic environment where one is solely responsible for himself, his own safety, livelihood, and necessities therein. From what I have learned through a well traveled acquaintance, strength rules in the realms of Dengland and beyond and one must adapt accordingly, making himself strong and feared lest he be succumbed by the wandering tyranny his weakness invites. So one must protect himself and his own. For those poor souls who cannot provide their own strength a life of forced servitude and victimization awaits. The clan has grown strong, venturing even to the seas and bringing thither their piracy, all in the name of some deific cause. Into other realms they roam, in search of what I don't yet know, even into my homeland and so imprisoned myself and my friend into forced servitude, generating wealth for their brotherhood. The signs, however, suggest the endeavors of the clan have a long history, before even the Ahga and his Brotherhood as we know it."

"Cannot they be confronted by an army of an aggrieved realm and so put an end to them?" Vadro asked.

"Not likely," Damian replied. "There is no suitable force to properly counter them on large scale. Demar could assume the task but they would likely be alone. The world is in a state of moral and organizational degradation. The numbers of the Kunn are too few, their chapters mobile, and their allegiance is only to themselves and their code. They are all but free to come and depart as they please. Their presence is more overt in the deserts where they originated, but have or do not need an established permanent residence. They have penetrated the west but keep themselves well concealed underground and their operations more secret. Their many henchmen are well trained, highly paid, and are more difficult to find here. It is difficult to wage war upon an underground gang of thugs who have safehouses and chapters in every city for they purchase the favor of the powerful and corrupt. Their residences must be discovered, their brotherhood penetrated, their commerce intercepted, their members eliminated, city by city until the Order is laid bare and disbanded. They can be destroyed, certainly, but it must be done singly and with small numbers."

"Yeah," interjected Cam, "two." He idly spun a blade between his fingers while he leaned on the hull of the vessel, slicing through the waves.

"And when we upset whatever the Kunn may be intending to achieve here we shall return to our homeland to continue our feud. It is to be hoped that you and your folk need not worry about further aggression toward you. Where these recent events in the Sea of Marán may be the isolated deeds of a small detachment of the Kunn, their presence is far greater on the mainland and it is there that we must return upon our completion here. It is with great anticipation and eagerness that I await my eventual arrival to the criminal cities there, Mod and elsewhere in Govannum and beyond where the Brotherhood is firmly entrenched, if that is where this journey takes me. It aches me to think that others are at the mercy of those clans and I cannot be there to assist. But a time will come. Meanwhile we have reason to believe the Kunn is attempting to establish an operating detachment in these parts for some filthy purpose of their own, simple piracy perhaps but maybe even something more, something which we have not considered, and for this reason our presence here is necessary."

"Yes," replied Vadro, "their purpose is to hunt the sea like jackals and murder my friends and rob them of their earned riches. I will not rest until they are expelled or destroyed, my brother and crew returned." So they spoke for a long while into the night, recounting news and histories of the world, pondering the present and future, and what may be in store therein.

They sailed onward and passed several islands of Marán along the north tip of the belt, and Vadro named them all for his guests and told them of their ways and cultures and the vital ties between the mainland and Dinitia as a whole. The alliance between Demar and Dinitia was strong and the news of pirating along the strait was disturbing. Damian and Cam passed news and stories to the crew at times, withholding more sensitive or personal information and keeping secret their small resistance. The two eagerly assisted with the sailing of the swift vessel and learned the ways of a sailor. The crew looked upon them with wonder. These two strangers who had voluntarily assumed duty with them on their ship seemed not of this earth but from another realm, for their speech was unlike most as were their faces and countenance, fair but deadly, holding a potency the observers had no doubt was being reserved, and from which they would flee when it was at last unleashed. They marveled especially at Cam who appeared to them little more than a young boy of about fourteen years, but such grace and speed and skill with hand and body was given him, abilities of the physical self one would be challenged to duplicate, that they smiled upon him and believed they had been blessed with beings of another world. They gaped in awe at his feats of dexterity which he proudly demonstrated on the ropes and masts of the vessel as if eager and restless to put them to use.

The wind was steadily athwartships and the clouds and rain from the night before departed to the south, and the sky to starboard made itself visible. The clear, cool night sky eventually stretched from all horizons and the stars shone. The night passed without event and it wasn't until late the next morning when the lookout finally heralded their destination.

Vadro looked upon Spen as they drew nearer and he gave a sigh of dismay. There were many ships about, including some Dinitian warships, far more than usual and he was approached by a pair of sentry vessels. His standards were present and his familiar brig easily recognizable, but Vadro knew something was amiss when he was stopped and boarded by his unexpectedly distrustful escorts. He and his crew had been to Spen harbor several times before and they had never seen a heightened paranoia and security such as this. He was finally allowed passage after some unusual scrutiny and due to his marked vessel of the Semári. They pulled their ship into the cove and docked. The harbor and boardwalks of lashed canes and logs were notably busier than usual. An unease could be felt. Guards were present all along the circular cove inlet, investigating the area all about, from the thick brush to the east of the looming cliff and the wharf and ships moored to the west, detained until allowed release. They were obviously searching for something and questioning the sailors and citizenry with earnestness. Vadro and his crew looked about them with confused stares. Damian and Cam quickly assessed the situation and exchanged knowing glances. They didn't need to be told that their fears and information were correct. As expected, they had arrived too late.

The crew was forbidden disembark temporarily due to security measures, but Vadro took with him his two guests onto the dock for he proposed to venture into the fort and inquire of the situation. Armed guards awaited them at the bottom of the gangplank. They hailed Vadro as a fellow defender but forbid the strangers and regarded them with distrust.

"They are friends of mine," Vadro proclaimed. "I will answer for them. They hail from the mainland and are familiar with this enemy, who, if I am not mistaken, have left their mark yet again."

"We know not of what you speak," answered one of them. "The enemy appears to be from Demar, with whom we have had longstanding alliance until now." They cast their unfriendly glances at the strangers who flanked the old captain.

Damian answered calmly. "The enemy you seek is not from Demar, though I perceive that it was designed to appear so. It is by some deception that this notion has been contrived. These thieves are far more elusive and wholly without honor. You need not fear one who has pledged their destruction. I will prove their culpability. Let me pass." They fell back before his command and some guards reluctantly escorted them all into the mouth of Spen which they reached by means of rowboat. The gate had been repaired, for the sabotage was simple, and they were rowed into the cave and up to the enclosed dock. The newcomers looked about them. They could see burnt wreckage still floating in the water within the great cave, the remains of the ships that were set ablaze. The gear on the floor of the dock had all been rummaged through and was spread out for search. The guests were halted by the stairs and told to await the officer who would admit them into the fortress. One of the guards departed to inform his superior of the newcomers. When their captain arrived shortly thereafter with some of his fellow officers he immediately recognized the sea captain. He was introduced to the guests who he was told claimed to be familiar with the phantoms, and was informed of their intentions to learn more of the crime and perhaps dispel the misconception as to the identity of its perpetrators. After a brief debate of few words he led all into the upper chambers and described in detail how the culprits accomplished the great theft. He brought them into the vault and showed them the emptiness on the wall where the Etar once sat. They could see much blood on the floor. It looked as though a great skirmish took place here. They then were led all the way upstairs to the bell room and lookout.

"And in the end," said the captain of the guard as they all gazed out into the harbor, "as I looked out into the night with hatred in my eyes I could clearly distinguish the blue and white standards of Demar on the culprit vessel as she sped out of the cove below the starlit sky, and the silhouette was that of a fully rigged ship of the line, undoubtedly from the northern country. The storm from the day before had slowly fled to the south and all was clear at that hour. I am loth to swear vengeance to an old ally, but this you say cannot be and I am deceived. But if this is not proof enough, my old friend, I still have this to show you."

He turned and crossed the long hall which brought them out to the fort's front main entrance on the other side of the cliff, high above the cove

268

behind it. The guards threw open the heavy double doors for their captain and they walked out onto the dirt road. Bodies there were, set in two groups, lined on the ground to the side. One looked as though they were esteemed diplomats and men of stature and nobility from Dinitia and the mainland territories, attired well and seeming venerable and wealthy, now heartlessly murdered. The other group evidently comprised of the guards of Spen killed in action.

"These bodies we found in the vault," said the guard captain, pointing to the fallen diplomats, "obviously slain by the valiant sentry within before he, too, met his fate." The captain pointed to one of the slain guards. "And as you can see the guilty are mostly from Kandar, as was their ship which our escorts easily recognized when the treasonous villains first arrived two nights ago. The Tarsh of Marán has been informed of the events, and his council even now considers action that must be taken. Our enemy is acknowledged. We are mustering a force for a mass search and possible counterattack."

"That will not be necessary," Vadro protested. "I know the foe that we must hunt. I of all sailors should know."

"You have been blind, Vadro," answered the captain. "This whole time you have wasted chasing your phantoms when you should have directed your attention to the real criminals. Then perhaps we would not have suffered this loss."

Damian and Cam approached the dead and examined them closely. They looked upon their hewn bodies and disfigured faces, though they doubted not that they had once been fair and held memories of a productive life and a devotion to their just duties. They had been removed from this world without consent, a world which would no longer receive the gift of their continued presence and blessings. Damian wondered what they could possibly have done to deserve this hideous end. He doubted not the real perpetrators and vowed to avenge the deaths of these men, not for them or himself alone, but for all those who have or may suffer the same fate in time to come. The Kunn has struck again, he thought. Only those bloodthirsty and professional murderers would commit such a despicable act of unwarranted terror. His memories of his own sorrow and hardships again came to mind and he gritted his teeth in anger, cursing their tardiness in preventing the atrocity. He closed the eyes of the slain and whispered blessings upon them. Then he stood and faced the guard.

"These men were not slain in battle," he said. "They bear wounds spread about them to deceive, wounds received after they were murdered. These men had their throats slit, an infliction I find difficult believing the lone heroic guard had either the inclination or ability to accomplish in a struggle against many. These men were probably murdered before or during the attack and placed to guise the identity of the real culprits, a deed certainly within the character of those we hunt."

Cam was still probing over the bodies with a grim look on his face when he suddenly gave a shout. Upon a certain portion of clothing of one of the dead his attention was drawn. They all ran over and attempted to discover what it was. On the two shoulder garments of the corpse, written in blood and evidently in haste for it was barely discernible, were painted two words, one on each side: EAGLE ISLAND. At first they appeared simply to be stains from wounds for there were many, but upon closer examination even the captain of the guard could not deny the inscription. There was a moment of silence and they all looked at each other.

Vadro was the first to speak. "I find it too much of a coincidence that the whereabouts of these thieves is still a mystery and after another of their deeds we find this inscription. These words, written in blood and in haste for the writer obviously had no other tools or instruments at his disposal, pertain to this mysterious island of which I believe I am familiar. He was also desperate for he had not time to write a more complete message. Perhaps they still have with them a prisoner or slave seeking our assistance."

"Maybe he is even still alive and is leaving us a clue in the hopes of us affecting a rescue," offered Cam.

"It could mean anything," the captain protested. "Are you saying that you actually believe this is related to the treason at hand? These men all had insignia of sorts upon them for they were of royalty and held rank. It will take more than a crude image to absolve these men of their guilt. Why, one can barely read it."

"A crude image written in blood?" Damian asked and looked at him. "It reinforces the idea that whoever did this had not time or better means and was probably well guarded. It seems to me it was written in desperation."

"I know of this island," Vadro insisted and became noticeably hopeful, even excited. "It cannot be mistaken with others. It is not a location that is inhabited that we know of, indeed it is avoided. My instinct tells me this is no accident or mere fanciful image of dried blood. Perhaps we have a breakthrough in this long hunt at last. And as we have no other leads to follow and only time to lose, I will make the journey there without delay."

"You'll be chasing another phantom of your imagination and vengeance, old man," the unconvinced captain called out as his guests began to depart. They stopped at these words. "Your search is in vain and your journeys plagued with misfortune and failure. Many times you have returned from your ghost hunt empty-handed though we have waited long for the success you promised when the Tarsh granted your wish to captain

270

his vessel, for an end you said would be to our mutual benefit but really was for your own satisfaction. The dungeon of Spen still eagerly awaits the arrival of your hunters of the sea. You are a disgrace to the Semáris who were once proud and competent. The Semáris will be redeployed very soon and you will be called to return to their ranks. But I see it is your doom to pursue ghosts and villains of your fancy. The Tarsh has even offered a handsome bounty for the return of your imaginary culprits. And here, for once, we have real proof as to the identity of those who have been secretly assailing us but you choose again to continue to follow the delusions bred by your anger, as is your wont. Go again, Captain, if you wish to desert us, but you will not be victorious. The curse of Agon is on you."

Vadro seemed to fall dead at these painful words. His head dropped as he considered them and felt the guilt of his failures weigh him like lead. He relived all his small journeys in his mind and the dismal ends they all seemed to amount to. He always felt personally responsible for the fate of his ship and crew, especially his brother, and these failures spoken of openly in the presence of others confirmed his own incompetence and cowardice to himself. He breathed deeply, besieged with guilt and disappointment. But there was something that told him his moment of delivery and justice had finally come. He made no return to the proud captain behind him who regarded him disapprovingly, but again looked up, as though purging himself of all doubt and castigation, and continued on his way with renewed hope. Damian and Cam remained, however, and the former placed his hand on the shoulder of the latter to restrain him for fire was in his eyes.

"What is your name?" Damian asked him. Cam eyed him angrily.

"Telachus," the guard captain replied, undaunted, flanked by two of his lieutenants.

"Well, Telachus, you may judge us anew when we return," Damian told him. "I warn you that your words, spoken solely from your own frustration and impatience, will betray you. I will bring to you a gift when I return that will remind you of your foolish words spoken here today." He turned and followed after Vadro with Cam in his wake, who looked over his shoulder at the obstinate guards and their doubtful stares.

"What did he say his name was?" one of them asked.

"Ratarra," answered the captain and they returned to their duties.

* * *

They returned immediately to their vessel moored along the boardwalk. Vadro avoided contact with the other guards and officers for he desired to escape without any of their interruptions. He knew the captain and his men would inform their superiors of Vadro's intention to ignore his orders to rejoin his fellow guardians of the sea and assume a new responsibility against their wishes. Vadro had no intention of receiving or obeying that order which he knew would come. He knew his opportunity for redemption had at last arrived to save him from all disgrace and finally enable him to complete the task he originally began, and he could barely contain his excitement to capitalize on this lead. It all seemed so suddenly obvious to him though he concealed his thoughts and designs from the crew until he was ready. He quietly issued some orders to his men who quickly responded. They only needed a new supply of water for they had still plenty of rations from their stop in Prova. Damian helped the first mate with this task to hasten the process and together they rolled new barrels from the supply house nearby and onto the vessel. The crew made immediate preparations for departure, aided by Cam who swung like an ape from sail to sail, and after a few final arrangements they were ready. With some blank looks from those on the dock the *Cardela* was speeding out of the harbor when the group of officers from Spen finally arrived at the mooring to arrest the rebellious captain. They failed in their mission to prevent his inevitable desertion.

The steady breeze from the northwest pushed the ship southward. The afternoon wore on and the sun shone bright and hot though the seas picked up under the wind. It was a perfect stern wind and Vadro took advantage, running with all speed to his destination which he knew would be at least a two day sail away. They were racing against time again, for their enemy possessed the great prize and the captain was sure they would not delay delivering such an artifact. The Etar itself must be beyond price, he thought, though he also knew there would be no shortage of offers for such a mighty and renowned heirloom. The Kunn must be powerful indeed, thought the captain, standing on the bowdeck as he gazed at the horizons through his glass and pondered the new mission. He couldn't believe this organization he hardly knew and virtually never heard of until recently was able to penetrate the almighty fortress of Spen Mala and succeed in such an infamous and daring scheme. It was only now that he could fully appreciate and respect the enemy he has been pursuing these past few months and could no longer question their success. This new suspicion of his, if proved correct, only added more to his disbelief at his enemy's incredible initiative. This newfound respect did not cause him greater fear, however, rather it strengthened his resolve. He thought of his own grievance at their hands, but with the help of his new friends they would suffer their redemption.

When the ship was well beyond the interfering grasp of the island and its sentries and was well under way, Damian and Cam approached Vadro for counsel, as expected, and he brought them below to his quarters, passing control of the ship to his first mate for the time. They placed themselves around his small table and he produced rolled maps from a case for them to review.

"What is this Eagle Island," asked Damian, "and what cause do you have to believe this may be the hideout we've been looking for?"

"It is not called Eagle Island," replied the captain, searching through his scrolls and leaves until he found the one he sought. He finally found it and placed it atop the rest and they looked upon it with interest. "It is called Cara Rock. It is named after the great seabird of Marán for a great projection of stone exists on the southern face of the cliff which naturally resembles that of the bill of the famous bird. It is the location of the legendary Sunken City of Cara, where the natives there were all killed in a massive earthquake centuries ago which was so powerful the island itself plunged partially into the sea, flooding the great city within as if Agon himself shoved the earth with his massive hands in a fury. The old city was built in the bowl of the highlands which surround it on all sides. It was grand indeed, according to old tales, for the folk that dwelt there were an offshoot of the great Maranisian civilization. But ingress into the island is virtually impossible for the island and its city are sealed by a completely encompassing high cliff, resulting from the land shift which closed the narrow gap into the inlet, denying one access to the ruins beyond. This is why no one has been able to explore the city and retrieve its riches, this perhaps being a design of the deity himself, if one believes in such things. He has kept them all safely for his own, all locked within the entombed city. I cannot think how our enemies infiltrated it, if they have, unless they discovered some opening in the impenetrable wall of rock which protects it. Perhaps the island has decayed enough in a certain location to admit a small vessel into its secret and undisturbed precincts. Though it has been hundreds of years since the Great Shift and has been mostly dormant, it is common knowledge that Cara Rock is slowly breaking from underneath and is sinking further into the sea. We must be cautious indeed when we arrive there."

"Whoever wrote the inscription could not have known its real name, then," observed Cam aloud as he studied the old map.

"No," agreed Vadro, "the writer called it by its most obvious and recognizable feature. The great stone bill of the Cara on the face of the cliff is singular indeed, and can be seen from afar. One will not find another similar resemblance anywhere in this sea. It is without any doubt that I seek it."

"And it is conceivable that this brave writer is still alive."

"Possibly," responded the captain. "And obviously a foreigner, if he is not familiar with the name. All Maranisians know of the legendary island of Cara."

"This city and its riches would also inevitably draw the Kunn thither," Damian added. "A city full of wealth undisturbed will be an attraction for the Ahga and his clan, always eager to accomplish the impossible. Maybe there is something of particular interest buried there. But this earthquake you speak of...perhaps there is something more. Agon indeed..." Damian's voice faltered as his thought drifted.

"The Kunn has beaten the greatness of Spen," acknowledged Vadro. "I now have little doubt of their capabilities. They are cunning and determined indeed, beyond anything I could have predicted even after experiencing their prowess some months ago. I am afraid you are right, Ratarra, this code they follow has delivered them greatness and reward."

Damian growled to himself. "More properly what they consider to be reward. It is then their duty to become more powerful than others to ensure success and overthrow of the inferior, as is called for by their code."

"Then we must put an end to that belief," Vadro said, and they pieced together a plan.

The next day was spent running with the breeze which showed no sign of abating, but pushed the heaving vessel along with all haste. They passed many more islands on either side, but they could not name them all for they rarely traveled this far south and the islands became smaller and rocky. The traffic seemed also to have been left behind for all sightings of and encounters with other vessels ceased rapidly. With no one about they immediately decided to enhance their skill and expertise with their heavy weapons before the engagement which they all hoped would come to pass. They readied their pitch and powders and loaded the shot into the metal carriers which were retracted for launch by means of a winch, and ignited the round missile ball. They fired all the ballistae several times each in teams of two and performed well and with satisfactory speed. Their captain seemed pleased.

When they finished they ran practice drills, rapidly tacking and turning in a simulated battle. Damian could haul and brace the yards of the mainmast himself, so mighty was he, and he felt as though he was riding and controlling the vessel under his own power, pulling the sheets and collecting the wind as if it were his obedient subject and propelling the ship like an arrow through the sea. The lines they rerouted and adapted for his solo use. This freed most of the small crew from their sailing duties, though several would still have to man the yards of the foremast, and it was devised that they should fight and man the weapons while Damian did most of the sailing. The compact ship proved especially maneuverable and would do well in combat. He felt not a little satisfaction and invigoration from the propulsion he commanded, and the execution of the responsive ship heaving under him as the result of his efforts was gratifying. The whole experience reminded him of riding his horse, who he hoped was well. There was little that could compare to this exhilaration. With the wind in his hair he shouted confidently to the crew who obeyed him as he constantly adjusted the sails, and the ship came rapidly about with Vadro at the helm behind him steering. They felt the sea spray on their faces as they sliced through the water and the men held onto the stays and chainplates for stability while they manned their weapon stations.

Cam was placed in the crow's nest high above on the mainmast for he had by far the best eyesight and could climb the rigging more rapidly than the others, even in a gale, and he shouted below to the captain the positions of rocks or landmasses, or heralded any change in the activity of the wind and sea in the distance. He could easily distinguish a duck from a gull a mile off without the aid of a glass and Vadro was glad to have such a sharp lookout. He executed his new duties delightfully and with the vigor of a child on his first fishing trip. And so the day passed quickly and with few sightings, and they covered much distance, feeling the rewards that teamwork and a productive day can bring, and they all smiled on each other and felt like brothers.

The next morning brought a brief rain which quickly gave way to clear skies, though the wind remained steady from the north and west. They changed their course and headed more to the southwest to avoid the worst of the cluster of rock islands and lengths of reef commonly known as the Kunga Teeth, for these grouped rocks were part of an underwater ridge which reached only just higher than sea level and were barely visible until a vessel was upon them. They had to steer through them, however, for encircling the huge reef would divert them too far and delay their arrival at least a day, an unacceptable option in their need of haste. During storms these rocks could be impossible to detect, though normally the belt of surf and foam enveloping the deadly teeth made this possible. Many unfortunate hulls were torn open as they unknowingly ran across the hidden predators and many victims were pulled under the surface to rest among like company in the graveyard far below. Sailors have long since avoided the Path of the Teeth and steered wide around, though these were few since little commerce flowed this way. The traffic this far south and west was mostly minimal, save for an occasional fishing vessel or adventurer from Dinitia's southern town of Sedini, about eighty miles west of their position. Cam kept an especially sharp lookout for these rocks which Vadro was sure to warn him about as they drew closer to this perilous geological feature. The perpetually excitable lookout shouted instructions below and he guided them confidently through the winding lanes of teeth. They assumed battle ready posture and the deck weapons were manned and prepared henceforth per orders, for they were drawing closer to their destination and expected encounter any time with an enemy ship which would be in this vicinity if their assumptions proved correct. Cam scanned the horizons in earnest, but all he could see were small islands dotting the ocean in all directions. Good area to hide a ship, he thought. They passed tediously but safely through the Teeth and saw no vessels that day or into the night and they pushed ever southward, alert but without event.

The next morning brought clouds and a stiffer breeze from the west and as a consequence the seas increased slightly. The ship rocked and heaved side to side on the churning water. The warm breeze from the day before cooled somewhat. Damian strode the deck and looked southward. Vadro came up beside him.

"We will not be able to identify the island from the north," he said gazing ahead of him. "The bill is on the southern face of the cliff. We won't see it until we've almost passed it."

They passed through an empty stretch of sea space all morning and finally came upon another large cluster of islands, higher and taller as though part of what seemed to be an ominous, sheer-faced mountain range and its family of detached offspring. Into this unique maze they plunged. It seemed as though they were floating through a hallway of chiseled rock. The wind and the din created by it and the choppy seas seemed to subside somewhat as the ship took refuge in this valley of tall, silent hills and it became eerily quiet. Their footsteps upon the wooden deck seemed to echo between the high cliff walls and they took pains to reduce noise. They felt as though they were creeping cat-like to a hidden enemy fortress which they knew could be around the next rock. They passed several islands and circled to the fronts to identify them but had not as yet found Cara Rock. The captain expected it any time and they kept a sharp, quiet watch all day. Cam communicated by hand signal to maintain silence, using colored pieces of scrap sailcloth and old flags. With such a collection of small islands and tall rocks here it would be easy to conceal a ship or even establish a point of ambush. They proceeded more slowly and carefully. The loneliness and desolation of these uninhabited islands and craggy rock features this far south created a feeling of dread and watchfulness. They seemed to watch the ship below them as it passed under their unfriendly and ghostly stares. The crew became uneasy and Vadro searched the area with an almost maniacal eagerness and impatience, darting back and forth from all points of the ship with haste, peering through his glass at phantom ships hiding among the clutter. This tense waiting and fear continued slowly and painfully into the afternoon when Cam suddenly waved the black cloth above in urgency.

"We have a sighting, captain," one of the crew uttered below a shout. Vadro and Damian ran over to the port bow. They soon saw an island ahead, to the southeast, separated from its siblings and across a short channel where the wind and seas again resumed their siege and the relative calm dwelling between the hills was forbidden entry. At the southern tip of this distant island they could plainly perceive a ship which seemed to head directly for it. They couldn't identify the ship at this distance, no one had seen this silhouette before and they all felt that sickening feeling they had come to expect. Cam was waving his flag in terror and excitement and throwing his hands madly. He had no doubt. Yes, this was the one.

The crew readied their weapons and prepared their missiles. Damian resumed his post as sole yard-hauler and gripped the lines, ready for action. Vadro was at the helm behind him, replacing the helmsman who helped the others with the loading and firing of the heavy ballistae. The strong northwest wind took them suddenly as they departed the shelter of cliff and the sleek ship sped like a dart eastward, across the channel. The enemy vessel was heading north, almost on opposite bearing as the *Cardela*, and convergence was inevitable. Cam judged that the two ships were equidistant from the island but with the enemy ship struggling and tacking close-hauled into the wind and the *Cardela* running strong at true broad, the Kunn ship was indubitably within the jaws of the attacker armed with the weather gauge. He jumped up and down with excitement in his high seat. Engagement was certain.

The gap between the converging ships drew smaller. Cam could see the pirates upon the deck, readying their catapults and deck ballistae. The alarm was up. This ship was not powered by rowers but by sails only, being of comparable rigging to the *Cardela*. The Kunn ship was slightly larger than its adversary with a broader beam as well and boasted a much fuller crew and compliment of weapons. All the better to board victim vessels with, thought Cam. The servants of the Ahga were watching this strange new ship approach them very intently for they did not know what to expect or whether it was friend or foe. The mog captain was strong and cruel looking, shouting to his men and pacing the deck angrily, closely scrutinizing the approaching vessel through his scope. They had produced their fire-powders and pitch and mixtures from below and distributed them about the deck. Melee and missile weapons were stacked and placed for rapid availability. When the mog captain recognized the colors of green and black waving to stern he gave a shout of dismay. He knew what that meant. The pirates rushed about, ready for battle. Cam relayed every move to Damian below, shouting for stealth was no longer a factor. The ships stared at each other like charging beasts across the water.

"Ready weapons!" shouted Damian and he gripped the lines for quick adjustment, his great voice easily making itself heard over the din of the wind and spray. The men and captain chorused in answer. He looked ahead, to port and starboard, ensuring their preparedness. He knew this first pass would be critical and they had to capitalize on their advantage. There was no doubt of the identity of the other ship now. He could see the figures rushing about the deck and their familiar bandanas and rank insignias without a lens. The demeanor of the mog captain alone and his obedient, disciplined crew were further confirmation of their despised secret allegiance and he growled aloud. Perhaps they were even out looking for easy prey, a fishing vessel or merchant seeking to cross peacefully. Maybe one that would rescue a drifting sailor, captain Vadro thought. These heathen Kunn pirates will pay.

"All ahead!" Damian shouted angrily. "Ready first volley! Remember the crimes these villains have aggrieved you with! Make safe the Strait! Let's send these scum into the cold depths where they belong!" The men shouted and threw their arms into the air, chanting death to these merciless approaching wolves. They remembered the disasters at sea suffered at the hands of this clan, and finally beholding them riding the waves before their eyes confirmed the existence of these elusive, phantom brigands to the increasingly doubtful but loyal crew. Old shipmates and brothers they were, taken or killed by ruthless pirates driven by greed and desire of that which belonged to others, heedless of honor or respect for laws and principles of moral behavior. This plague would be resolved here and now with little remorse.

They bore down quickly on the Kunn ship, struggling against the headwind. The wind was strong and the waves mirrored its anger. The ships tossed and heaved on the rolling seas. Within moments the ships were within a hundred yards of each other.

"Remember the *Phelidan*!" Damian shouted and the men yelled in unison. "Come to port!" The captain turned her ten degrees and sought to come alongside to expose the broadside for attack. The mog captain, perceiving this, also brought his vessel slightly to port to align the barrage. The ships were almost parallel. The crew ignited the round shots waiting in their drawn carriers. Cam could see the mog pirates also preparing their volley and he shouted a warning below. Damian waited a moment for the right time. "LOOSE!" he yelled in fury. All four ballistae fired at once, the two on the starboard side amidships and the ones to bow and stern which could pivot sufficiently for a broadside shot. One hit the hull below the gunwale with a thud, one landed on the deck and started a small fire which was immediately tended to before the fire-chemicals ignited. One missed completely, sailing across the deck, but the last shot penetrated one of the lower main sails, blowing a sizable hole right through it and setting the sail afire.

The pirates loosed their volley almost simultaneously and the air was filled with glowing balls and their trails of smoke. Two landed on the *Cardela's* deck and some crewmembers immediately dumped sea water to douse them. Some darts and arrows flew across the deck or stuck into the hull and the crew crouched for cover. But the last shot came from the stern of the Kunn ship. It was a steel-tipped heavy bolt, and with the ships' sterns and helms aligned perfectly near the end of the pass, the mog archers aimed a shot at the helmsman. The *Cardela* straked low to port in the tossing seas, bringing the starboard side high. The careening missile struck the armor plate on the gunwale at an angle, deflecting it upwards with a shriek of metal on metal. The bolt continued past, striking the head of Captain Vadro in a glancing trajectory as it flew over the ship and into the sea. The captain was thrown to the slick deck unconscious, blood running down the side of his head from a deep gash. The mog captain clenched his fist in triumph as he sped past.

"Bring the captain below!" shouted Damian. Two men immediately picked him up and clumsily carried him belowdecks. The first mate resumed the helm. Furious, Damian pulled the halyards and the sails pivoted. "Come to starboard! Make ready for another pass!" The crew did not question his authority in the stead of their captain's but hastily made ready the weapons, running along the slippery deck to assist those now under-manned. One of them slipped on the way to the bow and fell hard into the bulwark as the ship turned rapidly and bounced on the waves. Damian cursed aloud.

The Kunn vessel came slowly to port, coming about with the wind now behind her. The pirates were reloading the deck weapons and preparing for another pass. Well, the mog captain thought, it looks like I have a real fight on my hands at last. These merchant vessels he usually ambushed were like toothless sheep by comparison. Now he could put his crew to the test on a more worthy opponent. He leveled off the ship's turn, anticipating the next route of his enemy. He was now running before the wind, almost parallel again with his adversary who had brought their ship around to the same bearing. They had both made a half-circle for each other and were now flying southeast before the wind.

The *Cardela* completed her turn and was now chasing the Kunn ship. One thing was for sure, Damian immediately noticed. His ship was definitely faster and much more agile than his prey, though they were shamefully under-manned. He wondered how he could put it to use as he quickly gained the enemy vessel, looming close enough to starboard one could almost leap aboard. The pirate ship turned to port to again align the broadside for another volley.

"Aim for the sails! LOOSE!" Damian yelled again and the air was filled with smoke and fireballs from the simultaneous volleys. Several punched holes in the sails of the pirate vessel, causing them to burn. The Kunn aimed for the deck and landed several missiles. And again the crew worked frantically to extinguish the flames before the powders caught fire. The pirates on deck drew their bows and aimed their crossbows for a volley. They'll all be killed in the barrage, thought Damian, hearing the warnings and desperate cries from Cam above. He saw his crew running about, stamping out fires, taking cover in the hail, and making an attempt to assist one another to reload the weapons for another shot. He needed more time to ready his vessel.

"Hard to port!" he cried to the helm behind him. Damian swung the sails again and the ship ruddered, abruptly bolting away to the east slightly to put some distance between the ships as the pirates released their hail of darts. This maneuver undoubtedly saved his men from the worst of it as they branched away. Many arrows and bolts thudded into the hull and masts and whined over the heads of the crew, though a few found a mark. Damian saw two of his men fall with arrows in their backs.

"Prepare to bring her about on my mark!" Damian shouted. He sped eastward for a few moments, putting some distance between the ships and giving his diminishing crew more time to ready the weapons for another pass. The Kunn ship remained steadily on course, heading southeast, watching the *Cardela* closely and trying to guess its next move. The pirates were throwing water on the sails in a fruitless attempt to douse the flames which were slowly gaining in strength and ferocity in one particular sail and beyond reach, the maintopsail. This threatened the sails around and in close proximity of it, and the captain immediately ordered a host to climb the rigging and beat the flames down before it enveloped the whole assembly. His vessel becoming victim to fire and therefore unsailable was unacceptable. His enemy was relatively unscathed in regards to her hull. He issued a new order.

"Hard to starboard!" Damian shouted. "Bring her about!" He swung the sails again and the ship spun hard, back to the south. The Kunn ship turned to port to engage and the ships again were on converging courses. "Make ready!" Damian barked. Only a few more seconds…

Cam's voice could be heard again from high above. "Damian!" he cried and pointed. "HARPOON!!"

Damian gritted his teeth. A small party of mogs and Turuks could be seen preparing their gangplanks and melee weapons. *They're going to board us.* "LOOSE!" This time the volley struck a keg of powder and the deck of the Kunn ship quickly caught fire. But at the same time the volley of the Kunn came screeching in response. Two more of the *Cardela's* crew fell to arrows and darts. Damian howled with rage but what happened next filled them all with even greater terror. A single crack and whistle could be heard as the harpoon launched from its great mounted engine of black steel.

The sickening whisper of the unwinding rope seemed to pronounce doom to the cowering crew aboard the *Cardela* as the heavy spear hurled its way to its target. It found a weak gap between the armor plates and crashed into the upper port side, splintering wood as it pierced clean through.

Damian watched the Kunn captain shout and clench his fists in triumph. He looked ahead, to the sea and the activity of the waves, his broken crew sprawled upon the soaked and heaving deck among the wooden splinters and dead and wounded, the Kunn ship and its behavior and how it was sailing with its continuing damage due to the strengthening fire. The pirates began the turning of the capstan, a girthy drum which drew in their harpooned vessels. The drum revolved and coiled the rope but Damian could see that he had several moments to take matters further into his own hands.

The ships were slowly passing each other though the thick rope connecting them pulled taut. Damian tied the lines of the sails quickly to the belaying pins in a matter of seconds, angling the yards for a turn to port. He drew his bow and fitted an arrow. *Wave! Wave!* came the cries from above. He glanced one last time at the approaching waves rising before the headwind which he was now coming across as the ship came to port, approaching a southerly bearing. The mog captain was hissing with laughter and satisfaction as he slowly drew the *Cardela* closer, heedless of the frantic crew and flames which surrounded him. He saw victory beyond all doubt. This crippled crew he was up against could not withstand boarding and he would take possession of their ship. With only a moment left in the pass Damian drew back his great bow with one last look at this detested captain who returned his own disdainful expression to this persevering but doomed sailor. The garvonite arrow shot across the water and pierced through the leather-armored torso of the mog, dropping him to the burning deck. *I find your laughter disturbing.* He drew again quickly and shot the helmsman. The wheel spun free.

"Bring her to port... NOW!" Damian yelled to the steadfast helmsman behind him. The *Cardela* rode a sizable wave perfectly as she turned about again. "Drag her in!" The taut rope pulled the Kunn vessel abruptly around to the north, into the wind. The pirate vessel caught the wave badly in its unmanned, wild turn and broached in the headwind, snapping the top half of the foremast which fell backwards with its members still climbing the ratlines, shouting as they descended into the angry sea. At the same moment Damian drew his sword and with one swing cut the impaling harpoon which held them in half, releasing them. The Kunn ship was released and thrown sideways by the wave and capsized, floating on the water a flaming hulk. The sea enveloped it, a mass of fire and wreckage which was quickly pulled under before their eyes.

CHAPTER 5
THE DEAD CITY

Damian and the rest of the crew tended to the fallen. Including the captain there were three wounded and two dead. They were brought below where one of the crew most familiar in treating wounds tended them. Damian produced from his pack below a vial which he gave to the crewman to administer to the hurt. Then he went above. Only six crewmen remained to sail the vessel under Damian's command. They cleaned the deck, tossing overboard the splintered and broken wood. The dead were wrapped in sail cloth to be given a ceremonial burial at sea later. They took some food and water but did not have time to rest. Cam's cries above brought them back to their duties and peril.

"Damian!" he cried. "That's it! That's the island!" He pointed north, back to the same island the Kunn ship was approaching earlier. They could clearly see the distinguishing shape of rock in the likeness of a large bill jutting outwards on the southern face of the cliff which was coming around and in view. They brought the ship around to the north. With the wind now off the port bow the *Cardela* slowly sailed toward it.

Damian and the crew looked upon this island of haunting legend. It seemed to withhold dark secrets it did not wish disclosed to the world around it, animate or otherwise. This island of mystery seemed to emanate a life force of its own, a will and purpose independent and regardless of the laws other forces and masses of the world adhered to. An unfriendliness and opposition could be felt by all the crew, especially Damian, a resistance put forth by the angry and isolated domain of lifeless rock that could be felt, and the crew grew pale and withdrawn. They remembered what their captain said about the land itself and the disaster of epic proportions caused by the moving earth. The legend of the Sunken City was well known among the Maranisians and was passed down through the generations. The hostile island brought death, they knew, and could not be trusted. It harbored a hatred of mankind and all it created and devised. Even as they gazed upon its approaching shape of menace, seething with volatility, they perceived a distant rumble and unrest, as if the rock still slept uneasily and fitful. Something had disturbed its long slumber and vexed its dreams, provoking its eventual and deadly resurrection, and the crew stirred uneasily. As if in confirmation of these fancies they beheld several large chunks of rock slide off the face of the cliff below the great hill and crash into the sea below. This foreboding of peril drew their scrutinizing attention and they could discern what appeared to be a minute gap in the impenetrable wall of rock, a fissure partially extending to the high roof of the otherwise unyielding barrier, created by the wrath of the island or by force of unknown craft, large enough perhaps to allow entry of a vessel, though had it not been for the revealing activity of the loose boulders this fissure was virtually impossible to detect from afar for it divided the rock at an angle invisible to observers at sea.

"If we are not killed by these pirates we shall be crushed by this ruthless and accursed island of rock," growled the first mate, Erius, standing beside Damian on the bow.

"Nay," replied Damian, "only those who seek to disturb or wrest the treasures within. The land itself speaks to me. I feel a great lamentation spoken from the ghosts of people who once dwelt here, a song of sorrow and shame. It is as if they reaped their fate and their greatness is withheld from them forever, for they diverted themselves down a wayward and corrupt path in their latter years of life and were no longer worthy of the splendor they created. Their folliness was their downfall but they know it is too late to redeem themselves."

"Then there must be wealth within indeed," said Erius, "enough to fill an armada of ships. It is little wonder our pirate friends are making such a venture. And if we are victorious over them then it is our merit to remove that which was taken from us and rightfully stow the wealth in our own vessel for transport back home, and for ourselves, I might add."

"No," protested Damian. "Removal of treasures will undoubtedly result in our own destruction. They must remain undisturbed, even that which the Kunn villains may have unearthed. The rescue of any prisoners and the destruction of the pirates is our primary objective. The Etar, I believe, we may also be permitted to retrieve, if it is there, for it was not crafted by this people. Nothing more." Erius sighed audibly at this and muttered something to one of the crew as he strode away but resumed his duty at the helm.

The ominous rock island drew slowly closer. The fissure became more visible as the ship came around to its southernmost point. It appeared to be a prodigious crack in the rock face, extending vertically from below the waterline where it was widest, narrowing to the crest of the cliff some five or six hundred feet straight up, though it failed to achieve the precipice which formed a high but obviously unstable bridge over the narrow gap beneath the divided cliffsides. This aperture undoubtedly was the unintentional result of some natural phenomenon for they could all now plainly perceive the instability of the land mass itself. The bill of the Cara projected from the cliff directly above this hidden point of entry and seemed to them to be a sentinel or guardian of the island. It filled the crew with foreboding for it seemed to watch them approach below with a sentiment they felt sure was an indiscriminate disapproval and repulsion for all beings of the earth. An unknown doom could be felt, one that would inevitably come to pass but was yet restrained until a certain fateful moment.

They turned aside from these reveries and resumed their duties aboard their ship. They immediately reefed the sails for what would prove to be a careful and tedious entry into the hidden realm beyond the concealing cliff face. The strength of the wind against full sails would have dashed them on the rocks as they attempted the careful maneuver. The rock above formed an arched ceiling high overhead for this narrow point of entry and cast the deep tunnel into darkness. They slowly ruddered the ship toward the dark and widening gap. Cam kept quiet now but pointed and signaled, watchful and intent. The uncanny sculpture of menacing rock passed slowly above them as they plunged carefully into the dim tunnel, but they did not dare look upon it. They felt sure they had entered, without invite, into a forbidden and guarded realm. The sound of the elements fell dead as the world of fury was left behind and an echo could soon be heard. It seemed as though they were sailing through a dark and winding subterranean lake under an unfriendly archway of steep rock. The sound of stones falling into the water could be heard in places, sometimes near, sometimes far. They fancied that they heard the moaning of the earth around them at times and they looked up in fear. Damian took command and led them deep into the tunnel, lifting their spirits with fearless words and courage.

Before long the tunnel widened and the archway of rock above began to thin and recede until it opened completely, allowing the sun and sky to light the chasm. The ship took a few more turns and they could see what must be the exit from this confining cavern for the rock finally separated altogether and revealed the mystery beyond. They all ran forward to look with eyes unblinking and mouths agape. There, as they made the last turn, under the sun lay the city of death they had all heard much rumor of, though they would all agree the words they had heard were exceedingly feeble in describing the spectacle. The foolish myths and tales failed to convey the eerie dread the City of Cara produced in he who beheld this phenomenon of unparalleled death and destruction. Even Cam stood silent and dumbstruck in his high perch. Like a vast graveyard in a wide rippling swamp lay the doomed civilization of these bygone people, stretched out for miles in the enclosure. The innumerable stone buildings thrust out their heads in endless rows of tombstones before them at the bottom of a vast bowl of high encircling rock which shielded the inhabitants below it from the perils of the earth. The empty windows stared out at the newcomers like a thousand eyes searching sadly in all directions, forever cold and lifeless. The speechless onlookers could not doubt the greatness this legendary city once boasted with its obelisks and grand temples and wide amphitheaters visible in the distance. Domes of structures revealed their round crests above the conquering liquid which surrounded and consumed all. Mighty pillars and roofs of skilled and appealing architecture still floated above the stone-paved streets resting below. The dwellings of these beings, whoever they were, stood in rank upon rank, as far as the eye could see, like an army of ghosts that seemed to whisper of the departed, and a voice could almost be heard as if the desperate inhabitants endeavored in vain to speak of their fate but were hushed by an unseen hand. Only the seabirds inhabited them now, their haunting shapes and voices the only break in the silence and stillness. Great boulders of fallen rock could be seen vaguely along the far end and along the sides and all throughout the flooded city. Paths and avenues were created by their destructive descents, and artful buildings and structures that once stood proud were crushed or toppled in their rampage. No imaginings of a more destructive force of nature could any hope to conceive, and they all gazed with speechless horror.

It was Damian who revived them all from the terror which held them immovable. They resumed their positions on deck. Damian held the glass to his eye and strove to view the more distant parts of the great city and searched for anything that might yield signs of enemy presence or activity. The tall masts of the ship were also a concern for it would reveal their presence so he sought for a place to possibly conceal the vessel while they formulated an attack plan. All of a sudden Cam was signaling with excitement and pointing. The enemy had been sighted. They pulled their ship behind a huge boulder which landed in front of the city on the southeast corner, large enough to anchor their vessel safely behind for the moment, though they could only hope they had not been sighted themselves yet. Damian ordered the unfurling of the sails while they were anchored and idle for there was little wind here and he felt a hasty withdrawal was inevitable. Cam slid down the rigging and he and Damian leaped overboard onto a climbable and flat portion of the boulder to have a better look at the city. Erius joined them.

"You can see them at work now," Cam said pointing to the north. "Those maggots are busy in the area of that huge temple and the surrounding buildings."

"I see nothing but fallen stones there," Damian replied, peering through his glass. "Looks like that whole side of the mountain fell in."

"No, closer in, toward the middle. They've built some kind of walkway right on the water, you can see them crossing on them. Looks like they've been here awhile. They've got that whole area boarded, like raised streets of wood and staging built right on the water, winding around the blocks."

"You're right, Cam," Damian acknowledged and adjusted the lens. "They put their prisoners to work, that's obvious enough. They're hauling loot across the walkways and onto their…ships. Now I see them, they must be at least a mile off. I count two of them."

"Yeah, one of them is the *Advent* by the looks of it. Big bastard. The one moored beside it is just as big. Must be a transport or cargo cog by the looks of it, for hauling all the loot back to their Ahga. We made it here before they bolted, it seems. Got lucky on that one, maybe the Etar is still on it. Oh! There's two more, attack ships by their silhouette, farther off, to the east by that domed structure. Must have taken a hundred years to build that." Cam paused a moment to appreciate the work and years undertaken to construct this wonder and the power its people once possessed. "Damian this is one major operation they have going on here. The Ahga must be serious about this place and it's no wonder. You can see the cranes and tripods hoisting booty from the depths. Looks like an excavation. There must be a score of prisoners over there, and who knows how many underwater roping it all up."

"And they will have plenty to spare, then," said Erius. "Those they have aggrieved will at least receive some recompense. I will enjoy confiscating their treasures."

"No!" Damian said as loudly as he dared and with urgency. "Do not touch anything! There is something at work here, a will bent on vengeance and destruction to those who disturb the relics and secrets within. Already I perceive a rising wrath and it is like a branch about to snap under the weight of many stones. We have little time. We have to board the prisoners as quickly as possible and sail out of here like the wind. Can't think of anything too elaborate, either. It's all open and time is against us. Maybe I'll just sail right in there and introduce myself. We should have a few moments before they can identify us. I don't think they will see us approach until we're right on them."

"Too late!" cried Cam. He spied an errant scout observing them from atop the nearest structure, not far from where they were anchored. Apparently he was about, searching or keeping lookout at the farthest and southernmost extremities of the city and spied the vessel as it drifted into the realm. He recognized the colors of the ship and was now endeavoring to alert his friends of the intrusion. Cam leaped from the boulder onto the rooftop of the first of the buildings right in front of him and began his pursuit.

"Go!" he cried over his shoulder as he fled. "Just go in! Take the ship in! I'll catch up!"

Damian hissed and cursed and he leapt back onto the deck of the *Cardela* followed by Erius. "Raise anchor!" he yelled and the men sprung into action. "Ready weapons! Take her in!" Without waiting he grabbed hold of the capstan and wound the anchor in a matter of seconds, for it was not deep. The breeze was light under the cliff but with the use of poles in the shallow water the men propelled the ship into the floating city and caught the wind. There was an obvious avenue for vessels which wound through the flooded ruins and led to the further depths and docking area which the Kunn had constructed and moored their ships to, and this is what they followed. It seemed to Damian that the entirety of this pirating detachment was present, with the exception of their lost ship, and he was fortunate enough to arrive with the rest of them all here. There certainly was a fair amount of activity over there and a small handful of ships. *I'll bring an end to the piracy of the seas now, in one fatal blow,* he thought to himself as he angrily shoved the ship along. Silent, half-submerged buildings in various stages of disintegration passed them on either side as they crept inward like water snakes of the river moving in on prey before the pounce.

Badai of the Mak-Baccád was keeping lookout on the roof of the southernmost building, expecting the return of their patrol ship. It wasn't safe or wise to send one out in broad daylight like that but Mellinak insisted. With the arrival of their supply ship from Serabat and the *Advent* bearing the prize, the possibility of discovery or attack in the wake of the great heist was too high. Dinitian ships would be on the prowl, he said, and the good fortune they experienced with their prolonged concealment would eventually give way to discovery. Mellinak was definitely impatient and anxious, especially now that he achieved his goal and was nearing the final stages of its completion. He loathed every minute his treasure was delayed delivery. He felt like a beast with its prey between its teeth, eyed enviously by scavengers which surrounded him. If he didn't move soon it would be stolen from him by other opportunists interested in his hoarded wealth. It was just a matter of time before they were pinned in their seclusion with no escape and he could not assume that his ruse was executed wholly without flaw or chance of penetration. The simple mystery may have been unraveled by now though it was sufficient at the time to facilitate his escape.

But there was a certain relic discovered in one of the buildings they explored just this morning which must be brought to their Baccád superiors on the mainland, and it was upon this that Mellinak waited as he strode the deck of the *Advent* with obvious impatience. The removal operation was taking far longer than expected for this valuable piece was fastened to its base of stone, prolonging the extraction. Badai couldn't agree more, believing that moving lightly and secretly and fleeing with pockets only half full was far more valuable than risking being exposed with greater wealth and destroyed, a sentiment he shared with his captain. And this accursed island was certainly making him uncomfortable. Why one could almost feel something was going to happen here any minute; an indescribable tension brewed to the point of breaking and they would be caught in the middle. The island didn't seem to want to give up the ancient Stone. The lean-statured Turuk looked at the cliffs around him with distrust and unease, as if he expected them to crumble on top of him and his idle comrades any moment. But one of Mellinak's lieutenants insisted the wait would prove more than compensatory and the find imperative to the cause of the clan. Badai growled with fury. This was taking too long.

He watched the incoming ship wind through the narrow tunnel. At first he was relieved. Our ship has returned. There must not be anyone about, he thought, and relaxed somewhat. But this immediately gave way to disbelief when his sharp eyes caught sight of the sailors and markings as they pulled in closer. His fears came true. They had been discovered at last. He needed to sound the alarm which consisted of nothing more than a heavy, oversized construction rod of iron and a length of old steel hung from some beams, salvaged from the destruction for this use. Being restless and angry, though, he wandered and left them a few buildings away. He began to run back across the buildingtops.

Cam leaped onto the buildingtop and chased his enemy. He appeared to be much leaner and swifter than most of the Kunn scum he had contested with in the past, and apparently well trained. This Turuk, roughly his own size, lightly armored for stealth, jumped fully from roof to roof, clearing the spans of water beneath him, perceiving his pursuer who was surprisingly close on his tail. Cam saw him look over his shoulder and caught a cunning gleam in his eye as he was obviously trying to reach a certain destination. There it was, some crude alarm improvisation on that next rooftop. Badai made the leap but looked back and knew he would only have time for one swing at the sonorous plate of steel before this capable and agile adversary was upon him. He absolutely had to alert his friends, but they all had their heads buried in that unnecessary venture deeper in the city. But as he reached for the iron Cam let loose with a volley of spikes even as he leaped onto the roof to prevent the sounding. Badai was forced to evade and he dove onto the floor, dropping the hammer and jumping back onto his feet.

"Can't let you do that," Cam said as he drew his sword. "Your business here is over."

Badai stood before him with his own sword drawn and regarded this strange new foe condescendingly. An arrogant smile spread about on his lips as he brandished his sword. He would enjoy the challenge leading to this daring fool's destruction.

"Is it now?" he asked and his voice hissed with evidence of insult. "What, do you think you can stop us? You know nothing of what you are up against, little fool, nothing at all. One must have the favor of the Divine One, and be strong and swift indeed and bear much pain, more than you can know to bear the marks of the Mak-Baccád!" Badai laughed and pointed to his proud hash marks on his neck and flexed his ripped musculature. Only a select few could claim that title.

"I know as much as I need to," Cam replied and drew his other sword, swinging them in unison faster than sight. "I have all I need to bring you down, and I think you'll find me quite capable of doing it." Cam grinned angrily and returned the insult.

"Indeed? I would like to see you accomplish that," Badai said with a face that spoke his hatred. "Let's see how you do." With that he ran across the rooftop and Cam began the chase, one that led over and through the many structures, their rooftops and third and fourth stories beneath serving as their battlefield, a lengthy and dangerous chase of prolonged intensity requiring all his abilities, patience, and endurance, a chase Cam would never forget. Cam kept close behind, succeeding giant, twenty-five foot leaps from building to building in all directions, now leaping down through windows of lower levels, now atop balconies and crumbling staircases which broke below and crashed into the water close underneath them, all the time moving at immortal speeds in a great pursuit through a floating, dead city. And anon, Badai would stop quickly and fence with his adept foe, exchanging blows with sword and body in a coordinated and skillful attack and defense utilizing multiple weapons simultaneously, skills he had trained for before the Ahga. Then Badai would bolt again in another direction, leading the chaser up wide and once beautiful steps of stone or across raised courtyards with statues upon them, and turn for duel atop chiseled railways and crumbling archways or dried garden beds and bath halls. Their forms could be seen from afar, if one had a moment to fix his eye upon their tireless figures which moved swiftly about like two dueling birds of prey, fighting over territory.

Cam was at loss for a moment. He chased Badai into the third level of a wide hall which led outside to the roof, and the whole was open, save for a dividing and engraved partition running the middle. It was extensive, as though it once accommodated many guests on many festive and perverse nights of recklessness and corruption unspeakable under the moon which bore witness long ago. Now it was silent and empty and littered in places with decay. Bones lay about, mingled with flotsam. He entered quickly but carefully, alert for attack. He began to case the area, swords drawn, staying close to the outside walls which wrapped around the center partition in an oval shape. Sweat dripped steadily from his glistening forehead as he shuffled lightly onward. Suddenly Badai emerged from hiding and drove Cam backwards with an onslaught of fury.

"You've done well!" he cried angrily as he came down on Cam with heavy blows, and Cam could sense the hint of insult and hate in his voice for the foe he failed to lose in his challenging pursuit. "Almost as well as any of the Baccád could have done. I must say your skills almost impress me! But now I must be done with you, for you are a hindrance. I have no further time for your dull company. Rest among the dead in the cold water!" Badai managed to slash Cam's leg, drawing some blood before kicking him out the window. Cam fell backwards into the water outside two levels below with a curse and a splash. Badai sped off to the north toward his friends. He didn't see his enraged pursuer climb up the portholes like an ape and follow him.

Damian and his crew sailed the vessel through the valley between the old stone buildings which served as the mountains on either side. All an onlooker would have seen were the masts moving oddly through the city as if floating down the winding avenues paved by the dead. Damian looked below and could see, as they floated slowly by, remnants of the dead civilization: bones and fossils covering the paved streets below, left where their keepers perished; great statues and sculptures of stone, toppled and split, covered in growths; tools and wagons and other creations, barely discernible due to decay, pored over by small schools of fish. The stories of their culture and life could be read merely by passing over the remains. But Damian had little sympathy for them. He did not need to be told of the reason for their destruction. For everything he gazed upon resting in the shallow depths spoke of a people who became giddy with their obsessive wealth and possession and enamored with corrupt and unguarded behavior. They had embraced an existence of unreserved gluttony and indulgence, devoid of principle or discipline, and for this reason their greatness was confiscated. With free will comes responsibility and reward–or punishment. Damian cast his glance upwards again and looked once more at the surrounding cliffs and he paused unmoving as the boat moved forward, as if listening to powers beyond the sight of mortals and gauging their potency. He could still perceive a thunder and rumble within the depths. Soon it would burst, he thought. It cannot be withheld for much longer.

Cam ran across the buildingtops. His foe was only two buildings ahead of him, running like the wind northward. Cam could see the attack ships of the Kunn now less than a mile away and the area of excavation which they were moored around. The pirates had built stagings and raised walkways of planks and beams around the relic, structures to facilitate the withdrawal of treasure hoarded within or below water. He could see Kunn thugs and prisoners traversing them with tools and gear, or chests and sacks laden with loot. At his current and relentless pace Badai would reach his associates in a matter of minutes and pass the alarm. Cam looked back quickly as he leaped across a wide space over rippling water and could see the masts of his ship moving steadily toward the docking area of the *Advent* and the supply ship. It would only be a few more minutes before engagement. Cam wanted this fox for himself anyway. He seethed with anger and pushed himself to even greater speed, driven by his own wrath and determination for justice. Rooftop after rooftop fled from underneath him until his enemy, perceiving him, slowed to counter. He stopped atop the flat stone roof of what must have once been some kind of governmental or civil establishment or gathering hall for it was vast, measuring some hundreds of feet across, consuming two blocks, and was higher than its counterparts below which peered up at it. This was a capital building.

"So you've come back for more?" Badai said and turned, planting himself firmly on the stone floor. He drew his sword again and it rang as it was unsheathed from his back. He pointed it at Cam threateningly. "Not satisfied with my generosity at sparing your life? This time I will finish the job."

Cam said nothing in reply but with a yell and the ferocity of a raging beast unleashed an attack on his opponent. Swords clashed and rang like bells on the roof. He could not now doubt the skill this Turuk clearly demonstrated in fighting and discipline. The Kunn worshipped and trained steadfastly until perfection and invulnerability had been achieved as called for by the code, and here was proof of a true student, indomitable and virtually omnipotent. The Ahga must be proud of the fruit he has produced here. His speed and strength were impressive indeed, close to his own, though Cam was about to prove his true and superior abilities in this final bout. He drove Badai downstairs where he turned and fled.

Cam chased him below into what seemed to be a large room of many divisions. This apartment was almost as large as the roof above and consisted of uniform rooms, or halls, which were partially divided by many walls running parallel to each other, but rather than terminating at their extremities fell short by design and an archway was built, thus enabling one easy access to all subdivisions without the necessity of doors. An arcade of windows or cutouts there were in all the walls which aligned themselves perfectly so that one could see the far ends of the building from anywhere he stood, though the inner recesses were dim. Badai led him on another chase through this maze, seeking somehow to use these halls to hide himself and eliminate his enemy. He plunged into the shadows and disappeared.

Cam ran through the halls, searching for his hidden foe. His head turned each way, looking through the windows across the wide room. He could see Badai at times running in different directions, his shape appearing in the windows, sometimes nearer, sometimes farther, trying to outwit his enemy. Swords clashed at times through openings when encounter was finally achieved, after which Badai would speed off and disappear to further frustrate Cam. He seemed to be enjoying his torment and sought for new ways to intensify this anger in his foe to exacerbate his defeat, through not only physical breakdown but psychological as well. Badai intended to demonstrate the superior beliefs and training that his religion preached to this nonconforming and unworthy *insal* who dared challenge him. And for a time Cam was at a loss, seemingly always one step behind his elusive opponent who ambushed him around corners and through windows.

Cam could hear Badai's voice from somewhere in the lengthy, divided hall. He seemed to be taunting Cam, inviting him to find him and insulting him with demeaning words. All was silent in the vast room save for this voice which Cam had come to despise far more than he could have imagined, almost to the point of demoniacal rage. His desire to destroy Badai was so intense he shook with uncontrollable anger. This enemy had insulted him not only with words but with his virtual invincibility. All Cam's efforts to slay him failed, desperate though they were, and his usual confident and spirited demeanor gave way to hatred and growing discouragement which fueled his frustration. His breath came heavily. Cam's inability to vanquish this foe which took delight in this intolerable torment drove Cam to madness. But Cam knew this approach would not deliver him the success he sought. He was through playing this game. It was time for a new tactic. He slowed his pacings and lowered his weapons, even as his enemy continued his mockings which echoed through the halls, and with inhuman resolution calmed and withdrew himself. Cam closed his eyes and hid under a window somewhere in the middle of the dim room.

"Come, come," came the voice which seemed to be drawing nearer, and it echoed and reverberated throughout the halls so they seemed to come from everywhere, "come and taste a little more. You think your feeble skills are a match for the Ahga's chosen? Come, put them to the test."

Cam waited patiently in his dark huddle and could hear the voice approach steadily. He crouched against the wall and listened, restraining his wrath for his moment of attack. Badai paced the silent halls cautiously, attempting to draw out his enemy as he searched.

"My brothers will have to wait for my return, for by now they are aware of your friends who are now undoubtedly undergoing their own destruction. But that can wait, for at present I am engaged in a most entertaining diversion. I have enjoyed my game with you and intend to stay and see it through, since you have demonstrated ingratitude and stubbornness. Your vindictiveness is an easy defect to use against you. The Mari teaches subordination to those you know are superior in the eyes of the Divine One, but this gesture of humility does not commend itself to you. Predictable for a rash fool such as yourself. *Insal,* you are; unbeliever. There is no room in the world for haughtiness and pride of your degree and I am allowed and honored the task of your justified destruction. Your friends are of little concern. Two full ships of fighters are hidden. Your pathetic crew and companion are no match for this superior force of the Ahga. And who is this friend of yours who sails into the claimed land of the Father so proudly, as though he is more deserving of the vast riches than the Kunn? The tokens of the Divine are rightfully ours and not to be pored over by the unworthy. I will lay you both among the rotting corpses which litter the watery–" His last words were cut short. A sword suddenly swung out from a window in front of him as he passed unaware and with the speed of light beheaded the Turuk in one fell stroke.

The dock was within view, and Damian and the crew prepared for their attack. Bows were readied and shot was loaded. The two ships lay still, moored side by side to the makeshift wharf. Damian could see several mog, Turuk and Hidari pirates upon the *Advent* pacing impatiently but none atop its brother beside it, quiet and unmanned. The running boardwalk could now be seen, snaking its way around certain buildings, bobbing and tossing slightly in the moving water. Hoists and cranes had been erected in places for the retrieval of submerged booty. Large A-frames and tripods of sturdy logs stood atop adapted structures of wood and beams of salvaged materials. Many folk could be seen working upon one of them, hoisting heavy goods from underwater, lashed and hooked to ropes and chains by men in the water. They were attempting to lift some great artifact even now and shouting was heard as the huge, netted bundle was raised from the water with much difficulty. Many hands reached to assist the load in its slow and careful ascension. All attention seemed to be focused on this crucial endeavor and Damian approached virtually undetected by the occupied work party. The idle ships were right in front of him. It would only be a few more moments. Damian fitted an arrow into his bow. They prepared to fire.

Mellinak stood upon the deck of the *Advent,* pacing impatiently. The artifact was at last exhumed from its watery resting place. He paused in his frustrations to gaze upon it as the crew clumsily raised the heavy load. It was brought slowly to the raised walkway and lowered. The men began to unwrap it and remove the sea-growths that had despoiled it. Mellinak placed the lens to his eye. Well, he thought as he watched them clean it. This promised to be an heirloom of value indeed, a mighty tool of Adin. A large black stone it seemed to be, perfectly spherical in shape, with ancient carvings of a lost tongue etched upon it. He wondered what secrets or powers it contained. Objects from that land of mystery possessed wonders and gifts forbidden ordinary mortals. But the Kunn, he thought, the rightful heirs and soldiers of that legacy, wielded the power and authority to unlock those mysteries and use them to their advantage to achieve their purpose. The clan had invested considerable time and resources to acquire this piece and now it was his. As he watched the unraveling of that mystical orb he knew he had earned the favor of the Unseen. He held his breath…

"NOW!" shouted Damian. Mellinak almost dropped his glass when he spun around. Fireballs shot from the intruder ship he was seeing for the first time. Arrows and darts filled the air. Pirates dropped where they stood or fell backwards dead into the water, unprepared and jolted out of their enchantment on their floating walkways. The glimmering prize was immediately and painfully forgotten. Hoists fell over and crashed and caught fire. Armed Kunn pirates still alive ran about, routed and confused. A great clamor and shouting broke out. The prisoners working in the water and laboring in places revolted, seeing their moment of escape and rebelling against their captors with anything they could use. Men and Achellan of Dinitia and seafaring cities of Vidia they were, captured sailors and merchants though there were not many, perhaps thirty in all. Mellinak shouted to his now outnumbered men, furious at the situation. He knew this would happen if he didn't seize his opportunity to flee and now his fears proved justified. He who sits idly on a hoard of gold will be inevitably relieved of it by a more competent keeper. What happened to his prized lookout? Why wasn't the alarm sounded? It was impossible that Badai had failed him. He cursed aloud, then remembered the rest of his force on the other side of the city only a mile away.

Damian pulled the ship to the dock and leaped off, sword in hand, followed by Erius and two others who stormed upon the walk. The remainder guarded the ship and manned the weapons, searching for targets among the small throng which ran chaotically about in front of them. Damian slew the few remaining pirates with a vengeance, sending them to join the host of dead beneath the shallow water with many splashes and noise of yelling.

Damian then ran aboard the *Advent* for he could see several pirates upon it, firing their arrows into the mass of rebelling prisoners, felling some of them. He stormed the moored ship, followed by a host of prisoners, perceiving the Kunn captain and his three bodyguards who dropped their bows and stood to defend him. There was a pause as Damian faced them upon the deck. Fell they were, strong and mighty indeed, hand picked fighters of the Ahga assigned to the protection of his great sea captain: thick black armor of leather and hide was upon them; bracers of steel girded their thick wrists; cold, steel swords of the Kunn were in their powerful, trained hands; bandanas waved in the breeze upon their foreheads of iron; prestigious hash marks, earned through pain and blood, were branded proudly upon their necksides.

The host halted behind Damian with fear and a silence fell. The unarmed and haggard men dared not approach these deadly henchmen, heavily armed and strong, defending their captain who stood upon the raised poopdeck to the rear with a defiant smile upon his black lips. Though there were only three of them the score of prisoners hesitated upon the deck behind their strange and mighty deliverer who they regarded with wonder, and they formed a half circle with the four of them in the midst. Mellinak chuckled at the sight but this brought an unforeseen consequence. Damian heard the laugh and looked up at who he doubted not was responsible for the savage piracy of the seas and the murders and theft at Spen. But he was in haste. The compliment of the Kunn force he could see and hear in the far distance, fast approaching toward them on their last two ships for they had been alerted by the noise and distraction, and he allowed himself only a brief but necessary glance before he let out a yell of fury and rage. He rushed forward, charging the fearsome guards. His sword rose and fell. One by one he slew them in a rapid storm of anger and covered the deck in their dark blood to the amazement of the onlookers. He clove through the sword of the last and beheaded him. Mellinak stood alone and resigned himself to capture.

CHAPTER 6
ESCAPE FROM CARA

Damian sheathed his sword and grabbed the mog chief by the throat. "I will take you as a prize," he growled in his face, and motioned to some men to disarm and tie him. "Prepare for sail! Move! We leave immediately! Make it ready!" he shouted with authority that they had not inclination nor desire to question. Damian sent a portion to assist with the *Cardela,* waiting nearby, and they all jumped to with haste and fear, for they could see that escape had not yet been achieved. The remainder of the Kunn force, some thirty or forty strong they reckoned upon their ships, was drawing nearer and they pointed in fear. Damian made a hasty inspection of the vessel and ventured below. There he encountered a man tied to one of the beams above the bulkhead.

The man turned excitedly upon the entrance of the stranger. He had an expectant look in his eyes which lit when he saw the stranger enter. "So someone interpreted my message? Ha! It seemed to be beyond hope, but yes, you found me. I heard all the commotion above. You must have brought half the Semáris with you."

"Ralen?" Damian asked.

"How did you know?" he asked.

"I suspected it would be unwise for them to murder you, you're too valuable." Damian said. "The others are dead, hideously murdered by the Kunn. You must have left the clever inscription."

"It was tricky work writing that message in the middle of the action at Spen. Yes, Mellinak brought me along everywhere, wouldn't let me out of his sight. He intended to utilize me again in the future to get him through customs and searches. Thug. He and his boys have been here awhile, though, and I think they're all here. The Kunn has been conducting excavations, digging for artifacts at several sites, here and elsewhere. The Ahga has a sweet spot for old treasures and such, but for what reason I can't say. But I think he chose the wrong place to dig for loot. There's something uncanny at work on this accursed rock."

"There's no time to explain," said Damian, feeling he had wasted enough time and he impatiently cut the cords around his wrists. "Where is the Etar?"

"Yes, it's here," Ralen said and pointed to the massive round treasure lashed securely in the storage bay. Damian only took a quick glance to confirm it and they both ran topside.

Damian came above decks but felt something was not right in the tumultuous moments before their departure. He frantically ran to and fro among the crew and took account of everyone. He ran to the bulwark of the *Advent* and looked about him. His thoughts strayed to Cam who he had not seen since he fled but for him he had only passing concern. His trusty adept comrade was quite capable of his own survival. But someone else was missing and he yelled to the *Cardela* in distress.

"Erius!" he cried. "Where is Erius!" Some of them came forward and pointed to the Kunn supply ship which waited quietly beside them, almost forgotten. There had been no enemy activity aboard it, no sign of life whatever during the short struggle. The shape of the vessel seemed to make its presence suddenly known to Damian and he cursed in anger. The realization of the intentions of his first mate dawned on him. He knew what Erius was doing there. He had no time for this foolishness. The enemy approached. Damian leaped off the deck, ran along the wharf, and up the gangplank of the ship calling his name.

Erius emerged from below, hearing his name called. He and two of his comrades from the *Cardela* were in the process of looting the treasure-laden ship. Small piles of wealth lay upon the deck, ready for transfer to their vessel. They had not even assisted with the preparation for their hasty flight but seized the moment during the confusion to relieve the pirates of some of their loot for themselves. Damian was beside himself with wrath. Erius did not wait for his scolding.

"We are simply taking that which rightfully belongs to those who have been wronged," he said. "My people are deserving of this as recompense. Surely you can see that."

"I warned you such a motion would lead to your own deaths!" Damian cried impatiently. "Nothing may be removed from this abode of ghosts, for it is doomed to remain forever and only with your lives will it be bought. It is the property of Cara. Do not give cause for its reawakening! The enemy comes and the rock itself shakes. It is not safe to stay! It is our lives that are at stake." Damian looked at the cliffsides again in fear.

"Do not attempt to dissuade us, Ratarra," Erius responded. "I take my leave of you. I will not be satisfied with the Etar only. Not when there is far more to gain from our success."

Damian could hear the men on his ships calling his name in earnestness. They were ready. "I leave you to your fate." Damian said and without delay flew from the doomed ship and boarded the *Advent.* They shoved off and headed back to the fissure.

The ships sped through the winding avenue of dead structures that led to the exit. The men looked about them in fear. A thunder beneath the water could be heard and a rumble felt. Some boulders fell from the cliff face in the distance and crashed onto the city, crushing some buildings. The smaller Kunn ships, they could see, were quickly gaining and closing the distance behind them. The fell crew aboard were waving their weapons in anticipation. The wind was light, too light to escape.

"Set the studding sails!" Damain ordered, and the experienced sailors set immediately to work. In a few moments they were catching the wind which seemed to be increasing. Damian scanned the buildingtops for now he was worried. His friend should have been here by now. Where was Cam?

As if in answer to his question he could faintly perceive a small figure in the distance making its way across the city, leaping from the rooftops with great speed toward the vessel. Damian watched his progress closely and when they reached the southernmost extremity of the city, where they first entered, he risked a momentary halt to retrieve his dear friend. They pulled alongside one of the buildings and Cam leaped aboard in a crumpled heap and everyone turned in their stations to look.

"If I didn't know better I'd say you are tired," Damian remarked. His companion seemed more noticeably spent than usual, even after action, and his attire bore evidence of struggle. His smile was gone.

Cam slowly pulled himself up on the deck and leaned on the gunwale, looking into the distance. "It was worth it," was all he could manage to say.

But the short delay cost them dearly and Damian could see that escape without another fight would be impossible, a fight that would be dangerous. The attack ships of the Kunn were better armed and manned, and faster, though they were without rowers. His men were mostly weaponless. Even if they reached the open sea they were doomed. He searched about him a moment. He thought of an alternative and wondered if he could make use of it. It was time to arouse a greater force around him.

"Sail on!" he shouted to his men. "Do not wait for me! Make for the gap!" He pointed to the great fissure in the rock face and he jumped off the ship and onto the rooftop of the building. The ships sailed away and Damian found the heavy rod of iron that the lookout was using as a hammer for the alarm. He lifted it and leaped onto the rocks, for this building was adjacent to the outer bowl of the circular cliff. He ran up the incline with his burden. Higher and higher he climbed, seeking the pinnacle. He didn't

298

have much time. The pirate ships were close on the tail of the trailing *Advent*. His men would be captured. The path to the peak was straight, but the ships now far below him still had to follow a winding path through the ruins to navigate before they reached the openness and he judged that he could arrive in time. He ran ever faster, driven by desperation.

The strange stone was left alone, abandoned on the dock. Corpses surrounded it. As it sat with its still concealed secrets it seemed to sink, indeed the whole of the structure in the vicinity of the ancient orb slowly gave way under the weight of it all, from the destabilizing effect of the earlier struggle upon the crude construction or perhaps due to some other force. It all began to crumble imperceptibly downward, even as Erius and his men sailed slowly past almost within reach upon the ship of which they now assumed control, making for the fissure. The bodies of the dead upon it were slowly consumed. Ripples and bubbles soon enveloped the mystical black stone as it slowly returned to its resting place under the water, and when it finally reached bottom a tremor could be felt by all.

Damian soon reached the top. He placed himself directly over the fragile apex of the great fissure where the cliffsides conjoined. He held himself fast and poised for a moment upon that point of ultimate vulnerability, fixed and unmoving. Tremors shook the cliff and he perceived a will and an anger, a wrath about to burst. He looked up. The sky was brilliantly blue and the sun shone clear and powerful overhead without a single cloud to mask its face, and Damian had almost to shield his eyes from the strength of it. The ships were some hundreds of feet directly below him, racing for the gap in file and he could discern the supply vessel which Erius was compelled to flee upon, struggling slowly behind. He cast his gaze to the sides. He could see the island in its entirety and from where he stood felt it under his command, and in his hand held the mighty rod to which it would obey. The city below looked like small, crumbling spikes sticking out of a vast bowl half-filled with water, a long-forsaken victim of some unearthly catastrophe. He was counting on that.

He raised the weighty rod over his head for a blow and felt the powers of the earth draw themselves up. The wind increased and the tension of doom in the air felt like a rising storm, held yet in check for one last moment before it was released. He turned his head up to the sky as if in reverence and humility. Power became in his possession and at his discretion to unleash, as though a force was given, or shared with an earthly and worthy keeper, and he acknowledged the blessing. He only needed timely cooperation. His ships below were almost overtaken. Waiting no longer he finally drove the great rod with all his might onto the rock surface, emitting a great shout that echoed throughout the vast enclosure.

The cliff split at his feet with the deafening crack of a thousand thunders upon impact. The island shook fitfully, the noise of which drowned all other sound and thought. Rocks from the cliffsides all around gave way and fell. The wind quickly increased and the ships below heeled under the ferocity of its strength. The fleeing sailors shook with fright and panicked. But it wasn't enough.

Again he raised the rod and let it fall. He yelled with impatience, as though the wrathful giant he summoned was reluctant to fully waken, though he knocked with all earnestness upon its door, and he feared that when it did it would be too late. He drove the massive hammer again upon the crumbling rock face. The split under Damian's feet widened. The earth quaked with increasing violence and fury. The great archway under which the *Cardela* and the *Advent* now sped through began to collapse behind them. Great boulders dislodged themselves in fury and crashed all around the fleeing vessels and the men wailed in terror and threw themselves onto the deck out of fear for their lives, covering their faces from death. A fierce wind came suddenly from the north in answer of the call, over the distant cliff wall, and the driving force of it blew the studding sails off the vessels. The ships heeled and gaffs snapped and lines were fouled as the ships were pushed through the fissure, as if being expelled from the domain by the breath of an angry beast. Against rocks the ships were violently tossed and spun in their turbulent exodus through the collapsing tunnel.

As if to hasten and thoroughly complete the destruction and produce the final devastating effect the woken monster would deliver, Damian raised the rod and drove it upon the quaking rock one last time. The cliff, already greatly destabilized beneath him, finally and utterly gave way with a great thunder and cracking and he cast the rod into the water far below and fled down the hillside. The whole of the island rocked and heaved unceasingly with a deafening ferocity. What remained of the city began to tumble and sink further into the depths, buried by the sinking and disintegrating cliffs around which followed it to its doom below the sea. The whole of Cara Rock seemed to submerge, engulfing the last of its unfortunate and despised inhabitants which dared wrong it again. Down, down it went, shaking the earth and sea in its plunge. The great Bill of Cara disintegrated and was the last to be consumed. A great water rushed in as if in conquest and swallowed all in its ravenous hunger and vengeance. The last of the great and once proud structures was quickly consumed, claimed fully, at last and forever.

When Captain Vadro awoke, resting in his cot below the *Cardela* and shaken from his state of unconsciousness by the chaos and clatter around him, he immediately went topside to learn of the events. He ran to the stern where a crowd was strangely gathered, gazing in awe and fear at an unfathomable scene. He found himself witnessing the final existence of some great island mass, victim to some pronouncement of ultimate doom or other, nothing like he had ever seen, and he stood awestruck. But even as he gazed with the likewise spellbound throng which did not notice his unexpected arrival, he could faintly perceive a figure upon the last of the sinking cliffs, running as if for his life along the crumbling peaks. He rubbed his weary eyes clear, for he could not believe it, and thought he saw this figure, doomed to certain death, plunge into the foamy and frothing water which formed a raging vortex around the rapidly disappearing mass, the gravitational strength of which this determined survivor had to desperately swim against. The destruction seemed to engulf this poor doomed soul, despite his heroic attempts to save himself, and the captain's eyes searched frantically for this struggling figure. But it was in vain. Nowhere in the swirling midst could anyone see any sign of him. They had almost resigned him to his unimaginable and unavoidable fate when one of the onlookers of the strange ship beside them, perched rearmost, smaller than many but sharp-eyed as an eagle, gave a shout. There, outside the whirlpool and just beyond its grip swam he for whom all had forsaken any hope. He lived. Many shouts went up. The deckhands jumped to stations. They brought the ship about and drew him in.

When Damian finally dropped prostrate upon the deck of the *Advent,* soaked and exhausted, breathing heavily, he was met with a familiar figure who came to his side and he looked up. It was Cam, peering into his eyes with a faint smile.

"If I didn't know better I'd say you are tired," he said.

Damian drew himself up slowly and scanned the ocean to view the results of the aftermath. Of the other ships which pursued them earlier there was no sign. Only the *Cardela* sailed beside them under the bright sun. He managed a grin. "It was worth it."

* * *

They arrived at Spen four days later to find officers of Dinitia and Demar in a heated counsel or debate in the fort's main function hall. There was little doubt in Damian's mind as to the nature of the animated disagreement: Demar was being put on trial. When Captain Vadro, Cam, and another guest by Damian's side were admitted through the guarded double doors along with the Etar, borne victoriously by the last of the survivors of the *Cardela,* a hush fell among the assembly and all turned curiously to behold the newcomers. Vadro's brother followed in as well, rescued and delivered from his captors along with the surviving crew. Ralen also entered with them and was immediately recognized by most.

One of the questioning officers, apparently in the throes of deep persecution of the defendants who were seated before him, was the last to cease his virulence and turn and acknowledge them. Damian recognized him as Telachus who beheld them astonished. There was the old captain with a bloody cloth wrapped around his forehead and his two strange friends, returned from some venture of questionable worth and sanity. His head then turned upon the wonders before him without speaking. He doubted what his eyes revealed to him and a tense moment passed as he assured himself of his rationality. In addition to retrieving the prized ancient artifact, to his utter disbelief, and the apparent rescue of the missing crewmen, they also had in their custody a certain individual no one had the displeasure of before meeting. He had an ill-favored look in his malicious eyes. His hands were tied behind him with a cord. Damian grabbed him by the back of his branded neck and shoved Mellinak into the midst of the assembled which stood and gasped. His distinguishing marks were recognized by some, and not with favor.

Telachus approached him slowly. He eyed the prisoner a moment then looked at Damian, then at Vadro.

"Is this, then, the phantom you promised us?" Telachus asked doubtfully but not without surprise and astonishment. His guests offered no response but held their gaze upon the captive. A moment of brief silence ensued, but the courtiers could no longer restrain themselves. The court erupted into a loud frenzy and motions were immediately made to absolve the defendants. All charges were dropped. Praises of the guests were made. Guards were ushered in to apprehend the criminal who was brought below into the prison-hold. Again the court was hushed and the guests were addressed.

"As reward for your service, then, we offer the bounty," Telachus said hesitantly and with a note of wounded pride. A chest was produced and placed before them. But Damian objected.

"I said I would bring you a gift," he said. "I do not accept payment for my services. I hunt this enemy of my own free will and their destruction is payment enough. But you may instead offer this to Captain Vadro, of whom is deserving many thanks for his steadfast loyalty and devotion, without which this would have been impossible." Damian gave Telachus an expectant look and waited. The reluctant guard faced Vadro and made a silent gesture of amends before the witnesses, and the injured captain accepted both payment and apology. After, Telachus again turned to Damian.

"And what of you?" he asked. "Who are you and what is your intent?"

"To leave immediately," Damian answered. "I must return to the mainland. It goes ill there. But this venture was not without merit. The Kunn has lost something of great value. I will soon learn what." With that

302

he and Cam departed. The doors were thrown open for them and they returned to the *Advent.* They sailed off, taking all the grateful prisoners with them who needed transport across the Strait.

A small gathering watched the great ship sail out of the cove. "What did he say his name was?" one of them asked the man next to him.

"Ratarra," came the reply.

EPISODE 4
THE CODE OF THE KUNN

CHAPTER 1
SHADOWS OF MOD

It was well past midnight on the dark streets of Mod. The once robust music heard from all points of the lively city had finally subsided and even the most fervent of the revelers had at last returned to their chambers, or fell prostrate in alleys or on corners succeeding their throes of debauchery, or passed along walkways aimlessly only to collapse in a stupor of infamy, when a dark figure emerged upon the scene of exhausted carousal. Out of place he seemed, ignorant of the intoxication which surrounded him and unaffected by its false allure, the breath of which poured forth from entryways and holes all around him. Unhindered he passed like a shadow along the now silent and dense avenues of stone buildings and dark windows under the starry sky. And those few who had still sufficient presence of mind to observe the stealthy movements of this cloaked apparition had not strength or ability left for inquiry or pursuit which might reveal its identity or intentions. When this stalker had completed the length of a street or walk before the dreamy-eyed observers and finally turned a corner and became lost to sight, all at once, as if succumbing to an enchantment, they fell back into their induced delusions and reveries. And in his silent wake this retreating figure left all in a state of blinking paralysis, leaving only the quiet darkness behind him as he passed.

Past throngs of stone or clay huts he stalked like a shadow. Their arched windows were open to allow the entry of the cool night breeze, though the doors below were locked to forbid the many thugs of this lawless desert city. He was aware of the foul folk which dealt corruptively among themselves in alleyways or in high halls above, and he cast his keen glance imperceptibly about him in all directions. His pace was steady and determined and his presence not a little intriguing. Though strange folk and villains from all over were not an unusual sight here, something about this one aroused intense curiosity. No doubt there were secrets concealed beneath the cloak of this strange but foolish individual, secrets worth investigating. This irresistible possibility drew the attention of a certain opportunist who made the mistake of emerging from his usual perch in the shadows and engaged the stranger with a drawn blade.

The dark figure paused a moment in his steps to regard the threat. Of his features the assailant was still not able to discern for his hood covered him almost completely, though a gleam in his eyes could be seen as he slowly raised his head, the reflection of the bright moon. A moment of silence ensued, the sickly smile upon the assailant very evident as he held his latest victim before him. But nothing from the cloaked stranger was forthcoming, not a quiver of the muscle could be detected. The obvious intent and demand of the assailant seemed not to even present itself to the reason of the victim. The stranger stood stone-still, his dark eyes fixed, and for a moment the thief felt a twinge of fear and doubt at the obvious lack of retreat. He looked about him, sensing a trick. At last, furious at his hesitation, the assailant thrust forward his blade. Quicker than eyesight the cloaked figure dodged to the side and with gloved hands wrapped a noosed metal cord around the neck of the thief. It had been equipped with a uni-directional, sliding crimp, mercilessly cinched in a twinkling. With the same measured step the figure continued on his way, ignoring the thief's silent and voiceless thrashings on the dusty street as he was quickly strangled to death. He didn't have much further to go.

He turned another corner. The street was dim and quiet. This area was more residential and bore evidence of better care. The dense cantinas and bazaars became more distant behind him. A deeper quiet dwelt here, though the rhythmic and muffled sounds of night insects could now be faintly heard. He passed several larger estates and mansions on either side, gated and walled. A person could make a fair amount of money here if he knew how and had the power and means to achieve it. He reached the entryway at last. This was the private back entrance to the estate of the renowned gangster Rash-Haba, to whom he had to pay an uninvited visit. On either side of the sculpted pylons which led into the dome-enshrouded and canopied street burned a brazier of fire, placed on tripods and illuminating the motionless road before it. He nonchalantly placed a small object within the flames and proceeded to the outside and shaded far end of the walled entrance. He drew out a length of rope and silently heaved it over the shallow roof. He glanced around. There was no one in sight, though he knew there were guards within the foyer, alert at all hours. The mansion on the other side was not within view, being obstructed by the encircling wall which was about twelve feet high. He began his climb. The arched roof which sheltered the small street beneath had a large, rectangular cutout in the center which served as a skylight. When he reached the top he peered in and waited. It should be any moment now.

A ball of fire suddenly lit the night at the top of the private lane with an audible blast, and the guards standing idle within immediately fled their post to investigate the curious disturbance at the gate. Utilizing the diversion, the figure on the roof dropped to the street within when the sentries rushed past, and like a shadow slipped unnoticed inside the compound.

He placed himself under the outside balcony of the mansion which was three floors above. There seemed to be no one atop it now. He again drew his rope and flung it over the stone railing which encircled the entire rectangular roof. The hook caught and he began his ascent. Upon arrival at the top he immediately scanned the roof area. No doubt the host with whom he sought verbal exchange held many banquets upon this open and elaborate function hall beneath the sky. Many bribes and coercions of ill nature had taken place here, and many guests either welcomed or murdered. He hopped over the railing and withdrew the rope, even as another sentry rounded the corner on the ground below who missed the slowly ascending line in front of him. He circled around the kitchen and open dining area and approached the door which led below, but it was locked. He instead went over to the large square opening which allowed for the intake of fresh rain water to the storage cisterns in the grand atrium below which lay in a spacious, enclosed courtyard. He could see another sentry pacing slowly, well below him on the first level within the mansion. He looped the rope around the railing and waited for the sentry to pass out of sight before he dropped it below.

Quieter than the cool night breeze he glided down the rope but halted halfway down to survey the interior. The sentry had almost completed his dreary circle within the dark, quiet courtyard, and was slowly approaching the suspended and poised intruder directly in front of him, unseen. Several moments passed where the very breath of the unwary watchman could be heard between his slow footsteps which echoed slightly on the smooth, marble floor. Like a spider the dark figure dropped to the floor in front of him and before he could even shout, the wide-eyed guard's face was smothered by a rag which had been doused in some lethal solution, and as soon as it was breathed he fell to the floor a corpse. A small loss for the host to pay. Replacement thugs were readily available in this despot. The intruder proceeded within and found the staircase which led to the inner chambers and cubicula on the second floor. He climbed stealthily up and passed numerous doors, the quarters of his servants and henchmen, all closed and lifeless. There was no one else about and all was silent. He finally reached the last chamber which was furthest away and promised to be the largest of them. The door was locked, as expected, and he set to work on the knob with some small tools which he produced from somewhere within his concealed person. The door eventually opened and he pushed it noiselessly inward.

As soon as he had quietly shut the door behind him the inhabitant within, by some reflex of perpetual paranoia, leaped up from his position of repose and sought the dagger he kept by his bedside. But it was too late. The dark intruder sprung inside and the keen blade of his sword was pressed against the throat of the host. He froze and instinctively sought the eyes of his captor. His head slowly turned to regard him.

"I advise you to remain very still," the intruder said in just above a whisper. "And don't bother to shout, for it will be the last thing your wretched throat ever cries again. You may drop the weapon."

Without looking, Rash released his grip on the blade. He was a large, ugly creature, of mixed race and origin, though in this dim light he looked mostly to be of a dark green color, something like a blend of Mogoli and Harikan. He didn't look as though he hailed from this side of the Ash Mountains but from the other, though creatures and races of many unique kinds were commonplace in this realm. He looked into the face of his guest but could only discern his dark eyes, though he caught a hint of a beard from within the folds of his hood.

The intruder spoke first. "Some weeks ago a certain shipment of smuggled goods never made it into the hands of its purchaser. The value of this delivery was staggering, and though it was escorted by your associates it was inexplicably confiscated by some daring rogues and diverted elsewhither." He lowered his blade slightly as he spoke and Rash relaxed somewhat, his large eyes searching as he ingested this information. "I can see you know something of this."

"Perhaps," Rash replied softly. He had many such abrupt and dramatic encounters with characters of all sorts, and this determined fellow had already won his respect. Some dialog, he supposed, he could allow himself to be inconvenienced with at this hour. Maybe it would be useful and even informative. "Though it is unapparent to me why I should divulge information on this matter to a vagabond as yourself. Such things are always a possibility in this trade, and not wholly unexpected."

"Running the River is becoming ever more difficult, perhaps?"

"Her Highness tightens her grip on those lands though they are not rightfully hers, as no doubt you know my inquisitive friend," Rash replied. "The witch strengthens her forces and the Tanga is more heavily patrolled. Getting anything through requires far more planning and drives the risk and fees much higher. Any shipment successfully crossed is prime fodder. I don't know by what miracle or foolishness she was handed her power but she has obviously run away with her ridiculous and flexed influence. But perhaps it is of little matter. With the price on her head she won't hold it much longer and things will be as they were." He chuckled to himself. "We need only be patient. In the meantime I sustain my losses without recompense or retribution," he ended, implying innocence.

"Ah, but this time there is reason for you to fear," responded the stranger. "The individuals responsible seek to depose you as chief runner. You and your black operation are in peril."

"And who may you be referring to?" Rash posed, being elusive and withholding. "Our difficulties of late have been addressed and will not be repeated, I assure you. These cunning thieves are common pirates and highwaymen, nothing more. Or perhaps some rogue element of Her design. Ever She seeks vengeance against these clans and thieves of the lands. I daresay before long I and many others may be seeking a new profession if her proud tactics persevere. But somehow I doubt that will come to pass." He ended with a smile.

"Nay," replied the stranger, "your danger does not come from her, but the Ahga. The Kunn is in the process of wresting from you your goods and services. Too long have you been a nuisance to him, and with the recent discovery of a certain new commodity–" the stranger paused and allowed his prisoner a moment to appreciate the insinuation "–I am sure the Ahga will find new reasons to fulfill his long desire to eliminate you at last."

Rash burst out laughing. "The Kunn!" he scoffed, unable to contain himself. "Surely you jest! The Ahga doesn't touch me, who do you think brings him half his loot? If it wasn't for me those fools and their cult wouldn't have their precious crystals and lost stones of the ghost realm. Where do you think it all comes from? If it crosses the Tanga my friend, I know about it."

"As does Thuliak," answered the stranger, "to whom you have very close ties, do you not? And, with the value of your operation suddenly seeing an envious and noticeable increase in profit, due to this rare bit of new and secret treasure, the Ahga, who I think you'll agree has no admiration for you or your greedy friend in the Harásh, may find it more than beneficial to finally relieve you of your service and take all for himself."

"I think you must be weary from a long night's intoxication," Rash objected, but with a hint of concern he could not hide. "I cannot believe even the Ahga could possibly have dreamed something as this. I know of no such secret. Ha! Surely you are a madman." He drew some liquor from a large goblet near his bedside.

The stranger reached into his cloak and produced a unique and large gold ingot, obviously different from the norm in color and density. It was of an improved composition, brighter and harder, rare and valuable. Few had ever even seen this new material. The smile on Rash's face quickly disappeared as he gazed at it.

"I think you'll agree that for me to acquire a piece such as this I would have had to purchase it of yourself," the stranger said, "for one cannot find it anywhere else, and it is too new."

The blank look on Rash's face could not conceal his befuddlement. His momentary silence confirmed his concurrence, but his ignorant front quickly resumed. "An interesting specimen," he finally said. "And what is your interest with it, and me, might I ask?"

"I stole this from one of the Ahga's agents very recently, here, within this very city. A small band of Kunn bandits pulled in this morning. They made the mistake of stopping in to see one of their fellow agents before returning to their leader in the Harásh. They seemed to be in a hurry. As I was charged with the retrieval of my master's lost goods and the discovery of the thieves, I found this interesting and decided to have a closer look."

"So Thuliak sent you," Rash said.

"Nay, my master and I work independently and have no ties," the stranger replied. "But we share the same injuries due to your failures. As for my Kunn friends this morning, I infiltrated the apartment in very much the same manner I did yours just now, though perhaps with a little less grace for I had not time. I found a case in their possession which contained some very interesting nuggets, the likes of which few had ever seen, even myself, and I knew that I had found my master's culprits and some valuable goods which I shall retain for myself as compensation for past losses. Now you and I both know this was not to land in the hands of those your primary employer has, shall we say, a delicate relationship with. I have no longer time to listen to your ignorance. The one on whose behalf I speak has no desire to conduct his transactions through the Kunn for the obvious reasons that they tend to draw their clients too close and increase their fees and grip when control has been achieved. I suppose you could say he favors the loose and accommodating relationship your particular service provides but fears for your continued existence. My advice to you, my careless and foolish friend, is to secure what you have with your chief purchaser and prevent this inevitable overthrow which awaits you. The Ahga is not as ignorant and slow as you are, and a bloody conflict with the Kunn would bear serious consequences for you."

With that he deliberately placed the ingot on a table within the room, the sound and presence of which produced an intended effect, and with a last look of exhortation leaped out the chamber window and disappeared.

CHAPTER 2
TOWERS OF DISCORD

The vast palace of Mod, or the Harásh, as it was known unofficially by the folk of the desert city, was built on a low rise with the miles of urban development surrounding it, depreciating in value and condition as the distance increased from the beautiful epicenter which stood in stark contrast to the rot and filth enveloping it. It looked like a vast, pointed crown with walls of white and gray marble, elevated in the midst of an urban sea, its many tall obelisks pointing upwards like the fangs of the open mouth of an upturned beast. The name stood not only for the structures or dwellings within but for the abode as a whole, and when one mentioned the word it signified all that dwelt and transpired within the grand walls. It was of a stretched hexagonal shape, the Harásh, and guarded at each angled point by a tall obelisk which reached eagerly toward the sky like a spike seeking the heavens. They each had four smooth and tapered sides, unadorned, without mark or device, which ultimately terminated at the pinnacles in a pyramidal shape. There were two main structures within the enclosing and white-hued, battlemented walls, named after the founding rulers of old: the Alad, which was where Thuliak resided in his vast splendor, and the Olóbid, which was recently given over to the Ahga and his cabinet, or Baccád. The former was far greater in shape and size than its lesser counterpart which struggled to make itself visible over the fifty-foot walls. One could only view the topmost storey of the dwelling of the Ahga as he gazed upon the breathtaking but agreeably impractical monument from a position on the ground before it. Both the predecessors and current occupier of the Harásh had desire only for the vanity and boastfulness of architecture and craft of their dwelling, placing value in appearance rather than principle and pragmatism, and believing its splendor alone would deliver the successive regime the respect and awe it demanded. Ever would Thuliak seek to envelop himself in vain riches, having little real strength and leadership of his own, but attempting to rectify this deficiency with craft and sculpture he constantly purchased from afar to compensate for weakness within.

As soon as one was admitted through the lengthy gatehouse, after search and questioning, and proof of invitation, verified by authorities, he entered the main courtyard. This was artfully tiled with stone masonry which changed in hue according to the décor or theme of a particular section, and amidst the many structures and monuments paved its way in paths through lengths of well-tended patches of colorful flowers or grass, or exotic desert shrubs and trees of the eccentric taste of the lord who dwelt here, though he would not dare consider working these with his own smooth hands. A large circular fountain was visible to the far left, in the midst of a terraced garden. Upon the colossal tower in front of him, arranged in ascending rows, were windows of stained glass that looked out upon the city beyond. The high crest of the palace was crowned with an array of smaller turrets whose pointed tips mirrored the obelisks around it. The lower walls of the Alad presented an impressive arcade of archways within the encircling façade of polished white marble, admitting guests through a wide and grand hall succeeding their easy stride through the garden and over the broad, marble threshold before it, bedecked in places with sculptures and statues of antiquity and craft, and other lavish or exotic embellishments. In all places one would find himself in awe of the majesty and beauty of the magnificent wonder, an oasis among a sea of destitution. And so the impression and promise of virtue and justice upon the ignorant succeeded in imposing itself.

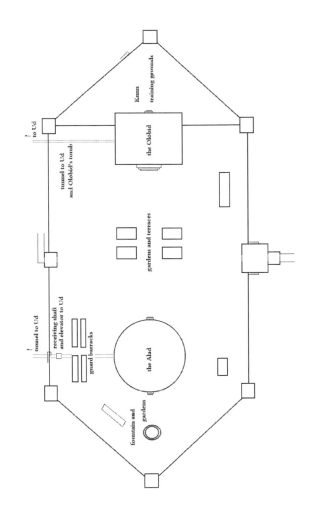

To the right of the towering Alad, slightly distant and across another courtyard, one beheld the lesser keep, the Olóbid. The absence of comparable artwork and devices of this noticeably plain and unadorned structure left one with a dissimilar impression than did its splendorous and inviting counterpart. This suited the Ahga well, for he had not inclination or time to follow the vain desires of his foolish landlord and adhere to his unnecessary standards of aestheticism. The differences in construction and color of the Olóbid were testament to the differences in the founding brothers of old, and they insisted upon these in the original design. The rectangular walls were smooth and of a duller grey color, virtually windowless until the eye reached the top levels, the chambers of the Ahga and his henchmen. Flanking and elbowed staircases led to thick, wooden entryways on either side of the grim domain, closed and guarded. A low marble staircase led to the main front entrance. Walls enclosed a separate and large courtyard, sealed from both view and access for the private use of the Kunn. This area had been modified and refitted for the specific purpose of training the Ahga's deadly henchmen. Ever the sounds of melee combat and physical training and shouts in unison would resonate forth from behind the dark curtain, and one could only wonder in fear of what transpired behind it. Ranks of the Ahga's finest would hone their skills within in methods the unbelievers outside would consider unthinkable. Upon completion of these tests, the members would disperse to their assignments or reassemble inside their tower for counsel or instruction.

This was the dark hall of the Ahga and the current but temporary base of operations for the Kunn. Some years ago this feared clan leader purchased his way into the recently vacated dwelling with the promise of a mutually beneficial relationship with the host. And the promise was surpassingly delivered, much to the satisfaction of the landlord. A generous percentage of income earned by the clan was reverted to the holdings of the host, as agreed upon, though the sentiments between the two leaders grew notably strained of late. The host of the palace, the Lord Thuliak, had begun to regret his agreement with the zealous warlord with whom he felt he had made an increasingly unfortunate and foolish alliance. The questionable ways and livelihood of this ideological following gnawed at his reason, insulted his taste, belittled his rulership, contested his judgment, challenged and even mocked his beliefs, until his fragile sanity gave way to an impatience and disgust he could no longer conceal. His questionable affiliation with the clan tainted his reputation among his fellow governing counterparts of foreign states with whom he had to maintain relations and commerce. He would look down upon that hideous tower from his high dwelling in the Alad with an expression of disdain, his face contorting with detestation as he continually bore witness to the frugal cult which abutted his grandeur. There they were again, he thought in his obsessive mind, plagued with intolerable paranoia, those twisted fools are outside performing their insane rituals. Their lack of adherence to the décor and courtesies he demanded of these animalistic tenants infuriated him. He felt sure the Ahga only humored him when confronted with his legitimate requests to conform to standards of the royal codes of behavior and dress. Their barbaric rituals and ways from which he could not distance himself tested his patience though he dared not put into effect the desires his volatile emotions urged him. One thing even this ruler, consumed with pettiness, knew, and that was that this warlord and his small band of loyal and devout followers were not to be crossed. But for how much longer his sentiments could be restrained he did not know.

* * *

The Ahga's followers lined themselves in numerous ranks within their concealed courtyard. Fighting staffs called *haran-chos* were in their hands and they held themselves unmoving until the command was given. These were not the expendable servants of the Ahga, the *suchuks*, which performed his more mundane duties on the streets of cities or labored elsewhere in the lands in various ways for the profit of the Kunn, but the elite fighters of the Mak-Baccád, some forty strong, fell and silent, waiting for the command to commence the next series of movements. They held themselves in a low, crouched, squatted position, fighting staffs held outward at arm's length in front of them for so long a time that most would have long since quitted from the agony. But the Ahga believed in discipline and strength, tenets of the code, and such practices were only too common for these veteran fighters. They accepted pain like a dear friend, for pain, like hunger, cleanses the soul of indulgent desires, realigns thought and purges it of the foolish and tempting ideas a weak mind and soul create for itself and which are barraged daily by these other petty cultures and their vain pursuits. Pain made them stronger, more fell, and delivered them more closely to that which cannot be seen but lie within. Pain brought the spirit to the forefront of consciousness, leaving the physical form and its earthly necessities behind to explore lesser-sought realms of mortal possibilities. By achieving this level of spiritual enlightenment such hardships of the body were forgotten, obstacles of the flesh once considered impossible overcome, an unknown strength of both mind and body developed, an enduring discipline which would carry the being like a faithful steed through any struggle honed, creating a virtually new mortal: powerful, superior, ethereal.

This was the code of the Mari and the reward it promised to those brave and sacrificing enough to endure the rituals and trials it demanded. Its origins were largely unknown in the contemporary world, save by the loremasters and historians, and of course its nucleus of adherents, and there was controversy and mystery regarding its conception and introduction among the few who still pursued what many would consider a heathenistic and unattainable religion. The loremasters would have testified that it had been passed down by Adin himself, the great warlord of Shomeneria long ago who founded it, claiming the code bestowed one with extramortal abilities if one was devout and chosen of the Divine. A ridiculous assertion, many thought. The folk of Tog, the Hakai, could certainly claim some credit for its cross-cultural inception in recent centuries. But anything brought forth from that race of ghosts under the mountains must be ill indeed, folk thought, and the strange beliefs of that alien world were quickly dismissed and mocked. One can perceive an idea in any manner that suits his desire, they said, and it is subject to mortal contamination like anything else. Claims of achieving a greater inner power were but oft spewed nonsense. Ideas such as this were nothing new, and one must be wary. But there were those to whom the code appealed, those within the clan who felt the Mari spoke to them, those who needed to belong and felt worthy of the promises others claimed were beyond achievability.

Few indeed were invited to subject themselves to its painful tests though, and the Ahga and his Baccád chose their applicants with great care. Only to members of this higher order within the clan, especially and personally chosen, would the wondrous and long-sought secrets of the code be revealed. This was the great pursuit of the Kunn, to achieve this higher existence and power and therefore propel the clan to earthly superiority. But the chosen would be bound to painful death should they fail to adhere to the Ahga's strict order of silence. So the mysteries of the code remained largely preserved, much to the satisfaction of the Baccád. Tog, however, and those few like him who possessed this level of abilities virtually no other follower could claim to have, even the Ahga himself, would look upon most adherents of the Mari with disgust, feeling that the true rewards were forever beyond the reach and capability of these spiritually deficient fools. For this reason the seldom-seen but much rumored champion chose to disassociate himself with their doings and presence, feeling that his religion was being improperly followed by the weak and incompetent, and though they made a commendable attempt at an honorable achievement, their failure and intolerable incapability of full earthly withdrawal surely only enraged him. But he needed the Kunn as an appendage to his own mission. His patience held out only for the purpose for which he needed them. His was a task carried out upon other plane.

But those who held themselves in deep meditation on the prestigious grounds of the Ahga below the shadow of the shorter but girthy Olóbid could be regarded almost with respect, even in Tog's cruel eyes, eyes that found fault with all. Sweat dripped from their grim faces under the morning Mod sun, already hot; honed muscles held themselves like arms of machines, their closed eyes focused and searching within, their long black hair pulled tightly and banded uniformly in the ceremonial black and crimson wraps of the feared Mak-Baccád. Robes of black enshrouded the trainees who entranced themselves under the agony of the ritual. The fell instructor whom they obeyed paced condemningly among the ranks. Finally satisfied, he bellowed the anticipated command. A series of movements immediately commenced and the once still and quiet courtyard erupted with acrobatics and skillful, uniformed, execution of weaponry and fighting tactics, accompanied anon with shouts in chorus. When the form reached its termination another command was given and the fighters obediently lined themselves across from each other in two facing files. A tense moment passed. At the command, the fighters, haran-cho staffs in hand, began viciously fencing their paired opponent in an impressive display of skill and expertise. Many shouts could be heard from the other side of the curtain wall along with the terrifying snaps and cracks of staff upon staff, and Thuliak's guards on duty in the decorated courtyard without looked up yet again at the sound they knew so well from beyond that hated wall but to which they failed to adequately accustom themselves. Though these men-at-arms also trained regularly, none would honestly yearn to be pitted against the Ahga's well-trained and ambitious fighters, imbued with the belief that they were under divine sanction. Every morning at this hour the yells that blasted forth from that secret domain were found to be unnerving at the least, and even the most veteran of them would shift uneasily at his idle post.

At last, when the deaths of them all would be reasonably assumed by any sane individual making his way into the Alad by the level of thunder they produced nearby, another shout was given. Total silence then commenced. Another mode of training was begun, and they divided into smaller groups. The staffs were dropped in formation and projectile weapons were assumed. Targets of wooden beams had been built, all in various degrees of decomposition resulting from frequent use. They were pockmarked and splintered greatly. Arrows, bolts of crossbows, throwing stars and knives, darts, a large hand-held throwing blade called a *gullick*, had all made their imprints on these sacrificed pieces of wood, even javelins. The gullick was the preferred throwing weapon of these killers for it had two ends, both bladed, and its distance of flight was remarkable, owing to its unique design, returning to the thrower should it fail to impact with anything. Catching it required much practice of course, which was another feat exercised here. Many hands had been impaled due to improper seizure of the weapon in flight, but one would witness no such inability here. Skillful handling of the weapon was demonstrated profoundly on the grounds, along with any other melee or projectile weapon which they sought eagerly to master. This weapon in the hands of an untrained opponent was of little concern for the stranger would find it unwieldy and alien, another reason for its preference among the secret society which solely used it.

Other exercises were also performed: fists were driven deep into barrels of sand; chunks of wood were broken over heads and knees; flips and airborne somersaults were accomplished through hoops or over poles and beams, some of which were moved by handlers to increase difficulty; ropes were climbed upside down and with hands tied behind them; followers fought hand-to-hand while prone or blindfold or practiced the bow also deprived of sight; high leaps were made onto cords suspended over pits; fired missiles of bow weapons were caught by open hand; staffs and boards were broken over exposed ribcages of muscle and skin of iron; blades were swung at throats and arrested by bare hand; stacks of stone blocks broke and cracked from various bodily impacts, crumbling to the ground in accumulating heaps of debris; walls of virtually smooth composition were climbed by naked hand and foot; all these and other harsh modes of universal honing and mastery considered barbaric and impossible by unbelievers, conducted beyond the sight and knowledge of those outside. Indeed many could only guess as to the dark rituals and events performed on the other side of that oft-pondered and feared wall, for the grim and silent members which came forth from its doors and departed with equal mystery for weeks at a time would divulge nothing of their secret activities upon their return.

Today brought a special diversion from the usual routine, however, and when the training had reached its completion the members formed themselves on either side of the area for viewing a rare event. The students stood still and silent in rows as the esteemed members of the Baccád filed out in order from the Olóbid doors and onto the grounds in a place of honor to also witness. They all wore the coveted sleeveless black shirts of canvas, flared outwards at the shoulders, with four scarlet hash marks on their necks and black bracers worn upon their wrists, and loose red trousers upon their thick legs of steel. These mogs were huge and powerful, and experienced. The mere look on their faces and their mighty frames induced fear and humility, and even the most fell, well-trained and disciplined students of the Mak-Baccád were constrained to cast their eyes downward as their superiors strode slowly past. Several of the Baccád had actually been recalled from their distant posts to witness the crucial event. The Ahga and his *ghad-hesh*, Gathmug, followed them out lastly.

Three particular students had been separated from the rest for the occasion and brought into the middle of the assembly. This was the beginning of the *chun-vok*, the deadly ritual one must succeed to enter the Baccád, and some candidates had indeed been chosen, for there was a state of vacancy in the Order. For most of them present this was the first viewing, and upon none of the observers would one find so much as a hint of a smile for the mere thought or mention of the ritual brought an indescribable respect and seriousness. Unfortunately for the Ahga, his Baccád had suffered two recent losses: Azag, his captain who was murdered by one of his own in the Khala mines; and Mozep who also fell at the hands of his disgruntled subject, Draga. News of his most recent loss and the failure in Hera had indeed reached his ears, but his wrath was almost quelled when he concluded that his two elusive new enemies could conveniently claim credit for the annihilation of his rogue lieutenant and his followers. Disloyalty will result in death, and can be brought about by myself or our own enemies, he thought. He had some empty positions to fill, and today may bring one who qualified.

The first test was called the *ruk-mesh*, where the candidate had his upper back pierced by large teeth of beasts. His bones were hooked sufficiently to lend strength and grasp to the ropes that would suspend him several feet off the ground for many minutes. This ritual was performed before the others for the pain and horrible trial of it would bring the victim closer to his spiritual side, and he would need this difficult connection to complete the remaining tasks. It was believed among the adherents of their order that only such an extremity of exertion could stimulate that inner essence into usable function, to urge that inner being and perception into greater and superior vitality, a power ordinarily suppressed and rejected by unbelieving mortals. It was performed simultaneously on all three. A handful of members made the necessary arrangements and performed the piercings, scars that would remain proudly forever on their bodies as testament to the fearful undertaking. They grimaced as they lay face down on the ground when the deep punctures were made through thick and powerful muscle, honed through long training. The cords were strung through a sturdy framework of high wooden beams. Within moments the three were hoisted into their suspended positions. The attendants tied the ropes in place, locking them. Without a word the assembly watched in honor as the trio wrestled and struggled with the immortal pain, fading in and out of consciousness, reality and illusions exchanging predominance in their crying souls. An otherwise unattainable level of meditation was slowly achieved. All that one could hear as he watched breathless and paralyzed with awe and horror was the low and rhythmic humming and moaning of the victims as mortality was overcome.

Already the Ahga could perceive which had achieved the deepest level of meditation and which had not. He had witnessed the ruk-mesh scores of times, for he demanded it of his followers and believed in it and the profit which it produced in his loyal men. He watched them all closely with a scrutinizing eye as they hung motionless before him and sought another power within themselves, one which was elusive and difficult to find but required activation. The Mari called for this vital inception which the code termed *emergence* and its followers constantly strived for its achievement, though most were only partially successful at best. For the Ahga and those like him, recognizing emergence was easily done, and he could even now perceive the levels reached by the candidates simply by studying them. He had a good guess already as to which would succeed the trial and the two that would fail.

The test had finally reached its completion and they were lowered back to the ground. They were quickly disconnected from their machine of pain. The onlookers, however, did not recognize their comrades standing unmoving on the bloodstained ground. Their faces seemed strangely tranquil, their bodies fixed and focused. An iron rigidity pervaded their frames. An expression of ignorance of the world around them could be read in their faces for they seemed to be elsewhere. A fixed look remained in their unseeing eyes for their souls had taken partial flight from their physical bodies, elevating them to a higher state of existence. This was only for a moment for they were immediately hooded to preserve this state. Blindness aided emergence; sight impeded it. This blindness would be tested in the next trial.

They were aligned in a row, spread apart from each other. Black hoods were upon their heads. The witnesses lined themselves before the three to observe the next phase. This was called the *gok-armok,* palms of steel. Gathmug strode forward before the rows of silent observers bearing a large, unsheathed sword, the coveted *kodara.* He placed himself in front of the first of the three contestants. They looked as prisoners awaiting execution and before them strode the executioner. A short pause followed in which all was silent. No one moved or made a sound. All watched intensely as the ghad-hesh prepared to swing at the entranced candidate who stood completely motionless before him. He was in deep meditation, his emergence activated. The objects of the earth were almost visible to him as he listened and concentrated intently. His ability to control and utilize his emergence was about to be tested. Failure at the gok-armok would result in death. Gathmug studied him for a time before bringing the keen blade upon him. Finally, quicker than sight, Gathmug swung the sword at his throat. This stroke would have been instantly fatal had it proceeded as desired, but was caught between the palms of the blinded contestant who sprang suddenly to life, arresting the destroying weapon. The blade was held fast in front of him, unmoving in the clasped palms of his hands. In a moment it was released, and the contestant withdrew into his state of motionlessness, and the Tester moved on to his next victim. Again the blade was caught before its lethal impact, and a breath of relief and blinking awe could be discerned from the observers as they relaxed almost imperceptibly each time. He moved on to the last. Another moment of silent tension, the level of concentration and physical removal critically studied by the executioner. Death waited only seconds away, and relied on but a small miscalculation or distraction on the part of the victim to wrest its soul away. Breath ceased. Time halted its revolutions. Thought and energy became predominant, the earth far away. All were seized with immovability. And with the swift stroke and arrest of the sword, all had resumed. The world returned with a sudden jolt that was almost audible. They had succeeded the gok-armok.

They were then led singly from the grounds to the inside of the keep. They marched up the short ramp and through the large wooden doors and were brought into the great hall of the Ahga on the ground floor, the Hall of the Kunn. The esteemed competitors were placed onto a platform which would lower them into the dreaded and dark chamber below for the next part of the trial. This platform comprised of three sturdy and closed metal cages which prevented the candidates from any physical access to each other for they were now being inducted into the renowned and feared *Uden-Khan,* or Chamber of Death. The doors of the cages were arranged in such a way that the extremities faced outwards from each other and the middle faced forward. In this manner the participants could only exit in one unique direction when he reached the destination below. Only one could emerge from the unknown trials of the deep the victor, the one who proved he possessed the favor of the Divine One, and premature elimination was an undesired outcome of the Testers. Of these trials there had been rumors, all beyond imaginings, but the secrets of what really transpired in the depths under the keep were closely guarded. The assembled could only guess at the death and agonies which awaited them in that feared and dark domain right below their sandaled feet.

There was a pause. The Ahga strode to the center of the ranked assembly and spoke. His words echoed in the great hall and his booming voice resonated so that all shook. "Let the trial begin," he thundered. No other words were necessary. They all knew why they were here.

The contenders were each closed inside their respective cages and with a word the platform was slowly lowered into the dreaded darkness below by pulleys and chains above. The platform solemnly disappeared from sight. After several moments the descent had ceased and the chains hung motionless–the bottom had been reached. The assembly watched with a mixture of horror and honor as the heavy, slotted plates were put back into place covering the large rectangular hole in the floor of the hall. They all knew that there would be no return for two of them, perhaps even all three if things went completely ill, and with the sound of the grates thrust upon the stone floor they had resigned their old mates to their honorable fate. But the look upon the face of the Ahga was proud and content, indeed it seemed satisfied and pleased with the endeavor. The successor had already been determined in his mind, though witness to the trials and horrors below was impossible. The Ahga intended it that way. Report of his designs would never reach the ears of anyone not in his Baccád, and for those that failed the chun-vok it was impossible to reveal the secrets that dwelt beneath the halls of the Ahga: they were all dead, still in their cold repose below. Those who had not been invited and had never experienced the worst the Ahga could conceive could busy themselves with their wild conjectures. Affectation and manipulation of the mind was a necessary part of the training and selection. They all waited quietly and proudly in the great hall for the outcome, wondering of their fates below and each hoping he would be one day called upon for the prestigious undertaking.

* * *

That morning, while the Ahga was occupied with his men in the Olóbid, in the throes of what those outside could only vaguely guess at, a certain well-known guest and his escorts had unexpectedly arrived at the front gate of the Harásh. Apparently he was a frequent visitor for he was admitted almost immediately and with little question. He seemed to be in haste. The many guards quickly made way at the command of their captain and the series of heavy gates were lifted upwards in sequential order. The visitor rode through on his desert kelgan, followed by his handful of armed escorts. The gates immediately closed behind them.

The Lord Thuliak was pacing about impatiently in one of his suites on the topmost floor of his lofty residence. He was of a race close to what one would consider to be a half-mog. He was shorter and slighter of build than his more physical mog relatives, and squint-eyed, the result of his incurable paranoia and suspicion. A distrust could be read in those snake-like eyes behind which lay much perception but little strength or wisdom or any other value worth respect. His hands trembled constantly as though he suppressed a gnawing fear or doubt, as though it were a disease, and he was seen to fidget and handle small objects compulsively. He spoke rapidly and in hurried tone and with dramatic gesticulations of the arms. He was in ill humor, as was his wont, and his many servants endeavored in vain to afford him some alleviation of his present vexation.

Suddenly there was a knock at his great wooden door and his guards escorted the guest into the presence of their master. It was Rash-Haba, coming to inquire about the delay of his latest payment no doubt. Thuliak had enlisted the services of this professional smuggler to bring him the rarest and most expensive of commodities from abroad. Due to his knowledge of the criminal underground in every city and his valuable connection to it, it was little wonder Thuliak and others sought the assistance of his network to deliver precious goods anywhere—stolen, counterfeited, or otherwise, without the unfortunate drawback of the intrusions, tariffs, and fees imposed by governances upon open traffic. His services were especially useful if one desired his transaction to remain secret from any authorities with which perhaps the purchaser had a less than favorable relationship. Rash certainly developed the network and abilities to deliver these valuable goods and Thuliak was one of his prime employers.

But Rash did not approach demanding some kind of monetary transaction, much to the surprise of the master, though he had suffered great loss of late which vexed him not a little. He secretly vowed he would not depart the palace today without something of value. His losses bore him great injury and this intolerable sustainment could not continue. One way or another he was going to get his own back and he had something suitable in mind, but for it he would have to work alone. He need only be patient. Rash entered boldly, which was unlike him considering his sentiments for the ruler, and striding hastily to the feet of the one he sought speech with he immediately stated the reason for his presence. Thuliak dismissed everyone in the room and the door closed. Only the bodyguards of the two accompanied them at a distance.

"We have a problem," he grunted.

"No, you have a problem," Thuliak looked at him. "I have nothing to do with your failures and if they continue I will be forced to seek help elsewhere."

Rash withdrew a large and unusual gold ingot from his pouch which he held before them. Thuliak's eyes widened with anger and disbelief.

"How did you acquire that?" he demanded and Rash could have sworn he made a motion for his dagger when he asked. "I gave instructions that I was to be the only one on this side of the river with ownership to that item! It was mine, mine alone! Or is this because of you? Must I do everything myself? I thought I had an agreement with Peng. That fool has been bought, as I suspected he would in time. I invest thousands and this is how he compensates me, by dipping it into the black market for his own gain. He has now cost me untold fortunes with his foolishness. Does he not see what could have been were it not for his incompetence? Cut all ties with that swine!" His voice and anger echoed in the spacious room. Thuliak picked up a metallic ornament nearby and threw it against a wall in a rage, creating a clatter which echoed in the hall. Thuliak breathed heavily and paced around the room. "What has happened to my shipment?" Thuliak asked calmly after a moment, composing himself.

"Intercepted," Rash answered. "Our network was penetrated yet again and our entire code and routes are compromised. We are finished."

Thuliak looked incredulous. He walked over to a table and poured himself some drink. He did not offer any to his guest. After a drought he again faced him.

"How does a rag-tag band of river bandits manage to eliminate my men and take goods so well guarded, the secret of which alone is known only to a few and entrusted to yourself? I would be loth to imprison and hang one who was once such an ally but now has betrayed me. You can be added to my proud collection in the dungeon. There are more than a handful of interesting characters down there, festering. My men are at my call. Must I make such a move?"

"Your villains have a name," Rash said, ignoring his threat. Rash was also familiar with some of the imprisoned. "And they certainly are not mere bandits, not anymore."

"You cannot mean the Bará," Thuliak said. "Even they should know I have no real alliance with the Ahga. Hallév does not believe that lie and would not seek to assuage his own vengeance with my demise. I cannot fathom how Peng would seek injury against me either, I offered him the greatest of sums. Though perhaps Her Highness may have some involvement in this. She is quite a revolutionary."

"It is not of the Bará or Peng Goshek which I speak," Rash replied. "And She will not have the means yet to achieve a profile disruption such as this. She has too little loyalty and power. Though you should know Hallév has more than reason to have you assassinated, but whether he could fulfill such a task is questionable. Why, you have his greatest enemy housed within your own walls." Rash looked out the window. Something was happening in the tower across the yard. Thuliak looked at him disapprovingly and almost struck him. How dare he speak such things in his presence. Rash continued. "Nay, the ones who have undermined your every move for years and plagued your estate and rulership are none other than the Kunn."

Thuliak stopped dead. His hand gravitated toward the wall in an instinctive motion for support. He looked ill. His eyes widened with disbelief, then understanding, then fury. It began to make sense. Only the Kunn could have done this, and with relative ease. His fists clenched and his twisted face reddened with the realization of his blindness. His wrath was about to burst with this as yet unconfirmed inference. If this were true the Ahga and his men will meet their bloody destruction. Even after all his vows of compliance and obedience to his face as prerequisites for his tenancy, they would dare betray him so deeply. His spies assigned to keep strict surveillance over his increasingly ambitious and untrustworthy neighbor had failed. Yes, it was them, it had to be, they were right here, allowed into his precious domain by his own accord. The proof had been procured right before his eyes. The Baccád must know his every move, every dark alliance penetrated, and every transaction monitored before it even took place, and he looked about the room speechless as though there were spies hidden in corners. He couldn't believe these heathenistic barbarians had outwitted him. This was not possible, but then it began to make perfect sense. It was time for them to go. He had had enough of this zealot and his band of mindless followers. He immediately fled the room and sought counsel with his advisers.

CHAPTER 3
THE CHUN-VOK

The heavy platform reached the bottom of its descent. The clang of the impact echoed at the termination of the vault. It was not overly far, maybe forty feet. None of the three were able to see above or around them at all, even if they had removed their hoods. The cages in which they placed were completely enclosed to prevent any visual distraction. But if this were not enough the eternal darkness of the hole they now found themselves in revealed little, even to their Mari-adapted eyes. When the time came, all three removed their hoods.

The doors opened before them as if by magic. Each beheld a dim corridor at his feet, cut into the earth in a different direction than the others, and lit sparsely by the small light of candles that burned in niches on the rock walls. The lights were so distantly spread that it actually enfeebled and impeded their eyesight, perhaps by design. Night vision enjoyed greater effectiveness without lucid interference. The visibility was reduced to little to none. There were three corridors which made up the trial area, each heading in a separate direction: one rounded to the east, one to the west, and the last south, the extremities forming a semi-circle which purported to ultimately reach a common destination, unknown of course to the venturers who tread separately. The platform-cage specially designed by the Ahga and his engineers fit in the shaft closely and in such a way that the occupants would be released in their intended direction at the bottom and restricted to tread his assigned path alone. There was also a fourth and little used chamber, at the other far end of this wide circle, which led to the *Gahg-Morga,* the Hall of Horrors. The Ahga reserved this one for his most special trials and was not normally used in the chun-vok due to its mortal severity. This, like many of the Ahga's designs, remained enveloped in mystery. There were many things he preferred withheld from knowledge, especially about his secret trials. What madness transpired in the underworld of the Ahga was a source of unlimited rumor and conjecture in the world beyond.

There were three contestants, all weaponless, and each stepped from his restraint: Babla, Narnak, and Klintuk. Each was a mog of feared repute, all proven and loyal members of the Kunn, all vying for the ultimate title of superiority and favor of the Mari. They had all served the Ahga well for many years and had succeeded the various trials and tests put forth by his fatherhood. All had excelled upon not only the grounds of the Ahga but in his actual services and demands in the field. They had each earned the elusive trust of the Ahga through blood, pain, sacrifice, and unquestioning dedication to his will. Each was a hand-picked student and servant, chosen for skill and loyalty, and all had received the invitation with honor.

But there was also an understanding among them: only one would be the victor. They all knew that elimination of his brother would be called upon, in some unknown manner within the trial. The Ahga oftentimes required eliminations of his own followers, even within the Brotherhood, and the possibility of one day receiving this dreaded assignment was very real. For this reason the essential fratricide was incorporated into the trial, even at the expense of some of his best men.

Babla proceeded slowly down the dim, arching corridor. Not a sound could he hear, even in his enhanced state of awareness, unless it was the small candles quietly burning in their lonely niches along the damp rock wall. He looked about him, even behind him as he crept. His steps came deliberately, one slow, silent, well-placed foot in front of the other. He knew that traps or pits awaited him in this subterranean tunnel along with some death of hideous conception, though in what manner he was to meet it he could not fathom. Already the sweat dripped from his face, from the heat of the dungeon but also the incredible anticipation. The tension seemed to press on him from all sides so that his movements felt restricted, as though he was walking through water. He felt as though he had left the familiar world behind him and he had been spawned into this unknown subterranean realm of darkness and fear to conquer some feat of his worst imaginings. He held his powerful hands out in front of him, ready, his fingers twitching with expectation, his breath coming heavy but controlled. One by one the candles passed slowly and silently behind him and the tunnel continued onward.

He did not actually travel a great distance, though the heaviness of the dread around him made it seem so, when he perceived a single door at the end of the tunnel. He paused in his steps. He trusted nothing. The rumors he had heard in the world of light he left behind stirred immense distrust within. This was the chun-vok, the personal trial of the Ahga, not some petty field exercise or melee training. Nothing would surprise him here. He knew his chances of survival were slim at best. There were many names that had made the descent in the past, never to be called again except to be remembered in honor. The candles burned softly to either side, whispering doom in his ears, and they seemed like silent watchers that would bear witness to his horrible destruction even as they guided him to it. He continued onward.

The door was of iron, heavy but unlocked. It opened without a sound and with little effort and he drew cautiously aside as it swung. Nothing. He left it open and moved inward. The hall, it seemed, continued for a short distance before it opened into a larger chamber though what it held could not be ascertained in this mixed light and at this distance. After a few more cautious steps he noticed several bones lying on the ground to the side, spread and rummaged by something. He wondered again what lay in store for him. *Some vicious trick conceived by the Ahga one must succeed to gain full admittance.* But it was all necessary and he believed in it wholeheartedly. He would not have it any other way. The reward of the Mari was his goal. He peered again into the distance when suddenly he jumped to the side, alerted by a perceived motion and sound to the rear or above him. A portcullis gate of heavy steel had closed behind him with such virulence and rapidity that it undoubtedly would have crushed anyone under it. His heart pounded. He accredited his successful evasion to his meditative emergence level. Full awareness, fully alive, fear subdued. The gate sealed the way shut, preventing escape, striking the solid floor with a clang that rent the still air and shocked his mind.

Immediately succeeding this abruption he thought he heard, in the distance, some rustling and scraping, as if from some other creature or being who shared his presence in this solitary realm and was alerted to the familiar noise. But whatever it was he could perceive its readiness, for the muffled sounds continued for several seconds before they quickly stopped and silence again resumed, though he thought he could now hear a faint whispering sound beyond which puzzled him. It did not cease but continued with the same low and monotonous hum, the identity of which greatly occupied his struggling thought. He gritted his teeth. His enemy possessed the distinct advantage of the familiarity of its domain and Babla knew it waited for him, patiently, quietly, hidden in the shadows in its customary vantage of superiority. He perceived its existence in the thick gloom ahead though it remained well out of sight. He readied himself and continued into the distant and mysterious chamber at the end of the hall.

The walls to his sides seemed to suddenly vanish and he stepped onto a small ledge which jutted out into the center of a lengthy and broad pit of oval shape. All was still dim and quiet though the humming continued, waxing in intensity, but it seemed now to come from beneath. The darkness at his feet was impenetrable and even his night-eyes could reveal little of certainty. The few candles burning tranquilly along the far sides impeded and confused his vision. He wished them gone. He cast his glance upwards and thought he could make out a great wheel of steel affixed parallel to the flat roof which was not overly high here, under twenty feet he guessed it was, though the dimness of the huge vault made this difficult to determine. Many sturdy chains hung loosely a brief length from this strange wheel, all placed in equal distances around its great circumference. It appeared to him that this great wheel was capable of revolving but was not as yet in motion. In the far distance, well across the black gulf before him and almost beyond sight, he thought he could discern the small and shadowy shape of a door on the landing illuminated by torches on either side.

He began to ponder how the Ahga could have possibly created such a place under the earth, even from the labyrinth of existing tunnels and miles of under-ways of the ancient Harásh, the palace of ages, but the time for reflection had suddenly come to an end. He heard the growling of a monster, or maybe more, somewhere within the enclosure and he stiffened. Then all thought was completely extinguished and his eyes widened for the many lights hidden in the crevices along the side of the hall illuminated themselves simultaneously, as if by spell, and at the same time the great wheel above labored itself into motion by some unseen force. The many chains, as a natural consequence of this rotation, began to spread further apart from each other as the speed increased and to angle themselves more distantly from that of their vertical, original position of idle. A low and audible beat was produced by its regulated revolutions, like a muffled drum, the haunting sound of which drove the blood and adrenaline upon him. He could now also see that this was not the only wheel in the room but there were in fact two, the other located further on the roof, closer to what he guessed must be the far exit. The nearer of the great wheels revolved clockwise, the other counter-clockwise.

The pit below him and all its horror now became visible. Raised and isolated platforms of stone seemed to make a broken and staggered path to his destination, spread about distantly with the obvious intent to require the contender to somehow jump across this chasm, utilizing these minute portals of safety to reach the other side. The source of the strange humming was now revealed. All about the floor of the pit, below the platforms, writhed a host of vipers, the deadly Black *Ráka* of the Marak Desert and beyond, swarming about and slithering along the distant floor and attempting to climb the solitary columns which supported the circular platforms above them. They seemed to lick the smooth surfaces with their tongues and reptilian hide in their endless attempts to climb them. The contender could see them wrapping themselves around the skeletal remains of failed and fallen brethren. The whole of the pit seemed to take on animate qualities as it twisted and burned with a sickening black flame, and the hissing and spitting that occurred in that unimaginable hell grew louder, and seemed in joint collaboration with the rhythmic beat of the great wheels above. It all intensified to such a degree that all thought was drowned by its smothering and deafening effect. A knowledge of what was about to be seemed apparent as the pit and indeed the whole chamber came suddenly to life. Upon two of the round platforms, in the center of the pit and directly across from each other, poised for attack, crouched a pair of *karkua,* the great brown hunting cats of the Al-Akat Mountains to the east.

Babla no longer wondered his fate. For a moment he froze on the brink with disbelief. In the next the hunters leaped for him. The huge cats with fangs like daggers made the twenty-foot leaps between platforms in their deadly approach. They looked as though much time had passed since they had last eaten. Their mouths dripped with anticipation. Their growls were muffled by the ceaseless whisperings and hellish drumbeat which announced his inescapable doom. The rhythmic hum seemed a voice chanting his destruction, gaining in strength and intensity. He spun around and saw another gate had closed behind him. There was no escape but the door on the far side of the chasm. He made a frantic look about before he made a move.

The portals on which he had to leap were arranged in a staggered formation; first a pair across each other about twenty feet apart in front of him, then a solo landing in the middle some distance behind them; then again a pair, then one, pair, then one, and so on until the deadly path became within reach of the far landing. He could also tell that these portals did not provide much of a running start, having a diameter of only about eight feet, and a long jump between them would be difficult indeed even without the disadvantage of being chased relentlessly by two beasts that could. These portals of safety were dangerously small, without ledge or rail, all by design to allow the contender an easy drop to peril below. He perceived the slowly revolving chains above to be his vehicle that would deliver him to his perilous destination, but even with that help the journey would be difficult. Even the initial leap would require him to become airborne over the lethal pit for the extremities of the whirling chains at this point were well beyond reach.

Without further hesitation he leaped from the landing. For one perilous moment he hovered over certain death with nothing beneath him that would prevent his final plunge to doom. He succeeded in grasping one of the chains that sped his way even as the cats moved in closer. The hunters had just reached the portal he intended to swing to so he remained clutching the chain until it carried him back to his starting point. One of the cats moved in to attack, the other remained on the solo portal as if guarding against escape. They were working together, coordinating their attack to prevent their prey from gaining the exit. They had obviously done this before.

One of the cats leaped from the side onto the portal Babla currently inhabited after dropping from his chain. The other came from the portal in front to assist simultaneously, attacking from two sides, but the hardened fighter from the Mak-Baccád made a desperate leap unassisted to the lone portal ahead, directly into the path of the airborne hunter approaching him who passed within inches of his projecting frame. The cat made an attempt to grab his prey as it passed unexpectedly but only managed to rend some of its flesh in the pass. Amazingly, Babla made the great jump, catching the ledge with his outstretched hands. He pulled himself up in a twinkling of terror, ignoring his wounds which stretched the length of the majority of his left side, lacerated by the beast. Surprised at such a bold move, the two cats leaped in pursuit with a vengeance.

Being now in the lone center the chains were out of reach. Babla had not time for a measured jump anyway. With his hunters already crossing the gap behind him he made what he could for a running start and propelled himself to the next row of portals, right side. The exercise was not dissimilar with what he was familiar with in the training and fighting pits of the Ahga in his original home of recruitment with the Kunn in the city of Kadr, though in this dungeon that seemed a world away. That training had come in useful for the challenge at hand. Without it he would have surely been killed here. Again he completed the leap, catching the ledge. He wasted no time. His killers, with superior speed, were already right behind him. Saliva dripped from their knife-like teeth. He pulled himself up. Trusting to faith, he immediately made a hasty vertical leap, catching one of the chains hurtling by. This swung him to the next level and he made a landing on the lone platform. He had now reached the halfway point.

But his pursuers had grown weary and frustrated with the agility and success of their elusive prey. He attempted again a free leap to the next platform, a paired one, but the lead cat had gained on him. The speed of the predators was too great even for this great warrior and he was about to meet his bloody fate. In mid-flight the cat tore at its prey's feet and legs, turning it and disrupting its trajectory. He only caught the ledge sideways with one hand and almost slipped into the abyss, becoming instead the victim for the mass of heathens below. That would have been counterproductive. The skilled cats could not allow such a mistake to occur. One of them pulled the victim onto the ledge by his grasping hand to preserve it for themselves, the other bypassed the engagement to cut off escape, making a double jump ahead to the next platform.

Babla found himself dragged upwards by his enemy. Faced with destruction he became an animal himself. Back and forth they tossed about the small round portal for a perilous time, trading blows, drawing blood, the drumbeat becoming more intense as they exchanged predominance, matching their prodigious strength in a hideous struggle for survival, mog vs. beast. Most any other being would have easily been killed by this great beast and its vast strength. When a moment of freedom had come, and recognizing an opportunity, Babla reached again for his revolving deliverers which turned now in an opposing direction. There were to be no more struggles with these foes. The time for evading was over. He allowed himself to be carried to another point to enact his idea. When he gained the surface he immediately turned and used the pursuing momentum of his enemy, who leaped in behind him, to knock him from the platform. Not expecting this, the great roaring cat was caught off guard and thrown beyond the ledge, clinging for its life. With one last blow Babla sent it to its doom. The hissing demons below vied with one another for the prize. They wasted no time consuming it.

In desperation and rage, the remaining beast leaped headlong for its prey with a growl of fury. Babla clung to the chains and swung to the next level to evade. There was only one more portal in front of him, then the ledge of freedom. This ledge was even further away, impossible to reach by the looks, but had been equipped with a metal ladder which stretched some six feet below the lip, allowing one to climb it to gain the surface. Considering its distance it was evident that it could only be reached with one running motion, by utilizing the interim platform as a springboard to reach the ledge. With the beast close on his tail he summoned a greater strength within himself. This great leap would be the one that determined his life. With a yell, he made the leap to the last of the platforms and without stopping leaped again onto the far ladder, barely succeeding. He lifted his legs up just in time. The great cat made the jump but missed the leg of its prey. Instead it clung to the lowest rung by its teeth. Babla climbed up and stood on the ledge in exhausted triumph. He bore many wounds. He paused to catch his breath and watched his enemy claw and struggle for many minutes in vain to improve its grip. At last he turned toward the door, ignoring the cries of the beast as it fell to its hideous fate. Babla wondered how his competitors were faring as he headed down the hall beyond.

* * *

Narnak stepped boldly from his cage. He had reached the bottom and immediately cast aside his hood which held him blind. He needed no impediments but also no assistance. He was by far the strongest and greatest of the Mogoli in the Mak-Baccád. All feared him. His services had been enlisted for the purposes of the Kunn some years ago in the city of Bahrag. His strength and brutality on the streets were renowned, being an undefeated fighter and contender and earning his keep in this filthy underground profession. There were those who would pay for such a gift and proficiency, and this carried him to higher aspirations. The scum he later became affiliated with were glad to have him as their strong man but he could not be content only with these small gangsters and their closet operations. Another place awaited him, something more befitting one of his rare and much-sought capabilities. When an informed representative of the Kunn finally had counsel with him, sharing the gifts of the code, he was only too glad to oblige. This clan of high and fearsome repute held the future he sought and the power he craved, and the creed which called to him, a code other pursuits could not claim to have. To slay for the Divine One was his desire, to remove possession of the weak he had been gifted with overpowering, to have illimitable respect and fear and therefore satisfaction, these he yearned for, and being in the service of the Ahga would finally deliver it.

The door he stepped from was in the center of the three and faced the middle corridor. Though he could not see them he knew his competitors had also embarked on their trial. This was the sort of thing he yearned for, a test, a competition, a means to prove himself more able than all others, and he was finally taking part in what he hoped would be the greatest test of his life. All others had been disappointments, all easily overcome. Everything he had heard of this particular trial seemed but the unfounded rumors of those who dared not venture thither, those who would undoubtedly fail. He did not. Nor did he heed the cautions of his clanmates. They were unnecessary in the past, and were surely not needed now. And the requirement that he eliminate his brothers troubled him not at all. He had done this many times before, and for many superiors. He half smiled as he strode without fear down the dark, candle-lit tunnel which bore its way slightly downward without turn or lateral angle.

The tunnel ended with a single door of heavy iron. He easily pulled it open and entered. The door shut behind him, for it was weighted for self-closure. He continued boldly down a short hall until it opened into a larger vault, rectangular in shape and darkened, dimly illuminated by small torches along the way to the extremity which was beyond sight here. The floor, however, had been altered, causing him to pause. Just beyond the lip of the hall the floor had noticeably dropped. This new surface seemed to be metallic in composition. Many protrusions of short iron shafts reared their rounded heads through this odd floor, as though many thick nails had been poked through the metal beneath. This impeding array of spikes covered the path completely for about thirty feet distant, making it impossible to leap or circumvent. Looking more closely at the floor, he noticed that it had been divided into barely perceptible squares about a foot across and it was at the corners of these squares that the shafts protruded. Placing his hand upon one of the squares directly in front of him, he felt it depress under the pressure and a dart from the side wall shot from a hole he didn't notice and pierced his arm. It was sprung at a low height, the target area being the lower leg of a prospective walker. He jerked his arm back from the sudden impact and withdrew the projectile. Having no weapons or armor, a small puncture wound was made.

He stood up and cleared himself of the setback. The matter was but trivial. It was, after all, only a minor wound, and it would take more than such a pin-prick to bring this giant down. The solution seemed obvious enough and a faint grin again developed on his face. Very carefully he placed his foot on one of the iron prods. Nothing happened. He balanced himself on its small, rounded tip, placing his other sandaled foot on another prod nearby to evenly distribute his great weight. He carefully departed the stone floor of safety and began his slow, tedious traverse.

When he had taken only two or three successful steps, he heard a rumbling and looked up. The rock floor seemed to quake. It seemed to come from all sides but the source was quickly revealed. To his astonishment a wall further ahead, beyond the booby-trapped floor, and another one behind him, began to move simultaneously from their perched positions to the side and seemed to both slide along a provided path or track in the rock beneath and above them, with the apparent intent to seal him in. To worsen matters, the iron prods poking through the perilous floor providing his relative safety began to slowly recede, sinking into their retracted positions below it, seemingly in synchronicity with the moving walls to front and back which crept steadily to their destinations. With the distance he still had yet to cover and the speed at which these heavy walls ground along in progress, coupled with the disappearing buffer at his feet, Narnak could easily see he had little time to complete his traverse, this obviously done by intent to hasten the walker along the deadly floor. The grumbling with which the rock walls pushed closer to their entrapping terminations seemed to proclaim doom.

With greater urgency and a feeling all unfamiliar to him that others would call fear, he attempted his hastened traverse. Balancing his great frame on those small tips was no easy feat, even for a trained fighter as him, and with the pressure of time against him he stumbled often. He was pierced numerous times from sprung darts each time his weight unintentionally fell upon the deadly squares beneath. The sliding walls ahead had only a small gap remaining. With the end now finally within reach he made a dive for the finish as the last of the prods disappeared at his feet and this desperate maneuver cost him some more wounds. He lunged forward, throwing himself through the last two feet of space the wall still had left. He pulled his legs in before they were crushed by its immense and grinding weight.

But he was not allowed a moment to assess himself. The inertia of his hasty escape was his undoing. The instant his prone frame gained the floor on the other side he felt himself spiraling headlong down a slick surface, inclined fairly steeply, similar to a funnel. All attempts to halt his descent were fruitless. The floor above became distant. A moment later he splashed into a thick, murky substance which consumed the entirety of the chamber he now inhabited. He pulled himself up out of the unknown matter which now covered him completely. Standing, the thick mud was about waist deep, and it slowly dripped from his body like ooze. It looked almost grey in this mixed light. The rays of a distant torch found their way to portions of the depression. All was silent and dim. He looked about, trying to determine where or what he had fallen into. He seemed to have landed in a narrow well shaft, the shape of which was tapered, or funneled slightly toward the mouth above which was distinctly wider there than at the bottom, which was narrower. A veritable oubliette, with the bottom filled with some kind of mud of high viscosity. The sides of this narrow chasm were of a smooth but seemingly climbable rock, this mode of escape being the first to enter his mind. Making a more thorough examination of his environment he determined this to be the only available method at hand. There were no hand rails and no objects whatever, only the solid rock walls which seemed to suffocate and surround him in a fairly close circle. He first spent a few moments removing the many darts which had pierced him before attempting his escape. He was disgusted with himself and his performance thus far and he cursed as he cast them away.

Looking up again before his climb he noticed a rope or cord hanging from the gloom high above, directly over the center of the hole. It was well out of reach but he determined that if he succeeded in climbing a portion of the way, as was intended, he may just be able to reach it with difficulty. The smooth walls were angled in such a way that one could 'walk' his way to the top, using his arms and legs to press against the sides and inch along with tremendous outward thrust. But as he gained height this would become even more difficult, for the sides grew farther apart, and eventually impossible. The height at which the rope hung would seem to offer escape at the highest possible point of reach.

Narnak growled. The genius of the Ahga was obvious, and he did not look forward to taking part in it. He knew there was more to the trial and that he had only made it part of the way and was now pitifully stuck. He had underestimated the test thus far, and cursed at his predicament. This ascent would not be easy. He yelled in fury and threw his arms. He took a breath and made efforts to gather himself. Finally he placed his arms on the walls on either side and began to heave himself upward, inch by inch, pressing against them. The weight of the mud seemed to offer some resistance against his upward attempt as his legs followed. He made it a short way before his hand slipped on the smooth rock surface and he fell back in. He couldn't believe this. A great fighter like him with the strength of giants, trapped in a hole of slime. Again he attempted the ascent, again he fell.

Upon the fourth or fifth try, and again landing in the medium below, he perceived that the density of the mud had clearly *increased*. The effort at which he withdrew his sturdy limbs and body grew each time he reattempted his arduous ascent. The weight of the ooze which clung to his frame dragged him downward with more vigor each time. They seemed like fingers pulling him into their hideous midst, and he could not break free of their stiffening grip. To further complicate his plight, he swore he could feel the onset of a faint dizziness from outside the realm of his own body. He felt his concentration enfeebled. His emergence was corrupted by something without. The great limbs with which he exerted his prodigious strength numbed, almost imperceptibly, but intensified so that he had to shake them to reacquire sensation.

He gasped for breath. He grit his fierce teeth. His adrenaline increased with the onslaught of fear. Those darts he thought nothing but pins must have been poisoned or drugged. His movements became slower and his surroundings dim. He had never faced threat like this before. The reality exploded upon his thought like the tolling of a bell in an empty hall of stone. If he couldn't succeed in climbing out he would be frozen in this accursed chasm, reduced to a fossil as he slowly wasted away, claimed by something as simple as thickening mortar. He reeled.

With renewed vigor he again climbed, indeed his leap would have won him recognition so great was his effort, and the chasm echoed with his frustration. But the world had taken on strange hues, and the rope above became an unreachable face which mocked him, laughed at his humbled greatness, and the sides of the shaft seemed to move so that his grip was often misplaced, and his judgment and reach underestimated. The echoes in the shaft sounded like the wailings of his many victims who returned to witness his downfall. The rope above tortured his mind as he reached for it. Many times more he failed, and again attempted the ascent, but the grip of the monster below had ultimately denied him egress until he fainted with exhaustion. He cowered and placed his hands on his head in defeat. He could not believe one so mighty as he was humbled by a handful of pins and a well-placed narrow hole of mud.

All one could see of Narnak, when he peered into that chasm weeks later, was the form of a giant, half consumed by rock, his torso laying prone on his conqueror with outspread arms as though he embraced death and gave honor to the one who delivered it.

* * *

Klintuk crept cautiously down the dark tunnel. His banked slightly to the right in what appeared to be a half-circle. He couldn't tell that the outlying tunnels formed a wide circle and finally met again at some middle point further on. But that matter was trivial. He focused on the perilous deed at hand. He followed the candles carefully down the quiet hall, his head turning and his limbs of steel ready.

He came to a juncture in the corridor. On one side a thick door barred the way, on the other a narrow tunnel branched off to his left and seemed to descend deeper into the earth. He tried the door and it was locked. This heavy door of steel was completely unmovable, try as he would to force it open. He knew he was intended for the other way. He peered into the tunnel. It was roughly cut and narrow, unlike the smooth and spacious main tunnel, and pitch black. It looked like a hole to death, for it headed downward at a sharp angle. He had to squat to enter it. He immediately could perceive the greater presence of moisture, on the rough walls and in the close air. Slowly he crawled down the worm-hole head first, his night eyes feebly piercing the thick darkness. The direction did not change but held its course steadily downward for some time.

He almost placed his hand in the water before he saw it, so still and silent it was. The tunnel was completely filled with water here. His progress was impeded. He had arrived at an underground well, and paused a moment to consider his next move. The water did not smell foul. He tasted it and it was good, fresh. There was nothing else around him and no other means of progress available. Only the hole in front of him and the tunnel back.

He couldn't fathom how something like this could be part of a test, a requirement for admittance into the Baccád, but he readied himself for anything. The chun-vok wasn't expected to be easy or predictable. It would put all his skills to the test: strength, intellect, emergence. He knew it would be nothing like he had ever done before. Riding abroad with the Kunn on his steed with his warring brethren in the early days of his recruitment, spreading terror among the weak where needed for the profit of the clan, or fighting the Bará in the south to claim regional dominance, or stealing from the Hōsh to gain control of shipping routes in Dakachi was business as usual compared to this. This would be far different from anything he had ever done. His long involvements with the suchuks, the lower order of the Kunn, were but the duties of an obedient follower. He had moved on from that fundamental level of service. The secret and difficult tasks required of a Mak-Baccád brother, some years later after proving himself and his loyalties, took his abilities to a higher level of expectation and satisfaction. His skills as an effective extortionist and later a tyrant and educator earned him the trust of the Ahga. His favor within the code was remarkable, even being only an elite soldier. He exhibited the signs of having the blessing of the Divine One, and this was rare, even within the Brotherhood which sought this enviable and difficult achievement. To have this fabled favor was the dream of every member of this strict, zealous organization, blending worldly gain with the tapped power of the spirit. But in the end only few possessed the blessing the Mari promised, and it was believed that these few individuals had been chosen by a power or force which dwelt elsewhere, and it was upon these that this power bestowed supermortal abilities to do his will, aligning to ultimate completion and potency: mind, body, spirit, the trihedral of emergence. These beings were the Baccád, the highest order of the Ahga and proven possessors of the Mari. Klintuk certainly exhibited these abilities and had been under the eye of the Ahga for a long time. The time had come, and he was invited to undergo the trial.

He knelt at the brink of the depression. He summoned his strength and filled his chest with air, and plunged into the water-filled tunnel. His eyes could penetrate the murkiness enough to enable navigation. It held its course in a controlled, downward descent. His high emergence level allowed him to swim without air for far longer than was possible for others. This mortal impediment became less necessary as he attuned himself to his new environment. After some time the tunnel opened into a larger chamber which became level again. He swam to the top where there was a significant gap between the water and the ceiling and drew breath.

He found himself in a cavernous opening, roughly oval in shape. It appeared to be a subterranean lake, or holding cell which had been filled in with water. Klintuk knew the labyrinths under the Olóbid had been altered over the recent decades to suit the shifting purposes of its inhabitants. The Baccád only allowed certain members into the secret chambers and ways beneath, these recesses being reserved for the purposes of the Ahga. The sides of this one were only about thirty feet apart and the roof pressed low. There was only about five feet of space between the surface of the lake and the rocky overhead. All about him were the echoing sounds of water dripping from holes in the walls. Looking more closely he could see three distinct, door-like openings cut into the right side of the vault. These three openings, spread apart some ten feet each, had been barred with gates of steel to prevent access. He could see no other means of egress at hand. All was silent save for the dripping of water all about, and he paused while he ingested the strange stimuli.

He did see something of interest: looking up and further away in the chamber, shoved blade first deeply into a recessed niche in the ceiling, was a long dagger. It was out of reach, try as he would to acquire it. There was no ledge or shelf in the pool to stand on. Something told him he would need this, but all his strength could not propel him sufficiently out of the water to grip it.

Before he could decide what his next course of exploration would be he heard a monstrous groan which seemed to shake the cave, followed by a rushing or shifting of some unknown movement or vomit of the earth beneath, or above. Something of great proportions approached with unstoppable ferocity and he searched about him in frantic expectation. He looked toward the openings with their forbidding bars of steel, for it was from these that the destroyer of the underworld seemed to approach. He grasped the bars in eager anticipation, trying to discover the cause of the impending doom. Before he could move he was knocked deep into the pool by the onset of a great rushing of water which suddenly and simultaneously poured forth with a fury from these holes of death.

He quickly swam to the turbulent surface, now frothing and heaving with virulence under the tremendous pressure. The noise of it all was deafening. The greatly agitated water beat against the walls in a rage, and visibility within its violent depths was now impossible. He instinctively returned to his point of entry deep under the pool with some difficulty but found that it had been sealed mysteriously. A gate of bars had closed firmly shut, locking him in. He flew back up to the surface. Already he could perceive the rising level of the water in the chamber. With the incredible rate of incoming water from the three openings it would not be long before he was trapped in and killed by drowning. He turned his head frantically. Again, not perceiving any other means of escape, he returned to the underwater entrance. He pulled at one of the bars in desperation. Slowly it started to bend. But something grabbed his leg and dragged him under. He was not alone.

In the depths of the earth, far under the surface of mortals which walked the sun-soaked plain, dwell the *madidi*, a great eel of the underworld. The city of Mod was watered by many underground springs and streams which were channeled or pumped upward to the great municipality. This water source originated in the Ash Mountains and flowed under the caverns and tunnels of the earth forming a lengthy aquifer of many miles, passing through the secret Khala mine, northeast of Mod, and then south through the city. Beyond the city, where the earth began its decline toward the coast, the hidden river burst forth from its place of concealment and flowed openly until it met the sea near Bamidia. This unique subterranean habitation brought forth a small pool of underground life, opportunist carnivores mostly, preying on the unwary in the dark or even land creatures that stumbled into this vital water source. As the victim paused to drink, or as the blind fish wandered too close, its life was suddenly ended by the grip of the hidden madidi and it was dragged to its doom. This river was feared, and the inhabitants of the lands called it Karkana, or River of Ghosts. The madidi were renowned for being the hunters of the depths, but also as a food source. The dwellers along the river trapped the great but rare eels in the wells and sold them, for their value was high. The Ahga also partook in this common but rarely successful practice by baiting this cell with meat until he caught one, and a large one to his delight and surprise, drawn in through the many winding tunnels of the city until it found the chamber under the palace. But his purpose was different.

Bearing several thick tentacles with which to draw in prey, the creature pulled its long-sought sustenance under the water and dragged it downward to the hole at the bottom of the chamber where it hid. Klintuk's legs were tightly wrapped, being caught off guard. He pounded the snake-like dweller repeatedly with his fists. He finally managed to break free and sped for the surface. He needed that knife, but he couldn't get it until the water level had risen sufficiently. His head surfaced just long enough to take a breath. He could see that he was now able to reach the knife, if he could grab it. The cell was filling quickly and there was not much air space left. But his position in the well had changed in the struggle and he surfaced too far away from the weapon. He caught a glimpse of it, perched in wait. He didn't have an opportunity to swim to it. Again he was dragged under and with greater vigor. With desperate strength he grappled with the arms of the creature in an underwater contest of survival. He could see its hideous face emerging from a chasm at the far bottom of the cave, its mouth opening in preparation. But he also saw the unmistakable outline of a round metal door behind the creature, closed and affixed directly to the distant floor. The exertion to free himself spent his air quickly. The mouth of the eel found its mark on the leg of the prey and the water was tainted with blood. With fury Klintuk struck at the face of his enemy. Dismayed, the madidi released its grip.

The water level was now so high the dagger which once hung well out of reach now penetrated the surface. Less than a foot of space remained in the chamber. With his sharp eyes the trained mog of the Mak-Baccád succeeded in gaining the weapon amid the tumult of the violent water. He had not time to lose. He needed to get to the door on the bottom, it was his only way out. He immediately sought the creature which had dared lay wound to his flesh. Now he had the upper hand and he descended. The onslaught was fierce. Many times he was wrapped and bitten, many times he plunged the blade into the demon. The water had turned into a pool of frothing red wine. He severed one tentacle, then another. Finally the beast surrendered and withdrew into a far corner.

Klintuk resurfaced for more air. The struggle cost him precious breath. He would only have time for one more. He swam directly to the far floor and tried the door. It must have been about thirty feet deep by his vague reckoning. The bottom half of the cell declined in shape toward the floor, forming that of a smooth and wide funnel, and angled easily toward the door. The door was sealed by means of a wheel which he twisted with all his might and desperation. He had to open this door, or drown in the well and become the pitiful sustenance of the beast, he would. Only moments remained. Death breathed its proclamation on his soul. At last the lock released. He returned to the surface for his last breath. The capacity of the cell had all but reached its limitation. To breathe he had to turn his head upwards and press his lips to the rock ceiling. One last time he made the plunge.

He gripped the handle and pulled, but the immense weight of the liquid pressed upon it and kept it shut. The space behind must be empty, he thought. There was no equal pressure behind it to facilitate its opening, but the weighty consequences of that did not occur to him in that moment of desperation. Maddening with the ferocity of a titan, he spent his last strength and breath, shaking the cave with his voice until it opened. And when the door pivoted upon its steel hinges the water, as a natural consequence, made a mad and sudden rush for the vacancy which opened below, and the monstrous weight and sudden force of it caused the breathless contender to fall instantly to the floor, crushed. He couldn't move, not even lift his hand upwards. He was pinned underwater by the hands of a giant that wouldn't release him for breath. The abrupt redirection of energy resulted in a vortex which pulled all into the conical abyss beneath. Any loose objects were lifted or pried from their places of rest and thrown into the whirlpool. Small stones and cave debris whipped about and struck him. The maimed madidi whirled round and round, making attempts to halt the crushing expulsion. The twisting force was so strong that Klintuk, clawing for grip on the inclined rock surface, had to fit his hands into crevices and hold with all his remaining might lest he be dragged into the hole and to death unknown. His legs and body hovered parallel with the spinning motion and massive pull of the blood-soaked water. Several times he lost his grip and was sucked into the madness until he miraculously found another hold for his fingertips.

In the midst of it all, between the lack of air and the monstrous force which pulled and threw him, he felt a distinct loss of sensibility as though the world of revolving ferocity was becoming more distant and quiet, and his mind and soul grew numb. He knew he was losing consciousness and struggled to maintain his grip on the world which seemed to be disintegrating and collapsing around him in a whirlwind that grew in power. He could hear the beast which alone accompanied him finally give up its life and depart the chamber, disappearing in the round hole beneath. It was gone. Klintuk clutched the uneven floor desperately. He knew he had been successful, relatively speaking, and that he just needed to hold onto life for another moment. If he could, he stood a fair chance of proceeding on to the next level of the chun-vok.

The intake of water above the surface must have stopped for the vortex was finally diminishing in strength. Gradually the angle of the water lessened as the last of it found its way to the bottom. At last Klintuk lost consciousness and became victim to the ebbing vortex. Round and round he spun, like a toy at the mercy of its master, but its wrath was spent. His body was thrust and beat against the aperture but failed to make entry. The whirlpool gave up its soul in one loud, long, and monstrous shriek which shook the chamber and rocked the earth until it at last disappeared, consumed by the darkness below. Then all fell silent.

Klintuk drew himself up ever so slowly, coughing and sputtering weakly. He couldn't tell for what length of time he had remained senseless. It took a considerable time before he had purged himself of water and had strength again even to stand. Never before had he undergone such a struggle, never had death whispered so closely in his ear. He was amazed to be alive. His eyesight was slow to recover and everything looked grey and hazy. He crawled back up the funnel awkwardly and finally landed on the level floor, breathing heavily. He remained on the floor for some duration, breathless and exhausted. When he again came to he looked around him. The water inlets on the wall had fallen empty and silent save for the persistent dripping. The tunnel at the low far end of the chamber was still barred but empty. He turned around to the opposite end. Outlined against the wall, low so that it rested on the floor, appeared what could only be another exit. He slowly approached, as one who is recovering from a stupor of intoxication and struggles to rid himself of its hindrance and see through the fog it produced. He placed his hands upon the almost invisible protrusions and ridges and discovered that it indeed was a door of sorts, small and round, without handles, concealed from discovery and inaccessible when the chamber was full for the weight pressed the close-fitting hatch firmly shut. It had partially opened for this pressure was now absent and it stood ajar. He pulled it open completely and staggered down the dry tunnel beyond.

* * *

Babla and Klintuk opened the doors which met them at the end of their respective tunnels and entered the vast chamber beyond. Their eyes met across what appeared to be some kind of fighting arena. The two looked weary and bore the scars of an intense struggle. Blood coated much of their bodies. They looked as if they had been rent and mauled, almost to death, and appeared fatigued, far different from the way they looked when first they began the trial. Then, they seemed to emanate strength and power, and fearlessness. Domination radiated about them like a glow. Now they seemed more than half beaten: their frames dipped slightly; their breath came heavier; their eyes lost much of their gleam; their garments hung on them in ribands. Each wondered what mode of torture and trial the other had undergone. But one thing was common in both of the eyes that glared across the open room: survival.

This wide, open, torch-lit chamber was hexagonal in shape, domed of ceiling, with a beam of about fifty feet from any point on the surrounding walls to the center. But it was not flat. There were low rises strategically placed, as well as shallow depressions, forming many flat surfaces throughout the room at different heights from which one could attack his enemy. These dips or rises carved out of the smooth stone floor were symmetrically positioned and well crafted to create different angles and vantage points for the contenders within. About the room were placed objects to assist them in their attempt to secure the victory. Directly at the feet of them both was a gullick, the bladed throwing weapon of the Kunn. Somewhere toward the middle were bladed pole arms. Several fighting staffs were within easy range. Apparently the expected number of contestants was four, for there were four doors of entry, all on opposite and facing sides of the vault. But two of the doors remained silent and closed, and they wondered at the absence of their friend, Narnak, the third of their party. They looked upon the fourth and furthest door with curiosity, wondering where it led, for it was different from the other three and seemed to breathe of death. Immediately there came to their minds the possibility that this could lead to the much feared and rumored Gahg-Morga, the Ahga's Hall of Horrors. Dismissing this possibility, they focused their attention to the other objects in the room.

Upon the walls on all six sides were placed small platforms at different heights which jutted outwards, only accessible by jumping or leaping. To complement this arrangement of altitude combat, several poles had been affixed either to the ceiling or the floor, providing lateral or vertical attack and evade options. They looked around and scrutinized every aspect and detail of what was an enormous and ingeniously modified arena. Were it not for the grim requirements of the circumstances, this room promised to be an excellent means of physical training, not unlike the grounds outside the keep.

As their eyes wandered back toward the middle again they noticed a small dais directly in the center upon which was locked what could only be the honorable sword of the Kunn, the *kodara,* the strongest and keenest of all swords, displayed proudly on its mount of silver as a gift to the victor. This required a unique set of keys to open, and they could see the placement of a single key above each door of entry. Each one latched to the other three and when assembled formed a singular unlocking mechanism designed to fit through the four fingers of the holder when held in a fist. The four prongs, when assembled and locked together, could be fitted into the four holes of the custom-crafted lock to extract the grand and coveted award.

342

The doors closed behind them and the sound echoed. It was like a bell tolling doom. Only one would emerge alive. The elimination had begun. One would rise to greatness and glory and be honored with carrying out the will of the Brotherhood, the other eternally silenced. All over the arena they fought in a desperate and secret duel under the earth, concealed from all eyes, leaping onto the platforms, swinging from the poles in the air, throwing the returnable gullicks and evading their deadly arcs, trading blows with both staff and hand. Their skills for which they trained were utilized, and one would have been impressed indeed. Like acrobats they leaped and somersaulted through the air in a perilous chase and attack. But in the end it was Babla who was victorious. After an exemplary and extensive performance Klintuk heaved his throwing blade only to have it caught by his enemy unexpectedly who returned it with deadly accuracy. Klintuk had gotten this far in the service of the Father only to fall at the bitter end. The Ahga would mourn the heavy loss of this great servant, but in his wisdom the expense was well worth the respect and command received in turn by his subjects that his establishment demanded. These were the reasons his men were so disciplined and fully committed to him and his cause: his followers feared and revered him but also gave their lives to him. A command issued was service received.

Babla saluted his fallen comrade. Then he looked upwards and gave a long shout of triumph which echoed in the wide and empty hall. His energy was too great to be restrained. He had completed the chun-vok. In moments he would receive his honorary induction into the Baccád before his comrades. The favor of the Divine One was certainly upon him. He quickly gathered all the keys and unlocked the case, gratefully withdrawing his own new sword, the kodara. This weapon was forged by the best engineers the Ahga had abducted or coerced into his service, for it indeed was made of garvonite, that increasingly rare and valuable material and the product of the tedious crafting process which made the blade so great. Only those of the Baccád had a weapon of this strength and make. Around the arena he paraded with his prize, gesticulating toward the sky with gratitude to the Divine, and throwing his hands and voice in the wild energies of his victory. A door soon opened and in stepped the Ahga and his Baccád for his ceremonial induction. The Ahga offered his congratulations and welcome. He had been correct in his prediction and was pleased with the outcome. Narnak's fate was predictable but necessary. Klintuk was a sore loss, but there was no doubt that his new successor, Babla, was chosen by the Divine One to commence a greater duty, one that would prove fruitful to the cause. He it was that possessed the favor of the Mari and he was rightfully elevated to his proper plane of service. It was a good day for the Kunn.

The gatehouse of the Harásh was busy most of the time, and the many guards on duty there were usually occupied with the aspiring guests or visitors, many of whom were denied entry due to the contagious distrust of the lord. This was a large chamber, the gatehouse, and was amply equipped for the task of the careful admission and discharge of folk and goods onto or from the grounds of the estate. A large and lengthy ramp led up to it from the low street below, on which were placed many guards who encircled the entirety of the mighty dwelling to quell the frequent unrest and send a message of intimidation to the passers-by. The unjust rule of the tyrant bred resentment among the ruled which in turn aggravated the distrust and paranoia of the lord, such that his guards were almost always busy. The Harásh was built upon a higher elevation than the dense urban sea which surrounded and pressed upon it, and the task of keeping unwanted folk at a safe distance was a constant priority. The streets in the immediate area underneath the palace were sealed off and heavily guarded. Any shipments or guests had first to pass through the main guard post on the ground who would question and demand proof of identity or invite of the prospective visitors. They then would begin the ascent up the ramp, upon which passed daily many wagons and steeds to and from the huge guardhouse at the pinnacle which was also paved with stone and leveled to accommodate a sizable and mounted host. When one reached this point he had a moment to look about him for there was usually a wait. The position above the street commanded a view of the city on the southern side and the multitudes treading upon the narrow avenues. The helmeted centurions in the red and brown garb of Mod paced everywhere, above and below, the tips of their spears shone brightly in the potent sun.

If one was permitted access and whose invitation was honored, he then proceeded through the main inlet which was divided into two avenues to accommodate the heavy traffic, one for ingress, one for egress. A large portcullis drew itself up and led into a wide, arched, antechamber. Two heavy doors at the end of this were thrown open and he at last tread upon the grand grounds of the Harásh and was escorted thence to his destination.

Among the assortment of individuals and vans before the gatehouse appeared the stranger from the night before, waiting inconspicuously by his steed. His character name here was known by some but his real name would draw suspicion at the least and more probably sturdy guards to arrest him. He had just paid an unexpected visit to a renowned gangster the previous night under other guise and was now attempting something else of daring, all part of his plot. He had started the fire, now he came to see the outcome–and see about one more thing. This mysterious individual was proclaimed the foremost enemy of the Kunn, a renowned spy or traitor of sorts, but who he really was or what he did or who he worked for was beyond the knowledge of most familiar with his name and association. But that was trivial. The price offered by the Ahga for this cunning and elusive shadow of many guises marginalized his real importance. He was probably just another vigilante seeking vengeance upon these gangsters known as the Kunn. There were not a few of those, but none possessed his level of daring. As it was widely suspected that he traveled abroad frequently, especially to Mod, Thuliak's men had been informed of this man and to be on the constant watch for him, not so much for the bounty but to utilize this figure as a tool to pressure and manipulate the Ahga and his following. With his capture Thuliak could make the Ahga talk, squirm even, and beg for mercy. His patience with his neighbor was wearing thin, and though Thuliak assured this King of Thugs that he would do all he could to affect the capture of one of his most wanted, he did not mention that the prisoner would be kept for himself to bring about the Ahga's immolation. His captains and henchmen, who also shared no loyalty with that clan, had been earnestly informed of this individual and to keep an especially sharp eye, for their lord greatly desired the apprehension of this covert enemy of the Kunn for his own profitable purposes.

This valuable stranger bore the presence of a skilled and renowned craftsman, wearing fairly plain clothes, which were dirty and worn from having seen a fair amount of use, and enabled him to work freely without hindrance. He stood beside his mule of burden which pulled a small cart of tools, pieces of material to be cut and fit, stones for grinding and shaping, and other paraphernalia of a busy but rather disorganized veteran tradesman. His graying beard suited his persona for the day, along with the stuffing in his midsection which protruded sufficiently to mask his slender build. A filthy bandana around his forehead added to the deception and his hair was tied back. His hands and face were dirty as were other areas about his person. He walked with a bit of a limp and the perpetual smile on his face and quick, loud, and friendly laugh dispelled any suspicion or fear of what appeared to be a commoner of the middle class, here by special invitation. He had an approachable aspect about him, very welcoming and outspoken. Just another hired tool or locksmith, they thought, here to repair or add to the ever-growing construction and maintenance of the palace. We see many of those.

When he reached the pinnacle and was approached by the guards they looked at him and let out a familiar laugh.

"Back again, Jesper?" they said. "You must be well off for a craftsman of your kind. I'll wager he pays handsomely for your work. Maybe I should change my line of work and be called by lords all over every time their bahndas break a wheel and their spoons need polishing. Then I could make some real loot."

Jesper laughed heartily and with a wide smile, as one who welcomes the jests of old and daily companions. His open mouth was sufficiently hideous to deceive and it revealed some missing teeth. "Aye, His Highness always has something special for me, you know how he is, there's just no satisfying the old dog. Why just last month he wanted those new stained glass windows replaced on the south turrets, the ones I just put in last year! Those pretty pieces must have cost a barrel of loot, but what's that to him? But I don't complain, I need the work, though I think all this haulin's taking a toll on my mule here." He then slapped the mule who half jumped. "I believe I will need a new one. Maybe His Highness could pay me in mules instead! Har, har, har," he laughed so overtly that he bent backwards to such a degree that he looked foolish, and this was chorused in turn by the guards, who didn't know whether to laugh at him or his pitiful behavior and appearance. They waved him through and returned some jests of their own. He was led through the gates and was released without escort into the courtyard. Old Jesper knew his business.

CHAPTER 4
MUTINY SIMMERS

The Ahga and his Baccád filed into the upper chambers of the Olóbid immediately succeeding the ritual. His subjects he had dismissed to assume their guard duties until further instruction. Babla had been briefly treated for his wounds and given sustenance, for he was to attend the meeting. He was now an official member of the Baccád, he had just received his fourth shukk mark only moments ago, and the Ahga expected his presence. He had been given a personal debrief by the Ahga and Gathmug concerning his new expectations and duties. Any other secrets and pertinent information would be disclosed in due time. A burning issue was at hand and the Ahga wished to waste no more time in the delay of its contemplation. They seated themselves in their assigned chairs of iron which formed an oval around a large wooden table, thirteen in all though one still remained empty. They were arranged in order of superiority, succeeding in distance away from the Ahga who sat at the head with his Gahd-hesh by his side. Babla took his new place at the far end. He looked around at the venerable and fearsome figures seated beside him and could scarcely believe he was now among them. The Ahga began to speak and all listened. The wide and vaulted chamber echoed with his voice.

"The issue of the prisoner Gadrin has not yet been resolved. This spy was aware of our deeds against Thuliak. The last he was seen alive was in Hera, and Mozep's remaining force informed us of our failure to reacquire him and of Draga's success. He took the spy for himself, for his own purposes no doubt. The details concerning the fallout of our old friend Draga have been made available to us. Our scouts have returned with tidings. The old tower in the hills was thoroughly searched. There was evidence of a great struggle. Draga and all his followers were killed, but of the perpetrators there was no sign. The inner chambers of the cave had been badly damaged and much of his stored wealth destroyed. The giant kunga which he keeps housed beneath the tower was still alive, but all else was destroyed or plundered."

"Could it not have been the deed of Hera, for there are many under the hills of that tower who are still loyal to Karius, nobles and wealthymen, and perhaps took it upon themselves to flush out Draga and his servants?" offered Mesahalat, the likely replacement for Mozep in that city. He had great familiarity with the city and its geopolitics. "The Guards of Karius have regrouped perhaps. It was feared to be so. In which case we have them to thank for destroying our enemy, the traitor Draga."

Gathmug spoke. "Nay," he answered. "That is unlikely. The attack looked too personal, as though it were carried out by only a few." There were some looks with this insinuation. Thoughts of their elusive new enemies, which none here had even yet seen, came to mind. Little did they know of the great loss they were about to suffer at their hands again. Even now Damian and Cam were sailing their vessel across the Strait to halt Kunn pirating in the Vidian Sea.

"What of the adept who was dispatched for their elimination?" said Gōz, chapter leader in Kadr. He had traveled the past three days to be present for the occasion. He was referring to Tog, their secretive mentor, but this agent of mystery was only alluded to and never mentioned by name. The business of the Consortium was beyond their parameters. Even speaking about that leader openly before the Ahga took courage. They thought Tog immortal and able to commune with ghosts. It was widely believed that he did not originate in this world, and this Baccád member was no exception to that myth. Gōz was an especially vicious mog, high of standing and trust, and was adorned with a unique jeweled bandolier which hailed from Barikash, beyond the mountains to the east. He killed a notorious gangster in that city in an unarmed duel and won the respectable and valuable ornament as a prize. The Ahga allowed him to wear it as proof of supremacy.

The Ahga made no sign. "He is responsible to himself," he replied evasively. "Of his designs we are not privy. The doings of the Consortium are not ours in which to meddle." Their trusted champion had been delayed and disrupted before, but in the end he never failed to succeed, and with more than customary expectations. The Ahga would not bring discredit to the greatest and most mysterious of his followers in front of his men, even if he did have his own suspicions or doubts.

"No sign of him could we find within the grounds of the tower," replied Ushep. This mog had a much more sinister look to him. His presence suggested that he was more of a swindler and negotiator for his eyes were especially keen and perceptive. He was older among them but his eyes and thought missed little, and the Ahga valued that highly. Ushep was the main advisor and overseer of the political and subversive penetration of the northern lands, Hera and Gyla and currently the cities of Kandar. He was knowledgeable of rulers there and provided the Ahga with educated plots for infiltration. "We believe he is still in pursuit of his objective," he ended.

"And what of the prisoner?" asked Hemetek, changing the subject. That matter was best left alone. Hemetek was chief overseer of commerce, which was great. Hemetek was of high rank and status, even within the Baccád, and he had numerous subjects at his disposal. "Draga had succeeded in taking this man for himself. And he was knowledgeable of our operations against Thuliak. It is possible that Draga extracted this information from him."

"And perhaps passed it on before he was killed," suggested Rug-Adda in his booming voice, a huge Mogoli with fists like barrels and a hideous scar on one side of his head which deprived it of the usual black hair. This mog was given responsibility of management of the kuth trade and other commodities originating in the far south and west of the great Tanga River with the help of his brother, Kassét, clan leader in Mulda. This included knowledge and containment of competing clans in the area and the elimination therein. He was somewhat arrogant for the Ahga's taste but his success rate and obedience earned him respect and position regardless. "Are we sure that all his men were eliminated?"

"How can we be sure our scouts found everything?" posed another mog, Vekk, clan leader in Bahrag. "The ulaks cannot be wholly trusted. They have brought erroneous reports before. And despite our efforts to instill loyalty, their adherence can waver and they are subject to bribery, as has been proven in the case of our fallen brother, Draga."

"Which means we cannot count on containment of the secret!" burst out Bazi, clan leader in Darhúk, and his fists met with the thick table in fury. He was an especially rash member of the Baccád, known for his questionable sanity and quick temper. Outbursts of anger and rage brought him happiness, and the objects of his hideous murders were oftentimes the undeserving and helpless victims who fell under his restless fists and uncontrollable fury. His explosive demeanor made even the most fearsome of the Kunn avoid him. Tog thought him a mindless fool. He would love to destroy this ape. An unworthy specimen of the Mari and what it stood for. Strength and ferocity do not supplant the powers of the mind but are to be utilized in conjunction to achieve ultimate existence with the forces of the earth. Bazi had a look in his dark eyes that spoke of dangerous instability within, and they were wild with energy. He was a dangerous character to be sure. "We must assume there were survivors and this volatile information passed on, perhaps to our enemies who will use this against us!"

Some discussion broke out. Gathmug held up his hand and silence ensued. "The body of the prisoner was found, chained to the walls and executed. It is probable that he was forced to divulge his secrets before his death. We must assume that our new enemy, Ratarra, was present at Draga's tower, has been made aware of the secret, and has found a way to inform Thuliak. Ratarra is no fool. This information can be used against us. He has connections and a network of spies with whom he and his friend consort. His presence in Hera has been confirmed. He and his friend are identifiable; they are no longer secret. Bounties have been offered for their heads. Our chapter there is ordered to seek him out and destroy him, though we are in need of a new leader there (here he nodded to Mesahalat). It is possible that Thuliak is at last aware of us and preparing his revenge as we speak."

The assembled exchanged some looks. After a moment one of them voiced common concern and opinion. "And are we then to wait for him to imprison us singly, or lay ambush to our keep while we are unaware?" asked Zodd, overseer of ground operations right here in Mod. "We dwell in the heart of his strength. Though I despise the worthless slug, his forces, however inferior to us, outnumber us many times. His garrison is at his call. We do not have the upper hand in his domain, even if we recalled all our strength from the city below. We have not acquired the Greater Mari yet, my brothers. For the gift of Azandium we still search. In the meantime we cannot wait until he formulates a plan to arrange a raid and apprehend all of us. His destruction will do us no good if it also causes our own. It will be the end of the Brotherhood."

"We must assume that he is now aware of us and that we are in peril," one of them said.

"That is why we will attack him first," said the Ahga. A moment of stunned silence followed.

Mesahalat finally broke the silence. Much thought transpired with these last words of the Ahga. "And what if we succeed?" he asked. "Are we to assume the throne? How do we intend to reestablish rule if by some miracle we are victorious against Thuliak? I, like my fellow brothers assembled here, share the same sentiments regarding the fool. But I am also prudent. We have not the strength yet to subdue his superior garrison."

"Nor do we have the full support of the citizenry, but more importantly the soldiers of the city," added Hemetek. "If we are to attempt a coup, as I perceive that we are, and I am not opposed to it my brothers, we need to foresee and prepare for all ends. Much is at stake here. This is not something to be taken lightly." The Ahga and Gathmug waited patiently for them to voice their concerns. It was best if they all knew the volatility of the situation.

"And we must ask ourselves," posed Zodd, "is this the direction we desire for the Order to tread upon? Actual rulership and governance of a city? I have enjoyed our freedom. We move about at will, manipulating lords all over, and it has always proved profitable. Do we wish to be tied by the tedious demands of a bureaucratic rule? Being locked immovable in the quagmire of governing may not be the wisest choice in the long run. It is not here in Mod that the destiny of the Brotherhood lies."

"But imagine the riches the Order would bring then!" spouted Bazi. "And the power! All would bow to the Kunn. These small bands of rebels and clans which have opposed us would flee, for they would be crushed, like we did to Kadkade's Raiders at Kuyala Canyon [he referred to the notorious victory at the Drop in the Vora Gorga where the Kunn forced their enemy's bahnda chariots right over the cliff edge]. Now it is our time to reign. We are no longer the band of desert warriors that we once were, hiding in obscurity, but an organization, one that the citizens recognize as the supreme clan in the region. We need not hide any longer. It is time to openly embrace our true and greater purpose, for which we are ready. All hail the Kunn down in the city. Our takeover would be welcomed and our ranks would grow enough to bring our objective to the next stage." He was liking this idea and held up his fists.

"We control much of the movement of goods in the whole realm," added Ushep, "and have asserted control over much of the piracy in the Gulf. We wield great power within the governments of many of our cities. Our presence is felt in all corners of the realm, save Kadr which is lost. All fear us. It is time to finally seize what we have the power to control, and to openly declare to the lords of the lands and our enemies alike what kind of force we are. Let us now take what is deserving of us. We need not be hesitant in this undertaking, nor should we continue to obscure our presence with our usual clandestine methods. A bold move as this will render them no longer necessary."

"And with the seizure of this capital city we will have a point of strength from which to strike the hated northern and western realms," added Ulgash, clan diplomat to western cities, Prova and Bren, "without the hindrance of this overseer we all despise. She grows powerful in the east. Let us not forget the prophecy: *In the first city the enemy will be destroyed and the new realm will begin.* According to the Book the time grows near. After Mod, Hera will easily fall, and therein lies our ultimate destiny."

"And we would have a force strong enough to counter this new revolutionary in Kadr," said Gōz. "Do not believe what they say about her. I see the influence she has there. Mark my words, my brothers, she will be a force to contend with. It would be foolish to overlook and underestimate the power she musters in what was once our home city from which we have been essentially driven. And now would be the time to overthrow her, before she has acquired her full strength, for not all support her. Can we not find someone to replace her after we have assassinated her as well? It can be accomplished quite easily there, our networks are still in place."

351

"I think you have all overestimated our chances of success," Vekk said, attempting to revive them from their stupor and delusions of reign. "Though I agree that it would be a privilege and an honor to die in an open strife against the fool, Thuliak. But I am inclined to agree with my brother Zodd. Why do we desire this course of action? I question whether the income we gain will be worth the trouble of assuming full power and exposing ourselves prematurely. Let these other fools rule their cities, it is far easier manipulating the weak and undermining their authority to suit our needs, and depart when necessary. We need not be troubled with the tediousness of governing, it has never been in our creed, nor is it necessarily demanded of our task. Strength to wrest what power we need is all that is needed. Kane will fall beneath the tide we are creating by the policy in place. Governing is the part of others under our watchful yoke. Remember, it is not in these territories that we intend to one day rule."

"And who exactly is to rule in Mod?" posed Rugg-Adda. "Are we to replace the entire infrastructure of the city? And how long will that take? This is very short notice to accomplish all that we must. I don't think we all appreciate the undertaking that is at stake. Is any of Thuliak's cabinet to be kept in place, or are we to expel or execute all of them, as I feel will be necessary. Removing all disloyalties will be imperative."

"The result of which will be unpredictable," said Zodd. "We may even have a full-scale mutiny on our hands and riots in the streets."

The Ahga finally held up his hand and intervened. "We shall only establish a puppet government, to serve our needs in the meantime. The city and its policies will be subject to our demands. We must recognize the opportunity before us. It is time to seize that which the Divine One has proffered. We will maintain our status and level of organization for the time but with a greater portion of earned funds allocated to ourselves as a result of the ousting. No longer will we have to sacrifice a disproportionate sum of wealth to our host as agreement of our residence, for this will be a requirement of the new ruler's instatement, among other things which we desire. Most of what you are implying will not even be necessary. The transition of power will be very smooth indeed."

"Then," Mesahalat uttered with difficulty, "you are not to rule?"

Gathmug finished the briefing. He was the Ahga's closest confidant. Whatever he knew, all that he considered or intended was shared with his most trusted of all the Baccád. There were no secrets between them. "As Vekk has said, the throne of the Father will not ultimately be located here. It is elsewhere that the banner of the Kunn must fly. Kane will be confronted again in due time. But this is a necessary step toward our ultimate goal: challenging Demar, and the time has come to bring our great task to its next level, to emerge from the shadows and make a declaration of sovereignty and purpose. Mod can be our footstool. The appointed one the Father is referring to dwells here, below this very palace. A certain prisoner is held in the dungeons below who was once a high-standing member of the Kunn for a considerable amount of time. He eventually left to seek advancement as a political contender for this state. He, not unlike ourselves, despised the ruler Thuliak and instead of seeking to strive with him from the outside he manipulated his way into the lower cabinet and sought to overthrow him in this manner. His power grew and he developed a following among many of his cohorts who shared his sentiments. There is even much discontent among Thuliak's garrisons and officers still. Thuliak perceived the threat and seized him and his conspirators before any further strength was gained, and to convey a message to the rest of the Council. They still occupy several of the cells to this day, and their loyalty remains intact."

"Salzan!" said Hemetek abruptly, and they all acknowledged their old former brother. Their faces became alight with the understanding. The success of the coup seemed possible after all. Fists pounded the table in fervor.

"Salzan Karpoli and his conspirators will assume the rulership of Mod," the Ahga concluded, "and will be our hand here. Considering the impending circumstances we have little choice regardless. Thuliak is undoubtedly on the move already. We fight, or we will be destroyed. There are many who despise Thuliak. His rule will end and all will hail the Kunn as their victors." With that they all stood and threw their arms in the air, chanting and yelling slogans of the clan, celebrating what would either be a great achievement or deaths with honor and the end of the Order.

* * *

Thuliak's hastily arranged counsel had quickly reached conclusion. The lords and officers of his city who were available at the inconvenient hour of mid-day had obeyed the strange and urgent summons, and found themselves in the midst of a wrath they had seldom witnessed, even from this ill-tempered dictator. They all stood dumbstruck. Proof had been presented beyond doubt: the Kunn was responsible for all their failures of late and had cost them untold wealth in loss, loss in which they all had a stake. That rare and unusual gold ingot had been presented as the painful truth. Only Thuliak had a sample stash of that rare piece in his possession. And somehow the Kunn had acquired some of it and it found its way right back to its owner. Rash could no longer be trusted. He had failed him again. Thuliak's secrets, his treasury perhaps, his dark alliances–all were presumed laid bare. All those shipments sacked, all those important purchases lost, and he and his men were never able to discover the cunning and obviously well-informed thieves behind it. After all the assistance he gave the Ahga and his Order, offering them a substantial and adequate satellite in a western city since their virtual eviction from Kadr, even to pursue their dubious objective, it had been met with treason. This past year must have been the worst Thuliak had ever experienced. All this time it was believed that it was the combined work of the new ruler in Kadr, Her Highness, and the Bará, who had probably made an unofficial alliance for mutual benefit and undoubtedly sought vengeance on Thuliak's regime for fostering those bitter rivals, the Kunn, and offering them his support and favor.

Thuliak quietly ordered the entire premises sealed off and every available soldier was mustered for a raid, one that would undoubtedly prove costly. The Kunn will be destroyed, not succeeding long council and meditation during which time and indecision eroded opportunity and initiative, but here and now, and the Ahga will hang. The Kunn was strong to be sure, but they could not fight a whole army. A multitude of centurions immediately surrounded the compound. No one was leaving.

An alcove existed in the far wall where Thuliak and Rash-Haba had their encounter in the Alad earlier in the day. This cutout, which served as one of the many architectural decorations throughout the splendorous dwelling, extended beyond the floor and ceiling of the room of its origination, and had been adopted as a shrine of Thuliak's. Plates of gold and statuettes had been placed in here for presentational purposes to please the eyes of his guests who seated themselves here in comfort for counsel with the lord, though this was not the only means of décor in this parlor. The openness and shape of this forgotten alcove provided an advantageous medium of acoustics that a certain resourceful servant of the Ahga had, in time, found good use for. Not only did it allow him an excellent mode of eavesdropping in the parlor but in the meeting room below as well. A thin layer of masonry on the floor of this recess was all that separated it from the large counsel room below and the sound of discourse and debate traveled and reverberated easily within its narrow and hollow enclosure.

His name was Sebuda, and he had been a servant at the Alad for several years. Being a Turuk of keen wit and slighter frame than the mogs, half-mogs, Hidari, and Humans who dwelt here and which also comprised the bulk of Thuliak's soldiers, his proficiency in stealth and delivery of information was profound. He was actually a member of the Mak-Baccád, expertly trained in espionage and assassination, but Thuliak and those in the Alad would never have suspected this. The Ahga had him specifically chosen for what the Kunn leader considered to be a position of vital importance and necessity. A spy in the Alad was absolutely imperative, indeed it would be foolish not to have eyes and ears in that corrupt labyrinth, seething with foul folk seeking their own gain who would not hesitate to drive a dagger into the heart of a dear friend if it meant some ascent in power. The Ahga immediately sought to fill this post when he initially brought his Brotherhood into the capital to increase his enterprise in these western cities. He did not trust the lord of the city, though the latter eagerly accepted the clan leader's offer for wealth in return for residence, and deployed a trusted servant to monitor his doings. Sebuda was a follower of unquestionable loyalty and had serviced the Father for many years, usually in the field of reconnaissance and espionage. He it was who the Ahga dispatched many times to discover any useful information about clients or clan members, oppositional entities, or even politicians and lawmakers. The Ahga knew the importance of a valuable bit of information and he did not overlook this necessity.

Sebuda was summoned in secret from his duties somewhere in the east, before his new placement in the palace. He had received his new orders and he understood. No one in the territory was familiar with him at the time, none had seen him before. He had never been in the city of Mod. He was a perfect candidate. An agent arranged his hire in the dwelling some time preceding the anticipated arrival of the Brotherhood, and this was done with the intent to scout the area undercover and study the people, the nobilities, their allegiances or lack thereof, intentions of the lord, etc., and send report of anything of interest back to the clan for analysis. His very identity was concealed from all. There were only four others knew of his existence: the Ahga, Gathmug, his contact, and a secondary. Perhaps there were a few within the clan who might have succeeded in recognizing him, having worked or trained with him before, and for this reason his features had been altered to disguise him. His contact who worked in conjunction with him was a bribed official who worked openly in the palace, coming and going regularly on business, and merely delivered the correspondence as an easy means of supplemental income though he was carefully watched. Sebuda placed messages in a number of unique places, dispersed throughout the domain to avoid routine and to accommodate the contact's ever-changing movements. In a vast dwelling such as the Harásh this was not overly difficult. He retrieved the coded messages which Sebuda wrote carefully in a special ink that could only be read when doused in a certain secret chemical mixture in the possession of the Ahga, and simply included the scroll with the host of others he had at all times. As the small page appeared blank, suspicion was not aroused should it be observed. Never once did he return to the Olóbid, however. That would be too obvious. He swiftly departed for the city below where concealment was easy, and convened with his secondary who in turn delivered the precious document to the Ahga. And this had been done routinely for many months.

Gathmug approached the Ahga with the message. They never called him Sebuda by name, only *makuru,* which meant 'worm', and this word became associated with their spy and his messages. Anything regarding the worm was strictly concealed and handled with extreme care. Even most of the Baccád didn't know about him. The repercussions against the Kunn if Thuliak discovered that his confidentiality had been compromised would be devastating, and that indeed was the issue at hand: the Ahga and his men had been discovered as the grand thieves. The Father had dismissed his cabinet after proposing his daring plan and now they were hastening its preparation per his orders. They didn't have much time. Every hand had been informed of the impending disaster and had gone below to assist with the desperate preparations, though the guards at the main doors had been doubled. All his men were recalled inside. The message that the Ahga was now decrypting intensified and confirmed this once suspected but now imminent confrontation. He immediately went below with Gathmug. The Ahga was right. Thuliak was mustering. They had less time than they thought.

Tension brewed between the two towers, an enmity conceived not by mutual declaration but by perception, gaining speed and wrath so much that one could almost see a force at work between the two, pulling and wrestling with one another in a strained silence. Sounds of activity ordinarily heard seemed muted. The dwellings stared at each other menacingly. And though no outward sign or token was forthcoming from either camp which might reveal the secret intentions of the two contenders, even the most ignorant began to perceive an unspoken contention within the walls. The faces that moved about the elaborate courtyards outside were unusually grim and expectant, and the solemn workers in the gardens and upon the grounds or the walls were constrained to pause and hearken to the whispering peril; a hastier step was noticed among those who strode; a countenance of unease and foreboding took its place upon all who passed or waited outside; a heavy silence like that of death pervaded; a doom was about to fall.

CHAPTER 5
SECRETS OF THE DEAD

Jesper managed his way inside the Harásh earlier that morning. He clumsily carried the tools he would need for the maintenance of the day, laughing pathetically as he went, accompanied by a centurion of Mod as escort. Thuliak was not available, being detained by a most pressing issue at hand, but old Jesper was quietly directed to design plans for a certain new trap door in a room within the palace, and thither he was led. Jesper was an expert locksmith and inventor, known to the dictator for he had been here before, and had been recalled some time ago to help finish this unique installation on a particular portion of the domain intended to be sealed. It was a minor request, nothing of major import was to be placed within this new vault, the lord assured him. Probably more acquired heirlooms or statuettes, or other items of vanity, or simply more worthless possessions, thought Jesper, who held little respect for the monarch inwardly though he did offer his gratitude. Thuliak was protective of his possessions and that of the palace and was particularly selective of the one doing the work. Jesper assured him that he would return as soon as he was able. In reality, Jesper had ventured there some time ago with the intent to penetrate the Harásh where the clan known as the Kunn had assumed a recent residence. He needed a means of access to the compound in order to conduct his espionage and sabotage against them. At first he offered his services to the lord for mere crumbs, begging for work and some paltry mode of income to 'feed his poor, starved family'. The lord of the dwelling was always in need of good craftsmen so it was an easy bargain to accept, even for a dictator who had no interest in the struggles of the lower class.

In a short time he succeeded in impressing the lord of the dwelling with his knowledge of craftsmanship, masonry work, and the design and engineering of parts and mechanisms so much that he named him the 'trickmaster' for his expertise in installing hidden trap doors and spring devices, necessary for the lord's insidious character and intentions. Thuliak actually implored him to return, for he wished him to personally install his unique locking devices for some of his interior gates and vaults. The humble but friendly old man accepted the offer gratefully and returned when he could, but it was always with an ulterior motive and when it served his purpose. Jesper created and installed Thuliak's personal safe in the wall of his very suite, one that opened only to the correct alignment of an array of knobs on the door. Thuliak had no understanding of the mechanics of such a device and nor would he express such a thing. He cared only for extravagance and that which brought him further worship and reverence. Jesper was paid handsomely but he did not service the lord for his money. His charade was a vital key into the domain of a ruler and an advantageous means of information gathering. Knowledge of secrets that could be used to aid the destruction of his enemy was his purpose. The poor craftsman could not refuse such an invitation or opportunity. His presence in the Harásh was like that of a rat in the home of his enemy, eating his crumbs, learning his secrets and weaknesses, acquiring vital information and tidings of events in the region. Though he did not actually return regularly, for his real work lie elsewhere, Jesper was always well received when he did, and the lord always had some task pending which required his genius. And so he achieved a privileged guest residence in the capital, indeed within the very castle. One could be assured that he would maintain his hold on this unique circumstance.

The purpose of his return today was two-fold: to witness what he hoped would be a destructive and devastating outcome for the Kunn, precipitated by his revelation of the Brotherhood's covert operations against Thuliak, aided by proven theft of this new and secret commodity; and, if things went ill and as a last resort, somehow prevent the Ahga or his agents from acquiring the vast wealth of Thuliak which he had hidden in his domain. Jesper did not underestimate the abilities of the Kunn under the Ahga, however out-manned by Thuliak and his regime. He knew the well-trained fighters of the Baccád were far superior to the lord's mediocre and untrustworthy garrison of guards. And though Thuliak was certainly no ally or trustworthy friend of this phantom, he was, at least, a potential enemy of and weapon against the Kunn, the clan that the injured craftsman had sworn vengeance upon. He had provided the weapon with the necessary ammunition. He returned to see the weapon at work. Old Jesper lumbered blissfully along, making his way through the palace to his destination.

On his way below, the Ahga pulled one of his men aside. He gave him a special order, one that he did not fully understand. The Ahga had an emergency code of flight prepared for his spy in the Alad. Should the cover of the worm be compromised or his life in imminent danger due to discovery, or for any reason of vital import and desperation in which the worm must make immediate flight from his place of eavesdrop, it was agreed that a small red banner of the Kunn would be tied to a ring outside the topmost wall of the Olóbid to signal this greatest of warnings in an inconspicuous manner. This was arranged as the quickest means of communication to the worm across the yard for the banner would be in full view of the windows of the Alad and he could not fail to see it. Though this symbol had never been displayed before outside the Olóbid, for it was forbidden, the seriousness that it conveyed would be taken as a sign of danger. If the futile but oft pondered became a reality, if the Ahga was finally committing to some kind of open aggression against Thuliak, as he had at times alluded, Sebuda's life would be spilled on the polished floors along with the rest of Thuliak's men. The fierce servants of the Kunn were not aware of him and he was indistinguishable from the rest of the weak scum of the Brotherhood's detestation. The Ahga handed his associate the banner with the order that it be hung topside. It may arouse suspicion but that was irrelevant. After today the worm would be unnecessary.

Deep under the palace, and throughout the low, rocky, plateau that it stood upon, lay an extensive underground labyrinth. This arrangement of burrowing tunnels had been excavated and constantly extended over the centuries to accommodate the ever-growing needs of the rulers of these old standing bastions of power and art. Many vaults and secret chambers there were, locked behind doors of iron, or immovable stone, or secreted behind the many family heirlooms and treasures passed down through generations and tenures of succeeding tyrants who once dwelt here, exerting their power and ruthlessness on the weak and common folk of the realm. Lengths of catacombs had been dug in symmetrical chambers separated by long tunnels, and the remains of rulers and their families had been placed forever within in reverence and dignity. Many rows of sarcophagi lined the floors and walls of the inner chambers, all covered in the dust of the earth despite the constant labors of the attendants to maintain presentability. This elaborate burrow of housing and burial was given the name of Ud, which meant simply 'the dead'.

The tombs of the founding brothers, Alad and Olóbid, were separate and placed deepest within the labyrinth and with the greatest honor. They each had two chambers: one for their raised and engraved tombs of stone, placed with honor in the center and free from obstruction; the other chamber held their personal possessions and any wealth or belongings afforded them in their death. Impressed upon the walls were images in bas-relief, carved with skill, symbols and ancient words praising or telling a false history of the fallen with the intent to elevate his legacy to something that was greater than in life, seeking an emulative sentiment in those who stood in awe within the grandiose chamber. But in truth they were to be loathed and despised, for these rulers were plagued with greed and corruption and so also were their regimes. The dungeons within the Ud held many political dissidents or criminals of the regime, some real, some perceived, all imprisoned because they posed a direct threat to power or dared speak out against the unjust ruler, whoever it was at the time. Thuliak had only been in power for a short time but still retained many that had been apprehended during his tyrannical uncle's rule. Those that rebelled with violence against the ruler and his men were summarily executed before the walls for all to see, and their bodies were removed to the catacombs and dumped in a deep shaft called Potep-Ud, or Pit of the Whispering Dead. The number of those which had been tortured and murdered unjustly over the centuries and placed within this mass grave could not be counted. But their spirits still cried out from below the depths. Those who routinely ventured into the crypt silently swore to themselves that voices could be heard, deep within the shaft of Potep-Ud, the bottom of which could not be seen for it plunged into the cavernous and gnawed earth of the Karkana River, flowing far below and carving out the depths in its slow and ever-changing passage to the sea far away.

To the west of the tombs and north past the dungeons lay Thuliak's vault, and this is where he housed the greatest bulk of his wealth, all hoarded safely within his especially locked and situated keepsafe. It was actually located within the shaft of the mass grave and could only be reached by an ascending bridge of rock which projected outwards from the tunnel and over the haunted chasm below. The vault beyond looked like a lone turret of encapsulating rock that protruded from the tunnel and into the middle of the darkness and emptiness of the shaft with a short avenue of rock to reach it. The rulers wanted their treasures well protected and accessible only to themselves, and had adopted this accommodating feature of the cavern for their purposes. Entry into the vault required the correct arrangement of a unique puzzle of locks on the wall which one must decipher to unlock the heavy stone door which opened to the bridge.

The remainder of the labyrinth wound its way north and eastward, toward the Olóbid and the various chambers of the Uden-Khan where the Ahga had transformed that large undercroft for his unusual training purposes. The four chambers of the chun-vok were surrounded in a circle by tunnelways which ultimately led into the main fighting arena. The veins of the Karkana ran noisily below, and this water-course was utilized in the aforementioned Pit of the Madidi. It also ran directly below the tomb of Olóbid, which was almost directly across that of his brother, Alad. And so the two tombs nearly faced each other in the lengthy passageway. East beyond Olóbid's tomb the main tunnel had collapsed due to erosion of the cavern underneath caused by the river. This corridor once led to the Uden-Khan and the keep of Olóbid from the north, but was now completely inaccessible. The Ahga used this to his advantage and created his own vault beneath his keep, on the other side of the arena, safe from Thuliak or anyone else venturing into the Ud from the Alad side. The Ahga, by contrast, had his own way to reach Thuliak's side and the Alad, but it remained secret.

There were only three ways to enter the Ud: from the supply shaft, which was a vertical access hole, safely housed outside and at ground level right inside the compound. This was used to lower materials, supplies, stone coffins, corpses, loot, or anything else that required an improved means of placement into or out of the dungeons by utilizing the sturdy crane and pulley elevator system constructed above ground. It was usually guarded and the rotunda which enshrouded the accessway was locked to prevent unwarranted infiltration by thieves, etc. The dome of this structure was high enough to shelter most of the tall frame of the elevating system required, and all was concealed within its appealing and sculpted walls. The excess of the crane protruded through the small round oculus of the dome. The other means of ingress were located within the separate palaces: one in the Alad, one in the Olóbid. One designated hallway of each presiding tower descended into the labyrinth, locked behind doors of iron. Entry was strictly and closely monitored. Admission for most was forbidden. The Alad was positioned on the left, or west side of the Harásh, the Olóbid, the right, or east. With the two palaces located across each other in this manner entry into the Ud came from their respective and opposite sides, though access to the Olóbid from beneath was forever destroyed as far as Thuliak knew. It was deep in the Ud that the Ahga intended to make his stand, and there he was overseeing the preparations for the execution of his plans.

* * *

Sebuda inconspicuously made his way about the palace, pretending not to notice the tenseness of the surroundings. Guards came and went at a noticeably quicker pace than was the norm, whispering to superiors and reporting to the lord of the house before departing with no further words. The worm could easily perceive the stealthy evacuation of the Alad which Thuliak was attempting to achieve with as little arousement as to the nature of the events as possible. His many guests or diplomats from afar and businessmen which frequented the palace were quietly ushered from the premises, with ill humor and health of the lord provided as the reason for their premature expulsion. All laborers and craftsman working upon the grounds were ordered to their places of residence for the day. Thuliak feared for his reputation and desired for what he hoped would be a minor and swift altercation to be witnessed only by a few. A coup or strife of this degree within his own home would not represent his rule well with those of whom he meant to secure commerce. No, this petty misunderstanding would be resolved with barely a wince to be heard, and word of it would not reach the ears of those outside, not until it was well under control and overwith. And at such time the crafty ruler would carefully arrange the appropriate propaganda to be delivered as explanation of the strange events to satisfy the curious, but also for his own aggrandizement among the influential he intended to intimidate and impress. The destruction of the greatest clan in the region would bring him respect realmwide. Thuliak's obsessive thought altered between his current rage and future grandeur. Guards with spears and swords took their places everywhere and seemed only to be awaiting the order to commence their raid.

The worm was fully aware of the events, of course. He made efforts to avoid sight and contact with Thuliak and his men as he carried on with his mundane duties of servanthood. He knew his time had come. Thuliak's men were occupied with their preparations and he was overlooked. He didn't need to see the banner of the Kunn hanging from that high ring outside the Olóbid to understand the peril of the situation. But there it was, as if in confirmation of his assumptions: a black fist in a field of red, visible through one of the tall, stained windows of the palace. He was alone, forgotten it seemed, in one of the grand halls of the lower level and he paused to regard it. Not only did the signal confirm to him his necessity of flight in any manner he deemed suitable, provided it was timely, but it also recalled to his mind the words of the Ahga to him the first days of his important assignment to the Alad. The Ahga impressed upon him repeatedly that Thuliak had a secret and locked vault under the palace and it should be the ultimate endeavor of the worm to acquire the secret to its access. Sebuda was to discover this secret as a final deed of worth to the Ahga, and should an end arrive such as this where the outcome is beyond assurance, he must infiltrate this cache of wealth and return with a prize of stature. And this would be done not so much for the desire of gold but for revenge and sabotage. If the Ahga and Thuliak ever had a fatal disagreement, if the continued existence of the Baccád was undoubtedly jeopardized, the Ahga wanted to have a means of piercing the heart of his enemy from behind, assuring his vindication and insult should he suffer defeat. The Ahga liked to be remembered.

Over time the worm discovered a clue to the entry of this vault, which he had in fact seen on a rare and chance occasion. The vault, in fact, did not rely upon a key but the correct arrangement of a multitude of sliding squares, or coffers, upon the walls in a chamber immediately preceding the bridge to the vault. The alignment of course was impossible to decipher on his own, for it would require too much time and descent into the Ud was closely guarded. Nothing could he discover in his months in the Alad regarding the combination or any further steps necessary for its disclosure. The Lord Thuliak was far too careful with its secret. He was the only one

362

with the knowledge, and he would die with it rather than pass it to another who would not be his successor. He made it quite clear many times to all: *the treasure is in a place where only myself and the dead can get it.* Even his chief advisors knew nothing of its secret and they were wise enough to believe the sincerity of the tyrant in his promise. Thuliak left little doubt as to the possessor of the wealth and should it threaten to fall into the hands of another, a victorious conqueror perhaps, he had an emergency means of final exclusion and sanctuary for his precious wealth, a failsafe should events go ill.

There was one thing the worm was able to discover, however, through his relentless eavesdrop of the lord and his closest advisors. A year ago some curious character, acting on his own, succeeded in gaining access to the Ud and was able to decipher the secret to the vault. Apparently he had invested a great amount of time researching and preparing the heist. Pressed by his own inclination to discover the solutions of mysteries, for this thief was skilled in the unraveling of puzzles, he opened the vault and beheld the riches within but was captured before he could escape. Thuliak caught him alone by fortunate chance when he descended below to gaze upon or add to his stash, which he did at times. Enraged but also intrigued, Thuliak pressed this wayward mastermind to divulge his method for unlocking his prized safe but he refused. Without giving reason to his men, he ordered him placed in solitary confinement within the dungeon until the thief finally felt the time had come to 'loosen his tongue'. Thuliak found this character interesting and actually respected him for his accomplishment. He was the one who actually broke the code. But for this, strict orders were given that the door to the cell would only be opened for the master alone. He was not to speak to anyone. The tyrant would not grant his execution but rather found his genius intriguing and kept him alive just to speak with on occasion, hoping in the process to increase the desperation of 'his favorite prisoner' with his sporadic ventures below. Time in solitary drives one to madness and he will come to crave his only means of social interaction. The guard would admit his lord into the dark chamber at the far end, which was not unusual for he had many conversations with his prisoners on occasion, mostly to torment them in their state of helplessness for his own entertainment no doubt, and leave them a moment to converse. And none could make a guess as to the reasoning for this character's especially severe incarceration. No one would have thought that one had come so close to stealing the heart of their lord and was considered so dangerous to warrant this strict, silent treatment. But over time the rumors of the secret trickled out and found their way to inquisitive ears.

This interesting prisoner was the key to the vault. Before Sebuda fled the palace he would be the first to make contact with this code breaker. He knew where he was held. The worm made ready for his flight. It will be one to be remembered. He quit his duties and inconspicuously but hastily headed downstairs where he knew the doorway to the Ud lay.

It was now well into the afternoon and Jesper had worked his way into the dark reaches of the palace. He was initially directed to some other portion of the estate which required some attention, but abandoned this order as soon as he was left alone. He had his own ideas. He was successful in his prevention of being ushered from the palace in all the rising tumult and avoided chance confrontation along the way which might divert him from gaining his desired destination. There were many halls and turns in the palace and concealment was easy. When he finally reached his vantage point, deep in the castle and well beyond where anyone of his insignificance should belong, he began performing some work on the lock and traverse mechanism on a certain door which led to a room across a balcony overlooking the guarded doorway of the Ud one level beneath him. A lone guard was there who took little notice of the old man. He looked harmless enough and was probably half drunk by his shabby appearance, thought the guard. Jesper chose this as his station of reconnaissance due to its close proximity of the great door and worked this into his plan, for the possibility might arise that he should have to enter it. An advantageous view of the foyer below was afforded him from his lonely position in the dark corner above it. He had been down in the tunnels of the Ud himself once to advise Thuliak about some dilemma requiring architectural skill some years ago, but he also had with him a map of the labyrinth, a worthwhile tip purchased from an agent he knew in the bazaar. He hoped it was accurate or he would return to find him. He folded it for the meantime and tucked it back into his pocket.

He made himself familiar with his new surroundings. There was the dark hallway to his right from which he came. To the left of that was a stairwell leading up to the second level, dim and empty. The whole area was dark and quiet. Everyone who was left in the palace seemed to be on the southern portion. He hoped he was now forgotten, his passing face but one of many on business in the palace, blending with the host of others. But while he made his tricky ingress he certainly took notice of the tense goings-on and obvious preparations for what must be some act of organized aggression or defense, despite the lord's attempts to prevent the arousal of suspicion. It was apparent that this vigilante's volatile message had gotten through, thanks to his exploited messenger Rash-Haba, and far more quickly than he anticipated. The wrath of Thuliak waited for nothing. He only pretended to work as he kept his ears and eyes open for anything. He made sure his own hidden weapons were ready and adjusted his belt for action. An engagement between the Baccád and Thuliak could get very ugly and he wasn't sure how it would end. He wanted to be here for it. And if his plan backfired there was one matter of import that would require his expertise to prevent total failure, and this was his backup: he would need to enter the Ud should things go ill, and he prepared and placed himself for the possibility of forced entry. The storm he contrived himself was already about to burst and he made ready. Just then he thought he heard something from around the corner and froze.

Sebuda stealthily arrived on the landing overlooking the doorway. He could see the guard there. Good, there was only one. No one else was in sight, nothing more could he hear in the open chamber. This apartment was located in the northern lower corner of the palace, on the west side, so there were few if any occupants here now. The garrison had been deployed to the eastern and southern sides of the palace, within and amid the courtyard outside where attack was to be expected. This far corner had been almost left completely alone. Thuliak obviously intended to rush the Olóbid from above and outside. Sebuda knew the location of the secret tunnel in the Ud which led to the Olóbid from underneath. The original tunnel was destroyed. Though it was unknown to Thuliak and his men, the Ahga made sure his worm was aware of his alternative should a desperate occasion as this arise.

The stone baluster of the floor circled the lower chamber almost completely. Three sides were railed and the door and guard were directly below. The guard obviously hadn't seen the newcomer, for he stood still, idling and dull. He had been left alone to assume this dull duty while his more capable comrades were deployed elsewhere of greater import. Sebuda circled the floor until he was directly above the guard. His eyes were downward, watching his target intently below, so he did not notice the quiet blacksmith in the corner behind him, silently watching him with equal interest. The shukk marks on his neck were just visible. That was a giveaway. It must be a servant who removed his ordinary collar and tunic, being released from duty or other, but Jesper thought it odd that Thuliak would have a member of the Mak-Baccád as a servant. Without breathing in his corner to the side, he watched this curious Turuk even more closely. Sebuda stood on the balcony and withdrew a length of cord from his pocket and readied it in his hands. This would be a silent kill. He cast a final glance upstairs before he jumped over the railing. He landed on the guard with a muffled thud and both crashed to the ground. In a moment the strangulation was complete. It made little noise. The worm removed the keys from the belt of the victim and set to work on the door. In a moment it was unlocked. He removed the large bolt which held it fast and it swung open with a slight creak. Sebuda hastily withdrew the body into the tunnel beyond and closed the door. Not a clue was left behind as to what just transpired in the foyer of the Ud; of the guard there was no sign.

But what the old blacksmith saw next confounded him even more. Before he was able to pursue this curious character, who he concluded could not possibly have allegiance to Thuliak and yet was infiltrating his precious vault with probable intent, yet another figure approached from the stairs above like a phantom descending from the darkness. Out of place he seemed, as though he pursued something of his own interest and was not affiliated with Thuliak or his affairs, was not one of his soldiers, but rather sought to use the confusion of the environment to his advantage as the Turuk had. He also seemed to have witnessed the assassination of the guard. Perhaps he had been casing the inner chambers of the palace in search of items of value to pilfer or merely waited for some chance opportunity to achieve his sinister ends. And he found it. Without noticing the forgotten and silent stranger in the far upper corner, crouched against the wall and irrelevant, this newcomer approached the door to the Ud and carefully followed in after the Turuk. This was all too much of a coincidence for Jesper. The volatile situation at hand that was beyond doubt brewing, a Mak-Baccád Turuk killing Thuliak's guard and entering the forbidden chambers of the Ud, only to be followed in by another with unknown intent–all spoke of theft and espionage. The resourceful seemed indeed to be aware of what was going on and made their simultaneous moves to reach the cache below. Jesper had competition.

The hoard was not to fall into the hands of the Kunn or their agents. This was his mission and it was threatened. Jesper withdrew himself from his secluded work area and looked carefully about. He could not afford for his plan to fail. He needed to see what these two were up to. It was very possible that they were all seeking the same thing and he decided he had to move. He stealthily crept over to the open doorway and he, too, plunged in.

CHAPTER 6
THE CLEANSING OF THE HARÁSH

Thuliak paced about impatiently on the main ground level of the Alad. His men were in place. The grounds had been sealed off. All unaffiliated personnel had been evacuated, hopefully without arousing suspicion. He hoped they had all been accounted for. The tyrant strode back and forth from one of his officers to another, inquiring as to the status of his men and also the activity of the Ahga and the Olóbid. All had been strangely quiet over there, a silence that did not produce a sense of ease in the guards garbed in red and brown, watchful of that isolated domain, or even suggest ignorance or unpreparedness of those they intended to surprise. Throughout the tense afternoon hours they kept sharp watch on the Tower of the Baccád, listening and waiting for any to come forth from its heavy wooden doors for routine business and interaction. But not a sound was forthcoming, not a token of life even could be detected from within the foreboding walls and darkened archways. No indication of presence whatsoever was given, no feel of foot or sound of call, and the guards outside stood ill at ease. The Olóbid stood like a cold tombstone, silent and lifeless. The only token which gave any proof of activity, the one none could remove his eyes from for it was never before observed in its current display of obstinacy, was the banner of the Kunn hanging from the ring high above, stirring gently in the late breeze. The westering sun shone its diminishing rays upon its scarlet face and it seemed to those who gazed upon it that it ran with blood, and all were stricken with a mood of peril and death. The ominous face of this prohibited placard of doom spread fear and apprehension as the silence grew deeper and night approached with its shadows, and was taken inwardly as a sign of some fate or evil foreboding. The thin clouds above seemed to speed past in the reddening sky behind an ominous tower of darkness. The faces of the soldiers grew pale with the heaviness and their spears lay feebly in their hands. And again, as if unwillingly, they would turn to regard the scarlet banner high up on the wall and could not help but to be in awe and dread of it.

Thuliak's plan was to wait for the inevitable return of the Ahga's men in the field, his suchuks of this riotous city, who were due to ride in at any moment. At this time the great doors of the Olóbid would predictably open to allow their return, and at this time Thuliak would make his great arrest. Every eve his troop of thugs would return from their routine duties of thievery, extortion, collection of payments, delivery of shipments to faithful clientele, murders and executions of those who were not, or who, because of aggression toward them or allegiance to another clan, or any other reason deemed necessary by the Mak-Baccád superior who led them, needed removal. Normally they departed and returned several times per day, but for whatever reason had not as yet rode up the ramp with their tidings which they would immediately relay to their Ahga-Rosh for further instruction. Perhaps the city kept them too occupied and delayed their return. Perhaps a skirmish with the Bará on the southern outskirts of the city weakened their force, or maybe they were slain by one of those fabled and mysterious Kadali Monks. Thuliak could only hope. But when these riders did return on their swift desert steeds and kelgan-drawn chariots, or *bahndas*, his men would allow them entry into the courtyard where he would arrest them before they could swell the thin ranks of the Ahga, and call for his surrender when they surrounded and seized his tower.

Ah, here they come now, he thought as he searched the streets below. A commotion went up by the dusty road leading to the Harásh and the mounted fighters climbed the inclined path to the gatehouse. The guards were instructed to allow them entry without harassment and the gates quickly made way.

Hachek rode with his dusty troop of suchuk fighters up the ramp to the Harásh. Their duties to the Ahga were complete for the day. Almost. This mog of the Mak-Baccád had just finished routing some Harikans in Saipa, the notoriously dangerous slum of southwest Mod, and was about to continue surveillance and patrol of the area and the enforcement of clan territory when a familiar brother unexpectedly arrived on the scene. He looked as though he rode in great haste for he was breathless. The two spoke alone and the urgent message was brief. Those that rode with Hachek did not know the words that were spoken at the time, only that a smile crossed the face of their leader as he listened on his trusty steed. The messenger departed but Hachek kept his secret until the time was right. So, he thought as he pondered this new and interesting information, the Ahga is plotting a coup up there, and we will be honored with special participation. Hachek's well-trained kelgan would play a key role in the affray. *We will be ready*, he thought. The Baccád certainly was swift with communication. All he could say about the whole thing was, it was about time. He tried to conceal his smile as he rode in through the gates. This should be interesting…

The troop passed under the open gates, some thirty of them in all with Hachek aforemost, hardened mogs, Turuks, and Hidari coated with a layer of dust. The pounding of the kelgan and the rolling bahndas shook the earth and rent the air, drawing dust in their wake. The guards who were posted in areas of the grounds within and the captains watching them from balconies above noticed that the eyes of the newcomers were not feeble and dim from a long day's work, as expected, but perceptive and keen with attentiveness, scanning the area with their eyes from beneath their light helms. Their heads were held low but the eyes of the riders moved from left to right and above, suspicious, ready for a mutiny and ambush, one that they would initiate this very moment, analyzing all within sight: the officers upon the balcony above the colonnaded façade of the huge entryway, more than normal and watchful, accompanied by Thuliak himself with an evil smile who monitored all carefully–his moment of revenge had come; the numerous guards pretending to pace in the paths of the garden in the center of the vast courtyard, out of routine; the doubled guard force manning the huge gatehouse behind them and the heads turning with the incoming host, silent, apprehensive; the notable absence of workers and dignitaries anywhere, the unusual stillness of the court and the ominous clang of the gates behind them–all spoke of danger and entrapment. Hachek and his force passed inside without a word and seemed to head for the great stone staircase of the Olóbid.

All was proceeding as Thuliak hoped. The squad passed through the courtyard and headed for the doors which would open momentarily. His many men were armed and ready. He was about to give the signal for the arrest. Suddenly the sound of the crack of wood jolted the air.

Thuliak's smile vanished and his eyes reddened. *No...*

Right for the Alad drove the host of Hachek with a yell. They abruptly turned their steeds and bahndas about at the signal. The doors of the Olóbid opened behind them with a loud crack and out poured another mounted force led by none other than three mighty warriors of the Baccád: Babla, Bazi, and mighty Rugg-Adda, their bandanas of red upon their foreheads, charging the startled guards of the palace. They did not expect this. Behind them rushed a force of some twenty well trained Mak-Baccád. Thuliak's men were caught in a counterattack they weren't ready for, an attack within the royal compound itself. Such a thing hadn't happened since Sazuzu's Rebellion in 522. Out from their hiding places behind the columns of the palace charged the garrison of Mod. The situation had changed drastically. The force which had been deployed for the seizure of the Olóbid found themselves instead chasing their foes. The attackers became the attacked. Like a cavalry of desert thugs pouring from the dunes the Ahga's men charged them, pounding the ground with thunder and shouting as they rode. A tumult instantly went up; the brooding silence was expelled. The Kunn cut right through the soldiers, caught slightly unaware. Gullicks and spears filled the air, arrows and darts shot forth from the mounted host and the ground was quickly littered with bodies. Statuettes of stone, trees and exotic plants, small monuments of marble and granite, all were toppled or trampled in the sudden melee. The stone tiles that made up the winding paths through the courtyard were stained with blood. The air was loud with the roar of the Kunn, and the soldiers quailed at the sudden and bold onslaught.

Thuliak ground his teeth in a rage. He pounded the balustrade of the balcony. This rabble he thought would be an easy capture drove right through his struggling force and, inconceivably, actually headed straight for the foyer of his precious domain. *They are going to attack the palace?* It was not possible, not even thinkable. The glaze of disbelief and confusion veiled over his wide eyes and pallid face. The cavalry right below him, tearing and ripping his landscape and beauty and hewing his men like gini trees, split into two groups: one went for the gatehouse to seize it, the other sped for the Alad, driving through his guards before the hidden reinforcements were in position. The Baccád had obviously planned this. They had not time to mount a counterattack, so sudden was the ambush. He actually felt a twinge of fear as the villains set their filthy feet near his domain, and he found himself taking a step back in retreat. He could see the marks upon several of them–Baccád elites, fierce, deadly, powerful. His pathetic guard force fell before them like sticks. He ground his teeth in frustration. They drew closer.

"Seal the gates!" he shouted and his men leaped into action, aroused from their shock. Thuliak couldn't believe such an order actually became necessary. This wasn't part of the plan. "Lock the doors on the first level, NOW!" he shouted with furious impatience. He gripped the rail. His men below acknowledged the order and immediately moved for the doorways. But there were many, one for each facing of the octagonal palace, ringed with columns succeeding wide and encompassing steps of marble. His men weren't quick enough. Those foul slugs of the Ahga were actually going to set foot in his dwelling. He looked up to the gatehouse to see the progress of his men upon it and on the street beyond. It wasn't getting better. He began to tear his hair.

The mounted force of the Kunn, about fifty strong altogether, drove upon the foot soldiers of Thuliak like a wave. When they reached the halfway point between the two towers they broke apart into two groups. Babla and Hachek with their force sped madly for the Alad, trying to break inside before the soldiers mustered themselves. Theirs was a special mission. Arrows and spears flew at them as they rushed. The hides of the kelgan were stricken with splinters, blades bounced off shoulder plates or

370

stuck in their dusty leather armor, but they ran on, their riders leaning low through the strengthening hail. Thuliak's men finally organized themselves and began to fight back. His shrill voice could be heard over the din, growing with impatience and frustration.

Rugg-Adda and Bazi turned south with their force and galloped for the gatehouse. This capture was imperative to prevent the reinforcement of Thuliak's troops within the Harásh from those that were still outside maintaining perimeter security on the street. Rugg and Bazi stormed upon the house and their small force dismounted. They ran into this vital keypoint like beasts, hacking and slaying the guards in front of them. This was the only entry into the compound, the other was a smaller and seldom-used postern on the northern opposite side. The guards in the gatehouse, perceiving the intent of the Kunn raiders, immediately attempted to open the gates again to allow the force from the streets to assist with the struggle. But it was too late. Bazi and Rugg beheaded the last of the resistors and seized the controls to the gates even as the reinforcements threw themselves upon the descending portcullis. The rest of the clansters secured the structure, locking themselves inside. Now they were attacked from both sides, arrows and bolts from both front and back gates flew into the large, open hall of stone and the mutinous occupiers took cover behind what they could. They divided themselves into two small groups—one defending the south gate, the other the north. Including Bazi and Rugg there were a total of fifteen holding the ground inside. They had to hold the gatehouse. They drew their bows and took careful aim, conserving their shots. The angry soldiers outside yelled and beat against the gate with hammers. Some ran off to find some oil or burning powder to drive out the entrenched occupiers. Bazi wasn't about to wait for that.

"I'm going topside!" he yelled to Rugg across the hall. They hid behind the rows of columns supporting the roof. Arrows flew past their heads. One of the Kunn mogs fell to an arrow and two of the kelgan had already dropped. Their corpses were collecting projectiles as they lay. They wouldn't last forever. Soldiers were massing on either end. When one dropped from a well aimed bolt, another took his place. Rugg acknowledged the idea of an alternative and also sped up the staircase, for there was one on his side as well and both led to the castellated roof. Bazi braved the hail and ran up the stairs on his side to seek a better attack point. He wasn't about to let these slugs set the place ablaze. They needed to hold the gates at all cost, a direct order from the Ahga. Fight to the last member, die with honor, hold the gate. *Uden og Kabba.*

The roof of the two-story gatehouse was encircled with crenellations and overlooked the rampway and streets below to the south and the compound within to the north. Guards normally kept watch here to monitor the traffic. Bazi and Rugg reached the top at the same time. They ran to the

371

southern edge and looked at the writhing mass under them. A few darts were shot upwards and whistled past their heads. They looked about and saw a pile of stone and refuse masonry in a corner, the remnants of some recent repair work conducted on the building. Without a moment's hesitation they heaved the chunks at the soldiers. They looked like green giants hurling massive stones at an enemy trying to capture their mountain. Some found a mark and crushed the heads of those it struck. Rocks bounced off shields and broke spears and shoulders. The soldiers drew back to evade the barrage but returned fire.

Their supply of stones quickly depleted and the two ran to the northern side to see things there. Chaos overtook the whole of the grounds within. The madness of melee transformed the elaborate courtyard into the wreck of a passing windstorm. The once fair paths and ways were overturned and despoiled. Bodies were strewn everywhere. Braziers of fire had tipped in the melee and spilled their flammable contents all over the paths and fires were left to spread and burn, lighting the darkening sky and illuminating the shocking spectacle. Soldiers and captains were shouting in desperation. Figures were running in all directions. They looked upon the Olóbid and saw a group attempting to ram down the thick doors with hammers. Babla and Hachek must have made it inside the Alad for there was no sign of them in the fiery courtyard, unless they were killed. From the streets below the Harásh it must have looked like Thuliak was having a feast of unusual magnificence, or else his precious dwelling was burning down. A red glow lit up the dusk above the palace.

Bazi could see some soldiers approaching, pulling some heavy-looking barrels rolled on wagons, undoubtedly some kind of pyrotechnic compound. Thuliak's soldiers below seemed to part and make way for it, but there were not many of them. Most of the remaining force seemed to retreat back into the Alad. They drew closer with their explosive weapon. They would all be burned or blown out. Bazi and Rugg were left with an obvious option. They could not fail their Ahga. They threw their arms into the air with a yell and dove down upon their enemies, leaping from the battlements, kodara swords in hand. *Baccád ak Kunn!* they cried, *Baccád! Baccád! Uden og Kabba!* (order of the fist, death with honor). *Al-Medu!* These two giant, rugged killers of the Ahga felled the guards before the gate with ease and terror. Their fellow mutineers behind them in the hall ceased their fire in that direction and faced the south, praising their captains and chorusing their cry. All one could see from the windows of the Alad was two enraged hulks felling the guards by the gate, by sword, hand, foot, daggers, heaving bodies of the fallen–any way available to them. These pathetic unbelievers were no match for the skill and toughness of the Ahga's chosen, favored by the Mari with their indomitable power and strength of immortals. Blows and darts seemed to bounce off their iron skin

372

like they were made of steel and felt no pain. This gift they had earned with discipline others did not have, and the Baccád brothers felt the emergence of the Mari come upon them. This was what they trained so ruthlessly for. These muscled monsters destroyed all in their path and the few guards left in front of them fled in terror of their might. Bazi and Rugg's monstrous voices drowned all with their rage and fury. Wild with hysteria and a heightened energy that refused to wane, they grabbed the abandoned cart of combustible substance, spun it around, and drove it straight for the Alad, yelling as they pushed it quickly forward. Thuliak would have this fiery poison shoved right down his throat.

Babla and Hachek sped for the Alad. They had to take advantage of their surprise, using the feebleness and shock of Thuliak's men to gain entry into the palace before they completely sealed themselves inside. Their mission was twofold and split between them: to capture and hold the main council and throne room, and Babla, being the newest of the Baccád, had been honored with this vital task to further prove himself; and to draw Thuliak's forces into the Ud where the Ahga had a special greeting awaiting them, and Hachek with his kelgan was charged with this feint. The Harásh would fall from within, and the Kunn would claim control. They charged upon the pale soldiers and hewed those that stood in their way, leaving the others to chase them. The riders leaped upon the porticoed façade of the ground level of the Alad and succeeded in reaching the archways before they were closed. These were held open only long enough for the remainder of the Kunn force, some thirty mounted fighters, to burst through. They did not divert themselves from their objective–all else was ignored and bypassed as they raced for their respective locations within the palace. Speed and surprise were key.

They were wild with freedom and disbelief as they burst fully upon the polished floors of their hated mentor and held back not for concern or etiquette. They rode without restrictions or regard for the décor and embellishments of the grand domain. The kelgan beasts of the desert bared their fangs and dripped at the mouth as they raced down beautiful halls of shining marble, leaping upon stairwells only the dignified could tread, knocking over pieces of art and sculpture and other vanities of the ruler's eccentric taste, tearing carpets of antiquity and value in their wild haste beneath paintings and wall-reliefs of craft only the wealthy corrupt were privileged to see. Pots and vessels were spilled upon the floor along the violent path and their contents ruined in the thundering stampede and chase. Pendants and streamers bearing the colors of red and brown were thrown to the floor wantonly in the passage. Babla led the way, following the directions given him by the Ahga and Gathmug. He could still hear the pursuit, racing down the halls and shouting after them to halt their unbelievable but undeniable and obvious objective: they were going to seize the palace as well. This was not a mere token of protest to some petty arrest or dispute but a full-fledged coup, and the men of the Alad were too slow to appreciate it. Thuliak must be collapsed onto the floor with disbelief, thought Babla. He may be new to the Baccád but he was certainly a veteran with the Ahga in Mod, and was very familiar with Thuliak and his foolishness. Overthrowing this fool would be an honor and a privilege.

Thuliak's personal guards and Keepers of Quarters posted along the halls of the upper levels of the palace had been alerted to the sounds of unrest outside. They had adhered to their orders to remain on guard inside, keeping watch over the throne room and main counsel hall where Thuliak and his officers conducted their governing. Dressed in the royal garb of Mod, they obediently manned their posts just outside this iconic and important function room with strict orders to stay. Their lord and his men had merely gone outside to make some arrest or other or settle some dispute with the Ahga next door. It should not take long. But some disquieting sounds could be heard from beneath, or even within the palace, sounds of destruction, yelling, and what they thought must be galloping, though their better judgment dispelled this unrealistic possibility. The sounds drew nearer and brought forth with them a malice that could not be ignored. A feeling of curiosity, then dread, began to wax. What is this? Have the horses been let loose upon the palace floors? The guards finally began to stir and look about. The sounds were coming closer and all heads turned to the far turn in the hallway.

Babla's detachment galloped up the second set of stairs. This was a symmetrical and curving staircase, with one on either side of the wide open chamber leading to the floor above in an arched trajectory. Dual rounding staircases under them also descended into the lower levels. Here Hachek branched off with his group and bolted downstairs to reach the inner Ud entrance. Half of Babla's force went up one set of stairs, half the other to attack from both sides. They quickly reached the top and rounded the corners with a yell. This vaulted and adorned corridor led to the throne room and main counsel hall. Along this esteemed hall were placed many ornaments and memorials of sorts pertaining to rulers of the past, including the original, Alad himself, to which there was dedicated much wall space to his honor and memory though in truth he was an unjust and selfish lord, consumed with greed and power. This wide and decorated length of chamber was called The Hall of Alad. The Guards of Mod, Keepers of Quarters detachment, stood watch here and were charged with the defense of the throne room in which entered many persons of stature to further

374

corrupt the city for their own ends and undermine others under the guise of governing.

When a troop of mounted Kunn warriors flew around the corner brandishing swords and spears, their eyes wild with battle and teeth glaring, this handful of guards shrank back in alarm. Never before was such a host seen descending upon a hall of power, aye, within the palace itself. This could not be happening. Disbelief held them unmoving for one moment. They shook their paralysis and put forth a good defense, however, for these were some of Thuliak's best and dedicated. The affray was sharp and quick, and Babla actually lost two of his fighters and two steeds to these guards, but ultimately secured a rapid victory. The once grand hall was littered with blood and bodies. Weapons and debris were strewn about. They didn't have much time. The soldiers were not far behind. Even now they could hear them just beyond the stairs on the lower level, shouting as they came.

"Take your positions!" shouted Babla to his men. "Move!" and they drew their crossbows to defend the two opposite staircases. Holding these two narrow avenues against the onslaught of soldiers was their priority. The throne room must be held until total control was achieved. They removed the packs from their steeds which contained a large number of bolts for their weapons, packed for this purpose of prolonged defense, and threw them down the hall to each of the two groups of defenders. Altogether Babla had still eighteen fellow brothers fighting under him and they loaded their weapons. The soldiers should come around that corner on the landing below any second. They were making a great noise as they approached. All weapons were aimed for the entryway.

Hachek rushed down the stairs on his kelgan to the first level. He proceeded more slowly for he wished for the soldiers to follow him downward. He made sure he made a fair amount of noise as he went, knocking things over, slaying any stray guard or servant, making a clatter to attract pursuit. His trailers to the rear signaled to him that they indeed were being pursued by a force. Good. The troop made their way to the Ud entrance, below the ground level. They were surprised to find it already open and the guard from whom the keys would be wrested was nowhere in sight. Perhaps this great deed was favored by the Divine One. Hachek perceived this as a good sign until he discovered the body of the guard tucked inside the passageway within. It seemed someone else was down here, too.

Thuliak proclaimed the palace and grounds under attempt of coup and takeover. His shrill voice could be heard yelling in fury and fear from anywhere in the tumultuous compound. Night had all but fallen and his precious dwelling was under attack by this mutinous organization within his own burning walls. His surprise attack failed. He cursed and raved ceaselessly and his officers fled his wrath. He ran back and forth in the confusion, shouting orders and cursing his men. They still hadn't recaptured the gatehouse and his fools were still banging on the door of the Olóbid across the yard. His enemies seemed to have all gone underground for none of them could be seen in the open now. The courtyard was a shambles but empty. His soldiers, what he had left on hand, he ordered back into the palace to defend it for these heathen vultures had actually just set foot inside it. Due to the seizure of the gatehouse he was not able to send dispatches to the city to recall his dormant militia for the purpose of helping to quell this flame of rebellion which seemed to have spread beyond containment. A design of the Ahga's no doubt. Thuliak's tongue was tied. Things had gotten thoroughly out of control. He couldn't believe his very rule was in real jeopardy of being wrested from him by these cultists. He rallied a few of his men and darted inside to oversee the recapture and restoration of his palace.

He followed the wreckage and the dead to the inner open hall which led either up to the Hall of Alad and his throne room, or else down to the lower levels and the Ud. He cursed at the destruction in his domain which added further insult to his injury. Have those foul slugs no regard for art and antiquity? One way or another he was going to be the victor here. The Ahga's men could not last much longer. His failure here was only a matter of time and Thuliak need only to wear down the mutineers. A strong contingent of his men was up ahead, attempting to retake the throne room. They were taking cover from the hail of arrows and darts which filled the air of the wide chamber. The beautiful staircases were covered with debris, blood, and bodies, mostly his but he did notice a few dead mogs and Hidari of the Kunn among the carrion. It was as he thought. They were holding their position upstairs well but would not last forever. Soon all their arrows would be spent and they would be forced into melee combat against a foe of far greater numbers. His men returned fire and advanced into the room, making ground, though the narrow opening the Kunn thugs held was difficult to advance upon. Torches had been thrown upstairs along with vials of oil to intensify the small fires that burned there and drive back the occupiers. Another accursed Kunn mog just fell to a dart and rolled down the stairs. He looked as though he had been pierced by many. A smile crossed Thuliak's face as he watched from the rear. It would all be over soon.

Babla and his force had held their position well. With only eighteen fighters, he held the far numerically superior soldiers at bay and littered the floors and stairs on both sides with their bodies. He had lost a few to darts, but for every one he lost they paid with far more. His men were strong indeed and would have made the Ahga proud. Their training had definitely paid off. The lack of training and discipline in their enemies was very evident. He ran back and forth among his men, shouting inspiration and assisting where the advance was hottest. They would hold this position or die in the attempt. This was a coup, and one strike only would they have. This could not fail, there would be no second try.

This battle had waged now for some time and Babla was sustaining losses. They were almost completely out of bolts for their small crossbows. The soldiers had thrown many torches and oil up into his lofty defense and fires had sprung up, making it more difficult to shoot upon the enemy. Smoke began to fill the air. He felt he would have to retreat to the throne room to make his final stand with his remaining force. He was about to give the order to retreat. One of his mog fighters had just caught fire in his valiant attempt to use his weapon. Seeing this, the Mod soldiers threw another vial and torch. A flame leaped up and the area was completely afire. This poor mog was now covered in burning oil and screaming. His whole body was alight with flames. Too proud to retreat, he made ready to leap down the stairs at his enemy in a final attempt at vengeance. He reached the ledge and cast himself off.

Just then a commotion went up downstairs. The soldiers seemed to flee in a forward direction. Something was coming up behind, something that wielded a great destructive power. A yelling preceded this mysterious approaching anomaly. From around the corner, knocking over men in their wake, came Rugg and Bazi, eyes alive with fire and madness, pushing their wagon of death before them into the crowd of soldiers. They had pushed their explosive load right into the heart of the palace to blow it up. The timing couldn't have been better. All they had time to see was a flaming hulk of a body falling from the balcony above. They had sought for a torch but there was no need. The Divine provided. Rugg and Bazi shoved the volatile wagon in its path and dove headlong down the stairs. The descending fireball seemed to instinctively seek out its method of destructive catalysis and landed directly on the barrels which contained the volatile substance. The resulting explosion blew the wall apart behind it, cracked and ripped the balcony above which fell bodily to the floor, sent chunks of stone and masonry everywhere, and rocked the whole palace. The large, ornamental chandelier stationed on the vaulted ceiling fell in a multitude of showering fragments. Soldiers reeled and fell from the devastation. Splinters and death shot into all corners. Thuliak, who had been observing from the side, was blown down the stairs and into the lower levels. Seizing their opportunity, Babla and his men, who had taken cover behind the wall upstairs, leaped out from their place of refuge and stormed below. Rugg-Adda and Bazi stood up and joined them. Whatever Mod soldiers were left alive were surrounded by their Kunn captors. They threw their weapons on the floor in defeat. *Baccád ak Kunn!*

* * *

Sebuda sped stealthily down the passageway. The tunnel to the Ud led straight and in a northward direction. Sparse lanterns along the walls illuminated his path. The tunnel was dim but he soon could see some more light ahead, as though a larger room loomed nearer. He stepped quickly but cautiously forward. He reached the bored elevator shaft and looked up. He could barely see the sturdy platform in its station of readiness not far above, maybe two stories up. No one seemed to be in the large open receiving room, the area where supplies were brought into the housed structure at ground level and lowered below by means of this elaborate crane system. He passed through this opening and proceeded into the tunnel beyond which continued further and deeper into the earth. He needed to reach the dungeons deep within and initiate his plot. For all that he had to do he didn't have much time. He passed several smaller chambers to either side containing various antiquities and heirlooms of bygone generations, each one devoted to a particular ruling family or dynasty. He paid these no heed but sped onward, looking over his shoulder for any pursuit. The prison-hold was not much farther ahead.

Down under the earth the chaos above seemed far away and irrelevant. The rock walls insulated this underworld from all that transpired above. The world of violence and hysteria became distant and almost forgotten in this subterranean dwelling. All was quiet and strangely still and the worm advanced slowly and carefully. The tunnel continued without turn. Through the gloom he could soon discern another hallway farther ahead that branched off to the left. Echoes of what could only be a slowly pacing sentinel reverberated in the quiet tunnel. The sounds of chains and the clink of metal came to his ears. Sebuda approached more slowly and could now see shadows in motion up ahead. Along the walls they moved as the sentinel paced down the torch-lit tunnel, out of sight to his left. Without a sound the light and slender Turuk hugged the wall and drew alongside the corner of the junction and halted. The footsteps of the sentinel drew closer. His slow pace reached almost to the corner and stopped, just before the turn. His heavy, dull breath could be heard. Probably a mog. He paused a moment just before the junction and Sebuda froze. Without even breathing he waited as the sentinel idled in the quiet hallway. He fumbled with his gear as if simply wasting time. Sebuda was weaponless except for a dagger hidden in his clothing and his garrot. He wanted to avoid confrontation if possible. There may be more than one guard down here, and the worm probably wouldn't do well against those odds. His specialty was stealth, not strength. He was about to put it to use.

Finally the guard resumed his route. He turned around, passed through an open door, and went back into the dungeon area. Sebuda peered around the corner and watched him disappear further down the hall. The guard turned left. That was good. The cell the worm had to reach was on the right. There were two symmetrical dungeon-rows, or blocks, one which split to the left, the other right. He knew there had to be another guard down there somewhere, probably on the right side. He also knew that he didn't have an abundance of time. Hostilities above may have even commenced by now, he thought. He had to succeed in this mission. If the Kunn was successful in their coup, Thuliak would be down here in a twinkling to secure his wealth and make an escape. The Ud was the first place he would go in such a circumstance. The Ahga was counting on his master saboteur and spy to prevent that from happening. Thuliak was to be captured and his vast wealth preserved for the Kunn. The Ahga was looking forward to obtaining this sizable hoard and placed it in the hands of one of his top agents. If the Ahga failed and Thuliak was victorious, Sebuda stood a fair chance of being arrested and executed as a spy. His presence in the Ud would be suspicious indeed. Without wasting another moment he strode down the hall and into the dungeon.

He passed through the open door and reached the cell blocks. This was not a large dungeon-keep, altogether there were only about a dozen cells to either side of each of the two tunnels, and a larger, common hold for numerous, short-term prisoners. He could hear some of them, moaning or talking to the darkness. One of them banged on a wall or door somewhere. A few torches in the walls cast their sad light into this oppressive world of darkness and depression. The poor souls held here unjustly, past and present, added to the gloomy and despondent atmosphere common in the dungeons of tyrants, but this was not his concern. The hold of solitary confinement was at the far end of the row. That's where his mastermind prisoner was being held. The individual behind that seldom-opened door of cold iron was his deliverer. All he needed was the key from the guard. Not usually a problem with the right amount of time. This time-constrained circumstance, however, would require a far more direct approach. He couldn't see the jailor from his position at the entryway. He must be at the far end, in the guard shack half-asleep, he thought. He wondered at the lack of more security down here but concluded that all available personnel were deployed to the palace. There were not a few characters of repute and danger in these holds, but then there were few people ever down here anyway. Sebuda stealthily paced past the closed and locked cells to either side until he reached the extremity. There was a small room to his right from which came forth some stronger light. The door was open and someone was inside. Directly across from this was another locked door, the target holding cell. The worm approached the door to the guard shack and looked inside.

There he was, asleep on a chair, his back to the door. Perfect. His associate must be manning the mundane post and performing his rounds while the other utilized the lack of supervision and fewer hands for a more advantageous purpose. *Characteristic of the regime bereft of any belief.* It was benefitting him indeed, the fellow was snoring. Sebuda half smiled in his fortune. Removing the ring of keys from the clasp on his belt was work for an amateur. The worm stepped back into the hall. The other guard must still be on the other side. He faced the door and tried several keys before the lock turned. He looked behind him and checked the sleeping guard. All clear. He pulled the heavy door open just far enough for him to enter. It creaked and groaned slightly. Still no response from the opposition. He passed through this door, strode across a short antechamber, and came to the next. A moment later he had the door open. He took a torch off the wall and entered the cell.

A lean, haggard, half-starved and filthy creature of unknown race lay within on a pile of straw. He recoiled from the sudden intrusion and shielded his eyes from the powerful light, then slowly stood. He began to curse and whine, thinking this was another routine visit from his tormentor, but the Turuk clasped his own hand to his face and hushed him. He shone the light on his features to reveal his identity. The prisoner calmed and stood still.

"You are the one called Bellick?" Sebuda asked. The prisoner nodded. Sebuda continued. "There is a certain vault down the hall from here, you know the one. We're breaking into it. I think you know the way. Let's go." He didn't have time for introductions or explanations. He grabbed Bellick by his slender arm and pulled him out.

Sebuda cautiously peered around the second door and into the hall. He froze in his steps when he saw the other guard in the distance just about to turn the corner into the cell block. A primitive but effective plan immediately came to mind. With the instant he had he darted across the hall and into the guard shack, pushing the prisoner ahead of him. The sentinel must have thought he heard something because he quickened his pace toward the far end. He looked side to side at the cells as he came, all quiet, secure. He reached the last one on the left and saw the door open. He paused a moment in doubt. He looked into the guard shack and saw his companion still asleep. He stood before the cell, confused. He drew his sword and entered the hold.

"Golog, hey?" he called as he went inside. His voice echoed in the chamber beyond the door. "Have you been–" but he didn't finish his thought. Sebuda rushed out from his place of concealment within the shadows of the guard shack, crossed the hall, and heaved the door of the holding cell shut, locking the curious sentinel inside. The yelling and pounding that succeeded his abrupt and unexpected imprisonment would have undoubtedly woken his sleeping companion, but a quick strike over his exposed head with a nearby loose chain prevented this possibility. Sebuda grabbed Bellick and fled down the hall. The tumult caused by the furious sentinel aroused all in the cell block and the escapees took flight amid a great noise and shouting. The yelling and banging that followed them out seemed to waken everything. But it was of no concern now. The worm had what he needed. Stealth was no longer a necessity. He bolted down the hall and out of the dungeon, joining the main tunnel into the Ud, dragging his prize behind him. In his rush he didn't know he was being followed. He wasn't the only one seeking injury against Thuliak.

Sebuda and Bellick ran down the tunnel. It delved deeper into the earth at a slight gradient. They looked behind them constantly for pursuit but they saw or heard no one yet. All was silent in the dim tunnels but a feeling of dread grew. Sebuda cared no longer for a slow and careful progression but hastened at full speed. They had given themselves away and it would only be a small matter of time before they were sought out and captured, or killed in the chaos which was undoubtedly beginning above ground. Thuliak's soldiers would be deployed to the Ud to secure it and purge it of any intruders. They must have discovered the murder of the guard in the lower palace by now and Sebuda expected the tunnels to be swarming with soldiers any minute. Fortunately the difficult part was over; the next should be quick and easy. As for the prisoner, Bellick, he felt he had nothing to lose so he more or less cooperated with his captor for the time. This flight was far preferable to his captivity and he also felt not a little vengeful against his tormentor. By the way things were going even he could tell that something of import was under way, some great transpiration of events that would warrant this daring and unexpected heist and rescue. Everything seemed to be out on its limb. Either this would end with great benefit and victory or failure and execution. Both sides in this strange conflict had everything to lose. There was no point in holding anything back now. He would still retain one vital piece of information from his strange captor should things go ill, or his deliverer turn against him in the end. This bit of knowledge may save his life. He kept this secret and would play this as his last and desperate act of survival if necessary.

After a while they turned a corner to the left and came to a three-way junction. The main way turned to the right, east, and continued toward the inner tombs and catacombs. The other two branched off to the left. One of them plunged lower into the earth, to Potep-Ud, the deep and feared chasm of the dead with its fabled endless whisperings of the deceased who were removed from memory. The other went straight to Thuliak's vault, the *Vog-Khana*, Chamber of Treasures. Sebuda pushed his prisoner in front and Bellick led the way.

Hachek and his host sped down the tunnels of the Ud. He made sure that he didn't lose his pursuit. The Ahga had a little surprise for them within the deep. He didn't know exactly what but that was not for him to ponder. *Make sure they find their way to Alad's tomb,* were his instructions from the Ahga himself. Being on swift steeds, he had to slow his advance often. The footfalls of the kelgan thundered in the narrow passageways. He soon reached the turn to the dungeons on the left. He slowed for he thought he saw something of interest within the hall. A guard emerged slowly from the gloom in the distance, staggering as though he were drunk, holding a rag on his head which was evidently bleeding from a substantial wound. His vision must have been impaired as well for he held one arm out in front as though he had difficulty seeing the way before him. Perceiving the host halted in front of him he began to cry out, but his words were slurred and almost incomprehensible. Hachek and his men allowed themselves a short pause to ingest his words though they regarded him incredulously.

"They've gone," he said slowly and with difficulty, his words broken with hisses of pain, "he escaped... you know the one," he worked to form his thoughts and words. Hachek struggled to decipher his tedious speech. "Ah, they took him out. They, I think, got away... Not here... Tell Thuliak, ah, not here... His favorite...escaped... Can still catch them..." He said no more but stumbled and remained unmoving where he lay.

The mog chief stared at him a moment then resumed his flight. The soldiers were getting closer. Their booted feet and shouts could be heard echoing in the tunnel. He could only assume that Thuliak's dungeon guard knew not to whom he spoke when he sought to pass his important message to his fellows. Hachek could discern nothing of relevance from his broken speech. He knew little of those Thuliak had locked in his cells, and though the ways of the Ud were fairly familiar to him, for he had ventured here on special errands before for the Ahga, Thuliak's affairs and incarcerated dissidents were not. But one thing of import perhaps could be learned from his babble, Hachek thought as he rode onward. Someone escaped and was probably here in the tunnels still. The door to the Ud in the palace which was strangely open came to his mind. That bumbling fellow was probably right. There is something else going on down here.

* * *

Thuliak drew himself up. The explosion in the great hall threw him downstairs to the first level. It took him a moment for his sight to return but his hearing was still drowned in a persistent ringing. He pieced the events of the past hour in his mind as quickly as he could. The failed seizure and arrest, the counterattack, the flight back into the palace, the captured throne room, the blast–all these returned to his memory. He looked around. He was behind the stairwell below the great hall. He could hear activity up there and he looked more closely. It had been overrun with those filthy goons of the Kunn. They were everywhere, going up the stairs to the throne room, *his* throne room, back down the stairs again, out into the hall and its further chambers. There was no sign of his soldiers anywhere. He stood dumbstruck. He couldn't believe his failure. It was not possible that the Ahga's men had ousted him and taken control of his palace. But that was just what happened, and the realization that those slugs had succeeded in subduing the last of his garrison and seized the palace poured over him like burning oil and almost made him swoon with fury. He would have run up the stairs and slaughtered all those miserable Kunn maggots in ordinary circumstances where he had a host of guards at his call, but he was becoming aware of another realization, one that made him cower, one that withdrew his hasty and grasping hands, one that extinguished his immeasurable temper and pride: the invaders were searching the premises, scouring it top to bottom in earnestness, for *him*. They must have overlooked him in the dark corner under the stairs or mistook him for the dead. He could see and hear them only a short stride away up the stairs now, their blood-stained weapons and clothing, their victorious and merciless eyes, their shouts in haste.

Different they seemed. He had never known them to be so fell and deadly and yet so obedient and organized, so dedicated to the cause and willing to give their lives in its attempt, and he felt himself withdraw. For the first time he truly acknowledged the enemy he had foolishly invited into his domain and strength, and felt his peril. They represented a power that did not come from numbers, or rule of territory, or political organization such as he knew it to be. It had come from a loyalty, a dedication, a belief, a Brotherhood, one that prided itself in skill and discipline, and a questionable faith he could never understand or subject himself to. The pettiness of his rule was eclipsed by a greatness he had ignored and defied, and this greatness he at last acknowledged in his defeat. But even as he retreated out of sight he felt his pride swell along with his vindictiveness. It was time to finally secure what he had and flee, time to play his last trick. The Ahga would not claim total victory. He fled down the halls out of sight and found the entrance to the Ud. But when he discovered the absence of the guard and the open door, a fury not even a beast of the mountains could possibly duplicate possessed him. They were after his gold as well. With a hiss and a face that would terrify a kelgan he discarded his cloak, drew his sword, and bolted inside.

CHAPTER 7
REDRESS OF THE UD

Sebuda and Bellick reached the large, open chamber before the closed door of Thuliak's vault. This was the *Gahg-Ajtak,* the Hall of Secrets, the master lock for opening the Chamber. They looked around them. The hall was straight and lengthy, adorned at intervals with statues of ruling figures of the past with their names inscribed in the base. The huge stone door at the far end was closed shut. No sign of a handle or grip of any kind was upon its smooth surface. All around them were inscriptions and images in relief upon the wall, placed there by others who once assumed the throne of this city, or sought to impart upon the observer something pertaining to a certain period of time such as an event or accomplishment of the tyrant it intended to glorify. This seemed to be a hall strictly for and about the rulers, for it was solely theirs, and everything in it spoke of their legacy. They felt in the midst of the city's tainted and tumultuous history. But there was one thing in it that was not to be revealed, and that was the secret to the locked chamber beyond which contained the vast wealth of the city, passed down from ruler to ruler, accumulating with each successive generation.

Upon the wall to their left was an arrangement of square coffers, or tiles, which were designed to slide on their tracks and into a particular pattern or order within a certain limited space. Each of the coffers had some unique inscription or insignia chiseled upon it, distinguishing it from the otherwise identical host of others. Not every available square space within the puzzle was occupied. Only two were not, allowing for the movement of the others to be slid into the desired positions. Within these two bare, unoccupied slots, straight lines were visible cutting deep into the rock which was smooth here like polished glass. The track lines upon which the squares moved along they seemed to be, perhaps shifting the position of some connecting rod or linkage behind the wall. Some kind of complicated, ingenius lock mechanism must exist beyond the rock which all these rods purported to attach to, turning the lock within as they traversed upon their perpendicular grids. The lines seemed to intersect in a criss-cross pattern so that all these squares were able to be slid into any position on the board. A staff which pivoted in the hand of the statue right beside the immovable door appeared to be a lever which one must pull, or push, when the desired arrangement of coffers was achieved. But if the combination of the tiles was incorrect, the thief would be locked inside this hall by the ensnaring gate near the only entrance, activated by the lever, and to be left here to await his arrest.

Sebuda stood Bellick before the puzzle. "We don't have much time," Sebuda snarled when he shoved him into position. "Now you can open this door for me, or I'll find a most unpleasant way for you to spend your last moments on this earth. You'll wish you were back in that accursed cell of yours." The Turuk drew his dagger. Bellick met his fiery eyes with his own, then set to work on the puzzle.

It was a full year since he last put his cleverness to work on this particular enigma but he could never forget these squares. A long time he had studied them as he sat alone in this chamber, to which he reached by climbing the rotting chasm of Potep-Ud and so came from underneath. He had mapped the labyrinth of the Karkana Caverns over the course of many secret and tedious adventures into its depths and found his way, with great risk, up to the Hall of Secrets. As he ascended the great chasm he was able to see the capsule of rock above him where the treasure was cunningly housed, floating like a boat it seemed, at a higher elevation in the shaft with nothing below it but the emptiness of the pit. But to reach this was next to impossible for it jutted outwards from the cave wall and the undercut was too steep to attempt. The short tunnel which led from the hall to the chamber was completely enveloped in rock anyway, making entry virtually impossible, but even if he could somehow chisel his way in, teetering dangerously over certain death from a fall of hundreds of feet, extraction of the treasure inside was unthinkable with that solid stone door to the tunnel sealed shut. He thought it best to simply put his analytical skills to use on the lock inside, and within the silent hall and for days he pored over it, shifting the squares carefully until he had it solved. He did not put his solution to the test on that occasion but waited until his next venture. He knew that if he was unsuccessful he would be trapped inside, but sure enough, when he returned for what he thought would be the last time, to his relief, the huge door opened and in he went. But that happened to be a night of unrest for the tyrant of the palace, who was wont to be ill at ease, and he strode into his favorite chamber at that late hour perhaps to find some solace in the presence of his beloved possessions and coincidentally came upon the clever thief, but not before Bellick was able to discover his other secret. After his imprisonment, the injured lord ordered the shaft underneath sealed by a gate to prevent other crafty and ambitious characters from again accessing his secret vault. But he was unable as yet to wrest from the thief his means of solving the lock, and this vexed the lord greatly.

Bellick slid the squares along the board. With only two spaces vacant in the two-dimensional puzzle of many pieces, it took some time for them all to be in the proper order. Sebuda watched him closely, his dagger ready, his head turning uneasily from the puzzle to the tunnel behind them. When Bellick finally had them in position he studied the arrangement carefully to ensure its accuracy. He began to pant and shake with an almost cataleptic fit as he neared its completion, a nervous habit of the ingenius but excitable puzzler whenever he solved any puzzle or mystery. The suspense and rapture of solution always seized him thus, rendering him somewhat incapacitated and breathless for a time. He composed himself and moved over to the staff lever and placed his hand upon it. His captor stiffened and raised his weapon to the throat of the thief.

"Carefully my unsteady friend," Sebuda warned. "If we are trapped inside because you felt it wise instead to ensnare me, you will simply be removed again to your vile hole of habitation back in the dungeon to rot. I myself have Thuliak's trust, and he is more than familiar with you to doubt the reason for your presence here. It will not be difficult convincing him that I was abducted by the escaped thief to lend him aid in his renewed attempt to complete what he began. I hope for your sake you have it correct."

Bellick made no reply but returned his attention to the lever. He felt that in the end he could only be the victor here and this palace snake would meet his doom within.

Jesper quickly ran down the main tunnel into the Ud, following the scent of the two other intruders. He had no doubt what these two were after and he had to fulfill his mission on this point. He was sure the Turuk was a spy of the Baccád, but he didn't know who the other intruder was. Maybe this character would do his dirty work for him. Either way, if he felt things turned against Thuliak, anyone attempting entry into the Chamber of Treasures would have to be neutralized. And this covert operator had a tip that such a thing could be done with the help of a certain mastermind locked in the Ud. It was not difficult to see that this was the intent of those he quietly pursued. Not only would he have to deal with them but he would also have to disable the fabled puzzle within to deny access forever. Being an expert assassin and designer of sorts for unique locks and contraptions a means of sabotage would likely present itself to him, and he had a certain adapted mechanism in his possession that would aid him in this. He adjusted his disguise to facilitate his movement and made ready his weapons as he sped deeper into the earth. Confrontation was inevitable. He abandoned his charade as a cheerful commoner for the moment and resumed his stern and scrutinizing demeanor, though when his deed was accomplished he would make his way back to the surface to again resume his disguise and find a way to leave without his true motive being discovered. He did not know how things were going topside or in what direction success would tilt, but the issue of the vault had to be resolved. He was the protector. It was not to fall into the hands of the Kunn.

He reached the halls to the dungeons. A loud clatter and noise could be heard within and he approached slowly, guessing what could have caused a disruption as this. There was still no sign of his phantom intruders but he was sure that they must have had something to do with this unusual tumult. There were no signs of guards either, and that was also strange with this riot taking place. These events left him with little doubt: they had been here already. They must have broken the prisoner out and even now were unlocking the vault. His suspicions proved correct. He wasted no more time but hastened down the descending tunnel.

Bellick pushed the staff lever and the very ground began to shake. The immense door of rock began to grind and grumble along its track and slide slowly to the left. It revealed to them a short tunnel which led slightly upwards to a circular vault in which were placed many items high in value and some great in age including gold, rare potteries from distant lands, silver plates and vessels, chests of coins and jewels, and other items of excessive worth. But they did not gaze upon it long. Before the door even reached its place of rest in the wall, Sebuda suddenly seized his assistant and attempted to bind his hands with a short length of rope hidden in his clothing. Bellick resisted and a short scuffle ensued, but it was short-lived. The strong Turuk of the Mak-Baccád quickly beat down his quaking opponent, nearly breaking the weak prisoner's arms in the process. He strung the rope through one of the legs of a near statue, confining Bellick to the ground immovable. He groaned in pain as the Turuk bound his wrists tightly.

"Now you just stay here," Sebuda growled. "I can't sift through Thuliak's filth with an untrustworthy sneak like you behind me." With that he ventured into the short hall and up into the chamber.

Among the wealth stored in here by Thuliak and his predecessors was a small stash of an uncommon form of gold, locked in its own large case, and it was this for which the worm sought fervently. It contained many ingots of the secret element Akalium, or by some called *plate gold* for its harder composition. It was discovered to be suitable for uses like armor, for it was stronger and yet lighter than ordinary gold but no less appealing. This rare and improved form of the precious metal was mined in secret somewhere in the mountains and gorges of Adovia and had only made its introduction into the black market for the first time a few months ago. This mysterious material aroused the interest and curiosity of the wealthy and powerful, but the resourceful runner who presented it to them in their halls of stone and iron was wise to suppress and withhold it from mainstream distribution, for it drove its value ever higher. When Thuliak heard of this new item he not only purchased some of the supplier but bribed him with a small fortune to provide the Akalium only to himself, that Thuliak would be his chief and sole sponsor to whom this prize would be delivered, and this was agreed upon. Thuliak desired the prestige of being the only power with claim to this coveted item and he would pay whatever it took to achieve this. Lords from all over would offer him wealth untold for a small supply of it and his investment would be returned a hundredfold. But the real target of humiliation and subjection was the Ahga and the Kunn, those material misers of the east to whom all must pay not only gold but usually loyalty as well. An item came finally to light that only Thuliak could claim possession to, and he grasped the opportunity. He would enjoy watching the Ahga beg for this item.

But, like all that Thuliak devised, the Ahga found a way to seize it from him without his knowledge. His worm discovered Thuliak's new secret and sent word over. The Ahga sent his trusted followers to intercept this item somehow, which they did, with the help of his spy. The Baccád always found Thuliak's attempts at secrecy humorous but also capitalized on them. That fool should know there were no secrets in that loose-tongued and undisciplined pit called the Alad. The Ahga was aware that a small but valuable amount of the Akalium was locked within the vault, and along with the overthrow, as if to claim a total and insulting victory, he determined to have this as well.

Sebuda found the case. He gloated over his prize for a moment. He turned and was about to flee with it when he was confronted suddenly by someone else and he froze in his steps. The figure stood upon the threshold of the vault with a drawn sword. It was Rash-Haba.

When Jesper finally strode down the tunnel to the Hall of Secrets and set foot upon its sacred floor, the sounds of an altercation from within came vaguely to his ears. The agent drew a small bow weapon from the folds of his dirty shirt, a star-shooter of custom design or modified crossbow it looked to be. He crept within the hall and beheld the prisoner on the floor, tied by the wrists and evidently unaware of the stranger. He writhed about, struggling with his bonds. He looked weak and pale, shaking somewhat from some fit of fatigue or excitement. His breaths came in gasps. The stranger stepped to within a pace of the prisoner and the latter stopped his struggle and looked up.

"Who are you and what is happening?" Jesper asked.

"It would take too long to explain," Bellick answered feebly. He was a slender, inquisitive fellow, shaking in his frail limbs. He couldn't stand up to a stiff breeze by his appearance. "But we are both in peril. Thuliak's men will be here soon. He has no mercy for those who tread in this hall. It is a serious crime merely to be here and he will not bother to hear your pleas. You do not want to be prisoner here, they are ruthless. I don't know who you are but release me and I will save you from this capture. I must escape." Bellick tugged desperately at the rope.

Jesper studied him a moment with his scrutinizing eyes. "You must be the puzzle breaker. Someone broke you out to get him into the chamber."

Bellick nodded. "I know a shortcut out of here. I will show it to you. Hurry before we are captured or killed. They are coming!" The sounds of fierce fighting came from the vault ahead. There was definitely a struggle to the death going on up there. A great crashing and banging gushed forth from the opening. Jesper also fancied he heard a rumbling or galloping approaching from down the hall behind him. It seemed they were here. He, too, was now fair game for capture with nowhere to go. He thought a moment, seeking some possible alternative course of action. There seemed little other choice but nothing to lose in the endeavor anyway. Without further hesitation he cut the bonds around Bellick's wrists and followed him up the short slope into the open vault.

Within they found two figures grappling and rolling amid a room of strewn gold and broken pottery. The place appeared completely ransacked. Sebuda and Rash both held the blade of the other from piercing his throat. Rash had broken into the Ud when his moment of opportunity came, boldly seeking the recompense his superior refused to offer him. The losses of that gangster had more than injured him of late and he would not be subjected to this unacceptable denial of funds. He did not come today to inform his master of his problems alone, but to exact his own revenge. Rash was not leaving the premises without a fair payback in gold. He knew Thuliak had a considerable stash under the palace, and, seizing the chance opportunity in the chaos to venture underground to wrest greater riches than those upstairs, decided it would be a worthwhile attempt and diverted himself thither. The Akalium which he himself helped run would be suitable indeed. But there was only one case of it, so rare it was, and neither of these thieves was about to allow it to fall into the hands of another. Back and forth and from wall to wall crashed the two of them, knocking over piles of coins and shelves of wealth in their struggle to the death.

Bellick and Jesper paused a moment upon the threshold for their opportunity. Bellick told him there was a tunnel on the other side of the vault with a secret exit. But this of course meant that they would have to cross the length of the vault with its two combatants who were as yet unaware of the observers only a few strides away. Both of them clasped the case of Akalium by its metal handle, vying for possession. Jesper could make out an opening on the far side of the chamber and what looked from here like another short hallway leading out to the other side. Bellick was probably right then. They would have to make a break for it. They turned around suddenly for they heard the approach of riders, and sure enough a troop of Kunn fighters burst into the hallway upon their steeds. This unexpected display of force by the Kunn in this territory seemed to confirm to the stranger the shift of power that was taking place. His plan failed. He knew he had no choice now but to flee. The Ahga's men had reached the vault deep within the Ud. It was Hachek, and he gave a shout. On they came.

Bellick and Jesper bolted across the span of floor, Bellick in front leading weakly. At that moment the case of Akalium came free from the grasp of the contenders who fell again to the floor in their throes of death. Bellick was ahead, but Jesper seized the chance in mid-sprint. He abruptly halted and grabbed the case from the surprised fighters. Sebuda reached for it desperately but being prone on the floor with Rash on top of him he was unable to get a sufficient grip. But just as Jesper grabbed the case away from him their eyes met, and for a moment time seemed to stand still for the two actually recognized each other and they both froze agape. In the next instant Jesper turned and followed his anxious comrade who was calling him in earnest. He reached the extremity of the chamber and fled down the succeeding tunnel on the other side. Seeing their mutual failure, Rash and Sebuda made attempts to disengage themselves and pursue. Bellick quickly reached the end of the tunnel and came to the rock landing. He immediately set to work on his escape. There was one more secret of Thuliak's he discovered.

The Chamber of Treasures, or the Vog-Khana, was a spherical portal of hollowed rock supported in its place of virtual suspension over the broad chasm of Potep-Ud by two rock tunnels which formed an arched bridge with the chamber being the keystone. The rulers of old wanted not only a safe and secure location to store their most precious of possessions, but they also desired a means of sole extraction of this wealth and an advantageous and quick means of escape, all being made available to the monarch should some event of catastrophic implications or ultimate doom arise which demanded the hasty flight of the lord this arrangement accommodated. Two massive rods, or girders, were driven into carved holes in the base of the chamber and into opposite sides of the connecting escape tunnel. Once the girders were in place and safely supporting the weight of the chamber, the connecting tunnel was severed neatly from it top to bottom, making these massive rods the sole supporters of the whole suspended vault. These girders were able to be drawn back and forth by means of a wheel in the escape tunnel which turned a heavy screw in the floor, retracting them. With the retraction of the supporting girders the destructive descent of the chamber into the chasm was assured, destroying not only all the wealth but allowing the fleeing monarch to escape down the tunnel beyond without pursuit.

Bellick spun the wheel as fast as his weak arms could. He was shaking violently and panting from the excitement. He didn't have time to wait for Jesper to fully achieve the safe landing before he began his act of devastation but called to him in haste. The two still in the chamber scrambled to their feet and bolted for the escape tunnel, perceiving their destruction. But they were too late. Just as Jesper dove for safety on the landing behind Bellick there was a loud crack which echoed in the chasm. The chamber convulsed and rocked on its fragile and weakening supports, throwing its occupants inside back to the unsteady floor. Their attempts to regain their feet were fruitless and the tunnels resounded with their shouts in anger and fear. The chamber was falling. Sebuda and Rash tripped and fumbled over one another as they attempted to flee back to the Hall of Secrets. There was another crack and the chamber rocked again, dropping slightly on its vanishing support, and the objects inside made a unanimous lunge for the lower end, making a great noise and clamor of crashing metal. Rash was knocked over by spilled gold but Sebuda managed to get a handhold on the angled floor and began crawling back to the tunnel on the other side as fast as he could. It would all be over in the next moment and Rash's desperation and anger consumed the vault with its wild echoes. He knew he was doomed and as soon as he could made a fruitless lunge for the escape tunnel where Bellick frantically spun the wheel of doom. But Bellick suddenly collapsed with fatigue. Jesper quickly came to his aid and finished it. There was one more massive crack and it was over. The orb and all its vast wealth dropped from its suspended perch, dragging the two tunnels with it as it fell. The whole structure crumbled and dashed against the sides of the chasm with a thunderous and deafening roar. The cries of the once notorious gangster Rash-Haba could be heard for the last time echoing in the chasm as he made his descent to doom. He went down to join the dead at the far bottom of Potep-Ud, and the watchers upon the broken ledge could have sworn they heard a wailing sound comingled almost imperceptibly with the many ghastly resonations coming from the depths that was not from the cascading rock. It lingered for some time after the silence fell and echoed in the chasm. Perhaps the dead found some vindication in the confiscation of the legendary hoard of those who had perpetrated the gross injustices upon them.

* * *

Jesper brought Bellick to his feet and they stood only a moment upon the broken ledge which protruded outward into the chasm like the trunk of a tree which had been snapped off. They then turned and ran back down the tunnel. Hachek and his riders, on the opposite side of the gulf, had not been idle. When the chamber before them disappeared and made its final plunge they dismounted and fired their arrows across the Pit at the retreating figures, but it was in vain. The two fugitives quickly disappeared into the darkness on the other side. Hachek cursed and peered over the ledge for a moment before turning back to his mission. He failed to see a figure in the shadows only a few yards below him, clutching the rough edges of the chasm in desperation. This figure wouldn't finish the climb or even move a muscle until the ulak turned around and left. If he was seen, he would have been shot. But his discipline held, and when the mog departed with his troop he crawled back up the shaft like a spider and back into the hall.

Hachek rode further into the Ud with the last force of Thuliak close behind him. He had lost time when he detoured from his route to investigate the strange goings-on in the Gahg-Ajtak. His fighters, trained well in mounted combat, had to turn on their steeds to shoot behind them at the far superior pursuing force but it aided their charade of retreating. They were heading with all speed to the Tomb of Alad, which was not much further down the tunnel, and as far as Thuliak's men knew there was no way out down there. The Ahga's men would be trapped and slain with their backs against the wall, the defenders thought, and the vengeful soldiers of Mod chased them wildly and with renewed spirit. The Kunn riders had passed several more smaller chambers to either side, lesser rooms for storage or inhumation. A moment later they entered a wider chamber, the end of which was not visible for it was too far to discern. They had come to the catacombs deep in the Ud, but they did not slow. They knew this is where the Kunn would make its last stand against the palace garrison. If they succeeded here, total seizure of power was all but theirs.

To either side of this vast chamber were many rows of smaller halls, each containing many sarcophagi and sepulchral tombs. Most of these were inhabited, but others remained empty until occupied by the rightful deceased. The air was dank and thick in this ancient underground mausoleum, though a strange, sweet smell mysteriously pervaded the

392

chamber, and light from torches and lanterns struggled noticeably. The moisture from the Karkana below eased its way up through cracks in the rock walls. Scant, mossy growths and webs of unseen insects established their presence in places here despite the attempts of the attendants who routinely kept a cursory maintenance. These were but the tombs of the succeeding rulers and their kin, the great catacombs before one reached the doors of the grand Tomb of Alad further down the hall.

As Hachek and his troop passed through this wide stretch of hallway he was greeted by eyes which peered out from under the loose lids of stone coffins, or looked around the many corners of the apartment to either side, or watched them from spaces and niches above their heads as they rode under them. These were his brothers, he saw, the fighters of the Kunn, aye, even the esteemed members of the ruling Baccád seemed to be present for this moment of glory. This indeed was a privilege. He recognized some of them as his eyes searched about and he secretly saluted them as he passed them in their places of concealment. Evidently they had emptied many of these hallowed sepulchers of the remains of the deceased, despoiling them by order of the Ahga, and casting them with reverence deserving of swine into a heap of bones and rotting, worthless devices and heirlooms. And it was with great joy that they committed the violation, too, as if allowing themselves this indulgence to finally avenge themselves of the one they unanimously despised and exact further insult upon him and his pathetic and petty family of rulers. It was here that the Ahga directed them strategically to take places suitable for ambush, and they made all preparations and disposed of what they needed to for this great encounter, taking concealment in the coffins and devices of the chamber. The Ahga warned them that they were greatly outnumbered, that they would each have to slay many before his own life was taken, and this only drove the eager fighters to greater ambition. Their moment of success and greater renown was upon them and they were more than willing to take part. Either a greater dawn or an eternal twilight awaited. Here it was that the fate of the Brotherhood was to be decided.

Thuliak finally reached his precious Hall of Secrets, panting in anger and brandishing his sword. The invaders seemed to have branched off elsewhere in the tunnels. So let them be. All he wanted now was his vault. Without any hesitation he would have killed without mercy any he found even poking about his grand vault. He could have sworn that someone had just been here, however, that he missed them and was too late. He cursed, perceiving that he had been beaten to his domain of secrecy. But what he saw next as he fell inward upon the chamber nearly made him swoon with disbelief. He halted as if stunned by a spell. The sword fell from his hands and he stumbled a pace. He blinked in an attempt to expel the delirium that seemed to have overcome his senses. There, in lieu of his private and inaccessible keepsafe of stone, was nothing but the empty and gaping space of the now open chasm of Potep-Ud. The broken ledge which once led up to it was all that remained, jutting outwards into the vacant shaft where his vast wealth for ages was stored. The opposite ledge which led to his escape door was across the chasm and well out of reach. It looked as though a giant of the underworld had reached up from the depths of the Karkana and tore his precious and floating house down into the abyss, to be consumed unjustly by his rotting victims. His unique means of sabotage had been used against him. He stood upon the brink and fell to his knees and seemed to plead with fate, as if by some miracle or chance it was all a merely a vision and he could possibly save some small remnant of his lost hoard. His own prophetic words seemed to drift upward from the bottom of the gulf and he fancied he heard them within his ears though they came not from him: *the treasure is in a place where only myself and the dead can get it.* He wailed as these words came unbidden from elsewhere, and the deep and mysterious Potep-Ud, teeming with sorrow, resonated with his cries.

Hachek's troop reached the far end at almost the same moment the Mod soldiers entered the near end of the chamber. He feigned a desperate look around and his mounted troop of suchuks halted and stirred as if lost and trapped. The soldiers saw them in the distance. Trapped they were, like cattle in a pen, and in the soldiers ran with a yell. Their captain would finish this little rebellion down here, once and for all. But upon their rushed entry a lone figure suddenly appeared at just past the midway of the vault. The clansters on their steeds behind him became forgotten for the moment. They became lost in the gloom and the room seemed to fall silent. All eyes were fixed on this lone figure who seemed to appear from nowhere. The captain of Mod couldn't discern the identity of that courageous newcomer, standing irresolutely before a storm as though he had no fear. It was Gathmug, the reputed warlord of the Baccád, his mighty frame looking like a column of iron, and he was holding aloft a longbow with an arrow that was alight with a small flame. He drew it back and aimed it over the heads of the oncomers.

At that moment there was a grumbling as the door of entry behind them closed shut and the great door to Alad's Tomb was opened at the extremity of the chamber. A great rushing of air from the opened vault almost lifted them from their feet. All the lights in the chamber which were dim almost to extinction suddenly became alight with an anger and ferocity from the gust. The arrow which sped over the heads of the now pallid and disconcerted soldiers appeared to them to be like the hand of some deity of the stars, reaching over them with his hand like an arc of flame. The entryway of the chamber and well into the hall itself had been doused with much oil and the soldiers realized their doom. Like a fresh torch the chamber blazed with its imperiled host in the midst. From above in compartments and below in coffins jumped the waiting and concealed assailants. The last few of the Ahga's Mak-Baccád on site leaped out. Hachek and his suchuks turned and rode forth with a cry. They all seized the moment of advantage and crashed upon the reeling soldiers like a stampede, filling the air with their cries of *Uden og Kabba! Baccád! Baccád!* Among them were the rest of the Baccád: Mesahalat, Vekk, Gōz, Ushep, Hemetek, Zodd, Kassét, and Ulgash–all leaped into the fray with their kodara swords aloft. The blazing air was filled with throwing stars and knives. None could resist their terrifying onslaught. Like trees in a heavy gale they fell into the fire and were consumed.

What became known as the Massacre in the Ud was over in a matter of moments, and the perpetrators quickly prepared the chamber for the last part. The dead were left as they were, still smoldering in their destruction. The entry door was reopened for their last guest and the great door to Alad's Tomb was also left in its position of retraction. The Kunn made haste to depart. Gathmug ordered the chamber emptied and they all sped into the tomb, proceeding past this eastward and into the secret passageway which led back to the Olóbid. Gathmug remained to oversee this last part. This was to be an especial favorite for the Ahga and he paused to ensure its success. Here he comes now, thought Gathmug. A lone figure just rushed into the vault. He couldn't quite tell who it was exactly at this distance but judging by his evident hysteria there was little doubt. Gathmug idled a moment in the chamber before he finally withdrew.

CHAPTER 8
THE DEPOSITION OF THULIAK

Thuliak burst into the catacombs like a beast seeking to avenge itself upon the one that had slain its offspring. His reddened eyes were wild with fury, his teeth ground, his breath coming in gasps. His sword was in his hand and it shook with the uncontrollable vengeance of its master. He looked beaten and his clothes were tattered, as though he had survived a great storm on the world above. His embroidered and scarlet garments hung off his bent frame like drapes which had been torn by a great wind. When he happened in upon the cruel and hideous scene of destruction of the last of his men he stopped only a moment to regard them. There they were, corpses strewn about the floor, vapors still twisting from their scorched and hewn bodies, lying like beasts of a fiery slaughter. The last of his garrison in the palace they were, but he paid them little heed. His wrath was too great to be concerned for them. All his cares and responsibilities, any regard for his or anyone else's life had been long since abandoned. His rule was finished, but this brought a heretofore unknown savagery into his soul. His life and all he held dear in this world had been cast into the pit of the earth to be consumed by the demons which dwelt in its unreachable shadows, forever beyond his grasp. Now, with nothing to lose but his own life he felt a rage and insanity that was free from all bond and restraint. The heavy cage of even his sparse reason had been lifted and he felt energized by its release. His anger increased all the more with the freedom and his eyes were filled with such malice that even the doughtiest warrior of the Kunn would have had to draw back in fear of them. There was only one thing he lived for now, and that was revenge. He would have it or die in the attempt. Not only had he been defeated in his endeavor to expel what he thought was merely a growing nuisance within his domain which he grossly underestimated, he was intentionally humiliated by them with an unusual and unprecedented bitterness which surpassed even his reputed callousness and cruelty. He looked upon the spoiled tombs of his predecessors and their mingled remains, all heaped in a careless pile of filth. But almost he cared not for them and he rejoiced at the absence of any conscious concern. He felt now free to do whatever act of abomination his soul demanded of him and to commit to the wildest and most hideous indulgences of his raging fancy. He dismissed his surroundings and cast his glance in front of him.

He could vaguely discern the door to the great tomb beyond, lying at the far end of the scorched rows of sepulchers. It was open, and the light of the moon which the oculus of the tomb's high domed ceiling permitted entry cast its feeble rays through the circular aperture. This cold, white light rested momentarily upon a certain figure in the threshold of the doorway whose shadow lingered upon the floor of the crypt before it retreated into the chamber beyond. A growl escaped through Thuliak's clenched teeth. His hand gripped his sword. Like a man intoxicated with the hatred of a demon he strode forward. Almost he staggered with the potency. Death was in his eyes.

"AHGA!" he shouted as he came and the walls echoed with his monstrous wrath and insanity. "COME NOW AND SETTLE IT WITH ME! YOU HAVE TAKEN ALL THAT WAS MINE, COME AND TAKE MY LIFE AS WELL! OR ARE YOU TOO AFRAID TO LOWER YOURSELF TO SUCH A DAUNTING TASK! FOR YOU CANNOT TRIUMPH OVER ME! AHGAAA!" his pace quickened to a run. There was no response but the figure fled around a corner and out of sight. Through the Tomb of Alad Thuliak passed. The moonlight which streamed in from above focused its beams on the large, stone monument in the center of the rectangular and open chamber. The eye of the distant ceiling had been enshrouded in a low dome structure on the surface, designed to maximize light intake. It was oval in shape and cut in a convex manner, aligned with the cosmos in such a way as to afford an advantageous inlet of light from celestial bodies to shine upon the great tomb, night and day. Thuliak did not pause to witness the wonder but sped through this and down the succeeding passageway which led to the Tomb of Olóbid.

He turned a corner, hearkening to the retreating footsteps ahead of him which seemed to have quickened slightly. The original hallway continued eastward, toward the Ahga's citadel, but it had been long since impassable. The tunnels over the Karkana were always unstable. He detoured to the right at the junction instead and headed south. There was the large doorway to the tomb, slightly further ahead, and open. The shadow of his enemy could be seen slithering upon the floor and walls as it disappeared within. This was the Tomb of Olóbid, however. There was no escape from this chamber, Thuliak knew. The old passageway out had long since collapsed. Whoever it was that fled him would meet his doom within. He was trapped and Thuliak laughed with glee.

"Ha, ha, ha!" the vengeful pursuer cried out. "Now I have you! Come and face me, for there is no escape! You are mine, now, you filth!" But suddenly he fell silent and the grin on his twisted face disappeared when he thought he saw what could only be an opening in the far wall. Many sarcophagi lined the walls all around, placed upright against them and in such a way that they seemed to look upon the great tomb in the center and offer their reverence to the fallen ruler, though there was no light of splendor here to match the chamber of the brother. Only torches illuminated the room, placed in a ring all about the circular vault. And the light of these fell upon an open and empty sarcophagus and amazingly, a narrow tunnel beyond.

Thuliak blinked his eyes as he gazed upon it. Here indeed was the source of all his woes brought upon him by the Ahga and his cohorts. This was the avenue that the Kunn used to infiltrate his domain and learn all his secrets. He had been played for a fool all along. All his failures with all their mysteries had at last been explained. Even the secrets of the mastermind he caught by fortunate chance began to make sense. He was a fool for not executing him immediately, for he had undoubtedly been used to break into his vault. One with a secret as volatile as that cannot be preserved for another to seize as a powerful weapon against you. All these villains had dug right under him. He began to wonder how else he had been exploited but his wrath and vengeance superseded these trivialities. These things were of little matter now. Only one thing was certain now, and that was death.

So, this is the secret entrance to the Ahga's keep, he thought. That fool must not have had time to properly close the door behind him, being chased. He was nowhere in sight and must have gone in seeking refuge. Fool. There was no refuge against this wrath. They would all die and Thuliak would burn all their corpses and use their accursed bandanas to clean the mess. He plunged inside the secret tunnel, his fury and delight returning.

He followed the rough-cut tunnelway which appeared to have been used by the thugs recently. Without a doubt they used this passage to conduct their coup and ambush his garrison. It headed east but soon turned south toward the Olóbid. He could hear the running of water up ahead and the walls and ceiling opened to all sides. He soon stepped upon the ledge of an underground bridge, constructed of wood planks and rope. Below him ran the noisy Karkana River, the great river of the underworld, flowing through a large, open cavern below. There was no sign of his enemy but this was the only route he could have taken. Thuliak crossed the rift and reached the other side. The river flowed in a southerly direction, toward the Olóbid, and he reckoned himself to be close to the destination. He couldn't have much farther to go.

The tunnel banked slightly to his right and he lost his sense of direction. Perhaps his reckoning was amiss. He thought for sure he must be directly under the Olóbid by now, having traveled back to the south for some time, but the passage arced in a semi-circle as though it circumvented another chamber or area which must lie to his left. Anyone subjected to the lethal chun-vok trial would have been able to tell him where he was. He began to become impatient and curses escaped his clenched and grinding teeth. This venture underground had gone too long. Just as he was about to burst out with the agony of his suspense he perceived a light ahead, that which undoubtedly came from something above and illuminated a larger room. With his sword drawn and the smile of revenge he burst into this chamber. It seemed to be rectangular in shape with a lofty ceiling which he could not see clearly in this light. There was still no sign of the phantom he had been chasing and he looked about wildly. Where had he gone? But just as he set foot into the chamber a stone door closed behind him, trapping him in. All was silent for a moment until he heard a voice coming from above and he looked up.

"I was hoping you would join us," the voice said, and the strength of it echoed in the wide vault. It was a voice all too familiar to Thuliak and he shouted curses so that the walls shook. It was the voice of the Ahga, coming from somewhere in the darkness high above, though Thuliak fancied he could see his face somewhere in the gloom, peering over a ledge or balcony at him.

"AHGA!!" Thuliak shouted in rage and swung his sword in helpless fury. He repeated his shouts of madness several times over accompanied by wild gesticulations and then became silent again.

"You are but the last loose end to be settled in our great design of takeover," the voice of the Ahga continued, almost passively, ignoring his cries and with a hint of pleasure. "I have saved you for this final role of honor. We of the Kunn, you understand, have need of your reign here to settle some of our own larger issues and embark upon greater, and you were an obstruction to that end. This is my city now, to be added to the host of others under my authority. I will no longer be subservient to you. The time has come for the Brotherhood to move beyond that which it once was. It is time for the Kunn to rise and assume its divine inheritance. Our kingdom awaits. For these reasons it has become necessary to permanently remove you from our society. But you need not fear for your realm. Your pitiful authority will be handed over to one whom I deem more capable to sit on your throne and carry out my wishes as needed. Mod will be a supporting sister city for the next great venture of the clan and I need one upon whose obedience I can rely. Surely you can guess of whom I speak. Why you have been sitting on one in your own dungeon who had also plotted your ruin is beyond my capability of understanding. He has still quite a following and I intend to use it."

Thuliak was incredulous and his rage increased with these revelations. "Salzan!" he shouted upwards with disbelief and shook his fists, his wrath plain to see. "Salzan! That fool?!" He twisted with anger. These words pierced him like a dagger. This inept conspirator who plotted Thuliak's demise was to replace him! "You are as blind and foolish as he is, Ahga. Azandium is a futile pursuit. The Slovidars couldn't find it and neither will their bastard child, the Kunn. You will soon meet your end here, though it will come in a way unforeseen by even you. But then I suppose with all my wealth in your possession you will get all that you desire. I am sure the Akalium will fetch you all the volia and Ceneaen glass and Adovian crystal your filthy hut can hold. And take from me all my loyal friends, to bow to you in my stead, much to your delight. Come, tell me, how does it feel to now have all the wealth of centuries in your halls? Does it bring you greater pleasure knowing that it was once mine, one who offered you the greatest of generosity? Swine! And what do you intend to do, keep me locked in this filthy little hole of yours to gnaw the ages with my sorrow and entertain you with my trifles?" Thuliak began to laugh with a shrill shriek, half of humor, half of madness. "Will you come to visit me often in this pit to relieve me of my solitude and misery? Why it smells like rotting corpses in here."

The Ahga ignored his rambling. *Corpses indeed.* "Nay, you will serve a greater purpose," he said and paused a moment for effect. Thuliak was silent. "My servants call this room the Gahg-Morga. Surely you know what that means." Thuliak's smile disappeared. His face went deathly white. The Ahga said no more but left him to his kindled imaginings and terror. The distant form of the Ahga retreated slowly out of sight, his footsteps echoing in the vault.

"AHGA!" Thuliak thundered. Only echoes.

"AHGAA!!" Thuliak bellowed again with greater stress and fury. The Ahga closed a heavy metal door behind him, shutting out the noise of his cries. And with the clang of the door, as if by spell, all at once the lights went out and the chamber fell into complete darkness. Thuliak's muffled cries shook the ground with his anger.

* * *

It was deep night, and the city had fallen again into its reveries and dreams under the starry sky. The palace of Mod had lost its glow as if the fire of unrest that had burned for a time within its forbidding walls had been quenched, and the rise upon which the vast domain rested fell quiet and dark once more. Shadows settled back into crevices and folds of the earth and wrapped the incline in darkness. So it was that no one could notice two figures emerge from a small round door in the face of the ascending rockside, a door no one ever saw before for it was made to resemble the surface upon which it had been built in secret. These two strange figures

400

seemed to be carrying something as though it were valuable. They stole away into the night and disappeared into the city below.

Sometime later that night, or perhaps it was the next morning, Sebuda succeeded, with difficulty, in bringing himself into the presence of his master. The Ahga was seated upon his throne of iron, surrounded by a few of his elites who were not presently consumed with the duties of security outside but awaited orders or sought counsel. The coup was complete and his servants now were engaging in the final necessary operations of securing the palace compound and apprehending any remaining personnel. The city of Mod was now essentially in the hands of the Kunn, their new base city established, and to its machine the resources would pour. Sebuda anticipated a favorable reception from the great one he served, having provided him with the most devastating of secrets which proved instrumental in this latest and boldest of operations. But despite his stunning success it appeared the Ahga was in ill humor. The loss of the hoard had been brought to his attention and he could not conceal his wrath. It was impossible that such a thing could happen. The Ahga counted heavily on confiscating the hoard for its wealth was great indeed, and he was anxious for its reception. The Akalium alone was worth a fortune. The astounding success of the coup did not satisfy him sufficiently to allow this failure to pass forgotten and unavenged. When Sebuda approached he was forced to give an account of his actions, for in this matter the worm was directly responsible.

"Perhaps you can tell me something of my lost money," the Ahga posed in a tone that suggested he was about to mangle something with his bare hands. His eyes would have bored holes through a stone wall. The worm shifted on his weary feet before him. "And who is responsible. For even Thuliak would not have done this in his madness."

"It was not Thuliak or one of his agents who has deprived us of the hoard," Sebuda answered steadily.

The Ahga leaped to his feet in a sudden fit of rage and drove his hammer-like fist right through the huge wooden table in front of him. It exploded with a great crash in their midst, completely and utterly destroyed in one fell stroke. Splinters and debris scattered over the floor were all that remained of it. His pale subjects instinctively fell back several paces at this outburst. Sebuda somehow managed to stand firm.

"Then I demand to know who did!" shouted the Ahga and the hall shook. "For I will hunt him to the ends of the earth for this outrage and hang his bloody corpse from the castle walls for all to see!"

There was a pause. Sebuda composed himself.

"Riman," came the reply.

APPENDICES, BOOK 1

PEOPLE

Azag – Kunn ulak intended to replace Kurg at Khala due to incompetence; slain by Kurg

Balinus – lieutenant to Helbek

Bellick Madrudo – locksmith, puzzler, rescued by Riman under the Harásh; works for Riman after rescue

Cam of Bren – boy enslaved by Kunn who also receives divine blessing with his best friend Damian. Empowered with speed and acrobatic abilities

Damian of Tirien – boy enslaved by Kunn who receives divine blessing to fight the clan. Empowered with strength

Draga – mog ulak of the Kunn; rejection of induction into Baccád results in his roguery and treachery against Mozep, his competitor, who he slays

Erius – first mate of the *Cardela* under captain Vadro

Haj Osavius – lord of Bren

Hallév – leader of the Bará clan

Helbek – lord of Hera, puppet of Kunn

Kane – lord of Kandar

Klavéc – freelance mercenary who captures escapee of Khala to sell to Kunn in Hera

Kom – lord of sister city Gyla, also subject to Kunn

Kurg – Kunn warden at Khala mines

Marcus Galnum – agent working for Riman in Palace of Hera; member of the Hera Council

Mavili Veshtoli – lord of Prova

Mozep – Baccád mog of the Kunn, clan ulak of Hera; is slain by Draga

Peng Goshek – freelance merchant, smuggler, supplier of material and valuables, including relics; deals with clans and Thuliak

Rash-Haba – gangster in Mod, runner of the Tanga River, cooperating with Thuliak in acquiring Akalium nuggets

Riman – craftsman forced to work for Kunn, exploited of his engineering abilities. Meets with Damian and Cam and the three form a resistance. Riman, however, dubious of mythical conjecture. Aliases: Jesper, Stal, Hamlad of Capetibi

Sadru-Yen – tarsh, or ruler, of Dinitia, island country to west of Vidia

Salzan Karpoli – prisoner of Thuliak, held in the Ud; made to replace Thuliak as ruler of Mod after Kunn takeover

Telachus – captain of guard at Spen Mala

Thuliak – ruler in Mod, uses Kunn as monetary prop to support his corrupt regime; is overthrown by Baccád to establish Kunn city

Tog – leader of the Consortium, bearer of the rumjad, the token of dominion

Tura – ranking human agent working for Kunn in Hera; Kunn liaison to Helbek

Vadro Alladakis – Achellan of Dinitia, captain of the *Cardela;* helps Damian and Cam in their hunt of Kunn pirates in the Dinitian Sea

Vid Markuso – beleaguered senator of Second Pillar in the Hera Council, opposition to Helbek and Kunn who are taking over his city; implements revolution in Hera

PROVINCES

Dinitia

Island nation to the southwest of the mainland Vidia including the islands of Marán. Hot, tropical climate. Achellan is the main race which dwell there. Have standing alliance with Kandar. The colors of Dinitia are black and green

The Govánnum
Home to capital city Mod. Clans have some reign here, somewhat chaotic and corrupt. Marak Desert to the south and Govan Wastes to the north. Land becomes more barren here in contrast to Nadea. The Khala mines are located in northeastern Govannum

Kandar
Actually a country, solidly united and organized. Well defended with strong border watch maintained on north side of Brown Hills in the lowlands between Nadea and Kandar

Nadea
Home of capital cities Hera and Gyla. Once prosperous and just, now penetrated by agents of the Kunn and has fallen into corruption. Not a solidly unified country, comprised of city-states, hence only considered a province, but commerce commences throughout territory. The birthplace of Damian is Tirien, a small farming village to the southeast of Hera, on the border with Govannum. Bren is the birthplace of Cam, a small coastal town along the Ella River far to the south in Nadea

Thecenea
Country south of Adovia, hot, coastal, more fertile than the lands to its north and east. Peninsula jutting out into Vidian Sea, many ports, seafaring, mountainous. The colors of Thecenea are red

These were the original five provinces of the Old Alliance

Bhull
Country on east side of Ash Mountains, divided into realms of Shomenria to the south, Katzatan to the north

Marán
Hot island country of Dinitia. Ruler called a Tarsh. The colors of Marán are yellow and red

CITIES

Demar

Main capital city of Kandar where dwells the Lord Kane. The colors of Demar are blue and white. Other cities of Kandar under the umbrella of Demar are Pomay, Veccenberg, and Casten. The Vastila is the palace stronghold. The Pentagrid is an extension of this where the Demarian spy network, the Hattél, is stationed

Hera and Gyla
Large capital cities of Nadea built on the volatile Plateau of Hera. The previous rulers were Karius and Alos, allied brothers whose prosperous, if reclusive, rule was cut short by assassination due to their obstructionism and harshness in dealing with despotic clans. Among the many creations of the two lords is the Ascension, a great staircase cut into the Plateau. Current rulers are Helbek of Hera and Kom of Gyla. The flag of Hera is a great seabird decked with five stars, one for each of the original five united territories of the Old Alliance

Kadr
City in Dengland, home to the creation of the Kunn and the Baccád. Formerly under the rule of Illidrab, power recently given over to new ruler, a woman, who revolutionizes and revitalizes the city to create an opposing force to counter the Kunn

Mod
Capital city of Govannum province, original home to the Lord Thuliak. The predecessor was ousted in a coup and the Kunn established Mod as a supporting appendage. The colors of Mod are brown and red

Prova
Strong and great coastal city of Nadea. The City on the Sea, it is home and port to seafarers. Independent, sharing marginal allegiance with Hera and Gyla though free from clan influence or presence. Mavili Veshtoli ruler here

RACES

Achellan
Dark-skinned, dwelling mostly in island country of Dinitia. Good folk, allied with Demar with whom they trade. The colors of Dinitia are black and green

Gaden (the Gades)
Short, sturdy folk

Harikans
Blue-hued humanoids, black hair and eyes

Hakai
Dark-skinned, spiritual tribal race dwelling in the mountains, the offspring of Agal. Feared by others as strange and untrustworthy, belonging to another world. Connected to the unseen, dwelling on other plane. True believers in the Mari and able to extract greater gifts if one is devout

Hidari
Black-haired, light-skinned, thick and sturdy

Humans

Mogoli
Tough, green-skinned, fanged, black-haired beings

Turuks
Green-skinned, slighter and shorter than their mog relatives

THE CLANS

The Kunn
Made up of the Ahga and his followers. Ranks are comprised of Baccád elites, Mak-Baccád, and suchuk fighters. Follow a strict code of discipline and physical training. The Mari grants superiority and reward to its most devout followers but the weak are expelled. Only the strongest and most adherent are allowed practice and admission into the brotherhood. Powerful and organized, following the demands of their creed to achieve dominance in the world through application

The Bará
Made up mostly of Harikans of Thecenea, the main enemy of the Kunn. Can be found in Mod and in other suburbs and cities to the south. Hold sway in coastal city of Daldune. Hallév the clan leader. Insignia of black stripe under right eye, the slash of Darr. Pressed and routed by the far superior Kunn.

The Hōsh
Can be found operating mostly to the south and east, in Thecenea and Hepesh. Often feud with the Bará in the southern territories. Standard is of a victim's head being crushed between the fangs of a black serpent, all on a field of green

THE BACCÁD

Made up of thirteen members. Must accomplish certain rituals and tasks to qualify, one of which is the chun-vok. Members of the Kunn receive hash marks on their necks called shukk marks to denote insignia of rank. These members make up the Ahga's highest order. This is, in fact, what Baccád means, 'order', and they are most trusted and proven. Members of the Baccád have four shukk marks

The Baccád, in order of rank:

1. The Ahga-Rosh, or Father

2. Gathmug
ghad-hesh, or second man

3. Hemetek
Overseer of commerce, high of rank and responsibility

4. Ulgash
Clan diplomat to western cities, Prova and Bren

5. Vekk
Clan leader in Bahrag

6. Gōz
Leader in Vurg, jeweled bandolier. Once belonged to a gang lord there who he killed in a duel. Is beset by opposing revolutionary who threatens his existence, the Queen of Kadr

7. Ushep
Overseer of espionage and penetration of gov't in northern areas, Hera and Gyla. Supplemental officer in these two newly penetrated cities. Makes bribes, coercions, etc of politicians and businessmen to help cause of Kunn

8. Zodd
Overseer of ground ops in Mod and suchuks

9. Mesahalat
Becomes clan ulak in Hera

10. Rugg-Adda

Overseer of southern commodities, kuth, rare stones, etc. Also elimination of competing clans in southern territories. Extraordinarily large and arrogant, strong, even for Baccád

11. Bazi
Insane, rash. Clan leader in Darhúk

12. Kassét
Clan leader in Mulda

13. Mozep
Clan ulak in Hera, slain by Draga

Mak-Baccád (under order)
These are the super soldiers of the Ahga. Very well trained, experts in fighting and covert ops, well equipped. Wear black bandanas with three shukk marks

Suchuks (lesser order)
These are the foot soldiers of the Kunn. Cause most of the terror on the street and countryside

SLOVIAD SPEAK

Al-Medu – for the Divine

Chun-vok – trial of the Baccád

Gok-armok – palms of steel

Hakim-Razsda – submission of body ritual, the cutting off of one's shukk marks to retain some level of honor

Iim-chai – the Viper's Nest, secret underground vault occupied by the Kunn in Hera

Kada-ud – suicide of dishonor

Kochok Uden – self immolation

Kumitam – shrine of worship for the Kunn

Ruk-mesh – ritual of pain

Stalat uruz al-Medu – work for the Divine

Tarral – submission bar for Kunn servants

HERA NOTES

The Hera Council
Made up of eleven members. 6 votes necessary for majority

1st Pillar
Helbek (former officer of high rank under Karius)
Balinus (second in command, aid to Helbek and his confidant)
Malkor Bethúluket
Narsech of Halkád

2nd Pillar
Desh-Mandreni
Vid Markuso
Marcus Galnum
Arthelius Napibi

3rd Pillar
Garen Durél
Hon-Miladvik
Naricius

CREATURES

Arlick – wild pig of the south

Belkan deer – deer of the jungle

Boros – huge, four legged reptiles used to carry goods across the deserts

Delling – delicacy of desert, rodent of the desert

Dendu – swift reptiles of the desert, used by Kunn for speed

Derrician Drifters – large carnivorous birds used to carry messages long distances

Gurdu lizards – crocodile-like reptiles of the Vora Gorga Wastes

Jarella – small, featherless bird

Karkua – large brown hunting cat of the east, found in Al-Akat Mountains

Karpi pigs – man-eating pigs of the Palmwood jungle

Kunga – beast of vast bulk, mammal of the far north

Madidi – large, dangerous and carnivorous eel of the underground, subterranean river of Karkana, River of Ghosts

Pelera – vicious ape of Marán

Ráka – extremely venomous snake of the desert

Red Runners – small poisonous snakes of the jungle

Ribi flies – biting flies of palmwood

Rovola – large, brown, reptilian creature of the mountains to the north and east. Venomous bite

Sardina bats – wailing bats

Talpin monkey – small ape

OTHER WORDS OF IMPORT

Agon's Fury – pyrotechnic composition
Akalium gold – rare form of gold mined secretly in the Al-Akat Mountains to the east
Balsan crystals – pyrotechnic ingredient
Bazinite – mineral ingredient used in construction, forging, metallurgy, composites
Cabskins – animal skins used to make tough fabrics, armor lining in conj w/kunga oil
Darhindi berries – poisonous berries of same plant
Figwine – drink delicacy
Galnaberries – berry delicacy
Garvonite – prized metal for making weapons. Called Peplag in the east
Geluda gum – pyrotechnic ingredient
Gini sticks – stick made of same wood

Golianthus oil – great fish of the sea from which oil is derived; valuable

Hataba smoke – mixture which burns to create fatal smoke

Hypsan Cane – sugar stick, Riman's particular fancy

Hyr – healing liquor, expensive

Ido – pirate currency, outlawed by authorities. Can be used for armor, plating, weapon tips

Kinsweed – herb for making healing liquor

Kira silver – valuable silver mined in the Al-Akat Mountains, Mt. Kira, also called Adovia silver

Ku mortar – special, harder blend of mortar, commodity of Hera

Kunga oil – used in tanning, lubrication, many uses with cabskins

Lunacrystal – gem that produces faint light in the dark

Molgite shavings – used to make hataba smoke

Mona nuts – large nut with hard rind, used for containment of liquids

Murahellin – drug that induces deep sleep

Potan paste – creamy, poisonous plant extract

Saisa dust – powder ignited by fire creating unbreathable circumstances

Si-si dates – dates grown in Dinitia, delicacy

Sodin powder – tacky substance that burns underwater hot enough to melt steel (Cerion's Candles)

Tempra parchment – a decomposing paper

Tilnian granules – ingredient used to make fatal hataba smoke

Tylia – herb for making healing liquor, found in Palmwood

Vella-beer – liquor indigenous to Thecenea, made from the vella berries there

Volia – silk made from the same plant in Adovia and northern Dengland

Volkyrian grain – burn powder, explosive, created in Artos, Thecenea

Zuki poison – granules of the plant which can be ingested through the skin; fatal

Zūl-fire – blue flame used for decoding encrypted, doused messages

Michael Schwartz spent his youth involved with karate training and dragon slaying in the woods of New Hampshire. He was fond of role-playing games such as Dungeons and Dragons, and even created his own written adventures and modifications. At the young age of eighteen he fell in love with and married his neighbor and high school sweetheart, Kimberly. Shortly thereafter he earned his black belt in martial arts. After graduating high school he embarked on a short term of service in the United States Marine Corps, during which his two sons were born. He returned to the simple working life at the grocery store, adding a daughter to the household, raising a family of three children with his wife. Their children are grown and Michael and Kimberly have been married happily for twenty-two years. They are now kept company by a small host of furry animals.

The September 11, 2001 terrorist attacks had a profound effect on Michael's outlook of life, God, and His purpose for mankind. He was moved to study theology and philosophy, in particular religiously inspired warfare. Trying to discover the answer to divinely justified murder, and man's eager claim to it, he wrote this book series.

Visit the Ratarra website at ratarra.com
Facebook: facebook.com/ratarra.bookseries

Made in the USA
San Bernardino, CA
30 May 2014